The Adventures of Harry Richmond

THE ADVENTURES OF

HARRY RICHMOND

by George Meredith

Edited with an introduction by L. T. Hergenhan

UNIVERSITY OF NEBRASKA PRESS • LINCOLN

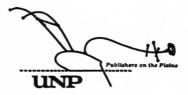

Copyright © 1970 by the University of Nebraska Press

Quotations from Meredith's manuscripts copyright © 1970 by the Trustees of the Estate of the late George Meredith

Standard Book Number 8032–0712–3

Library of Congress Catalog Card Number 78–88088

Manufactured in the United States of America

...fireworks. He rose about, interrogating the servants, & grooms holding horses & dogs. They could tell us that the cattle were safe, not a word of my father; & amid shrieks of women at fresh falls of timber & ceiling into the pit of flame, & warnings from them, we ran the circle of the doomed building to find a loophole & offer aid if a living soul should be left, the night around us bright as day, busier than day, & a human now added to elemental horror. I could not quit her place. She sent her carriage-horses to Bulsted, & sat in the carriage to see the last of Riversley. Each time that I came to her she folded her arms on my neck & kissed me silently. She wept more when little Riomi was found after a winter night stretched over the grave of her child frozen dead; now when news came to us that our friend Heriot had fallen on an Indian battlefield. My father was never seen again.

The last page of Meredith's handwritten draft of *The Adventures of Harry Richmond.*

CONTENTS

Introduction by L. T. Hergenhan xi

Selected Bibliography xxxv

THE ADVENTURES OF HARRY RICHMOND

Chap.

    I.   I Am a Subject of Contention 1

    II.   An Adventure on My Own Account 12

    III.   Dipwell Farm 21

    IV.   I Have a Taste of Grandeur 27

    V.   I Make a Dear Friend 37

    VI.   A Tale of a Goose 55

    VII.   A Free Life on the Road 66

    VIII.   Janet Ilchester 81

    IX.   An Evening with Captain Bulsted 88

    X.   An Expedition 101

    XI.   The Great Fog and the Fire at Midnight 107

    XII.   We Find Ourselves Bound on a Voyage 115

    XIII.   We Conduct Several Learned Arguments with the Captain of the Priscilla 124

    XIV.   I Meet Old Friends 131

    XV.   We Are Accosted by a Beautiful Little Lady in the Forest 138

    XVI.   The Statue on the Promontory 148

    XVII.   My Father Breathes, Moves, and Speaks 157

XVIII.	We Pass a Delightful Evening, and I Have a Morning Vision	161
XIX.	Our Return Homeward	171
XX.	News of a Fresh Conquest of My Father's	179
XXI.	A Promenade in Bath	186
XXII.	Conclusion of the Bath Episode	196
XXIII.	My Twenty-First Birthday	205
XXIV.	I Meet the Princess	215
XXV.	On Board a Yacht	221
XXVI.	In View of the Hohenzollern's Birthplace	227
XXVII.	The Time of Roses	232
XXVIII.	Ottilia	242
XXIX.	An Evening with Dr. Julius Von Karsteg	246
XXX.	A Summer Storm, and Love	253
XXXI.	Princess Ottilia's Letter	260
XXXII.	An Interview with Prince Ernest and a Meeting with Prince Otto	264
XXXIII.	What Came of a Shilling	272
XXXIV.	I Gain a Perception of Princely State	287
XXXV.	The Scene in the Lake-Palace Library	303
XXXVI.	Homeward and Home Again	310
XXXVII.	Janet Renounces Me	321
XXXVIII.	My Banker's Book	331
XXXIX.	I See My Father Taking the Tide and Am Carried on It Myself	347
XL.	My Father's Meeting with My Grandfather	362
XLI.	Commencement of the Splendours and Perplexities of My Father's Grand Parade	367
XLII.	The Marquis of Edbury and His Puppet	381
XLIII.	I Become One of the Chosen of the Nation	394

XLIV.   My Father Is Miraculously Relieved by
        Fortune 405

XLV.   Within an Inch of My Life.........................415

XLVI.   Among Gipsy Women.............................419

XLVII. My Father Acts the Charmer Again.............428

XLVIII. The Princess Entrapped.........................440

XLIX.   Which Foreshadows a General Gathering.....452

L.   We Are All in My Father's Net..................457

LI.   An Encounter Showing My Father's Genius
        in a Strong Light.................................473

LII.   Strange Revelations, and My Grandfather
        Has His Last Outburst...........................489

LIII.   The Heiress Proves That She Inherits the
        Feud and I Go Drifting..........................503

LIV.   My Return to England............................517

LV.   I Meet My First Playfellow and Take My
        Punishment 522

LVI.   Conclusion 533

APPENDIXES

Appendix A:

A Note on the Text.....................................547

Appendix B:

Revisions of the Original Printed Text.............573

Appendix C:

Misprints, Punctuation, and Author's Errors in the
Present Edition Corrected for the Finally Revised
de Luxe Edition of 1897..............................610

Acknowledgments 613

INTRODUCTION

DURING his lifetime Meredith had to wait longer for recognition than his Victorian contemporaries, and after achieving wide acclaim and adulation as novelist and sage around the turn of the century his reputation went into an eclipse from which it has never fully emerged. Though to some extent he is at present accepted as a major novelist, this recognition has not been vital enough to win him the wider readership, with its sense of rediscovery, that has been extended to his nineteenth-century compeers. Various explanations have been offered for his neglect: that his "philosophy has not worn well";[1] that his scenes and characters are artificial, his style and commentary strained by "airs of intellectual superiority."[2]

Granted that Meredith's novels have their weaknesses, perhaps the neglect during his earlier career and after his death was partly due to the fact that he is a difficult and challengingly original novelist, not sufficiently accessible to be ever "popular," but having a great deal to offer the serious modern reader: moral complexity and psychological depth, often realized with poetic force and vividness; a sophisticated, innovatory craftsmanship; and an individual vision. The case for the continuing interest of Meredith's novels must go beyond generalities and be presented at some length, but another way of inviting attention to his work is to reissue his best novels in accessible editions.

It is true that the three novels that probably mark the peak of his achievement, *The Ordeal of Richard Feverel, Beauchamp's Career,* and *The Egoist* have been kept in print

[1] E. M. Forster, *Aspects of the Novel* (Harmonsworth, 1962), p. 97.
[2] Virginia Woolf, *The Common Reader*, Second Series (London, 1932), p. 233.

(though apparently *Beauchamp's Career* has not always been available in America); but valuable as these works are, they may prove daunting to anyone approaching Meredith for the first time—rather like presenting a climber with the highest peaks of a challenging new range without allowing him practice on the neighboring slopes. *The Adventures of Harry Richmond* is Meredith's most readable novel as well as one of his finest achievements. Later in life Meredith himself gave it a high place among his works: "Sometimes *Harry Richmond* is my favourite, but I am inclined to give the palm to *Beauchamp's Career*."[3]

The purpose of this present edition is to offer *Harry Richmond* as an introduction to his work, or in the case of more experienced readers, as an opportunity to renew or make acquaintance with a novel that has not been in print for some time. Meredith looked on each of his novels as "an experiment,"[4] and certainly even in an age of great productivity and individuality they offer an impressive range; but at the same time certain recognizable Meredithian qualities and concerns inevitably run through his work.

Considerable care has been taken to study the textual history of *Harry Richmond* and to make the present text a reliable and full one, if not definitive, so a special Note on the Text has been appended for those interested, and textual details are only mentioned in this critical introduction when they are especially relevant.

The kind of novel Meredith attempted in *Harry Richmond* may be better grasped by placing it briefly in the context of his other works and of their contemporary reception.[5] *Richard*

---

[3] Quoted by Lionel Stevenson, *The Ordeal of George Meredith* (London, 1954), p. 199.

[4] C. L. Cline, ed., *The Letters of George Meredith*, 3 vols. (Oxford, in press), I, 468; hereafter referred to as *Letters*.

[5] For a fuller treatment of the effects of the reception of Meredith's novels on his work see the present writer's articles: "The Reception of George Meredith's Novels," *Nineteenth-Century Fiction*, IX (June 1964), 213–235; "Meredith's Attempts to Win Popularity," *Studies in English Literature*, IV (Autumn 1964), 637–651; "Meredith's Revisions of *Harry Richmond*," *Review of English Studies*, XIV (February 1963), 24–32; and "Meredith Achieves Recognition: The Reception of *Beauchamp's Career* and *The Egoist*," *Texas Studies in Literature* (forthcoming).

Feverel (1859), Meredith's first real novel, may have established him with the reading public, but disapproval on moral grounds led to its being banned from Mudie's circulating library. (His second and best volume of poems, *Modern Love* [1862], suffered a similar fate). In *Evan Harrington* (1861), and *Emilia in England* (1864, later renamed *Sandra Belloni*) Meredith resisted advice to emulate the exciting action of Smollett and Wilkie Collins (*The Woman in White* appeared contemporaneously with *Evan Harrington*), attempting instead a close comic study of character and society: "Interest, not to be false and evanescent, must kindle slowly, and ought to centre more in character—out of which incidents should grow."[6] Unfortunately these novels did not attract much notice.

To win a wider readership Meredith next wrote three novels that depended more on a chain of external events, involving mystery and excitement (Meredith's idea of "plot"), and unimpeded by analysis and commentary: *Rhoda Fleming* (1865), *Vittoria* (1866), and *Harry Richmond* (1871). The result was that the first two were even less successful with the public than their predecessors, mainly because the demands of an elaborate plot and Meredith's deeper purpose tended to pull in different directions instead of being fused together.

In *Harry Richmond*, however, Meredith did largely succeed in reconciling what seemed to him conflicting interests. But although achieving some success as a serial in the popular *Cornhill Magazine*, it was not much liked by reviewers, who ironically found it difficult rather than straightforward, and were puzzled rather than pleased by its originality. In his next two novels, *Beauchamp's Career* (1875) and *The Egoist*, (1879), Meredith refused to have his characters "boxed in a plot,"[7] and found unexpectedly that these were the works which carried him into more general favor.

Meredith's letters show that he began planning the novel that was to become *Harry Richmond* in 1861, nine years before it was published. It is first mentioned as "an autobiographic [first-person] story"[8] along with other works simmer-

---

[6] Letter to Samuel Lucas 1859, *Letters*, I, 49.
[7] Letter to George Bainton, 1887, *Letters*, II, 888.
[8] *Letters*, I, 95.

ing in his mind. It is referred to again in letters of March and May, 1864, along with several other works on hand, the novels *Rhoda Fleming* and *Vittoria*, and some verse.[9] When mentioned again it has become *"The Adventures of Richmond Roy and His Friend Contrivance Jack . . .* a spanking bid for popularity,"[10] but a manuscript sketch of it at this stage bears little relation to the final version (see A Note on the Text, p. 547). When Meredith was writing the novel he resented restrictions that seemed to be forced on him:

> The general public will not let me probe deeply into humanity. You must not paint either woman or man: a surface view of the species flat as a wafer is acceptable. I have not plucked at any of the highest and deepest chords. (Hence possibly) those who have heard some of the chapters [the early childhood ones?] say it must be the best novel I have written.[11]

Later he felt that he had not sacrificed his principles as a novelist, for he had followed his "scheme as a workman" to

> show the action of minds as well as of fortunes—of here and there men and women vitally animated by their brains at different periods of their lives—and of men and women with something of a look-out on the world and its destinies:—the mortal ones: the divine I leave to Doctors of D[ivinity].[12]

Apparently Meredith had revised the novel after first submitting it for *Cornhill* publication so "as to make it an almost entirely different thing,"[13] and all the suggestions are that if meant to be "popular," it was not meant to be a potboiler.

In reconciling "the action of minds as well as of fortunes" Meredith achieved an individual adaptation of the *Bildungsroman*, the moral education of the protagonist in his journey from childhood to maturity, the broad category into which *Harry Richmond* falls. In such a novel, the hero is launched on travels and adventures which serve to develop his nature. It is in keeping with Meredith's original mind that he chose

---

[9] *Letters*, I, 250, 254.

[10] *Letters*, I, 255.

[11] *Letters*, I, 412–413.

[12] *Letters*, I, 451. Meredith's correspondent, Augustus Jessopp, had just received an honorary Doctorate of Divinity from Oxford.

[13] *Letters*, I, 457.

a kind of unheroic hero who seems least likely to fit this demand of varied scene and action; for Harry is basically a passive, at the most a vacillating, character condemned to follow at the heels of others rather than call the tune himself. In fact his wavering unease and inability to act decisively at critical moments bring him closer to Arnold's Empedocles and Clough's "hero," Claude, from *Amours de Voyages* than his fictional autobiographic forerunners, so far as problems of dramatic presentation are concerned. Harry is Meredith's version of the ninetenth-century irresolute, self-divided, and self-conscious mind; but the emphasis is more on a personal drama (which of course does not make Harry's career un-typical) than one rooted in the intellectual and social currents of the day, though these currents do play a subsidiary part.

If Harry does not initiate action, he is tied to a father whose personal recklessness and grandiose aspirations ensure a brisk variation of scene, often on a "grand" scale. Indeed, action is an opiate for Roy, who deflates when denied an outlet for his amibitious scheming. Harry's comfort, on the other hand, is "the drug of passion," which absorbs his energies and delays action. For Harry (and Meredith), "the pleasant narrator in the first person is the happy babbling fool, not the philosopher who has come to know himself and his relations towards the Universe," whose "mind is bent upon the causes of events rather than their progress" (p. 536). Harry aims to stand "some-where between the two," but what is really attempted in the novel is a compromise between the critical and probing point of view congenial to Meredith and a simpler recording of people and events such as one finds in Esther Summerson's narrative. The exaggerated irony of "happy babbling fool" is directed at the reading public's lazy preference for more super-ficial novels. *Harry Richmond* thus depends more on drama-tization than, say, *The Egoist*, with its long passages of analysis and commentary, though Harry has felt it his duty to "expose the mechanism [of himself as autobiographer] when out of action."

If coupling Harry to such a father solved the problem of providing an eventful action (though I am not suggesting that Meredith himself saw the priorities this way), it served a more serious purpose by providing an opportunity to study a youth's education from a point of view not yet explored by other novelists. Harry's basic problem is to free himself from his dependence on his family—here reduced to his father, and to some extent his grandfather—which has sapped his growth as an individual. The other notable first-person heroes and heroines of Victorian fiction, Jane Eyre, David Copperfield, and Pip, had been orphans from the beginning, or near-beginning, of their careers. In *Harry Richmond* Meredith saw that one of the crucial tests of youth, perhaps *the* test, is to develop an individual self. In such a case as Harry's, where the child has become too involved with one parent (the father, in contrast to *Sons and Lovers*), this step can only be taken painfully and at the cost of at least a partial rejection. Meredith had treated this problem in *Richard Feverel* in a different way, but the only other Victorian novel to focus on it was Butler's *The Way of All Flesh*, published posthumously in 1903. But one of Harry's main appeals to our sympathy is that he is concerned to understand his father and can retain some love for him in the face of the total disapproval of others, instead of indulging in the more selfish and distorting rejection of Ernest in *The Way of All Flesh*. Harry lacks the touches of nobility to be found in Richard Feverel and Beauchamp, erring as they are, and in spite of his unusual situations he is closer to ordinary youth.

If one perceives, then, that the backbone of the novel is Harry's growth, or in Meredith's own term, close evolution,[14] it becomes a satisfying and intricate study of the "action of minds" that can underlie external adventures, though Harry's dominating father may deflect one's attention, as happened with the novel's first readers. Harry's growth is painfully slow and incomplete, and challengingly devious, lacking the more simplified linear development, with the clear-cut stages and final reach of achievement of its forerunners. In all his work Meredith showed a deeper understanding of character as a fluid process than any of his contemporaries, except George Eliot.

Harry's development has a distinctive movement which at times strains the basic need of the novel form for narrative

---

14 *Letters*, I, 415.

progression. As early as the end of Chapter II, Harry thinks of himself as "a kind of shuttlecock flying between two battle-dores," his father and his grandfather. (Later in the novel Harry is to play an actual game of shuttlecock with Janet as a partner.) This image refers not simply to the continuing battle for physical possession of Harry but for the shaping influence over him and his emotional allegiance, and it implies in Harry himself a lack of volition, a dependence restricting him to an oscillation that seems closer to repetition than progression. This movement characterizes Harry's moral direction for much of the novel and is aided by his continual relapses. The oscillation between grandfather and father is echoed by his later waverings between Ottilia and Janet, a wheel-within-a-wheel movement. So time and time again, to the very end, we see him resubmit to his dependence on his father, unhealthy as he knows it to be, to hanker after Ottilia even when he realizes in his heart that Janet is his more equal mate. Continually he falls victim to the blandishments of his pride and egotism, which he acknowledges and disavows to no apparent avail. Harry's fluctuations are also described through the figures of a "magnet" (Ottilia's rank) that both repels and attracts, and a "whirlwind." The "whirlwind" refers to Harry's inner turmoil and to its external counterpart: the momentum of Roy's final campaign which for the third time is to end in his "eclipse on the Continent" after "blazing over London" (p. 506).

Yet although Harry's moral career does seem to depend on the patterns of a closed circuit, if we read closely we can see that this movement more closely characterizes Roy, who, with his "unteachable spirit," can only travel in circles, no matter how rapid and varied his movements. Harry does achieve some growth, minimal though it may seem to be. Another figure, mentioned in Harry's talk with Dr. Julius Karsteg, is useful in describing Harry's career. The Professor opposes the stagnation of the English to the movement of the world, which

". . . moves by computation some considerable sum upwards of sixty thousand miles an hour."

"Not on a fresh journey—a recurring course!" said I.

> ". . . I grant you the physical illustration," the Professor con-
> tinued. . . . "The mind journeys somewhat in that way, and we in
> our old Germany hold that the mind advances notwithstanding.
> Astronomers condescending to earthly philosophy may admit that
> advance in the physical universe is computable though not per-
> ceptible. Somewhither we tend, shell and spirit." [P. 249]

Though Harry's course is for much of the time an apparently
oscillating or circular one, we may feel that he "advances
notwithstanding" through this mode, even if at times the
advance be virtually "not perceptible." This movement is a
part of the progress, as in an eddy or the most gradual of
spiral staircases.

Such a hero is likely to try the patience of a reader (as he
did that of the otherwise perceptive R. H. Hutton in the
Spectator in 1872[15]) unless he understands that the creation
of a nature like Harry's for the central role is an act of sympathy and understanding for which Meredith is not always
credited, though it is somewhat concealed by the self-censoring
eye of the narrator reflecting back over his life as a means of
subduing his pride, and inclined to be over-rigorous. If we
wonder at Harry's failing so often to seize his opportunities,
we must distinguish between the awareness of a self in process
of being formed, often trapped in ignorance or self-deception,
and his later detached awareness. Furthermore, behind Harry's conscious lapses is the compulsion of the past, rather than
willfulness, as he realizes later and expresses in a passage
striking for its perception of the interrelation of past, present,
and future:

> I see that I might have acted wisely, and did not; but that is
> a speculation taken apart from my capabilities. If a man's fate
> were as a forbidden fruit, detached from him, and in front of
> him, he might hesitate fortunately before plucking it; but, as
> most of us are aware, the vital half of it lies in the seed-paths he
> has traversed. We are sons of yesterday, not of the morning. The
> past is our mortal mother, no dead thing. Our future constantly
> reflects her to the soul. Nor is it ever the new man of today
> which grasps his future, good or ill. We are pushed to it by the

---

[15] *Spectator*, July 8, 1871, p. 839; reprinted in M. B. Forman, ed., *George
Meredith: Some Early Appreciations* (London, 1909).

hundreds of days we have buried, eager ghosts. And if you have
not a habit of taking counsel with them, you are but an instrument in their hands. [Pp. 269–270]

Harry to some extent escapes from the past in the only way—by
understanding and accepting ("taking counsel with") it. In
contrast, Roy, and the squire also, are tied to the past in a way
that predetermines their present and future.

Meredith feared with some reason that the unusually small
scale on which he developed Harry might dissipate the interest
of the general reader: "I fear I am evolving his personality too
closely for the public, but a man must work by the light of
his conscience if he's to do anything worth reading."[16] Elsewhere he writes:

> Note as you read the gradual changes of the growing Harry in
> the manner of regarding his father and the world. I have carried
> it so far as to make it perhaps dull during adolescence and young
> manhood, except to one *studying* [Meredith's italics] the narrative
> —as in the scenes with Dr. Julius.[17]

A sampling of some of the details of the novel may serve to
suggest the intricate and perceptive working out of Harry's
development. Early in Chapter I the child's point of view is
arrestingly declared in its simplicity and freshness when Harry
confronts his father for the first time:

> It appeared to him that the stranger was of enormous size,
> like the giants of fairybooks: for as he stood a little out of the
> doorway there was a peep of night sky and trees behind him and
> the trees looked very much smaller, and hardly any sky was to
> be seen except over his shoulders. [P. 8]

Along with its literal meaning this passage foreshadows how
Roy is to dominate Harry's life. Similarly proleptic is Roy's
injunction: "You must learn at any cost to know and love
your papa" (p. 9). Harry's love is of rapid growth, accelerated
rather than retarded by Roy's tantalizing absences; knowledge
is obscured and complicated, as well as guided, by the deep-
seated love.

The opening childhood chapters, besides offering the ap-

---

[16] *Letters*, I, 415.
[17] *Letters*, I, 453.

peal of a boy's wonder and excitement, provide a forcible picture of the way Roy's real charm as "magician" and "enchanter" captivates his son, weaning him away from any tentative grasp of the realities of his situation by encouraging him to live a great deal of his life in self-flattering fantasy. Harry's fantasies and dreams go beyond the romantic imaginings common to most children (including the fictional ones of the time), and express in a complex way the distorting effect of father on son. Roy's fantastic schemes, both imagined and realized, such as his grand London house with kings-of-England windows, build up dangerous expectancies that he can transform realities to suit his son's wishes. Harry's habit of living "out of myself in extreme flights of the imagination," of sliding easily from reality to fantasy, gives to his youthful, and to some extent, his later, life a kaleidoscopic effect, the process being speeded up by a freely roving and selective memory and the enforced changes of scene:

> I remember a pang I had when she [Mrs. Waddy] spoke of his exposure to the risk of marrying again; it added a conscious romantic tenderness to my adoration of him, and made me feel that he and I stood against the world. To have his hand in mine was my delight. Then it was that I could think earnestly of Prince Ahmed and the kind and beautiful Peribanou, whom I would not have minded his marrying. My favourite dream was to see him shooting an arrow in a match for a prize, and losing the prize because of not finding the arrow, and wondering where the arrow had flown to, and wandering after it till he passed out of green fields to grassy rocks, and to a stony desert, where at last he found his arrow at an enormous distance from the shooting line, and there was the desert all about him. . . . In his absence I really hungered for him and was jealous. During this Arabian life, we sat on a carpet that flew to the Continent, where I fell sick and was cured by smelling at an apple; and my father directed our movements through the end of a telescope. . . . As for the cities and cathedrals, the hot meadows under mountains, the rivers and the castles—they were little more than an animated book of geography, opening and shutting at random; and travelling from place to place must have seemed so much like the life I had led, that I was generally as quick to cry as to laugh, and was never at peace between any two emotions. By-and-by I lay in a gondola with a young lady. . . . [Pp. 31–32]

Here the fact and fantasy, so brilliantly interwoven by Meredith's adaptable style, jostle one another so closely that a reader may be forgiven for thinking at first that the "magic carpet" trip to the Continent is imaginary, and one wonders whether such rapid transitions contributed to the difficulty contemporary readers had in holding on to any central thread.[18] In the above passage Harry's developing inner life is not forgotten: the abrupt changes of scene are shown to have inwardly divisive, unsettling effects, echoed by his later oscillations.

The early part of the novel is notable for its brisk pace and rapidity of style, as Harry is subjected to dizzying changes: "'One minute I was curriously perusing the soft shade of a moustache on my aunt's upper lip; the next, we jumped into the carriage, and she was my dear Aunt Dorothy again, and the world began rolling another way" (p. 81).

Harry's growing independence of his father is represented as a gradual, at first unconscious, loosening of the bonds, rather than any sudden rupture. The first seeds of doubt appear in one of the vivid, darting glimpses into Harry's consciousness by means of metaphor that is one of Meredith's great skills, and which he varies with passages of slower but equally brilliant elaboration: "The intelligence [of Rippenger's criticism of his father for not paying Harry's school fees] filled my head like the buzz of a fly, occupying my meditations without leading them anywhere" (p. 50). Harry's brooding fit is dispersed in typical fashion by a leap of fantasy: "I was sure my father was a fountain of gold and only happened to be travelling."

When Harry finds his "lost" father "impersonating" a royal statue after an "odyssey" of search, we reach one of the climactic scenes of the novel marking the first definite stage in Harry's growing away from Roy. (Here the novel moves surely on its two levels, though when we come to the duel, event is more curtailed in favor of its consequences for Harry.) In handling the statue scene Meredith was well aware of the

---

[18] Meredith wrote to John Morley of "a lady—a great novel-reader—who finds *Harry Richmond* quite unintelligible in parts" (*Letters*, I, 432). See also contemporary reviews discussed in the articles referred to in footnote 5, above.

possibilities of the first-person point of view: "I resisted every temptation to produce great and startling effects (after the scene of the statue which was permissable in art, as coming from a boy and coloured by a boy's wonder)."[19] Yet the interest of the scene is not so much in the startling revelation of Roy when the statue comes alive as in the unexpected and subtle effects on Harry. His immediate emotional reaction is given with simplicity and economy suitable to a youth's feelings, yet it carries deeper, only partly conscious overtones:

> My head was like a ringing pan. I knew it was my father, but my father with death and strangeness, earth, metal about him; and his voice was like a human cry contending with earth and metal—mine was stifled. I saw him descend. I dismounted. We met at the ropes and embraced. All his figure was stiff, smooth, cold. My arms slid on him. Each time he spoke I thought it an unnatural thing. I myself had not spoken once. . . . There was no warmth to revive me in the gauntlet I clasped. I looked up at the sky, thinking it had fallen dark. [Pp. 156–157]

Here for the first time Harry feels a troubling separateness, a barrier between him and his father, without letting himself become fully aware of it. The association of death derives partly from Roy's appearance as a memorial-statue, but it carries suggestions of the hero's mortality (Roy is Harry's hero) and presages the death of Harry's ideal conception of their relationship. The "strangeness" reinforces the idea of separation, while "earth," probably suggested by the color of the paint and plaster, is an echo of death and at the same time an intimation that Harry's idol has feet of clay. The repetition of "metal" carries suggestions of the artificial as against straightforwardly human flesh. In his relentless pursuit of his delusion Roy does to some extent become dehumanized, a kind of heedless machine, especially towards the end. The impression of its having fallen dark foreshadows the eclipse of Harry's ideal.

Meredith skillfully pursues Harry's unusual, shocked state of mind, a kind of suspension of ordered thought and feeling: The "powers of my heart and will were frozen; I thought and felt at random," registering "trifling phenomena of sensa-

---

[19] *Letters*, I, 453.

tions," some apparently irrational, instead of a full picture. (Harry calls attention to Temple's account of the scene as a "truer historical picture" but questions even its complete truth.) But amid the apparently random thoughts is a key one he accepts but doesn't question, as the sky partakes further of his disappointment: "I thought to myself: this is my father and I am not overjoyed or grateful. In the same way I felt the sky was bronze, and I did not wonder at it" (p. 157). Though the whole scene is a moving one, it has an underlying irony, for the "enacting" of the romantically heroic image of the father leads not to joy but to disillusion and a sense of loss.

Harry's fears and conflicting feelings are conveyed at the end of the statue episode in one of the memorable dreams that Meredith can make so vivid and meaningful:

> My dreams led me wandering with a ship's diver under the sea, where we walked in a light of pearls and exploded old wrecks. I was assuring the glassy man that it was almost as clear beneath the waves as above, when I awoke to see my father standing over me in daylight; and in an ecstacy I burst into sobs. [P. 170]

Earlier, at Venice, Clara Goodwin had seemed to Harry like "rest and dreams . . . soft sea and pearls" (p. 32), a kind of oasis in his restless world. In his dream the sea and pearls suggest the security and happiness of the old life of romantic glamour that he wishes to recapture with his father, but there are hints of uncertainty: besides the ambiguous "exploded wrecks," both a romantic and a foreshadowing image, his father has been transformed into a diver, a "glassy man," a variation of the bronze-statue image and not his usual accessible self. In his assurances to the diver Harry is affirming that their relationship is still intact, or almost so: "I was assuring the glassy man that it was almost as clear beneath the glassy waves as above." Then suddenly the dreamer wakes into real daylight, all barriers drop away as his father's newly regained physical presence is confirmed, melting all doubts and fears in an ecstacy of relieved happiness. A later dim and ironic echo of the dream occurs when, running up against Roy's embarrassingly deluded inflexibility, Harry wishes "we two were at the bottom of the sea" (p. 357).

The process of Harry's growth is traced with the same psychological penetration, the same subtlety and richness in exploring and realizing his feelings and attitudes, as we have glimpsed in its beginnings. His oscillation between Ottilia and Janet is a further means of education, echoing and complementing what becomes his "struggle" with his father; but because the emphasis is perforce on father and son, these two women characters cannot emerge with the same fullness as Roy and Harry. Meredith himself defended on this ground the extent to which Ottilia is a partial portrait,[20] but the demands of the theme, of the first-person point of view, and of plot were also restricting. In curtailing these characters (and Heriot and Kiomi, who would have been allowed a subplot by other novelists) in the interests of the main theme, Meredith's method looks forward to the exclusions of the methods of James rather than backwards to the amplitude which allowed subsidiary characters more of a "separate" life in the novels of other Victorian contemporaries and predecessors. The numerous minor characters dotted along Harry's path, and all relevant to his growth and fortunes, do not spring into such instantaneous and memorable life as those in *David Copperfield*, but Meredith, being more intent on the intracacies and development of character than Dickens, needed a less eventful scene to build up a wider assemblage of notable characters than the few principals. In *Beauchamp's Career* he was able to take advantage of such freedom. But if one accepts Meredith's purpose, Ottilia and Janet are satisfying in their roles, and we can be content with occasional glimpses of the Heriot-Kiomi, Mabel Sweetwinter–Edbury, stories rather than a fuller tracing of them, as contributing to the thematic frame of reference and to some density of milieu. The relationships of seducer and seduced represent old ground in the Victorian novel (there are echoes of Steerforth and Emily), but Meredith makes his own sparing and unsentimental use of them without involving himself in mere imitation.

If at first sight Ottilia seems too shadowy and idealized, we must make allowance for Harry's romantic veneration of her rank and his awe of her capabilities for rational and inde-

---

[20] *Letters*, I, 468.

pendent choice—the qualities in which he himself is so lacking. In addition, Ottilia herself, for all her strengths, shows the inexperience and fervours of youth, as in her "child's enthusiasm for England" which encourages her in thinking Harry "superior to the passions of other men" (p. 307). She too moves towards responsible independence instead of possessing it from the start, though she moves more surely than Harry. As he acknowledges, hers is an "impulsive over-generous heart" which, along with her youth and romanticism, serves sufficiently to make her human and to offset Harry's tendency to idolize her as a "touchstone, a relentless mirror, a piercing eye, a mind severe as the Goddess of the God's head . . . a remorseless intellect" (p. 442). Ottilia is a "touchstone," a mirror, in showing up Harry's weakness, but never a "relentless" one, except in *his* mind—even under great provocation and disappointment she never reproaches him or shows regret.

Nevertheless, Ottilia has to experience her own "successive shocks of discernment" (p. 458), which further emphasize the near-circular nature of Harry's growth. In three climactic scenes, partly repetitive but cumulative, they are brought to realize one another's limitations, though Ottilia emerges as the stronger character. Ottilia is faced with Harry's inability to speak out manfully and claim her on the basis of clear-sighted love rather than romantic passion. Two of the testing scenes occur when Harry is convalescent: after the duel and after the gypsy attack. In between these is a scene in the Lake Palace library where the lovers reach an understanding, only to have it shattered by the violent interference of Roy. Although the scenes expose the same weaknesses and illusions in the lovers, through them Harry comes increasingly to recognize that Ottilia is too rational and self-reliant to conform to his romantic fantasies, and he is able in the end to accept her inevitable loss without the bitterness and wounded pride that have in the past placed him in the hands of his father. Indeed after the library scene it gradually emerges that Harry maintains only a token lover's allegiance; one of the interesting phases of his development is his regretting the loss, but at the same time unconsciously accepting it in advance, and even assisting it by refraining from the obvious positive steps until it is too late. As usual Harry is slow in making his growing attitudes conscious. It is the lovers' moral inequality that drives them apart, not so much the social disparity, which could have been overcome. In aspiring to Ottilia, Harry realizes at last that he is demanding too much of his own nature, just as his father strained to act a part as a statue of royalty, and later as social meteor in London. Yet Ottilia is far from being an idealized guiding angel like Agnes Wickfield, and it might be remarked that Dickens does not allow David Copperfield to offend convention by consciously oscillating between Dora and Agnes. Instead he is able to accept each in "proper" sequence.

Janet Ilchester has even less room than Ottilia to move and display her nature independently of Harry's biased vision. She moves for most part in the shadow of the squire. Perhaps there is some weakness in Meredith's craftsmanship here, for later she has to step forth to play a major role. Janet alienates Harry's sympathies from the start because she joins "the mysterious league" against his father, but his changing attitude towards her, devious as usual, is delicately intimated and foreshadowed. Her "orderly simple unpretendingness of nature," and her "straightforward intellect," both attract and repel him because they make her unamenable to his romantic wishes and hold the mirror up to his weaknesses. Furthermore, Janet lacks the glamour of rank and of the reach of intellect that helps to attract Harry to Ottilia. It is unnecessary and beyond the scope of the novel to reconcile Janet as a spoiled child with the mature woman; we can accept the change, and for a large part we can allow for Harry's obvious prejudice, replaced by his later condescension and complacent ownership. We should note also the opinion of other characters and his open intimations of his biased view. When Janet has more opportunity to act, as in the four chapters deleted in revision, she becomes a more substantial figure, especially at the end where it is most necessary. This is one of the reasons why the original version may be preferred.

Harry's loss of Ottilia has a further educative effect that is developed, if not completed, by his later relationship with Janet in scenes which again bring out the novel's characteristic movement. In the scene where Ottilia shelters under the boat in the storm, and in the library meeting, Harry manages to achieve a real, if transitory, sense of release from self, through a wordless but strongly felt communication with another person, respecting rather than seeking to extinguish her personality. These occasions gain Harry his few moments of peace and poise.

The final reconciliation of Harry and Janet, following a greater turbulence of feeling than perhaps he has ever experienced before, develops this series of self-victories in another wordless scene of felt understanding occurring in the deleted chapter LVIII, "My Subjection":

> Janet and I sat long into the night, not uttering one word of love.
>
> "Morning's outside," I said.
>
> She answered, "I don't know what morning is."
>
> "You have a dark line under your eyes."
>
> "My own doing."
>
> "Mine."
>
> "Then it will not disfigure me."
>
> We gazed at the clock on the mantlepiece, named the hour and forgot the hour.
>
> When we parted she kissed me—she bent over to me at half-arm's length, and put her lips to my cheek.
>
> Might I then have overcome her resolution [of marrying Edbury] by taking advantage of the thankful tenderness which blessed me for respecting her?
>
> Forms of violation that trample down another's will are pardonable—can well be justified in the broad working world, considering what it is composed of. If you admit the existence of a more delicate and higher world, you understand that I did not lose by abnegation . . . .

The liberation of Harry's sexuality following his break with his father and Ottilia is part of the background of this scene and has been evident in a growing, but suppressed, appreciation of Janet's physical attractiveness, a reversal in Harry's feelings that is typically developed in a series of small touches. This release is expressed in Harry's affair with Jenny Chassediane shown in glimpses that are even more fragmentary—insufficiently so, in the revised version. Though mindful of conventions in this brief, indirect treatment, Meredith has broken with them to some extent and thereby extended the presentation of the Victorian autobiographic hero in the interests of truthfulness.

Harry's outburst of freedom is more directly shown when he returns to make "hot love" to the betrothed Janet, forcing his attentions and caresses upon her in a way that scandalized contemporary readers. It is out of such reaction to the curbs placed unavailingly and unrealistically on his nature that he rises to the moment of self-conquest quoted above. It is not presented as a big scene or as a final victory, but given its placing in the series and its nature, one may well feel that such moments will become more accessible in the future after Harry returns from his wanderings still true to the pledge of this moment. For the novel offers us more the beginnings, or first painful foundations, of self-education than a finished process as previous novels had done. The reader's sympathy is maintained, like that of Ottilia's, Harry's "keenest reader," by a perception of "what could be wrought out of him," and we leave him at the end showing only qualified promise, "still subject to the relapses of a not perfectly right nature." Perhaps the main confirmation that Harry has developed is the cumulatively forceful, if indirect, evidence of his whole narrative: the unshrinking honesty that he brings to his review of the past, guaranteeing that he "can no longer have much of the hard grain of pride in him" (p. 275).

Harry's evolution typifies Meredith's predominantly rational view of life: human nature can develop through self-knowledge and self-effort. But the process is not made alluringly easy or universal: it is not short-lived but life-long, and counterbalanced by the picture of the "unteachable" Roy, who is neither a "progressive comedy" nor a tragic victim of circumstances, but something of both. It is unnecessary to dwell on Roy's nature and its great appeal for the reader, as it has been discussed by many commentators and is so palpable that he has tended to steal the limelight, as Falstaff (with whom we are implicitly invited to compare him, for example, on p. 63) did for some critics in *Henry IV*. Harry is sometimes called "Hal" and implicitly compared with the Prince Hal of that play, who, unlike Harry, is able to renounce the companions who are bad influences and accept responsibility without protracted struggle. When Roy, in one of his unbalanced outbursts bids his audience at the City Banquet to "beware of princes, beware of idle princes" (p. 532), his advice is an ironic inversion of Henry IV's warning to his son and of Roy's own life-long reverence for royalty. At other moments Roy has provided a parody of Tamburlaine ("To avoid swelling talk, I tell you, Richie, I have my hand on the world's wheel," p. 396), and even, though this is more tenuous, of Lear.[21]

While in my reading of *Harry Richmond* I have stressed the centrality of Harry's personal (but not untypical) growth, it does have its social aspects. Hereditary rank is looked upon as one of the false props which individuals blindly lean on instead of developing a positive, rational independence of mind and involvement with mankind. Alternatively, rank can be destructive not only through neglect of others but through resorting to rights and privileges as "forms of violation that trample down another's will." The novel makes it clear that Ottilia is prepared to step outside the restrictions of her privileged position in defiance of tradition, but instead of rising to meet her on her own rational grounds, Harry wavers because he puts a false value on rank and confuses her independence with condescension. Ironically, he deserves Prince Hermann's aristocratic judgment of being a "nullity" in "point of your individual will" (pp. 266–267), not because he is lowborn, but because of his limitations as a person. Rank

---

[21] The comparable passage from *Tamburlaine* is:
    I hold the Fates bound fast in iron chains,
    And with my hand turn Fortune's wheel about . . . .
                                   (I.2)
The more tenuous *King Lear* comparison is with the reunion of Lear with Cordelia (IV.7):

LEAR: Pray do not mock me.

But though Roy is to become "broken" in mind as well as in spirit and fortune like Lear, the pathos of Lear's humility and gropings towards sanity contrasts with Roy's compulsion to play the actor with "inveterate fancifulness," even in defeat, and to plead some self-justification. However, the squire's vindictive shattering of Roy's delusion, reducing him to childish helplessness and inconsequent wanderings about "Waddy's monument," is not without its touch of pathos.

is largely seen as opposed to human and social development in the novel because it is self-absorbed, backward-looking, and inflexible. The squire's case is similar: "a curious study to me of the Tory mind in its attachment to solidity, fixity, certainty, its unmatched generosity within a limit, its devotion to the family and the family eye for the country" (p. 332). Roy's social parades and intrigues in Bath and London carry an implied criticism of the pettiness and falsities of upper-class life, though we may agree with Hutton that the "vast detail" with which they are developed does not always maintain our interest. The political election is a satirical parody. However the social criticism of the novel, including both praise of England and attacks on her, is meant to support the central theme rather than to exert much separable interest, a point underlined by the fact that in the manuscript Meredith pruned it down. In his next novel, *Beauchamp's Career*, he was to concentrate on political and social issues as the main means of developing the destinies of his characters and of suggesting "the state of the country." Some of the social criticism of *Harry Richmond* looks forward to this novel, as do two of its images: horsewhipping images occur in Roy's first (p. 11) and last (pp. 494–495) clash with the squire, whereas this violence achieves a reverberating, if indirect, enactment in the next novel; the imagery of gourds or pumpkins applied to the aristocracy in Roy's speech at the City Banquet and previously by Karsteg is also echoed.

One of Harry's aids in looking at his past honestly is to try "to shape his style to harmonize with every development of his nature" (p. 275). Though understandably not as thoroughgoing in the adaptation of style to narrator as some twentieth-century novels, Meredith is more aware of the problem and more successful in overcoming it than any other novelist up to his time. This harmonizing was all the more challenging to a writer with a developed personal style running to mannerisms that act like trademarks. Meredith also had to balance the claims of maintaining a complicated narrative of external events, which does not leave as much room for modulations of style as narratives based more exclusively on a single consciousness and more dependent on impressions. Nevertheless, the attuning of style to attitude, consciousness, and mood

frequently delights the reader of *Harry Richmond*. Virginia
Woolf pays tribute to the way

> the story bowls smoothly along the road . . . of autobiographical
> narrative. It is a boy speaking, a boy thinking, a boy adventuring.
> For that reason, no doubt, the author has curbed his redundance
> and pruned his speech. The style is the most rapid possible. It
> runs smooth without a kink in it . . . with its precise adroit
> phrases, its exact quick glance at visible things.[22]

We have already noticed other qualities of style in sampling
aspects of Harry's early development. Even external adventures can have the vividness and excitement of dream when
viewed through Harry's transforming imagination, as with
the adventures in the fog, in the country, and in London.

An interesting example of Meredith's subtle use of detail
that one savors on rereadings occurs in the scene of the fire
at the Bench prison, an occasion for one of Harry's imaginative flights. Here his wonder and excitement yield momentarily to a "painful" glimpse of Lear's "unaccommodated
man," in the form of a "poor half-naked old woman" looking
"like a singed turkey" as she jumps to safety with the help of
Harry and Temple, who are disturbed by her plight while
onlookers laugh. When Harry goes to sleep that night aboard
the *Priscilla* the old woman with her "fowl-like cry and limbs
in the air" flashes briefly into his dreams, jostling other impressions of the eventful day. During the duel some years
later Harry's "vividest" thought is a picture of the same old
woman. Though unaccountably random to Harry we may see
it as a deflating image called to mind at the beginning of
Harry's revulsion against the senseless vanity of the duel.

It is not only in the boyhood sections of the novel that Meredith's style is so flexible and expressive. The attuning of
landscape to feeling, as in Harry's feverish ride through the
heat in Germany, or the yachting scenes, is usually done with
tact and economy that avoids the lumpiness of the set-piece,
such as the "Ferdinand and Miranda" scene in *Richard
Feverel* and the cherry tree in *The Egoist*. The freneticism of
Harry's uncertain amorous adventures in Germany is well
caught:

---

[22] *The Common Reader*, p. 230.

> Off I flew, tearing through dry underwood, and round the
> bend of the lake, determined to confront her, wave the man aside,
> and have my say with the false woman. . . . Blood was inflamed,
> brain bare of vision: "He takes her hand, she jumps from the
> boat; he keeps her hands, she feigns to withdraw [them]. . . ."
> [P. 257]

The staccato movement conveys Harry's jealousy, but the
phrases about "blood" and "brain" may sound closer to
Meredithian doctrine than to interpolations of Harry's reflective mind. Similarly, the compulsive Meredithian epigram
sometimes obtrudes in Harry's reflections, though generally
it occurs in dramatized form in the speech of Roy and De
Witt, often dubiously witty and strained, even if intentionally
so. But it would be a carping critic who would single out
Meredith's lapses in harmonizing style and narrator in this
novel.

The imaginative resources of Meredith's style, so skillful
in capturing finer shades of mood and feeling here as in his
other novels, may be seen in the evocation of Harry's strange
mood of self-protective, assumed calm:

> . . . the strange mood, half stupor, half the folding-in of pas-
> sion; it was such magical happiness. Not to be awake, yet vividly
> sensible; to lie calm and reflect, and only to reflect; to be satisfied
> with each succeeding hour and the privations of the hour, and, as
> if in the depths of a smooth water, to gather fold over patient fold
> of the submerged self, safe from wounds; the happiness was not
> noble, but it breathed and was harmless, and it gave me rest
> when the alternative was folly and bitterness. [Pp. 253–254]

One final point to be mentioned is the truthfulness of the
scenes and characters, which has been questioned in this and
other Meredith novels by a critic as perceptive as Virginia
Woolf. There is little point in describing *Harry Richmond*
as a romance, as contemporaries classified it, except in drawing
attention to the greater liberties with probability Meredith
takes here than in, say, *Beauchamp's Career* and *The Egoist*.
Instead of being restricted in their humanity, the two main
characters have more room to develop in strict accord with
psychological and moral, if not "outer," realities. Roy, for all
his unusual circumstances, in fact because of them, emerges

with a memorable largeness and animation. Though he threatens to overshadow Harry, Roy really serves to throw Harry's problems—to a large extent the problems of youth—into greater relief, for the scale and vitality of his own infectious delusion magnifies Harry's egoism. Pip's weaknesses, encouraged by "great expectations," are similarly magnified by the unusual, and it might be noted in passing that in both novels a secret gift of money encourages delusions and plays a part in destroying them. But if *Harry Richmond* takes liberties with probabilities, many of the occasions of chance and coincidence are only apparently random; for as Barbara Hardy has shown,[23] it is an anti-Providence novel, in contrast to *Jane Eyre*. Part of Harry's bitter self-discovery is to realize that what he or his father have considered as chance occurrences are usually the result of the "actions of minds," not of an unfriendly fate or a protective Providence. Harry's beating at the hands of the gypsies is the result of mistaken identity, but Harry makes himself vulnerable by his self-immersion, his readiness to fight a second duel, again out of wounded pride, and to deny the promptings of his heart in going straight to Heriot instead of Riversley and Janet. So in a sense Harry "deserves" the beating, though ironically its deflating effects are short-lived as usual. Along with this thematic and ironic use of chance, *Harry Richmond* consistently exposes the falseness and excesses of one kind of romantic vision, so that in a sense it is an anti-romantic novel, even an anti-romance, as well as an anti-Providence novel.

The novel may also seem somewhat unreal to readers not used to Meredith because he neglects one of the more usual ways of achieving "solidity of specification." The realistic particulars of environment, including a high degree of ordinary detail, are thin compared with their density in other Victorian novels. Meredith was impatient with such aids to credulity that rely on the "impressionable senses" and introduce "the dust of the struggling outer world" (*The Egoist*), and instead concentrated his attention on what he thought mattered most: the particulars of inner character in all its dynamic complexity, gradually revealed. Here he is able to

---

[23] *The Appropriate Form* (London, 1964), p. 85.

work with detailed insight and yet with intensity. If we grant the grounds of his appeal, as we should do with all novelists, Meredith offers rewards. It is not wholly true, as Virginia Woolf says, that *Harry Richmond* "bowls smoothly along the road which Dickens has already trodden of autobiographical narrative";[24] to a great extent Meredith pioneers his own route, here as elsewhere, and one of his enduring appeals is an individuality of mind that does not date or become mannered, because its adventurousness is guided by honesty and insight.

L. T. Hergenhan

University of Tasmania

---

[24] *The Common Reader*, p. 230.

SELECTED BIBLIOGRAPHY

Cline, C. L., ed. *The Letters of George Meredith*. 3 vols. Oxford, in press.

Hardy, Barbara. " 'A Way to Your Hearts through Fire and Water': The Structure of Imagery in *Harry Richmond*," *Essays in Criticism*, X (April 1960), 163–180. Reprinted in Barbara Hardy, *The Appropriate Form* (London, 1964).

Hergenhan, L. T. "Meredith's Attempts to Win Popularity," *Studies in English Literature*, IV (Autumn 1964), 637–651.

———. "Meredith's Revisions of *Harry Richmond*," *Review of English Studies*, XIV (February 1963), 24–32.

Hudson, Richard B. "Meredith's Autobiography and 'The Adventures of Harry Richmond,' " *Nineteenth-Century Fiction*, IX (June 1954), 38–49.

Hutton, R. H. *Spectator*, July 8, 1871, p. 839. Reprinted in M. B. Forman, ed., *George Meredith: Some Early Appreciations* (London, 1909).

Kelvin, Norman. *A Troubled Eden: Nature and Society in the Works of George Meredith*. Edinburgh and Stanford, 1961.

Lindsay, Jack. *George Meredith: His Life and Work*. London, 1956.

Photiades, Constantin. *George Meredith*. Paris, 1910; London, 1911.

Priestley, J. B. *George Meredith*. London, 1926.

Sasson, Siegfried. *Meredith*. London, 1948.

Stevenson, Lionel. *The Ordeal of George Meredith*. London, 1954; New York, 1953.

Woolf, Virginia. *The Common Reader*. Second series. London and New York, 1932.

———. *Granite and Rainbow*. London, 1958.

Wright, Walter F. *Art and Substance in George Meredith*. Lincoln, Nebr., 1953.

The Adventures of Harry Richmond

THE ADVENTURES

OF

HARRY RICHMOND.

CHAPTER I.

I AM A SUBJECT OF CONTENTION.

ONE midnight of a winter month the sleepers in Riversley Grange were awakened by a ringing of the outer bell and blows upon the great hall-doors. Squire Beltham was master there: the other members of the household were, his daughter Dorothy Beltham; a married daughter Mrs. Richmond; Benjamin Sewis, an old half-caste butler; various domestic servants; and a little boy, christened Harry Lepel Richmond, the squire's grandson. Riversley Grange lay in a rich watered hollow of the Hampshire heath-country; a lonely circle of enclosed brook and pasture, within view of some of its dependent farms, but out of hail of them, or any dwelling except the stables and the head-gardener's cottage. Traditions of audacious highwaymen, together with the gloomy surrounding fir-scenery, kept it alive to fears of solitude and the night; and there was that in the determined violence of the knocks and repeated bell-peals which assured all those who had ever listened in the servants' hall to prognostications of a possible night attack, that the robbers had come at last most awfully. A crowd of maids gathered along the upper corridor of the main body of the building: two or three footmen hung lower down, bold in attitude. Suddenly the noise ended, and soon after the voice of old Sewis commanded them to scatter away to their beds; whereupon the footmen took agile leaps to the post of danger, while the women, in whose bosoms intense curiosity now supplanted terror, proceeded to a vacant room overlooking the front entrance, and spied from the window.

Meanwhile Sewis stood by his master's bedside. The squire was a hunter of the old sort: a hard rider, deep drinker, and heavy slumberer. Before venturing to shake his arm Sewis struck a light and flashed it over the squire's eyelids to make the task of rousing him easier. At the first touch the squire sprang up, swearing by his Lord Harry he had just dreamed of fire, and muttering of buckets.

"Sewis! you're the man, are you: where has it broken out?"

"No, sir; no fire," said Sewis; "you be cool, sir."

"Cool, sir! confound it, Sewis, haven't I heard a whole town of steeples at work? I don't sleep so thick but I can hear, you dog! Fellow comes here, gives me a start, tells me to be cool; what the deuce! nobody hurt, then? all right!"

The squire had fallen back on his pillow and was relapsing to sleep

Sewis spoke impressively: "There's a gentleman downstairs; a gentleman downstairs, sir. He has come rather late"

"Gentleman downstairs come rather late." The squire recapitulated the intelligence to possess it thoroughly. "Rather late, eh? Oh! Shove him into a bed, and give him hot brandy and water, and be hanged to him!"

Sewis had the office of tempering a severely distasteful announcement to the squire.

He resumed: "The gentleman doesn't talk of staying. That is not his business. It's rather late for him to arrive."

"Rather late!" roared the squire. "Why, what's it o'clock?"

Reaching a hand to the watch over his head, he caught sight of the unearthly hour. "A quarter to two? Gentleman downstairs? Can't be that infernal apothecary who broke 's engagement to dine with me last night? By George, if it is I'll souse him; I'll drench him from head to heel as though the rascal 'd been drawn through the duckpond. Two o'clock in the morning? Why, the man's drunk. Tell him I'm a magistrate, and I'll commit him, deuce take him; give him fourteen days for a sot; another fourteen for impudence. I've given a month 'fore now. Comes to me, a Justice of the peace!—man's mad! Tell him he's in peril of a lunatic asylum. And doesn't talk of staying? Lift him out o' the house on the top o' your boot, Sewis, and say it's mine; you've my leave."

Sewis withdrew a step from the bedside. At a safe distance he fronted his master steadily; almost admonishingly. "It's Mr. Richmond, sir," he said.

"Mr. . . . ." The squire checked his breath. That was a name never uttered at the Grange. "The scoundrel?" he inquired harshly, half in the tone of one assuring himself, and his rigid dropped jaw shut.

The fact had to be denied or affirmed instantly, and Sewis was silent.

Grasping his bedclothes in a lump, the squire cried: "Downstairs? downstairs, Sewis? You've admitted him into my house!"

"No, sir."

"You have!"

"He is not in the house, sir."

"You have! How did you speak to him, then?"

"Out of my window, sir."

"What place here is the scoundrel soiling now?"

"He is on the doorstep outside the house."

"Outside, is he? and the door's locked?"

"Yes, sir."

"Let him rot there!"

By this time the midnight visitor's patience had become exhausted. A renewal of his clamour for immediate attention fell on the squire's ear, amazing him to stupefaction at such challenging insolence.

"Hand me my breeches," he called to Sewis; "I can't think brisk out of my breeches."

Sewis held the garment ready. The squire jumped from the bed, fuming speechlessly, chafing at gaiters and braces, cravat and coat, and allowed his buttons to be fitted neatly on his calves; the hammering at the hall-door and plucking at the bell going on without intermission. He wore the aspect of one who assumes a forced composure under the infliction of outrages on his character in a Court of Law, where he must of necessity listen and lock his boiling replies within his indignant bosom.

"Now, Sewis, now my horsewhip," he remarked, as if it had been a simple adjunct of his equipment.

"Your hat, sir?"

"My horsewhip, I said."

"Your hat is in the hall," Sewis observed gravely.

"I asked you for my horsewhip."

"That is not to be found anywhere," said Sewis.

The squire was diverted from his objurgations against this piece of servitorial defiance by his daughter Dorothy's timid appeal for permission to come in. Sewis left the room. Presently the squire descended, fully clad, and breathing sharply from his nostrils. Servants were warned off out of hearing; none but Sewis stood by.

The squire himself unbolted the door, and threw it open to the limit of the chain.

"Who's there?" he demanded.

A response followed promptly from outside: "I take you to be Mr. Harry Lepel Beltham. Correct me if I err. Accept my apologies for disturbing you at a late hour of the night, I pray."

"Your name?"

"Is plain Augustus Fitz-George Roy Richmond at this moment, Mr. Beltham. You will recognize me better by opening your door entirely: voices are deceptive. You were born a gentleman, Mr. Beltham, and will not reduce me to request you to behave like one. I am now in the position, as it were, of addressing a badger in his den. It is on both sides unsatisfactory. It reflects egregious discredit upon you, the householder."

The squire hastily bade Sewis see that the passages to the sleeping apartments were barred, and flung the great chain loose. He was acting under strong control of his temper.

It was a quiet grey night, and as the doors flew open, a largely-built man, dressed in a high-collared great-coat and fashionable hat of the time, stood clearly defined to view. He carried a light cane, with the point of the silver handle against his under lip. There was nothing formidable in his appearance, and his manner was affectedly affable. He lifted his hat as soon as he found himself face to face with the squire, disclosing a partially bald head, though his

whiskering was luxuriant, and a robust condition of manhood was indicated by his erect attitude and the immense
swell of his furred greatcoat at the chest. His features
were exceedingly frank and cheerful. From his superior
height, he was enabled to look down quite royally on the
man whose repose he had disturbed.

The following conversation passed between them.

"You now behold who it is, Mr. Beltham, that acknowledges to the misfortune of arousing you at an unseemly
hour—unbetimes, as our gossips in mother Saxon might say
—and with profound regret, sir, though my habit is to take
it lightly."

"Have you any accomplices lurking about here ?"

"I am alone."

"What's your business ?"

"I have no business."

"You have no business to be here, no. I ask you what's
the object of your visit ?"

"Permit me first to speak of the cause of my protracted
arrival, sir. The ridicule of casting it on the post-boys will
strike you, Mr. Beltham, as it does me. Nevertheless, I
must do it; I have no resource. Owing to a rascal of the
genus, incontinent in liquor, I have this night walked seven
miles from Ewling. My complaint against him is not on
my own account."

"What brought you here at all ?"

"Can you ask me ?"

"I ask you what brought you to my house at all ?"

"True, I might have slept at Ewling."

"Why didn't you ?"

"For the reason, Mr. Beltham, which brought me here
originally. I could not wait—not a single minute. So far
advanced to the neighbourhood, I would not be retarded, and
I came on. I crave your excuses for the hour of my arrival.
The grounds for my coming at all you will very well understand, and you will applaud me when I declare to you that
I come to her penitent; to exculpate myself, certainly, but
despising self-justification. I love my wife, Mr. Beltham.
Yes; hear me out, sir. I can point to my unhappy star,
and say, blame that more than me. That star of my birth
and most disastrous fortunes should plead on my behalf to
you ; to my wife at least it will."

" You've come to see my daughter Marian, have you ?"

" My wife, sir."

" You don't cross my threshold while I live."

" You compel her to come out to me ?"

" She stays where she is, poor wretch, till the grave takes her. You've done your worst ; be off."

" Mr. Beltham, I am not to be restrained from the sight of my wife."

" Scamp !"

" By no scurrilous epithets from a man I am bound to respect will I be deterred or exasperated."

" Damned scamp, I say !" The squire having exploded his wrath gave it free way. " I've stopped my tongue all this while before a scoundrel 'd corkscrew the best-bottled temper right or left, go where you will one end o' the world to the other, by God ! And here's a scoundrel stinks of villany, and I've proclaimed him 'ware my gates as a common trespasser, and deserves hanging if ever rook did nailed hard and fast to my barn doors ! comes here for my daughter, when he got her by stealing her, scenting his carcase, and talking 'bout his birth, singing what not sort o' foreign mewin' stuff, and she found him out a liar and a beast, by God ! And she turned home. My doors are open to my flesh and blood. And here she halts, I say, 'gainst the law, if the law's against me. She's crazed : you've made her mad ; she knows none of us, not even her boy. Be off ; you've done your worst; the light's gone clean out in her ; and hear me, you Richmond, or Roy, or whatever you call yourself, I tell you I thank the Lord she has lost her senses. See her or not, you've no hold on her, and see her you shan't while I go by the name of a man."

Mr. Richmond succeeded in preserving an air of serious deliberation under the torrent of this tremendous outburst, which was marked by scarce a pause in the delivery.

He said, " My wife deranged ! I might presume it too truly an inherited disease. Do you trifle with me, sir ? Her reason unseated ! and can you pretend to the right of dividing us ? If this be as you say—Oh ! ten thousand times stronger my claim, my absolute claim, to cherish her. Make way for me, Mr. Beltham. I solicit humbly the holiest privilege sorrow can crave of humanity. My wife ! my wife ! Make way for me, sir."

His figure was bent to advance. The squire shouted an order to Sewis to run round to the stables and slip the dogs loose.

"Is it your final decision?" Mr. Richmond asked.

"Damn your fine words! Yes, it is. I keep my flock clear of a foul sheep."

"Mr. Beltham, I implore you, be merciful. I submit to any conditions : only let me see her. I will walk the park till morning, but say that an interview shall be granted in the morning. Frankly, sir, it is not my intention to employ force : I throw myself utterly on your mercy. I love the woman; I have much to repent of. I see her, and I go; but once I must see her. So far I also speak positively."

"Speak as positively as you like," said the squire.

"By the laws of nature and the laws of man, Marian Richmond is mine to support and comfort, and none can hinder me, Mr. Beltham; none, if I resolve to take her to myself."

"Can't they!" said the squire.

"A curse be on him, heaven's lightnings descend on him, who keeps husband from wife in calamity!"

The squire whistled for his dogs.

As if wounded to the quick by this cold-blooded action, Mr. Richmond stood to his fullest height.

"Nor, sir, on my application during to-morrow's daylight shall I see her?"

"Nor, sir, on your application"—the squire drawled in uncontrollable mimicking contempt of the other's florid forms of speech, ending in his own style,—"no, you won't."

"You claim a paternal right to refuse me : my wife is your child. Good. I wish to see my son."

On that point the squire was equally decided. "You can't. He's asleep."

"I insist."

"Nonsense : I tell you he's a-bed and asleep."

"I repeat, I insist."

"When the boy's fast asleep, man!"

"The boy is my flesh and blood. You have spoken for your daughter—I speak for my son. I will see him, though I have to batter at your doors till sunrise."

Some minutes later the boy was taken out of his bed by his aunt Dorothy, who dressed him by the dark window-light, crying bitterly, while she said, "Hush, hush!" and fastened on his small garments between tender huggings of his body and kissings of his cheeks. He was told that he had nothing to be afraid of. A gentleman wanted to see him: nothing more. Whether the gentleman was a good gentleman, and not a robber, he could not learn: but his aunt Dorothy, having wrapped him warm in shawl and comforter, and tremblingly tied his hat-strings under his chin, assured him, with convulsive caresses, that it would soon be over, and he would soon be lying again snug and happy in his dear little bed. She handed him to Sewis on the stairs, keeping his fingers for an instant to kiss them: after which, old Sewis, the lord of the pantry, where all sweet things were stored, deposited him on the floor of the hall, and he found himself facing the man of the night. It appeared to him that the stranger was of enormous size, like the giants of fairy books: for as he stood a little out of the doorway there was a peep of night sky and trees behind him, and the trees looked very much smaller, and hardly any sky was to be seen except over his shoulders.

The squire seized one of the boy's hands to present him and retain him at the same time: but the stranger plucked him from his grandfather's hold, and swinging him high, exclaimed, "Here he is! This is Harry Richmond. He has grown a grenadier."

"Kiss the little chap and back to bed with him," growled the squire.

The boy was heartily kissed and asked if he had forgotten his papa. He replied that he had no papa: he had a mama and a grandpapa. The stranger gave a deep groan.

"You see what you have done; you have cut me off from my own," he said terribly to the squire; but tried immediately to soothe the urchin with nursery talk and the pats on the shoulder which encourage a little boy to grow fast and tall. "Four years of separation," he resumed, "and my son taught to think that he has no father. By heavens! it is infamous, it is a curst piece of inhumanity. Mr. Beltham, if I do not see my wife, I carry off my son."

"You may ask till you're hoarse, you shall never see her in this house while I am here to command," said the squire.

"Very well; then Harry Richmond changes homes. I take him. The affair is concluded."

"You take him from his mother?" the squire sang out.

"You swear to me she has lost her wits; she cannot suffer. I can. I shall not expect from you, Mr. Beltham, the minutest particle of comprehension of a father's feelings. You are earthy; you are an animal."

The squire saw that he was about to lift the boy, and said, "Stop, never mind that. Stop, look at the case. You can call again to-morrow, and you can see me and talk it over."

"Shall I see my wife?"

"No, you shan't."

"You remain faithful to your word, sir, do you?"

"I do."

"Then I do similarly."

"What! Stop! Not to take a child like that out of a comfortable house at night in Winter, man?"

"Oh, the night is temperate and warm; he shall not remain in a house where his father is dishonoured."

"Stop! not a bit of it," cried the squire. "No one speaks of you. I give you my word, you're never mentioned by man, woman or child in the house."

"Silence concerning a father insinuates dishonour, Mr. Beltham."

"Damn your fine speeches, and keep your blackguardly hands off that boy," the squire thundered. "Mind, if you take him, he goes for good. He doesn't get a penny from me if you have the bringing of him up. You've done for him, if you decide that way. He may stand here a beggar in a stolen coat like you, and I won't own him. Here, Harry, come to me; come to your grandad."

Mr. Richmond caught the boy just when he was turning to run.

"That gentleman," he said, pointing to the squire, "is your grandpapa. I am your papa. You must learn at any cost to know and love your papa. If I call for you to-morrow or next day they will have played tricks with Harry Richmond, and hid him. Mr. Beltham, I request you, for the final time, to accord me your promise—observe, I accept your promise—that I shall, at my demand, to-morrow or the next day, obtain an interview with my wife."

The squire coughed out an emphatic "Never!" and fortified it with an oath as he repeated it upon a fuller breath.

"Sir, I will condescend to entreat you to grant this permission," said Mr. Richmond, urgently.

"No, never: I won't!" rejoined the squire, red in the face from a fit of angry coughing. "I won't; but stop, put down that boy; listen to me, you Richmond! I'll tell you what I'll do. I'll—if you swear on a Bible, like a cadger before a bench of magistrates, you'll never show your face within a circuit o' ten miles hereabouts, and won't trouble the boy if you meet him, or my daughter, or me, or any one of us— harkye, I'll do this: let go the boy, and I'll give ye five hundred—I'll give ye a cheque on my banker for a thousand pounds; and, hark me out, you do this, you swear, as I said, on the servants' Bible, in the presence of my butler and me, 'Strike you dead as Ananias and t'other one if you don't keep to it,' do that now, here, on the spot, and I'll engage to see you paid fifty pounds a year into the bargain. Stop! and I'll pay your debts under two or three hundred. For God's sake, let go the boy! You shall have fifty guineas on account this minute. Let go the boy! And your son— there, I call him your son—your son, Harry Richmond, shall inherit from me; he shall have Riversley and the best part of my property, if not every bit of it. Is it a bargain! Will you swear? Don't, and the boy's a beggar, he's a stranger here as much as you. Take him, and by the Lord, you ruin him. There now, never mind, stay, down with him. He's got a cold already; ought to be in his bed; let the boy down!"

"You offer me money," Mr. Richmond answered. "That is one of the indignities belonging to a connection with a man like you. You would have me sell my son. To see my afflicted wife I would forfeit my heart's yearnings for my son; your money, sir, I toss to the winds; and I am under the necessity of informing you that I despise and loathe you. I shrink from the thought of exposing my son to your besotted selfish example. The boy is mine; I have him, and he shall traverse the wilderness with me. By heaven! his destiny is brilliant. He shall be hailed for what he is, the rightful claimant of a place among the proudest in the land; and mark me, Mr. Beltham, obstinate sensual old man that you are! I take the boy, and I consecrate my life to the duty of establishing him in his proper rank and station, and there, if you live and I live, you shall behold him and bow your grovelling pig's head to the earth, and bemoan the day, by heaven! when you,—a common country squire, a man of no origin, a creature with whose blood we have mixed ours —and he is stone-blind to the honour conferred on him— when you in your besotted stupidity threatened to disinherit Harry Richmond."

The door slammed violently on such further speech as he had in him to utter. He seemed at first astonished; but finding the terrified boy about to sob, he drew a pretty box from one of his pockets and thrust a delicious sweetmeat between the whimpering lips. Then, after some moments of irresolution, during which he struck his chest soundingly and gazed down, talked alternately to himself and the boy, and cast his eyes along the windows of the house, he at last dropped on one knee and swaddled the boy in the folds of the shawl. Raising him in a business-like way, he settled him on an arm and stepped briskly across gravel-walk and lawn, like a horse to whose neck a smart touch of the whip has been applied.

The soft mild night had a moon behind it somewhere; and here and there a light-blue space of sky showed small rayless stars; 'the breeze smelt fresh of roots and heath.' It was more a May-night than one of February. So strange an aspect had all these quiet hill-lines and larch and fir-tree tops in the half-dark stillness, that the boy's terrors were overlaid and almost subdued by his wonderment; he had never before been out in the night, and he must have feared to cry in it, for his sobs were not loud. On a rise of the park-road where a fir-plantation began, he heard his name called faintly from the house by a woman's voice that he knew to be his aunt Dorothy's. It came after him only once: "Harry Richmond;" but he was soon out of hearing, beyond the park, among the hollows that run dipping for miles beside the great high-road toward London. Sometimes his father whistled to him, or held him high and nodded a salutation to him, as though they had just discovered one another; and his perpetual accessibility to the influences of spicy sugar-plums, notwithstanding his grief, caused his father to prognosticate hopefully of his future wisdom. So, when obedient to command he had given his father a kiss, the boy fell asleep on his shoulder, ceasing to know that he was a wandering infant: and, if I remember rightly, he dreamed he was in a ship of cinnamon-wood upon a sea that rolled mightily, but smooth immense broad waves, and tore thing from thing without a sound or a hurt.

CHAPTER II.

AN ADVENTURE ON MY OWN ACCOUNT.

THAT night stands up without any clear traces about it or near it, like the brazen castle of romance round which the sea-tide flows. My father must have borne me miles along the road; he must have procured food for me; I have an idea of feeling a damp forehead and drinking new milk, and by-and-by hearing a roar of voices or vehicles, and seeing a dog that went alone through crowded streets without a master, doing as he pleased, and stopping every other dog he met. He took his turning, and my father and I took ours. We were in a house that, to my senses, had the smell of dark corners, in a street where all the house-doors were painted black, and shut with a bang. Italian organ-men and milk-men paraded the street regularly, and made it sound hollow to their music. Milk, and no cows anywhere; numbers of people, and no acquaintances among them;—my thoughts were occupied by the singularity of such things.

My father could soon make me forget that I was transplanted; he could act dog, tame rabbit, fox, pony, and a whole nursery collection alive, but he was sometimes absent for days, and I was not of a temper to be on friendly terms with those who were unable to captivate my imagination as he had done. When he was at home I rode him all round the room and upstairs to bed, I lashed him with a whip till he frightened me, so real was his barking; if I said "Menagerie" he became a caravan of wild beasts; I undid a button of his waistcoat, and it was a lion that made a spring, roaring at me; I pulled his coat-tails and off I went tugging at an old bear that swung a hind leg as he turned, in the queerest way, and then sat up and beating his breast sent out a mew-moan. Our room was richer to me than all the Grange while these performances were going forward. His monkey was almost as wonderful as his bear, only he was too big for it, and was obliged to aim at reality in his representation of this animal by means of a number of breakages; a defect that brought our landlady on the scene. The enchantment of my father's companionship caused me to suffer proportionately in his absence. During that period of solitude, my nursemaid had to order me to play, and I would stumble about and squat in the middle of the floor, struck suddenly by the marvel of the difference between my present and my other home. My father entered into arrangements with a Punch and Judy man for him to pay me regular morning visits opposite our window; yet here again his genius defeated his kind intentions; for happening once to stand by my side during the progress of the show, he made it so vivid to me by what he said and did, that I saw no fun in it without him: I used to dread the heralding crow of Punch if he was away, and cared no longer for wooden heads being knocked ever so hard. On Sundays we walked to the cathedral, and this was a day with a delight of its own for me. He was never away on the Sunday. Both of us attired in our best, we walked along the streets hand in hand; my father led me before the cathedral monuments, talking in a low tone of British victories, and commending the heroes to my undivided attention. I understood very early that it was my duty to imitate them. While we remained in the cathedral he talked of glory and Old England, and dropped his voice in the middle of a murmured chant to introduce Nelson's name or some other great man's: and this recurred regularly. "What are we for now?" he would ask me as we left our house. I had to decide whether we took a hero or an author, which I soon learnt to do with capricious resolution. We were one Sunday for Shakespeare; another for Nelson or Pitt. "Nelson, papa," was my most frequent rejoinder, and he never dissented, but turned his steps toward Nelson's cathedral dome, and uncovered his head there, and said: "Nelson, then, to-day;" and we went straight to his monument to perform the act of homage. I chose Nelson in preference to the others because near bed-time in the evening my father told me stories of our hero of the day, and neither Pitt nor Shakespeare lost an eye, or an arm, or fought with a huge white bear on the ice to make himself interesting. I named them occasionally out of compassion, and to please my father, who said that they ought to have a turn. They were, he told me, in the habit of paying him a visit, whenever I had particularly neglected them, to learn the grounds for my disregard of their claims, and they urged him to intercede with me, and imparted many of their unpublished adventures, so that I should be tempted to give them a chance on the following Sunday.

"Great Will," my father called Shakespeare, and "Slender Billy," Pitt. The scene where Great Will killed the deer, dragging Falstaff all over the park after it by the light of Bardolph's nose, upon which they put an extinguisher if they heard any of the keepers, and so left everybody groping about and catching the wrong person, was the most wonderful mixture of fun and tears. Great Will was extremely youthful, but everybody in the park called him, "Father William;" and when he wanted to know which way the deer had gone, King Lear (or else my memory deceives me) punned, and Lady Macbeth waved a handkerchief for it to be steeped in the blood of the deer; Shylock ordered one pound of the carcase; Hamlet (I cannot say why, but the fact was impressed on me) offered him a three-legged stool; and a number of kings and knights and ladies lit their torches from Bardolph; and away they flew, distracting the keepers and leaving Will and his troop to the deer. That poor thing died from a different weapon at each recital, though always with a flow of blood and a successful dash of his antlers into Falstaff; and to hear Falstaff bellow! But it was mournful to hear how sorry Great Will was over the animal he had slain. He spoke like music. I found it pathetic in spite of my knowing that the whole scene was lighted up by Bardolph's nose. When 1 was just bursting out crying—for the deer's tongue was lolling out and quick pantings were at his side; he had little ones at home—Great Will remembered his engagement to sell Shylock a pound of the carcase; determined that no Jew should eat of it, he bethought him that Falstaff could well spare a pound, and he said the Jew would not see the difference: Falstaff only got off by hard running and roaring out that he knew his unclean life would make him taste like pork and thus let the Jew into the trick.

My father related all this with such a veritable matter-of-fact air, and such liveliness—he sounded the chase and its cries, and showed King Lear tottering, and Hamlet standing dark, and the vast substance of Falstaff—that I followed the incidents excitedly, and really saw them, which was better than understanding them. I required some help from him to see that Hamlet's offer of a three-legged stool at a feverish moment of the chase, was laughable. He taught me what to think of it by pitching Great Will's voice high, and Hamlet's very low. By degrees I got some unconscious knowledge of the characters of Shakespeare. There never was so fascinating a father as mine for a boy anything under eight or ten years old. He could guess on Saturday whether I should name William Pitt on the Sunday; for, on those occasions, "Slender Billy," as I hope I am not irreverent in calling him, made up for the dulness of his high career with a raspberry-jam tart, for which, my father told me solemnly, the illustrious Minister had in his day a passion. If I named him, my father would say, "W. P., otherwise S. B., was born in the year so-and-so; now," and he went to the cupboard, "in the name of Politics, take this and meditate upon him." The shops being all shut on Sunday, he certainly bought it, anticipating me unerringly, on the Saturday, and, as soon as the tart appeared, we both shouted. I fancy I remember his repeating a couplet,

> Billy Pitt took a cake and a raspberry jam,
> When he heard they had taken Seringapatam.

At any rate, the rumour of his having done so at periods of strong excitement, led to the inexplicable display of foresight on my father's part. My meditations upon Pitt were, under this influence, favourable to the post of a Prime Minister, but it was merely appetite that induced me to choose him; I never could imagine a grandeur in his office, notwithstanding my father's eloquent talk of ruling a realm, shepherding a people, hurling British thunderbolts. The day's discipline was, that its selected hero should reign the undisputed monarch of it, so when I was for Pitt, I had my tart as he used to have it, and no story, for he had none, and I think my idea of the ruler of a realm presented him to me as a sort of shadow about a pastrycook's shop. But I surprised people by speaking of him. I made remarks to our landlady which caused her to throw up her hands and exclaim that I was astonishing. She would always add a mysterious word or two in the hearing of my nursemaid or any friend of hers who looked into my room to see me. After my father had got me forward with instructions on the piano, and exercises in early English history and the book of the Peerage, I became the wonder of the house. I was put up on the stool to play "In my Cottage near a Wood," or "Cherry Ripe," and then, to show the range of my accomplishments, I was asked, "And who married the Dowager Duchess of Dewlap?" and I answered, "John Gregg Wetherall, Esquire, and disgraced the family." Then they asked me how I accounted for her behaviour. "It was because the Duke married a dairymaid," I replied, always tossing up my chin at that. My father had concocted the questions and prepared me for the responses, but the effect was striking, both upon his visitors and the landlady's. Gradually my ear grew accustomed to her invariable whisper on these occasions. "Blood Rile," she said; and her friends all said "No!" like the run of a finger down a fiddlestring.

A gentleman of his acquaintance called on him one evening to take him out for a walk. My father happened to be playing with me when this gentlemen entered our room: and he jumped up from his hands and knees, and abused him for intruding on his privacy, but afterwards he introduced him to me as Shylock's great-great-great-grandson, and said that Shylock was satisfied with a pound, and his descendant wanted two hundred pounds, or else all his body: and this, he said, came of the emigration of the family from Venice to England. My father only seemed angry, for he went off with Shylock's very great grandson arm-in-arm, exclaiming, "To the Rialto!" When I told Mrs. Waddy about the visitor, she said, "Oh, dear! oh, dear! then I'm afraid your sweet papa won't return very soon, my pretty pet." We waited a number of days, until Mrs. Waddy received a letter from him. She came full-dressed into my room, requesting me to give her twenty kisses for papa, and I looked on while she arranged her blue bonnet at the glass. The bonnet would not fix in its place. At last she sank down crying in a chair, and was all brown silk, and said that how to appear before a parcel of dreadful men, and perhaps a live duke into the bargain, was more than she knew, and more than could be expected of a lone widow woman. "Not for worlds!" she answered my petition to accompany her. She would not, she said, have me go to my papa *there* for anything on earth; my papa would perish at the sight of me; I was not even to wish to go. And then she exclaimed, "Oh, the blessed child's poor papa!" and that people were cruel to him, and would never take into account his lovely temper, and that everybody was his enemy, when he ought to be sitting with the highest in the land. I had realized the extremity of my forlorn state on a Sunday that passed empty of my father, which felt like his having gone for ever. My nursemaid came in to assist in settling Mrs. Waddy's bonnet above the six crisp curls, and while they were about it I sat quiet, plucking now and then at the brown silk, partly to beg to go with it, partly in jealousy and love at the thought of its seeing him from whom I was so awfully separated. Mrs. Waddy took fresh kisses off my lips, assuring me that my father would have them in twenty minutes, and I was to sit and count the time. My nursemaid let her out. I pretended to be absorbed in counting, till I saw Mrs. Waddy pass by the window. My heart gave a leap of pain. I found the street-door open and no one in the passage, and I ran out, thinking that Mrs. Waddy would be obliged to take me if she discovered me by her side in the street.

I was by no means disconcerted at not seeing her immediately. Running on from one street to another, I took the turnings with unhesitating boldness, as if I had a destination in view. I must have been out an hour before I understood that Mrs. Waddy had eluded me; so I resolved to enjoy the shop-windows with the luxurious freedom of one whose speculations on those glorious things all up for show are no longer distracted by the run of time and a nursemaid. Little more than a glance was enough, now that I knew I could stay as long as I liked. If I stopped at all, it was rather to exhibit the bravado of liberty than to distinguish any particular shop with my preference: all were equally beautiful; so were the carriages; so were the people. Ladies frequently turned to look at me, perhaps because I had no covering on my head; but they did not interest me in the least. I should have been willing to ask them or any one where the Peerage lived, only my mind was quite full, and I did not care. I felt sure that a great deal of walking

would ultimately bring me to St. Paul's or Westminster
Abbey; to anything else I was indifferent.

Toward sunset my frame was struck as with an arrow by
the sensations of hunger on passing a cook's-shop. I faltered along, hoping to reach a second one, without knowing
why I had dragged my limbs from the first. There was a
boy in ragged breeches, no taller than myself, standing
tiptoe by the window of a very large and brilliant pastrycook's. He persuaded me to go into the shop and ask for a
cake. I thought it perfectly natural to do so, being hungry;
but when I reached the counter and felt the size of the
shop, I was slightly abashed, and had to repeat the nature
of my petition twice to the young woman presiding there.

" *Give* you a cake, little boy?" she said. "We don't give
cakes, we sell them."

" Because I am hungry," said I, pursuing my request.

Another young woman came, laughing and shaking lots
of ringlets.

" Don't you see he's not a common boy? he doesn't
whine," she remarked, and handed me a stale bun, saying,
" Here, Master Charles, and you needn't say thank you."

" My name is Harry Richmond, and I thank you very
much," I replied.

I heard her say, as I went out, "You can see he's a gentleman's son." The ragged boy was awaiting me eagerly.
" Gemini! you're a lucky one," he cried: " here, come along,
curly-poll." I believe that I meant to share the bun with
him, but of course he could not be aware of my beneficent
intentions: so he treated me as he thought I was for treating
him, and making one snatch at the bun, ran off cramming it
into his mouth. I stood looking at my hand. I learnt in
that instant what thieving was, and begging, and hunger,
for I would have perished rather than have asked for
another cake, and as I yearned for it in absolute want of
food, the boy's ungenerous treatment of me came down in a
cloud on my reason. I found myself being led through the
crush of people, by an old gentleman, to whom I must have
related an extraordinary rigmarole. He shook his head,
saying that I was unintelligible; but the questions he put
to me, "Why had I no hat on in the open street?—Where
did my mother live?—What was I doing out alone in
London?" were so many incitements to autobiographical

composition to an infant mind, and I tumbled out my history afresh each time that he spoke. He led me into a square, stooping his head to listen all the while; but when I perceived that we had quitted the region of shops, I made myself quite intelligible by stopping short and crying: "I *am* so hungry." He nodded and said, "It's no use cross-examining an empty stomach. You'll do me the favour to dine with me, my little man. We'll talk over your affairs by-and-by." My alarm at having left the savoury street of shops was not soothed until I found myself sitting at table with him, and a nice young lady, and an old one who wore a cap, and made loud remarks on my garments and everything I did. I was introduced to them as the little boy dropped from the sky. The old gentleman would not allow me to be questioned before I had eaten. It was a memorable feast. I had soup, fish, meat and pastry, and, for the first time in my life, a glass of wine. How they laughed to see me blink and cough after I had swallowed half the glass like water. At once my tongue was unloosed. I seemed to rise right above the roofs of London, beneath which I had been but a wandering atom a few minutes ago. I talked of my wonderful father, and Great Will, and Pitt, and the Peerage. I amazed them with my knowledge. When I finished a long recital of Great Will's chase of the deer, by saying that I did not care about politics (I meant, in my own mind, that Pitt was dull in comparison), they laughed enormously, as if I had fired them off.

"Do you know what you are, sir?" said the old gentleman; he had frowning eyebrows and a merry mouth: "you're a comical character."

I felt interested in him, and asked him what he was. He informed me that he was a lawyer, and ready to be pantaloon to my clown, if I would engage him.

"Are you in the Peerage?" said I.

"Not yet," he replied.

"Well, then," said I, "I know nothing about you."

The young lady screamed with laughter. "Oh, you funny little boy; you killing little creature!" she said, and coming round to me, lifted me out of my chair, and wanted to know if I knew how to kiss.

"Oh, yes; I've been taught that," said I, giving the salute without waiting for the invitation: "but," I added, "I don't care about it much." She was indignant, and told me she was going to be offended, so I let her understand that I liked being kissed and played with in the morning before I was up, and if she would come to my house ever so early, she would find me lying next the wall and ready for her.

"And who lies outside?" she asked.

"That's my papa," I was beginning to say, but broke the words with a sob, for I seemed to be separated from him now by the sea itself. They petted me tenderly. My story was extracted by alternate leading questions from the old gentleman and timely caresses from the ladies. I could tell them everything except the name of the street where I lived. My midnight excursion from the house of my grandfather excited them chiefly; also my having a mother alive who perpetually fanned her face and wore a ball-dress and a wreath; things that I remembered of my mother. The ladies observed that it was clear I was a romantic child. I noticed that the old gentleman said "Humph," very often, and his eyebrows were like a rook's nest in a tree when I spoke of my father walking away with Shylock's descendant and not since returning to me. A big book was fetched out of his library, in which he read my grandfather's name. I heard him mention it aloud. I had been placed on a stool beside a tea-tray near the fire, and there I saw the old red house of Riversley, and my mother dressed in white, and my aunt Dorothy; and they all complained that I had ceased to love them, and must go to bed, to which I had no objection. Somebody carried me up and undressed me, and promised me a great game of kissing in the morning.

The next day in the strange house I heard that the old gentleman had sent one of his clerks down to my grandfather at Riversley, and communicated with the constables in London; and, by-and-by, Mrs. Waddy arrived, having likewise visited those authorities, one of whom supported her claims upon me. But the old gentleman wished to keep me until his messenger returned from Riversley. He made all sorts of pretexts. In the end, he insisted on seeing my father, and Mrs. Waddy, after much hesitation, and even weeping, furnished the address: upon hearing which, spoken aside to him, he said, "I thought so." Mrs. Waddy entreated him to be respectful to my father, who was, she declared, his superior, and, begging everybody's pardon present, the superior of us all, through no sin of his own, that caused him to be so unfortunate; and a real Christian and pattern, in spite of outsides, though as true a gentleman as ever walked, and by rights should be amongst the highest. She repeated " amongst the highest " reprovingly, with the ears of barley in her blue bonnet shaking, and her hands clasped tight in her lap. Old Mr. Bannerbridge (that was the old gentleman's name) came back very late from his visit to my father, so late that he said it would be cruel to let me go out in the street after my bed-time. Mrs. Waddy consented to my remaining, on the condition of my being surrendered to her at nine o'clock, and no later, the following morning. I was assured by Mr. Bannerbridge that my father's health and appetite were excellent; he gave me a number of unsatisfying messages, all the rest concerning his interview he whispered to his daughter and his sister, Miss Bannerbridge, who said they hoped they would have news from Hampshire very early, so that the poor child might be taken away by the friends of his infancy. I could understand that my father was disapproved of by them, and that I was a kind of shuttlecock flying between two battledores, but why they pitied me I could not understand. There was a great battle about me when Mrs. Waddy appeared punctual to her appointed hour. The victory was hers, and I, her prize, passed a whole day in different conveyances, the last of which landed us miles away from London, at the gates of an old drooping, mossed and streaked farmhouse, that was like a wall-flower in colour.

CHAPTER III.

DIPWELL FARM.

In rain or in sunshine this old farmhouse had a constant resemblance to a wall-flower; and it had the same moist earthy smell, except in the kitchen, where John and Martha Thresher lived apart from their furniture. All the fresh eggs, and the butter stamped with three bees, and the pots of honey, the fowls, and the hare lifted out of the hamper by his hind legs, and the country loaves smelling heavenly, which used to come to Mrs. Waddy's address in London, and appear on my father's table, were products of Dipwell farm, and presents from her sister, Martha Thresher. On receiving this information I felt at home in a moment, and asked right off, " How long am I to stay here ?—Am I going away to-morrow ?—What's going to be done with me ?" The women found these questions of a youthful wanderer touching. Between kissings and promises of hens to feed, and eggs that were to come of it, I settled into contentment. A strong impression was made on me by Mrs. Waddy's saying, " Here, Master Harry, your own papa will come for you; and you may be sure he will, for I have his word he will, and he's not one to break it, unless his country's against him; and for his darling boy he'd march against cannons. So here you'll sit and wait for him, won't you?" I sat down immediately, looking up. Mrs. Waddy and Mrs. Thresher raised their hands. I had given them some extraordinary proof of my love for my father. The impression I received was that sitting was the thing to conjure him to me.

" Where his heart's not concerned," Mrs. Waddy remarked of me flatteringly, " he's shrewd as a little schoolmaster."

" He've a bird's-nesting eye," said Mrs. Thresher, whose face I was studying.

John Thresher wagered I would be a man before either of them reached that goal. But whenever he spoke he suffered correction on account of his English.

" More than his eating and his drinking, that child's father worrits about his learning to speak the language of a British gentleman," Mrs. Waddy exclaimed. " Before that child your *h*'s must be like the panting of an engine—to please his father. He'd stop me carrying the dinner-tray on meat-dish hot, and I'm to repeat what I said, to make sure the child haven't heard anything ungrammatical. The child's nursemaid he'd lecture so, the poor girl would come down to me ready to bend double, like a bundle of nothing, his observations so took the pride out of her. That's because he's a father who knows his duty to the child :—' Child!' says he, ' man! ma'am.' It's just as you, John, when you sow your seed you think of your harvest. So don't take it ill of me, John; I beg of you be careful of your English. Turn it over as you're about to speak."

"Change loads on the road, you mean," said John Thresher. "Na, na, he's come to settle nigh a weedy field, if you like, but his crop ain't nigh reaping yet. Hark you, Mary Waddy, who're a widde, which's as much as say, an unocc'pied mind, there's cockney, and there's country, and there's school. Mix the three, strain, and throw away the sediment. Now, yon's my view."

His wife and Mrs. Waddy said reflectively, in a breath, "True!"

"Drink or no, that's the trick o' brewery," he added.

They assented. They began praising him, too, like meek creatures.

"What John says is worth listening to, Mary. You may be over-careful. A stew's a stew, and not a boiling to shreds, and you want a steady fire, and not a furnace."

"Oh, I quite agree with John, Martha: we must take the good and the evil in a world like this."

"Then I'm no scholar, and you're at ease," said John.

Mrs. Waddy put her mouth to his ear.

Up went his eyebrows, wrinkling arches over a petrified stare.

In some way she had regained her advantage. "Are't sure of it?" he inquired.

"Pray don't offend me by expressing a doubt of it," she replied, bowing.

John Thresher poised me in the very centre of his gaze. He declared he would never have guessed that, and was reproved, inasmuch as he might have guessed it. He then said that I could not associate with any of the children thereabout, and my dwelling in the kitchen was not to be thought of. The idea of my dwelling in the kitchen seemed to be a serious consideration with Mrs. Martha likewise. I was led into the rooms of state. The sight of them was enough. I stamped my feet for the kitchen, and rarely in my life have been happier than there, dining and supping with John and Martha and the farm-labourers, expecting my father across the hills, and yet satisfied with the sun. To hope, and not be impatient, is really to believe, and this was my feeling in my father's absence. I knew he would come, without wishing to hurry him. He had the world beyond the hills; I this one, where a slow full river flowed from the sounding mill under our garden wall, through long meadows. In Winter the wild ducks made letters of the alphabet flying.

On the other side of the copses bounding our home, there was a park containing trees old as the History of England, John Thresher said, and the thought of their venerable age enclosed me comfortably. He could not tell me whether he meant as old as the book of English History; he fancied he did, for the furrow-track follows the plough close upon; but no one exactly could swear when that (the book) was put together. At my suggestion, he fixed the trees to the date of the Heptarchy, a period of heavy ploughing. Thus begirt by Saxon times, I regarded Riversley as a place of extreme baldness, a Greenland, untrodden by my Alfred and my Harold. These heroes lived in the circle of Dipwell, confidently awaiting the arrival of my father. He sent me once a glorious letter. Mrs. Waddy took one of John Thresher's pigeons to London, and in the evening we beheld the bird cut the sky like an arrow, bringing round his neck a letter warm from him I loved. Planet communicating with planet would be not more wonderful to men than words of his to me, travelling in such a manner. I went to sleep, and awoke imagining the bird bursting out of heaven.

Meanwhile there was an attempt to set me moving again. A strange young man was noticed in the neighbourhood of the farm, and he accosted me at Leckham fair. " I say, don't we know one another ? How about your grandfather the squire, and your aunt, and Mr. Bannerbridge ? I've got news for you."

Not unwilling to hear him, I took his hand, leaving my companion, the miller's little girl, Mabel Sweetwinter, at a toy-stand, while Bob, her brother and our guardian, was shying sticks in a fine attitude. " Yes, and your father, too," said the young man; " come along and see him; you can run ?" I showed him how fast. We were pursued by Bob, who fought for me, and won me, and my allegiance instantly returned to him. He carried me almost the whole of the way back to Dipwell. Women must feel for the lucky heroes who win them something of what I felt for mine; I kissed his bloody face, refusing to let him wipe it. John Thresher said to me at night, " Ay, now you've got a notion of boxing; and will you believe it, Master Harry there's people fools enough to want to tread that ther' first-rate pastime under foot ? I speak truth, and my word for 't, they'd better go in petticoats. Let clergymen preach as in duty bound; you and I'll uphold a manful sport, we will, and a cheer for Bob!" He assured me, and he had my entire faith, that boxing was England's natural protection from the foe. The comfort of having one like Bob to defend our country from invasion struck me as inexpressible. Lighted by John Thresher's burning patriotism, I entered the book of the History of England at about the pace of a cart-horse, with a huge waggon at my heels in the shape of John. There was no moving on until he was filled. His process of receiving historical knowledge was to fight over again the personages who did injury to our honour as a nation, then shake hands and be proud of them. "For where we ain't quite successful we're cunning," he said; "and we not being able to get rid of William the Conqueror, because he's got a will of his own and he won't budge, why, we takes and makes him one of ourselves; and no disgrace in that, I should hope! He paid us a compliment, don't you see, Master Harry? he wanted to be an Englishman. 'Can you this?' says we, sparrin' up to him. 'Pretty middlin,' says he, 'and does it well.' 'Well then,' says we, 'then you're one of us, and we'll beat the world;' and did so." John Thresher had a laborious mind; it cost him beads on his forehead to mount to these satisfactory heights of meditation. He told me once that he thought one's country was like one's wife: you were born in the first, and married to the second, and had to learn all about them afterwards, ay, and make the best of them. He recommended me to mix, strain, and throw away the sediment, for that was the trick o' brewery. Every puzzle that beset him in life resolved to this cheerful precept, the value of which, he said, was shown by clear brown ale, the drink of the land. Even as a child I felt that he was peculiarly an Englishman. Tales of injustice done on the Niger river would flush him in a heat of wrath till he cried out for fresh taxes to chastise the villains. Yet at the sight of the beggars at his gates he groaned at the taxes existing, and enjoined me to have pity on the poor taxpayer when I lent a hand to patch the laws. I promised him I would unreservedly, with a laugh, but with a sincere intention to legislate in a direct manner on his behalf. He, too, though he laughed, thanked me kindly.

I was clad in black for my distant mother. Mrs. Waddy brought down a young man from London to measure me, so that my mourning attire might be in the perfect cut of fashion. "The child's papa would strip him if he saw him in a country tailor's funeral suit," she said, and seemed to blow a wind of changes on me that made me sure my father had begun to stir up his part of the world. He sent me a prayer in his own handwriting to say for my mother in heaven. I saw it flying up between black edges whenever I shut my eyes. Martha Thresher dosed me for liver. Mrs. Waddy found me pale by the fireside, and prescribed iron. Both agreed upon high-feeding, and the apothecary agreed with both in everything, which reconciled them, for both good women loved me so heartily they were near upon disputing over the medicines I was to consume. Under such affectionate treatment I betrayed the alarming symptom that my imagination was set more on my mother than on my father: I could not help thinking that for any one to go to heaven was stranger than to drive to Dipwell, and I had this idea when my father was clasping me in his arms; but he melted it like snow off the fields. He came with postillions in advance of him wearing crape rosettes, as did the horses. We were in the cricket-field, where Dipwell was playing its first match of the season, and a Dipwell lad, furious to see the elevens commit such a breach of the rules and decency as to troop away while the game was hot, and surround my father, flung the cricket-ball into the midst and hit two or three of the men hard. My father had to shield him from the consequences. He said he liked that boy; and he pleaded for him so winningly and funnily that the man who was hurt most laughed loudest. Standing up in the carriage, and holding me by the hand, he addressed them by their names: "Sweetwinter, I thank you for your attention to my son; and you, Thribble; and you, my man; and you, Baker; Rippengale, and you; and you, Jupp;" as if he knew them personally. It was true he nodded at random. Then he delivered a short speech and named himself a regular subscriber to their innocent pleasures. He gave them money, and scattered silver coin among the boys and girls, and praised John Thresher, and Martha, his wife, for their care of me, and pointing to the chimneys of the farm, said that the house there was holy to him from henceforth, and he should visit it annually if possible, but always in the month of May, and in the shape of his subscription, as certain as the cowslip. The men, after their fit of cheering, appeared unwilling to recommence their play, so he alighted and delivered the first ball, and then walked away with my hand in his, saying: " Yes, my son, we will return to them tenfold what they have done for you. The eleventh day of May shall be a day of pleasure for Dipwell while I last, and you will keep it in memory of me when I am gone. And now to see the bed you have slept in."

Martha Thresher showed him the bed, showed him flowers I had planted, and a Spanish chestnut tree just peeping.

" Ha !" said he, beaming at every fresh sight of my doings : " madam, I am your life-long debtor and friend !" He kissed her on the cheek.

John Thresher cried out: " Why, dame, you trembles like a maid."

She spoke very faintly, and was red in the face up to the time of our departure. John stood like a soldier. We drove away from a cheering crowd of cricketers and farm-labourers, as if discharged from a great gun. " A royal salvo !" said my father, and asked me earnestly whether I had forgotten to reward and take a particular farewell of any one of my friends. I told him I had forgotten no one, and thought it was true, until on our way up the sandy lane, which offered us a last close view of the old wall-flower farm front, I saw little Mabel Sweetwinter, often my playfellow and bedfellow, a curly-headed girl, who would have danced on Sunday for a fairing, and eaten gingerbread nuts during a ghost-story. She was sitting by a furze-bush in flower, cherishing in her lap a lamb that had been worried. She looked half up at me, and kept looking so, but would not nod. Then good-bye, thought I, and remembered her look when I had forgotten that of all the others.

CHAPTER IV.

I HAVE A TASTE OF GRANDEUR.

THOUGH I had not previously seen a postillion in my life, I gazed on the pair bobbing regularly on their horses before me, without a thought upon the marvel of their sudden

apparition and connection with my fortunes. I could not
tire of hearing the pleasant music of the many feet at the
trot, and tried to explain to my father that the men going
up and down made it like a piano that played of itself.   He
laughed and kissed me ; he remembered having once shown
me the inside of a piano when the keys were knocked.   My
love for him as we drove into London had a recognised footing : I perceived that he was .my best friend and only true
companion, besides his being my hero.   The wicked men
who had parted us were no longer able to do harm, he said.
I forgot, in my gladness at their defeat, to ask what had
become of Shylock's descendant.

Mrs. Waddy welcomed us when we alighted.   Do not
imagine that it was at the door of her old house.   It was in
a wide street opening on a splendid square, and pillars were
before the houses, and inside there was the enchantment of
a little fountain playing thin as whipcord, among ferns, in a
rock-basin under a window that glowed with kings of
England, copied from boys' history books.   All the servants
were drawn up in the hall to do homage to me.   They
seemed less real and living than the wonder of the sweet-
smelling chairs, the birds, and the elegant dogs.   Richest
of treats, a monkey was introduced to me.   "It's your papa's
whim," Mrs. Waddy said, resignedly ; " he says he must
have his jester.   Indeed it is no joke to me."   Yet she
smiled happily, though her voice was melancholy.   From
her I now learnt that my name was Richmond Roy, and not
Harry Richmond.   I said, "Very well," for I was used to
change.   Everybody in the house wore a happy expression
of countenance, except the monkey, who was too busy.   As
we mounted the stairs I saw more kings of England painted
on the back-windows.   Mrs. Waddy said : "It is considered
to give a monarchical effect,"—she coughed modestly after
the long word, and pursued : "as it should."   I insisted
upon going to the top-floor, where I expected to find William
the Conqueror, and found him ; but that strong connecting
link between John Thresher and me presented himself only
to carry my recollections of the Dipwell of yesterday as far
back into the past as the old Norman days.

"And down go all the kings, downstairs," I said, survey-
ing them consecutively.

"Yes," she replied, in a tone that might lead one to

think it their lamentable fate. "And did the people look at you as you drove along through the streets, Master Richmond?"

I said, "Yes," in turn; and then we left off answering, but questioned one another, which is a quicker way of getting at facts; I know it is with boys and women. Mrs. Waddy cared much less to hear of Dipwell and its inhabitants than of the sensation created everywhere by our equipage. I noticed that when her voice was not melancholy her face was. She showed me a beautiful little pink bed, having a crown over it, in a room opening to my father's. Twenty thousand magnificent dreams seemed to flash their golden doors when I knew that the bed was mine. I thought it almost as nice as a place by my father's side.

"Don't you like it, Mrs. Waddy?" I said.

She smiled and sighed. "Like it? Oh! yes, my dear, to be sure I do. I only hope it won't vanish." She simpered and looked sad.

I had too many distractions, or I should have asked her whether my amazing and delightful new home had ever shown symptoms of vanishing; it appeared to me, judging from my experience, that nothing moved violently except myself, and my principal concern was lest any one should carry me away at a moment's notice. In the evening I was introduced to a company of gentlemen who were drinking wine after dinner with my father. They clapped their hands and laughed immoderately on my telling them that I thought those kings of England who could not find room on the windows must have gone down to the cellars.

"They are going," my father said. He drank off a glassful of wine and sighed prodigiously. "They are going, gentlemen, going there, like good wine, like old Port, which they tell us is going also. Favour me by drinking to the health of Richmond Roy the younger."

They drank to me heartily, but my father had fallen mournful before I left the room.

Pony-riding, and lessons in boxing and wrestling, and lessons in French from a French governess, at whose appearance my father always seemed to be beginning to dance a minuet, so exuberantly courteous was he; and lessons in Latin from a tutor, whom my father invited to dinner once a fortnight, but did not distinguish otherwise than occasionally to take down Latin sentences in a note-book from his dictation, occupied my mornings. My father told the man who instructed me in the art of self-defence that our family had always patronized his profession. I wrestled ten minutes every day with this man's son, and was regularly thrown. On fine afternoons I was dressed in black velvet for a drive in the park, where my father uncovered his head to numbers of people, and was much looked at. " It is our duty, my son, never to forget names and persons; I beg you to bear that in mind, my dearest Richie," he said. We used to go to his opera-box; and we visited the House of Lords and the House of Commons; and my father, though he complained of the decay of British eloquence, and mourned for the days of Chatham, and William Pitt (our old friend of the cake and the raspberry jam), and Burke, and Sheridan, encouraged the orators with approving murmurs. My father no longer laid stress on my studies' of the Peerage. " Now I have you in the very atmosphere, *that* will come of itself," he said. I wished to know whether I was likely to be transported suddenly to some other place. He assured me that nothing save a convulsion of the earth would do it, which comforted me, for I took the firmness of the earth in perfect trust. We spoke of our old Sunday walks to St. Paul's and Westminster Abbey as of a day that had its charm. Our pew among a fashionable congregation pleased him better. The pew-opener curtseyed to none as she did to him. For my part, I missed the monuments and the chants, and something besides that had gone—I knew not what. At the first indication of gloom in me, my father became alarmed, and, after making me stand with my tongue out before himself and Mrs. Waddy, like a dragon in a piece of tapestry, would resume his old playfulness, and try to be the same that he had been in Mrs. Waddy's lodgings. Then we read the Arabian Nights together, or, rather, he read them to me, often acting out the incidents as we rode or drove abroad. An omission to perform a duty was the fatal forgetfulness to sprinkle pepper on the cream-tarts; if my father subjected me to an interrogation concerning my lessons, he was the dread African magician to whom must be surrendered my acquisition of the ring and the musty old lamp. We were quite in the habit of meeting fair Persians. He would frequently ejaculate that he resembled the Three

Calendars in more respects than one. To divert me during my recovery from measles, he one day hired an actor in a theatre, and put a cloth round his neck, and seated him in a chair, rubbed his chin with soap, and played the part of the Barber over him, and I have never laughed so much in my life. Poor Mrs. Waddy got her hands at her sides, and kept on gasping, "Oh, sir! oh!" while the Barber hurried away from the half-shaved young man to consult his pretended astrolabe in the next room, where we heard him shouting the sun's altitude, and consulting its willingness for the impatient young man to be further shaved; and back he came, seeming refreshed to have learnt the sun's favourable opinion, and gabbling at an immense rate, full of barber's business. The servants were allowed to be spectators; but as soon as the young man was shaved, my father dismissed them with the tone of a master. No wonder they loved him. Mrs. Waddy asked who could help it? I remember a pang I had when she spoke of his exposure to the risk of marrying again; it added a curious romantic tenderness to my adoration of him, and made me feel that he and I stood against the world. To have his hand in mine was my delight. Then it was that I could think earnestly of Prince Ahmed and the kind and beautiful Peribanou, whom I would not have minded his marrying. My favourite dream was to see him shooting an arrow in a match for a prize, and losing the prize because of not finding his arrow, and wondering where the arrow had flown to, and wandering after it till he passed out of green fields to grassy rocks, and to a stony desert, where at last he found his arrow at an enormous distance from the shooting line, and there was the desert all about him, and the sweetest fairy ever imagined going to show herself to him in the ground under his feet. In his absence I really hungered for him, and was jealous. During this Arabian life, we sat on a carpet that flew to the Continent, where I fell sick, and was cured by smelling at an apple; and my father directed our movements through the aid of a telescope, which told us the titles of the hotels ready to receive us. As for the cities and cathedrals, the hot meadows under mountains, the rivers and the castles—they were little more to me than an animated book of geography, opening and shutting at random; and travelling from place to place must have seemed to me so much like the life I had led, that I was generally as quick to cry as to laugh, and was never at peace between any two emotions. By-and-by I lay in a gondola with a young lady. My father made friends fast on our travels: her parents were among the number, and she fell in love with me and enjoyed having the name of Peribanou, which I bestowed on her for her delicious talk of the blue and red-striped posts that would spout up fountains of pearls if they were plucked from their beds, and the palaces that had flown out of the farthest corners of the world, and the city that would some night or other vanish suddenly, leaving bare sea-ripple to say "Where? where?" as they rolled over. I would have seen her marry my father happily. She was like rest and dreams to me, soft sea and pearls. We entered into an arrangement to correspond for life. Her name was Clara Goodwin; she requested me to go always to the Horse Guards to discover in what part of the world Colonel Goodwin might be serving when I wanted to write to her. I, in return, could give no permanent address, so I related my history from the beginning. "To write to you would be the same as writing to a river," she said; and insisted that I should drop the odious name of Roy when I grew a man. My father quarelled with Colonel Goodwin. Months after I felt as if I had only just been torn from Clara, but she stood in a mist, irrecoverably distant. I had no other friend.

Twelve dozen of splendid Burgundy were the fruit of our tour, to be laid down at Dipwell farm for my arrival at my majority, when I should be a legal man, embarked in my own ship, as my father said. I did not taste the wine. "Porter for me that day, please God!" cried Mrs. Waddy, who did. My father eyed her with pity, and ordered her to send the wine down to Dipwell, which was done. He took me between his knees, and said impressively, "Now, Richie, twelve dozen of the best that man can drink await you at the gates of manhood. Few fathers can say that to their sons, my boy! If we drink it together, blessings on the day! If I'm gone, Richie, shut up in the long box," his voice shook, and he added, "gone to Peribanou underneath, you know, remember that your dada saw that the wine was a good vintage, and bought it and had it bottled in his own presence while you were asleep in the Emperor's room in the fine old Burgundy city, and swore that, whatever came to

them both, his son should drink the wine of princes on the
day of his majority." Here my father's tone was highly
exalted, and he sat in a great flush. I promised him I would
bend my steps toward Dipwell to be there on my twenty-
first birthday, and he pledged himself to be there in spirit
at least, bodily if possible. We sealed the subject with some
tears. He often talked of commissioning a poet to compose
verses about that wonderful coming day at Dipwell. The
thought of the day in store for us sent me strutting as
though I had been in the presence of my drill-master. Mrs.
Waddy, however, grew extremely melancholy at the mention
of it. "Lord only knows where we shall all be by that
time!" she sighed. "She is a dewy woman," said my father,
disdainfully. They appeared always to be at variance, notwithstanding her absolute devotion to him. My father
threatened to have her married to somebody immediately if
she afflicted him with what he called her Waddyism. She
had got the habit of exclaiming at the end of her remarks,
"No matter; our clock strikes soon!" in a way that communicated to me an obscure idea of a door going to open
unexpectedly in one of the walls, and conduct us, by subterranean passages, into a new country. My father's method
of rebuking her anxious nature was to summon his cook,
the funniest of Frenchmen, Monsieur Alphonse, and issue
orders for a succession of six dinner-parties. "And now,
ma'am, you have occupation for your mind," he would say.
To judge by the instantaneous composure of her whole appearance, he did produce a temporary abatement of her
malady. The good soul bustled out of the room in attendance upon M. Alphonse, and never complained while the
dinners lasted, but it was whispered that she had fits in the
upper part of the house. No sooner did my father hear
the rumour than he accused her to her face of this enormity,
telling her that he was determined to effect a permanent
cure, even though she should drive him to unlimited expense.
We had a Ball party and an Aladdin supper, and for a fortnight my father hired postillions; we flashed through London.
My father backed a horse to run in the races on Epsom
Downs named Prince Royal, only for the reason that his
name was Prince Royal, and the horse won, which was, he
said, a proof to me that in our country it was common prudence to stick to royalty; and he bade me note that if he

went in a carriage and two, he was comparatively unnoticed, whereas when he was beheld in a carriage and four, with postillions, at a glance from him the country people tugged their forelocks, and would like, if he would let them, to kiss his hand. "We will try the scarlet livery on one of our drives, Richie," said he. Mrs. Waddy heard him. "It is unlawful, sir," she said. "For whom, ma'am?" asked my father. "None but royal . . . ." she was explaining, but stopped, for he showed her an awful frown, and she cried so that my heart ached for her. My father went out to order the livery on the spot. He was very excited. Then it was that Mrs. Waddy, embracing me, said, "My dear, my own Master Richmond, my little Harry, prepare your poor child's heart for evil days." I construed her unintelligible speech as an attack upon my father, and abused her violently. While I was in this state of wrathful championship, the hall-door was opened. I ran out and caught sight of my aunt Dorothy, in company with old Mr. Bannerbridge. I was kissed and hugged for I know not how long, until the smell of Riversley took entire possession of me, and my old home seemed nearer than the one I lived in; but my aunt, seeing tears on my cheeks, asked me what was my cause of sorrow. In a moment I poured out a flood of complaints against Mrs. Waddy for vexing my father. When she heard of the scarlet livery, my aunt lifted her hands. "The man is near the end of his wits and his money together," said Mr. Bannerbridge; and she said to me, "My darling Harry will come back to his own nice little room, and see his grandpapa soon, won't you, my pet? All is ready for him there as it used to be, except poor mama. 'Kiss my boy, my Harry—Harry Richmond.' Those were her last words on her death-bed, before she went to God, Harry, my own! There is Sampson the pony, and Harry's dog Prince, and his lamb Daisy, grown a sheep, and the ploughboy, Dick, with the big boots." Much more sweet talk of the same current that made my face cloudy and bright, and filled me with desire for Riversley, to see my mother's grave and my friends.

Aunt Dorothy looked at me. "Come now," she said; "come with me, Harry." Her trembling seized on me like a fire. I said, "Yes," though my heart sank as if I had lost my father with the word. She caught me in her arms

tight, murmuring, " And dry our tears and make our house
laugh. Oh! since the night that Harry went . . . And I
am now Harry's mama, he has me."

I looked on her forehead for the wreath of white flowers
my mother used to wear, and thought of my father's letter
with the prayer written on the black-bordered page. I said
I would go, but my joy in going was gone. We were stopped
in the doorway by Mrs. Waddy. Nothing would tempt her
to surrender me. Mr. Bannerbridge tried reasoning with
her, and, as he said, put the case, which seemed to have
perched on his forefinger. He talked of my prospects, of
my sole chance of being educated morally and virtuously as
became the grandson of an English gentleman of a good old
family, and of my father having spent my mother's estate,
and of the danger of his doing so with mine, and of religious
duty and the awfulness of the position Mrs. Waddy stood in.
He certainly subdued me to very silent breathing, but did
not affect me as my aunt Dorothy's picturing of Riversley
had done; and when Mrs. Waddy, reduced to an apparent
submissiveness, addressed me piteously, " Master Richmond,
would you leave papa?" I cried out, " No, no, never leave
my papa," and twisted away from my aunt's keeping. My
father's arrival caused me to be withdrawn, but I heard his
offer of his hospitality and all that was his; and subsequently
there was loud talking on his part. I was kissed by my
aunt before she went. She whispered, " Come to us when
you are free; think of us when you pray." She was full
of tears. Mr. Bannerbridge patted my head. The door
closed on them and I thought it was a vision that had passed.
But now my father set my heart panting with questions as
to the terrible possibility of us two ever being separated.
In some way he painted my grandfather so black that I
declared earnestly I would rather die than go to Riversley;
I would never utter the name of the place where there was
evil speaking of the one I loved dearest. " Do not, my son,"
he said solemnly, " or it parts us two." I repeated after him,
" I am a Roy and not a Beltham." It was enough to hear
that insult and shame had been cast on him at Riversley for
me to hate the name of the place. We cried and then
laughed together, and I must have delivered myself with
amazing eloquence, for my father held me at arms' length
and said, " Richie, the notion of training you for a General

commandership of the British army is a good one, but if you have got the winning tongue, the woolsack will do as well for a whisper in the ear of the throne. That is our aim, my son. We say,—you will not acknowledge our birth, you shall acknowledge our worth." He complained bitterly of my aunt Dorothy bringing a lawyer to our house. The sins of Mrs. Waddy were forgiven her, owing to her noble resistance to the legal gentleman's seductive speech. So I walked up and down stairs with the kings of England looking at me out of the coloured windows quietly for a week; and then two ugly men entered the house, causing me to suffer a fearful oppression, though my father was exceedingly kind to them and had beds provided for them, saying that they were very old retainers of his. But the next day our scarlet livery appeared. After exacting particular attention to his commands, my father quitted Mrs. Waddy, and we mounted the carriage, laughing at her deplorable eyes and prim lips, which he imitated for my amusement. "A load is off my head," he remarked. He asked me if splendour did not fatigue me also. I caught the answer from his face and replied that it did, and that I should like to go right on to Dipwell. "The Burgundy sleeps safe there," said my father and thought over it. We had an extraordinary day. People stood fast to gaze at us; in the country some pulled off their hats and set up a cheer. The landlords of the inns where we baited remained bare-headed until we started afresh, and I, according to my father's example, bowed and lifted my cap gravely to persons saluting us along the roads. Nor did I seek to know the reason for this excess of respectfulness; I was beginning to take to it naturally. At the end of a dusty high-road, where it descends the hill into a town, we drew up close by a high red wall, behind which I heard boys shouting at play. We went among them, accompanied by their master. My father tipped the head boy for the benefit of the school, and following lunch with the master and his daughter, to whom I gave a kiss at her request, a half-holiday was granted to the boys in my name. How they cheered! The young lady saw my delight, and held me at the window while my father talked with hers; and for a long time after I beheld them in imagination talking: that is to say, my father issuing his instructions and Mr. Rippenger receiving them like a pliant hodman; for the

result of it was that two days later, without seeing my kings
of England, my home again, or London, I was Julia Rippenger's intimate friend and the youngest pupil of the school.
My father told me subsequently that we slept at an hotel
those two nights intervening. Memory transplants me
from the coach and scarlet livery straight to my place of
imprisonment.

CHAPTER V.

I MAKE A DEAR FRIEND.

HERIOT was the name of the head-boy of the school. Boddy
was the name of one of the ushers. They were both in love
with Julia Rippenger. It was my fortune to outrun them
in her favour for a considerable period, during which time,
though I had ceased to live in state, and was wearing out
my suits of velvet, and had neither visit nor letter from my
father, I was in tolerable bliss. Julia's kisses were showered
on me for almost anything I said or did, but her admiration
of heroism and daring was so fervent that I was in no greater
danger of becoming effeminate than Achilles when he wore
girl's clothes. She was seventeen, an age bewitching for
boys to look up to and men to look down on. The puzzle of
the school was how to account for her close relationship to
old Rippenger. Such an apple on such a crab-tree seemed
monstrous. Heriot said that he hoped Boddy would marry
old Rippenger's real daughter, and, said he, that's birch-
twigs. I related his sparkling speech to Julia, who laughed,
accusing him, however, of impudence. She let me see a
portrait of her dead mother, an Irish lady raising dark
eyelashes, whom she resembled. I talked of the portrait to
Heriot, and as I had privileges accorded to none of the other
boys and could go to her at any hour of the day after lessons,
he made me beg for him to have a sight of it. She considered awhile, but refused. On hearing of the unkind
refusal, Heriot stuck his hands into his pockets and gave up
cricketing. We saw him leaning against a wall in full view
of her window, while the boys crowded round him trying to
get him to practise a school-match of an important character

coming off with a rival academy; and it was only through
fear of our school being beaten if she did not relent that
Julia handed me the portrait, charging me solemnly to bring
it back.   I promised, of course.   Heriot went into his
favourite corner of the playground, and there looked at it
and kissed it, and then buttoned his jacket over it tight,
growling when I asked him to return it.   Julia grew
frightened.   She sent me with numbers of petitions to
him.

"Look here, young un," said Heriot; "you're a good little
fellow, and I like you, but just tell her I believe in nothing
but handwriting, and if she writes to me for it humbly and
nicely she shall have it back.   Say I only want to get a
copy taken by a first-rate painter."

Julia shed tears at his cruelty, called him cruel, wicked,
false to his word.   She wrote, but the letter did not please
him, and his reply was scornful.   At prayers morning and
evening, it was pitiful to observe her glance of entreaty and
her downfallen eyelashes.   I guessed that in Heriot's letters
to her he wanted to make her confess something, which she
would not do.   "Now I write to him no more; let him know
it, my darling," she said, and the consequence of Heriot's
ungrateful obstinacy was that we all beheld her, at the
ceremony of the consecration of the new church, place her
hand on Mr. Boddy's arm and allow him to lead her about.
Heriot kept his eyes on them; his mouth was sharp, and his
arms stiff by his sides.   I was the bearer of a long letter to
her that evening.   She tore it to pieces without reading it.
Next day Heriot walked slowly past Mr. Boddy holding the
portrait in his hands.   The usher called to him!—

"What have you there, Heriot?"

My hero stared.   "Only a family portrait," he answered,
thrusting it safe in his pocket and fixing his gaze on Julia's
window.

"Permit me to look at it," said Mr. Boddy.

"Permit me to decline to let you," said Heriot.

"Look at me, sir," cried Boddy.

"I prefer to look elsewhere, sir," replied Heriot, and there
was Julia visible at her window.

"I asked you, sir, civilly," quoth Boddy, "for permission
to look,—I used the word intentionally; I say I asked you
for permission . . ."

" No, you didn't," Heriot retorted, quite cool; "inferentially you did; but you did not use the word permission."

" And you turned upon me impudently," pursued Boddy, whose colour was thunder: "you quibbled, sir; you prevaricated; you concealed what you were carrying . . ."

" Am carrying," Heriot corrected his tense; "and mean to, in spite of every Boddy," he murmured audibly.

" Like a rascal detected in an act of felony," roared Boddy, " you concealed it, sir . . ."

" Conceal it, sir."

" And I demand, in obedience to my duty, that you instantly exhibit it for my inspection, now, here, at once; no parleying; unbutton, or I call Mr. Rippenger to compel you."

I was standing close by my brave Heriot, rather trembling, studious of his manfulness though I was. His left foot was firmly in advance, as he said, just in the manner to start an usher furious :—

" I concealed it, I conceal it; I was carrying it, I carry it : you demand *that* I exhibit for your inspection what I mean no Boddy to see ? I have to assure you respectfully, sir, that family portraits are sacred things with the sons of gentlemen. Here, Richie, off !"

I found the portrait in my hand, and Heriot between me and the usher, in the attitude of a fellow keeping another out of his home at prisoner's-base. He had spied Mr. Rippenger's head at the playground gate. I had just time to see Heriot and the usher in collision before I ran through the gate and into Julia's arms in her garden, whither the dreadful prospect of an approaching catastrophe had attracted her.

Heriot was merely reported guilty of insolence. He took his five hundred lines of Virgil with his usual sarcastic dignity : all he said to Mr. Rippenger was, " Let it be about Dido, sir," which set several of the boys upon Dido's history, but Heriot was condemned to the battles with Turnus. My share in this event secured Heriot's friendship to me without costing me the slightest inconvenience. " Papa would never punish you," Julia said; and I felt my rank. Nor was it wonderful I should when Mr. Rippenger was constantly speaking of my father's magnificence in my presence before company. Allowed to draw on him largely for pocket-money, I maintained my father's princely reputation in the school.   At times, especially when the holidays arrived and I was left alone with Julia, I had fits of mournfulness, and almost thought the boys happier than I was.   Going home began to seem an unattainable thing to me.   Having a father, too, a regular father, instead of a dazzling angel that appeared at intervals, I considered a benefaction, in its way, some recompense to the boy ;for their not possessing one like mine.   My anxiety was relieved by my writing letters to my father, addressed to the care of Miss Julia Rippenger, and posting them in her work-basket.   She favoured me with very funny replies, signed, "Your own ever-loving Papa," about his being engaged killing Bengal tigers and capturing white elephants, a noble occupation that gave me exciting and consolatory dreams of him.   We had at last a real letter of his, dated from a foreign city; but he mentioned nothing of coming to me.   I understood that Mr. Rippenger was disappointed with it.   Gradually a kind of cloud stole over me.   I no longer liked to ask for pocket-money.; I was clad in a suit of plain cloth; I was banished from the parlour, and only on Sunday was I permitted to go to Julia.   I ceased to live in myself.   Through the whole course of lessons, at play-time, in my bed, and round to morning bell, I was hunting my father in an unknown country, generally with the sun setting before me : I ran out of a wood almost into a brook to see it sink as if I had again lost sight of him, and then a sense of darkness brought me back to my natural consciousness, without afflicting me much, but astonishing me.   Why was I away from him? I could repeat my lessons in the midst of these dreams quite fairly ; it was the awakening among the circle of the boys that made me falter during a recital and ask myself why I was there and he absent?   They had given over speculating on another holiday and treat from my father; yet he had produced such an impression in the school that even when I had descended to the level of a total equality with them, they continued to have some consideration for me.   I was able to talk of foreign cities and could tell stories, and I was, besides, under the immediate protection of Heriot.   But now the shadow of a great calamity fell on me, for my dear Heriot announced his intention of leaving the school next half.

"I can't stand being prayed at, morning and evening, by

a fellow who hasn't the pluck to strike me like a man," he said. Mr. Rippenger had the habit of signalizing offenders, in his public prayers, as boys whose hearts he wished to be turned from callousness. He perpetually suspected plots; and to hear him allude to some deep, long-hatched school conspiracy while we knelt motionless on the forms, and fetch a big breath to bring out, "May the heart of Walter Heriot be turned and he comprehend the multitudinous blessings," &c., was intensely distressing. Together with Walter Heriot, Andrew Saddlebank, our best bowler, the drollest fellow in the world, John Salter, and little Gus Temple, were oftenest cited. They declared that they invariably uttered "Amen," as Heriot did, but we none of us heard this defiant murmur of assent from their lips. Heriot pronounced it clearly and cheerfully, causing Julia's figure to shrink as she knelt with her face in the chair hard by her father's desk-pulpit. I received the hearty congratulations of my comrades for singing out "Amen" louder than Heriot, like a chorister, though not in so prolonged a note, on hearing to my stupefaction Mr. Rippenger implore that the heart of "him we know as Richmond Roy" might be turned. I did it spontaneously. Mr. Rippenger gazed at me in descending from his desk; Julia, too, looking grieved. For my part, I exulted in having done a thing that gave me a likeness to Heriot.

"Little Richmond, you're a little hero," he said caressing me. "I saw old Rippenger whisper to that beast, Boddy. Never mind; they won't hurt you as long as I'm here. Grow tough, that's what you've got to do. I'd like to see you horsed, only to see whether you're game to take it without wincing—if it didn't hurt you much, little lad."

He hugged me up to him.

"I'd take anything for you, Heriot," said I.

"All right," he answered, never meaning me to suffer on his account. He had an inimitable manner of sweet-speaking that endeared him to younger boys capable of appreciating it, with the supernatural power of music. It endeared him, I suppose, to young women also. Julia repeated his phrases, as for instance, "Silly boy, silly boy," spoken with a wave of his hand, when a little fellow thanked him for a kindness. She was angry at his approval of what

she called my defiance of her father, and insisted that I was
the catspaw of one of Heriot's plots to vex him.

"Tell Heriot you have my command to say you belong to
me and must not be misled," she said.   His answer was
that he wanted it in writing.   She requested him to deliver
up her previous letters.   Thereupon he charged me with a
lengthy epistle, which plunged us into boiling water.   Mr.
Boddy sat in the schoolroom while Heriot's pen was at
work, on the wet Sunday afternoon.   His keen little eyes
were busy in his flat bird's head all the time Heriot continued writing.   He saw no more than that Heriot gave me
a book ; but as I was marching away to Julia he called to
know where I was going.

"To Miss Rippenger," I replied.

"What have you there ?"

"A book, sir."

"Show me the book."

I stood fast.

"It's a book I have lent him, sir," said Heriot, rising.

"I shall see if it's a fit book for a young boy," said Boddy ;
and before Heriot could interpose, he had knocked the book
on the floor, and out fell the letter.   Both sprang down to
seize it : their heads encountered, but Heriot had the quicker
hand ; he caught the letter, and cried "Off!" to me, as on
another occasion.   This time, however, he was not between
me and the usher.   I was seized by the collar, and shaken
roughly.

"You will now understand that you are on a footing with
the rest of the boys, you Roy," said Boddy.   "Little scoun-
drelly spoilt urchins, upsetting the discipline of the school,
won't do here.   Heriot, here is your book.   I regret," he
added, sneering, "that a leaf is torn."

"I regret, sir, that the poor boy was so savagely handled,"
said Heriot.

He was warned to avoid insolence.

"Oh, as much Virgil as you like," Heriot retorted; "I
know him by heart."

It was past the hour of my customary visit to Julia, and
she came to discover the reason of my delay.   Boddy stood
up to explain.   Heriot went forward, saying, "I think I'm
the one who ought to speak, Miss Rippenger.   The fact is,
I hear from little Roy that you are fond of tales of Indian

adventure, and I gave him a book for you to read, if you like it. Mr. Boddy objected, and treated the youngster rather rigorously. It must have been quite a misunderstanding on his part. Here is the book: it's extremely amusing."

Julia blushed very red. She accepted the book with a soft murmur, and the sallow usher had not a word.

" Stay," said Heriot. " I took the liberty to write some notes. My father is an Indian officer, you know, and some of the terms in the book are difficult without notes. Richie, hand that paper. Here they are, Miss Rippenger, if you'll be so kind as to place them in the book."

I was hoping with all my might that she would not deny him. She did, and my heart sank.

" Oh, I can read it without notes," she said, cheerfully.

After that, I listened with indifference to her petition to Boddy that I might be allowed to accompany her, and was not at all chagrined by his refusal. She laid down the book, saying that I could bring it to her when I was out of disgrace.

In the evening we walked in the playground, where Heriot asked me to do a brave thing, which he would never forget. This was that I should take a sharp run right past Boddy, who was pacing up and down before the gate leading into Julia's garden, and force her to receive the letter. I went bounding like a ball. The usher, suspecting only that I hurried to speak to him, let me see how indignant he was with my behaviour by striding all the faster as I drew near, and so he passed the gate, and I rushed in. I had just time to say to Julia, " Hide it, or I'm in such a scrape."

The next minute she was addressing my enemy: " Surely you would not punish him because he loves me?" and he, though he spoke of insubordination, merited chastisement, and other usher phrases, seemed to melt, and I had what I believe was a primary conception of the power of woman. She led him to talk in the gentlest way possible of how the rain had refreshed her flowers, and of this and that poor rose.

I could think of nothing but the darling letter, which had flashed out of sight as a rabbit pops into burrows. Boddy departed with a rose.

" Ah, Richie," she said, " I have to pay to have you with me now."

We walked to the summer-house, where she read Heriot's letter through. "But he is a boy! How old is Heriot? He is not so old as I am!"

These were her words, and she read the letter anew, and read it again after she had placed it in her bosom, I meanwhile pouring out praises of Heriot.

"You speak of him as if you were in love with him, Richmond," said she.

" And I do love him," I answered.

" Not with me?" she asked.

"Yes, I do love you too, if you will not make him angry."

" But do you know what it is he wants of me?"

I guessed: " Yes; he wants you to let him sit close to you for half-an-hour."

She said that he sat very near her in church.

" Ah," said I, " but he mustn't interrupt the sermon."

She laughed, and mouthed me over with laughing kisses. " There's very little he hasn't daring enough for!"

We talked of his courage.

" Is he good as well?" said Julia, more to herself than to me; but I sang out,—

" Good! Oh, so kind!"

This appeared to convince her.

"Very generous to you and every one, is he not?" she said; and from that moment was all questions concerning his kind treatment of the boys, and as to their looking up to him.

I quitted her, taking her message to Heriot: " You may tell him—tell him that I can't write."

Heriot frowned on hearing me repeat it.

" Humph!" he went, and was bright in a twinkling: " that means she'll come!" He smacked his hands together, grew black, and asked, " Did she give that beast Boddy a rose?"

I had to confess she did; and feeling a twinge of my treason to her, felt hers to Heriot.

" Humph!" he went; " she shall suffer for that."

All this was like music going on until the curtain should lift and reveal my father to me.

There was soon a secret to be read in Heriot's face for one who loved it as I did. Julia's betrayed nothing. I was not taken into their confidence, and luckily not; otherwise I fear I should have served them ill, I was so poor a dissembler and was so hotly plied with interrogations by the suspicious usher. I felt sure that Heriot and Julia met. His eyes were on her all through prayer-time, and hers wandered over the boys' heads till they rested on him, when they gave a short flutter and dropped, like a bird shot dead. The boys must have had some knowledge that love was busy in their midst, for they spoke of Heriot and Julia as a jolly couple, and of Boddy as one meaning to play the part of old Nick the first opportunity. She was kinder to them than ever. It was not a new thing that she should send in cakes of her own making, but it was extraordinary that we should get these thoughtful presents as often as once a fortnight, and it became usual to hear a boy exclaim, either among a knot of fellows or to himself, "By jingo, she is a pretty girl!" on her passing out of the room, and sometimes entirely of his own idea. I am persuaded that if she had consented to marry Boddy, the boys would have been seriously disposed to conspire to jump up in the church and forbid the banns. We should have preferred to hand her to the junior usher Catman, of whom the rumour ran in the school that he once drank a bottle of wine and was sick after it, and he was therefore a weak creature to our minds; the truth of the rumour being confirmed by his pale complexion. That we would have handed our blooming princess to him was full proof of our abhorrence of Boddy. I might have thought with the other boys that she was growing prettier, only I never could imagine her so delicious as when she smiled at my father.

The consequence of the enlistment of the whole school in Heriot's interests was that at cricket-matches, picnics on the hills, and boating on the canal, Mr. Boddy was begirt with spies, and little Temple reported to Heriot a conversation that he, lying hidden in tall grass, had heard between Boddy and Julia. Boddy asked her to take private lessons in French from him. Heriot listened to the monstrous tale as he was on the point of entering Julia's boat, where Boddy sat beside her, and Heriot rowed stroke-oar. He dipped his blade, and said, loud enough to be heard by me in Catman's boat,—

" Do you think French useful in a military education, sir ?"

And Boddy said : " Yes, of course it is."

Says Heriot : " Then I think I shall take lessons."

Boddy told him he was taking lessons in the school.

" Oh !" says Heriot, " I mean private lessons ;" and here he repeated one of Temple's pieces of communication : " so much more can be imparted in a private lesson !"

Boddy sprang half up from his seat. " Row, sir, and don't talk," he growled.

" Sit, sir, and don't dance in the boat, if you please, or the lady will be overset," said Heriot.

Julia requested to be allowed to land and walk home. Boddy caught the rudder lines and leapt on the bank to hand her out ; then all the boys in her boat and in Catman's shouted, " Miss Julia ! dear Miss Julia, don't leave us !" and we heard wheedling voices : " Don't go off with him alone !" Julia bade us behave well or she would not be able to come out with us. At her entreaty Boddy stepped back to his post, and the two boats went forward like swans that have done ruffling their feathers.

The boys were exceedingly disappointed that no catastrophe followed the events of the day. Heriot, they thought, might have upset the boat, saved Julia, and drowned Boddy, and given us a feast of pleasurable excitement : instead of which Boddy lived to harass us with his tyrannical impositions and spiteful slaps, and it was to him, not to our Heriot, that Julia was most gracious. Some of us discussed her conduct.

" She's a coquette," said little Temple. I went off to the French dictionary.

" Is Julia Rippenger a coquette, Heriot ?" I asked him.

" Keep girls out of your heads, you little fellows," said he, dealing me a smart thump.

" Is a coquette a nasty girl ?" I persisted.

" No, a nice one, as it happens," was his answer.

My only feeling was jealousy of the superior knowledge of the sex possessed by Temple, for I could not fathom the meaning of coquette ; but he had sisters. Temple and I walked the grounds together, mutually declaring how much we would forfeit for Heriot's sake. By this time my Sunday visits to Julia had been interdicted : I was plunged, as it were, in the pit of the school, and my dreams of my father were losing distinctness. A series of boxes on the ears from Boddy began to astound and transform me. Mr. Rippenger, too, threatened me with canings, though my offences were slight. "Yes," said Temple and I, in chorus, "but you daren't strike Heriot!" This was our consolation, and the sentiment of the school. Fancy, then, our amazement to behold him laying the cane on Heriot's shoulders as fiercely as he could, and Boddy seconding him. The scene was terrible. We were all at our desks doing evening tasks for the morrow, a great match-day at cricket, Boddy watching over us, and bellowing, "Silence, at your work, you lazy fellows, if you want lessons to be finished at ten in the morning!" A noise came growing up to us from below, up the stairs from the wet-weather shed, and Heriot burst into the room, old Rippenger after him, panting.

"Mr. Boddy, you were right," he cried; "I find him a prowler, breaking all rules of discipline. A perverted, impudent rascal! An example shall be set to my school, sir. We have been falling lax. What! I find the puppy in my garden, whistling—he confesses—for one of my servants . . . . here, Mr. Boddy, if you please. My school shall see that none insult me with impunity!" He laid on Heriot like a wind on a bulrush. Heriot bent his shoulders a trifle, not his head.

"Hit away, sir," he said, during the storm of blows, and I, through my tears, imagined him (or I do now) a young eagle forced to bear the thunder, but with his face to it. Then we saw Boddy lay hands on him, and in a twinkling down pitched the usher, and the boys cheered—chirped, I should say, they exulted so, and merely sang out like birds, without any wilfulness of delight or defiance. After the fall of Boddy we had no sense of our hero suffering shame. Temple and I clutched fingers tight as long as the blows went on. We hoped for Boddy to make another attempt to touch Heriot; he held near the master, looking ready to spring, like a sallow panther; we kept hoping he would, in our horror of the murderous slashes of the cane; and not a syllable did Heriot utter. Temple and I started up, unaware of what we were going to do, or of anything until we had got a blow a-piece, and were in the thick of it, and Boddy had us both by the collars, and was knocking our heads together, as he dragged us back to our seats. But the boys told us we stopped the execution. Mr. Rippenger addressed us before he left the school-room. Saddlebank, Salter, and a good many others, plugged their ears with their fists. That night Boddy and Catman paced in the bed-chambers, to prevent plotting and conspiracy, they said. I longed to get my arms about Heriot, and thought of him, and dreamed of blood, and woke in the morning wondering what made me cry, and my arms and back very stiff. Heriot was gay as ever, but had fits of reserve; the word passed round that we were not to talk of yesterday evening. We feared he would refuse to play in the match.

" Why not ?" said he, staring at us angrily. " Has Saddlebank broken his arm, and can't bowl ?"

No, Saddlebank was in excellent trim, though shamefaced, as was Salter, and most of the big boys were. They begged Heriot to let them shake his hand.

" Wait till we win our match," said Heriot.

Julia did not appear at morning prayers.

" Ah," said Temple, " it'd make her sick to hear old Massacre praying." It had nearly made him sick, he added, and I immediately felt that it had nearly made me sick.

We supposed we should not see Julia at the match. She came, however, and talked to everybody. I could not contain myself, I wanted so to tell her what had befallen Heriot overnight, while he was batting, and the whole ground cheering his hits. I on one side of her whispered—

" I say, Julia, my dear, I say, do you know . . . ."

And Temple on the other: " Miss Julia, I wish you'd let me tell you . . . ."

We longed to arouse her pity for Heriot at the moment she was admiring him, but she checked us, and as she was surrounded by ladies and gentlemen of the town, and particular friends of hers, we could not speak out. Heriot brought his bat to the booth for eighty-nine runs. His sleeve happened to be unbuttoned, and there, on his arm was a mark of the cane.

" Look !" I said to Julia. But she looked at me.

" Richie, are you ill ?"

She assured me I was very pale, and I felt her trembling excessively, and her parasol was covering us.

"Here, Roy, Temple," we heard Heriot call; "here, come here and bowl to me."

I went and bowled till I thought my head was flying after the ball and getting knocks, it swam and throbbed so horribly.

Temple related that I fell, and was carried all the way from the cricket-field home by Heriot, who would not give me up to the usher. I was in Julia's charge three days. Every time I spoke of her father and Heriot, she cried, "Oh, hush!" and had tears on her eyelids. When I was quite strong again, I made her hear me out. She held me and rocked over me like a green tree in the wind and rain.

"Was any name mentioned?" she asked, with her mouth working, and to my "No," said "No, she knew there was none," and seemed to drink and choke, and was one minute calm, all but a trembling hanging underlip, next smiling on me, and next having her face carved in grimaces by the jerking little tugs of her mouth, which I disliked to see, for she would say nothing of what she thought of Heriot, and I thought to myself, though I forbore to speak unkindly, "It's no use your making yourself look ugly, Julia." If she had talked of Heriot, I should have thought that crying persons' kisses were agreeable.

On my return into the school, I found it in a convulsion of excitement, owing to Heriot's sending Boddy a challenge to fight a duel with pistols. Mr. Rippenger preached a sermon to the boys concerning the un-Christian spirit and hideous moral perversity of one who would even consent to fight a duel. How much more reprehensible, then, was one that could bring himself to defy a fellow-creature to mortal combat! We were not of his opinion; and as these questions are carried by majorities, we decided that Boddy was a coward, and approved the idea that Heriot would have to shoot or scourge him when the holidays came. Mr. Rippenger concluded his observations by remarking that the sharpest punishment he could inflict upon Heriot was to leave him to his own conscience; which he did for three days, and then asked him if he was in a fit state of mind to beg Mr. Boddy's pardon publicly.

"I'm quite prepared to tell him what I think of him publicly, sir," said Heriot.

A murmur of exultation passed through the school. Mr. Rippenger seized little Temple, and flogged him. Far from dreading the rod, now that Heriot and Temple had tasted it, I thought of punishment as a mad pleasure, not a bit more awful than the burning furze-bush plunged into by our fellows in a follow-my-leader scamper on the common; so I caught Temple's hand as he went by me, and said, eagerly, " Shall I sing out hurrah ?"

" Bother it !" was Temple's answer, for he had taken a stinging dozen, and had a tender skin.

Mr. Rippenger called me up to him, to inform me that, whoever I was, and whatever I was, and I might be a little impostor foisted on his benevolence, yet he would bring me to a knowledge of myself : he gave me warning of it ; and if my father objected to his method, my father must write word to that effect, and attend punctually to business duties, for Surrey House was not an almshouse, either for the sons of gentlemen of high connection, or of the sons of vagabonds. Mr. Rippenger added a spurning shove on my shoulder to his recommendation to me to resume my seat. I did not understand him at all. I was, in fact, indebted to a boy named Drew, a known sneak, for the explanation, in itself difficult to comprehend. It was, that Mr. Rippenger was losing patience because he had received no money on account of my boarding and schooling. The intelligence filled my head like the buzz of a fly, occupying my meditations without leading them anywhere. I spoke on the subject to Heriot.

" Oh, the sordid old brute !" said he of Mr. Rippenger. " How can he know the habits and feelings of gentlemen ? Your father's travelling, and can't write, of course. My father's in India, and I get a letter from him about once a year. We know one another, and I know he's one of the best officers in the British army. It's just the way with schoolmasters and tradesmen : they don't care whether a man is doing his duty to his country ; he must attend to them, settle accounts with them—hang them ! I'll send you money, dear little lad, after I've left."

He dispersed my brooding fit. I was sure my father was a fountain of gold, and only happened to be travelling. Besides, Heriot's love for Julia, whom none of us saw now, was an incessant distraction. She did not appear at prayers. She sat up in the gallery at church, hardly to be spied. A letter that Heriot flung over the garden-wall for her was returned to him, open, enclosed by post.

"A letter for Walter Heriot," exclaimed Mr. Boddy, lifting it high for Heriot to walk and fetch it; and his small eyes blinked when Heriot said aloud on his way, cheerfully,—

"A letter from the colonel in India!"

Boddy waited a minute, and then said, "Is your father in good health?"

Heriot's face was scarlet. At first he stuttered, "My father!—I hope so! What have you in common with him, sir?"

"You stated that the letter was from your father," said Boddy.

"What if it is, sir?"

"Oh, in that case, nothing whatever to me."

They talked on, and the youngest of us could perceive Boddy was bursting with devilish glee. Heriot got a letter posted to Julia. It was laid on his desk, with her name scratched completely out, and his put in its place. He grew pale and sad, but did his work, playing his games, and only letting his friends speak to him of lessons and play. His counsel to me was that, in spite of everything, I was always to stick to my tasks and my cricket. His sadness he could not conceal. He looked like an old lamp with a poor light in it. Not a boy in the school missed seeing how Boddy's flat head perpetually had a side-eye on him.

All this came to an end. John Salter's father lived on the other side of the downs, and invited three of us to spend a day at his house. The selection included Heriot, Saddlebank, and me. Mr. Rippenger, not liking to refuse Mr. Salter, consented to our going, but pretended that I was too young. Salter said his mother and sisters very much wished to make my acquaintance. We went in his father's carriage. A jolly wind blew clouds and dust and leaves: I could have fancied I was going to my own father. The sensation of freedom had a magical effect on me, so that I was the wildest talker of them all. Even in the middle of the family I led the conversation; and I did not leave Salter's house without receiving an assurance from his elder sisters that they were in love with me. We drove home—back to prison, we called it—full of good things, talking of Salter's

father's cellar of wine and of my majority Burgundy, which
I said, believing it was true, amounted to twelve hundred
dozen; and an appointment was made for us to meet at
Dipwell Farm, to assist in consuming it, in my honour and
my father's. That matter settled, I felt myself rolling over
and over at a great rate, and clasping a juniper tree. The
horses had trenched from the chalk road on to the downs.
I had been shot out. Heriot and Salter had jumped out—
Heriot to look after me; but Saddlebank and the coachman
were driving at a great rate over the dark slope. Salter felt
some anxiety concerning his father's horses, so we left him
to pursue them, and walked on laughing, Heriot praising
me for my pluck.

"I say good-bye to you to-night, Richie," said he. "We're
certain to meet again. I shall go to a military school. Mind
you enter a cavalry regiment when you're man enough. Look
in the *Army List*, you'll find me there. My aunt shall make
a journey and call on you while you're at Rippenger's, so
you shan't be quite lonely."

To my grief, I discovered that Heriot had resolved he
would not return to school.

"You'll get thrashed," he said; "I can't help it: I hope
you've grown tough by this time. I can't stay here. I feel
more like a dog than a man in that house now. I'll see you
back safe. No crying, young cornet!"

We had lost the sound of the carriage. Heriot fell to
musing. He remarked that the accident took away from
Mr. Salter the responsibility of delivering him at Surrey
House, but that he, Heriot, was bound, for Mr. Salter's sake,
to conduct me to the doors; an unintelligible refinement of
reasoning to my wits. We reached our town between two
and three in the morning. There was a ladder leaning
against one of the houses in repair near the school. "You
are here, are you!" said Heriot, speaking to the ladder:
"you'll do me a service—the last I shall want in the neighbourhood." He managed to poise the ladder on his shoulder,
and moved forward.

"Are we going in through the window?" I asked, seeing
him fix the ladder against the school-house wall.

He said, "Hush; keep a look-out."

I saw him mount high. When he tapped at the window

I remembered it was Julia's; I heard her cry out inside. The window rose slowly. Heriot spoke:—

"I have come to say good-bye to you, Julia, dear girl: don't be afraid of me." She answered inaudibly to my ears. He begged her to come to him once, only once, and hear him and take his hand. She was timid; he had her fingers first, then her whole arm, and she leaned over him. "Julia, my sweet, dear girl," he said; and she—

"Heriot, Walter, don't go—don't go; you do not care for me if you go. Oh, don't go."

"We've come to it," said Heriot.

She asked why he was not in bed, and moaned on: "Don't go." I was speechless with wonder at the night and the scene. They whispered; I saw their faces close together, and Heriot's arms round her neck. "Oh, Heriot, my darling, my Walter," she said, crying, I knew by the sound of her voice.

"Tell me you love me," said Heriot.

"I do, I do, only don't go," she answered.

"Will you love me faithfully?"

"I will; I do."

"Say, 'I love you, Walter.'"

"I love you, Walter."

"For ever."

"For ever. Oh! what a morning for me. Do you smell my honeysuckle? Oh, don't go away from me, Walter. Do you love me so?"

"I'd go through a regiment of sabres to get at you."

"But smell the night air; how sweet! oh, how sweet! No, not kiss me, if you are going to leave me; not kiss me, if you can be so cruel!"

"Do you dream of me in your bed?"

"Yes, every night."

"God bless the bed!"

"Every night I dream of you. Oh! brave Heriot; dear dear Walter, you did not betray me; my father struck you, and you let him for my sake. Every night I pray heaven to make you forgive him: I thought you would hate me. I cried till I was glad you could not see me. Look at those two little stars; no, they hurt me, I can't look at them ever again. But no, you are not going; you want to frighten me. Do smell the flowers. Don't make them poison to me.

Oh, what a morning for me when you're lost! And me, to look out on the night alone! No, no more kisses! Oh, yes, I will kiss you, dear."

Heriot said: "Your mother was Irish, Julia."

"Yes. She would have loved you."

"I've Irish blood too. Give me her portrait. It's the image of you."

"To take away? Walter! not to take it away?"

"You darling! to keep me sure of you."

"Part with my mother's portrait?"

"Why, yes, if you love me one bit."

"But you are younger than me, Heriot."

"Then good-night, good-bye, Julia."

"Walter, I will fetch it."

Heriot now told her I was below, and she looked down on me and called my name softly, sending kisses from her fingers while he gave the cause for our late return.

"Some one must be sitting up for you—are we safe?" she said.

Heriot laughed, and pressed for the portrait.

"It is all I have. Why should you not have it? I want to be remembered."

She sobbed as she said this and disappeared. Heriot still talked into her room. I thought I heard a noise of the garden-door opening. A man came out rushing at the ladder. I called in terror: "Mr. Boddy, stop, sir." He pushed me savagely aside, pitching his whole force against the ladder. Heriot pulled down Julia's window; he fell with a heavy thump on the ground, and I heard a shriek above. He tried to spring to his feet but dropped, supported himself on one of his hands, and cried:—

"All right; no harm done; how do you do, Mr. Boddy? I thought I'd try one of the attics, as we were late, not to disturb the house. I'm not hurt, I tell you," he cried as loud as he could.

The usher's words were in a confusion of rage and inquiries. He commanded Heriot to stand on his legs, abused him, asked what he meant by it, accused him of depravity, of crime, of disgraceful conduct, and attempted to pluck him from the spot.

"Hands off me," said Heriot; "I can help myself. The youngster'll help me, and we'll go round to the front door.

I hope, sir, you will behave like a gentleman; make no row here, Mr. Boddy, if you've any respect for people inside. We were upset by Mr. Salter's carriage; it's damaged my leg, I believe. Have the goodness, sir, to go in by your road, and we'll go round and knock at the front door in the proper way. We shall have to disturb the house after all."

Heriot insisted. I was astonished to see Boddy obey him and leave us, after my dear Heriot had hopped with his hand on my shoulder to the corner of the house fronting the road. While we were standing alone a light cart drove by. Heriot hailed it, and hopped up to the driver.

"Take me to London, there's a good fellow," he said; "I'm a gentleman; you needn't look fixed. I'll pay you well and thank you. But quick. Haul me up, up; here's my hand. By jingo! this is pain."

The man said, "Scamped it out of school, sir?"

Heriot replied: "Mum. Rely on me when I tell you I'm a gentleman."

"Well, if I pick up a gentleman I can't be doing a bad business," said the man, hauling him in tenderly.

Heriot sung to me in his sweet manner: "Good-bye, little Richie. Knock when five minutes are over. God bless you, dear little lad! Leg'll get well by morning, never fear for me; and we'll meet somehow; we'll drink the Burgundy. No crying. Kiss your hand to me."

I kissed my hand to him. I had no tears to shed; my chest kept heaving enormously. My friend was gone. I stood in the road straining to hear the last of the wheels after they had long been silent.

CHAPTER VI.

A TALE OF A GOOSE.

From that hour till the day Heriot's aunt came to see me, I lived systematically out of myself in extreme flights of imagination, locking my doors up, as it were, all the faster for the extremest strokes of Mr. Rippenger's rod. He remarked justly that I grew an impenetrably sullen boy, a constitutional rebel, a callous lump: and assured me that if

my father would not pay for me, I at least should not escape
my debts. The title of little impostor, transmitted from the
master's mouth to the school in designation of one who had
come to him as a young prince, and for whom he had not
received one penny's indemnification, naturally caused me to
have fights with several of the boys. Whereupon I was
reported: I was prayed at to move my spirit, and flogged to
exercise my flesh. The prayers I soon learnt to laugh to
scorn. The floggings, after they were over, crowned me
with delicious sensations of martyrdom. Even while the
sting lasted I could say, it's for Heriot and Julia! and it
gave me a wonderful penetration into the mournful ecstasy
of love. Julia was sent away to a relative by the sea-side,
because, one of the housemaids told me, she could not bear
to hear of my being beaten. Mr. Rippenger summoned me
to his private room to bid me inform him whether I had
other relatives besides my father, such as grandfather,
grandmother, uncles, or aunts, or a mother. I dare say
Julia would have led me to break my word to my father by
speaking of old Riversley, a place I half longed for since my
father had grown so distant and dim to me; but confession
to Mr. Rippenger seemed, as he said of Heriot's behaviour
to him, a gross breach of trust to my father; so I refused
steadily to answer, and suffered the consequences now on
my dear father's behalf.

Heriot's aunt brought me a cake, and in a letter from him
an extraordinary sum of money for a boy of my age. He
wrote that he knew I should want it to pay my debts for
treats to the boys and keep them in good humour. He believed
also that his people meant to have me for the Christmas
holidays. The sum he sent me was five pounds, carefully
enclosed. I felt myself a prince again. The money was
like a golden gate through which freedom twinkled a finger.
Forthwith I paid my debts, amounting to two pounds twelve
shillings, and instructed a couple of day-boarders, commercial fellows, whose heavy and mysterious charges for com-
missions ran up a bill in no time, to prepare to bring us
materials for a feast on Saturday. Temple abominated the
trading propensities of these boys. "They never get licked
and they've always got money, at least I know they always
get mine," said he; "but you and I and Heriot despise
them." Our position toward them was that of an encum-

bered aristocracy, and really they paid us great respect.
The fact was that, when they had trusted us, they were
compelled to continue obsequious, for Heriot had instilled
the sentiment in the school that gentlemen never failed to
wipe out debts in the long run, so it was their interest to
make us feel they knew us to be gentlemen, who were at
some time or other sure to pay, and thus also they operated
on our consciences. From which it followed that one title
of superiority among us, ranking next in the order of nobility
to the dignity conferred by Mr. Rippenger's rod, was the
being down in their books. Temple and I walked in the
halo of unlimited credit like more than mortal twins. I
gave an order for four bottles of champagne.

On the Friday evening Catman walked out with us. His
studious habits endeared him to us immensely, owing to his
having his head in his book on all occasions, and a walk
under his superintendence was first cousin to liberty. Some
boys roamed ahead, some lagged behind, while Catman
turned over his pages, sounding the return only when it
grew dark. The rumour of the champagne had already
intoxicated the boys. There was a companion and most
auspicious rumour that Boddy was going to be absent on
Saturday. If so, we said, we may drink our champagne
under Catman's nose and he be none the wiser. Saddlebank
undertook to manage our feast for us. Coming home over
the downs, just upon twilight, Temple and I saw Saddlebank carrying a long withy upright. We asked him what
it was for. He shouted back: "It's for fortune. You keep
the rearguard." Then we saw him following a man and a
flock of geese, and imitating the action of the man with his
green wand. As we were ready to laugh at anything
Saddlebank did, we laughed at this. The man walked like
one half asleep, and appeared to wake up now and then to
find that he was right in the middle of his geese, and then
he waited, and Saddlebank waited behind him. Presently
the geese passed a lane leading off the downs. We saw
Saddlebank duck his wand in a coaxing way, like an angler
dropping his fly for fish; he made all sorts of curious easy
flourishes against the sky and branched up the lane. We
struck after him, little suspecting that he had a goose in
front, but he had; he had cut one of the loiterers off from
the flock; and to see him handle his wand on either side his

goose, encouraging it to go forward, and remonstrating, and addressing it in bits of Latin, and the creature pattering stiff and astonished, sent us in a dance of laughter.

" What have you done, old Saddle ?" said Temple, though it was perfectly clear what Saddlebank had done.

" I've carved off a slice of Michaelmas," said Saddlebank, and he hewed the air to flick delicately at his goose's head.

" What do you mean—a slice ?" said we.

We wanted to be certain the goose was captured booty. Saddlebank would talk nothing but his fun. Temple fetched a roaring sigh :

" Oh ! how good this goose 'd be with our champagne."

The idea seized and enraptured me. " Saddlebank, I'll buy him of you," I said.

" Chink won't flavour him," said Saddlebank, still at his business : " here, you two, cut back by the down and try all your might to get a dozen apples before Catman counts heads at the door, and you hold your tongues."

We shot past the man with the geese—I pitied him— clipped a corner of the down, and by dint of hard running reached the main street, mad for apples, before Catman appeared there. Apples, champagne, and cakes were now provided ; all that was left to think of was the goose. We glorified Saddlebank's cleverness to the boys.

" By jingo ! what a treat you'll have," Temple said among them, bursting with our secret.

Saddlebank pleaded that he had missed his way on presenting himself ten minutes after time. To me and Temple he breathed of goose, but he shunned us ; he had no fun in him till Saturday afternoon, when Catman called out to hear if we were for cricket or a walk.

" A walk on the downs," said Saddlebank.

Temple and I echoed him, and Saddlebank motioned his hand as though he were wheedling his goose along. Saddlebank spoke a word to my commissioners. I was to leave the arrangements for the feast to him, he said. John Salter was at home unwell, so Saddlebank was chief. No sooner did we stand on the downs than he gathered us all in a circle, and taking off his cap threw in it some slips of paper. We had to draw lots who should keep by Catman out of twenty-seven ; fifteen blanks were marked. Temple dashed his hand into the cap first. " Like my luck," he remarked,

and pocketed both fists as he began strutting away to hide
his desperation at drawing a blank. I bought a substitute
for him at the price of half-a-crown,—Drew, a fellow we
were glad to get rid of; he wanted five shillings. The
feast was worth fifty, but to haggle about prices showed the
sneak. He begged us to put by a taste for him; he was
groaned out of hearing. The fifteen looked so wretched
when they saw themselves divided from us that I gave them
a shilling a-piece to console them. They took their instructions from Saddlebank as to how they were to surround
Catman, and make him fancy us to be all in his neighbourhood; and then we shook hands, they requesting us feebly
to drink their healths, and we saying, ay, that we would.
Temple was in distress of spirits because of his having been
ignominiously bought off. Saddlebank, however, put on
such a pace that no one had leisure for melancholy. "I'll
get you fellows up to boiling point," said he. There was a
tremendously hot sun overhead. On a sudden he halted,
exclaiming: "Cooks and gridirons! what about sage and
onions?" Only Temple and I jumped at the meaning of
this. We drew lots for a messenger, and it was miserable
to behold an unfortunate fellow touch Saddlebank's hand
containing the notched bit of stick, and find himself condemned to go and buy sage and onions somewhere, without
knowing what it was for:—how could he guess we were
going to cook a raw goose! The lot fell to a boy named
Barnshed, a big slow boy, half way up every class he was
in, but utterly stupid out of school; which made Saddlebank say: "They'll take it he's the bird that wants stuff-
ing." Barnshed was directed where to rejoin us. The
others asked why he was trotted after sage and onions.
"Because he's an awful goose," said Saddlebank. Temple
and I thought the word was out and hurrahed, and back
came Barnshed. We had a task in persuading him to
resume his expedition, as well as Saddlebank to forgive us.
Saddlebank's anger was excessive. We conciliated him by
calling him captain, and pretending to swear an oath of
allegiance. He now led us through a wood on to some
fields down to a shady dell, where we were to hold the feast
in privacy. He did not descend it himself. Vexatious as
it was to see a tramp's tent there, we nevertheless acknowledged the respectful greeting of the women and the man

with a few questions about tent-pegs, pots, and tin mugs. Saddlebank remained aloft, keeping a look-out for the day-school fellows, Chaunter, Davis, and Bystop, my commissioners. They did not keep us waiting long. They had driven to the spot in a cart, according to Saddlebank's directions. Our provisions were in three large hampers. We praised their forethought loudly at the sight of an extra bottle of champagne, with two bottles of ginger-wine, two of currant, two of raisin, four pint bottles of ale, six of gingerbeer, a Dutch cheese, a heap of tarts, three sally-lunns, and four shillingsworth of toffy. Temple and I joined our apples to the mass: a sight at which some of the boys exulted aloud. The tramp-women insisted on spreading things out for us: ten yards off their children squatted staring: the man smoked and chaffed us.

At last Saddlebank came running over the hill-side, making as if he meant to bowl down what looked a black body of a baby against the sky, and shouting, "See, you fellows, here's a find!" He ran through us, swinging his goose up to the hampers, saying that he had found the goose under a furze-bush. While the words were coming out of his mouth, he saw the tramps, and the male tramp's eyes and his met.

The man had one eyebrow and his lips at one corner screwed in a queer lift: he winked slowly, "Odd! ain't it?" he said.

Saddlebank shouldered round on us, and cried, "Confound you fellows! here's a beastly place you've pitched upon." His face was the colour of scarlet in patches.

"Now, I call it a beautiful place," said the man, "and if you finds goosies hereabouts growing ready for the fire, all but plucking, why, it's a bountiful place, I call it."

The women tried to keep him silent. But for them we should have moved our encampment. "Why, of course, young gentlemen, if you want to eat the goose, we'll pluck it for you and cook it for you, all nice," they said. "How can young gentlemen do that for theirselves?"

It was clear to us we must have a fire for the goose. Certain observations current among us about the necessity to remove the goose's inside, and not to lose the giblets, which even the boy who named them confessed his inability to recognize, inclined the majority to accept the woman's proposal. Saddlebank said it was on our heads, then.

To revive his good humour, Temple uncorked a bottle of champagne. The tramp-woman lent us a tin mug, and round it went. One boy said, "That's a commencement;" another said, "Hang old Rippenger." Temple snapped his fingers, and Bystop, a farmer's son, said, "Well, now I've drunk champagne; I meant to before I died!" Most of the boys seemed puzzled by it. As for me, my heart sprang up in me like a colt turned out of stables to graze. I determined that the humblest of my retainers should feed from my table, and drink to my father's and Heriot's honour, and I poured out champagne for the women, who just sipped, and the man, who vowed he preferred beer. A spoonful of the mashed tarts I sent to each of the children. Only one, the eldest, a girl about a year older than me, or younger, with black eyebrows and rough black hair, refused to eat or drink.

"Let her bide, young gentlemen," said a woman; "she's a regular obstinate, once she sets in for it."

"Ah!" said the man, "I've seen pigs druv, and I've seen iron bent double. She's harder 'n both, once she takes 't into her head."

"By jingo, she's pig-iron!" cried Temple, and sighed, "Oh, dear old Heriot!"

I flung myself beside him to talk of our lost friend.

A great commotion stirred the boys. They shrieked at beholding their goose vanish in a pot for stewing. They wanted roast-goose, they exclaimed, not boiled; who cared for boiled goose! But the women asked them how it was possible to roast a goose on the top of wood-flames, where there was nothing to hang it by, and nothing would come of it except smoked bones!

The boys groaned in consternation, and Saddlebank sowed discontent by grumbling, "Now you see what your jolly new acquaintances have done for you."

So we played at catch with the Dutch cheese, and afterwards bowled it for long-stopping, when, to the disgust of Saddlebank and others, down ran the black-haired girl and caught the ball clean at wicket-distance. As soon as she had done it she was ashamed, and slunk away.

The boys called out, "Now then, pig-iron!"

One fellow enraged me by throwing an apple that hit her in the back. We exchanged half-a-dozen blows, whereupon he consented to apologize, and roared, "Hulloa, pig-iron, sorry if I hurt you."

Temple urged me to insist on the rascal's going on his knees for flinging at a girl.

"Why," said Chaunter, "you were the first to call her pig-iron."

Temple declared he was a blackguard if he said that. I made the girl take a piece of toffy.

"Aha!" Saddlebank grumbled, "this comes of the precious company you would keep in spite of my caution."

The man told us to go it, for he liked to observe young gentlemen enjoying themselves. Temple tossed him a pint bottle of beer, with an injunction to him to shut his trap.

"Now, you talk my mother tongue," said the man; "you're what goes by the name of a learned gentleman. Thank ye, sir. You'll be a counsellor some day."

"I won't get off thieves, I can tell you," said Temple. He was the son of a barrister.

"Nor you won't help cook their gooses for them, may be," said the man. "Well, kindness is kindness, all over the world."

The women stormed at him to command him not to anger the young gentlemen, for Saddlebank was swearing awfully in an undertone. He answered them that he was the mildest lamb afloat.

Despairing of the goose, we resolved to finish the cold repast awaiting us. The Dutch cheese had been bowled into bits. With a portion of the mashed tarts on it, and champagne, it tasted excellently; toffy to follow. Those boys who chose ginger-wine had it, and drank, despised. The ginger-beer and ale, apples and sally-lunns, were reserved for supper. My mind became like a driving sky, with glimpses of my father and Heriot bursting through.

"If I'm not a prince, I'm a nobleman," I said to Temple.

He replied, "Army or Navy. I don't much care which. We're sure of a foreign war some time. Then you'll see fellows rise: lieutenant, captain, colonel, General—quick as barrels popping at a bird. I should like to be Governor of Gibraltar."

"I'll come and see you, Temple," said I.

" Done ! old Richie," he said, grasping my hand warmly,

" The truth is, Temple," I confided to him, " I've an uncle—I mean a grandfather—of enormous property ; he owns half Hampshire, I believe, and hates my father like poison. I won't stand it. You've seen my father, haven't you ? Gentlemen never forget their servants, Temple. Let's drink lots more champagne. I wish you and I were knights riding across that country there, as they used to, and you saying, ' I wonder whether your father's at home in the castle expecting our arrival.' "

" The Baron !" said Temple. " He's like a Baron, too. His health. Your health, sir ! It's just the wine to drink it in, Richie. He's one of the men I look up to. It's odd he never comes to see you, because he's fond of you ; the right sort of father ! Big men can't be always looking after little boys. Not that we're so young though, now. Lots of fellows of our age have done things fellows write about. I feel——" Temple sat up swelling his chest to deliver an important sentiment ; " I feel uncommonly·thirsty."

So did I. We attributed it to the air of the place, Temple going so far as to say that it came off the chalk, which somehow stuck in the throat.

" Saddlebank, don't look glum," said Temple. " Lord, Richie, you should hear my father plead in Court with his wig on. They used to say at home I was a clever boy when I was a baby. Saddlebank, you've looked glum all the afternoon."

" Treat your superiors respectfully," Saddlebank retorted.

The tramp was irritating him. That tramp had never left off smoking and leaning on his arm since we first saw him. Two boys named Hackman and Montague, not bad fellows, grew desirous of a whiff from his pipe. They had it, and lay down silent, back to back. Bystop was led away in a wretched plight. Two others, Paynter and Ashworth, attacked the apples, rendered desperate by thirst. Saddlebank repelled them furiously. He harangued those who might care to listen.

" You fellows, by George ! you shall eat the goose, I tell you. You've spoilt everything, and I tell you, whether you like it or not, you shall have apples with it, and sage and onions too. I don't ask for thanks. And I propose to post outposts in the wood to keep watch."

He wanted us to draw lots again. His fun had entirely departed from him; all he thought of was seeing the goose out of the pot. I had a feeling next to hatred for one who could talk of goose. Temple must have shared it.

" We've no real captain now dear old Heriot's gone," he said. " The school's topsy-turvy : we're like a lot of things rattled in a box. Oh, dear! how I do like a good commander. On he goes you after him, never mind what happens."

A pair of inseparable friends, Happitt and Larkins, nick-named Happy-go-Lucky, were rolling arm-in-arm, declaring they were perfectly sober, and, for a proof of it, trying to direct their feet upon a lump of chalk, and marching, and missing it. Up came Chaunter to them : " Fat goose !" he said—no more. Both the boys rushed straight as far as they could go; both sung out, " I'm done !" and they were.

Temple and I contemplated these proceedings as matters belonging to the ordinary phenomena of feasting. We agreed that gentlemen were always the last to drop, and were assured, therefore, of our living out the field ; but I dreaded the moment of the goose's appearance, and I think he did also. Saddlebank's pertinacity · in withholding the cool ginger-beer and the apples offended us deeply ; we should have conspired against him had we reposed confidence in our legs and our tongues. Twilight was around us. The tramp-children lay in little bundles in one tent; another was being built by the women and the girl. Overhead I counted numbers of stars, all small ; and lights in the valley —lights of palaces to my imagination. Stars and tramps seemed to me to go together. Houses imprisoned us, I thought : a lost father was never to be discovered by re-maining in them. Plunged among dark green leaves, smell-ing wood-smoke, at night; at morning waking up, and the world alight, and you standing high, and marking the hills where you will see the next morning and the next, morning after morning, and one morning the dearest person in the world surprising you just before you wake : I thought this a heavenly pleasure. But, observing the narrowness of the tents, it struck me there would be snoring companions. I felt so intensely sensitive, that the very idea of a snore gave me tremours and qualms : it was associated with the sense of fat. Saddlebank had the lid of the pot in his hand ; we smelt the goose, and he cried, " Now for supper ; now for it ! Halloa, you fellows !"

" Bother it, Saddlebank, you'll make Catman hear you," said Temple, wiping his forehead.

I perspired coldly.

" Catman ! He's been at it for the last hour and a half," Saddlebank replied.

One boy ran up : he was ready, and the only one who was. Presently Chaunter rushed by.

" Barnshed's in custody; I'm away home," he said, passing.

We stared at the black opening of the dell.

" Oh, it's Catman ; we don't mind him," Saddlebank reassured us ; but we heard ominous voices, and perceived people standing over a prostrate figure. Then we heard a voice too well known to us. It said, " The explanation of a pupil in your charge, Mr. Catman, being sent barefaced into the town—a scholar of mine—for sage and onions . . . ."

" Old Rippenger !" breathed Temple.

We sat paralyzed. Now we understood the folly of despatching a donkey like Barnshed for sage and onions.

" Oh, what asses we have been !" Temple continued. " Come along – we run for it ! Come along, Richie ! They're picking up the fellows like windfalls."

I told him I would not run for it; in fact, I distrusted my legs ; and he was staggering, answering Saddlebank's reproaches for having come among tramps.

" Temple, I see you, sir !" called Mr. Rippenger. Poor Temple had advanced into the firelight.

With the instinct to defeat the master, I crawled in the line of the shadows to the farther side of a tent, where I felt a hand clutch mine. " Hide me," said I ; and the curtain of the tent was raised. After squeezing through boxes and straw, I lay flat, covered by a mat smelling of abominable cheese, and felt a head outside it on my chest. Several times Mr. Rippenger pronounced my name in the way habitual to him in anger : " Rye !"

Temple's answer was inaudible to me. Saddlebank spoke, and other boys, and the man and the woman. Then a light was thrust in the tent, and the man said, " Me deceive you, sir ! See for yourself, to satisfy yourself. Here's our little uns laid warm, and a girl there, head on the mat, going down to join her tribe at Lipcombe, and one of our women sleeps here, and all told. But for you to suspect me of combining——Thank ye, sir. You've got my word as a man."

The light went away. My chest was relieved of the weight on it. I sat up, and the creature who had been kind to me laid mat and straw on the ground, and drew my head on her shoulder, where I slept fast.

CHAPTER VII.

A FREE LIFE ON THE ROAD.

I WOKE very early, though I had taken kindly to my pillow, as I found by my having an arm round my companion's neck, and her fingers intertwisted with mine. For awhile I lay looking at her eyes, which had every imaginable light and signification in them; they advised me to lie quiet, they laughed at my wonder, they said, "Dear little fellow!" they flashed as from under a cloud, darkened, flashed out of it, seemed to dip in water and shine, and were sometimes like a view into a forest, sometimes intensely sunny, never quite still. I trusted her, and could have slept again, but the sight of the tent stupefied me; I fancied the sky had fallen, and gasped for air; my head was extremely dizzy, too; not one idea in it was kept from wheeling. This confusion of my head flew to my legs when, imitating her, I rose to go forth. In a fit of horror I thought, "I've forgotten how to walk!"

Summoning my manful resolution, I made the attempt to step across the children swaddled in matting and straw and old gowns or petticoats. The necessity for doing it with a rush seized me after the first step. I pitched over one little bundle, right on to the figure of a sleeping woman. All she did was to turn round, murmuring, "Naughty Jackie." My companion pulled me along gravely, and once in the air, with a good breath of it in my chest, I felt tall and strong, and knew what had occurred. The tent where I had slept struck me as more curious than my own circumstances. I lifted my face to the sky; it was just sunrise, beautiful;

bits of long and curling cloud brushed any way close on the blue, and rosy, and white, deliciously cool; the grass was all grey, our dell in shadow, and the tops of the trees burning, a few birds twittering.

I sucked a blade of grass.

" I wish it was all water here," I said.

" Come and have a drink and a bathe," said my companion.

We went down the dell and over a juniper slope, reminding me of my day at John Salter's house and the last of dear Heriot. Rather to my shame, my companion beat me at running; she was very swift, and my legs were stiff.

" Can you swim ?" she asked me.

" I can row, and swim, and fence, and ride, and fire a pistol," I said.

" Oh, dear," said she, after eyeing me enviously. I could see that I had checked a recital of her accomplishments.

We arrived at a clear stream in a gentleman's park, where grass rolled smooth as sea-water on a fine day, and cows and horses were feeding.

" I can catch that horse and mount him," she said.

I was astonished.

" Straddle ?"

She nodded down for " Yes."

" No saddle ?"

She nodded level for " No."

My respect for her returned. But she could not swim.

" Only up to my knees," she confessed.

" Have a look at me," said I; and I stripped and shot into the water, happy as a fish, and thinking how much nicer it was than champagne. My enjoyment made her so envious that she plucked off her stockings, and came in as far as she dared. I called to her, " You're like a cow," and she showed her teeth, bidding me not say that.

" A cow! a cow!" I repeated, in my superior pleasure.

She spun out in a breath: " If you say that, I'll run away with every bit of your clothes, and you'll come out and run about naked, you will."

" Now I float," was my answer, " now I dive;" and when I came up she welcomed me with a big bright grin.

A smart run in the heat dried me. I dressed, finding half my money on the grass. She asked me to give her one of those bits—a shilling. I gave her two, upon which she asked me, invitingly, if ever I tossed. I replied that 1 never tossed for money ; but she had caught a shilling, and I could not resist guessing "heads," and won; the same with her second shilling. She handed them to me sullenly, sobbing, yet she would not take them back.

"By-and-by you give me another two," she said, growing lively again.

We agreed that it would be a good thing if we entered the village and bought something. None of the shops were open. We walked through the churchyard. I said, "Here's where dead people are buried."

"I'll dance if you talk about dead people," said she, and began whooping at the pitch of her voice. On my wishing to know why she did it, her reply was that it was to make the dead people hear. My feelings were strange : the shops not open, and no living people to be seen. We climbed trees, and sat on a branch talking of birds' eggs till hunger drove us to the village street, where, near the public-house, we met the man tramp, who whistled.

He was rather amusing. He remarked that he put no questions to me, because he put no question to anybody, because answers excited him about subjects that had no particular interest to him, and did not benefit him to the extent of a pipe of tobacco ; and all through not being inquisitive, yesterday afternoon he had obtained, as if it had been chucked into his lap, a fine-flavoured fat goose honourably for his supper, besides bottles of ale, bottles of ginger-pop, and a fair-earned half-crown. That was through his not being inquisitive, and he was not going to be inquisitive now, knowing me for a gentleman : my master had tipped him half-a-crown.

Fortunately for him, and perhaps for my liberty, he employed a verb marvellously enlightening to a school-boy. I tipped him another half-crown. He thanked me, observing that there were days when you lay on your back and the sky rained apples ; while there were other days when you wore your fingers down to the first joint to catch a flea. Such was Fortune !

In a friendly manner he advised me to go to school; if not there, then to go home. My idea, which I had only partly conceived, was to have a look at Riversley over a hedge, kiss my aunt Dorothy unaware, and fly subsequently in search of my father. Breakfast, however, was my immediate thought. He and the girl sat down to breakfast at the inn as my guests. We ate mutton-chops and eggs, and drank coffee. After it, though I had no suspicions, I noticed that the man grew thoughtful. He proposed to me, supposing I had no objection against slow travelling, to join company for a couple of days, if I was for Hampshire, which I stated was the county I meant to visit.

"Well then, here now, come along, d'ye see, look," said he, "I mustn't be pounced on, and no missing young gentle man in my society, and me took half-a-crown for his absence, that won't do. You get on pretty well with the gal, and that's a screaming farce: none of us do. Lord! she looks down on such scum as us. She's gipsy blood, true sort; everything's sausages that gets into their pockets, no matter what it was when it was out. Well then, now, here, you and the gal go t'other side o' Bed'lming, and you wait for us on the heath, and we'll be there to comfort ye 'fore dark. Is it a fister?"

He held out his hand; I agreed; and he remarked that he now counted a breakfast in the list of his gains from never asking questions.

I was glad enough to quit the village in a hurry, for the driver of the geese, or a man dreadfully resembling him, passed me near the public-house, and attacked my conscience on the cowardly side, which is, I fear, the first to awaken, and always the liveliest half while we are undisciplined. I would have paid him money, but the idea of a conversation with him indicated the road back to school. My companion related her history. She belonged to a Hampshire gipsy tribe, and had been on a visit to a relative down in the East counties, who died on the road, leaving her to be brought home by these tramps: she called them mumpers, and made faces when she spoke of them. Gipsies, she said, were a different sort: gipsies camped in gentlemen's parks; gipsies, horses, fiddles, and the wide world—that was what she liked. The wide world she described as a heath, where you looked and never saw the end of it. I let her talk on. For me to talk of my affairs to a girl without bonnet and boots would have been absurd. Otherwise, her society pleased me: she was so like a boy, and unlike any boy I knew.

My mental occupation on the road was to calculate how many hill-tops I should climb before I beheld Riversley. The Sunday bells sounded homely from village to village as soon as I was convinced that I heard no bells summoning boarders to Rippenger's school. The shops in the villages continued shut; however, I told the girl they should pay me for it next day, and we had an interesting topic in discussing as to the various things we would buy. She was for bright ribands and draper's stuff, I for pastry and letter-paper. The smell of people's dinners united our appetites. Going through a village I saw a man carrying a great baked pie, smelling overpoweringly, so that to ask him his price for it was a natural impulse with me. " What! sell my Sunday dinner," he said, and appeared ready to drop the dish. Nothing stopped his staring until we had finished a plateful a-piece and some beer in his cottage among his family. He wanted to take me in alone. " She's a common tramp," he said of the girl.

" That's a lie," she answered.

Of course I would not leave her hungry outside, so in the end he reluctantly invited us both, and introduced us to his wife.

" Here's a young gentleman asks a bit o' dinner, and a young I-d'n-know-what's after the same; I leaves it to you, missus."

His wife took it off his shoulders in good humour, saying it was lucky she made the pie big enough for her family and strays. They would not accept more than a shilling for our joint repast. The man said that was the account to a farthing, if I was too proud to be a poor man's guest, and insisted on treating him like a public. Perhaps I would shake hands at parting? I did cordially, and remembered him when people were not so civil. They wanted to know whether we had made a runaway match of it. The fun of passing a boys'-school and hearing the usher threaten to punish one fellow for straying from ranks, entertained me immensely. I laughed at them just as the stupid people we met laughed at me, which was unpleasant for the time; but I knew there was not a single boy who would not have changed places with me, only give him the chance, though my companion was a gipsy girl, and she certainly did look odd company for a gentleman's son in a tea-garden and public-house parlour. At nightfall, however, I was glad of her and she of me, and we walked hand in hand. I narrated tales of Roman history. It was very well for her to say, "I'll mother you," as we lay down to sleep; I discovered that she would never have hooted over churchyard graves in the night. She confessed she believed the devil went about in the night. Our bed was a cart under a shed, our bed-clothes fern-leaves and armfuls of straw. The shafts of the cart were down, so we lay between upright and level, and awakening in the early light I found our four legs hanging over the seat in front. "How you have been kicking!" said I. She accused me of the same. Next minute she pointed over the side of the cart, and I saw the tramp's horse and his tents beneath a broad roadside oak-tree. Her face was comical, just like a boy's who thinks he has escaped and is caught. "Let's run," she said. Preferring positive inde-pendence, I followed her, and then she told me that she had overheard the tramp last night swearing I was as good as a fistful of half-crowns lost to him if he missed me. The image of Rippenger's school overshadowed me at this com-munication. With some melancholy I said: "You'll join your friends, won't you?"

She snapped her fingers: "Mumpers!" and walked on carelessly.

We were now on the great heaths. They brought the memory of my father vividly; the smell of the air half inclined me to turn my steps toward London, I grew so full of longing for him. Nevertheless I resolved to have one gaze at Riversley, my aunt Dorothy, and Sewis, the old grey-brown butler, and the lamb that had grown a sheep; wonderful contrasts to my grand kings of England career. My first clear recollection of Riversley was here, like an outline of a hill seen miles away. I might have shed a tear or two out of love for my father, had not the thought that I was a very queer boy displaced his image. I could not but be a very queer boy, such a lot of things happened to me. Suppose I joined the gipsies? My companion wished me to. She had brothers horse-dealers, beautiful fiddlers. Suppose I learnt the fiddle? Suppose I learnt their lan-guage and went about with them and became king of the gipsies? My companion shook her head; she could not encourage this ambitious idea because she had never heard of a king of the gipsies or a queen either. "We fool people," she said, and offended me, for our school believed in a gipsy king, and one fellow, Hackman, used to sing a song of a gipsy king; and it was as much as to say that my school-fellows were fools, every one of them. I accused her of telling lies. She grinned angrily. "I don't tell 'em to friends," she said. We had a quarrel. The truth was, I was enraged at the sweeping out of my prospects of rising to distinction among the gipsies. After breakfast at an inn, where a waiter laughed at us to our faces, and we fed scowling, shy, and hungry, we had another quarrel. I informed her of my opinion that gipsies could not tell fortunes.

"They can, and you come to my mother and my aunt, and see if they can't tell your fortune," said she, in a fury.

"Yes, and that's how they fool people," said I. I enjoyed seeing the flash of her teeth. But my daring of her to look me in the eyes and swear on her oath she believed the fortunes true ones, sent her into a fit of sullenness.

"Go along, you nasty little fellow, your shadow isn't half a yard," she said, and I could smile at that; my shadow stretched half across the road. We had a quarrelsome day wherever we went; rarely walking close together till night-fall, when she edged up to my hand, with, "I say, I'll keep ɔu warm to-night, I will." She hugged me almost too tight, but it was warm and social, and helped to the triumph of a feeling I had that nothing made me regret running away from Rippenger's school.

An adventure befell us in the night. A farmer's wife, whom we asked for a drink of water after dark, lent us an old blanket to cover us in a dry ditch on receiving our promise not to rob the orchard. An old beggar came limping by us, and wanted to share our covering. My companion sank right under the blanket to peer at him through one of its holes. He stood enormous above me in the moonlight, like an apparition touching earth and sky.

"Cold, cold," he whined: "there's ne'er a worse off but there's a better off. Young un!" His words dispersed the fancy that he was something horrible, or else my father in disguise going to throw off his rags, and shine, and say he had found me. "Are ye one, or are ye two?" he asked.

I replied that we were two.

"Then I'll come and lie in the middle," said he.

"You can't; there's no room," I sang out.

"Lord," said he, "there's room for any reckoning o' empty stomachs in a ditch."

"No, I prefer to be alone : good-night," said I.

"Why!" he exclaimed, "where ha' you been t' learn language? Halloa!"

"Please, leave me alone; it's my intention to go to sleep," I said, vexed at having to conciliate him; he had a big stick.

"Oho!" went the beggar. Then he recommenced :—

"Tell me you've stole nothing in your life! You've stole a gentleman's tongue, I knows the ring o' that. How comes you out here? Who's your mate there down below? Now, see, I'm goin' to lift my stick."

At these menacing words the girl jumped out of the blanket, and I called to him that I would rouse the farmer.

"Why . . . because I'm goin' to knock down a apple or two on your head?" he inquired, in a tone of reproach. "It's a young woman you've got there, eh? Well, odd grows odder, like the man who turned three shillings into five. Now, you gi' me a lie under your blanket, I'll knock down a apple a-piece. If ever you've tasted gin, you'll say a apple at night's a cordial, though it don't intoxicate."

The girl whispered in my ear, "He's lame as ducks." Her meaning seized me at once; we both sprang out of the ditch and ran, dragging our blanket behind us. He pursued, but we eluded him, and dropped on a quiet sleeping-place among furzes. Next morning, when we took the blanket to the farm-house, we heard that the old wretch had traduced our characters, and got a breakfast through charging us with the robbery of the apple-tree. I proved our innocence to the farmer's wife by putting down a shilling. The sight of it satisfied her. She combed my hair, brought me a bowl of water and a towel, and then gave us a bowl of milk and bread, and dismissed us, telling me I had a fair face and dare-devil written on it : as for the girl, she said of her that she knew gipsies at a glance, and what God Almighty made them for there was no guessing. This set me thinking all through the day, "What can they have been made for?" I bought a red scarf for the girl, and other things she fixed her eyes on, but I lost a great deal of my feeling of fellowship with her. "I dare say they were made for fun," I thought, when people laughed at us

now, and I laughed also. I had a day of rollicking laughter,
puzzling the girl, who could only grin two or three seconds
at a time, and then stared like a dog that waits for his
master to send him off again running, the corners of her
mouth twitching for me to laugh or speak, exactly as a dog
might wag his tail. I studied her in the light of a harmless sort of unaccountable creature; witness at any rate for
the fact that I had escaped from school.

We loitered half the morning round a cricketer's booth
in a field, where there was moderately good cricketing.
The people thought it of first-rate quality. I told them I
knew a fellow who could bowl out either eleven in an hour
and a half. One of the men frightened me by saying, " By
Gearge! I'll in with you into a gig, and off with you after
that ther' faller." He pretended to mean it, and started
up. I watched him without flinching. He remarked that
if I " had not cut my lucky from school, and tossed my cap
for a free life, he was——" whatever may be expressed by a
slap on the thigh. We played a single-wicket side game,
he giving me six runs, and crestfallen he was to find himself
beaten; but, as I let him know, one who had bowled to
Heriot for hours and stood against Saddlebank's bowling,
was a tough customer, never mind his age.

This man offered me his friendship. He made me sit
and eat beside him at the afternoon dinner of the elevens,
and sent platefuls of food to the girl, where she was allowed
to squat; and said he, " You and I'll tie a knot, and be
friends for life."

I replied, " With pleasure."

We nodded over a glass of ale. In answer to his questions, I stated that I liked farms, I would come and see his
farm, I would stay with him two or three days, I would
give him my address if I had one, I was on my way to have
a look at Riversley Grange.

"Hey!" says he, " Riversley Grange! Well, to be sure
now! I'm a tenant of Squire Beltham's, and a right sort of
landlord, too."

"Oh!" says I, " he's my grandfather, but I don't care
much about him."

"Lord!" says he. "What! be you the little boy, why,
Master Harry Richmond that was carried off in the night,
and the old squire shut up doors for a fortnight, and made

out you was gone in a hearse ! Why, I know all about you,
you see. And back you are, hurrah ! The squire'll be
hearty, that he will. We've noticed a change in him ever
since you left. Gout's been at his leg, off and on, a deal
shrewder. But he rides to hounds, and dines his tenants
still, that he does; he's one o' th' old style. Everything
you eat and drink's off his estate, the day he dines his
tenants. No humbug 'bout old Squire Beltham."

I asked him if Sewis was alive.

"Why, old Sewis," says he, "you're acquainted with old
Sewis ? Why, of course you are. Yes, old Sewis's alive,
Master Harry. And you bet me at single-wicket ! That'll
be something to relate to 'em all. By Gearge, if I didn't
think I'd got a nettle in my fist when I saw you pitch into
my stumps. Dash it ! thinks I. But th' old squire'll be
proud of you, that he will. My farm lies three miles away.
You look at a crow flying due South-east five minutes from
Riversley, and he's over Throckham farm, and there I'll
drive ye to-night, and to-morrow, clean and tidy out o' my
wife's soap and water, straight to Riversley. Done, eh ?
My name's Eckerthy. No matter where you comes from,
here you are, eh, Master Harry ? And I see you last time
in a donkey-basket, and here you come in breeches and defy
me to single-wicket, and you bet me too !"

He laughed for jollity. An extraordinary number of
emotions had possession of me : the most intelligible one
being a restless vexation at myself, as the principal person
concerned, for not experiencing anything like the farmer's
happiness. I preferred a gipsy life to Riversley. Gipsies
were on the road, and that road led to my father. I endea-
voured to explain to Farmer Eckerthy that I was travelling
in this direction merely to have a short look at Riversley;
but it was impossible; he could not understand me. The
more I tried, the more he pressed me to finish my glass of
ale, which had nothing to do with it. I drank, nevertheless,
and I suppose said many funny things in my anxiety that
the farmer should know what I meant; he laughed enough.

While he was fielding against the opposite eleven, the
tramp came into the booth, and we had a match of cunning.

"Schoolmaster's out after you, young gentleman," said he,
advising me to hurry along the road if I sought to baffle
pursuit.

I pretended alarm, and then said, " Oh, you'll stand by me," and treated him to ale.

He assured me I left as many tracks behind me as if I went spilling a box of lucifer-matches. He was always for my hastening on until I ordered fresh ale for him. The girl and he grimaced at one another in contempt. So we remained seeing the game out. By the time the game ended, the tramp had drunk numbers of glasses of ale.

" A fine-flavoured fat goose," he counted his gains since the commencement of our acquaintance, " bottles of ale and ginger-pop, two half-crowns, more ale, and more to follow, let's hope. You only stick to your friends, young gentleman, won't you, sir ? It's a hard case for a poor man like me if you don't. We ain't got such chances every morning of our lives. Do you perceive, sir ? I request you to inform me, do you perceive, sir ? I'm muddled a bit, sir, but a man must look after his interests."

I perceived he was so muddled as to be unable to conceal that his interests were involved in my capture ; but I was merry too. Farmer Eckerthy dealt the tramp a scattering slap on the back when he returned to the booth, elated at having beaten the enemy by a single run.

" Master Harry Richmond go to Riversley to his grand-father in your company, you scoundrel !" he cried in a rage after listening to him. " I mean to drive him over. It's a comfortable ten-mile, and no more. But I say, Master Harry, what do you say to a peck o' supper ?"

He communicated to me confidentially that he did not like to seem to slink away from the others, who had made up their minds to stop and sup ; so we would drive home by moonlight, singing songs. And so we did. I sat beside the farmer, the girl scrambled into the hinder-part of the cart, and the tramp stood moaning, "Oh dear ! oh dear ! you goes away to Riversley without your best friend."

I tossed him a shilling. We sang beginnings and ends of songs. The farmer looked at the moon, and said, " Lord ! she stares at us !" Then he sang :—

> " The moon is shining on Latworth lea,
> And where'll she see such a jovial three
> As we, boys, we ? And why is she pale ?
> It's because she drinks water instead of ale.

Where's the remainder?   There's the song!—

> Oh ! handsome Miss Gammon
> Has married Lord Mammon,
> And jilted her suitors,
> All Cupid's sharpshooters,
> And gone in a carriage
> And six to her marriage,
> Singing hey ! for I've landed my salmon, my salmon !

Where's the remainder?   I heard it th' only time I ever was
in London town, never rested till I'd learnt it, and now it's
clean gone.   What's come to me?"

He sang to "Mary of Ellingmere" and another maid of
some place, and a loud song of Britons.

It was startling to me to wake up to twilight in the open
air and silence, for I was unaware that I had fallen asleep.
The girl had roused me, and we crept down from the cart.
Horse and farmer were quite motionless in a green hollow
beside the roadway.   Looking across fields and fir planta-
tions, I beheld a house in the strange light of the hour, and
my heart began beating; but I was overcome with shyness,
and said to myself, "No, no, that's not Riversley; I'm sure
it isn't;" though the certainty of it was, in my teeth, refuting
me.   I ran down the fields to the park and the bright little
river, and gazed.   When I could say, "Yes, it is Riversley!"
I turned away, hurt even to a sense of smarting pain, without knowing the cause.   I daresay it is true, as the girl
declared subsequently, that I behaved like one in a fit.   I
dropped, and I may have rolled my body and cried.   An in-
definite resentment at Riversley was the feeling I grew
conscious of after very fast walking.   I would not have
accepted breakfast there.

About midday, crossing a stubble-field, the girl met a
couple of her people—men.   Near evening we entered one of
their tents.   The women set up a cry, "Kiomi! Kiomi!"
like a rising rookery.   Their eyes and teeth made such a
flashing as when you dabble a hand in a dark waterpool.
The strange tongue they talked, with a kind of peck of the
voice at a word, rapid, never high or low, and then a slide
of similar tones all round,—not musical, but catching and
incessant,—gave me an idea that I had fallen upon a society
of birds, exceedingly curious ones.   They welcomed me
kindly, each of them looking me in the face a bright second

or so.   I had two helps from a splendid pot of broth that
hung over a fire in the middle of the tent.

Kiomi was my companion's name.   She had sisters Adeline
and Eveleen, and brothers Osric and William, and she had
a cousin a prize-fighter.   "That's what I'll be," said I.
Fiddling for money was not a prospect that charmed me,
though it was pleasant lying in Kiomi's arms to hear Osric
play us off to sleep; it was like floating down one of a number of visible rivers; I could see them converging and breaking away while I floated smoothly, and a wonderful fair
country nodded drowsy.   From that to cock-crow at a stride.
Sleep was no more than the passage through the arch of a
canal.   Kiomi and I were on the heath before sunrise, jumping gravel-pits, chasing sandpipers, mimicking pewits; it
seemed to me I had only just heard the last of Osric's fiddle
when yellow colour filled in along the sky over Riversley.
The curious dark thrill of the fiddle in the tent by night
seemed close up behind the sun, and my quiet fancies as I
lay dropping to sleep, followed me like unobtrusive shadows
during daylight, or, to speak truthfully, till about dinner-
time, when I thought of nothing but the great stew-pot.
We fed on plenty; nicer food than Rippenger's, minus
puddings.   After dinner I was ready for mischief.   My
sensations on seeing Kiomi beg of a gentleman were remarkable.   I reproached her.   She showed me sixpence
shining in the palm of her hand.   I gave her a shilling to
keep her from it.   She had now got one and sixpence, she
said—meaning, I supposed upon reflection, that her begging
had produced that sum, and therefore it was a good thing.
The money remaining in my pocket amounted to five shillings
and a penny.   I offered it to Kiomi's mother, who refused to
accept it; so did the father, and Osric also.   I might think
of them, they observed, on my return to my own house : they
pointed at Riversley.   "No," said I, "I shan't go there, you
may be sure."   The women grinned, and the men yawned.
The business of the men appeared to be to set to work about
everything as if they had a fire inside them, and then to
stretch out their legs and lie on their backs, exactly as if the
fire had gone out.   Excepting Osric's practice on the fiddle.
and the father's bringing in and leading away of horses, they
did little work in my sight but brown themselves in the sun.
One morning Osric's brother came to our camp with their

cousin the prize-fighter—a young man of lighter complexion, upon whom I gazed, remembering John Thresher's reverence for the heroical profession. Kiomi whispered some story concerning her brother having met the tramp. I did not listen; I was full of a tempest, owing to two causes: a studious admiration of the smart young prize-fighter's person, and wrathful disgust at him for calling Kiomi his wife, and telling her he was prepared to marry her as soon as she played her harp like King David. The intense folly of his asking a girl to play like David made me despise him, but he was splendidly handsome and strong, and to see him put on the gloves for a spar with big William, Kiomi's brother, and evade and ward the huge blows, would have been a treat to others besides old John of Dipwell farm. He had the agile grace of a leopard; his waistcoat reminded me of one; he was like a piece of machinery in free action. Pleased by my enthusiasm, he gave me a lesson, promising me more.

"He'll be champion some day," said Kiomi, at gnaw upon an apple he had given her.

I knocked the apple on the ground, and stamped on it. She slapped my cheek. In a minute we stood in a ring. I beheld the girl actually squaring at me.

"Fight away," I said, to conceal my shame, and imagining I could slip from her hits as easily as the prizefighter did from big William's. I was mistaken.

"Oh! you think I can't defend myself," said Kiomi; and rushed in with one, two, quick as a cat, and cool as a statue.

"Fight, my merry one; she takes punishment," the prizefighter sang out. "First blood to you, Kiomi; uncork his claret, my duck; straight at the nozzle, he sees more lamps than shine in London, I warrant. Make him lively, cook him; tell him who taught you; a downer to him, and I'll marry you to-morrow!"

I conceived a fury against her as though she had injured me by appearing the man's property—and I was getting the worst of it; her little fists shot straight and hard as bars of iron; she liked fighting; she was at least my match. To avoid the disgrace of seriously striking her, or of being beaten at an open exchange of blows, I made a feint, and caught her by the waist and threw her, not very neatly, for I fell myself in her grip. They had to pluck her from me by force.

" And you've gone a course of tuition in wrestling, squire ?"
the prizefighter said to me rather savagely.

The others were cordial, and did not snarl at me for going
to the ropes, as he called it. Kiomi desired to renew the
conflict. I said aloud:

" I never fight girls, and I tell you I don't like their licking
me."

" Then you come down to the river and wash your face,"
said she, and pulled me by the fingers, and when she had
washed my face clear of blood, kissed me. I thought she
tasted of the prizefighter.

Late in the afternoon Osric proposed that he and I and
the prizefighter should take a walk. I stipulated for Kiomi
to be of the party, which was allowed, and the gipsy-women
shook my hand as though I had been departing on a long
expedition, entreating me not to forget them, and never to
think evil of poor gipsy-folk.

" Why, I mean to stay with you," said I.

They grinned delightedly, and said I must be back to see
them break up camp in the evening. Every two or three
minutes Kiomi nudged my elbow and pointed behind, where
I saw the women waving their coloured neckerchiefs. Out of
sight of our tents we came in view of the tramp. Kiomi said
" Hide." I dived into a furze dell. The tramp approached,
calling out for news of me. Now at Rippenger's school,
thanks to Heriot, lying was not the fashion; still I had
heard boys lie, and they can let it out of their mouths like
a fish, so lively, simple, and solid, that you could fancy a
master had asked them for it and they answered, " There
it is." But boys cannot lie in one key spontaneously, a
number of them to the same effect, as my friends here did.
I was off, they said; all swung round to signify the direction of my steps; my plans were hinted at; particulars
were not stated on the plea that there should be no tellings;
it was remarked that I ought to have fair play and " law."
Kiomi said she hoped he would not catch me. The tramp
winced with vexation, and the gipsies chaffed him. I thanked
them in my heart for their loyal conduct. Creeping under
cover of the dell I passed round to the road over a knoll of
firs as quick as my feet could carry me, and had just cried,
" Now I'm safe;" when a lady stepping from a carriage on
the road, caught me in her arms and hugged me blind. It
was my aunt Dorothy.

CHAPTER VIII.

JANET ILCHESTER.

I was a prisoner, captured by fraud, and with five shillings and a penny still remaining to me for an assurance of my power to enjoy freedom. Osric and Kiomi did not show themselves on the road, they answered none of my shouts.

"She is afraid to look me in the face," I said, keeping my anger on Kiomi.

"Harry, Harry," said my aunt, "they must have seen me here; do you grieve, and you have me, dear ?"

Her eager brown eyes devoured me while I stood panting to be happy, if only I might fling my money at Kiomi's feet, and tell her: "There, take all I have; I hate you!" One minute I was curiously perusing the soft shade of a moustache on my aunt's upper lip ; the next, we jumped into the carriage, and she was my dear aunt Dorothy again, and the world began rolling another way.

The gipsies had made an appointment to deliver me over to my aunt; Farmer Eckerthy had spoken of me to my grandfather; the tramp had fetched Mr. Rippenger on the scene. Rippenger paid the tramp, I dare say; my grandfather paid Rippenger's bill and for Saddlebank's goose ; my aunt paid the gipsies, and I think it doubtful that they handed the tramp a share, so he came to the end of his list of benefits from not asking questions.

I returned to Riversley more of a man than most boys of my age, and more of a child. A small child would not have sulked as I did at Kiomi's behaviour; but I met my grandfather's ridiculous politeness with a man's indifference.

"So you're back, sir, are you !"

"I am, sir."

"Ran like a hare, 'stead of a fox, eh ?"

"I didn't run like either, sir."

"Do you ride ?"

"Yes, sir ; a horse."

That was his greeting and how I took it. I had not run away from him, so I had a quiet conscience.

He said, shortly after, "Look here; your name is Harry Richmond in my house—do you understand ? My servants have orders to call you Master Harry Richmond, according to your christening. You were born here, sir, you will please to recollect. I'll have no vagabond names here " —he puffed himself hot, muttering, " Nor vagabond airs neither."

1 knew very well what it meant. A sore spirit on my father's behalf kept me alive to any insult of him ; and feeling that we were immeasurably superior to the Beltham blood, I merely said, apart to old Sewis, shrugging my shoulders, " The squire expects me to recollect where I was born. I'm not likely to forget his nonsense."

Sewis, in reply, counselled me to direct a great deal of my attention to the stables, and drink claret with the squire in the evening, things so little difficult to do that I moralized reflectively, " Here's a way of gaining a relative's affection !" The squire's punctilious regard for payments impressed me, it is true. He had saved me from the disgrace of owing money to my detested schoolmaster ; and, besides, I was under his roof, eating of his bread. My late adventurous life taught me that I incurred an obligation by it. Kiomi was the sole victim of my anger that really seemed to lie down to be trampled on, as she deserved for her unpardonable treachery.

By degrees my grandfather got used to me, and commenced saying in approval of certain of my performances, " There's Beltham in that—Beltham in that !" Once out hunting, I took a nasty hedge and ditch in front of him ; he bawled proudly, " Beltham all over !" and praised me. At night, drinking claret, he said on a sudden, " And, egad, Harry, you must jump your *head* across hedges and ditches, my little fellow. It won't do, in these confounded days, to have you clever all at the wrong end. In my time, good in the saddle was good for everything ; but now you must get your brains where you can—pick here, pick there—and sell 'em like a huckster ; some do. Nature's gone—it's damned artifice rules, I tell ye ; and a squire of our country must be three parts lawyer to keep his own. You must learn ; by God, sir, you must cogitate ; you must stew at books and maps, or you'll have some infernal upstart taking the lead of you, and leaving you nothing but the whiff of his tail." He concluded, " I'm glad to see you toss down your claret, my boy."

Thus I grew in his favour, till I heard from him that I was to be the heir of Riversley and his estates, but on one condition, which he did not then mention. If I might have spoken to him of my father, I should have loved him. As it was, I liked old Sewis better, for he would talk to me of the night when my father carried me away, and though he never uttered the flattering words I longed to hear, he repeated the story often, and made the red hall glow with beams of my father's image. My walks and rides were divided between the road he must have followed toward London, bearing me in his arms, and the vacant place of Kiomi's camp. Kiomi stood for freedom, pointing into the darkness I wished to penetrate that I might find him. If I spoke of him to my aunt she trembled. She said, "Yes, Harry, tell me all you are thinking about, whatever you want to know;" but her excessive trembling checked me, and I kept my feelings to myself—a boy with a puzzle in his head and hunger in his heart. At times I rode out to the utmost limit of the hour giving me the proper number of minutes to race back and dress for dinner at the squire's table, and a great wrestling I had with myself to turn my little horse's head from hills and valleys lying East; they seemed to have the secret of my father. Blank enough they looked if ever I despaired of their knowing more than I. My Winter and Summer were the moods of my mind constantly shifting. I would have a week of the belief that he was near Riversley, calling for me; a week of the fear that he was dead; long dreams of him, as travelling through foreign countries, patting the foreheads of boys and girls on his way; or driving radiantly, and people bowing. Radiantly, I say: had there been touches of colour in these visions, I should have been lured off in pursuit of him. The dreams passed colourlessly; I put colouring touches to the figures seen in them afterward, when I was cooler, and could say, "What is the use of fancying things?" yet knew that fancying things was a consolation. By such means I came to paint the mystery surrounding my father in tender colours. I built up a fretted cathedral from what I imagined of him, and could pass entirely away out of the world by entering the doors.

Want of boys' society as well as hard head-work produced this mischief. My lessons were intermittent. Residenc tutors arrived to instruct me, one after another. They were clergymen, and they soon proposed to marry my aunt Dorothy, or they rebuked the squire for swearing. The devil was in the parsons, he said: in his time they were modest creatures and stuck to the bottle and heaven. My aunt was of the opinion of our neighbours, who sent their boys to school and thought I should be sent likewise.

"No, no," said the squire; "my life's short when the gout's marching up to my middle, and I'll see as much of my heir as I can. Why, the lad's my daughter's son! He shall grow up among his tenantry. We'll beat the country and start a man at last to drive his yard of learning into him without rolling sheep's eyes right and left."

Unfortunately the squire's description of man was not started. My aunt was handsome, an heiress (that is, she had money of her own coming from her mother's side of the family), and the tenderest woman alive, with a voice sweeter than flutes. There was a saying in the county that to marry a Beltham you must po'chay her.

A great-aunt of mine, the squire's sister, had been carried off. She died childless. A favourite young cousin of his likewise had run away with a poor baronet, Sir Roderick Ilchester, whose son Charles was now and then our playmate, and was a scapegrace. But for me he would have been selected by the squire for his heir, he said; and he often "confounded" me to my face on that account as he shook my hand, breaking out: "I'd as lief fetch you a cuff o' the head, Harry Richmond, upon my honour!" and cursing at his luck for having to study for his living, and be what he called a sloppy curate now that I had come to Riversley for good.

He informed me that I should have to marry his sister Janet; for that they could not allow the money to go out of the family. Janet Ilchester was a quaint girl, a favourite of my aunt Dorothy, and the squire's especial pet; red-cheeked, with a good upright figure in walking and riding, and willing to be friendly, but we always quarrelled: she detested hearing of Kiomi.

"Don't talk of creatures you met when you were a beggar, Harry Richmond," she said.

"I never was a beggar," I replied.

"Then she was a beggar," said Janet; and I could not

deny it; though the only difference I saw between Janet
and Kiomi was, that Janet continually begged favours and
gifts of people she knew, and Kiomi of people who were
strangers.

My allowance of pocket-money from the squire was fifty
pounds a year. I might have spent it all in satisfying Janet's
wishes for riding-whips, knives, pencil-cases, cairngorm buttons, and dogs. A large part of the money went that way.
She was always getting notice of fine dogs for sale. I bought
a mastiff for her, a brown retriever, and a little terrier. She
was permitted to keep the terrier at home, but I had to take
care of the mastiff and retriever. When Janet came to look
at them she called them by their names; of course they
followed me in preference to her; she cried with jealousy.
We had a downright quarrel. Lady Ilchester invited me
to spend a day at her house, Charley being home for his
Midsummer holidays. Charley, Janet, and I fished the river
for trout, and Janet, to flatter me (of which I was quite
aware), while I dressed her rod as if she was likely to catch
something, talked of Heriot, and then said: "Oh! dear, we
are good friends, aren't we? Charley says we shall marry
one another some day, but mama's such a proud woman she
won't much like your having such a father as you've got
unless he's dead by that time, and I needn't go up to him
to be kissed."

I stared at the girl in wonderment, but not too angrily,
for I guessed that she was merely repeating her brother's
candid speculations upon the future. I said: "Now mind
what I tell you, Janet: I forgive you this once, for you are
an ignorant little girl and know no better. Speak respectfully of my father or you never see me again."

Here Charley sang out: "Hulloa! you don't mean to say
you're talking of your father."

Janet whimpered that I had called her an ignorant little
girl. If she had been silent I should have pardoned her.
The meanness of the girl in turning on me when the glaring
offence was hers, struck me as contemptible beyond words.
Charley and I met half way. He advised me not to talk to
his sister of my father. They all knew, he said, that it was
no fault of mine, and for his part, had he a rascal for a
father, he should pension him and cut him; to tell the truth,
no objection against me existed in his family except on the

score of the sort of father I owned to, and I had better make
up my mind to shake him off before I grew a man; he spoke
as a friend. I might frown at him and clench my fists, but
he did speak as a friend.

Janet all the while was nibbling a biscuit, glancing
over it at me with mouse-eyes. Her short frock and her
greediness, contrasting with the talk of my marrying her,
filled me with renewed scorn, though my heart was sick at
the mention of my father. I asked her what she knew of
him. She nibbled her biscuit, mumbling, " He went to
Riversley, pretending he was a singing-master. I know
that's true, and more."

" Oh, and a drawing-master, and a professor of legerdemain," added her brother. " Expunge him, old fellow;
he's no good."

" No, I'm sure he's no good," said Janet.

I took her hand, and told her, " You don't know how you
hurt me; but you're a child: you don't know anything about
the world. I love my father, remember that, and what you
want me to do is mean and disgraceful; but you don't know
better. I would forfeit everything in the world for him.
And when you're of age to marry, marry anybody you like
—you won't marry me. And good-bye, Janet. Think of
learning your lessons, and not of marrying. I can't help
laughing." So I said, but without the laughter. Her
brother tried hard to get me to notice him.

Janet betook herself to the squire. Her prattle of our
marriage in days to come was excusable. It was the
squire's notion. He used to remark generally that he liked
to see things look safe and fast, and he had, as my aunt
confided to me, arranged with Lady Ilchester, in the girl's
hearing, that we should make a match. My grandfather
pledged his word to Janet that he would restore us to an
amicable footing. He thought it a light task. Invitations
were sent out to a large party at Riversley, and Janet came
with all my gifts on her dress or in her pockets. The squire
led the company to the gates of his stables; the gates opened,
and a beautiful pony, with a side-saddle on, was trotted forth,
amid cries of admiration. Then the squire put the bridle-
reins in my hands, bidding me present it myself. I asked
the name of the person. He pointed at Janet. I presented
the pony to Janet, and said, " It's from the squire."

She forgot, in her delight, our being at variance.

"No, no, you stupid Harry, I'm to thank you. He's a darling pony. I want to kiss you."

I retired promptly, but the squire had heard her.

"Back, sir!" he shouted, swearing by this and that. "You slink from a kiss, and you're Beltham blood? Back to her, lad. Take it. Up with her in your arms, or down on your knees. Take it manfully, somehow. See there, she's got it ready for you."

"I've got a letter ready for you, Harry, to say—oh! so sorry for offending you," Janet whispered, when I reached the pony's head; "and if you'd rather not be kissed before people, then by-and-by, but do shake hands."

"Pull the pony's mane," said I; "that will do as well. Observe—I pull, and now you pull."

Janet mechanically followed my actions. She grimaced, and whimpered, "I could pull the pony's mane right out."

"Don't treat animals like your dolls," said I.

She ran to the squire, and refused the pony. The squire's face changed from merry to black.

"Young man," he addressed me, "don't show that worse half of yours in genteel society, or, by the Lord! you won't carry Beltham buttons for long. This young lady, mind you, is a lady by birth both sides."

"She thinks she is marriageable," said I; and walked away, leaving loud laughter behind me.

But laughter did not console me for the public aspersion of him I loved. I walked off the grounds, and thought to myself it was quite time I should be moving. Wherever I stayed for any length of time, I was certain to hear abuse of my father. Why not wander over the country with Kiomi, go to sea, mount the Andes, enlist in a Prussian regiment, and hear the soldiers tell tales of Frederick the Great? I walked over Kiomi's heath till dark, when one of our grooms on horseback overtook me, saying that the squire begged me to jump on the horse and ride home as quick as possible. Two other lads and the coachman were out scouring the country to find me, and the squire was anxious, it appeared. I rode home like a wounded man made to feel proud by victory, but with no one to stop the bleeding of his wounds: and the more my pride rose, the more I suffered pain. There at home sat my grandfather, dejected, telling me that the loss of me a second time would kill him, begging me to overlook his roughness, calling me his little Harry and his heir, his brave-spirited boy; yet I was too sure that a word of my father to him would have brought him very near another ejaculation concerning Beltham buttons.

"You're a fiery young fellow, I suspect," he said, when he had recovered his natural temper. "I like you for it; pluck's Beltham. Have a will of your own. Sweat out the bad blood. Here, drink my health, Harry. You're three parts Beltham, at least, and it'll go hard if you're not all Beltham before I die. Old blood always wins that race, I swear. We're the oldest in the county. Damn the mixing. My father never let any of his daughters marry, if he could help it, nor'll I, bar rascals. Here's to you, young Squire Beltham. Harry Lepel Beltham—does that suit ye? Anon, anon, as they say in the play. Take my name, and drop the Richmond—no, drop the subject: we'll talk of it by-and-by."

So he wrestled to express his hatred of my father without offending me; and I studied him coldly, thinking that the sight of my father in beggar's clothes, raising a hand for me to follow his steps, would draw me forth, though Riversley should beseech me to remain clad in wealth.

CHAPTER IX.

AN EVENING WITH CAPTAIN BULSTED.

A DREAM that my father lay like a wax figure in a bed gave me thoughts of dying. I was ill and did not know it, and imagined that my despair at the foot of the stairs of ever reaching my room to lie down peacefully was the sign of death. My aunt Dorothy nursed me for a week: none but she and my dogs entered the room. I had only two faint wishes left in me: one that the squire should be kept out of my sight, the other that she would speak to me of my mother's love for my father. She happened to say, musing, " Harry, you have your mother's heart."

I said, " No, my father's."

From that we opened a conversation, the sweetest I had

ever had away from him, though she spoke shyly and told
me very little. It was enough for me in the narrow world
of my dogs' faces, and the red-leaved creeper at the window,
the fir-trees on the distant heath, and her hand clasping
mine. My father had many faults, she said, but he had
been cruelly used, or deceived, and he bore a grievous
burden; and then she said, "Yes," and "Yes," and "Yes,"
in the voice one supposes of a ghost retiring, to my questions
of his merits. I was refreshed and satisfied, like the parched
earth with dews when it gets no rain, and I was soon well.

When I walked among the household again, I found that
my week of seclusion had endowed me with a singular gift;
I found that I could see through everybody. Looking at
the squire, I thought to myself, "My father has faults, but
he has been cruelly used," and immediately I forgave the
old man; his antipathy to my father seemed a craze, and to
account for it I lay in wait for his numerous illogical acts
and words, and smiled visibly in contemplation of his rough
unreasonable nature, and of my magnanimity. He caught
the smile, and interpreted it.

"Grinning at me, Harry; have I made a slip in my grammar, eh?"

Who could feel any further sensitiveness at his fits of
irritation, reading him as I did? I saw through my aunt:
she was always in dread of a renewal of our conversation.
I could see her ideas flutter like birds to escape me. And I
penetrated the others who came in my way just as unerringly.
Farmer Eckerthy would acknowledge, astonished, his mind
was running on cricket when I taxed him with it.

"Crops was the cart-load of my thoughts, Master Harry,
but there was a bit o' cricket in it, too, ne'er a doubt."

My aunt's maid, Davis, was shocked by my discernment
of the fact that she was in love, and it was useless for her
to pretend the contrary, for I had seen her granting tender
liberties to Lady Ilchester's footman.

Old Sewis said gravely, "You've been to the witches,
Master Harry;" and others were sure "I had got it from
the gipsies off the common."

The maids were partly incredulous, but I perceived that
They disbelieved as readily as they believed. With my
latest tutor, the Rev. Simon Hart, I was not sufficiently
familiar to offer him proofs of my extraordinary power; so I

begged favours of him, and laid hot-house flowers on his
table in the name of my aunt, and had the gratification of
seeing him blush. His approval of my Latin exercise was
verbal, and weak praise in comparison; besides I cared
nothing for praises not referring to my grand natural accom-
plishment. "And my father now is thinking of me!" That
was easy to imagine, but the certainty of it confirmed me in
my conceit.

"How can you tell?—how is it possible for you to know
people's thoughts?" said Janet Ilchester, whose head was as
open to me as a hat. She pretended to be rather more
frightened of me than she was.

"And now you think you are flattering me!" I said.

She looked nervous.

"And now you're asking yourself what you can do better
than I can!"

She said, "Go on."

I stopped.

She charged me with being pulled up short.

I denied it.

"Guess, guess!" said she. "You can't."

My reply petrified her. "You were thinking that you
are a lady by birth on both sides."

At first she refused to admit it. "No, it wasn't that,
Harry, it wasn't really. I was thinking how clever you
are."

"Yes, after, not before."

"No, Harry, but you are clever. I wish I was half as
clever. Fancy reading people's ideas! I can read my pony's,
but that's different; I know by his ears. And as for my
being a lady, of course I am, and so are you—I mean, a
gentleman. I was thinking—now this is really what I was
thinking—I wished your father lived near, that we might
all be friends. I can't bear the squire when he talks . . . .
And you quite as good as me, and better. Don't shake me
off, Harry."

I shook her in the gentlest manner, not suspecting that
she had read my feelings fully as well as I her thoughts.
Janet and I fell to talking of my father incessantly, and
were constantly together. The squire caught one of my
smiles rising, when he applauded himself lustily for the
original idea of matching us; but the idea was no longer

distasteful to me. It appeared to me that if I must some day be married, a wife who would enjoy my narratives, and travel over the four quarters of the globe, as Janet promised to do, in search of him I loved, would be the preferable person. I swore her to secresy; she was not to tell her brother Charley the subject we conversed on.

"Oh dear, no!" said she, and told him straightway.

Charley, home for his winter holidays, blurted out at the squire's table: "So, Harry Richmond, you're the cleverest fellow in the world, are you? There's Janet telling everybody your father's the cleverest next to you, and she's never seen him!"

"How? hulloa, what's that?" sang out the squire.

"Charley was speaking of my father, sir," I said, prepared for thunder.

We all rose. The squire looked as though an apoplectic seizure were coming on.

"Don't sit at my table again," he said, after a terrible struggle to be articulate.

His hand was stretched at me. I swung round to depart. "No, no, not you; that fellow," he called, getting his arm level towards Charley.

I tried to intercede—the last who should have done it.

"You like to hear him, eh?" said the squire.

I was ready to say that I did, but my aunt, whose courage was up when occasion summoned it, hushed the scene by passing the decanter to the squire, and speaking to him in a low voice.

"Biter's bit. I've dished myself, that's clear," said Charley; and he spoke the truth, and such was his frankness that I forgave him.

He and Janet were staying at Riversley. They left next morning, for the squire would not speak to him, nor I to Janet.

"I'll tell you what; there's no doubt about one thing," said Charley; "Janet's right—some of those girls are tremendously deep: you're about the cleverest fellow I've ever met in my life. I thought of working into the squire in a sort of collateral manner, you know. A cornetcy in the Dragoon Guards in a year or two. I thought the squire might do that for me without much damaging you;—perhaps a couple of hundred a year, just to reconcile me to a nose out of joint. For, upon my honour, the squire spoke of making me his heir—or words to that effect neatly conjugated—before you came back; and rather than be a curate like that Reverend Hart of yours, who hands raisins and almonds, and orange-flower biscuits to your aunt—the way of all the Reverends who drop down on Riversley—I'd betray my bosom friend. I'm regularly ' hoist on my own petard,' as they say in the newspapers. I'm a curate and no mistake. You did it with a turn of the wrist, without striking out: and I like neat boxing. I bear no malice when I'm floored neatly."

Five minutes after he had spoken it would have been impossible for me to tell him that my simplicity and not my cleverness had caused his overthrow. From this I learnt that simplicity is the keenest weapon and a beautiful refinement of cleverness; and I affected it extremely. I pushed it so far that I could make the squire dance in his seat with suppressed fury and jealousy at my way of talking of Venice, and other Continental cities, which he knew I must have visited in my father's society; and though he raged at me and pshawed the Continent to the deuce, he was ready, out of sheer rivalry, to grant anything I pleased to covet. At every stage of my growth one or another of my passions was alert to twist me awry, and now I was getting a false self about me and becoming liker to the creature people supposed me to be, despising them for blockheads in my heart, as boys may who preserve a last trace of the ingenuousness denied to seasoned men. Happily my aunt wrote to Mr. Rippenger for the address of little Gus Temple's father, to invite my schoolfellow to stay a month at Riversley. Temple came, everybody liked him; as for me my delight was unbounded, and in spite of a feeling of superiority due to my penetrative capacity, and the suspicion it originated that Temple might be acting the plain well-bred schoolboy he was, I soon preferred his pattern to my own. He confessed he had found me changed at first. His father, it appeared, was working him as hard at Latin as Mr. Hart worked me, and he sat down beside me under my tutor and stumbled at Tacitus after his fluent Cicero. I offered excuses for him to Mr. Hart, saying he would soon prove himself the better scholar. " There's my old Richie !" said Temple, fondling me on the shoulder, and my nonsensical airs fell away from me at once. We roamed the neighbourhood talking old school days over, visiting houses, hunting and dancing, declaring every day we would write for Heriot to join us, instead of which we wrote a valentine to Julia Rippenger, and despatched a companion one composed in a very different spirit to her father. Lady Ilchester did us the favour to draw a sea-monster, an Andromeda, and a Perseus in the shape of a flying British hussar, for Julia's valentine. It seemed to us so successful that we scattered half-a-dozen over the neighbourhood, and rode round it on the morning of St. Valentine's Day to see the effect of them, meeting the postman on the road. He gave me two for myself. One was transparently from Janet, a provoking counterstroke of mine to her; but when I opened the other my heart began beating. The standard of Great Britain was painted in colours at the top; down each side, encircled in laurels, were kings and queens of England with their sceptres, and in the middle I read the initials, A. F-G. R. R., embedded in blue forget-me-nots. I could not doubt it was from my father. Riding out in the open air as I received it, I could fancy in my hot joy that it had dropped out of heaven.

"He's alive; I shall have him with me; I shall have him with me soon!" I cried to Temple. "Oh! why can't I answer him? where is he? what address? Let's ride to London. Don't you understand, Temple? This letter's from my father. He knows I'm here. I'll find him, never mind what happens."

"Yes, but," said Temple, "if he knows where you are, and you don't know where he is, there's no good in your going off adventuring. If a fellow wants to be hit, the best thing he can do is to stop still."

Struck by the perspicacity of his views, I turned homeward. Temple had been previously warned by me to avoid speaking of my father at Riversley; but I was now in such a boiling state of happiness, believing that my father would certainly appear as he had done at Dipwell farm, brilliant and cheerful, to bear me away to new scenes and his own dear society, that I tossed the valentine to my aunt across the breakfast-table, laughing and telling her to guess the name of the sender. My aunt flushed.

"Miss Bannerbridge?" she said.

A stranger was present. The squire introduced us.

" My grandson, Harry Richmond, Captain William Bulsted, frigate Polyphemus; Captain Bulsted, Master Augustus
Temple."

For the sake of conversation Temple asked him if his ship
was fully manned.

" All but a mate," said the captain.

I knew him by reputation as the brother of Squire Gregory
Bulsted of Bulsted, notorious for his attachment to my aunt,
and laughing-stock of the county.

" So you've got a valentine," the captain addressed me.
" I went on shore at Rio last year on this very day of the
month, just as lively as you youngsters for one. Salt-water
keeps a man's youth in pickle. No valentine for me! Paid
off my ship yesterday at Spithead, and here I am again on
Valentine's Day."

Temple and I stared hard at a big man with a bronzed
skin and a rubicund laugh who expected to receive valen-
tines.

My aunt thrust the letter back to me secretly. " It must
be from a lady," said she.

" Why, who'd have a valentine from any but a lady ?"
exclaimed the captain.

The squire winked at me to watch his guest. Captain
Bulsted fed heartily; he was thoroughly a sailor-gentleman,
between the old school and the new, and, as I perceived, as
far gone in love with my aunt as his brother was. Presently
Sewis entered carrying a foaming tankard of old ale, and he
and the captain exchanged a word or two upon Jamaica.

" Now, when you've finished that washy tea of yours, take
a draught of our October, brewed here long before you were
a lieutenant, captain," said the squire.

" Thank you, sir," the captain replied; " I know that ale;
a moment, and I will gladly. I wish to preserve my faculties; I don't wish to have it supposed that I speak under
fermenting influences. Sewis, hold by, if you please."

My aunt made an effort to retire.

" No, no, fair play; stay," said the squire, trying to
frown, but twinkling; my aunt tried to smile, and sat as if
on springs.

" Miss Beltham," the captain bowed to her, and to each
one as he spoke, " Squire Beltham, Mr. Harry Richmond,
Mr. Temple; my ship was paid off yesterday, and till a

captain's ship is paid off, he's not his own master, as you are aware. If you think my behaviour calls for comment, reflect, I beseech you, on the nature of a sailor's life. A three-years' cruise in a cabin is pretty much equivalent to the same amount of time spent in a coffin, I can assure you; with the difference that you're hard at work thinking all the time like the——hum."

"Ay, he thinks hard enough," the squire struck in.

"Pardon me, sir; like the—hum—plumb-line on a lee-shore, I meant to observe. This is now the third—the fourth occasion on which I have practised the observance of paying my first visit to Riversley to know my fate, that I might not have it on my conscience that I had missed a day, a minute, as soon as I was a free man on English terra firma. My brother Greg and I were brought up in close association with Riversley. One of the Beauties of Riversley we lost! One was left, and we both tried our luck with her; honourably, in turn, each of us, nothing underhand; above-board, on the quarter-deck, before all the company. I'll say it of my brother, I can say it of myself. Greg's chances, I need not remark, are superior to mine; he is always in port. If he wins, then I tell him—'God bless you, my boy; you've won the finest woman, the handsomest, and the best, in or out of Christendom!' But my chance is my property, though it may be value only one farthing coin of the realm, and there is always pity for poor sinners in the female bosom. Miss Beltham, I trespass on your kind attention. If I am to remain a bachelor and you a maiden lady, why, the will of heaven be done! If you marry another, never mind who the man, there's my stock to the fruit of the union, never mind what the sex. But, if you will have one so unworthy of you as me, my hand and heart are at your feet, ma'am, as I have lost no time in coming to tell you." So Captain Bulsted concluded. Our eyes were directed on my aunt. The squire bade her to speak out, for she had his sanction to act according to her judgement and liking.

She said, with a gracefulness that gave me a little aching of pity for the poor captain: "I am deeply honoured by you, Captain Bulsted, but it is not my intention to marry."

The captain stood up, and bowing humbly, replied: "I am ever your servant, ma'am."

My aunt quitted the room.

" Now for the tankard, Sewis," said the captain.

Gradually the bottom of the great tankard turned up to the ceiling. He drank to the last drop in it.

The squire asked him whether he found consolation in that.

The captain sighed prodigiously and said: " It's a commencement, sir."

" Egad, it's a commencement 'd be something like a final end to any dozen of our fellows round about here. I'll tell you what: if stout stomachs gained the day in love-affairs, I suspect you'd run a good race against the male half of our county, William. And a damned good test of a man's metal, I say it is ! What are you going to do to-day ?"

" I am going to get drunk, sir."

" Well, you might do worse. Then, stop here, William, and give my old Port the preference. No tongue in the morning, I promise you, and pleasant dreams at night." The captain thanked him cordially, but declined, saying that he would rather make a beast of himself in another place.

The squire vainly pressed his hospitality by assuring him of perfect secresy on our part, as regarded my aunt, and offering him Sewis and one of the footmen to lift him to bed. " You are very good, squire," said the captain; " nothing but a sense of duty restrains me. I am bound to convey the information to my brother that the coast is clear for him."

" Well, then, fall light, and for'ard," said the squire, shaking him by the hand. Forty years ago a gentleman, a baronet, had fallen on the back of his head and never recovered.

" Ay, ay, *launch* stern foremost if you like !" said th captain, nodding; " no, no, I don't go into port pulled by the tail, my word for it, squire; and good day to you, sir."

" No ill will about this bothering love-business of yours, William ?"

" On my soul, sir, I cherish none."

Temple and I followed him out of the house, fascinated by his manners and oddness. He invited us to jump into the chariot beside him. We were witnesses of the meeting between him and his brother, a little sniffling man, as like the captain as a withered nut is like a milky one.

"Same luck, William?" said Squire Gregory.

"Not a point of change in the wind, Greg," said the captain.

They wrenched hands thereupon, like two carpet-shakers, with a report, and much in a similar attitude.

"These young gentlemen will testify to you solemnly, Greg, that I took no unfair advantage," said the captain; "no whispering in passages, no appointments in gardens, no letters. I spoke out. Bravely, man! And now, Greg, referring to the state of your cellar, our young friends here mean to float with us to-night. It is now half-past eleven A.M. Your dinner-hour the same as usual, of course? Therefore at four P.M. the hour of execution. And come, Greg, you and I will visit the cellar. A dozen and half of light and half-a-dozen of the old family—that will be about the number of bottles to give me my quietus, and you yours —all of us! And you, young gentlemen, take your guns or your rods, and back and be dressed by the four bell, or you'll not find the same man in Billy Bulsted."

Temple was enraptured with him. He declared he had been thinking seriously for a long time of entering the Navy, and his admiration of the captain must have given him an intuition of his character, for he persuaded me to send to Riversley for our evening-dress clothes, appearing in which at the dinner-table, we received the captain's compliments, as being gentlemen who knew how to attire ourselves to suit an occasion. The occasion, Squire Gregory said, happened to him too often for him to distinguish it by the cut of his coat.

"I observe, nevertheless, Greg, that you have a black tie round your neck instead of a red one," said the captain.

"Then it came there by accident," said Squire Gregory.

"Accident! There's no such thing as accident. If I wander out of the house with a half dozen or so in me, and topple into the brook, am I accidentally drowned? If a squall upsets my ship, is she an accidental residue of spars and timber and old iron? If a woman refuses me, is that an accident? There's a cause for every disaster: too much cargo, want of foresight, want of pluck. Pooh! when I'm hauled prisoner into a foreign port in time of war, you may talk of accidents. Mr. Harry Richmond, Mr. Temple, I have the accidental happiness of drinking to your healths in a tumbler of hock wine. Nominative, hic, hæc, hoc."

Squire Gregory carried on the declension, not without pride. The Vocative confused him.

"Claret will do for the Vocative," said the captain, gravely; "the more so as there is plenty of it at your table, Greg. Ablative hoc, hac, hoc, which sounds as if the gentleman had become incapable of speech beyond the name of his wine. So we will abandon the declension of the article for a dash of champagne, which there's no declining, I hope. Wonderful men, those Romans! They fought their ships well, too. A question to you, Greg. Those heathen Pagan dogs had a religion that encouraged them to swear. Now, my experience of life pronounces it to be a human necessity to rap out an oath here and there. What do you say?"

Squire Gregory said: "Drinking, and no thinking, at dinner, William." The captain pledged him.

"I'll take the opportunity, as we're not on board ship, of drinking to you, sir, now," Temple addressed the captain, whose face was resplendent; and he bowed, and drank, and said,—

"As we are not on board ship? I like you!"

Temple thanked him for the compliment.

"No compliment, my lad. You see me in my weakness, and you have the discernment to know me for something better than I seem. You promise to respect me on my own quarter-deck. You are of the right stuff. Do I speak correctly, Mr. Harry?"

"Temple is my dear friend," I replied.

"And he would not be so if not of the right stuff! Good! That's a way of putting much in little. By Jove! a royal style."

"And Harry's a royal fellow!" said Temple.

We all drank to one another. The captain's eyes scrutinized me speculatingly.

"This boy might have been yours or mine, Greg," I heard him say in a faltering rough tone.

They forgot the presence of Temple and me, but spoke as if they thought they were whispering. The captain assured his brother that Squire Beltham had given him as much fair play as one who holds a balance. Squire Gregory doubted it, and sipped and kept his nose at his wineglass, crabbedly repeating his doubts of it. The captain then remarked that doubting it, his conscience permitted him to use stratagems, though he, the captain, not doubting it, had no such permission.

"I count I run away with her every night of my life," said Squire Gregory. "Nothing comes of it but empty bottles."

"Court her, serenade her," said the captain; "blockade the port, lay siege to the citadel. I'd give a year of service for your chances, Greg. Half a word from her, and you have your horses ready."

"She's past po'chaises," Squire Gregory sighed.

"She's to be won by a bold stroke, brother Greg."

"Oh, Lord, no! She's past po'chaises."

"Humph! it's come to be half-bottle, half-beauty, with your worship, Greg, I suspect."

"No. I tell you, William, she's got her mind on that fellow. You can't po'chay her."

"After he jilted her for her sister? Wrong, Greg, wrong. You are muddled. She has a fright about matrimony—a common thing at her age, I am told. Where's the man?"

"In the Bench, of course. Where'd you have him?"

"I, sir? If I knew my worst enemy to be there, I'd send him six dozen of the best in my cellar."

Temple shot a walnut at me. I pretended to be meditating carelessly, and I had the heat and roar of a conflagration round my head.

Presently the captain said: "Are you sure the man's in the Bench?"

"Cock," Squire Gregory replied.

"He had money from his wife."

"And he had the wheels to make it go." Here they whispered in earnest.

"Oh, the Billings were as rich as the Belthams," said the captain, aloud.

"Pretty nigh, William,"

"That's our curse, Greg. Money settled on their male issue, and money in hand; by the Lord! we've always had the look of a pair of highwaymen lurking for purses, when it was the woman, the woman, penniless, naked—I mean destitute; nothing but the woman we wanted. And there was one apiece for us. Greg, old boy, when will the old county show such another couple of Beauties! Greg, sir, you're not half a man, or you'd have carried her, with your opportunities. The fellow's in the Bench, you say? How are you cock-sure of that, Mr. Greg?"

"Company," was the answer; and the captain turned to Temple and me, apologizing profusely for talking over family matters with his brother after a separation of three years. I had guessed but hastily at the subject of their conversation until they mentioned the Billings, the family of my maternal grandmother. The name was like a tongue of fire shooting up in a cloud of smoke: I saw at once that the man in the Bench must be my father, though what the Bench was exactly, and where it was, I had no idea, and as I was left to imagination I became, as usual, childish in my notions, and brooded upon thoughts of the Man in the Iron Mask; things I dared not breathe to Temple, of whose manly sense I stood in awe when under these distracting influences.

"Remember our feast in the combe?" I sang across the table to him.

"Never forget it!" said he; and we repeated the tale of the goose at Rippenger's school to our entertainers, making them laugh.

"And next morning Richie ran off with a gipsy girl," said Temple; and I composed a narrative of my wanderings with Kiomi, much more amusing than the real one. The captain vowed he would like to have us both on board his ship, but that times were too bad for him to offer us a prospect of promotion. "Spin round the decanters," said he; "now's the hour for them to go like a humming-top, and each man lend a hand: whip hard, my lads. It's once in three years, hurrah! and the cause is a cruel woman. Toast her; but no name. Here's to the nameless Fair! For it's not my intention to marry, says she, and ma'am, I'm a man of honour: or I'd catch you tight, my nut-brown maid, and clap you into a cage, fal-lal, like a squirrel; to trot the wheel of mat—trimony. Shame to the first man down!"

"That won't be I," said Temple.

"Be me, sir, me," the captain corrected his grammar.

"Pardon me. Captain Bulsted; the verb 'To be' governs the nominative case in our climate," said Temple.

"Then I'm nominative hic . . . I say, sir, I'm in the

tropics, Mr. Tem . . . Mr. Tempus. Point of honour, not forget a man's name. Rippenger, your schoolmaster ? Mr. Rippenger, you've knocked some knowledge into this young gentleman." Temple and I took counsel together hastily; we cried in a breath: "Here's to Julia Rippenger, the prettiest, nicest girl living !" and we drank to her.

"Julia !" the captain echoed us. "I join your toast, gentlemen. Mr. Richmond, Mr. Tempus—Julia ! By all that's holy, she floats a sinking ship ! Julia consoles me for the fairest, cruellest woman alive. A rough sailor, Julia ! at your feet."

The captain fell commendably forward. Squire Gregory had already dropped. Temple and I tried to meet, but did not accomplish it till next morning at breakfast. A couple of footmen carried us each upstairs in turn, as if they were removing furniture.

Out of this strange evening came my discovery of my father, and the captain's winning of a wife.

CHAPTER X.

AN EXPEDITION.

I WONDERED audibly where the Bench was when Temple and I sat together alone at Squire Gregory's breakfast-table next morning, very thirsty for tea. He said it was a place in London, but did not add the sort of place, only that I should soon be coming to London with h m; and I remarked, "Shall I ?" and smiled at him as if in a fit of careless affection. Then he talked runningly of the theatres and pantomimes and London's charms.

The fear I had of this Bench made me passingly conscious of Temple's delicacy in not repeating its name, though why I feared it there was nothing to tell me. I must have dreamed of it just before waking, and I burned for reasonable information concerning it. Temple respected my father too much to speak out the extent of his knowledge on the subject, so we drank our tea with the grandeur of London for our theme, where, Temple assured me, you never had a head-ache after a carouse overnight : a communication that led me to think the country a far less favourable place of abode for gentlemen. We quitted the house without seeing our host or the captain, and greatly admired by the footmen, the maids, and the grooms for having drunk their masters under the table, which it could not be doubted that we had done, as Temple modestly observed while we sauntered off the grounds under the eyes of the establishment. We had done it fairly, too, with none of those Jack the Giant-Killer tricks my grandfather accused us of. The squire would not, and he could not, believe our story until he heard the confession from the mouth of the captain. After that he said we were men and heroes, and he tipped us both, much to Janet Ilchester's advantage, for the squire was a royal giver, and Temple's money had already begun to take the same road as mine.

Temple, in fact, was falling desperately in love; for this reason he shrank from quitting Riversley. I perceived it as clearly as a thing seen through a window-pane. He was always meditating upon dogs, and what might be the price of this dog or that, and whether lap-dogs were good travellers. The fashionable value of pugs filled him with a sort of despair. "My goodness!" he used an exclamation more suitable to women, "forty or fifty pounds you say one costs, Richie ?"

I pretended to estimate the probable cost of one. "Yes, about that ; but I'll buy you one, one day or other, Temple."

The dear little fellow coloured hot ; he was too much in earnest to laugh at the absurdity of his being supposed to want a pug for himself, and walked round me, throwing himself into attitudes with shrugs and loud breathings. "I don't . . . don't think that I . . . I care for nothing but Newfoundlands and mastiffs," said he. He went on shrugging and kicking up his heels.

"Girls like pugs," I remarked.

"I fancy they do," said Temple, with a snort of indifference. Then I suggested, "A pocket-knife for the hunting-field is a very good thing."

"Do you think so ?" was Temple's rejoinder, and I saw he was dreadfully afraid of my speaking the person's name for whom it would be such a very good thing.

"You can get one for thirty shillings. We'll get one

when we're in London. They're just as useful for women as they are for us, you know."

"Why, of course they are, if they hunt," said Temple.

"And we mustn't lose time," I drew him to the point I had at heart, "for hunting'll soon be over. It's February, mind!"

"Oh, lots of time!" Temple cried out, and on every occasion when I tried to make him understand that I was bursting to visit London, he kept evading me, simply because he hated saying good-bye to Janet Ilchester. His dulness of apprehension in not perceiving that I could not commit a breach of hospitality by begging him downright to start, struck me as extraordinary. And I was so acute. I saw every single idea in his head, every shift of his mind, and how he half knew that he profited by my shunning to say flatly I desired to set out upon the discovery of the Bench. He took the benefit of my shamefacedness, for which I daily punished his. I really felt that I was justified in giving my irritability an airing by curious allusions to Janet; yet, though I made him wince, it was impossible to touch his conscience. He admitted to having repeatedly spoken of London's charms, and "Oh, yes! you and I'll go back together, Richie," and saying that satisfied him: he doubled our engagements with Janet that afternoon, and it was a riding party, a dancing-party, and a drawing of a pond for carp, and we over to Janet, and Janet over to us, until I grew so sick of her I was incapable of summoning a spark of jealousy in order the better to torture Temple. Now, he was a quick-witted boy. Well, I one day heard Janet address my big dog, Ajax, in the style she usually employed to inform her hearers, and especially the proprietor, that she coveted a thing: "Oh, you own dear precious pet darling beauty! if I might only feed you every day of my life I should be happy! I curtsey to him every time I see him. If I were his master, the men should all off hats, and the women all curtsey, to Emperor Ajax, my dog! my own! my great, dear, irresistible love!" Then she nodded at me, "I would make them, though." And then at Temple, "You see if I wouldn't."

Ajax was a source of pride to me. However, I heard Temple murmur, in a tone totally unlike himself, "He would be a great protection to you;" and I said to him, "You know, Temple, I shall be going to London to-morrow or the next day, not later: I don't know when I shall be back. I wish you would dispose of the dog just as you like: get him a kind master or mistress, that's all."

I sacrificed my dog to bring Temple to his senses. I thought it would touch him to see how much I could sacrifice just to get an excuse for begging him to start. He did not even thank me. Ajax soon wore one of Janet's collars, like two or three other of the Riversley dogs; and I had the satisfaction of hearing Temple accept my grandfather's invitation for a further fortnight. And, meanwhile, I was the one who was charged with going about looking lovelorn! I smothered my feelings and my reflections on the wisdom of people.

At last my aunt Dorothy found the means of setting me at liberty on the road to London. We had related to her how Captain Bulsted toasted Julia Rippenger, and we had both declared in joke that we were sure the captain wished to be introduced to her. My aunt reserved her ideas on the subject, but by-and-by she proposed to us to ride over to Julia, and engage her to come and stay at Riversley for some days. Kissing me, my aunt said, "She was my Harry's friend when he was an outcast."

The words revived my affection for Julia. Strong in the sacred sense of gratitude, I turned on Temple, reproaching him with selfish forgetfulness of her good heart and pretty face. Without defending himself, as he might have done, he entreated me to postpone our journey for a day; he and Janet had some appointment. Here was given me a noble cause and matter I need not shrink from speaking of. I lashed Temple in my aunt's presence with a rod of real eloquence that astonished her, and him, and myself too; and as he had a sense of guilt not quite explicable in his mind, he consented to bear what was in reality my burden; for Julia had distinguished me and not him with all the signs of affection, and of the two I had the more thoroughly forgotten her; I believe Temple was first in toasting her at Squire Gregory's table. There is nothing like a pent-up secret of the heart for accumulating powers of speech; I mean in youth. The mental distilling process sets in later, and then you have irony instead of eloquence. From brooding on my father, and not daring to mention his name lest I should hear evil of it, my thoughts were a proud family, proud of their origin, proud of their isolation, and not to be able to

divine them was for the world to confess itself basely
beneath their level. But, when they did pour out, they
were tremendous, as Temple found. This oratorical display
of mine gave me an ascendancy over him. He adored
eloquence, not to say grandiloquence: he was the son of a
barrister. "Let's go and see her at once, Richie," he said
of Julia. "I'm ready to be off as soon as you like; I'm
ready to do anything that will please you;" which was
untrue, but it was useless to tell him so. I sighed at my
sad gift of penetration, and tossed the fresh example of it
into the treasury of vanity.

"Temple," said I, dissembling a little; "I tell you candidly: you won't please me by doing anything disagreeable
to you. A dog pulled by the collar is not much of a companion. I start for Julia to-morrow before daylight. If
you like your bed best, stop there; and mind you amuse
Janet for me during my absence."

"I'm not going to let any one make comparisons between
us," Temple muttered.

He dropped dozens of similar remarks, and sometimes
talked downright flattery, I had so deeply impressed him.

We breakfasted by candle-light, and rode away on a
frosty foggy morning, keeping our groom fifty yards to the
rear, a laughable sight, with both his coat-pockets bulging,
a couple of Riversley turnover pasties in one, and a bottle of
champagne in the other, for our lunch on the road. Now
and then, when near him, we galloped for the fun of seeing
him nurse the bottle-pocket. He was generally invisible.
Temple did not think it strange that we should be riding
out in an unknown world with only a little ring, half a
stone's-throw clear around us, and blots of copse, and queer
vanishing cottages, and hard grey meadows, fir-trees wonderfully magnified, and larches and birches rigged like fairy
ships, all starting up to us as we passed, and melting
instantly. One could have fancied the fir-trees black
torches. And here the shoulder of a hill invited us to race
up to the ridge: some way on we came to cross-roads,
careless of our luck in hitting the right one: yonder hung a
village church in the air, and church-steeple piercing ever
so high; and out of the heart of the mist leaped a brook,
and to hear it at one moment, and then to have the sharp
freezing silence in one's ear, was piercingly weird. It all

tossed the mind in my head like hay on a pitchfork. I forgot the existence of everything but what I loved passionately,—and that had no shape, was like a wind.

Up on a knoll of firs in the middle of a heath, glowing rosy in the frost, we dismounted to lunch, leaning against the warm saddles, Temple and I, and Uberly, our groom, who reminded me of a certain tramp of my acquaintance in his decided preference of beer to champagne; he drank, though, and sparkled after his draught. No sooner were we on horseback again—ere the flanks of the dear friendly brutes were in any way cool—then Temple shouted enthusiastically,—

"Richie, we shall do it yet! I've been funking, but now I'm sure we shall do it. Janet said, 'What's the use of my coming over to dine at Riversley if Harry Richmond and you don't come home before ten or eleven o'clock?' I told her we'd do it by dinner-time :—Don't you like Janet, Richie?—That is, if our horses' hic-hæc-hocks didn't get strained on this hard nominative-plural-masculine of the article road. Don't you fancy yourself dining with the captain, Richie? Dative huic, says old Squire Gregory. I like to see him at dinner because he loves the smell of his wine. Oh! it's nothing to boast of, but we did drink them under the table, it can't be denied. Janet heard of it. Hulloa! you talk of a hunting-knife. What do you say to a pair of skates? Here we are in for a frost of six weeks. It strikes me, a pair of skates . . ."

This was the champagne in Temple. In me it did not bubble to speech, and I soon drew him on at a pace that rendered conversation impossible. Uberly shouted after us to spare the horses' legs. We heard him twice out of the deepening fog. I called to Temple that he was right, we should do it. Temple hurrahed rather breathlessly. At the end of an hour I pulled up at an inn, where I left the horses to be groomed and fed, and walked away rapidly as if I knew the town, Temple following me with perfect confidence, and, indeed, I had no intention to deceive him. We entered a new station of a railway.

"Oh!" said Temple, "the rest of the way by rail."

When the railway clerk asked me what place I wanted tickets for, London sprang to my mouth promptly in a murmur, and taking the tickets I replied to Temple,—

" The rest of the way by rail. Uberly's sure to stop at that inn ;" but my heart beat as the carriages slid away with us ; an affectionate commiseration for Temple touched me when I heard him count on our being back at Riversley in time to dress for dinner.

He laughed aloud at the idea of our plumping down on Rippenger's school, getting a holiday for the boys, tipping them, and then off with Julia, exactly like two Gods of the mythology, Apollo and Mercury.

" I often used to think they had the jolliest lives that ever were lived," he said, and trying to catch glimpses of the country, and musing, and singing, he continued to feel like one of those blissful Gods until wonder at the passage of time supervened. Amazement, when he looked at my watch, struck him dumb. Ten minutes later we were in yellow fog, then in brown. Temple stared at both windows and at me ; he jumped from his seat and fell on it, muttering, " No ; nonsense ! I say !" but he had accurately recognized London's fog. I left him unanswered to bring up all his senses, which the railway had outstripped, for the contemplation of this fact, that we two were in the city of London.

CHAPTER XI.

THE GREAT FOG AND THE FIRE AT MIDNIGHT.

It was London city, and the Bench was the kernel of it to me. I throbbed with excitement, though I sat looking out of the windows into the subterranean atmosphere quite still and firm. When you think long undividedly of a single object it gathers light, and when you draw near it in person the strange thing to your mind is the absence of that light ; but I, approaching it in this dense fog, seemed to myself to be only thinking of it a little more warmly than usual, and instead of fading it reversed the process, and became, from light, luminous. Not being able, however, to imagine the Bench a happy place, I corrected the excess of brightness and gave its walls a pine-torch glow ; I set them in the middle of a great square, and hung the standard of England drooping over them in a sort of mournful family pride. Then, because I next conceived it a foreign kind of place, different altogether from that home growth of ours, the Tower of London, I topped it with a multitude of domes of pumpkin or turban shape, resembling the Kremlin of Moscow, which had once leapt up in the eye of Winter, glowing like a million pine-torches, and flung shadows of stretching red horses on the black smoke-drift. But what was the Kremlin, that had seen a city perish, to this Bench where my father languished! There was no comparing them for tragic horror. And the Kremlin had snow-fields around it; this Bench was caught out of sight, hemmed in by an atmosphere thick as Charon breathed; it might as well be underground.

"Oh! it's London," Temple went on, correcting his incorrigible doubts about it. He jumped on the platform; we had to call out not to lose one another. "I say, Richie, this is London," he said, linking his arm in mine: "you know by the size of the station; and besides, there's the fog. Oh! it's London. We've overshot it, we're positively in London."

I could spare no sympathy for his feelings, and I did not respond to his inquiring looks. Now that we were here I certainly wished myself away, though I would not have retreated, and for awhile I was glad of the discomforts besetting me; my step was hearty as I led on, meditating upon asking some one the direction to the Bench presently. We had to walk, and it was nothing but traversing on a slippery pavement atmospheric circles of black brown and brown red, and sometimes a larger circle of pale yellow; the colours of old bruised fruits, medlars, melons, and the smell of them; nothing is more desolate. Neither of us knew where we were, nor where we were going. We struggled through an interminable succession of squalid streets, from the one lamp visible to its neighbour in the darkness: you might have fancied yourself peering at the head of an old saint on a smoky canvas; it was like the painting of light rather than light. Figures rushed by; we saw no faces.

Temple spoke solemnly: "Our dinner-hour at home is half-past six."

A street-boy over heard him and chaffed him. Temple

got the worst of it, and it did him good, for he had the sweetest nature in the world. We declined to be attended by link-boys; they would have hurt our sense of independence. Possessed of a sovereign faith that, by dint of resolution, I should ultimately penetrate to the great square enclosing the Bench, I walked with the air of one who had the map of London in his eye and could thread it blindfold. Temple was thereby deceived into thinking that I must somehow have learnt the direction I meant to take, and knew my way, though at the slightest indication of my halting and glancing round his suspicions began to boil, and he was for asking some one the name of the ground we stood on: he murmured, " Fellows get lost in London." By this time he clearly understood that I had come to London on purpose : he could not but be aware of the object of my coming, and I was too proud, and he still too delicate, to allude to it.

The fog choked us. Perhaps it took away the sense of hunger by filling us as if we had eaten a dinner of soot. We had no craving to eat until long past the dinner-hour in Temple's house, and then I would rather have plunged into a bath and a bed than have been requested to sit at a feast; Temple too, I fancy. We knew we were astray without speaking of it. Temple said, " I wish we hadn't drunk that champagne." It seemed to me years since I had tasted the delicious crushing of the sweet bubbles in my mouth. But I did not blame them; I was after my father: he, dear little fellow, had no light ahead except his devotion to me: he must have had a touch of conscious guilt regarding his recent behaviour, enough to hold him from complaining formally. He complained of a London without shops and lights, wondered how any one could like to come to it in a fog, and so forth; and again regretted our having drunk champagne in the morning; a sort of involuntary whimpering easily forgiven to him, for I knew he had a gallant heart. I determined, as an act of signal condescension, to accost the first person we met, male or female, for Temple's sake. Having come to this resolve, which was to be an open confession that I had misled him, wounding to my pride, I hoped eagerly for the hearing of a footfall. We were in a labyrinth of dark streets where no one was astir. A wretched dog trotted up to us, followed at our heels a short distance, and left us as if he smelt no luck about us;

our cajoleries were unavailing to keep that miserable companion.

"Sinbad escaped from the pit by tracking a lynx," I happened to remark. Temple would not hear of Sinbad.

"Oh, come, we're not Mussulmen," said he; "I declare, Richie, if I saw a church open, I'd go in and sleep there. Were you thinking of tracking the dog, then? Beer may be had somewhere. We shall have to find an hotel. What can the time be?"

I owed it to him to tell him, so I climbed a lamp-post and spelt out the hour by my watch. When I descended we were three. A man had his hands on Temple's shoulders, examining his features.

"Now speak," the man said, roughly.

I was interposing, but Temple cried, "All right, Richie, we are two to one."

The man groaned. I asked him what he wanted.

"My son! I've lost my son," the man replied, and walked away; and he would give no answer to our questions.

I caught hold of the lamp-post, overcome. I meant to tell Temple, in response to the consoling touch of his hand, that I hoped the poor man would discover his son, but said instead, "I wish we could see the Bench to-night." Temple exclaimed, "Ah!" pretending by his tone of voice that we had recently discussed our chance of it, and then he ventured to inform me that he imagined he had heard of the place being shut up after a certain hour of the night.

My heart felt released, and gushed with love for him. "Very well, Temple," I said: "then we'll wait till to-morrow, and strike out for some hotel now."

Off we went at a furious pace. Saddlebank's goose was reverted to by both of us with an exchange of assurances that we should meet a dish the fellow to it before we slept.

"As for life," said I, as soon as the sharp pace had fetched my breathing to a regular measure, "adventures are what I call life."

Temple assented. "They're capital, if you only see the end of them."

We talked of Ulysses and Penelope. Temple blamed him for leaving Calypso. I thought Ulysses was right, otherwise we should have had no slaying of the Suitors: but Temple shyly urged that to have a Goddess caring for you (and she was handsomer than Penelope, who must have been an oldish woman) was something to make you feel as you do on a hunting morning, when there are half-a-dozen riding-habits speckling the field—a whole glorious day your own among them! This view appeared to me very captivating, save for an obstruction in my mind, which was, that Goddesses were always conceived by me as statues. They talked and they moved, it was true, but the touch of them was marble; and they smiled and frowned but they had no variety: they were never warm.

"If I thought that!" muttered Temple, puffing at the raw fog. He admitted he had thought just the contrary, and that the cold had suggested to him the absurdity of leaving a Goddess.

"Look here, Temple," said I, "has it never struck you? I won't say I'm like him. It's true I've always admired Ulysses; he could fight best, talk best, and plough, and box, and how clever he was! Take him all round, who wouldn't rather have had him for a father than Achilles? And there were just as many women in love with him."

"More," said Temple.

"Well then," I continued, thanking him in my heart, for it must have cost him something to let Ulysses be set above Achilles, "Telemachus is the one I mean. He was in search of his father. He found him at last. Upon my honour, Temple, when I think of it, I'm ashamed to have waited so long. I call that luxury I've lived in senseless. Yes! while I was uncertain whether my father had enough to eat or not."

"I say! hush!" Temple breathed, in pain at such allusions. "Richie, the squire has finished his bottle by about now; bottle number two. He won't miss us till the morning, but Miss Beltham will. She'll be at your bedroom door three or four times in the night, I know. It's getting darker and darker, we must be in some dreadful part of London."

The contrast he presented to my sensations between our pleasant home and this foggy solitude gave me a pang of dismay. I diverged from my favourite straight line, which seemed to pierce into the bowels of the earth, sharp to the right. Soon or late after, I cannot tell, we were in the midst of a thin stream of people, mostly composed of boys

and young women, going at double time, hooting and screaming with the delight of loosened animals, not quite so agreeably; but animals never hunted on a better scent. A dozen
turnings in their company brought us in front of a fire.
There we saw two houses preyed on by the flames, just as if
a lion had his paws on a couple of human creatures, devouring them; we heard his jaws, the cracking of bones, shrieks,
and the voracious in-and-out of his breath edged with anger.
A girl by my side exclaimed, "It's not the Bench, after all!
Would I have run to see a paltry two-story washerwoman's
mangling-shed flare up, when six penn'orth of squibs and
shavings and a cracker make twice the fun!"

I turned to her, hardly able to speak. "Where's the
Bench, if you please?" She pointed. I looked on an immense high wall. The blunt flames of the fire opposite
threw a sombre glow on it.

The girl said, "And don't you go hopping into debt, my
young cock-sparrow, or you'll know one side o' the turnkey
better than t'other." She had a friend with her who chid
her for speaking so freely.

"Is it too late to go in to-night?" I asked.

She answered that it was, and that she and her friend
were the persons to show me the way in there. Her friend
answered more sensibly: "Yes, you can't go in there before
some time in the morning."

I learnt from her that the Bench was a debtor's prison.
The saucy girl of the pair asked me for money. I handed
her a crown-piece.

"Now won't you give another big bit to my friend?" said
she.

I had no change, and the well-mannered girl bade me
never mind, the saucy one pressed for it, and for a treat.
She was amusing in her talk of the quantity of different
fires she had seen; she had also seen accidental-death corpses,
but never a suicide in the act; and here she regretted the
failure of her experiences. This conversation of a good-
looking girl amazed me. Presently Temple cried, "A third
house caught, and no engines yet! Richie, there's an old
woman in her night-dress; we can't stand by."

The saucy girl joked at the poor half-naked old woman.
Temple stood humping and agitating his shoulders like a cat
before it springs. Both the girls tried to stop us. The one

I liked best seized my watch, and said, "Leave this to me to take care of," and I had no time to wrestle for it. I had a glimpse of her face that let me think she was not fooling me, the watch-chain flew off my neck, Temple and I clove through the crowd of gapers. We got into the heat, which was in a minute scorching. Three men were under the window; they had sung out to the old woman above to drop a blanket—she tossed them a water-jug. She was saved by the blanket of a neighbour. Temple and I strained at one corner of it to catch her. She came down, the men said, like a singed turkey. The flames illuminated her as she descended. There was a great deal of laughter in the crowd, but I was shocked. Temple shared the painful impression produced on me. I cannot express my relief when the old woman was wrapped in the blanket which had broken her descent, and stood like a blot instead of a figure. I handed a sovereign to the three men, complimenting them on the humanity of their dispositions. They cheered us, and the crowd echoed the cheer, and Temple and I made our way back to the two girls: both of us lost our pocket-handkerchiefs, and Temple a penknife as well. Then the engines arrived and soused the burning houses. We were all in a crimson mist, boys smoking, girls laughing and staring, men hallooing, hats and caps flying about, fights going on, people throwing their furniture out of the windows. The great wall of the Bench was awful in its reflection of the labouring flames—it rose out of sight like the flame-tops till the columns of water brought them down. I thought of my father, and of my watch. The two girls were not visible "A glorious life a fireman's!" said Temple.

The firemen were on the roofs of the houses, handsome as Greek heroes, and it really did look as if they were engaged in slaying an enormous dragon, that hissed and tongued at them, and writhed its tail, paddling its broken big red wings in the pit of wreck and smoke, twisting and darkening— something fine to conquer, I felt with Temple.

A mutual disgust at the inconvenience created by the appropriation of our pocket-handkerchiefs by members of the crowd, induced us to disentangle ourselves from it without confiding to any one our perplexity for supper and a bed. We were now extremely thirsty. I had visions of my majority bottles of Burgundy, lying under John Thresher's care at

Dipwell, and would have abandoned them all for one on the spot. After ranging about the outskirts of the crowd, seeking the two girls, we walked away, not so melancholy but that a draught of porter would have cheered us. Temple punned on the loss of my watch, and excused himself for a joke neither of us had spirit to laugh at. Just as I was saying, with a last glance at the fire, " Anyhow, it would have gone in that crowd," the nice good girl ran up behind us, crying, " There!" as she put the watch-chain over my head.

. " There, Temple," said I, " didn't I tell you so?" and Temple kindly supposed so.

The girl said, " I was afraid I'd missed you, little fellow, and you'd take me for a thief, and thank God, I'm no thief yet. I rushed into the crowd to meet you after you caught that old creature, and I could have kissed you both, you're so brave."

" We always go in for it together," said Temple.

I made an offer to the girl of a piece of gold. " Oh, I'm poor," she cried, yet kept her hand off it like a bird alighting on ground, not on prey. When I compelled her to feel the money tight, she sighed, " If I wasn't so poor! I don't want your gold. Why are you out so late?"

We informed her of our arrival from the country, and wanderings in the fog.

" And you'll say you're not tired, I know," the girl remarked, and laughed to hear how correctly she had judged of our temper. Our thirst and hunger, however, filled her with concern, because of our not being used to it as she was, and no place was open to supply our wants. Her friend, the saucy one, accompanied by a man evidently a sailor, joined us, and the three had a consultation away from Temple and me, at the end of which the sailor, whose name was Joe, raised his leg dancingly, and smacked it. We gave him our hands to shake, and understood, without astonishment, that we were invited on board his ship to partake of refreshment. We should not have been astonished had he said on board his balloon. Down through thick fog of a lighter colour, we made our way to a narrow lane leading to the river-side, where two men stood thumping their arms across their breasts, smoking pipes, and swearing. We entered a boat and were rowed to a ship. I was not aware how frozen and befogged my mind and senses had become until I had taken a desperate and long gulp of smoking rum-and-water, and then the whole of our adventures from morning to midnight, with the fir-trees in the country fog, and the lamps in the London fog, and the man who had lost his son, the fire, the Bench, the old woman with her fowl-like cry and limbs in the air, and the row over the misty river, swam flashing before my eyes, and I cried out to the two girls, who were drinking out of one glass with the sailor Joe, my entertainer, "Well, I'm awake now!" and slept straight off the next instant.

CHAPTER XII.

WE FIND OURSELVES BOUND ON A VOYAGE.

It seemed to me that I had but taken a turn from right to left, or gone round a wheel, when I repeated the same words, and I heard Temple somewhere near me mumble something like them. He drew a long breath, so did I : we cleared our throats with a sort of whinny simultaneously. The enjoyment of lying perfectly still, refreshed, incurious, unexcited, yet having our minds animated, excursive, reaping all the incidents of our lives at leisure, and making a dream of our latest experiences, kept us tranquil and incommunicative. Occasionally we let fall a sigh fathoms deep, then by-and-by began blowing a bit of a wanton laugh at the end of it. I raised my foot and saw the boot on it, which accounted for an uneasy sensation setting in through my frame.

I said softly : "What a pleasure it must be for horses to be groomed!"

"Just what I was thinking!" said Temple.

We started up on our elbows, and one or the other cried, "There's a chart! These are bunks! Hark at the row overhead! We're in a ship! The ship's moving! Is it foggy this morning? It's time to get up! I've slept in my clothes! Oh, for a dip! How I smell of smoke! What a noise of a steamer! And the squire at Riversley! Fancy Uberly's tale!"

Temple, with averted face, asked me whether I meant to return to Riversley that day. I assured him I would, on my honour, if possible; and of course he also would have to return there. "Why, you've an appointment with Janet Ilchester," said I, "and we may find a pug; we'll buy the hunting-knife and the skates. And she shall know you saved an old woman's life."

"No, don't talk about that," Temple entreated me, biting his lip. "Richie, we're going fast through the water. It reminds me of breakfast. I should guess the hour to be nine A.M."

My watch was unable to assist us; the hands pointed to half-past four, and were fixed. We ran up on deck. Looking over the stern of the vessel, across a line of rippling eddying red gold, we saw the sun low upon cushions of beautiful cloud; no trace of fog anywhere; blue sky overhead, and a mild breeze blowing.

"Sunrise," I said.

Temple answered, "Yes," most uncertainly.

We looked round. A steam-tug was towing our ship out toward banks of red-reflecting cloud, and a smell of sea air.

"Why, that's the East, there!" cried Temple. We faced about to the sun, and behold, he was actually sinking!

"Nonsense!" we exclaimed in a breath. From seaward to this stupefying sunset we stood staring. The river stretched to broad lengths; gulls were on the grey water, knots of seaweed, and the sea-foam curled in advance of us.

"By jingo!" Temple spoke out, musing, "here's a whole day struck out of our existence."

"It can't be!" said I, for that any sensible being could be tricked of a piece of his life in that manner I thought a preposterous notion.

But the sight of a lessening windmill in the West, shadows eastward, the wide water, and the air now full salt, convinced me we two had slept through an entire day, and were passing rapidly out of hail of our native land.

"We must get these fellows to put us on shore at once," said Temple: "we won't stop to eat. There's a town; a boat will row us there in half-an-hour. Then we can wash, too. I've got an idea nothing's clean here. And confound these fellows for not having the civility to tell us they were going to start!"

We were rather angry, a little amused, not in the least alarmed at our position. A sailor, to whom we applied for an introduction to the captain, said he was busy. Another gave us a similar reply, with a monstrous grimace which was beyond our comprehension. The sailor Joe was nowhere to be seen. None of the sailors appeared willing to listen to us, though they stopped as they were running by to lend half an ear to what we had to say. Some particular movement was going on in the ship. Temple was the first to observe that the steam-tug was casting us loose, and cried he, " She'll take us on board and back to London Bridge. Let's hail her." He sang out, " Whoop! ahoy !" I meanwhile had caught sight of Joe.

" Well, young gentleman !" he accosted me, and he hoped I had slept well. My courteous request to him to bid the tug stand by to take us on board, only caused him to wear a look of awful gravity. " You're such a deuce of a sleeper," he said. " You see, we had to be off early to make up for forty hours lost by that there fog. I tried to wake you both; no good; so I let you snore away. We took up our captain mid-way down the river, and now you're in his hands, and he'll do what he likes with you, and that's a fact, and my opinion is you'll see a foreign shore before you're in the arms of your family again."

At these words I had the horrible sensation of being caged, and worse, transported into the bargain.

I insisted on seeing the captain. A big bright round moon was dancing over the vessel's bowsprit, and this, together with the tug thumping into the distance, and the land receding, gave me—coming on my wrath—suffocating emotions.

No difficulties were presented in my way. I was led up to a broad man in a pilot-coat, who stood square, and looked by the bend of his eyebrows as if he were always making head against a gale. He nodded to my respectful salute. " Cabin," he said, and turned his back to me.

I addressed him, " Excuse me, I want to go on shore, captain. I must and will go ! I am here by some accident; you have accidentally overlooked me here. I wish to treat you like a gentleman, but I won't be detained."

Joe spoke a word to the captain, who kept his back as

broad to me as a school-slate for geography and Euclid's propositions.

"Cabin, cabin," the captain repeated.

I tried to get round him to dash a furious sentence or so in his face, since there was no producing any impression on his back; but he occupied the whole of a way blocked with wire-coil, and rope, and boxes, and it would have been ridiculous to climb this barricade when by another right-about-face he could in a minute leave me volleying at the blank space between his shoulders.

Joe touched my arm, which, in as friendly a way as I could assume, I bade him not do a second time; for I could ill contain myself as it was, and beginning to think I had been duped and tricked I was ready for hostilities. I could hardly bear meeting Temple on my passage to the cabin. "Captain Jasper Welsh," he was reiterating, as if sounding it to discover whether it had an ominous ring: it was the captain's name, that he had learnt from one of the seamen.

Irritated by his repetition of it, I said, I know not why, or how the words came: "A highwayman notorious for his depredations in the vicinity of the city of Bristol."

This set Temple off laughing: "And so he bought a ship and had traps laid down to catch young fellows for ransom."

I was obliged to request Temple not to joke, but the next moment I had launched Captain Jasper Welsh on a piratical exploit; Temple lifted the veil from his history, revealing him amid the excesses of a cannibal feast. I dragged him before a British jury; Temple hanged him in view of an excited multitude. As he boasted that there was the end of Captain Welsh, I broke the rope. But Temple spoiled my triumph by depriving him of the use of his lower limbs after the fall, for he was a heavy man. I could not contradict it, and therefore pitched all his ship's crew upon the gallows in a rescue. Temple allowed him to be carried off by his faithful ruffians, only stipulating that the captain was never after able to release his neck from the hangman's slip-knot. The consequence was that he wore a shirt-collar up to his eyebrows for concealment by day, and a pillow-case over his head at night, and his wife said she was a deceived unhappy woman, and died of curiosity.

The talking of even such nonsense as this was a relief to us in our impatience and helplessness, with the lights of land heaving far distant to our fretful sight through the cabin windows.

When we had to talk reasonably we were not so success-ful. Captain Welsh was one of those men who show you, whether you care to see them or not, all the processes by which they arrive at an idea of you, upon which they forth-with shape their course. Thus, when he came to us in the cabin, he took the oil-lamp in his hand and examined our faces by its light; he had no reply to our remonstrances and petitions: all he said was, "Humph! well, I suppose you're both gentlemen born;" and he insisted on prosecuting his scrutiny without any reference to the tenour of our observa-tions.

We entreated him half imperiously to bring his ship to and put us on shore in a boat. He bunched up his mouth, remarking, "Know their grammar: habit o' speaking to grooms, eh?—humph." We offered to pay largely. "Loose o' their cash," was his comment, and so on; and he was the more exasperating to us because he did not look an evil-minded man; only he appeared to be cursed with an evil opinion of us. I tried to remove it; I spoke forbearingly. Temple, imitating me, was sugar-sweet. We exonerated the captain from blame, excused him for his error, named the case a mistake on both sides. That long sleep of ours, we said, was really something laughable; we laughed at the recollection of it, a lamentable piece of merriment.

Our artfulness and patience becoming exhausted, for the captain had vouchsafed us no direct answer, I said at last, "Captain Welsh, here we are on board your ship: will you tell us what you mean to do with us?"

He now said bluntly, "I will."

"You'll behave like a man of honour," said I, and to that he cried vehemently, "I will."

"Well, then," said I, "call out the boat, if you please; we're anxious to be home."

"So you shall!" the captain shouted, "and per ship—my barque Priscilla; and better men than you left, or I'm no Christian."

Temple said briskly: "Thank you, captain."

"You may wait awhile with that, my lad," he answered; and, to our astonishment, recommended us to go and clean our faces and prepare to drink some tea at his table.

" Thank you very much, captain, we'll do that when we're on shore," said we.

" You'll have black figure-heads and empty gizzards, then, by that time," he remarked. We beheld him turning over the leaves of a Bible.

Now, this sight of the Bible gave me a sense of personal security, and a notion of hypocrisy in his conduct as well; and perceiving that we had conjectured falsely as to his meaning to cast us on shore per ship, his barque Priscilla, I burst out in great heat, " What ! we are prisoners ? You dare to detain us ?"

Temple chimed in, in a similar strain. Fairly enraged, we flung at him without anything of what I thought eloquence.

The captain ruminated up and down the columns of his Bible.

I was stung to feel that we were like two small terriers baiting a huge mild bull. At last he said, " The story of the Prodigal Son."

" Oh !" groaned Temple, at the mention of this worn-out old fellow, who has gone in harness to tracts ever since he ate the fatted calf.

But the captain never heeded his interruption.

" Young gentlemen, I've finished it while you've been barking at me. If I'd had him early in life on board my vessel, I hope I'm not presumptuous in saying—the Lord forgive me if I be so !—I'd have stopped his downward career—ay, so !—with a trip in the right direction. The Lord, young gentlemen, has not thrown you into my hands for no purpose whatsoever. Thank him on your knees to-night, and thank Joseph Double, my mate, when you rise, for he was the instrument of saving you from bad company. If this was a vessel where you'd hear an oath or smell the smell of liquor, I'd have let you run when there was terra firma within stone's throw. I came on board, I found you both asleep, with those marks of dissipation round your eyes, and I swore—in the Lord's name, mind you—I'd help pluck you out of the pit while you had none but one leg in. It's said ! It's no use barking. I am not to be roused. The devil in me is chained by the waist, and a twenty-pound weight on his tongue. With your assistance, I'll do the same for the devil in you. Since you've had plenty of sleep, I'll trouble you to commit to memory the whole story of the

Prodigal Son 'twixt now and morrow's sunrise. We'll have
our commentary on it after labour done. Labour you will
in my vessel, for your soul's health. And let me advise you
not to talk; in your situation talking's temptation to lying.
You'll do me the obligation to feed at my table. And when
I hand you back to your parents, why, they'll thank me, if
you won't. But it's not thanks I look for : it's my bounden
Christian duty I look to. I reckon a couple o' stray lambs
equal to one lost sheep."

The captain uplifted his arm, ejaculating solemnly, "By!"
and faltered. "You were going to swear!" said Temple,
with savage disdain.

"By the blessing of Omnipotence! I'll save a pair o' pups
from turning wolves. And I'm a weak mortal man, that's
too true."

"He *was* going to swear," Temple muttered to me.

I considered the detection of Captain Welsh's hypocrisy
unnecessary, almost a condescension toward familiarity; but
the ire in my bosom was boiling so that I found it impossible
to roll out the flood of eloquence with which I was big.
Soon after, I was trying to bribe the man with all my money
and my watch.

"Who gave you that watch?" said he.

"Downright Church catechism!" muttered Temple.

"My grandfather," said I.

The captain's head went like a mechanical hammer, to
express something indescribable.

"My grandfather," I continued, "will pay you handsomely
for any service you do to me and my friend."

"Now that's not far off forgeing," said the captain, in a
tone as much as to say we were bad all over.

I saw the waters slide by his cabin-windows. My desolation, my humiliation, my chained fury, tumbled together.
Out it came—

"Captain, do behave to us like a gentleman, and you shall
never repent it. Our relatives will be miserable about us.
They—captain!—they don't know where we are. We
haven't even a change of clothes. Of course we know we're
at your mercy, but do behave like an honest man. You
shall be paid or not, just as you please, for putting us on
shore, but we shall be eternally grateful to you. Of course
you mean kindly to us ; we see that——"

" I thank the Lord for it !" he interposed.

"Only you really are under a delusion. It's extraordinary. You can't be quite in your right senses about us ; you must be—I don't mean to speak disrespectfully—what we call on shore, cracked about us . . ."

" Doddered, don't they say in one of the shires ?" he remarked.

Half-encouraged, and in the belief that I might be getting eloquent, I appealed to his manliness. Why should he take advantage of a couple of boys ? I struck the key of his possible fatherly feelings: What misery were not our friends suffering now. (" Ay, a bucketful now saves an ocean in time to come !" he flung in his word.) I bade him, with more pathetic dignity, reflect on the dreadful hiatus in our studies.

" Is that Latin or Greek ?" he asked.

I would not reply to the cold-blooded question. He said the New Testament was written in Greek, he knew, and happy were those who could read it in the original.

" Well, and how can we be learning to read it on board ship ?" said Temple, an observation that exasperated me because it seemed more to the point than my lengthy speech, and betrayed that he thought so ; however, I took it up :

" How can we be graduating for our sphere in life, Captain Welsh, on board your vessel ? Tell us that."

He played thumb and knuckles on his table. Just when I was hoping that good would come of the senseless tune, Temple cried,—

" Tell us what your exact intentions are, Captain Welsh. What do you mean to do with us ?"

" Mean to take you the voyage out and the voyage home, Providence willing," said the captain, and he rose.

We declined his offer of tea, though I fancy we could have gnawed at a bone.

" There's no compulsion in that matter," he said. " You share my cabin while you're my guests, shipmates, and apprentices in the path of living ; my cabin and my substance, the same as if you were what the North-countrymen call bairns o' mine : I've none o' my own. My wife was a barren woman. I've none but my old mother at home. Have your sulks out, lads ; you'll come round like the Priscilla on a tack, and discover you've made way by it."

We quitted his cabin, bowing stiffly.

Temple declared old Rippenger was better than this cant-ing rascal.

The sea was around us, a distant yellow twinkle telling of land.

"His wife a barren woman! what's that to us!" Temple went on, exploding at intervals. "So was Sarah. His cabin and his substance! He talks more like a preacher than a sailor. I should like to see him in a storm! He's no sailor at all. His men hate him. It wouldn't be difficult to get up a mutiny on board this ship. Richie, I under-stand the whole plot: he's in want of cabin-boys. The fellow has impressed us. We shall have to serve till we touch land. Thank God, there's a British consul every-where; I say that seriously. I love my country; may she always be powerful! My life is always at her——did you feel that pitch of the ship? Of all the names ever given to a vessel, I do think Priscilla is without exception the most utterly detestable. Oh! there again. No, it'll be too bad, Richie, if we're beaten in this way."

"If *you* are beaten," said I, scarcely venturing to speak lest I should cry or be sick.

We both felt that the vessel was conspiring to ruin our self-respect. I set my head to think as hard as possible on Latin verses (my instinct must have drawn me to them as to a species of intellectual biscuit steeped in spirit, tough, and comforting, and fundamentally opposed to existing circum-stances, otherwise I cannot account for the attraction). They helped me for a time; they kept off self-pity, and kept the machinery of the mind at work. They lifted me, as it were, to an upper floor removed from the treacherously sighing Priscilla. But I came down quickly with a crash; no dexterous management of my mental resources could save me from the hemp-like smell of the ship, nor would leaning over the taffrail, nor lying curled under a tarpaulin. The sailors heaped pilot-coats upon us. It was a bad ship, they said, to be sick on board of, for no such thing as brandy was allowed in the old Priscilla. Still I am sure I tasted some before I fell into a state of semi-insensibility. As in a trance I heard Temple's moans, and the captain's voice across the gusty wind, and the forlorn crunching of the ship down great waves. The captain's figure was sometimes

stooping over us, more great-coats were piled on us; sometimes the wind whistled thinner than one fancies the shrieks
of creatures dead of starvation and restless, that spend their
souls in a shriek as long as they can hold it on, say nursery-
maids; the ship made a truce with the waters and grunted;
we took two or three playful blows, we were drenched with
spray, uphill we laboured, we caught the moon in a net of
rigging, away we plunged; we mounted to plunge again
and again. I reproached the vessel in argument for some
imaginary inconsistency. Memory was like a heavy barrel
on my breast, rolling with the sea.

CHAPTER XIII.

WE CONDUCT SEVERAL LEARNED ARGUMENTS WITH THE CAPTAIN OF THE PRISCILLA.

CAPTAIN WELSH soon conquered us. The latest meal we
had eaten was on the frosty common under the fir-trees.
After a tremendous fast, with sea-sickness supervening, the
eggs and bacon, and pleasant benevolent-smelling tea on the
captain's table were things not to be resisted by two healthy
boys who had previously stripped and faced buckets of mad-
dening ice-cold salt-water, dashed at us by a jolly sailor.
An open mind for new impressions came with the warmth of
our clothes. We ate, bearing within us the souls of injured
innocents; nevertheless, we were thankful, and, to the
captain's grace, a long one, we bowed heads decently. It
was a glorious breakfast, for which land and sea had prepared us in about equal degrees: I confess, my feelings
when I jumped out of the cabin were almost those of one
born afresh to life and understanding. Temple and I took
counsel. We agreed that sulking would be ridiculous, un-
manly, ungentlemanly. The captain had us fast, as if we
were under a lion's paw; he was evidently a well-meaning
man, a fanatic deluded concerning our characters: the barque
Priscilla was bound for a German port, and should arrive
there in a few days,—why not run the voyage merrily since
we were treated with kindness? Neither the squire nor

Temple's father could complain of our conduct; we were simply victims of an error that was assisting us to a knowledge of the world, a youth's proper ambition. "And we're not going to be starved," said Temple.

I smiled, thinking I perceived the reason why I had failed in my oration over-night; so I determined that on no future occasion would I let pride stand in the way of provender. Breakfast had completely transformed us. We held it due to ourselves that we should demand explanations from Joseph Double, the mate, and then, after hearing him furnish them with a cordial alacrity to which we might have attached unlimited credence had he not protested against our dreaming him to have supplied hot rum-and-water on board, we wrote our names and addresses in the captain's log-book, and immediately asked permission to go to the mast-head. He laughed. Out of his cabin there was no smack of the preacher in him. His men said he was a stout seaman, mad on the subject of grog and girls. Why, it was on account of grog and girls that he was giving us this dish of salt-water to purify us! Grog and girls! cried we. We vowed upon our honour as gentlemen we had tasted grog for the first time in our lives on board the Priscilla., How about the girls? they asked. We informed them we knew none but girls who were ladies. Thereupon one sailor nodded, one sent up a crow, one said the misfortune of the case lay in all girls being such precious fine ladies; and one spoke in dreadfully blank language, he accused us of treating the Priscilla as a tavern for the entertainment of bad company, stating that he had helped to row me and my associates from the shore to the ship. "Poor Mr. Double!" says he; "there was only one way for him to jump you two young gentlemen out o' that snapdragon bowl you was in—or quashmire, call it; so he 'ticed you on board wi' the bait you was swallowing, which was making the devil serve the Lord's turn. And I'll remember that night, for I yielded to swearing, and drank too!" The other sailors roared with laughter.

I tipped them, not to appear offended by their suspicions. We thought them all hypocrites, and were as much in error as if we had thought them all honest.

Things went fairly well with the exception of the lessons in Scripture. Our work was mere playing at sailoring, helping furl sails, haul ropes, study charts, carry messages, and such like. Temple made his voice shrewdly emphatic to explain to the captain that we liked the work, but that such lessons as these out of Scripture were what the veriest youngsters were crammed with.

" Such lessons as these, maybe, don't have the meaning on land they get to have on the high seas," replied the captain : " and those youngsters you talk of were not called in to throw a light on passages : for I may teach you ship's business aboard my barque, but we're all children inside the Book."

He groaned heartily to hear that our learning lay in the direction of Pagan Gods and Goddesses, and heathen historians and poets ; adding, it was not new to him, and perhaps that was why the world was as it was. Nor did he wonder, he said, at our running from studies of those filthy writings loose upon London ; it was as natural as dunghill steam. Temple pretended he was forced by the captain's undue severity to defend Venus ; he said, I thought rather wittily, " Sailors ought to have a respect for her, for she was born in the middle of the sea, and she steered straight for land, so she must have had a pretty good idea of navigation."

But the captain answered none the less keenly, " She had her idea of navigating, as the devil of mischief always has, in the direction where there's most to corrupt ; and, my lad, she teaches the navigation that leads to the bottom beneath us."

He might be right, still our mien was evil in reciting the lessons from Scripture ; and though Captain Welsh had intelligence we could not draw into it the how and the why of the indignity we experienced. We had rather he had been a savage captain, to have braced our spirits to sturdy resistance, instead of a mild, good-humoured man of kind intentions, who lent us his linen to wear, fed us at his table, and taxed our most gentlemanly feelings to find excuses for him. Our way of revenging ourselves becomingly was to laud the heroes of antiquity, as if they had possession of our souls and touched the fountain of worship. Whenever Captain Welsh exclaimed, " Well done," or the equivalent, " That's an idea," we referred him to Plutarch for our great exemplar. It was Alcibiades gracefully consuming his black

broth that won the captain's thanks for theological acuteness, or the young Telemachus suiting his temper to the
dolphin's moods, since he must somehow get on shore on the
dolphin's back.   Captain Welsh could not perceive in Temple
the personifier of Alcibiades, nor Telemachus in me ; but he
was aware of an obstinate obstruction behind our compliance.
This he called the devil coiled like a snake in its Winter sleep.
He hurled texts at it openly, or slyly dropped a particularly
heavy one, in the hope of surprising it with a death-blow.
We beheld him poring over his Bible for texts that should
be sovereign medicines for us, deadly for the devil within
us.   Consequently, we were on the defensive : bits of Cicero,
bits of Seneca, soundly and nobly moral, did service on
behalf of Paganism ; we remembered them certainly almost
as if an imp had brought them from afar.   Nor had we any
desire to be in opposition to the cause he supported.   What
we were opposed to was the dogmatic arrogance of a just
but ignorant man, who had his one specific for everything,
and saw mortal sickness in all other remedies or recreations.
Temple said to him,—

"If the Archbishop of Canterbury were to tell me Greek
and Latin authors are bad for me, I should listen to his
remarks, because he's a scholar : he knows the languages,
and knows what they contain."

Captain Welsh replied,—

"If the Archbishop o' Canterbury sailed the sea, and
lived in Foul Alley, Waterside, when on shore, and so felt
what it is to toss on top of the waves o' perdition, he'd
understand the value of a big, clean, well-manned, well-
provisioned ship, instead o' your galliots wi' gaudy sails,
your barges that can't rise to a sea, your yachts that run to
port like mother's pets at first pipe o' the storm, your trim-
built wherries."

"So you'd have only one sort of vessel afloat !" said I.
"There's the difference of a man who's a scholar."

"I'd have," said the captain, "every lad like you, my lad,
trained in the big ship, and he wouldn't capsize, and be
found betrayed by his light timbers as I found you.   Serve
your apprenticeship in the Lord's three-decker ; then to
command what you may."

"No, no, Captain Welsh," says Temple : "you must grind
at Latin and Greek when you're a chick, or you won't ever

master the rudiments. Upon my honour, I declare it's the truth, you must. If you'd like to try, and are of a mind for a go at Greek, we'll do our best to help you through the aorists. It looks harder than Latin, but after a start it's easier. Only, I'm afraid your three-decker's apprenticeship 'll stand in your way."

"Greek's to be done for me; I can pay clever gentlemen for doing Greek for me," said the captain. "The knowledge and the love of virtue I must do for myself; and not to be wrecked, I must do it early."

"Well, that's neither learning nor human nature," said I.

"It's the knowledge o' the right rules for human nature, my lad."

"Would you kidnap youngsters to serve in your ship, captain?"

"I'd bless the wind that blew them there, foul or not, my lad."

"And there they'd stick when you had them, captain?"

"I'd think it was the Lord's will they should stick there awhile, my lad—yes."

And what of their parents?"

"Youngsters out like gossamers on a wind, their parents are where they sow themselves, my lad."

"I call that hard on the real parents, Captain Welsh," said Temple.

"It's harder on Providence when parents breed that kind o' light creature, my lad."

We were all getting excited, talking our best, such as it was; the captain leaning over his side of the table, clasping his hands unintentionally preacher-like; we on our side supporting our chins on our fists, quick to be at him. Temple was brilliant; he wanted to convert the captain, and avowed it.

"For," said he, "you're not like one of those tract-fellows. You're a man we can respect, a good seaman, master of your ship, and hearty, and no mewing sanctimoniousness, and we can see and excuse your mistake as to us two; but now, there's my father at home—he's a good man, but he's a man of the world, and reads his classics and his Bible. He's none the worse for it, I assure you,"

"Where was his son the night of the fog?" said the captain.

Well, he happened to be out in it.''

'' Where'd he be now but for one o' my men ?''

'' Who can answer that, Captain Welsh ?''

'' I can, my lad—stewing in an ante-room of hell-gates, I verily believe.''

Temple sighed at the captain's infatuation, and said,—

'' I'll tell you of a fellow at our school named Drew; he was old Rippenger's best theological scholar—always got the prize for theology. Well, he was a confirmed sneak. I've taken him into a corner and described the torments of dying to him, and his look was disgusting—he broke out in a clammy sweat. 'Don't, don't!' he'd cry. 'You're just the fellow to suffer intensely,' I told him. And what was his idea of escaping it ? Why, by learning the whole of Deuteronomy and the Acts of the Apostles by heart! His idea of Judgement Day was old Rippenger's half-yearly examination. These are facts, you know, Captain Welsh.''

I testified to them briefly.

The captain said a curious thing : '' I'll make an appointment with you in leviathan's jaws the night of a storm, my lad.''

'' With pleasure,'' said Temple.

'' The Lord send it !'' exclaimed the captain.

His head was bent forward, and he was gazing up into his eyebrows.

Before we knew that anything was coming, he was out on a narrative of a scholar of one of the Universities. Our ears were indifferent to the young man's career from the heights of fortune to delirium tremens down the cataract of brandy, until the captain spoke of a dark night on the Pool of the Thames ; and here his voice struggled, and we tried hard to catch the thread of the tale. Two men and ·a girl were in the boat. The men fought, the girl shrieked, the boat was upset, the three were drowned.

All this came so suddenly that nothing but the captain's heavy thump of his fist on the table kept us from laughing.

He was quite unable to relate the tale, and we had to gather it from his exclamations. One of the men was mate of a vessel lying in the Pool, having only cast anchor that evening ; the girl was his sweetheart ; the other man had once been a fine young University gentleman, and had become an outfitter's drunken agent. The brave sailor had nourished him often when on shore, and he, with the fluent tongue which his college had trimmed for him, had led the girl to sin during her lover's absence. Howsoever, they put off together to welcome him on his arrival, never suspecting that their secret had been whispered to Robert Welsh beforehand. Howsoever, Robert gave them hearty greeting, and down to the cabin they went, and there sat drinking up to midnight.

·" Three lost souls !" said the captain.

" See how they run," Temple sang, half audibly, and flushed hot, ashamed of himself.

" 'Twas I had to bear the news to his mother," the captain pursued ; " and it was a task, my lads, for I was then little more than your age, and the glass was Robert's only fault, and he was my only brother."

I offered my hand to the captain. He grasped it powerfully. " That crew in a boat, and wouldn't you know the devil'd be coxswain ?" he called loudly, and buried his face.

" No," he said, looking up at us, "I pray for no storm, but, by the Lord's mercy, for a way to your hearts through fire or water. And now on deck, my lads, while your beds are made up. Three blind things we verily are."

Captain Welsh showed he was sharp of hearing. His allusion to the humming of the tune of the mice gave Temple a fit of remorse, and he apologized.

" Ay," said the captain, " it is so ; own it : frivolity's the fruit of that training that's all for the flesh. But dip you into some o' my books on my shelves here, and learn to see living man half skeleton, like life and shadow, and never to living man need you pray forgiveness, my lad."

By sheer force of character he gained the command of our respect. Though we agreed on deck that he had bungled his story, it impressed us ; we felt less able to cope with him, and less willing to encounter a storm.

" We shall have one, of course," Temple said, affecting resignation, with a glance aloft.

I was superstitiously of the same opinion, and praised the vessel.

" Oh, Priscilla's the very name of a ship that founders with all hands and sends a bottle on shore," said Temple."

" There isn't a bottle on board," said I ; and this piece of nonsense helped us to sleep off our gloom.

CHAPTER XIV.

I MEET OLD FRIENDS.

NOTWITHSTANDING the prognostications it pleased us to indulge, we had a tolerably smooth voyage. On a clear cold Sunday morning we were sailing between a foreign river's banks, and Temple and I were alternately reading a chapter out of the Bible to the assembled ship's crew, in advance of the captain's short exhortation. We had ceased to look at ourselves inwardly, and we hardly thought it strange. But our hearts beat for a view of the great merchant city, which was called a free city, and therefore, Temple suggested, must bear certain portions of resemblance to old England; so we made up our minds to like it.

"A wonderful place for beer cellars," a sailor observed to us slyly, and hitched himself up from the breech to the scalp.

At all events, it was a place where we could buy linen. For that purpose, Captain Welsh handed us over to the care of his trusted mate Mr. Joseph Double, and we were soon in the streets of the city, desirous of purchasing half their contents. My supply of money was not enough for what I deemed necessary purchases. Temple had split his clothes, mine were tarred; we were appearing at a disadvantage, and we intended to dine at a good hotel and subsequently go to a theatre. Yet I had no wish to part with my watch. Mr. Double said it might be arranged. It was pawned at a shop for a sum equivalent in our money to about twelve pounds, and Temple obliged me by taking charge of the ticket. Thus we were enabled to dress suitably and dine pleasantly, and, as Mr. Double remarked, no one could rob me of my gold watch now. We visited a couple of beer-cellars to taste the drink of the people, and discovered three of our men engaged in a similar undertaking. I proposed that it should be done at my expense. They praised their captain, but asked us, as gentlemen and scholars, whether it was reasonable to object to liquor because your brother was carried out on a high tide? Mr. Double commended them to moderation. Their reply was to estimate an immoderate amount of liquor as due to them, with profound composure.

" Those rascals," Mr. Double informed us. " are not in the captain's confidence; they're tidy seamen. though, and they submit to the captain's laws on board and have their liberty ashore."

We inquired what the difference was between their privileges and his.

"Why," said he, " if they're so much as accused of a disobedient act, off they're scurried, and lose fair wages and a kind captain. And let any man Jack of 'em accuse me, and he bounds a indiarubber ball against a wall and gets it; all he meant to give he gets. Once you fix the confidence of your superior you're waterproof."

We held our peace, but we could have spoken.

Mr. Double had no moral hostility toward theatres. Supposing he did not relish the performance, he could enjoy a spell in the open air, he said, and this he speedily decided to do. Had we not been bound in honour to remain for him to fetch us, we also should have retired from a representation of which we understood only the word *ja*. It was tiresome to be perpetually waiting for the return of this word. We felt somewhat as dogs must feel when human speech is addressed to them. Accordingly, we professed, without concealment, to despise the whole performance. I reminded Temple of a saying of the Emperor Charles V. as to a knowledge of languages.

"Hem!" he went, critically; " it's all very well for a German to talk in that way, but you can't be five times an Englishman if you're a foreigner."

We heard English laughter near us. › Presently an English gentleman accosted us.

" Mr. Villiers, I believe ?"   He bowed at me.

" My name is Richmond."

He bowed again, with excuses, talked of the Play, and telegraphed to a lady sitting in a box fronting us. I saw that she wrote on a slip of paper; she beckoned; the gentleman quitted us, and soon after placed a twisted note in my hand. It ran:—

" Miss Goodwin (whose Christian name is Clara) wishes very much to know how it has fared with Mr. Harry Richmond since he left Venice."

I pushed past a number of discontented knees, trying, on my way to her box, to recollect her vividly, but I could barely recollect her at all, until I had sat beside her five minutes. Colonel Goodwin was asleep in a corner of the box. Awakened by the sound of his native tongue, he recognized me immediately.

"On your way to your father?" he said, as he shook my hand.

I thought it amazing he should guess that in Germany.

"Do you know where he is, sir?" I asked.

"We saw him," replied the colonel; "when was it, Clara? A week or ten days ago."

"Yes," said Miss Goodwin; "we will talk of that by-and-by." And she overflowed with comments on my personal appearance, and plied me with questions, but would answer none of mine.

I fetched Temple into the box to introduce him. We were introduced in turn to Captain Malet, the gentleman who had accosted me below.

"You understand German, then?" said Miss Goodwin.

She stared at hearing that we knew only the word *ja*, for it made our presence in Germany unaccountable.

"The most dangerous word of all," said Colonel Goodwin, and begged us always to repeat after it the negative *nein* for an antidote.

"You have both seen my father?" I whispered to Miss Goodwin; "both? We have been separated. Do tell me everything. Don't look at the stage—they speak such nonsense. How did you remember me? How happy I am to have met you! Oh! I haven't forgotten the gondolas and the striped posts, and *stali* and the other word; but soon after we were separated, and I haven't seen him since."

She touched her father's arm.

"At once, if you like," said he, jumping up erect.

"In Germany was it?" I persisted.

She nodded gravely and leaned softly on my arm while we marched out of the theatre to her hotel—I in such a state of happiness underlying bewilderment and strong expectation that I should have cried out loud had not pride in my partner restrained me. At her tea-table I narrated the whole of my adventure backwards to the time of our parting in Venice, hurrying it over as quick as I could, with the breathless termination, "And now?"

They had an incomprehensible reluctance to perform their

part of the implied compact. Miss Goodwin looked at Captain Malet. He took his leave. Then she said, " How glad I am you have dropped that odious name of Roy! Papa and I have talked of you frequently—latterly very often. I meant to write to you, Harry Richmond. I should have done it the moment we returned to England."

" You must know," said the colonel, " that I am an amateur inspector of fortresses, and my poor Clara has to trudge the Continent with me to pick up the latest inventions in artillery and other matters, for which I get no thanks at head-quarters—but it's one way of serving one's country when the steel lies rusting. We are now for home by way of Paris. I hope that you and your friend will give us your company. I will see this Captain Welsh of yours before we start. Clara, you decided on dragging me to the theatre to-night with your usual admirable instinct."

I reminded Miss Goodwin of my father being in Germany.

" Yes, he is at one of the Courts, a long distance from here," she said, rapidly. " And you came by accident in a merchant-ship! You are one of those who are marked for extraordinary adventures. Confess: you would have set eyes on me, and not known me. It's a miracle that I should meet my little friend Harry—little no longer: my friend all the same, are you not ?"

I hoped so ardently.

She with great urgency added, " Then come with us. Prove that you put faith in our friendship."

In desperation I exclaimed, " But I must, I must hear of my father."

She turned to consult the colonel's face.

" Certainly," he said, and eulogized a loving son. " Clara will talk to you. I'm for bed. What was the name of the play we saw this evening ? Oh! *Struensee*, to be sure. We missed the scaffold."

He wished us good-night on an appointment of the hour for breakfast, and ordered beds for us in the hotel.

Miss Goodwin commenced: " But really I have nothing to tell you, or very little. You know, papa has introductions everywhere; we are like Continental people, and speak a variety of languages, and I am almost a foreigner, we are so

much abroad; but I do think English boys should be
educated at home: I hope you'll go to an English college."

Noticing my painful look, "We saw him at the Court of
the Prince of Eppenwelzen," she said, as if her brows ached.
"He is very kindly treated there; he was there some weeks
ago. The place lies out in the Hanover direction, far from
here. He told us that you were with your grandfather, and
I must see Riversley Grange, and the truth is you must take
me there. I suspect you have your peace to make; perhaps
I shall help you, and be a true Peribanou. We go over
Amsterdam, the Hague, Brussels, and you shall see the
battlefield, Paris, straight to London. Yes, you are fickle;
you have not once called me Peribanou."

Her voluble rattling succeeded in fencing off my questions
before I could exactly shape them, as I staggered from blind
to blind idea, now thinking of the sombre red Bench, and
now of the German prince's Court.

"Won't you tell me any more to-night?" I said, when
she paused.

"Indeed, I have not any more to tell," she assured me.

It was clear to me that she had joined the mysterious
league against my father. I began to have a choking in the
throat. I thanked her and wished her good-night while I
was still capable of smiling.

At my next interview with Colonel Goodwin he spoke
promptly on the subject of my wanderings. I was of an
age, he said, to know my own interests. No doubt filial
affection was excellent in its way, but in fact it was highly
questionable whether my father was still at the Court of
this German prince; my father had stated that he meant
to visit England to obtain an interview with his son, and
I might miss him by a harum-scarum chase over Germany.
And besides, was I not offending my grandfather and my
aunt, to whom I owed so much? He appealed to my warmest
feelings on their behalf. This was just the moment, he said,
when there was a turning-point in my fortunes. He could
assure me most earnestly that I should do no good by
knocking at this prince's doors, and have nothing but bitterness if I did in the end discover my father. "Surely you
understand the advantages of being bred a gentleman?" he
wound up. "Under your grandfather's care you have a
career before you, a fine fortune in prospect, everything a

young man can wish for. And I must tell you candidly, you run great risk of missing all these things by hunting your father to earth. Give yourself a little time: reflect on it."

"I have," I cried. "I have come out to find him, and I must."

The colonel renewed his arguments and persuasions until he was worn out. I thanked him continually for his kindness. Clara Goodwin besought me in a surprising manner to accompany her to England, called herself Peribanou, and with that name conjured up my father to my eyes in his breathing form. She said as her father had done, that I was called on now to decide upon my future: she had a presentiment that evil would come to me of my unchecked, headstrong will, which she dignified by terming it a true but reckless affection: she believed she had been thrown in my path to prove herself a serviceable friend, a Peribanou of twenty-six who would not expect me to marry her when she had earned my gratitude.

They set Temple on me, and that was very funny. To hear him with his "I say, Richie, come, perhaps it's as well to know where a thing should stop; your father knows you're at Riversley, and he'll be after you when convenient; and just fancy the squire!" was laughable. He had some anxiety to be home again, or at least at Riversley. I offered him to Miss Goodwin.

She reproached me and coaxed me; she was exceedingly sweet. "Well," she said, in an odd, resigned fashion, "rest a day with us; will you refuse me that?"

I consented; she knew not with what fretfulness. We went out to gaze at the shops and edifices, and I bought two light bags for slinging over the shoulder, two nightshirts, tooth-brushes, and pocket-combs, and a large map of Germany. By dint of vehement entreaties I led her to point to the territory of the Prince of Eppenwelzen-Sarkeld. "His income is rather less than that of your grandfather, friend Harry," she remarked. I doated on the spot until I could have dropped my finger on it blindfold.

Two or three pitched battles brought us to a friendly arrangement. The colonel exacted my promise that if I saw my father at Sarkeld in Eppenwelzen I would not stay with him longer than seven days: and that if he was not there I would journey home forthwith. When I had yielded the promise frankly on my honour, he introduced me to a banker of the city, who agreed to furnish me money to carry me on to England in case I should require it. A diligence engaged to deliver me within a few miles of Sarkeld. I wrote a letter to my aunt Dorothy, telling her facts, and one to the squire, beginning, "We were caught on our arrival in London by the thickest fog ever remembered," as if it had been settled on my departure from Riversley that Temple and I were bound for London. Miss Goodwin was my post-bag. She said when we had dined, about two hours before the starting of the diligence, "Don't you think you ought to go and wish that captain of the vessel you sailed in good-bye?" I fell into her plot so far as to walk down to the quays on the river-side and reconnoitre the ship. But there I saw my prison. I kissed my hand to Captain Welsh's mainmast rather ironically, though not without regard for him. Miss Goodwin lifted her eyelids at our reappearance. As she made no confession of her treason I did not accuse her, and perhaps it was owing to a movement of her conscience that at our parting she drew me to her near enough for a kiss to come of itself.

Four-and-twenty German words of essential service to a traveller in Germany constituted our knowledge of the language, and these were on paper transcribed by Miss Goodwin's own hand. In the gloom of the diligence, packed between Germans of a size that not even Tacitus had prepared me for, smoked over from all sides, it was a fascinating study. Temple and I exchanged the paper half-hourly while the light lasted. When that had fled, nothing was left us to combat the sensation that we were in the depths of a manure-bed, for the windows were closed, the tobacco-smoke thickened, the hides of animals wrapping our immense companions reeked; fire occasionally glowed in their pipe-bowls; they were silent, and gave out smoke and heat incessantly, like inanimate forces of nature. I had most fantastic ideas,—that I had taken root and ripened, and must expect my head to drop off at any instant: that I was deep down, wedged in the solid mass of the earth. But I need not repeat them: they were accurately translated in imagination from my physical miseries. The dim revival of light, when I had well-nigh ceased to hope for it, showed us

all like malefactors imperfectly hanged, or drowned wretches
in a cabin under water. I had one Colossus bulging over
my shoulder! Temple was blotted out. His face, emerging
from beneath a block of curly bearskin, was like that of one
frozen in wonderment. Outside there was a melting snow
on the higher hills; the clouds over them grew steel-blue.
We were going through a valley in a fir-forest.

CHAPTER XV.

WE ARE ACCOSTED BY A BEAUTIFUL LITTLE LADY IN THE FOREST.

BOWLS of hot coffee and milk, with white rolls of bread
to dip in them, refreshed us at a forest inn. For some
minutes after the meal Temple and I talked like interchanging puffs of steam, but soon subsided to our staring
fit. The pipes were lit again. What we heard sounded
like a language of the rocks and caves, and roots plucked
up, a language of gluttons feasting; the word *ja* was like a
door always on the hinge in every mouth. Dumpy children,
bulky men, compressed old women with baked faces, and
comical squat dogs, kept the villages partly alive. We
observed one young urchin sitting on a stone opposite a dog,
and he and the dog took alternate bites off a platter-shaped
cake, big enough to require both his hands to hold it.
Whether the dog ever snapped more than his share was
matter of speculation to us. It was an education for him
in good manners, and when we were sitting at dinner we
wished our companions had enjoyed it. They fed with their
heads in their plates, splashed and clattered jaws, without
paying us any hospitable attention whatever, so that we had
the dish of Lazarus. They were perfectly kind, notwithstanding, and allowed a portion of my great map of Germany
to lie spread over their knees in the diligence, whilst Temple
and I pored along the lines of the rivers. One would thrust
his square-nailed finger to the name of a city and pronounce
it; one gave us lessons in the expression of the vowels, with
the softening of three of them, which seemed like a regulation drill movement for taking an egg into the mouth, and

showing repentance of the act. " Sarkeld," we exclaimed mutually, and they made a galloping motion of their hands, pointing beyond the hills. Sarkeld was to the right, Sarkeld to the left, as the road wound on. Sarkeld was straight in front of us when the conductor, according to directions he had received, requested us to alight and push through this endless fir-forest up a hilly branch road, and away his hand galloped beyond it, coming to a deep place, and then to grapes, then to a tip-toe station, and under it lay Sarkeld. The pantomime was not bad. We waved our hand to the diligence, and set out cheerfully, with our bags at our backs, entering a gorge in the fir-covered hills before sunset, after starting the proposition—Does the sun himself look foreign in a foreign country ?

" Yes, he does," said Temple ; and so I thought, but denied it, for by the sun's favour I hoped to see my father that night, and hail Apollo joyfully in the morning ; a hope that grew with exercise of my limbs. Beautiful cascades of dark bright water leaped down the gorge ; we chased an invisible animal. Suddenly one of us exclaimed, " We're in a German forest ;" and we remembered grim tales of these forests, their awful castles, barons, knights, ladies, long-bearded dwarfs, gnomes and thin people. I commenced a legend off-hand.

" No, no," said Temple, as if curdling; " let's call this place the mouth of Hades. Greek things don't make you feel funny."

I laughed louder than was necessary, and remarked that I never had cared so much for Greek as on board Captain Welsh's vessel.

" It's because he was all on the opposite tack I went on quoting," said Temple. " I used to read with my father in the holidays, and your Rev. Simon has kept you up to the mark ; so it was all fair. It's not on our consciences that we crammed the captain about our knowledge."

" No. I'm glad of it," said I.

Temple pursued, " Whatever happens to a fellow, he can meet anything so long as he can say—I've behaved like a man of honour. And those German tales—they only upset you. You don't see the reason of the thing. Why is a man to be haunted half his life ? Well, suppose he did commit a murder. But if he didn't, can't he walk through an old castle without meeting ghosts ? or a forest ?"

The dusky scenery of a strange land was influencing
Temple. It affected me, so I made the worst of it for a
cure.

"Fancy those pines saying, 'There go two more,' Temple.
Well; and fancy this—a little earth-dwarf as broad as I'm
long and high as my shoulder. One day he met the loveliest girl in the whole country, and she promised to marry
him in twenty years' time, in return for a sack of jewels
worth all Germany and half England. You should have
seen her dragging it home. People thought it full of char-
coal. She married the man she loved, and the twenty years
passed over, and at the stroke of the hour when she first met
the dwarf, thousands of bells began ringing through the
forest, and her husband cries out, 'What is the meaning of
it?' and they rode up to a garland of fresh flowers that
dropped on her head, and right into a gold ring that closed
on her finger, and—look, Temple, look!"

"Where?" asked the dear little fellow, looking in all
earnest, from which the gloom of the place may be imagined,
for, by suddenly mixing it with my absurd story, I discomposed his air of sovereign indifference as much as one does
the surface of a lake by casting a stone in it.

We rounded the rocky corner of the gorge at a slightly
accelerated pace in dead silence. It opened out to restorative daylight, and we breathed better and chaffed one another,
and, beholding a house with pendent gold grapes, applauded
the diligence conductor's expressive pantomime. The opportunity was offered for a draught of wine, but we held water
preferable, so we toasted the Priscilla out of the palms of
our hands in draughts of water from a rill that had the
sound of aspen-leaves, such as I used to listen to in the
Riversley meadows, pleasantly familiar.

Several commanding elevations were in sight, some wooded,
some bare. We chose the nearest, to observe the sunset, and
concurred in thinking it unlike English sunsets, though not
so very unlike the sunset we had taken for sunrise on board
the Priscilla. A tumbled, dark and light green country of
swelling forest-land and slopes of meadow ran to the West,
and the West from flaming yellow burned down to smoky
crimson across it. Temple bade me "catch the disc—that
was English enough." A glance at the sun's disc confirmed
the truth of his observation. Gazing on the outline of the

orb, one might have fancied oneself in England. Yet the moment it had sunk under the hill this feeling of ours vanished with it. The coloured clouds drew me ages away from the recollection of home.

A tower on a distant hill, white among pines, led us to suppose that Sarkeld must lie somewhere beneath it. We therefore descended straight toward the tower, instead of returning to the road, and struck confidently into a rugged path. Recent events had given me the assurance that in my search for my father I was subject to a special governing direction. I had aimed at the Bench—missed it—been shipped across sea and precipitated into the arms of friends who had seen him and could tell me I was on his actual track, only blindly, and no longer blindly now.

"Follow the path," I said, when Temple wanted to have a consultation.

"So we did in the London fog!" said he, with some gloom.

But my retort: "Hasn't it brought us here?" was a silencer.

Dark night came on. Every height stood for a ruin in our eyes; every dip an abyss. It grew bewilderingly dark, but the path did not forsake us, and we expected, at half-hour intervals, to perceive the lights of Sarkeld, soon to be thundering at one of the inns for admission and supper. I could hear Temple rehearsing his German vocabulary, "Brod, butter, wasser, fleisch, bett," as we stumbled along. Then it fell to "Brod, wasser, bett," and then, "Bett" by itself, his confession of fatigue. Our path had frequently the nature of a waterway, and was very fatiguing, more agreeable to mount than descend, for in mounting the knees and shins bore the brunt of it, and these sufferers are not such important servants of the footfarer as toes and ankles in danger of tripping and being turned.

I was walking on leveller ground, my head bent and eyes half-shut, when a flash of light in a brook at my feet caused me to look aloft. The tower we had marked after sunset was close above us, shining in a light of torches. We adopted the sensible explanation of this mysterious sight, but were rather in the grip of the superstitious absurd one, until we discerned a number of reddened men.

"Robbers!" exclaimed one of us. Our common thought

was, "No; robbers would never meet on a height in that manner;" and we were emboldened to mount and request their help.

Fronting the tower, which was of white marble, a high tent had been pitched on a green platform semicircled by pines. Torches were stuck in clefts of the trees, or in the fork of the branches, or held by boys and men, and there were clearly men at work beneath the tent at a busy rate. We could hear the paviour's breath escape from them. Outside the ring of torchbearers and others was a long cart with a dozen horses harnessed to it. All the men appeared occupied too much for chatter and laughter. What could be underneath the tent? Seeing a boy occasionally lift one of the flapping corners, we took licence from his example to appease our curiosity. It was the statue of a bronze horse rearing spiritedly. The workmen were engaged fixing its pedestal in the earth.

Our curiosity being satisfied, we held debate upon our immediate prospects. The difficulty of making sure of a bed when you are once detached from your home, was the philosophical reflection we arrived at, for nothing practical presented itself. To arm ourselves we pulled out Miss Goodwin's paper. "Gasthof is the word!" cried Temple. "Gasthof, zimmer, bett; that means inn, hot supper, and bed. We'll ask." We asked several of the men. Those in motion shot a stare at us; the torchbearers pointed at the tent and at an unseen height, muttering "Morgen." Referring to Miss Goodwin's paper we discovered this to signify the unintelligible word morning, which was no answer at all; but the men, apparently deeming our conduct suspicious, gave us to understand by rather menacing gestures that we were not wanted there, so we passed into the dusk of the trees, angry at their incivility. Had it been Summer we should have dropped and slept. The night air of a sharp season obliged us to keep active, yet we were not willing to get far away from the torches. But after a time they were hidden; then we saw one moving ahead. The holder of it proved to be a workman of the gang, and between us and him the strangest parley ensued. He repeated the word morgen, and we insisted on zimmer and bett.

"He takes us for twin Caspar Hausers," sighed Temple.

"Nein," said the man, and, perhaps enlightened by hearing a foreign tongue, beckoned for us to step at his heels.

His lodging was a woodman's hut. He offered us bread to eat, milk to drink, and straw to lie on: we desired nothing more, and were happy, though the bread was black, the milk sour, the straw mouldy.

Our breakfast was like a continuation of supper, but two little girls of our host, whose heads were cased in tight-fitting dirty linen caps, munched the black bread and drank the sour milk so thankfully, while fixing solemn eyes of wonder upon us, that to assure them we were the same sort of creature as themselves we pretended to relish the stuff. Rather to our amazement we did relish it. "Mutter!" I said to them. They pointed to the room overhead. Temple laid his cheek on his hand. One of the little girls laid hers on the table. I said "Doctor?" They nodded and answered "Princess," which seemed perfectly good English, and sent our conjectures as to the state of their mother's health astray. I shut a silver English coin in one of their fat little hands.

We now, with the name Sarkeld, craved of their father a direction to that place. At the door of his hut he waved his hand carelessly South for Sarkeld, and vigorously West where the tower stood, then swept both hands up to the tower, bellowed a fire of cannon, waved his hat, and stamped and cheered. Temple, glancing the way of the tower, performed on a trumpet of his joined fists to show we understood that prodigious attractions were presented by the tower; we said *ja* and *ja*, and nevertheless turned into the Sarkeld path.

Some minutes later the sound of hoofs led us to imagine he had despatched a messenger after us. A little lady on a pony, attended by a tawny-faced great square-shouldered groom on a tall horse, rode past, drew up on one side, and awaited our coming. She was dressed in a grey riding-habit and a warm winter-jacket of gleaming grey fur, a soft white boa loose round her neck, crossed at her waist, white gauntlets, and a pretty black felt hat with flowing rim and plume. There she passed us under review. It was a curious scene: the iron-faced great-sized groom on his bony black charger dead still: his mistress, a girl of about eleven or twelve or thirteen, with an arm bowed at her side, whip

and reins in one hand, and slips of golden brown hair straying on her flushed cheek; rocks and trees, high silver firs
rising behind her, and a slender water that fell from the
rocks running at her pony's feet. Half-a-dozen yards were
between the charger's head and the pony's flanks. She
waited for us to march by, without attempting to conceal
that we were the objects of her inspection, and we in good
easy swing of the feet gave her a look as we lifted our hats.
That look was to me like a net thrown into moonlighted
water: it brought nothing back but broken lights of a
miraculous beauty.

Burning to catch an excuse for another look over my
shoulder, I heard her voice:

"Young English gentlemen!"

We turned sharp round.

It was she without a doubt who had addressed us: she
spurred her pony to meet us, stopped him, and said with the
sweetest painful attempt at accuracy in pronouncing a
foreign tongue:—

"I sthink you go a wrong way?"

Our hats flew off again, and bareheaded, I seized the reply
before Temple could speak.

"Is not this, may I ask you, the way to Sarkeld?"

She gathered up her knowledge of English deliberately.

"Yes, one goes to Sarkeld by sthis way here, but to-day
goes everybody up to our Bella Vista, and I entreat you do
not miss it, for it is some-s-thing to write to your home of."

"Up at the tower, then? Oh, we were there last night,
and saw the bronze horse, mademoiselle."

"Yes, I know. I called on my poor sick woman in a hut
where you fell asleep, sirs. Her little ones are my lambs;
she has been of our household; she is good; and they said,
two young, strange, small gentlemen have gone for Sarkeld;
and I supposed, sthey cannot know all go to our Bella Vista
to-day."

"You knew at once we were English, mademoiselle?"

"Yes, I could read it off your backs, and truly too your
English eyes are quite open at a glance. It is of you both I
speak. If I but make my words plain! My 'th' I cannot
always. And to understand, your English is indeed heavy
speech! not so in books. I have my English governess. We
read English tales, English poetry—and sthat is your excel-

lence. And so, will you not come, sirs, up when a way is to be shown to you? It is my question."

Temple thanked her for the kindness of the offer.

I was hesitating, half conscious of surprise that I should ever be hesitating in doubt of taking the direction toward my father. Hearing Temple's boldness I thanked her also, and accepted. Then she said, bowing :—

"I beg you will cover your heads."

We passed the huge groom bolt upright on his towering horse; he raised two fingers to the level of his eyebrows in the form of a salute.

Temple murmured: "I shouldn't mind entering the German Army," just as after our interview with Captain Bulsted he had wished to enter the British Navy.

This was no more than a sign that he was highly pleased. For my part delight fluttered the words in my mouth, so that I had to repeat half I uttered to the attentive ears of our gracious new friend and guide :—

"Ah," she said, "one does sthink one knows almost all before experiment. I am ashamed, yet I will talk, for is it not so? experiment is a school. And you, if you please, will speak slow. For I say of you English gentlemen, silk you spin from your lips; it is not as a language of an alphabet; it is pleasant to hear when one would lull, but Italian can do that, and do it more—am I right?—soft?"

"Bella Vista, lovely view," said I.

"Lovely view," she repeated.

She ran on in the most musical tongue, to my thinking, ever heard:—

"And see my little pensioners' poor cottage, who are out up to Lovely View. Miles round go the people to it. Good, and I will tell you strangers :—sthe Prince von Eppenwelzen had his great ancestor, and his sister Markgräfin von Rippau said, 'Erect a statue of him, for he was a great warrior.' He could not, or he would not, we know not. So she said, 'I will,' she said, 'I will do it in seven days.' She does constantly amuse him everybody at de Court. Immense excitement! For suppose it!—a statue of a warrior on horseback, in perfect likeness, chapeau tricorne, perruque, all of bronze, and his marshal's bâton. Eh bien, well, a bronze horse is come at a gallop from Berlin; sthat we know.

By fortune a most exalted sculptor in Berlin has him ready,
—and many horses pulled him to here, to Lovely View, by
post-haste; sthat we know.   But we are in extremity of
puzzlement.   For where is the statue to ride him? where
—am I plain to you, sirs?—is sthe Marshal Fürst von
Eppenwelzen, our great ancestor?   Yet the Markgräfin says,
'It is right, wait!'   She nods, she smiles.   Our Court is all
at the lake-palace odder side sthe tower, and it is bets of
gems, of feathers, of lace, not to be numbered!   The Markgräfin says—sthere to-day you see him, Albrecht Wohlgemuth Fürst von Eppenwelzen!   But no sculptor can have cast
him in bronze—not copied him and cast him in a time of
seven days!   And we say sthis:—Has she given a secret
order to a sculptor—you understand me, sirs, commission—
where, how, has he sthe likeness copied?   Or did he come
to our speisesaal of our lake palace disguised?   Oh! but to
see, to copy, to model, to cast in bronze, to travel betwixt
Berlin and Sarkeld in a time of seven days?   No! so—oh!
we guess, we guess, we are in exhaustion.   And to-day is
like an eagle we have sent an arrow to shoot and know not
if he will come down.   For shall we see our ancestor on
horseback?   It will be a not-scribable joy!   Or not?   So
we guess, we are worried.   At near eleven o'clock a cannon
fires, sthe tent is lifted, and we see; but I am impatient wid
my breaths for the gun to go."

I said it would be a fine sight.

" For strangers, yes; you should be of the palace to know
what a fine sight! sthe finest!   And you are for Sarkeld?
You have friends in Sarkeld?"

" My father is in Sarkeld, mademoiselle.   I am told he is
at the palace."

"Indeed; and he is English, your fater?"

" Yes.   I have not seen him for years; I have come to
find him."

"Indeed; it is for love of him, your fater, sir, you come,
and not speak German?"

I signified that it was so.

She stroked her pony's neck musing.

" Because, of love is not much in de family in England, it
is said," she remarked very shyly, and in recovering her self-
possession asked the name of my father.

" His name, mademoiselle, is Mr. Richmond."

" Mr. Richmond ?"

" Mr. Richmond Roy."

She sprang in her saddle.

" You are son to Mr. Richmond Roy ? Oh! it is wonderful."

" Mademoiselle, then you have seen him lately ?"

" Yes, yes ! I have seen him. I have heard of his beautiful child, his son; and you it is ?"

She studied my countenance a moment.

" Tell me, is he well ? mademoiselle, is he quite well ?"

" Oh yes," she answered, and broke into smiles of merriment, and then seemed to bite her under-lip. " He is our fun-maker. He must always be well. I owe to him some of my English. You are his son? you were for Sarkeld? You will see him up at our Bella Vista. Quick, let us run."

She put her pony to a canter up the brown path between the fir-trees, crying that she should take our breath ; but we were tight runners, and I, though my heart beat wildly, was full of fire to reach the tower on the height; so when she slackened her pace, finding us close on her pony's hoofs, she laughed and called us brave boys. Temple's being no more than my friend, who had made the expedition with me out of friendship, surprised her. Not that she would not have expected it to be done by Germans ; further she was unable to explain her astonishment.

At a turning of the ascent she pointed her whip at the dark knots and lines of the multitude mounting by various paths to behold the ceremony of unveiling the monument.

I besought her to waste no time.

" You must, if you please, attend my pleasure, if I guide you," she said, tossing her chin.

" I thank you, I can't tell you how much, mademoiselle," said I.

She answered : " You were kind to my two pet lambs sir."

So we moved forward.

CHAPTER XVI.

THE STATUE ON THE PROMONTORY.

THE little lady was soon bowing to respectful salutations
from crowds of rustics and others on a broad carriage-way
circling level with the height. I could not help thinking
how doubly foreign I was to all the world here—I who was
about to set eyes on my lost living father, while these
people were tip-toe to gaze on a statue. But as my father
might also be taking an interest in the statue, I got myself
round to a moderate sentiment of curiosity and a partial
share of the general excitement. Temple and mademoiselle
did most of the conversation, which related to glimpses of
scenery, pine, oak, beech-wood, and lake-water, until we
gained the plateau where the tower stood, when the giant
groom trotted to the front, and worked a clear way for us
through a mass of travelling sight-seers, and she leaned to
me, talking quite inaudibly amid the laughter and chatting.
A band of wind instruments burst out. "This is glorious!"
I conceived Temple to cry like an open-mouthed mute. I
found it inspiriting. The rush of pride and pleasure produced by the music was irresistible. We marched past the
tower, all of us, I am sure, with splendid feelings. A stone's-
throw beyond it was the lofty tent; over it drooped a flag,
and flags were on poles round a wide ring of rope guarded
by foresters and gendarmes, mounted and afoot. The band,
dressed in green, with black plumes to their hats, played in
the middle of the ring. Outside were carriages, and ladies
and gentlemen on horseback, full of animation; rustics,
foresters, town and village people, men, women, and children, pressed against the ropes. It was a day of rays of
sunshine, now from off one edge, now from another of large
slow clouds, so that at times we and the tower were in a
blaze; next the lake-palace was illuminated, or the long
grey lake and the woods of pine and of bare brown twigs
making bays in it.

Several hands beckoned on our coming in sight of the
carriages. "There he is, then!" I thought; and it was like
swallowing my heart in one solid lump. Mademoiselle had
free space to trot ahead of us. We saw a tall-sitting lady,

attired in sables, raise a finger at her, and nip her chin. Away the little lady flew to a second carriage, and on again, as one may when alive with an inquiry. I observed to Temple, " I wonder whether she says in her German, ' It is my question;' do you remember?" There was no weight whatever in what I said or thought.

She rode back, exclaiming, " Nowhere. He is nowhere, and nobody knows. He will arrive. But he is not yet. Now," she bent coaxingly down to me, " can you not a few words of German ? Only the smallest sum ! It is the Markgräfin, my good aunt, would speak wid you, and she can no English—only she is eager to behold you, and come ! You will know, for my sake, some scrap of German—*ja ?* You will—*nicht wahr ?* Or French ? Make your plom-pudding of it, will you ?"

I made a shocking plum-pudding of it. Temple was no happier.

The margravine, a fine vigorous lady with a lively mouth and livelier eyes of a restless grey that rarely dwelt on you when she spoke, and constantly started off on a new idea, did me the honour to examine me much as if I had offered myself for service in her corps of grenadiers, and might do in time, but was decreed to be temporarily wanting in manly proportions.

She smiled a form of excuse of my bungling half-English horrid French, talked over me and at me, forgot me and recollected me, all within a minute, and fished poor Temple for intelligible replies to incomprehensible language in the same manner, then threw her head back to gather the pair of us in her sight, then eyed me alone.

" C'est peut-être le fils de son petit papa, et c'est tout dire."

Such was her summary comment.

But not satisfied with that, she leaned out of the carriage, and, making an extraordinary grimace appear the mother in labour of the difficult words, said,—" Doos yo' laff ?"

There was no helping it : I laughed like a madman, giving one outburst and a dead stop.

Far from looking displeased, she nodded. I was again put to the dreadful test.

" Can yo' mak' laff ?"

It spurred my wits. I had no speech to " mak' laff "

with. At the very instant of my dilemma I chanced to
see a soberly-clad old townsman hustled between two helpless women of the crowd, his pipe in his mouth, and his hat,
wig, and handkerchief sliding over his face, showing his
bald crown, and he not daring to cry out, for fear his pipe
should be trodden under foot.

" *He* can, your highness."

Her quick eyes caught the absurd scene. She turned to
one of her ladies and touched her forehead. Her hand was
reached out to me; Temple she patted on the shoulder.

" He can—*ja : du auch.*"

A grand gentleman rode up. They whispered, gazed at
the tent, and appeared to speak vehemently. All the men's
faces were foreign : none of them had the slightest resemblance to my father's. I fancied I might detect him disguised. I stared vainly. Temple, to judge by the expression
of his features, was thinking. Yes, thought I, we might as
well be at home at old Riversley, that distant spot! We're
as out of place here as frogs in the desert!

Riding to and fro, and chattering, and commotion, of
which the margravine was the centre, went on, and the band
played beautiful waltzes. The workmen in and out of the
tent were full of their business, like seamen under a storm.

" Fräulein Sibley," the margravine called.

I hoped it might be an English name. So it proved to
be; and the delight of hearing English spoken, and, what
was more, having English ears to speak to, was blissful as
the leap to daylight out of a nightmare.

" I have the honour to be your countrywoman," said a
lady, English all over to our struggling senses.

We became immediately attached to her as a pair of ship-
wrecked boats lacking provender of every sort are taken in
tow by a well-stored vessel. She knew my father, knew
him intimately. I related all I had to tell, and we learnt
that we had made acquaintance with her pupil, the Princess
Ottilia Wilhelmina Frederika Hedwig, only child of the
Prince of Eppenwelzen.

" Your father will certainly be here; he is generally the
margravine's right hand, and it's wonderful the margravine
can do without him so long," said Miss Sibley, and conversed with the margravine; after which she informed me

that she had been graciously directed to assure me my father would be on the field when the cannon sounded.

"Perhaps you know nothing of Court life?" she resumed. "We have very curious performances in Sarkeld, and we owe it to the margravine that we are frequently enlivened. You see the tall gentleman who is riding away from her. I mean the one with the black hussar jacket and thick brown moustache. That is the prince. Do you not think him handsome? He is very kind—rather capricious; but that is a way with princes. Indeed, I have no reason to complain. He has lost his wife, the Princess Frederika, and depends upon his sister the margravine for amusement. He has had it since she discovered your papa."

"Is the gun never going off?" I groaned.

"If they would only conduct their ceremonies without their guns!" exclaimed Miss Sibley. "The origin of the present ceremony is this: the margravine wished to have a statue erected to an ancestor, a renowned soldier—and I would infinitely prefer talking of England. But never mind. Oh, you won't understand what you gaze at. Well, the prince did not care to expend the money. Instead of urging that as the ground of his refusal, he declared there were no sculptors to do justice to Prince Albrecht Wohlgemuth, and one could not rely on their effecting a likeness. We have him in the dining-hall; he was strikingly handsome. Afterward he pretended — I'm speaking now of the existing Prince Ernest—that it would be ages before the statue was completed. One day the margravine induced him to agree to pay the sum stipulated for by the sculptor, on condition of the statue being completed for public inspection within eight days of the hour of their agreement. The whole Court was witness to it. They arranged for the statue, horse and man, to be exhibited for a quarter of an hour. Of course, the margravine did not signify it would be a perfectly finished work. We are kept at a great distance, that we may not scrutinize it too closely. They unveil it to show she has been as good as her word, and then cover it up to fix the rider to the horse,—a screw is employed, I imagine. For one thing we know about it, we know that the horse and the horseman travelled hither separately. In all probability, the margravine gave the order for the statue last autumn in Berlin. Now look at the prince. He has his eye on you. Look down. Now he has forgotten you. He is impatient to behold the statue. Our chief fear is that the statue will not maintain its balance. Fortunately, we have plenty of guards to keep the people from pushing against it. If all turns out well, I shall really say the margravine has done wonders. She does not look anxious; but then she is not one ever to show it. The prince does. Every other minute he is glancing at the tent and at his watch. Can you guess my idea? Your father's absence leads me to think—oh! only a passing glimmer of an idea —the statue has not arrived, and he is bringing it on. Otherwise, he would be sure to be here. The margravine beckons me."

"Don't go!" we cried simultaneously.

The Princess Ottilia supplied her place.

"I have sent to our stables for two little pretty Hungarian horses for you two to ride," she said. "No, I have not yet seen him. He is asked for, and de Markgräfin knows not at all. He bades in our lake; he has been seen since. The man is excitable; but he is so sensible. Oh, no. And he is full of laughter. We shall soon see him. Would he not ever be cautious of himself for a son like you?"

Her compliment raised a blush on me.

The patience of the people was creditable to their phlegm. The smoke of pipes curling over the numberless heads was the most stirring thing about them.

Temple observed to me,—

"We'll give the old statue a British cheer, won't we, Richie?"

"After coming all the way from England!" said I, in dejection.

"No, no, Richie; you're sure of him now. He's somewhere directing affairs, I suspect. I say, do let us show them we can ring out the right tune upon occasion. By jingo! there goes a fellow with a match."

We saw the cannonier march up to the margravine's carriage for orders. She summoned the prince to her side. Ladies in a dozen carriages were standing up, handkerchief in hand, and the gentlemen got their horses' heads on a line. Temple counted nearly sixty persons of quality stationed there. The workmen were trooping out of the tent.

Miss Sibley ran to us, saying,—

"The gun-horror has been commanded. Now then: the prince can scarcely contain himself. The gunner is ready near his gun; he has his frightful match lifted. See, the manager-superintendent is receiving the margravine's last injunctions. How firm women's nerves are! Now the margravine insists on the prince's reading the exact time by her watch. Everybody is doing it. Let us see. By my watch it is all but fifteen minutes to eleven, A.M. Dearest," she addressed the little princess; "would you not like to hold my hand until the gun is fired?"

"Dearest," replied the princess, whether in childish earnest or irony I could not divine, "if I would hold a hand it would be a gentleman's."

All eyes were on the Prince of Eppenwelzen, as he gazed toward the covered statue. With imposing deliberation his hand rose to his hat. We saw the hat raised. The cannon was fired and roared; the band struck up a pompous slow march: and the tent-veil broke apart and rolled off. It was like the dawn flying and sunrise mounting.

I confess I forgot all thought of my father for awhile; the shouts of the people, the braying of the brass instruments, the ladies cheering sweetly, the gentlemen giving short hearty expressions of applause, intoxicated me. And the statue was superb — horse and rider in new bronze polished by sunlight.

"It is life-like! it is really noble! it is a true Prince!" exclaimed Miss Sibley. She translated several exclamations of the ladies and gentlemen in German: they were entirely to the same effect. The horse gave us a gleam of his neck as he pawed a forefoot, just reined in. We knew him; he was a gallant horse; but it was the figure of the Prince Albrecht that was so fine. I had always laughed at sculptured figures on horseback. This one overawed me. The Marshal was acknowledging the salute of his army after a famous victory over the infidel Turks. He sat upright, almost imperceptibly but effectively bending his head in harmony with the curve of his horse's neck, and his bâton wept the air low in proud submission to the honours cast on him by his acclaiming soldiery. His three-cornered lace hat, curled wig, heavy-trimmed surcoat, and high boots, reminded me of Prince Eugene. No Prince Eugene—nay, nor Marlborough, had such a martial figure, such an animated

high old warrior's visage. The bronze features reeked of
battle.

Temple and I felt humiliated (without cause, I granted)
at the success of a work of Art that struck us as a new
military triumph of these Germans, and it was impossible not
to admire it. The little Princess Ottilia clapped hands by fits.
What words she addressed to me I know not. I dealt out
my stock of German—" *Ja, ja*"—to her English. We were
drawn by her to congratulate the margravine, whose hand
was then being kissed by the prince : he did it most
courteously and affectionately. Other gentlemen, counts
and barons, bowed over her hand. Ladies, according to
their rank and privileges, saluted her on the cheek or in
some graceful fashion. When our turn arrived, Miss Sibley
translated for us, and as we were at concert pitch we did
not acquit ourselves badly. Temple's remark was, that he
wished she and all her family had been English. Nothing
was left for me to say but that the margravine almost made
us wish we had been German.

Smiling cordially, the margravine spoke, Miss Sibley
translated :—

" Her Royal Highness asks you if you have seen your
father ?"

I shook my head.

The Princess Ottilia translated,—

" Her Highness, my good aunt, would know, would you
know him, did you see him ?"

" Yes, anywhere," I cried.

The margravine pushed me back with a gesture.

" Yes, your Highness, on my honour ; anywhere on
earth !"

She declined to hear the translation.

Her insulting disbelief in my ability to recognize the
father I had come so far to embrace would have vexed me
but for the wretched thought that I was losing him again.
We threaded the carriages ; gazed at the horsemen in a
way to pierce the hair on their faces. The little princess
came on us hurriedly.

" Here, see, are the horses. I will you to mount. Are
they not pretty animals ?" She whispered, " I believe your
fater have been hurt in his mind by something. It is only

perhaps. Now mount, for the Markgräfin says you are our good guests."

We mounted simply to show that we could mount, for we would rather have been on foot, and drew up close to the right of the margravine's carriage.

" Hush! a poet is reading his ode," said the princess. " It is Count Fretzel von Wolfenstein."

This ode was dreadful to us, and all the Court people pretended they liked it. When he waved his right hand toward the statue there was a shout from the rustic set; when he bowed to the margravine, the ladies and gentlemen murmured agreeably and smiled. We were convinced of its being downright hypocrisy, rustic stupidity, Court flattery. We would have argued our case, too. I proposed a gallop. Temple said,—

" No, we'll give the old statue our cheer as soon as this awful fellow has done. I don't care much for poetry, but don't let me ever have to stand and hear German poetry again for the remainder of my life."

We could not imagine why they should have poetry read out to them instead of their fine band playing, but supposed it was for the satisfaction of the margravine, with whom I grew particularly annoyed on hearing Miss Sibley say she conceived her Highness to mean that my father was actually on the ground, and that we neither of us, father and son, knew one another. I swore on my honour, on my life, he was not present; and the melancholy in my heart taking the form of extreme irritation, I spoke passionately. I rose in my stirrups, ready to shout, " Father! here's Harry Richmond come to see you. Where are you!" I did utter something—a syllable or two: " Make haste!" I think the words were. They sprang from my inmost bosom, addressed without forethought to that drawling mouthing poet. The margravine's face met mine like a challenge. She had her lips tight in a mere lip-smile, and her eyes gleamed with provocation.

" Her Highness," Miss Sibley translated, " asks whether you are prepared to bet that your father is *not* on the ground?"

" Beg her to wait two minutes, and I'll be prepared to bet any sum," said I.

Temple took one half the circle, I the other, riding through
the attentive horsemen and carriage-lines, and making sure
the face we sought was absent, more or less discomposing
everybody. The poet finished his ode; he was cheered, of
course. Mightily relieved, 1 beheld the band resuming their
instruments, for the cheering resembled a senseless beating
on brass shields. I felt that we English could do it better.
Temple from across the sector of the circle, running about
two feet in front of the statue, called aloud,—

"Richie! he's not here!"

"Not here!" cried I.

The people gazed up at us, wondering at the tongue we
talked.

"Richie! now let's lead these fellows off with a tip-top
cheer!"

Little Temple crowed lustily.

The head of the statue turned from Temple to me.

I found the people falling back with amazed exclamations.
I—so prepossessed was I—simply stared at the sudden-
flashing white of the statue's eyes. The eyes, from being
an instant ago dull carved balls, were animated. They were
fixed on me. I was unable to give out a breath. Its chest
heaved; both bronze hands struck against the bosom.

"Richmond! my son! Richie! Harry Richmond! Richmond Roy!"

That was what the statue gave forth.

My head was like a ringing pan. I knew it was my
father, but my father with death and strangeness, earth,
metal, about him; and his voice was like a human cry con-
tending with earth and metal—mine was stifled. I saw him
descend. I dismounted. We met at the ropes and embraced. All his figure was stiff, smooth, cold. My arms
slid on him. Each time he spoke I thought it an unnatural
thing: I myself had not spoken once.

After glancing by hazard at the empty saddle of the
bronze horse, I called to mind more clearly the appalling
circumstance which had stupefied the whole crowd. They
had heard a statue speak—had seen a figure of bronze walk.
For them it was the ancestor of their prince; it was the
famous dead old warrior of a hundred and seventy years ago
thus set in motion. Imagine the behaviour of people round
a slain tiger that does not compel them to fly, and may yet

stretch out a dreadful paw ! Much so they pressed for a
nearer sight of its walnut visage, and shrank in the act.
Perhaps I shared some of their sensations. I cannot tell:
my sensations were tranced. There was no warmth to
revive me in the gauntlet I clasped. I looked up at the sky,
thinking that it had fallen dark.

CHAPTER XVII.

MY FATHER BREATHES, MOVES, AND SPEAKS.

THE people broke away from us like furrowed water as we
advanced on each side of the ropes toward the margravine's
carriage.

I became a perfectly mechanical creature : incapable of
observing, just capable of taking an impression here and
there; and in such cases the impressions that come are
stamped on hot wax ; they keep the scene fresh ; they partly
pervert it as well. Temple's version is, I am sure, the
truer historical picture. He, however, could never repeat it
twice exactly alike, whereas I failed not to render image for
image in clear succession as they had struck me at the time.
I could perceive that the figure of the Prince Albrecht, in
its stiff condition, was debarred from vaulting, or striding,
or stooping, so that the ropes were a barrier between us. I
saw the little Princess Ottilia eyeing us with an absorbed
comprehensive air quite unlike the manner of a child. Dots
of heads, curious faces, peering and starting eyes, met my
vision. I heard sharp talk in German, and a rider flung his
arm, as if he wished to crash the universe, and flew off.
The margravine seemed to me more an implacable parrot
than a noble lady. I thought to myself : This is my father,
and I am not overjoyed or grateful. In the same way I felt
that the daylight was bronze, and I did not wonder at it:
nay, I reasoned on the probability of a composition of sun
and mould producing that colour. The truth was, the
powers of my heart and will were frozen; I thought and
felt at random. And I crave excuses for dwelling on such
trifling phenomena of the sensations, which have been useful
to me by helping me to realize the scene, even as at the time
they obscured it.

According to Temple's description, when the statue moved its head toward him, a shudder went through the crowd, and a number of fore-fingers were levelled at it, and the head moved toward me, marked of them all. Its voice was answered by a dull puling scream from women, and the men gaped. When it descended from the saddle, the act was not performed with one bound, as I fancied, but difficultly ; and it walked up to me like a figure dragging logs at its heels. Half-a-dozen workmen ran to arrest it ; some townswomen fainted. There was a heavy altercation in German between the statue and the superintendent of the arrangements. The sun shone brilliantly on our march to the line of carriages where the Prince of Eppenwelzen was talking to the margravine in a fury, and he dashed away on his horse, after bellowing certain directions to his foresters and the workmen, by whom we were surrounded; while the margravine talked loudly and amiably, as though everything had gone well. Her watch was out. She acknowledged my father's bow, and overlooked him. She seemed to have made her courtiers smile. The ladies and gentlemen obeyed the wave of her hand by quitting the ground ; the band headed a long line of the commoner sort, and a body of foresters gathered the remnants and joined them to the rear of the procession. A liveried groom led away Temple's horse and mine. Temple declared he could not sit after seeing the statue descend from its pedestal.

Her Highness's behaviour roughened as soon as the place was clear of company. She spoke at my father impetuously, with manifest scorn and reproach, struck her silver-mounted stick on the carriage panels, again and again stamped her foot, lifting a most variable emphatic countenance. Princess Ottilia tried to intercede. The margravine clenched her hands, and, to one not understanding her speech, appeared literally to blow the little lady off with the breath of her mouth. Her whole bearing consisted of volleys of abuse, closed by magisterial interrogations. Temple compared her highness's language to the running out of Captain Welsh's chain-cable, and my father's replies to the hauling in : his sentences were short, they sounded like manful protestations; I barely noticed them. Temple's version of it went : " And there was your father apologizing, and the margravine rating him," &c. My father, as it happened, was careful not to open his lips wide on account of the plaster, or thick coating of paint on his face. No one would have supposed that he was burning with indignation; the fact being that, to give vent to it, he would have had to exercise his muscular strength; he was plastered and painted from head to foot. The fixture of his wig and hat, too, constrained his skin, so that his looks were no index of his feelings. I longed gloomily for the moment to come when he would present himself to me in his natural form. He was not sensible of the touch of my hand, nor I of his. There we had to stand until the voluble portion of the margravine's anger came to an end. She shut her eyes and bowed curtly to our salute.

"You have seen the last of me, madam," my father said to her whirling carriage-wheels.

He tried to shake, and strained in his ponderous garments. Temple gazed abashed. I knew not how to act. My father kept lifting his knees on the spot as if practising a walk.

The tent was in its old place covering the bronze horse. A workman stepped ahead of us, and we all went at a strange leisurely pace down the hill through tall pine-trees to where a closed vehicle awaited us. Here were also a couple of lackeys, who deposited my father on a bed of moss, and with much effort pulled his huge boots off, leaving him in red silk stockings. Temple and I snatched his gauntlets; Temple fell backward, but we had no thought of laughter; people were seen approaching, and the three of us jumped into the carriage. I had my father's living hand in mine to squeeze; feeling him scarcely yet the living man I had sought, and with no great warmth of feeling. His hand was very moist. Often I said, "Dear father!—Papa, I'm so glad at last," in answer to his short-breathed "Richie, my little lad, my son Richmond! You found me out; you found me!" We were conscious that his thick case of varnished clothing was against us. One would have fancied from his way of speaking that he suffered from asthma. I was now gifted with a tenfold power of observation, and let nothing escape me.

Temple, sitting opposite, grinned cheerfully at times to encourage our spirits; he had not recovered from his wonderment, nor had I introduced him. My father, however, had caught his name. Temple (who might as well have talked,

I thought) was perpetually stealing secret glances of abstracted perusal at him with a pair of round infant's eyes. sucking his reflections the while. My father broke our silence.

"Mr. Temple, I have the honour," he said, as if about to cough; "the honour of making your acquaintance; I fear you must surrender the hope of making mine at present."

Temple started and reddened like a little fellow detected in straying from his spelling-book, which was the window-frame. In a minute or so the fascination proved too strong for him; his eyes wandered from the window and he renewed his shy inspection bit by bit as if casting up a column of figures.

"Yes, Mr. Temple, we are in high Germany," said my father.

It must have cost Temple cruel pain, for he was a thoroughly gentlemanly boy, and he could not resist it. Finally he surprised himself in his stealthy reckoning: arrived at the full-breech or buttoned waistband, about half-way up his ascent from the red silk stocking, he would pause and blink rapidly, sometimes jump and cough.

To put him at his ease my father exclaimed, "As to this exterior," he knocked his knuckles on the heaving hard surface, "I can only affirm that it was, on horseback—ahem!— particularly as the horse betrayed no restivity, pronounced perfect! The sole complaint of our interior concerns the resemblance we bear to a lobster. Human somewhere, I do believe myself to be. I shall have to be relieved of my shell before I can at all satisfactorily proclaim the fact. I am a human being, believe me."

He begged permission to take breath a minute.

"I know you for my son's friend, Mr. Temple: here is my son, my boy, Harry Lepel Richmond Roy. Have patience: I shall presently stand unshelled. I have much to relate; you likewise have your narrative in store. That you should have lit on me at the critical instant is one of those miracles which combine to produce overwhelming testimony—ay, Richie! without a doubt there is a hand directing our destiny." His speaking in such a strain, out of pure kindness to Temple, huskily, with his painful attempt to talk like himself, revived his image as the father of my heart and dreams, and stirred my torpid affection, though it was still torpid enough, as may be imagined, when I state that I remained plunged in contemplation of his stocking of red silk emerging from the full bronzed breech, considering whether his comparison of himself to a shell-fish might not be a really just one.   We neither of us regained our true natures until he was free of every vestige of the garb of Prince Albrecht Wohlgemuth.   Attendants were awaiting him at the garden-gate of a beautiful villa partly girdled by rising fir-woods on its footing of bright green meadow. They led him away, and us to bath-rooms.

CHAPTER XVIII.

WE PASS A DELIGHTFUL EVENING, AND I HAVE A MORNING VISION.

In a long saloon ornamented with stags' horns and instruments of the chase, tusks of boars, spear-staves, boar-knives, and silver horns, my father, I, and Temple sat down to a memorable breakfast, my father in his true form, dressed in black silken jacket and knee-breeches, purple-stockings and pumps; without a wig, I thanked heaven to see. How blithely he flung out his limbs and heaved his chest released from confinement! His face was stained brownish, but we drank old Rhine wine, and had no eye for appearances.

"So you could bear it no longer, Richie?" My father interrupted the narrative I doled out, anxious for his, and be began, and I interrupted him.

"You did think of me often, papa, didn't you?"

His eyes brimmed with tenderness.

"Think of you!" he sighed.

I gave him the account of my latest adventures in a few panting breaths, suppressing the Bench. He set my face to front him.

"We are two fools, Mr. Temple," he said.

"No, sir," said Temple.

"Now you speak, papa," said I.

He smiled warmly.

"Richie begins to remember me."

I gazed at him to show it was true.

" I do, papa—I'm not beginning to."

At his request I finished the tale of my life at school.

"Ah, well! that was bad fortune; this is good!" he exclaimed. " 'Tis your father, my son: 'tis day-light, though you look at it through a bed-curtain, and think you are half-dreaming. Now then for me, Richie."

My father went on in this wise excitedly:

" I was laying the foundation of your fortune here, my boy. Heavens! when I was in that bronze shell I was astonished only at my continence in not bursting. You have grown,—you have shot up and filled out. I register my thanks to your grandfather Beltham ;—the same, in a minor degree, to Captain Jasper Welsh. Between that man Rippenger and me there shall be dealings. He flogged you : let that pass. He exposed you to the contempt of your schoolfellows because of a breach in my correspondence with a base-born ferule-swinger. What are we coming to ? Richie, my son, I was building a future for you here. And Colonel Goodwin—Colonel Goodwin, you encountered him too, and his marriageable daughter—I owe it to them that I have you here! Well, in the event of my sitting out the period this morning as the presentment of Prince Albrecht, I was to have won something would have astonished that unimpressionable countryman of ours. Goodness gracious, my boy! when I heard your English shout, it went to my marrow. Could they expect me to look down on my own flesh and blood, on my son—my son Richmond—after a separation of years, and continue a statue ? Nay, I followed my paternal impulse. Grant that the show was spoilt, does the Markgräfin insist on my having a bronze *heart* to carry on her pastime ? Why, naturally, I deplore a failure, let the cause be what it will. Whose regrets can eclipse those of the principal actor ? Quotha! as our old Plays have it. Regrets ? Did I not for fifteen minutes and more of mortal time sit in view of a multitude, motionless, I ask you, like a chiselled block of stone,—and the compact was one quarter of an hour, and no farther ? That was my stipulation. I told her—I can hold out one quarter of an hour : I pledge myself to it. Who, then, is to blame ? I was exposed to view twenty-three minutes, odd seconds. Is there not some ancient story of a monstrous wretch baked in his own bull ?

My situation was as bad. If I recollect aright, he could roar; no such relief was allowed to me. And I give you my word, Richie, lads both, that while that most infernal Count Fretzel was pouring forth his execrable humdrum, I positively envied the privilege of an old palsied fellow, chief boatman of the forest lake, for, thinks I, hang him! he can nod his head and I can not. Let me assure you, twenty minutes of an ordeal like that,—one posture, mind you, no raising of your eyelids, taking your breath mechanically, and your heart beating—jumping like an enraged ballet-dancer boxed in your bosom—a literal description, upon my honour; and not only jumping, jumping every now and then, I may say, with a toe in your throat:—I was half-choked:—well, I say, twenty-minutes, twenty-seven minutes and a half of that, getting on, in fact, to half-an-hour, it is superhuman! —by heavens, it is heroical! And observe my reward: I have a son—my only one. I have been divided from him for years; I am establishing his fortune; I know he is provided with comforts:—Richie, you remember the woman Waddy? A faithful soul! She obtained my consent at last—previously I had objections; in fact, your address was withheld from the woman—to call at your school. She saw Miss Rippenger, a girl of considerable attractions. She heard you were located at Riversley:—I say, I know the boy is comfortably provided for; but we have been separated since he was a little creature with curls on his forehead, scarce breeched——"

I protested:

"Papa, I have been in jacket and trousers I don't know how long."

"Let me pursue," said my father. "And to show you, Richie, it is a golden age ever when you and I are together, and ever shall be till we lose our manly spirit,—and we cling to that,—till we lose our princely spirit, which we never will abandon—perish rather!—I drink to you, and challenge you; and, mind you, old Hock wine has charms. If Burgundy is the emperor of wines, Hock is the empress. For youngsters, perhaps, I should except the Hock that gets what they would fancy a trifle *piqué*, turned with age, so as to lose in their opinion its empress flavour."

Temple said modestly: "I should call that the margravine of wines."

My father beamed on him with great approving splendour.
" Join us, Mr. Temple ; you are a man of wit, and may
possibly find this specimen worthy of you. This wine has
a history. You are drinking wine with blood in it. Well,
I was saying, the darling of my heart has been torn from
me ; I am in a foreign land ; foreign, that is, by birth, and
on the whole foreign. Yes !—I am the cynosure of eyes ;
I am in a singular posture, a singular situation ; I hear a
cry in the tongue of my native land, and what I presume is
my boy's name : I look, I behold him, I follow a parent's
impulse. On my soul ! none but a fish-father could have
stood against it. Well, for this my reward is—and I should
have stepped from a cathedral spire just the same, if I had
been mounted on it—that I, I,—and the woman knows all
my secret—I have to submit to the foul tirade of a vixen.
She drew language, I protest, from the slums. And I
entreat you, Mr. Temple, with your ' margravine of wines'
—which was very neatly said, to be sure—note you this
curious point for the confusion of Radicals in your after
life ; her Highness's pleasure was to lend her tongue to
the language—or something like it—of a besotted fishwife ; so ! very well, and just as it is the case with that
particular old Hock you youngsters would disapprove of,
and we cunning oldsters know to contain more virtues in
maturity than a nunnery of May-blooming virgins, just so
the very faults of a royal lady—royal by birth and in temper
a termagant—impart a perfume ! a flavour ! You must age !
you must live in Courts, you must sound the human bosom,
rightly to appreciate it. She is a woman of the most
malicious fine wit imaginable. She is a generous woman, a
magnanimous woman ; wear her chains and she will not
brain you with her club. She is the light, the centre of
every society where she appears, like what shall I say ? like
the moon in a bowl of old Rhenish. And you will drain that
bowl to the bottom to seize her, as it were—catch a correct
idea of her ; ay, and your brains are drowned in the attempt.
Yes, Richie ; I was aware of your residence at Riversley.
Were you reminded of your wandering dada on Valentine's
day ? Come, my boy, we have each of us a thousand
things to relate. I may be dull—I do not understand
what started you on your journey in search of me. An
impulse ? An accident ? Say, a directing angel ! We rest

our legs here till evening, and then we sup. You will be
astonished to hear that you have dined. 'Tis the fashion
with the Germans. I promise you good wine shall make it
up to you for the return to school-habits. We sup, and we
pack our scanty baggage, and we start to-night. Brook no
insult at Courts if you are of material value : if not, it is unreservedly a question whether you like kickings."

My father paused, yawned and stretched, to be rid of the
remainder of his aches and stiffness. Out of a great yawn he
said :

" Dear lads, I have fallen into the custom of the country ;
I crave your permission that I may smoke. Wander, if you
choose, within hail of me, or sit by me, if you can bear it,
and talk of your school-life, and your studies. Your aunt
Dorothy, Richie ? She is well ? I know not her like. I
could bear to hear of any misfortune but that she suffered
pain ! "

My father smoked his cigar peacefully. He had laid a
guitar on his knees, and flipped a string, or chafed over all
the strings, and plucked and thrummed them as his mood
varied. We chatted, and watched the going down of the
sun, and amused ourselves idly, fermenting as we were.
Anything that gave pleasure to us two boys pleased and at
once occupied my father. It was without aid from Temple's
growing admiration of him that I recovered my active belief
and vivid delight in his presence. My younger days sprang
up beside me like brothers. No one talked, looked, flashed,
frowned, beamed, as he did ! had such prompt liveliness as
he ! such tenderness ! No one was ever so versatile in playfulness. He took the colour of the spirits of the people
about him. His vivacious or sedate man-of-the-world tone
shifted to playfellow's fun in a twinkling. I used as a little
fellow to think him larger than he really was, but he was of
good size, inclined to be stout ; his eyes were grey, rather
prominent, and his forehead sloped from arched eyebrows.
So conversational were his eyes and brows that he could
persuade you to imagine he was carrying on a dialogue without opening his mouth. His voice was charmingly clear ;
his laughter confident, fresh, catching, the outburst of his
very self, as laughter should be. Other sounds of laughter
were like echoes.

Strange to say, I lost the links of my familiarity with him

when he left us on a short visit to his trunks and portmanteaux, and had to lean on Temple, who tickled but rejoiced me by saying: "Richie, your father is just the one I should like to be secretary to."

We thought it a pity to have to leave this nice foreign place immediately. I liked the scenery, and the wine, and what I supposed to be the habit of the gentlemen here to dress in silks. On my father's return to us I asked him if we could not stay till morning.

"Till morning then," he said: "and to England with the first lark."

His complexion was ruddier; his valet had been at work to restore it; he was getting the sanguine hue which coloured my recollection of him. Wearing a black velvet cap and a Spanish furred cloak, he led us over the villa. In Sarkeld he resided at the palace, and generally at the lake-palace on the removal of the Court thither. The margravine had placed the villa, which was her own property, at his disposal, the better to work out their conspiracy.

"It would have been mine!" said my father, bending suddenly to my ear, and humming his philosophical "heigho," as he stepped on in minuet fashion. We went through apartments rich with gilded oak and pine panellings: in one was a rough pattern of a wooden horse opposite a mirror; by no means a figure of a horse, but apparently a number of pieces contributed by a carpenter's workshop, having a rueful seat in the middle. My father had practised the attitude of Prince Albrecht Wohlgemuth on it. "She timed me five and twenty minutes there only yesterday," he said; and he now supposed he had sat the bronze horse as a statue in public view exactly thirty-seven minutes and a quarter. Tubs full of colouring liquid to soak the garments of the prince, pots of paint, and paint and plaster brushes, hinted the magnitude of the preparations.

"Here," said my father in another apartment, "I was this morning apparelled at seven o'clock: and I would have staked my right arm up to the collar-bone on the success of the undertaking!"

"Weren't they sure to have found it out in the end, papa?" I inquired.

"I am not so certain of that," he rejoined: "I cannot quaff consolation from that source. I should have been

covered up after exhibition; I should have been pronounced imperfect in my fitting-apparatus; the sculptor
would have claimed me, and I should have been enjoying
the fruits of a brave and harmless conspiracy to do honour
to an illustrious prince, while he would have been moulding
and casting an indubitable bronze statue in my image.   A
fig for rumours! We show ourself; we are caught from
sight; we are again on show. Now this being successfully
done, do you see, royalty declines to listen to vulgar tattle.
Presumably, Richie, it was suspected by the Court that the
margravine had many months ago commanded the statue at
her own cost, and had set her mind on winning back the money.
The wonder of it was my magnificent resemblance to the defunct.
I sat some three hours before the old warrior's portraits in
the dining-saloon of the lake-palace.   Accord me one good
spell of meditation over a tolerable sketch, I warrant myself
to represent him to the life, provided that he was a personage :
I incline to stipulate for handsome as well.   On my word of
honour as a man and a gentleman, I pity the margravine—
my poor good Frau Feldmarschall! Now, here, Richie"—
my father opened a side-door out of an elegant little room
into a spacious dark place—" here is her cabinet-theatre,
where we act German and French comediettas in Spring and
Autumn.   I have superintended it during the two or more
years of my stay at the Court.   Humph! 'tis over."

He abruptly closed the door.   His dress belonged to the
part of a Spanish nobleman, personated by him in a Play
called *The Hidalgo Enraged*, he said, pointing a thumb over
his shoulder at the melancholy door, behind which gay
scenes had sparkled.

"Papa!" said I sadly, for consolation.

"You're change for a sovereign to the amount of four
hundred and forty-nine thousand shillings every time you
speak!" cried he, kissing my forehead.

He sparkled in good earnest on hearing that I had made
acquaintance with the little Princess Ottilia.   What I
thought of her, how she looked at me, what I said to her,
what words she answered, how the acquaintance began, who
were observers of it,—I had to repair my omission to mention
her by furnishing a precise description of the circumstances,
describing her face and style, repeating her pretty English.

My father nodded: he thought I exaggerated that foreign

English of hers ; but, as I said, I was new to it and noticed it. He admitted the greater keenness of attention awakened by novelty. " Only," said he, " I rather wonder——" and here he smiled at me inquiringly. " 'Tis true," he added, " a boy of fourteen or fifteen—ay, Richie, have your fun out. A youngster saw the comic side of her——. Do you know, that child has a remarkable character ? Her disposition is totally unfathomable. You are a deep reader of English poetry, I hope ; she adores it, and the English Navy. She informed me that if she had been the English people she would have made Nelson king. The royal family of England might see objections to that, I told her. Cries she : ' Oh ! anything for a sea-hero.' You will find these young princes and princesses astonishingly revolutionary when they entertain brains. Now at present, just at present, an English naval officer, and a poet, stand higher in the esteem of that young Princess Ottilia than dukes, kings, or emperors. So you have seen her !" my father ejaculated musingly, and hummed, and said, " By the way, we must be careful not to offend our grandpapa Beltham, Richie. Good acres—good anchorage; good coffers—good harbourage. Regarding poetry, my dear boy, you ought to be writing it, for I do—the diversion of leisure hours, impromptus. In poetry I would scorn anything but impromptus. I was saying, Richie, that if tremendous misfortune withholds from you your legitimate prestige, you must have the substantial element. 'Tis your spring-board to vault by, and cushions on the other side if you make a miss and fall. 'Tis the essence if you have not the odour."

I followed my father's meaning as the shadow of a bird follows it in sunlight ; it made no stronger an impression than a flying shadow on the grass ; still I could verify subsequently that I had penetrated him—I had caught the outline of his meaning—though I was little accustomed to his manner of communicating his ideas : I had no notion of what he touched on with the words, prestige, essence, and odour.

My efforts to gather the reason for his having left me neglected at school were fruitless. " Business, business ! sad necessity ! hurry, worry—the hounds !" was his nearest approach to an explicit answer ; and seeing I grieved his kind eyes, I abstained. Nor did I like to defend Mr. Rip-

penger for expecting to be paid. We came to that point
once or twice, when so sharply wronged did he appear, and
vehement and indignant, that I banished thoughts which
marred my luxurious contentment in hearing him talk and
sing, and behave in his old ways and new habits. Plain
velvet was his dress at dinner. We had a yellow Hock.
Temple's meditative face over it, to discover the margravine,
or something, in its flavour, was a picture. It was an evening of incessant talking; no telling of events straightforwardly, but all by fits—all here and there. My father
talked of Turkey, so I learnt he had been in that country;
Temple of the routine of our life at Riversley; I of Kiomi,
the gipsy girl; then we two of Captain Jasper Welsh; my
father of the Princess Ottilia. When I alluded to the margravine, he had a word to say of Mrs. Waddy; so I learnt
she had been in continual correspondence with him, and had
cried heavily about me, poor soul. Temple laughed out a
recollection of Captain Bulsted's " hic, hæc, hoc;" I jumped
Janet Ilchester up on the table; my father expatiated on
the comfort of a volume of Shakespeare to an exiled Englishman. We drank to one another, and heartily to the statue.
My father related the history of the margravine's plot in
duck-and-drake skips, and backward to his first introduction
to her at some Austrian Baths among the mountains. She
wanted amusement—he provided it; she never let him quit
her sight from that moment. " And now," he said, " she has
lost me !" He drew out of his pocket-book a number of
designs for the statue of Prince Albrecht, to which the
margravine's initials were appended, and shuffled them, and
sighed, and said :—" Most complete arrangements ! most
complete ! No body of men were ever so well drilled as
those fellows up at Bella Vista—could not have been ! And
at the climax, in steps the darling boy for whom I laboured
and sweated, and down we topple incontinently ! Nothing
would have shaken me but the apparition of my son ! I was
proof against everything but that ! I sat invincible for
close upon an hour—call it an hour ! Not a muscle of me
moved : I repeat, the heart in my bosom capered like an
independent organ ; had it all its own way, leaving me
mine, until—— Mr. Temple, take my word for it, there is a
guiding hand in some families ; believe it, and be serene in
adversity. The change of life at a merry Court to life in a

London alley will exercise our faith. But the essential thing is that Richie has been introduced here, and I intend him to play a part here. The grandson and heir of one of the richest commoners in England—I am not saying commoner as a term of reproach—possessed of a property that turns itself over and doubles itself every ten years, may—mind you, may—on such a solid foundation as that!—and as to birth, your Highness has only to grant us a private interview."

Temple was dazed by this mystifying address to him; nor could I understand it.

"Why, papa, you always wished for me to go into Parliament," said I.

"I do," he replied, "and I wish you to lead the London great world. Such topics are for by-and-by. Adieu to them!" He kissed his wafting finger-tips.

We fell upon our random talk again with a merry rattle.

I had to give him a specimen of my piano-playing and singing.

He shook his head. "The cricketer and the scholar have been developed at the expense of the musician; and music, Richie, music unlocks the chamber of satin-rose."

Late at night we separated. Temple and I slept in companion-rooms. Deadly drowsy, the dear little fellow sat on the edge of my bed chattering of his wonder. My dreams led me wandering with a ship's diver under the sea, where we walked in a light of pearls and exploded old wrecks. I was assuring the glassy man that it was almost as clear beneath the waves as above, when I awoke to see my father standing over me in daylight; and in an ecstasy I burst into sobs.

"Here, Richie"—he pressed fresh violets on my nostrils —"you have had a morning visitor. Quick out of bed, and you will see the little fairy crossing the meadow."

I leapt to the window in time to have in view the little Princess Ottilia, followed by her faithful gaunt groom, before she was lost in the shadow of the fir-trees.

CHAPTER XIX.

OUR RETURN HOMEWARD.

WE started for England at noon, much against my secret wishes; but my father would not afford the margravine time to repent of her violent language and injustice toward him. Reflection increased his indignation. Anything that went wrong on the first stages of the journey caused him to recapitulate her epithets and reply to them proudly. He confided to me in Cologne Cathedral that the entire course of his life was a grand plot, resembling an unfinished piece of architecture, which might, at a future day, prove the wonder of the world: and he had, therefore, packed two dozen of hoar old (*uralt :* he used comical German) Hock for a present to my grandfather Beltham, in the hope of its being found acceptable.

"For, Richie," said he, "you may not know—and it is not to win your thanks I inform you of it—that I labour unremittingly in my son's interests. I have established him, on his majority, in Germany, at a Court. My object now is to establish him in England. Promise me that it shall be the decided endeavour of your energies and talents to rise to the height I point out to you? You promise, I perceive," he added, sharp in detecting the unpleasant predicament of a boy who is asked to speak priggishly. So then I could easily promise with a firm voice. He dropped certain explosive hints, which reminded me of the funny ideas of my state and greatness I had when a child. I shrugged at them; I cared nothing for revelations to come by-and-by. My object was to unite my father and grandfather on terms of friendship. This was the view that now absorbed and fixed my mind. To have him a frequent visitor at Riversley, if not a resident in the house, enlivening them all, while I, perhaps, trifled a cavalry sabre, became one of my settled dreams. The difficult part of the scheme appeared to me the obtaining of my father's consent. I mentioned it, and he said immediately that he must have his freedom. "Now, for instance," said he, "what is my desire at this moment? I have always a big one perched on a rock in the distance: but I speak of my present desire. And let it be supposed that the squire is one of us : we are returning to England. Well, I want to show you a stork's nest. We are not far enough South for the stork to build here. It is a fact, Richie, that I do want to show you the bird for luck, and as a feature of the country. And in me, a desire to do a thing partakes of the impetus of steam. Well, you see we are jogging home to England. I resist myself for duty's sake : that I can do. But if the squire were here with his yea and his nay, by heavens ! I should be off to the top of the Rhine like a tornado. I submit to circumstances : I cannot, and I will not, be dictated to by men."

"That seems to me rather unreasonable," I remonstrated.

"It is ; I am ashamed of it," he answered. "Do as you will, Richie ; set me down at Riversley, but under no slight, mark you. I keep my honour intact, like a bottled cordial ; my unfailing comfort in adversity ! I hand it to you, my son, on my death-bed, and say, ' You have there the essence of my life. Never has it been known of me that I swallowed an insult.' "

"Then, papa, I shall have a talk with the squire."

"Make good your ground in the castle," said he. "I string a guitar outside. You toss me a key from the walls. If there is room, and I have leisure, I enter. If not, you know I am paving your way in other quarters. Riversley, my boy, is an excellent foothold and fortress : Riversley is not the world. At Riversley I should have to wear a double face, and, egad ! a double stomach-bag, like young Jack feeding with the giant—one full of ambition, the other of provender. That place is our touchstone to discover whether we have prudence. We have, I hope. And we will have, Mr. Temple, a pleasant day or two in Paris."

It was his habit to turn off the bent of these conversations by drawing Temple into them. Temple declared there was no feeling we were in a foreign country while he was our companion. We simply enjoyed strange scenes, looking idly out of our windows. Our recollection of the strangest scene ever witnessed filled us with I know not what scornful pleasure, and laughed in the background at any sight or marvel pretending to amuse us. Temple and I cantered over the great Belgian battle-field, talking of Bella Vista tower, the statue, the margravine, our sour milk and black-bread breakfast, the little Princess Ottilia, with her " It is my question," and "You were kind to my lambs, sir," thoughtless of glory and dead bones. My father was very differently impressed. He was in an exultant glow, far out-matching the bloom on our faces when we rejoined him. I cried,—

"Papa, if the prince won't pay for a real statue, I will, and I'll present it in your name!"

"To the nation?" cried he, staring, and arresting his arm in what seemed an orchestral movement.

"To the margravine!"

He heard, but had to gather his memory. He had been fighting the battle, and made light of Bella Vista. I found that incidents over which a day or two had rolled lost their features to him. He never smiled at recollections. If they were forced on him noisily by persons he liked, perhaps his face was gay, but only for a moment. The gaiety of his nature drew itself from hot-springs of hopefulness: our arrival in England, our interviews there, my majority Burgundy, my revisitation of Germany—these events to come gave him the aspect children wear out a-Maying or in an orchard. He discussed the circumstances connected with the statue as dry matter-of-fact, and unless it was his duty to be hilarious at the dinner-table, he was hardly able to respond to a call on his past life and mine. His future, too, was present tense: "We do this," not "we will do this;" so that, generally, no sooner did we speak of an anticipated scene than he was acting in it. I studied him eagerly, I know, and yet quite unconsciously, and I came to no conclusions. Boys are always putting down the ciphers of their observations of people beloved by them, but do not add up a sum total.

Our journey home occupied nearly eleven weeks, owing to stress of money on two occasions. In Brussels I beheld him with a little beggar-girl in his arms.

"She has asked me for a copper coin, Richie," he said, squeezing her fat cheeks to make cherries of her lips.

I recommended him to give her a silver one.

"Something, Richie, I must give the little wench, for I have kissed her, and, in my list of equivalents, gold would be the sole form of repayment after that. You must buy me off with honour, my boy."

I was compelled to receive a dab from the child's nose, by way of kiss, in return for buying him off with honour.

The child stumped away on the pavement fronting our hotel, staring at its fist that held the treasure.

"Poor pet wee drab of it!" exclaimed my father. "One is glad, Richie, to fill a creature out of one's emptiness. Now she toddles; she is digesting it rapidly. The last performance of one's purse is rarely so pleasant as that. I owe it to her that I made the discovery in time."

In this manner I also made the discovery that my father had no further supply of money, none whatever. How it had run out without his remarking it, he could not tell; he could only assure me that he had become aware of the fact while searching vainly for a coin to bestow on the beggar girl. I despatched a letter attested by a notary of the city, applying for money to the banker to whom Colonel Goodwin had introduced me on my arrival on the Continent. The money came, and in the meantime we had formed acquaintances and entertained them; they were chiefly half-pay English military officers, dashing men. One, a Major Dykes, my father established in our hotel, and we carried him on to Paris, where, consequent upon our hospitalities, the purse was again deficient. Two reasons for not regretting it were adduced by my father; firstly, that it taught me not to despise the importance of possessing money; secondly, that we had served our country by assisting Dykes, who was on the scent of a new and terrible weapon of destruction, which he believed to be in the hands of the French Government. Major Dykes disappeared on the scent, but we had the satisfaction of knowing that we had done our best toward saving the Navy of Great Britain from being blown out of water. Temple and I laughed over Major Dykes, and he became our puppet for by-play, on account of his enormous whiskers, his passion for strong drinks, and his air of secresy. My father's faith in his patriotic devotedness was sufficient to withhold me from suspicions of his character. Whenever my instinct, or common sense, would have led me to differ with my father in opinion fun supervened; I was willing that everything in the world should be as he would have it be, and took up with a spirit of laughter, too happy in having won him, in having fished him out of the deep sea at one fling of the net, as he said, to care for accuracy of sentiment in any other particular.

Our purse was at its lowest ebb; he suggested no means of replenishing it, and I thought of none. He had heard that it was possible to live in Paris upon next to nothing with very great luxury, so we tried it; we strolled through the lilac aisles among bonnes and babies, attended military spectacles, rode on omnibuses, dined on the country heights, went to theatres, and had a most pleasurable time, gaining everywhere front places, friendly smiles, kind little services, in a way that would have been incomprehensible to me but for my consciousness of the magical influence of my father's address, a mixture of the ceremonious and the affable such as the people could not withstand.

"The poet is perhaps, on the whole, more exhilarating than the alderman," he said.

These were the respective names given by him to the empty purse and the full purse. We vowed we preferred the poet.

"Ay," said he, "but for all that the alderman is lighter on his feet: I back him to be across the Channel first. The object of my instructions to you will be lost, Richie, if I find you despising the Alderman's Pegasus. On money you mount. We are literally chained here, you know, there is no doubt about it; and we are adding a nail to our fetters daily. True, you are accomplishing the Parisian accent. Paris has also this immense advantage over all other cities: 'tis the central hotel on the high-road of civilization. In Paris you meet your friends to a certainty; it catches them every one in turn; so now we must abroad early and late, and cut for trumps." A meeting with a friend of my father, Mr. Monterez Williams, was the result of our resolute adoption of this system. He helped us on to Boulogne, where my father met another friend, to whom he gave so sumptuous a dinner that we had not money enough to pay the hotel bill.

"Now observe the inconvenience of leaving Paris," said he. "Ten to one we shall have to return. We will try a week's whistling on the jetty; and if no luck comes, and you will admit, Richie—Mr. Temple, I call your attention to it—that luck will scarcely come in profuse expedition through the narrow neck of a solitary seaport, why, we must return to Paris."

I proposed to write to my aunt Dorothy for money, but

he would not hear of that.   After two or three days of whistling, I saw my old friend Mr. Bannerbridge step out of the packet-boat.   On condition of my writing to my aunt to say that I was coming home, he advanced me the sum we were in need of, grudgingly though, and with the prediction that we should break down again, which was verified.   It occurred only a stage from Riversley, where my grandfather's name was good as coin of the realm.   Besides, my father remained at the inn to guarantee the payment of the bill, while Temple and I pushed on in a fly with the two dozen of Hock.   It could hardly be called a break-down, but my father was not unwilling for me to regard it in that light. Among his parting remarks was an impressive adjuration to me to cultivate the squire's attachment at all costs.

" Do this," he said, " and I shall know that the lesson I have taught you on your journey homeward has not been thrown away.   My darling boy ! my curse through life has been that the sense of weight in money is a sense I am and was born utterly a stranger to.   The consequence is, my grandest edifices fall; there is no foundation for them.   Not that I am worse, understand me, than under a temporary cloud, and the blessing of heaven has endowed me with a magnificent constitution.   Heaven forefend that I should groan for myself, or you for me !   But digest what you have learnt, Richie; press nothing on the squire; be guided by the advice of that esteemed and admirable woman, your aunt Dorothy.   And, by the way, you may tell her confidentially of the progress of your friendship with the Princess Ottilia.   Here I shall employ my hours in a tranquil study of nature until I see you."   Thus he sped me forward.

We sighted Riversley about midday on a sunny June morning.   Compared with the view from Bella Vista, our firs looked scanty, our heath-tracts dull, as places having no page of history written on them, our fresh green meadows not more than commonly homely.   I was so full of my sense of triumph in my adventurous journey and the recovery of my father, that I gazed on the old Grange from a towering height.   The squire was on the lawn, surrounded by a full company : the Ilchesters, the Ambroses, the Wilfords, Captain and Squire Gregory Bulsted, the Rubreys, and others, all bending to roses, to admire, smell, or pluck.   Charming groups of ladies were here and there; and Temple whispered as we passed them:

" We beat foreigners in our women, Richie."

I, making it my business to talk with perfect unconcern, replied:

" Do you think so ? Perhaps. Not in all cases ;" all the while I was exulting at the sweet beams of England radiating from these dear early-morning-looking women.

My aunt Dorothy swam up to me, and, kissing me, murmured:

" Take no rebuff from your grandpapa, darling."

My answer was:

" I have found him !"

Captain Bulsted sang out our names; I caught sight of Julia Rippenger's face; the squire had his back turned to me, which reminded me of my first speech with Captain Jasper Welsh, and I thought to myself, I know something of the world now, and the thing is to keep a good temper. Here there was no wire-coil to intercept us, so I fronted him quickly.

" Hulloa !" he cried, and gave me his shoulder.

" Temple is your guest, sir," said I.

He was obliged to stretch out his hand to Temple.

A prompt instinct warned me that I must show him as much Beltham as I could summon.

" Dogs and horses all right, sir ?" I asked.

Captain Bulsted sauntered near.

" Here, William," said the squire, " tell this fellow about my stables."

" In excellent condition, Harry Richmond," returned the captain.

" Oh! he's got a new name, I'll swear," said the squire.

" Not I !"

" Then what have you got of your trip, eh ?"

" A sharper eye than I had, sir."

" You've been sharpening it in London, have you ?"

" I've been a little farther than London, squire."

" Well, you're not a liar."

" There, you see the lad can stand fire !" Captain Bulsted broke in. " Harry Richmond, I'm proud to shake your hand, but I'll wait till you're through the ceremony with your grandad."

The squire's hands were crossed behind him. I smiled boldly in his face.

"Shall I make the tour of you to get hold of one of them, sir?" He frowned and blinked.

"Shuffle in among the ladies; you seem to know how to make friends among them," he said, and pretended to disengage his right hand for the purpose of waving it toward one of the groups.

I seized it, saying heartily,—"Grandfather, upon my honour, I love you, and I'm glad to be home again."

"Mind you, you're not at home till you've begged Uberly's pardon in public, you know what for," he rejoined.

"Leaving the horse at that inn is on my conscience," said I.

The squire grumbled: "All the better; keep him there a bit."

"Suppose he kicks?" said I; and the captain laughed, and the squire too, and I was in such high spirits I thought of a dozen witty suggestions relative to the seat of the conscience, and grieved for a minute at going to the ladies.

Captain Bulsted convoyed me to pretty Irish-eyed Julia Rippenger. Temple had previously made discovery of Janet Ilchester. Relating our adventures on different parts of the lawn, we both heard that Colonel Goodwin and his daughter had journeyed down to Riversley to smooth the way for my return; so my easy conquest of the squire was not at all wonderful; nevertheless, I maintained my sense of triumph, and was assured in my secret heart that I had a singular masterfulness, and could, when I chose to put it forth, compel my grandfather to hold out his hand to my father as he had done to me.

Julia Rippenger was a guest at Riversley through a visit paid to her by my aunt Dorothy in alarm at my absence. The intention was to cause the squire a distraction. It succeeded; for the old man needed lively prattle of a less childish sort than Janet Ilchester's at his elbow, and that young lady, though true enough in her fashion, was the ardent friend of none but flourishing heads; whereas Julia, finding my name under a cloud at Riversley, spoke of me, I was led to imagine by Captain Bulsted, as a ballad hero, a gloriful fellow, a darling whose deeds were all pardonable—a mere puff of smoke in the splendour of his nature.

"To hear the young lady allude to *me* in that style!" he confided to my ear, with an ineffable heave of his big chest.

Certain good influences, at any rate, preserved the squire from threatening to disinherit me. Colonel Goodwin had spoken to him very manfully and wisely as to my relations with my father. The squire, it was assumed by my aunt, and by Captain Bulsted and Julia, had undertaken to wink at my father's claims on my affection. All three vehemently entreated me to make no mention of the present of Hock to him, and not to attempt to bring about an interview. Concerning the yellow wine I disregarded their advice, for I held it to be a point of filial duty, and an obligation religiously contracted beneath a cathedral dome; so I performed the task of offering the Hock, stating that it was of ancient birth. The squire bunched his features; he tutored his temper, and said not a word. I fancied all was well. Before I tried the second step, Captain Bulsted rode over to my father, who himself generously enjoined the prudent course, in accordance with his aforegone precepts. He was floated off, as he termed it, from the inn where he lay stranded, to London, by I knew not what heaven-sent gift of money, bidding me keep in view the grand career I was to commence at Dipwell on arriving at my majority. I would have gone with him had he beckoned a finger. The four-and-twenty bottles of Hock were ranged in a line for the stable-boys to cock-shy at them under the squire's supervision and my enforced attendance, just as revolutionary criminals are executed. I felt like the survivor of friends, who has seen their blood flow.

He handed me a cheque for the payment of debts incurred in my recent adventures. Who could help being grateful for it? And yet his remorseless spilling of the kindly wine full of mellow recollections of my father and the little princess, drove the sense of gratitude out of me.

CHAPTER XX.

NEWS OF A FRESH CONQUEST OF MY FATHER'S.

TEMPLE went to sea. The wonder is that I did not go with him: we were both in agreement that adventures were

the only things worth living for, and we despised English
fellows who had seen no place but England. I could not
bear the long separation from my father: that was my
reason for not insisting on the squire's consent to my becoming a midshipman. After passing a brilliant examination,
Temple had the good fortune to join Captain Bulsted's ship,
and there my honest-hearted friend dismally composed his
letter of confession, letting me know that he had been untrue to friendship, and had proposed to Janet Ilchester, and
interchanged vows with her. He begged my forgiveness,
but he did love her so !—he hoped I would not mind. I sent
him a reproachful answer; I never cared for him more
warmly than when I saw the letter shoot the slope of the
post-office mouth. Aunt Dorothy undertook to communicate
assurances of my undying affection for him. As for Janet—
Temple's letter, in which he spoke of her avowed preference
for Oriental presents, and declared his intention of accumulating them on his voyages, was a harpoon in her side. By
means of it I worried and terrified her until she was glad to
have it all out before the squire. What did he do? He
said that Margery, her mother, was niggardly ; a girl wanted
presents, and I did not act up to my duty; I ought to buy
Turkey and Tunis to please her, if she had a mind for them.
The further she was flattered the faster she cried ; she had
the face of an old setter with these hideous tears. The
squire promised her fifty pounds per annum in quarterly
payments, that she might buy what presents she liked, and
so tie herself to constancy. He said aside to me, as if he
had a knowledge of the sex—" Young ladies must have lots
of knickknacks, or their eyes 'll be caught right and left,
remember that." I should have been delighted to see her
caught. She talked of love in a ludicrous second-hand way,
sending me into fits of disgusted laughter. On other occasions her lips were not hypocritical, and her figure anything
but awkward. She was a bold, plump girl, fond of male
society. Heriot enraptured her. I believed at the time she
would have appointed a year to marry him in, had he put
the question. But too many women were in love with Heriot.
He and I met Kiomi on the road to the race-course on the
South-downs ; the prettiest race-course in England, shut
against gipsies. A barefooted swarthy girl ran beside our
carriage and tossed us flowers. He and a friend of his,

young Lord Destrier, son of the Marquis of Edbury, who
knew my father well, talked and laughed with her, and
thought her so very handsome that I likewise began to stare,
and I suddenly called "Kiomi!" She bounded back into the
hedge. This was our second meeting. It would have been
a pleasant one had not Heriot and Destrier pretended all
sorts of things about our previous acquaintance. Neither of
us, they said, had made a bad choice, but why had we
separated ? She snatched her hand out of mine with a grin
of anger like puss in a fury. We had wonderful fun with
her. They took her to a great house near the race-course,
and there, assisted by one of the young ladies, dressed her in
flowing silks, and so passed her through the gate of the
enclosure interdicted to bare feet. There they led her to
groups of fashionable ladies, and got themselves into pretty
scrapes. They said she was an Indian. Heriot lost his
wagers and called her a witch. She replied, "You'll find
I'm one, young man," and that was the only true thing she
spoke of the days to come. Owing to the hubbub around
the two who were guilty of this unmeasured joke upon con-
sequential ladies, I had to conduct her to the gate. Instantly,
and without a good-bye, she scrambled up her skirts and ran
at strides across the road and through the wood, out of sight.
She won her dress and a piece of jewelry.

With Heriot I went on a sad expedition, the same I had
set out upon with Temple. This time I saw my father
behind those high red walls, once so mysterious and terrible
to me. Heriot made light of prisons for debt. He insisted,
for my consolation, that they had but a temporary dishonourable signification ; very estimable gentlemen, as well
as scamps, inhabited them, he said. The impression produced by my visit—the feasting among ruined men who
believed in good luck the more the lower they fell from it,
and their fearful admiration of my imprisoned father—was
as if I had drunk a stupefying liquor. I was unable clearly
to reflect on it. Daily afterwards, until I released him, I
made journeys to usurers to get a loan on the faith of the
reversion of my mother's estate. Heriot, like the real friend
he was, helped me with his name to the bond. When my
father stood free, I had the proudest heart alive ; and as
soon as we had parted, the most amazed. For a long while,
for years, the thought of him was haunted by racket-balls

and bearded men in their shirt-sleeves; a scene sickening to one's pride. Yet it had grown impossible for me to think of him without pride. I delighted to hear him. We were happy when we were together. And, moreover, he swore to me on his honour, in Mrs. Waddy's presence, that he and the constable would henceforth keep an even pace. His exuberant cheerfulness and charming playfulness were always fascinating. His visions of our glorious future enchained me. How it was that something precious had gone out of my life, I could not comprehend.

Julia Rippenger's marriage with Captain Bulsted was an agreeable distraction. Unfortunately for my peace of mind, she went to the altar poignantly pale. My aunt Dorothy settled the match. She had schemed it, her silence and half downcast look seemed to confess, for the sake of her own repose, but neither to her nor to others did that come of it. I wrote a plain warning of the approaching catastrophe to Heriot, and received his reply after it was over, to this effect:—

"In my regiment we have a tolerable knowledge of women. They like change, old Richie, and we must be content to let them take their twenty shillings for a sovereign. I myself prefer the Navy to the Army; I have no right to complain. Once she swore one thing, now she has sworn another. We will hope the lady will stick to her choice, and not seek smaller change. 'I could not forgive coppers;' that's quoting your dad. I have no wish to see the uxorious object, though you praise him. His habit of falling under the table is middling old-fashioned; but she may like him the better, or she may cure him. Whatever she is as a woman, she was a very nice girl to enliven the atmosphere of the switch. I sometimes look at a portrait I have of J. R., which, I fancy, Mrs. William Bulsted has no right to demand of me; but supposing her husband thinks he has, why then I must consult my brother officers. We want a war, old Richie, and I wish you were sitting at our mess, and not mooning about girls and women."

I presumed from this that Heriot's passion for Julia was extinct. Aunt Dorothy disapproved of his tone, which I thought admirably philosophical and coxcombically imitable, an expression of the sort of thing I should feel on hearing of Janet Ilchester's nuptials.

The daring and success of that foreign adventure of mine had, with the aid of Colonel and Clara Goodwin, convinced the squire of the folly of standing between me and him I loved. It was considered the best sign possible that he should take me down on an inspection of his various estates and his great coal-mine, and introduce me as the heir who would soon relieve him of the task. Perhaps he thought the smell of wealth a promising cure for such fits of insubordination as I had exhibited. My occasional absences on my own account were winked at. On my return the squire was sour and snappish, I cheerful and complaisant; I grew cold, and he solicitous; he would drink my health with a challenge to heartiness, and I drank to him heartily and he relapsed to a fit of sulks, informing me that in his time young men knew when they were well off, and asking me whether I was up to any young men's villanies, had any concealed debts perchance, because, if so—Oh! he knew the ways of youngsters, especially when they fell into bad hands:—the list of bad titles rumbled on in an underbreath like cowardly thunder:—well, to cut the matter short, because, if so, his cheque-book was at my service; didn't I know that? eh? Not being immediately distressed by debt, I did not exhibit the gush of gratitude, and my sedate "Thank you, sir," confused his appeal for some sentimental show of affection. I am sure the poor old man suffered pangs of jealousy; I could even at times see into his breast and pity him. He wanted little more than to be managed; but a youth when he perceives absurdity in opposition to him chafes at it as much as if he were unaware that it is laughable. Had the squire talked to me in those days seriously and fairly of my father's character, I should have abandoned my system of defence to plead for him as before a judge. By that time I had gained the knowledge that my father was totally of a different construction from other men. I wished the squire to own simply to his loveable nature. I could have told him women did. Without citing my dear aunt Dorothy, or so humble a creature as the devoted Mrs. Waddy, he had sincere friends among women, who esteemed him, and were staunch adherents to his cause; and if the widow of the City knight, Lady Sampleman, aimed openly at being something more, she was not the less his friend.

Nor was it only his powerful animation, generosity, and grace that won them.

There occurred when I was a little past twenty, already much in his confidence, one of those strange crucial events which try a man publicly, and bring out whatever can be said for and against him. A young Welsh heiress fell in love with him. She was, I think, seven or eight months younger than myself, a handsome, intelligent, high-spirited girl, rather wanting in polish, and perhaps in the protecting sense of decorum. She was well-born, of course—she was Welsh. She was really well-bred too, though somewhat brusque. The young lady fell hopelessly in love with my father at Bath. She gave out that he was not to be for one moment accused of having encouraged her by secret addresses. It was her unsolicited avowal—thought by my aunt Dorothy immodest, not by me—that she preferred him to all living men. Her name was Anna Penrhys. The squire one morning received a letter from her family, requesting him to furnish them with information as to the antecedents of a gentleman calling himself Augustus Fitz-George Frederick William Richmond Guelph Roy, for purposes which would, they assured him, warrant the inquiry. He was for throwing the letter aside, shouting that he thanked his God he was unacquainted with anybody on earth with such an infernal list of names as that. Roy! Who knew anything of Roy ?"

" It happens to be my father's present name," said I.

" It sounds to me like the name of one of those blackguard adventurers who creep into families to catch the fools," pursued the squire, not hearing me with his eyes.

" The letter at least must be answered," my aunt Dorothy said.

"It shall be answered!" the squire worked himself up to roar.

He wrote a reply, the contents of which I could guess at from my aunt's refusal to let me be present at the discussion of it. The letter despatched was written by her, with his signature. Her eyes glittered for a whole day.

Then came a statement of the young lady's case from Bath.

" Look at that ! look at that !" cried the squire, and went

on, " Look at that !" in a muffled way. There was a touch
of dignity in his unforced anger.

My aunt winced displeasingly to my sight: " I see nothing
to astonish one."

" Nothing to astonish one !" The squire set his mouth in
imitation of her. " You see nothing to astonish one ? Well,
ma'am, when a man grows old enough to be a grandfather,
I do see something astonishing in a child of nineteen—
by George ! it's out o' nature. But you women like monstro-
sities.   Oh ! I understand.   Here's an heiress to fifteen
thousand a year.   It's not astonishing if every ruined
gambler and scapegrace in the kingdom's hunting her hot!
no, no ! that's not astonishing. I suppose she has her money
in a coal-mine."

The squire had some of his in a coal-mine; my mother
once had ; it was the delivery of a blow at my father, signi-
fying that he had the scent for this description of wealth.
I left the room. The squire then affected that my presence
had constrained him, by bellowing out epithets easy for me
to hear in the hall and out on the terrace. He vowed by
solemn oath he was determined to save this girl from ruin.
My aunt's speech was brief.

I was summoned to Bath by my father in a curious
peremptory tone implying the utmost urgent need of me.   I
handed the letter to the squire at breakfast, saying, " You
must spare me for a week or so, sir."

He spread the letter flat with his knife, and turned it
over with his fork.

" Harry," said he, half-kindly, and choking, " you're
better out of it."

" I'm the best friend he could have by him, sir."

" You're the best tool he could have handy, for you're a
gentleman."

" I hope I shan't offend you, grandfather, but I must go."

" Don't you see, Harry Richmond, you're in for an infernal
marriage ceremony there !"

" The young lady is not of age," interposed my aunt.

" Eh ? An infernal elopement, then.   It's clear the girl's
mad—head's cracked as a cocoa-nut bowled by a monkey,
brains nowhere. Harry, you're not a greenhorn ; you don't
suspect you're called down there to stop it, do you ? You
jump plump into a furious lot of the girl's relatives ; you

might as well take a header into a leech-pond. **Come!**
you're a man ; think for yourself. Don't have this affair on
your conscience, boy. I tell you, Harry Richmond, I'm
against your going. You go against my will; you offend me,
sir; you drag my name and blood into the mire. She's
Welsh, is she? Those Welsh are addle-pated, every one.
Poor girl!"

He threw a horrible tremour into his accent of pity.

My aunt expressed her view mildly, that I was sent for to
help cure the young lady of her delusion.

"And take her himself!" cried the squire. "Harry, you
wouldn't go and do that? Why, the law, man, the law—
the whole country 'd be up about it. You'll be stuck in a
coloured caricature!"

He was really alarmed lest this should be one of the consequences of my going, and described some of the scourging
caricatures of his day with an intense appreciation of their
awfulness as engines of the moral sense of the public. I
went nevertheless.

CHAPTER XXI.

A PROMENADE IN BATH.

I found my father at his hotel, sitting with his friend
Jorian DeWitt, whom I had met once before, and thought
clever. He was an ex-captain of dragoons, a martyr to gout,
and addicted to Burgundy, which necessitated his resorting
to the waters, causing him, as he said, between his appetites
and the penance he paid for them, to lead the life of a pen-
dulum. My father was in a tempered gay mood, examining
a couple of the county newspapers. One abused him viru-
lently; he was supported by the other. After embracing
me, he desired me to listen while he read out opposing sentences from the columns of these eminent journals :—

"The person calling himself 'Roy,' whose monstrously
absurd pretensions are supposed to be embodied in this
self-dubbed surname . . ."

"—The celebrated and courtly Mr. Richmond Roy, known
no less by the fascination of his manners than by his
romantic history . . ."

" —has very soon succeeded in making himself the talk of the town . . ."

" —has latterly become the theme of our tea-tables . . ."

" —which is always the adventurer's privilege . . ."

" —through no fault of his own . . ."

" —That we may throw light on the blushing aspirations of a crow-sconced Cupid, it will be as well to recall the antecedents of this (if no worse) preposterous imitation buck of the old school . . ."

" —Suffice it, without seeking to draw the veil from those affecting chapters of his earlier career which kindled for him the enthusiastic sympathy of all classes of his countrymen, that he is not yet free from a tender form of persecution . . ."

" —We think we are justified in entitling him the Perkin Warbeck of society . . ."

" —Reference might be made to mythological heroes . . ."

Hereat I cried out mercy.

Captain DeWitt (stretched nursing a leg) removed his silk handkerchief from his face to murmur,—

" The bass steadfastly drowns the treble, if this is meant for harmony."

My father rang up the landlord, and said to him,—

" The choicest of your cellar at dinner to-day, Mr. Lumley; and, mind you, I am your guest, and I exercise my right of compelling you to sit down with us and assist in consuming a doubtful quality of wine. We dine four. Lay for five, if your conscience is bad, and I excuse you."

The man smirked. He ventured to say he had never been so tempted to supply an inferior article.

My father smiled on him.

" You invite our editorial advocate ?" said Captain DeWitt.

" Our adversary," said my father.

I protested I would not sit at table with him. But he assured me he believed his advocate and his adversary to be one and the same, and referred me to the collated sentences.

" The man must earn his bread, Richie, boy ! To tell truth, it is the advocate I wish to rebuke, and to praise the adversary. It will confound him.

" It does me," said DeWitt.

"You perceive, Jorian, a policy in dining these men of the Press now and occasionally, considering their growing power, do you not?"

"Ay, ay! it's a great gossiping machine, mon Roy. I prefer to let it spout."

"I crave your permission to invite him in complimentary terms, cousin Jorian. He is in the town; remember, it is for the good of the nation that he and his like should have the opportunity of studying good society. As to myself personally, I give him carte blanche to fire his shots at me."

Near the fashionable hour of the afternoon my father took my arm, Captain DeWitt a stick, and we walked into the throng and buzz.

"Whenever you are, to quote our advocate, the theme of tea-tables, Richie," said my father, "walk through the crowd: it will wash you. It is doing us the honour to observe us. We in turn discover an interest in its general countenance."

He was received, as we passed, with much staring; here and there a lifting of hats, and some blunt nodding that incensed me, but he, feeling me bristle, squeezed my hand and talked of the scene, and ever and anon gathered a line of heads and shed an indulgent bow along them; so on to the Casino. Not once did he offend my taste and make my acute sense of self-respect shiver by appearing grateful for a recognition, or anxious to court it, though the curtest salute met his acknowledgment.

The interior of the Casino seemed more hostile. I remarked it to him. "A trifle more eye-glassy," he murmured. He was quite at his ease there.

"We walk up and down, my son," he said, in answer to a question of mine, "because there are very few who can; even walking is an art; and, if nobody does, the place is dull."

"The place is pretty well supplied with newspapers," said Captain DeWitt.

"And dowagers, friend Jorian. They are cousins. 'Tis the fashion to have our tattle done by machinery. They have their opportunity to compare the portrait with the original. Come, invent some scandal for us; let us make this place our social Exchange. I warrant a good bold piece

of invention will fit them, too, some of them. Madam,"—
My father bowed low to the beckoning of a fan,—"I trust
your ladyship did not chance to overhear that last remark
I made?"

The lady replied: "I should have shut my eyes if I had.
I called you to tell me, who is the young man?"

"For twenty years I have lived in the proud belief that
he is my son!"

"I would not disturb it for the world." She did me the
honour to inspect me from the lowest waistcoat button to
the eyebrows. "Bring him to me to-night. Captain DeWitt,
you have forsaken my whist-tables."

"Purely temporary fits of unworthiness, my lady."

"In English, gout?"

"Not gout in the conscience, I trust," said my father.

"Oh! that's curable," laughed the captain.

"You men of repartee would be nothing without your
wickedness," the lady observed.

"Man was supposed to be incomplete——" Captain
DeWitt affected a murmur.

She nodded "Yes, yes," and lifted eyes on my father.
"So you have not given up going to church?"

He bent and spoke low.

She humphed her lips. "Very well, I will see. It must
be a night in the early part of the week after next, then: I
really don't know why I should serve you; but I like your
courage."

"I cannot consent to accept your ladyship's favour on
account of one single virtue," said he, drooping.

She waved him to move forward.

During this frothy dialogue, I could see that the ear of the
assembly had been caught by the sound of it.

"That," my father informed me, "is the great Lady
Wilts. Now you will notice a curious thing. Lady Wilts
is not so old but that, as our Jorian here says of her, she is
marriageable. Hence, Richie, she is a queen to make the
masculine knee knock the ground. I fear the same is not
to be said of her rival, Lady Denewdney, whom our good
Jorian compares to an antiquated fledgeling emerging with
effort from a nest of ill construction and worse cement.
She is rich, she is sharp, she uses her quill; she is emphatically not marriageable. Bath might still accept her as a

rival queen, only she is always behindhand in seizing an occasion. Now you will catch sight of her fan working in a minute. She is envious and imitative. It would be undoubtedly better policy on her part to continue to cut me: she cannot, she is beginning to rustle like December's oaks. If Lady Wilts has me, why, she must. We refrain from noticing her until we have turned twice. Ay, Richie, there is this use in adversity; it teaches one to play sword and target with etiquette and retenue better than any crowned king in Europe. For me now to cross to her summons immediately would be a gross breach of homage to Lady Wilts, who was inspired to be the first to break through the fence of scandal environing me. But I must still show that I am independent. These people must not suppose that I have to cling to a party. Let them take sides; I am on fair terms with both the rivals. I show just such a nuance of a distinction in my treatment of them—just such—enough, I mean, to make the flattered one warm to me, and t'other be jealous of her. Ay, Richie, these things are trivial things beyond the grave; but here are we, my boy; and, by the way, I suspect the great campaign of my life is opening."

Captain DeWitt said that if so it would be the tenth, to his certain knowledge.

"Not *great* campaign!" my father insisted: "mere skirmishes before this."

They conversed in humorous undertones, each in turn seeming to turn over the earth of some amusing reminiscence, so rapt that, as far as regarded their perception of it, the assembly might have been nowhere. Perhaps, consequently, they became observed with all but undivided attention. My father's hand was on my shoulder, his head toward Captain DeWitt; instead of subduing his voice, he gave it a moderate pitch, at which it was not intrusive, and was musical, to my ear charming, especially when he continued talking through his soft laughter, like a hunter that would in good humour press for his game through links of water-nymphs.

Lady Denewdney's fan took to beating time meditatively. Two or three times she kept it elevated, and in vain: the flow of their interchanging speech was uninterrupted. At last my father bowed to her from a distance. She signalled: his eyelids pleaded short sight, awakening to the apprehension of a pleasant fact: the fan tapped, and he halted his march, leaning scarce perceptibly in her direction. The fan showed distress. Thereupon, his voice subsided in his conversation, with a concluding flash of animation across his features, like a brook that comes to the leap on a descent, and he left us.

Captain DeWitt and I were led by a common attraction to the portico, the truth being that we neither of us could pace easily nor talk with perfect abandonment under eye-fire any longer.

"Look," said he to me, pointing at the equipages and equestrians : " you'll see a sight like this in dozens—dozens of our cities and towns ! The wealth of this country is frightful."

My reply, addressed at the same time mentally to Temple at sea, was :

" Well, as long as we have the handsomest women, I don't care."

Captain DeWitt was not so sure that we had. The Provençal women, the women of a part of South Germany, and certain favoured spots of Italy, might challenge us, he thought. This was a point I could argue on, or, I should rather say, take up the cudgels, for I deemed such opinions treason to one's country and an outrage to common sense, and I embarked in controversy with the single-minded intention of knocking down the man who held them.

He accepted his thrashing complacently.

"Now here comes a young lady on horseback," he said; " do you spy her ? dark hair, thick eyebrows, rides well, followed by a groom. Is she a Beauty ?"

In the heat of patriotism I declared she was handsome, and repeated it, though I experienced a twinge of remorse like what I should have felt had I given Minerva the apple instead of Venus.

" Oh !" he commented, and stepped down to the road to meet her, beginning, in my hearing, " I am the bearer of a compliment——" Her thick eyebrows stood in a knot, then she glanced at me and hung pensive. She had not to wait a minute before my father came to her side.

" 1 knew you would face them," she said.

He threw back his head like a swimmer tossing spray from his locks.

" You have read the paper ?" he asked.

" You have horsewhipped the writer ?" she rejoined.

" Oh ! the poor *penster !*"

" Nay, we can't pretend to pity him !"

" Could we condescend to offer him satisfaction ?"

" Would he dare to demand it ?"

" We will lay the case before Lady Wilts to-night."

" You are there to-night ?"

" At Lady Denewdney's to-morrow night—if I may indulge a hope ?"

" Both ? Oh ! bravo, bravo ! Tell me nothing more just now. How did you manage it ? I must have a gallop. Yes, I shall be at both, be sure of that."

My father introduced me.

"Let me present to your notice my son, Harry Lepel Richmond, Miss Penrhys."

She touched my fingers, and nodded at me ; speaking to him :

" He has a boy's taste : I hear he esteems me moderately well-favoured."

" An inherited error certain to increase with age !"

" Now you have started me !" she exclaimed, and lashed the flanks of her horse.

We had evidently been enacting a part deeply interesting to the population of Bath, for the heads of all the strolling groups were bent on us ; and when Miss Penrhys cantered away, down dropped eyeglasses, and the promenade returned to activity. I fancied I perceived that my father was greeted more cordially on his way back to the hotel.

" You do well, Richie," he observed, " in preserving your composure until you have something to say. Wait for your opening ; it will come, and the right word will come with it. The main things are to be able to stand well, walk well, and look with an eye at home in its socket :—I put you my hand on any man or woman born of high blood.—Not a brazen eye ! —of the two extremes, I prefer the beaten spaniel sort.— Blindfold me, but I put you my hand on them. As to repartee, you must have it. Wait for that, too. Do not," he groaned, " do not force it ! Bless my soul, what is there in the world so bad ?" And rising to the upper notes of his groan : " Ignorance, density, total imbecility, is better ; I would rather any day of my life sit and carve for guests— the grossest of human trials—a detestable dinner, than be

doomed to hear some wretched fellow—and you hear the old
as well as the young—excruciate feelings which, where they
exist, cannot but be exquisitely delicate. Goodness gracious
me! to see the man pumping up his wit! For me, my visage
is of an unalterable gravity whenever I am present at one of
these exhibitions. I care not if I offend. Let them say I
wish to revolutionize society—I declare to you, Richie boy,
delightful to my heart though I find your keen stroke of
repartee, still your fellow who takes the thrust gracefully,
knows when he's traversed by a master-stroke, and yields
sign of it, instead of plunging like a spitted buffalo and
asking us to admire his agility—you follow me?—I say I
hold that man—and I delight vastly in ready wit; it is the
wine of language!—I regard that man as the superior being.
True, he is not so entertaining."

My father pressed on my arm to intimate, with a cavernous
significance of eyebrow, that Captain DeWitt had the gift of
repartee in perfection.

"Jorian," said he, "will you wager our editor declines to
dine with us?"

The answer struck me as only passable. I think it
was:—

"When rats smell death in toasted cheese."

Captain DeWitt sprang up the staircase of our hotel to
his bedroom.

"I should not have forced him," my father mused.
"Jorian DeWitt has at times brilliant genius, Richie—in
the way of rejoinders, I mean. This is his happy moment—
his one hour's dressing for dinner. I have watched him; he
most thoroughly enjoys it! I am myself a quick or slow
dresser, as the case may be. But to watch Jorian you cannot help entering into his enjoyment of it. He will have his
window with a view of the sunset; there is his fire, his
warmed linen, and his shirt-studs; his bath, his choice of a
dozen things he will or will not wear; the landlord's or
host's *menu* is up against the looking-glass, and the extremely
handsome miniature likeness of his wife, who is in the mad-
house, by a celebrated painter, I forget his name. Jorian
calls this, new birth—you catch his idea? He throws off
the old and is on with the new with a highly hopeful anticipation. His valet is a scoundrel, but never fails in extracting the *menu* from the cook, wherever he may be, and, in

fine, is too attentive to the hour's devotion to be discarded!
Poor Jorian. I know no man I pity so much."

I conceived him, I confessed, hardly pitiable, though not
enviable.

" He has but six hundred a year, and a passion for Burgundy," said my father.

We were four at table. The editor came and his timidity
soon wore off in the warmth of hospitality, He appeared a
kind excitable little man, glad of his dinner from the first,
and in due time proud of his entertainer. His response to
the toast of the Fourth Estate was an apology for its
behaviour to my father. He regretted it; he regretted it.
A vinous speech.

My father heard him out. Addressing him subsequently,—

" I would not interrupt you in the delivery of your sentiments," he said. " I must, however, man to man, candidly
tell you I should have wished to arrest your expressions of
regret. They convey to my mind an idea that, on receipt of
my letter of invitation, you attributed to me a design to
corrupt you. Protest nothing, I beg. Editors are human,
after all. Now, my object is that as you write of me, you
should have some knowledge of me ; and I naturally am
interested in one who does me so much honour. The facts
of my life are at your disposal for publication and comment.
Simply, I entreat you, say this one thing of me : I seek for
justice, but I never complain of my fortunes. Providence
decides :—that might be the motto engraven on my heart.
Nay, I may risk declaring it is! In the end I shall be
righted. Meanwhile you contribute to my happiness by
favouring me with your society."

" Ah, sir," replied the little man, " were all our great
people like you! In the country—the provinces—they treat
the representatives of the Fourth Estate as the squires a
couple of generations back used to treat the parsons."

" What! Have you got a place at their tables ?" inquired
Captain DeWitt.

" No, I cannot say that—not even below the salt. Mr.
Richmond—Mr. Roy, you may not be aware of it : I am the
proprietor of the opposition journals in this county. I tell
you in confidence, one by itself would not pay ; and I am a
printer, sir, and it is on my conscience to tell you I have, in

the course of business, been compelled this very morning to receive orders for the printing of various squibs and, I much fear, scurrilous things."

My father pacified him.

"You will do your duty to your family, Mr. Hickson."

Deeply moved, the little man pulled out proof-sheets and slips.

"Even now, at the eleventh hour," he urged, "there is time to correct any glaring falsehoods, insults, what not!"

My father accepted the copy of proofs.

"Not a word,—not a line! You spoke of the eleventh hour, Mr. Hickson. If we are at all near the eleventh, I must be on my way to make my bow to Lady Wilts; or it is Lady Denewdney's to-night? No, to-morrow night."

A light of satisfaction came over Mr. Hickson's face at the mention of my father's visiting both these sovereign ladies.

As soon as we were rid of him, Captain DeWitt exclaimed,—

"If that's the Fourth Estate, what's the Realm?"

"The Estate," pleaded my father, "is here in its infancy —on all fours——"

"Prehensile! Egad, it has the vices of the other three besides its own. Do you mean that by putting it on all fours?"

"Jorian, I have noticed that when you are malignant you are not witty. We have to thank the man for not subjecting us to a pledge of secresy. My Lady Wilts will find the proofs amusing. And mark, I do not examine their contents before submitting them to her inspection. You will testify to the fact."

I was unaware that my father played a master-stroke in handing these proof-sheets publicly to Lady Wilts for her perusal. The incident of the evening was the display of her character shown by Miss Penrhys in positively declining to quit the house until she likewise had cast her eye on them. One of her aunts wept. Their carriage was kept waiting an hour.

"You ask too much of me: I cannot turn her out," Lady Wilts said to her uncle. And aside to my father, "You will have to marry her."

" In heaven's name keep me from marriage, my lady !" I heard him reply.

There was sincerity in his tone when he said that.

CHAPTER XXII.

CONCLUSION OF THE BATH EPISODE.

THE friends of Miss Penrhys were ill advised in trying to cry down a man like my father.   Active persecution was the breath of life to him.   When untroubled he was apt to let both his ambition and his dignity slumber.   The squibs and scandal set afloat concerning him armed his wit, nerved his temper, touched him with the spirit of enterprise ; he became a new creature.   I lost sight of certain characteristics which I had begun to ponder over critically.   I believed with all my heart that circumstances were blameable for much that did not quite please me.   Upon the question of his magnanimity, as well as of his courage, there could not be two opinions. He would neither retort nor defend himself.   I perceived some grandeur in his conduct, without, however, appreciating it cordially, as I did a refinement of discretion about him that kept him from brushing good taste while launched in ostentatious displays.   He had a fine tact and a keen intui-tion.   He may have thought it necessary to throw a little dust in my eyes ; but I doubt his having done it, for he had only, as he knew, to make me jealous to blind me to his faults utterly, and he refrained.   In his allusions to the young lady he was apologetic, affectionate ; one might have fancied oneself listening to a gracious judge who had well weighed her case, and exculpated her from other excesses than that of a generous folly.   Jorian DeWitt, a competent critic, pronounced his behaviour consummate at all points.   For my behoof, he hinted antecedent reverses to the picture : meditating upon which, I traced them to the fatal want of money, and that I might be able to fortify him in case of need, I took my own counsel, and wrote to my aunt for the loan of as large a sum as she could afford to send.   Her eagerness for news of our doings was insatiable.   " You do not describe her," she replied, not naming Miss Penrhys ;

and again, " I can form no image of her. Your accounts of her are confusing. Tell me earnestly, do you like her? She must be very wilful, but is she really nice? I want to know how she appears to my Harry's mind."

My father borrowed these letters, and returning them tc me, said, " A good soul! the best of women! There—there is a treasure lost!" His forehead was clouded in speaking. He recommended me to assure my aunt that she would never have to take a family interest in Miss Penrhys. But this was not deemed perfectly satisfactory at Riversley. My aunt wrote: " Am I to understand that you, Harry, raise objections to her? Think first whether she is in herself objectionable. She is rich, she may be prudent, she may be a forethoughtful person. She may not be able to support a bitter shock of grief. She may be one who can *help*. She may not be one whose heart will bear it. Put your own feelings aside, my dearest. Our duties cannot ever be clear to us until we do. It is possible for headstrong wilfulness and secret tenderness to go together. Think whether she is capable of sacrifice before you compel her to it. Do not inflict misery wantonly. One would like to see her. Harry, I brood on your future; that is why I seem to you preternaturally anxious about you."

She seemed to me preternaturally anxious about Miss Penrhys.

My father listened in silence to my flippant satire on women's letters.

He answered after a pause,—

" Our Jorian says that women's letters must be read like anagrams. To put it familiarly, they are like a child's field of hop-scotch. You may have noticed the urchins at their game : a bit of tile, and a variety of compartmcnts to pass it through to the base, hopping. Or no, Richie,] ooh! 'tis an unworthy comparison, this hop-scotch. I mean, laddie, they write in zigzags; and so will you when your heart trumpets in your ear. Tell her, tell that dear noble good woman—say, we are happy, you and I, and alone, and shall be ; and do me the favour—she loves you, my son—address her ometimes— she has been it—call her ' mother'; she will like it: she deserves—nothing shall supplant her !"

He lost his voice.

She sent me three hundred pounds ; she must have supposed the occasion pressing. Thus fortified against paternal improvidence, I expended a hundred in the purchase of a horse, and staked the remainder on him in a match, and was beaten. Disgusted with the horse, I sold him for half his purchase-money, and with that sum paid a bill to maintain my father's credit in the town. Figuratively speaking, I looked at my hands as astonished as I had been when the poor little rascal in the street snatched my cake, and gave me the vision of him gorging it in the flurried alley of the London crowd.

"Money goes," I remarked.

" That is the general experience of the nature of money," said my father freshly ; " but nevertheless you will be surprised to find how extraordinarily few are the people to make allowance for particular cases. It plays the trick with everybody, and almost nobody lets it stand as a plea for the individual. Here is Jorian, and you, my son, and perhaps your aunt Dorothy, and upon my word, I think I have numbered all I know—or, ay, Sukey Sampleman, I should not omit her in an honourable list—and that makes positively all I know who would commiserate a man touched on the shoulder by a sheriff's officer—not that such an indignity is any longer done to me."

" I hope we have seen the last of Shylock's great-grand-nephew," said I emphatically.

" Merely to give you the instance, Richie. Ay ! I hope so, I hope so ! But it is the nature of money that you never can tell if the boarding's sound, once be dependent upon it. But this is talk for tradesmen."

Thinking it so myself, I had not attempted to discover the source of my father's income. Such as it was, it was paid half-yearly, and spent within a month of the receipt, for the most signal proof possible of its shameful insufficiency. Thus ten months of the year at least he lived protesting, and many with him, compulsorily. For two months he was a brilliant man. I penetrated his mystery enough to abstain from questioning him, and enough to determine that on my coming of age he should cease to be a pensioner, petitioner, and adventurer. He aimed at a manifest absurdity.

In the meantime, after the lesson I had received as to the nature of money, I saw with some alarm my father preparing to dig a great pit for it. He had no doubt performed wonders. Despite of scandal and tattle, and the deadly report of a penniless fortune-hunter having fascinated the young heiress, he commanded an entrance to the receptions of both the rival ladies dominant. These ladies, Lady Wilts and Lady Denewdney, who moved each in her select half-circle, and could heretofore be induced by none to meet in a common centre, had pledged themselves to honour with their presence a ball he proposed to give to the choice world here assembled on a certain illuminated day of the calendar.

"So I have now possession of Bath, Richie," said he, twinkling to propitiate me, lest I should suspect him of valuing his achievements highly. He had, he continued, promised Hickson of the Fourth Estate, that he would, before leaving the place, do his utmost to revive the ancient glories of Bath: Bath had once set the fashion to the king-dom; why not again? I might have asked him, why at all, or why at his expense; but his lead was irresistible. Captain DeWitt and his valet, and I, and a score of ladies, scores of tradesmen, were rushing, reluctant or not, on a torrent. My part was to show that I was an athlete, and primarily that I could fence and shoot. "It will do no harm to let it be known," said De Witt. He sat writing letters incessantly. My father made the tour of his fair stewardesses from noon to three, after receiving in audience his jewellers, linen-drapers, carpenters, confectioners, from nine in the morning till twelve. At three o'clock business ceased. Workmen then applying to him for instructions were despatched to the bar of the hotel, bearing the recommendation to the bar-maid not to supply them refreshment if they had ever in their lives been seen drunk. At four he dressed for after-noon parade. Nor could his enemy have said that he was not the chief voice and eye along his line of march. His tall full figure maintained a superior air without insolence, and there was a leaping beam in his large blue eyes, together with the signification of movement coming to his kindly lips, such as hardly ever failed to waken smiles of greeting. People smiled and bowed, and forgot their curiosity, forgot even to be critical, while he was in sight. I can say this, for I was acutely critical of their bearing; the atmosphere of the place was never perfectly pleasing to me. My attitude of watchful reserve, and my reputation as the heir of im-mense wealth, tended possibly to constrain a certain number of the inimical party to be ostensibly civil. Lady Wilts, who did me the honour to patronize me almost warmly, complimented me on my manner of backing him, as if I were the hero; but I felt his peculiar charm; she partly admitted it, making a whimsical mouth, saying, in allusion to Miss Penrhys, "I, you know, am past twenty. At twenty forty is charming; at forty twenty." Where I served him perhaps was in showing my resolution to protect him: he had been insulted before my arrival. The male relatives of Miss Penrhys did not repeat the insult; they went to Lady Wilts and groaned over their hard luck in not having the option of fighting me. I was, in her phrase, a new piece on the board, and checked them. Thus, if they provoked a challenge from me, they brought the destructive odour of powder about the headstrong creature's name. I was therefore of use to him so far. I leaned indolently across the rails of the promenade while she bent and chattered in his ear, and her attendant cousin and cavalier chewed vexation in the form of a young mustachio's curl. His horse fretted; he murmured deep notes, and his look was savage; but he was bound to wait on her, and she would not go until it suited her pleasure. She introduced him to me—as if conversation could be carried on between two young men feeling themselves simply pieces on the board, one giving check, and the other chafing under it! I need not say that I disliked my situation. It was worse when my father took to bowing to her from a distance, unobservant of her hand's prompt pull at the reins as soon as she saw him. Lady Wilts had assumed the right of a woman still possessing attractions to exert her influence with him on behalf of the family, for I had done my best to convince her that he entertained no serious thought of marrying, and decidedly would not marry without my approval. He acted on her advice to discourage the wilful girl.

"How is it I am so hateful to you?" Miss Penrhys accosted me abruptly. I fancied she must have gone mad, and an interrogative frown was my sole answer

"Oh! I hear that you pronounce me everywhere unendurable," she continued. "You are young, and you misjudge me in some way, and I should be glad if you knew me better. By-and-by, in Wales.—Are you fond of mountain scenery? We might be good friends; my temper is not bad—at least, I hope not. Heaven knows what one's relatives think of one! Will you visit us? I hear you have promised your confidante, Lady Wilts."

At a dancing party where we met, she was thrown on my hands by her ungovernable vehemence, and I, as I had told Lady Wilts, not being able to understand the liking of twenty for forty (fifty would have been nearer the actual mark, or sixty), offered her no lively sympathy. I believe she had requested my father to pay public court to her. If Captain DeWitt was to be trusted, she desired him to dance, and dance with her exclusively, and so confirm and defy the tattle of the town; but my father hovered between the dowagers. She in consequence declined to dance, which was the next worst thing she could do. An aunt, a miserable woman, was on her left; on her right she contrived, too frequently for my peace of mind, to reserve a vacant place for me, and she eyed me intently across the room, under her persistent brows, until perforce I was drawn to her side. I had to listen to a repetition of sharp queries and replies, and affect a flattered gaiety, feeling myself most uncomfortably, as Captain DeWitt (who watched us) said, Chip the son of Block the father. By fixing the son beside her, she defeated the father's scheme of coldness, and made it appear a concerted piece of policy. Even I saw that. I saw more than I grasped. Love for my father was to my mind a natural thing, a proof of taste and goodness; women might love him; but the love of a young girl with the morning's mystery about her! and for my progenitor!—a girl (as I reflected in the midst of my interjections) well-built, clear-eyed, animated, clever, with soft white hands and pretty feet; how could it be? She was sombre as a sunken fire until he at last came round to her, and then her sudden vivacity was surprising.

Affairs were no further advanced when I had to obey the squire's commands and return to Riversley, missing the night of the grand ball with no profound regret, except for my father's sake. He wrote soon after one of his characteristic letters, to tell me that the ball had been a success. Immediately upon this announcement, he indulged luxurious reflections, as his manner was :—

" To have stirred up the old place and given it something to dream of for the next half century, is a satisfaction, Richie.

I have a kindness for Bath. I leave it with its factions reconciled, its tea-tables furnished with inexhaustible supplies of the chief thing necessary, and the persuasion firmly established in my own bosom that it is impossible to revive the past, so we must march with the age. And let me add, all but every one of the bills happily discharged, to please you. Pray, fag at your German. If (as I myself confess to) you have enjoyment of old ways, habits, customs, and ceremonies, look to Court life. It is only in Courts that a man may now air a leg; and there the women are works of Art. If you are deficient in calves (which my boy, thank heaven! will never be charged with) you are there found out, and in fact every deficiency, every qualification, is at once in patent exhibition at a Court. I fancy Parliament for you still, and that is no impediment as a step. Jorian would have you sit and wallow in ease, and buy (by the way, we might think of it) a famous Burgundy vineyard (for an investment), devote the prime of your life to the discovery of a cook, your manhood to perfect the creature's education—so forth; I imagine you are to get five years of ample gratification (a promise hardly to be relied on) in the sere leaf, and so perish. Take poor Jorian for an example of what the absence of ambition brings men to. I treasure Jorian, I hoard the poor fellow, to have him for a lesson to my boy. Witty and shrewd, and a masterly tactician (I wager he would have won his spurs on the field of battle), you see him now living for one hour of the day—absolutely twenty-three hours of the man's life are chained slaves, beasts of burden, to the four-and-twentieth! So, I repeat, fag at your German.

"Miss Penrhys retires to her native Wales; Jorian and I on to London, to the Continent. Plinlimmon guard us all! I send you our local newspapers. That I cut entrechats is false. It happens to be a thing I could do, and not an Englishman in England except myself; only I did not do it. I did appear in what I was educated to believe was the evening suit of a gentleman, and I cannot perceive the immodesty of showing my leg. A dress that is not indecent, and is becoming to me, and is the dress of my fathers, I wear, and I impose it on the generation of my sex. However, I dined Hickson of the Fourth Estate (Jorian considers him hungry enough to eat up his twentieth before he dies—

I forget the wording of the *mot*), that he might know I was without rancour in the end, as originally I had been without any intention of purchasing his allegiance. He offered me his columns; he wished me luck with the heiress; by his Gods, he swore he worshipped entrechats, and held a silk leg the most admirable work of the manufactures. ' Sir, you're a gentleman,' says he; 'you're a nobleman, sir; you're a prince, you're a star of the first magnitude.'   Cries Jorian, ' Retract that, scum! you see nothing large but what you dare to think neighbours you,' and quarrels the inebriate dog.   And this is the maker and destroyer of reputations in his day!   I study Hickson as a miraculous engine of the very simplest contrivance; he is himself the epitome of a verdict on his period.   Next day he disclaimed in his opposition penny sheet the report of the entrechats, and ' the spectators laughing consumedly,' and sent me (as I had requested him to do) the names of his daughters, to whom I transmit little comforting presents, for if they are nice children such a parent must afflict them.

" Cultivate Lady Wilts.   You have made an impression. She puts you forward as a good specimen of our young men. 'Hem! madam.

" But, my dear boy, as I said, we cannot revive the past. I acknowledge it.   Bath rebukes my last fit of ambition, and the experience is very well worth the expense.   You have a mind, Richie, for discussing outlay, upon which I congratulate you, so long as you do not overlook equivalents. The system of the world is barter varied by robbery.   Show that you have something in hand, and you enjoy the satisfaction of knowing that you were not robbed.   I pledge you my word to it—I shall not repeat Bath.   And mark you, an heiress is never compromised.   I am not, I hope, responsible for every creature caught up in my circle of attraction. Believe me, dear boy, I should consult you, and another one, estimable beyond mortal speech! if I had become involved—impossible!   No; I am free of all fresh chains, because of the old ones.   Years will not be sufficient for us when you and I once begin to talk in earnest, when I open! To resume—so I leave Bath with a light conscience.   Mixed with pleasant recollections is the transient regret that you were not a spectator of the meeting of the Wilts and **Denewdney** streams.   Jorian compared them to the Rhone

and the—I forget the name of the river below Geneva—
dirtyish; for there was a transparent difference in the
Denewdney style of dress, and did I choose it I could sit
and rule those two factions as despotically as Buonaparte
his Frenchmen.   Ask me what I mean by scaling billows,
Richie.   I will some day tell you.   I have done it all my
life, and here I am.   But I thank heaven I have a son I
love, and I can match him against the best on earth, and
henceforward I live for him, to vindicate and right the boy,
and place him in his legitimate sphere.   From this time I
take to looking exclusively forward, and I labour diligently.
I have energies.

"Not to boast, darling old son, I tell truth; I am only
happy when my heart is beating near you.   Here comes
the mother in me pumping up.   Adieu.   Lebe wohl.   The
German!—the German!—may God in his Barmherzigkeit!
—Tell her I never encouraged the girl, have literally nothing
to trace a temporary wrinkle on my forehead as regards
conscience.   I say, may it please Providence to make you a
good German scholar by the day of your majority.   Hurrah
for it!   Present my humble warm respects to your aunt
Dorothy.   I pray to heaven nightly for one of its angels on
earth.   Kunst, Wissenschaft, Ehre, Liebe.   Die Liebe.   Quick
at the German poets.   Frau: Fräulein.   I am actually
dazzled at the prospect of our future.   To be candid, I no
longer see to write.   Grüss' dich herzlich.   From Vienna
to you next.   Lebe wohl!"

My aunt Dorothy sent a glance at the letter while I was
folding it, evidently thinking my unwillingness to offer it a
sign of bad news or fresh complications.   She spoke of Miss
Penrhys.

"Oh! that's over," said I.   "Heiresses soon get consoled."

She accused me of having picked up a vulgar idea.   I
maintained that it was my father's.

"It cannot be your father's," said she softly; and on
affirming that he had uttered it and written it, she replied
in the same tone, more effective than the ordinary language
of conviction, "He does not think it."

The rage of a youth to prove himself in the right of an
argument was insufficient to make me lay the letter out

before other eyes than my own, and I shrank from exposing it to compassionate gentle eyes that would have pleaded similar allowances to mine for the wildness of the style. I should have thanked, but despised the intelligence of one who framed my excuses for my father, just as the squire, by abusing him, would have made me a desperate partisan in a minute. The vitality of the delusion I cherished was therefore partly extinct; not so the love; yet the love of him could no longer shake itself free from oppressive shadows.

Out of his circle of attraction books were my resource.

CHAPTER XXIII.

MY TWENTY-FIRST BIRTHDAY.

Books and dreams, like the two rivers cited by my father, flowed side by side in me without mixing; and which the bright Rhone was, which the brown Arve, needs not to be told to those who know anything of youth; they were destined to intermingle soon enough. I read well, for I felt ground and had mounting views ; the real world, and the mind and passions of the world, grew visible to me. My tutor pleased the squire immensely by calling me matter-of-fact. In philosophy and history I hated speculation ; but nothing was too fantastic for my ideas of possible occurrences. Once away from books, I carried a head that shot rockets to the farthest hills. My dear friend Temple was at sea, or I should have had one near me to detect and control the springs of nonsense. I was deemed a remarkably quiet sober thoughtful young man, acquiescent in all schemes projected for my welfare. The squire would have liked to see me courting the girl of his heart, as he termed Janet Ilchester, a little more demonstratively. We had, however, come to the understanding that I was to travel before settling. Traditional notions of the importance of the Grand Tour in the education of gentlemen led him to consent to my taking a year on the Continent accompanied by my tutor. He wanted some one, he said, to represent *him* when I was out over there ; which signified that he wanted some one to keep my father in check; but as the Rev. Ambrose Peterborough, successor to the Rev. Simon Hart, was hazy and manageable, I did not object. Such faith had the quiet thoughtful young man at Riversley in the convulsions of the future, the whirlwinds and whirlpools spinning for him and all connected with him, that he did not object to hear his name and Janet's coupled, though he had not a spark of love for her. I tried to realize to myself the general opinion that she was handsome. Her eyebrows were thick and level and long; her eyes direct in their gaze, of a flinty blue, with dark lashes; her nose firm, her lips fullish, firm when joined; her shape straight, moderately flexible. But she had no softness; she could admire herself in my presence; she claimed possession of me openly, and at the same time openly provoked a siege from the remainder of my sex: she was not maidenly. 'She caught imagination by the sleeve, and shut it between square whitewashed walls.' Heriot thought her not only handsome, but comparable to Mrs. William Bulsted, our Julia Rippenger of old. At his meeting with Julia, her delicious loss of colour made her seem to me one of the loveliest women on earth. Janet never lost colour, rarely blushed; she touched neither nerve nor fancy.

"You want a rousing coquette," said Heriot; "you won't be happy till you've been racked by that nice instrument of torture, and the fair Bulsted will do it for you if you like. You don't want a snake or a common serpent, you want a Python."

I wanted bloom and mystery, a woman shifting like the light with evening and night and dawn, and sudden fire. Janet was bald to the heart inhabiting me then, as if quite shaven. She could speak her affectionate mind as plain as print, and it was dull print facing me, not the arches of the sunset. Julia had only to lisp, "my husband," to startle and agitate me beyond expression. She said simple things —"I slept well last night," or "I dreamed," or "I shivered," and plunged me headlong down impenetrable forests. The mould of her mouth to a reluctant "No," and her almost invariable drawing in of her breath with a "Yes," surcharged the every-day monosyllables with meanings of life and death. At last I was reduced to tell her, seeing that she reproached my coldness for Janet, how much I wished Janet resembled her. Her Irish eyes lightened: "Me! Harry;" then they shadowed: "She is worth ten of me."

Such pathetic humility tempted me to exalt her supremely. I talked like a boy, feeling like a man : she behaved like a woman, blushing like a girl.

"Julia ! I can never call you Mrs. Bulsted."

"You have an affection for my husband, have you not, Harry ?"

Of a season when this was adorable language to me, the indication is sufficient. Riding out perfectly crazed by it, I met Kiomi, and transferred my emotions. The squire had paid her people an annual sum to keep away from our neighbourhood, while there was a chance of my taking to gipsy life. They had come back to their old camping-ground, rather dissatisfied with the squire.

"Speak to him yourself, Kiomi," said I ; " whatever you ask for, he can't refuse anything to such eyes as yours."

"You !" she rallied me ; " why can't you talk sensible stuff !"

She had grown a superb savage, proof against weather and compliments. Her face was like an Egyptian sky fronting night. The strong old Eastern blood put ruddy flame for the red colour; tawny olive edged from the red ; rare vivid yellow, all but amber. The light that first looks down upon the fallen sun was her complexion above the brows, and round the cheeks, the neck's nape, the throat, and the firm bosom prompt to lift and sink with her vigour of speech, as her eyes were to flash and darken. Meeting her you swore she was the personification of wandering Asia. There was no question of beauty and grace, for these have laws. The curve of her brows broke like a beaten wave ; the lips and nostrils were wide, tragic in repose. But when she laughed she illuminated you; where she stepped she made the earth hers. She was as fresh of her East as the morning when her ancient people struck tents in the track of their shadows. I write of her in the style consonant to my ideas of her at the time. I would have carried her off on the impulse and lived her life, merely to have had such a picture moving in my sight, and call it mine.

"You're not married ?" I said, ludicrously faintly.

" I've not seen the man I'd marry," she answered, grinning scorn.

The prize-fighter had adopted drinking for his pursuit; one of her aunts was dead, and she was in quest of money to bury the dead woman with the conventional ceremonies and shows of respect dear to the hearts of gipsies, whose sense of propriety and adherence to customs are a sentiment indulged by them to a degree unknown to the stabled classes. In fact, they have no other which does not come under the definite title of pride;—pride in their physical prowess, their dexterity, ingenuity, and tricksiness, and their purity of blood. Kiomi confessed she had hoped to meet me; confessed next that she had been waiting to jump out on me: and next that she had sat in a tree watching the Grange yesterday for six hours; and all for money to do honour to her dead relative, poor little soul! Heriot and I joined the decent procession to the grave. Her people had some quarrel with the Durstan villagers, and she feared the scandal of being pelted on the way to the church. I knew that nothing of the sort would happen if I was present. Kiomi walked humbly, with her head bent, leaving me the thick rippling coarse black locks of her hair for a mark of observation. We were entertained at her camp in the afternoon. I saw no sign of intelligence between her and Heriot. On my asking her, the day before, if she remembered him, she said, " I do, I'm dangerous for that young man." Heriot's comment on her was impressed on me by his choosing to call her "a fine doe leopard," and maintaining that it was a defensible phrase.

She was swept from my amorous mind by Mabel Sweetwinter, the miller's daughter of Dipwell. This was a Saxon beauty in full bud, yellow as mid-May, with the eyes of opening June. Beauty, you will say, is easily painted in that style. But the sort of beauty suits the style, and the well-worn comparisons express the well-known type. Beside Kiomi she was like a rich meadow on the border of the heaths.

We saw them together on my twenty-first birthday. To my shame I awoke in the early morning at Riversley, forgetful of my father's old appointment for the great Dipwell feast. Not long after sunrise, when blackbirds peck the lawns, and swallows are out from under eaves to the flood's face, I was hailed by Janet Ilchester beneath my open windows. I knew she had a bet with the squire that she would be the first to hail me legal man, and was prepared for it. She sat on horseback alone in the hazy dewy Midsummer morning, giving clear note : "Whoop ! Harry Richmond! halloo!" To which I tossed her a fox's brush, having a jewelled bracelet pendant. She missed it and let it lie, and laughed.

"No, no ; it's foxie himself !—anybody may have the brush. You're dressed, are you, Harry ? You were sure I should come ? A thousand happy years to you, and me to see them, if you don't mind. I'm first to wish it, I'm certain ! I was awake at three, out at half-past, over Durstan heath, across Eckerthy's fields—we'll pay the old man for damage—down by the plantation, Bran and Sailor at my heels, and here I am. Crow, cocks ! bark, dogs ! up, larks ! I said I'd be first. And now I'm round to stables to stir up Uberly. Don't be tardy, Mr. Harry, and we'll be Commodore Anson and his crew before the world's awake."

We rode out for a couple of hours, and had to knock at a farmhouse for milk and bread. Possibly a sense of independence, owing to the snatching of a meal in mid flight away from home, made Janet exclaim that she would gladly be out all day. Such freaks were exceedingly to my taste. Then I remembered Dipwell, and sure that my father would be there, though he had not written of it, I proposed to ride over. She pleaded for the horses and the squire alternately. Feasting was arranged at Riversley, as well as at Dipwell, and she said musically,—

"Harry, the squire is a very old man, and you may not have many more chances of pleasing him. To-day do, do ! To-morrow, ride to your father, if you must : of course you must if you think it right; but don't go this day."

"Not upset my fortune, Janet ?"

"Don't hurt the kind old man's heart to-day."

"Oh ! you're the girl of his heart, I know."

"Well, Harry, you have first place, and I want you to keep it."

"But here's an oath I've sworn to my father."

"He should not have exacted it, I think."

"I promised him when I was a youngster."

"Then be wiser now, Harry."

"You have brilliant ideas of the sacredness of engagements."

"I think I have common sense, that's all."

"This is a matter of feeling."

" It seems that you forgot it though !"

Kiomi's tents on Durstan heath rose into view. I controlled my verbal retort upon Janet to lead her up to the gipsy girl, for whom she had an odd aversion, dating from childhood. Kiomi undertook to ride to Dipwell, a distance of thirty miles, and carry the message that I would be there by nightfall. Tears were on Janet's resolute face as we cantered home.

After breakfast the squire introduced me to his lawyer, Mr. Burgin, who, closeted alone with me, said formally,—

" Mr. Harry Richmond, you are Squire Beltham's grandson, his sole male descendant, and you are established at present, and as far as we can apprehend for the future, as the direct heir to the whole of his property, which is enormous now, and likely to increase so long as he lives. You may not be aware that your grandfather has a most sagacious eye for business. Had he not been born a rich man he would still have been one of our very greatest millionnaires. He has rarely invested but to double his capital ; never speculated but to succeed. He may not understand men quite so well, but then he trusts none entirely ; so if there is a chasm in his intelligence, there is a bridge thrown across it. The metaphor is obscure perhaps : you will doubtless see my meaning. He knows how to go on his road without being cheated. For himself, your grandfather, Mr. Harry, is the soul of honour. Now, I have to explain certain family matters. The squire's wife, your maternal grandmother, was a rich heiress. Part of her money was settled on her to descend to her children by reversion upon her death. What she herself possessed she bequeathed to them in reversion likewise to their children. Thus at your maternal grandmother's death, your mother and your aunt inherited money to use as their own, and the interest of money tied fast in reversion to their children (in case of marriage) after their death. Your grandfather, as your natural guardian, has left the annual interest of your money to accumulate, and now you are of age he hands it to you, as you see, without much delay. Thus you become this day the possessor of seventy thousand pounds, respecting the disposal of which I am here to take your orders. Ahem !— as to the remaining property of your mother's—the sum held by her for her own use, I mean, it devolved to her husband, your father, who, it is probable, will furnish you an account of it—ah!—at his leisure—ah! um! And now, in addition, Mr. Harry, I have the squire's commands to speak to you as a man of business, on what may be deemed a delicate subject, though from the business point of view, no peculiar delicacy should pertain to it. Your grandfather will settle on you estates and money to the value of twenty thousand pounds per annum on the day of your union with a young lady in this district, Miss Janet Ilchester. He undertakes likewise to provide her pin-money. Also, let me observe, that it is his request—but he makes no stipulation of it—that you will ultimately assume the name of Beltham, subscribing yourself Harry Lepel Richmond Beltham; or, if it pleases you, Richmond-Beltham, with the junction hyphen. Needless to say, he leaves it to your decision. And now, Mr. Harry, I have done, and may most cordially congratulate you on the blessings it has pleased a kind and discerning Providence to shower on your head."

None so grimly ironical as the obsequious! I thought of Burgin's "discerning" providence (he spoke with all professional sincerity) in after days.

On the occasion I thought of nothing but the squire's straightforwardness, and grieved to have to wound him. Janet helped me. She hinted with a bashfulness, quite new to her, that I must go through some ceremony. Guessing what it was, I saluted her on the cheek. The squire observed that a kiss of that sort might as well have been planted on her back hair. "But," said he, and wisely, "I'd rather have the girl worth ten of you, than you be more than her match. Girls like my girl here are precious." Owing to her intercession, he winked at my departure after I had done duty among the tenants; he barely betrayed his vexation, and it must have been excessive.

Heriot and I rode over to Dipwell. Next night we rode back by moonlight with matter for a year of laughter, singing like two Arabian poets praises of Dark and Fair, challenging one to rival the other. Kiomi! Mabel! we shouted separately. We had just seen the dregs of the last of the birthday Burgundy.

"Kiomi! what a splendid panther she is!" cries Heriot; and I: "Teeth and claws, and a skin like a burnt patch on a common! Mabel's like a wonderful sunflower."

"Butter and eggs! old Richie, and about as much fire as a rushlight. If the race were Fat she'd beat the world."

"Heriot, I give you my word of honour, the very look of her's eternal Summer. Kiomi rings thin—she tinkles; it's the difference between metal and flesh."

"Did she tinkle, as you call it, when that fellow Destrier, confound him! touched her?"

"The little cat! Did you notice Mabel's blush?"

"How could I help it? We've all had a dozen apiece. You saw little Kiomi curled up under the hop and briony?"

"I took her for a dead jackdaw."

"I took her for what she is, and she may slap, scream, tear, and bite, I'll take her yet—and all her tribe crying thief, by way of a diversion. She and I are footed a pair."

His impetuosity surpassed mine so much that I fell to brooding on the superior image of my charmer. The result was, I could not keep away from her. I managed to get home with leaden limbs. Next day I was back at Dipwell.

Such guilt as I have to answer for I may avow. I made violent love to this silly country beauty, and held every advantage over her other flatterers. She had met me on the evening of the great twenty-first, she and a line of damsels dressed in white and wearing wreaths, and I had claimed the privilege of saluting her. The chief superintendent of the festivities, my father's old cook, Monsieur Alphonse, turned twilight into noonday with a sheaf of rockets at the moment my lips brushed her cheek. It was a kiss marred; I claimed to amend it. Besides, we had been bosom friends in childhood. My wonder at the growth of the rose I had left but an insignificant thorny shoot was exquisite natural flattery, sweet reason, to which she could not say nonsense. At each step we trod on souvenirs, innocent in themselves, had they recurred to childish minds. The whisper, "Hark! it's sunset, Mabel, Martha Thresher calls," clouded her face with stormy sunset colours. I respected Martha even then for boldly speaking to me on the girl's behalf. Mrs. Waddy's courage failed. John Thresher and Mark Sweetwinter were overcome by my father's princely prodigality; their heads were turned, they appeared to have assumed that I could do no wrong. To cut short the episode, some one wrote to the squire in uncouth English, telling him I was courting a country lass, and he at once started me for the Continent. We had some conversation on money before parting. The squire allowed me a thousand a year, independent of my own income. He counselled prudence, warned me that I was on my trial, and giving me his word of honour that he should not spy into my Bank accounts, desired me to be worthy of the trust reposed in me. Speculation he forbade. I left him satisfied with the assurance that I meant to make my grand tour neither as a merchant, a gambler, nor a rake, but simply as a plain English gentleman.

"There's nothing better in the world than that," said he.

Arrived in London, I left my travelling companion, the Rev. Ambrose Peterborough, sipping his Port at the hotel, and rushed down to Dipwell, shot a pebble at Mabel's window by morning twilight, and soon had her face at the casement. But it was a cloudy and rain-beaten face. She pointed toward the farm, saying that my father was there.

"Has he grieved you, Mabel?" I asked softly.

"Oh, no, not he! he wouldn't, he couldn't; he talked right. Oh, go, go: for I haven't a foot to move. And don't speak so soft; I can't bear kindness."

My father in admonishing her had done it tenderly, I was sure. Tenderness was the weapon which had wounded her, and so she shrank from it; and if I had reproached and abused her she might, perhaps, have obeyed me by coming out, not to return. She was deaf. I kissed my hand to her regretfully; a condition of spirit gradually dissolved by the haunting phantom of her forehead and mouth crumpling up for fresh floods of tears. Had she concealed that vision with her handkerchief, I might have waited to see her before I saw my father. He soon changed the set of the current.

"Our little Mabel here," he said, "is an inflammable puss, I fear. By the way, talking of girls, I have a surprise for you. Remind me of it when we touch Ostend. We may want a yacht there to entertain high company. I have set inquiries afloat for the hire of a schooner. This child Mabel can read and write, I suppose? Best write no letters, boy. Do not make old Dipwell a thorny bed. I have a portrait to show you, Richie. A portrait! I think you will say the original was worthy of more than to be taken up and thrown away like a weed. You see, Richie, girls have only one chance in the world, and good God! to ruin that—

no, no. You shall see this portrait. A pretty little cow-like Mabel, I grant you. But to have her on the conscience! What a coronet to wear! My young Lord Destrier—you will remember him as one of our guests here; I brought him to make your acquaintance; well, *he* would not be scrupulous, it is possible. Ay, but compare yourself with him, Richie! and you and I, let us love one another and have no nettles."

He flourished me away to London, into new spheres of fancy. He was irresistible.

In a London Club I was led up to the miniature of a youthful woman, singular for her endearing beauty. Her cheeks were merry red, her lips lively with the spark of laughter, her eyes in good union with them, showing you the laughter was gentle; eyes of overflowing blue light.

"Who is she?" I asked.

The old-fashioned building of the powdered hair counselled me to add, "Who was she?"

Captain DeWitt, though a member of the Club, seemed unable to inform me. His glance consulted my father. He hummed and drawled, and said: "Mistress Anastasia Dewsbury; that was her name."

"She does not look a grandmother," said my father.

"She would be one by this time, I dare say," said I.

We gazed in silence.

"Yes!" he sighed. "She was a charming actress, and one of the best of women. A noble-minded young woman! A woman of cultivation and genius! Do you see a broken heart in that face? No? Very well. A walk will take us to her grave. She died early."

I was breathing "Who?" when he said, "She was my mother, my dear."

It was piteous.

We walked to an old worn flat stone in a London street, whereunder I had to imagine those features of beautiful humanity lying shut from us.

She had suffered in life miserably.

CHAPTER XXIV.

I MEET THE PRINCESS.

HEARING that I had not slept at the hotel, the Rev. Ambrose rushed down to Riversley with melancholy ejaculations, and was made to rebound by the squire's contemptuous recommendation to him to learn to know something of the spirit of young bloods, seeing that he had the nominal charge of one, and to preach his sermon in secret, if he would be sermonizing out of church. The good gentleman had not exactly understood his duties, or how to conduct them. Far from objecting to find me in company with my father, as he would otherwise have done by transmitting information of that fact to Riversley, he now congratulated himself on it, and after the two had conversed apart, cordially agreed to our scheme of travelling together. The squire had sickened him. I believe that by comparison he saw in my father a better friend of youth.

" We shall not be the worse for a ghostly adviser at hand," my father said to me with his quaintest air of gravity and humour mixed, which was not insincerely grave, for the humour was unconscious. "An accredited casuist may frequently be a treasure. And I avow it, I like to travel with my private chaplain."

Mr. Peterborough's temporary absence had allowed me time for getting ample funds placed at our disposal through the agency of my father's solicitors, Messrs. Dettermain and Newson, whom I already knew from certain transactions with them on his behalf. They were profoundly courteous to me, and showed me his box, and alluded to his Case—a long one, and a lamentable, I was taught to apprehend, by their lugubriously professional tone about it. The question was naturally prompted in me, " Why do you not go on with it ?"

" Want of funds."

" There's no necessity to name that now," I insisted. But my father desired them to postpone any further exposition of the case, saying " Pleasure first, business by-and-by, That, I take it, is in the order of our great mother Nature.

gentlemen. I will not have him help shoulder his father's pack until he has had his fill of entertainment."

A smooth voyage brought us in view of the towers of Ostend at sunrise. Standing with my father on deck, and gazing on this fringe of the grand romantic Continent, I remembered our old travels, and felt myself bound to him indissolubly, ashamed of my recent critical probings of his character. My boy's love for him returned in full force. I was sufficiently cognizant of his history to know that he kept his head erect, lighted by the fire of his robust heart in the thick of overhanging natal clouds. As the way is with men when they are too happy to be sentimental, I chattered of anything but my feelings.

"What a capital idea that was of yours to bring down old Alphonse to Dipwell! You should have heard old John Thresher and Mark Sweetwinter and the others grumbling at the interference of 'French frogs' with their beef, though Alphonse vowed he only ordered the ox to be turned faster, and he dressed their potatoes in six different ways. I doubt if Dipwell has composed itself yet. You know I sat for president in their tent while the beef went its first round; and Alphonse was in an awful hurry to drag me into what he called the royal tent. By the way, you should have hauled the standard down at sunset."

"Not when the *son* had not come down among us," said my father, smiling.

"Well, I forgot to tell you about Alphonse. By the way, we'll have him in our service. There was he plucking at me: 'Monsieur Henri-Richie, Monsieur Henri-Richie! milles complimens . . . et les potages, Monsieur!—à la Camérani, à la tortue, aux petits pois . . . c'est en vrai artiste que j'ai su tout retarder jusqu'au dernier moment. . . . Monsieur! cher Monsieur Henri-Richie, je vous en supplie, laissez-là ces planteurs de choux.' And John Thresher, as spokesman for the rest: 'Master Harry, we beg to say, in my name, we can't masticate comfortably while we've got a notion Mr. Frenchman he's present here to play his Frenchified tricks with our plain wholesome dishes. Our opinion is, he don't know beef from hedgehog; and let him trim 'em, and egg 'em, and breadcrumb 'em, and pound the mess all his might, and then tak' and roll 'em into balls, we say we wun't, for we can't make English muscle out o' that.'—And Alphonse, quite indifferent to the vulgar: 'Hé! mais pensez donc au Papa, Monsieur Henri-Richie, sans doute il a une santé de fer: mais encore faut-il lui ménager le suc gastrique, pancréatique. . . .''

"Ay, ay!" laughed my father; "what sets you thinking of Alphonse?"

"I suppose because I shall have to be speaking French in an hour."

"German, Richie, German."

"But these Belgians speak French."

"Such French as it is. You will, however, be engaged in a German conversation first, I suspect."

"Very well, I'll stumble on. I don't much like it."

"In six hours from this second of time, Richie, boy, I undertake to warrant you fonder of the German tongue than of any other spoken language."

I looked at him. He gave me a broad pleasant smile, without sign of a jest lurking in one corner.

The scene attracted me. Laughing fishwife faces radiant with sea-bloom in among the weedy pier-piles, and sombre blue-cheeked officers of the douane, with their double row of buttons extending the breadth of their shoulders. My father won Mr. Peterborough's approval by declaring cigars which he might easily have passed.

"And now, sir,"—he used the commanding unction of a lady's doctor,—"you to bed, and a short repose. We will, if it pleases you, breakfast at eight. I have a surprise for Mr. Richie. We are about to beat the drum in the market-place, and sing out for echoes."

"Indeed, sir?" said the simple man.

"I promise you we shall not disturb you, Mr. Peterborough. You have reached that middle age, have you not, when sleep is, so to put it, your capital? And your bodily and mental activity is the interest you draw from it to live on. You have three good hours. So, then, till we meet at the breakfast-table."

My father's first proceeding at the hotel was to examine the list of visitors. He questioned one of the waiters aside, took information from him, and seized my arm rather tremulously, saying,—

"They are here. 'Tis as I expected. And she is taking the morning breath of sea-air on the dunes. Come, Richie, come."

"Who's the 'she'?" I asked incuriously.

"Well, she is young, she is of high birth, she is charming. We have a crowned head or two here. I observe in you, Richie, an extraordinary deficiency of memory. She has had an illness; Neptune speed her recovery! Now for a turn at our German. Die Strasse ruhen; die Stadt schläft; aber dort, siehst Du, dort liegt das blaue Meer, das nimmer-schlafende! She is gazing on it, and breathing it, Richie. Ach! ihr jauchzende Seejungfern. On my soul, I expect to see the very loveliest of her sex! You must not be dismayed at pale cheeks—blasse Wangen. Her illness has been alarm-ing. Why, this air is the top of life; it will, and it shall, revive her. How will she address him?—'Freund,' in my presence, perchance: she has her invalid's privilege. 'Theure Prinzessin' you might venture on. No ice! Ay, there she is!"

Solitary, on the long level of the sand-bank, I perceived a group that became discernible as three persons attached to an invalid's chair, moving leisurely toward us. I was in the state of mind between divination and doubt when the riddle is not impossible to read, would but the heart cease its hurry an instant; a tumbled sky where the break is coming. It came. The dear old days of my wanderings with Temple framed her face. I knew her without need of pause or retro-spect. The crocus raising its cup pointed as when it pierced the earth, and the crocus stretched out on earth, wounded by frost, is the same flower. The face was the same, though the features were changed. Unaltered in expression, but wan, and the kind blue eyes large upon lean brows, her aspect was that of one who had been half caught away and still shook faintly in the relaxing invisible grasp.

We stopped at a distance of half-a-dozen paces to allow her time for recollection. She eyed us softly in a fixed manner, while the sea-wind blew her thick red-brown hair to threads on her cheek. Colour on the fair skin told us we were recognized.

"Princess Ottilia!" said my father.

"It is I, my friend," she answered. "And you?"

"With more health than I am in need of, dearest prin-cess."

"And he?"

"Harry Richmond! my son; now of age, commencing his

tour; and he has not forgotten the farewell bunch of violets."

Her eyelids gently lifted, asking me.

" Nor the mount you did me the honour to give me on the little Hungarian," said I.

" How nice this sea-air is!" she spoke in English. " England and sea go together in my thoughts. And you are here! I have been down very low, near the lowest. But your good old sea makes me breathe again. I want to toss on it. Have you yet seen the Markgräfin?"

My father explained that we had just landed from the boat.

" Is our meeting, then, an accident?"

" Dear princess, I heard of your being out by the shore."

" Ah! kind: and you walked to meet me? I love that as well, though I love chance. And it *is* chance that brings you here! I looked out on the boat from England while they were dressing me. I cannot have too much of the morning, for then I have all to myself: sea and sky and I. The night people are all asleep, and you come like an old Märchen."

Her eyelids dropped without closing.

" Speak no more to her just at present," said an English voice, Miss Sibley's. Schwartz, the huge dragoon, whose big black horse hung near him in my memory like a phantom, pulled the chair at a quiet pace, head downward. A young girl clad in plain black walked beside Miss Sibley, following the wheels.

" Danger is over," Miss Sibley answered my gaze. " She is convalescent. You see how weak she is."

I praised the lady for what I deemed her great merit in not having quitted the service of the princess.

" Oh!" said she, " my adieux to Sarkeld were uttered years ago. But when I heard of her fall from the horse I went and nursed her. We were once in dread of her leaving us. She sank as if she had taken some internal injury. It may have been only the shock to her system, and the cessation of her accustomed exercise. She has a little over-studied."

" The margravine?"

" The margravine is really very good and affectionate, and has won my esteem. So you and your father are united

at last? We have often talked of you. Oh! that day up
by the tower. But, do you know, the statue is positively
there now, and no one—no one who had the privilege of
beholding the first bronze Albrecht Wohlgemuth, Fürst von
Eppenwelzen-Sarkeld, no one will admit that the second is
half worthy of him. I can feel to this day the leap of the
heart in my mouth when the statue dismounted. The prince
sulked for a month: the margravine still longer at your
father's evasion. She could not make allowance for the
impulsive man : such a father ; *such* a son !"

"Thank you, thank you most humbly," said I, bowing to
her shadow of a mock curtsey.

The princess's hand appeared at a side of the chair. We
hastened to her.

"Let me laugh, too," she prayed.

Miss Sibley was about to reply, but stared, and delight
sprang to her lips in a quick cry.

"What medicine is this? Why, the light of morning has
come on you, my darling !"

"I am better, dearest, better."

"You sigh, my own."

"No; I breathe lots, lots of salt air now, and lift like a
boat. Ask him—he had a little friend, much shorter than
himself, who came the whole way with him out of true
friendship—ask him where is the friend ?"

Miss Sibley turned her head to me.

"Temple," said I; "Temple is a midshipman; he is at
sea."

"That is something to think of," the princess murmured,
and dropped her eyelids a moment. She resumed : " The
Grand Seigneur was at Vienna last year, and would not
come to Sarkeld, though he knew I was ill."

My father stooped low.

"The grand Seigneur, your servant, dear princess, was an
Ottoman Turk, and his Grand Vizier advised him to send
flowers in his place weekly."

"I had them, and when we could get those flowers nowhere
else," she replied. "So it was you! So my friends have
been about me."

During the remainder of the walk I was on one side of
the chair, and her little maid on the other, while my father
to rearward conversed with Miss Sibley. The princess took

a pleasure in telling me that this Aennchen of hers knew me well, and had known me before ever her mistress had seen me. Aennchen was the eldest of the two children Temple and I had eaten breakfast with in the forester's hut. I felt myself as if in the forest again, merely wondering at the growth of the trees, and the narrowness of my vision in those days.

At parting, the princess said,—

"Is my English improved? You smiled at it once. I will ask you when I meet you next."

" It is my question," I whispered to my own ears.

She caught the words.

" Why do you say—'It is my question' ?"

I was constrained to remind her of her old forms of English speech.

" You remember that? Adieu," she said.

My father considerately left me to carry on my promenade alone. I crossed the ground she had traversed, noting every feature surrounding it, the curving wheel-track, the thin prickly sand-herbage, the wave-mounds, the sparse wet shells and pebbles, the gleaming flatness of the water, and the vast horizon-boundary of pale flat land level with shore, looking like a dead sister of the sea. By a careful examination of my watch and the sun's altitude, I was able to calculate what would, in all likelihood, have been his height above yonder waves when her chair was turned toward the city, at a point I reached in the track. But of the matter then simultaneously occupying my mind, to recover which was the second supreme task I proposed to myself—of what I also was thinking upon the stroke of five o'clock, I could recollect nothing. I could not even recollect whether I happened to be looking on sun and waves when she must have had them full and glorious in her face.

CHAPTER XXV.

ON BOARD A YACHT.

WITH the heartiest consent I could give, and a blank cheque, my father returned to England to hire forthwith a commodious yacht, fitted and manned. Before going he discoursed of prudence in our expenditure; though not for the sake of the mere money in hand, which was a trifle, barely more than the half of my future income; but that the squire, should he by and by bethink him of inspecting our affairs, might perceive we were not spendthrifts.

"I promised you a surprise, Richie," said he, "and you have had it; whether at all equal to your expectations is for you to determine. I was aware of the margravine's intention to bring the princess to these sea-sands; they are famous on the Continent. It was bruited last Winter and Spring that she would be here in the season for bathing; so I held it likely we should meet. We have, you behold. In point of fact, we owe the good margravine some show of hospitality. The princess has a passion for tossing on the sea. To her a yacht is a thing dropped from the moon. His Highness the prince her father could as soon present her with one as with the moon itself. The illustrious Serenity's revenue is absorbed, my boy, in the state he has to support. As for his daughter's dowry, the young gentleman who anticipates getting one with her, I commend to the practise of his whistling. It will be among the sums you may count, if you are a moderate arithmetician, in groschen. The margravine's income I should reckon to approach twenty thousand per annum, and she proves her honourable sense that she holds it in trust for others by dispersing it rapidly. I fear she loves cards. So, then, I shall go and hire the yacht through Dettermain and Newson, furnish it with piano and swing-cot, &c.; and if the ladies shrink from a cruise they can have an occasional sail. Here are we at their service. I shall be seriously baffled by fortune if I am not back to you at the end of a week. You will take your early morning walk, I presume. On Sunday see that our chaplain, the excellent Mr. Peterborough, officiates for the assembled Protestants of all nations. It excites our English enthusiasm. In addition, son Richie, it is peculiarly our duty. I, at least, hold the view that it is a family duty. Think it over, Richie boy. Providence, you see, has sent us the man. As for me, I feel as if I were in the dawn of one life with all the mature experience of another. I am calm, I am perfectly unexcited, and I tell you, old son, I believe—pick among the highest—our destinies are about the most brilliant of any couple in Great Britain."

His absence relieved me in spite of my renewed pleasure in his talk; I may call it a thirsty craving to have him inflating me, puffing the deep unillumined treasure-pits of my nature with laborious hints, as mines are filled with air to keep the miners going. While he talked he made these inmost recesses habitable. But the pain lay in my having now and then to utter replies. The task of speaking was hateful. I found a sweetness in brooding unrealizingly over hopes and dreams and possibilities, and I let him go gladly that I might enjoy a week of silence, just taking impressions as they came, like the sands in the ebb-tide. The impression of the morning was always enough for a day's meditation. The green colour and the crimson athwart it, and higher up the pinky lights, flamingo feathers, on a warm half-circle of heaven, in hue between amethyst and milky opal; then the rim of the sun's disc not yet severe; and then the monstrous shadow of tall Schwartz darting at me along the sand, then the princess. This picture, seen at sunrise, lasted till I slept. It stirred no thoughts, conjured no images, it possessed me. In the afternoon the margravine accompanied the princess to a point facing seaward, within hearing of the military band. She did me the favour to tell me that she tolerated me until I should become efficient in German to amuse her, but the dulness of the Belgian city compared with her lively German watering-places compelled her to try my powers of fun in French, and in French I had to do duty, and failed in my office.

"Do you know," said she, "that your honourable papa is one in a million? He has the life of a regiment in his ten fingers. What astonishes me is that he does not make fury in that England of yours—that Lapland! Je ne puis me passer de cet homme! He offends me, he trifles, he outrages, he dares permit himself to be indignant. Bon! we part, and absence pleads for him with the eloquence of Satan. I am his victim. Does he, then, produce no stir whatever in your England? But what a people! But yes, you resemble us, as bottles bottles; seulement, you are emptied of your wine. Ce Monsieur Pétèrbooroo'! Il m'agace les nerfs. It cannot be blood in his veins. One longs to see him cuffed, to see if he has the English lion in him, one

knows not where. But you are so, you English, when not
intoxicated. And so censorious! You win your battles,
they say, upon beer and cordials: it is why you never can
follow up a success. Je tiens cela du Maréchal Prince
B——. Let that pass. One groans at your intolerable
tristesse. La vie en Angleterre est comme un marais. It is
a scandal to human nature. It blows fogs, foul vapours,
joint-stiffnesses, agues, pestilences, over us here,—yes, here!
That is your best side: but your worst is too atrocious!
Mon Dieu! Your men-rascals! Your women-rascals!"

" Good soul!" the princess arrested her, " I beg that you
will not abuse England."

" Have I abused England?" exclaimed the margravine.
" Nay, then, it was because England is shockingly unjust to
the most amusing, the most reviving, charming of men.
There is he fresh as a green bubbling well, and those
English decline to do honour to his source. Now tell me,
you!" She addressed me imperiously. " Are you prosecuting his claims? Are you besieging your Government?
What! you are in the season of generosity, an affectionate
son, wealthy as a Magyar prince of flocks, herds, mines, and
men, and you let him stand in the shade deprived of his
birthright? Are you a purse-proud commoner or an
imbecile?"

" My whimsy aunt!" the princess interposed again, " now
you have taken to abusing a defenceless Englishman."

"Nothing of the sort, child. I compliment him on his
looks and manners; he is the only one of his race who does
not appear to have marched out of a sentinel's box with a
pocket-mirror in his hand. I thank him from my soul for
not cultivating the national cat's whisker. None can
imagine what I suffer from the oppressive sight of his
Monsieur Pétèrbooroo'! And they are of one pattern—the
entire nation! He! no, he has the step of a trained blood-
horse. Only, as Kaunitz, or somebody, said of Joseph II.,
or somebody, he thinks or he chews. Englishmen's mouths
were clearly not made for more purposes than one. In
truth, I am so utterly wearied, I could pray for the diversion of a descent of rain. The life here is as bad as in
Rippau. I might just as well be in Rippau doing duty:
the silly people complain, I hear. I am gathering dust.

These, my dear, these are the experiences which age women at a prodigious rate. I feel chains on my limbs here."

"Madame, I would," said I, "that I were the Perseus to relieve you of your monster Ennui, but he is coming quickly."

"You see he has his pretty phrases!" cried the margravine; adding encouragingly: "S'il n'est pas tant soit peu impertinent?"

The advance of some German or Russian noblemen spared me further efforts.

We were on shore, listening to the band in the afternoon, when a sail like a spark of pure white stood on the purple black edge of a storm-cloud. It was the yacht. By sunset it was moored off shore, and at night hung with variegated lamps. Early next morning we went on board. The ladies were astonished at the extent of the vessel, and its luxurious fittings and cunning arrangements. My father, in fact, had negotiated for the hire of the yacht some weeks previously with his accustomed forethought.

"House and town and fortress provisioned, and moveable at will!" the margravine interjected repeatedly.

The princess was laid on raised pillows in her swing-cot under an awning aft, and watched the sailors, the splendid offspring of old sea-fights, as I could observe her spirited fancy conceiving them. They were a set of men to point to for an answer to the margravine's strictures on things English.

"Then, are you the captain, my good Herr Heilbrunn?" the margravine asked my father.

He was dressed in cheerful blue, wearing his cheerfullest air, and seemed strongly inclined for the part of captain, but presented the actual commander of the schooner-yacht, and helped him through the margravine's interrogations.

"All is excellent,—excellent for a day's sail," she said. I have no doubt you could nourish my system for a month, but to deal frankly with you—prepared meats and cold pies! —to face them once is as much as I am capable of."

"Dear Lady Field-Marshal," returned my father, "the sons of Neptune would be of poor account, if they could not furnish you cookery at sea."

They did, for Alphonse was on board. He and my father had a hot discussion about the margravine's dishes, Alphonse declaring that it was against his conscience to season them pungently, and my father preaching expediency. Alphonse spoke of the artist and his duty to his art, my father of the wise diplomatist who manipulated individuals without any sacrifice of principle. They were partly at play, of course, both having humour. It ended in the margravine's being enraptured. The delicacy of the invalid's dishes, was beyond praise. "So, then, we are absolutely better housed and accommodated than on shore!" the margravine made her wonder heard, and from that fell to enthusiasm for the vessel. After a couple of pleasant smooth-sailing days, she consented to cruise off the coasts of France and England. Adieu to the sands. Throughout the cruise she was placable, satisfied with earth and sea, and constantly eulogizing herself for this novel state of serenity. Cards, and a collection of tripping French books bound in yellow, danced the gavotte with time, which made the flying minutes endurable to her: and for relaxation there was here the view of a shining town dropped between green hills to dip in sea-water, yonder a ship of merchandise or war to speculate upon, trawlers, collier-brigs, sea-birds, wave over wave. No cloud on sun and moon. We had gold and silver in our track, like the believable children of fairyland. The princess, lying in her hammock-cot on deck, both day and night, or for the greater part of the night, let her eyes feast incessantly on a laughing sea: when she turned them to any of us, pure pleasure sparkled in them. The breezy salt hours were visible ecstasy to her blood. If she spoke it was but to utter a few hurried, happy words, and shrink as you see the lightning behind a cloud-rack, suggestive of fiery swift emotion within, and she gazed away overjoyed at the swoop and plunge of the gannet, the sunny spray, the waves curling crested or down-like. At night a couple of sailors, tender as women, moved her in the cot to her cabin. We heard her voice in the dark of the morning, and her little maid Aennchen came out and was met by me; and I at that hour had the privilege to help move her back to her favourite place, and strap the iron-stand fast, giving the warm-hooded cot room to swing. The keen sensations of a return to health amid unwonted scenes made things magical to her. When she beheld our low green Devon hills she signalled for help to rise, and " That is England !" she said, summoning to her

beautiful clear eyeballs the recollection of her first desire to
see my country. Her petition was that the yacht should go
in nearer and nearer to the land till she could discern men,
women, and children, and their occupations. A fisherman
and his wife sat in the porch above their hanging garden,
the woman knitting, the man mending his nets, barefooted
boys and girls astride the keel of a boat below them. The
princess eyed them and wept. "They give me happiness; I
can give them nothing," she said.

The margravine groaned impatiently at talk of such a
dieaway sort.

My father sent a couple of men on shore with a gift of
money to their family in the name of the Princess Ottilia.
How she thanked him for his prompt ideas! "It is because
you are generous you read one well."

She had never thanked me. I craved for that vibrating
music as of her deep heart penetrated and thrilling, but
shrank from grateful words which would have sounded payment. Running before the wind swiftly on a night of phos-
phorescent sea, when the waves opened to white hollows with
frayed white ridges, wreaths of hissing silver, her eyelids
closed, and her hand wandered over the silken coverlet to
the hammock-cloth, and up, in a blind effort to touch. Mine
joined to it. Little Aennchen was witness. Ottilia held
me softly till her slumber was deep.

CHAPTER XXVI.

IN VIEW OF THE HOHENZOLLERN'S BIRTHPLACE.

OUR cruise came to an end in time to save the margravine
from yawning. The last day of it was windless, and we
hung in sight of the colourless low Flemish coast for hours,
my father tasking his ingenuity to amuse her. He sang
with Miss Sibley, rallied Mr. Peterborough, played picquet
to lose, threw over the lead line to count the fathoms, and
whistling for the breeze, said to me, "We shall decidedly
have to offer her an exhibition of tipsy British seamen as
a final resource. The case is grave either way; but we
cannot allow the concluding impression to be a dull one."

It struck me with astonishment to see the vigilant watch

she kept over the princess this day, after having left her almost uninterruptedly to my care.

"You are better?" She addressed Ottilia. "You can sit up? You think you can walk? Then I have acted rightly, nay, judiciously,—I have not made a sacrifice for nothing. I took the cruise, mind you, on your account. You would study yourself to the bone, till you looked like a canary's quill, with that Herr Professor of yours. Now I've given you a dose of life. Yes, you begin to look like human flesh. Something has done you good."

The princess flushing scarlet, the margravine cried,—

"There's no occasion for you to have the whole British army in your cheeks. Goodness me! what's the meaning of it? Why, you answer me like flags, banners, uhlans' pennons, full-frocked cardinals!"

My father stepped in.

"Ah, yes," said the margravine. "But you little know, my good Roy, the burden of an unmarried princess; and heartily glad shall I be to hand her over to Baroness Turckems. That's her instituted governess, duenna, dragon, —what you will. She was born for responsibility, I was not; it makes me miserable. I have had no holiday. True, while she was like one of their wax virgins I had a respite. Fortunately, I hear of you English that, when you fall to sighing, you suck your thumbs and are consoled."

My father bowed her, and smiled her, and whirled her away from the subject. I heard him say, under his breath, that he had half a mind to issue orders for an allowance of grog to be served out to the sailors on the spot. I suggested, as I conceived in a similar spirit, the forcible ducking of Mr. Peterborough. He appeared to entertain and relish the notion in earnest.

"It might do. It would gratify her enormously," he said, and eyed the complacent clerical gentleman with transparent jealousy of his claims to decent treatment. "Otherwise, I must confess," he added, "I am at a loss. My wits are in the doldrums."

He went up to Mr. Peterborough, and, with an air of great sincerity and courtesy, requested him in French to create a diversion for her Highness the Margravine of Rippau during the extreme heat of the afternoon by precipitating himself headlong into forty fathoms, either attached or unattached. His art in baffling Mr. Peterborough's attempts to treat the unheard-of request as a jest was extraordinary. The ingenuity of his successive pleas for pressing such a request pertinaciously upon Mr. Peterborough in particular, his fixed eye, yet cordial deferential manner, and the stretch of his forefinger, and argumentative turn of the head—indicative of an armed disputant fully on the alert, and as if it were of profound and momentous importance that he should thoroughly defeat and convince his man—overwhelmed us. Mr. Peterborough, not being supple in French, fell back upon his English with a flickering smile of protestation; but even in his native tongue he could make no head against the tremendous volubility and brief eager pauses besetting him.

The farce was too evanescent for me to reproduce it.

Peterborough turned and fled to his cabin. Half the crew were on the broad grin. The margravine sprang to my father's arm, and entreated him to be her guest in her Austrian mountain summer-seat. Ottilia was now her darling and her comfort. Whether we English youth sucked our thumbs, or sighed furiously, she had evidently ceased to care. Mr. Peterborough assured me at night that he had still a difficulty in persuading himself of my father's absolute sanity, so urgent was the fire of his eye in seconding his preposterous proposition; and, as my father invariably treated with the utmost reserve a farce played out, they never arrived at an understanding about it, beyond a sententious agreement once, in the extreme heat of an Austrian highland valley, that the option of taking a header into seawater would there be divine.

Our yacht winged her way home. Prince Ernest of Eppenwelzen-Sarkeld, accompanied by Baroness Turckems, and Prince Otto, his nephew, son of the Prince of Eisenberg, a captain of Austrian lancers, joined the margravine in Würtemberg, and we felt immediately that domestic affairs were under a different management. Baroness Turckems relieved the margravine of her guard. She took the princess into custody. Prince Ernest greeted us with some affability; but it was communicated to my father that he expected an apology before he could allow himself to be as absolutely unclouded toward us as the blaze of his titles. My father declined to submit; so the prince inquired of us what our

destination was.   Down the Danube to the Black Sea and
Asia Minor, Greece, Egypt, the Nile, the Desert, India,
possibly, and the Himalayas, my father said.   The prince
bowed.   The highest personages, if they cannot travel, are
conscious of a sort of airy majesty pertaining to one who
can command so wide and far a flight.   We were supplicated by the margravine to appease her brother's pride
with half a word.   My father was firm.   The margravine
reached her two hands to him.   He kissed over them each
in turn.   They interchanged smart semi-flattering or cutting
sentences.

" Good !" she concluded ; " now I sulk you for five years."

" You would decapitate me, madam, and weep over my
astonished head, would you not ?"

" Upon my honour, I would," she shook herself to reply.

He smiled rather sadly.

" No pathos !" she implored him.

" Not while I live, madam," said he.

At this her countenance underwent a tremour.

" And when that ends . . . . friend ! well, I shall have
had my last laugh in the world."

Both seemed affected.   My father murmured some soothing word.

" Then you *do* mean to stay with me ?" the margravine
caught him up.

" Not in livery, your Highness."

" To the deuce with you !" would be a fair translation of
the exalted lady's reply.   She railed at his insufferable
pride.

" And you were wrong, wrong," she pursued.   " You
offended the prince mightily : you travestied his most
noble ancestor——"

" In your service, may it please you."

" You offended, offended him, I say, and you haven't the
courage to make reparation.   And when I tell you the prince
is manageable as your ship, if you will only take and handle
the rudder.   Do you perceive ?"

She turned to me.

" Hither, Mr. Harry ; come, persuade him.   Why, you do
not desire to leave me, do you ?"

Much the reverse.   But I had to congratulate myself
subsequently on having been moderate in the expression of

my wishes; for, as my father explained to me, with sufficient lucidity to enlighten my dulness, the margravine was tempting him grossly. She saw more than I did of his plans. She could actually affect to wink at them that she might gain her point, and have her amusement, and live for the hour, treacherously beguiling a hoodwinked pair to suppose her partially blind or wholly complaisant. My father knew her and fenced her.

"Had I yielded," he said, when my heart was low after the parting, "I should have shown her my hand. I do not choose to manage the prince that the margravine may manage me. I pose my pride—immolate my son to it, Richie? I hope not. No. At Vienna we shall receive an invitation to Sarkeld for the winter, if we hear nothing of entreaties to turn aside to Ischl at Munich. She is sure to entreat me to accompany her on her annual visit to her territory of Rippau, which she detests; and, indeed, there is not a vine in the length and breadth of it. She thought herself broad awake, and I have dosed her with an opiate."

He squeezed my fingers tenderly. I was in want both of consolation and very delicate handling when we drove out of the little Würtemberg town: I had not taken any farewell from Ottilia. Baroness Turckems was already exercising her functions of dragon. With the terrible forbidding word "Repose" she had wafted the princess to her chamber in the evening, and folded her inextricably round and round in the morning. The margravine huffed, the prince icy, Ottilia invisible, I found myself shooting down from the heights of a dream among shattered fragments of my cloud-palace before I well knew that I had left off treading common earth. All my selfish nature cried out to accuse Ottilia. We drove along a dusty country road that lay like a glaring shaft of the desert between vineyards and hills.

"There," said my father, waving his hand where the hills on our left fell to a distance and threw up a lofty head and neck cut with one white line, "your Hohenzollerns shot up there. Their castle looks like a tight military stock. Upon my word, their native mountain has the air of a drum major. Mr. Peterborough, have you a mind to climb it? We are at your disposal."

"Thank you, thank you, sir," said the Rev. Ambrose,

gazing enthusiastically, but daunted by the heat: "if it is your wish?"

"We have none that is not yours, Mr. Peterborough. You love ruins, and we are adrift just now. I presume we can drive to the foot of the ascent. I should wish my son perhaps to see the source of great houses."

Here it was that my arm was touched by old Schwartz. He saluted stiffly, and leaning from the saddle on the trot of his horse at an even pace with our postilion, stretched out a bouquet of roses. I seized it palpitating, smelt the roses, and wondered. May a man write of his foolishness?—tears rushed to my eyes. Schwartz was far behind us when my father caught sight of the magical flowers.

"Come!" said he, glowing, "we will toast the Hohen-staufens and the Hohenzollerns to-night, Richie."

Later, when I was revelling in fancies sweeter than the perfume of the roses, he pressed their stems reflectively, unbound them, and disclosed a slip of crested paper. On it was written:

" Violets are over."

Plain words; but a princess had written them, and never did so golden a halo enclose any piece of human handi-work.

CHAPTER XXVII.

THE TIME OF ROSES.

I SAT and thrilled from head to foot with a deeper emotion than joy. Not I, but a detached self allied to the careering universe and having life in it.

" Violets are over."

The first strenuous effort of my mind was to grasp the meaning, subtle as odour, in these words. Innumerable meanings wreathed away unattainable to thought. The finer senses could just perceive them ere they vanished. Then as I grew material two camps were pitched and two armies prepared to fight to establish one distinct meaning. 'Violets are over, so I send you roses;' she writes you simple fact. Nay, 'Our time of violets is over, now for us the roses;' she gives you heavenly symbolism.

'From violets to roses, so run the seasons.'

Or is it,—

'From violets to roses, thus far have we two travelled?'

But would she merely say, 'I have not this kind of flower, and I send you another?'

True, but would she dare to say, 'The violets no longer express my heart; take the roses?'

'Maidenly, and a Princess, yet sweet and grateful, she gives you the gracefullest good speed.'

'Noble above all human distinctions, she binds you to herself, if you will it.'

The two armies came into collision, the luck of the day going to the one I sided with.

But it was curiously observable that the opposing force recovered energy from defeat, while mine languished in victory. I headed them alternately, and it invariably happened so.

" She cannot mean so much as this."

" She must mean more than that."

Thus the Absolute and the Symbolical factions struggled on. A princess drew them as the moon the tides.

By degrees they subsided and united, each reserving its view; a point at which I imagined myself to have regained my proper humility. " The princess has sent you these flowers out of her homely friendliness; not seeing you to speak her farewell, she, for the very reason that she can do it innocent of any meaning whatsoever, bids you be sure you carry her esteem with you. Is the sun of blue heavens guilty of the shadow it casts? Clear your mind. She means nothing. Warmth and beauty come from her, and are on you for the moment.—But full surely she is a thing to be won: she is human: did not her hand like a gentle snake seek yours, and detain it, and bear it away into the heart of her sleep?—Be moderate. Let not a thought or a dream spring from her condescension, lest you do outrage to her noble simplicity. Look on that high Hohenzollern hilltop: she also is of the line of those who help to found illustrious Houses: what are you?"

I turned to my father and stared him in the face. What was he? Were we not losing precious time in not prosecut-

ing his suit? I put this question to him, believing that it
would sound as too remote from my thoughts to betray
them. He glanced at the roses, and answered gladly,—

"Yes!—no, no! we must have our holiday. Mr. Peterborough is for exploring a battle-field in the neighbourhood
of Munich. He shall. I wish him to see the Salzkammergut,
and have a taste of German Court-life. Allow me to be
captain, Richie, will you? I will show you how battles are
gained and mountains are scaled. That young Prince Otto
of Eisenberg is a fine young fellow. Those Austrian cavalry
regiments are good training-schools for the carriage of a
young man's head and limbs. I would match my boy
against him in the exercises—fencing, shooting, riding."

"As you did at Bath," said I.

He replied promptly: "We might give him Anna Penrhys
to marry. English wives are liked here—adored if they
fetch a dowry. Concerning my suit, Richie, enough if it
keeps pace with us: and we are not going slow. It is a
thing certain. Dettermain and Newson have repeatedly
said, 'Money, money! hand us money, and we guarantee
you a public recognition.' Money we now have. But we
cannot be in two fields at once. Is it your desire to return
to England?"

"Not at all," said I, with a chill at the prospect.

"If it is—— ?" he pressed me, and relenting added: "I
confess I enjoy this Suabian land as much as you do. Indolence is occasionally charming. I am at work, nevertheless. But, Richie, determine not to think little of yourself:
there is the main point; believe me, that is half the battle.
You, sir, are one of the wealthiest gentlemen in Europe.
You are pronouncedly a gentleman. That is what we can
say of you at present, as you appear in the world's eye.
And you are by descent illustrious. Well, no more of that,
but consider if you kneel down, who will decline to put a
foot on you? Princes have the habit, and they do it as a
matter of course. *Challenge* them. And they, Richie, are
particularly susceptible to pity for the misfortunes of their
class—kind, I should say, for class it is not; now I have
done. All I tell you is, I intend you, under my guidance, to
be happy."

I thought his remarks the acutest worldly wisdom I had
ever heard,—his veiled method of treating my case the

shrewdest, delicatest, and most consoling, most inspiring. It had something of the mystical power of the Oracles,—the power which belongs to anonymous writing. Had he disposed of my apparent rival, and exalted me to the level of a princely family, in open speech, he would have conveyed no balm to me—I should have classed it as one confident man's opinion. Disguised and vague, but emphatic, and interpreted by the fine beam of his eye, it was intoxicating ; and when he said subsequently, " Our majority Burgundy was good emperor wine, Richie. You approved it ? I laid that vintage down to give you a lesson to show you that my plans come safe to maturity,"—I credited him with a large share of foresight, though I well knew his habit of antedating his sagacity, and could not but smile at the illustration of it.

You perceive my state without rendering it necessary for me to label myself.

I saw her next in a pinewood between Ischl and the Traun. I had climbed the steep hill alone, while my father and Mr. Peterborough drove round the carriage-road to the margravine's white villa. Ottilia was leaning on the arm of Baroness Turckems, walking—a miracle that disentangled her cruelly from my net of fancies. The baroness placed a second hand upon her as soon as I was seen standing in the path. Ottilia's face coloured like the cyclamen at her feet.

" You !" she said.

" I might ask, is it you, princess ?"

" Some wonder has been worked, you see."

" I thank heaven."

" You had a part in it."

" The poorest possible."

" Yet I shall presume to call you Doctor Oceanus."

" Will you repeat his medicine ? The yacht awaits you always."

" When I am well I study. Do not you ?"

" I have never studied in my life."

" Ah, lose no more time. The yacht is delicious idleness, but it is idleness. I am longing for it now, I am still so very weak. My dear Sibley has left me to be married. She marries a Hanoverian officer. We change countries—I mean," the princess caught back her tongue, "she will become German, not compatriot of your ships of war. My

English rebukes me. I cease to express . . . It is like my walking, done half for pride, I think. Baroness, lower me, and let me rest."

The baroness laid her gently on the dry brown pine-sheddings, and blew a whistle that hung at her girdle, by which old Schwartz, kept out of sight to encourage the princess's delusion of pride in her walking, was summoned. Ottilia had fainted. The baroness shot a suspicious glance at me. "It comes of this everlasting English talk," I heard her mutter. She was quick to interpose between me and the form I had once raised and borne undisputedly.

"Schwartz is the princess's attendant, sir," she said. "In future, may I request you to talk German?"

The Prince of Eppenwelzen and Prince Otto were shooting in the mountains. The margravine, after conversing with the baroness, received me stiffly. She seemed eager to be rid of us; was barely hospitable. My mind was too confused to take much note of words and signs. I made an appointment to meet my father the day following, and walked away and returned at night, encountered Schwartz and fed on the crumbs of tidings I got from him, a good, rough old faithful fellow, far past the age for sympathy, but he had carried Ottilia when she was an infant, and meant to die in her service. I thought him enviable above most creatures. His principal anxiety was about my finding sleeping quarters. When he had delivered himself three times over of all that I could lead him to say, I left him still puffing at his pipe. He continued on guard to be in readiness to run for a doctor should one be wanted. Twice in the night I came across his path. The night was quiet, dark blue, and starry; the morning soft and fragrant. The burden of the night was bearable, but that of daylight I fled from, and all day I was like one expecting a crisis. Laughter, with so much to arouse it, hardly had any foothold within me to stir my wits. For if I said "Folly!" I did not feel it, and what I felt I did not understand. My heart and head were positively divided. Days and weeks were spent in reconciling them a little; days passed with a pencil and scribbled slips of paper—the lines written with regular commencements and irregular terminations; you know them. Why had Ottilia fainted? She recommended hard study—thinks me idle, worthless; she has a grave intelligence, a serious estimation of life; she thinks me intrinsically of the value of a summer fly. But why did she say, "We change countries," and immediately flush, break and falter, lose command of her English, grow pale and swoon; why? With this question my disastrous big heart came thundering up to the closed doors of comprehension. It was unanswerable. "We change countries." That is, she and Miss Sibley change countries, because the English-woman marries a German, and the German princess—oh! enormous folly. Pierce it, slay it, trample it under. Is that what the insane heart is big with? Throughout my night-watch I had been free of it, as one who walks meditating in cloisters on a sentence that once issued from divine lips. There was no relief, save in those pencilled lines which gave honest laughter a chance, they stood like such a hasty levy of raw recruits raised for war, going through the goose-step, with pretty accurate shoulders, and feet of distracting de-grees of extension, enough to craze a rhythmical drill-sergeant. I exulted at the first reading, shuddered at the second, and at the third felt desperate, destroyed them and sat staring at vacancy as if I had now lost the power of speech.

At last I flung away idleness and came to a good resolution; and I carried it through. I studied at a famous German university, not far from Hanover. My father, after discus-sing my project with me from the point of view of amaze-ment, settled himself in the University town, a place of hopeless dulness, where the stones of the streets and the houses seemed to have got their knotty problem to brood over, and never knew holiday. A fire for acquisition pos-sessed me, and soon an ungovernable scorn for English systems of teaching — sound enough for the producing of gentlemen, and perhaps of merchants; but gentlemen rather bare ·of graces, and merchants not too scientific in finance. Mr. Peterborough conducted the argument against me until my stout display of facts, or it may have been my insolence, combined with the ponderous pressure of the atmosphere upon one who was not imbibing a counteracting force, drove him on a tour among German cathedrals. Letters from Riversley informed me that my proceedings were approved, though the squire wanted me near him. We offered enter-tainments to the students on a vast scale. The local news-paper spoke of my father as the great Lord Roy. So it happened that the margravine at Sarkeld heard of us. Returning from a visit to the prince's palace, my father told me that he saw an opportunity for our being useful to the prince, who wanted money to work a newly-discovered coal-mine in his narrow dominions, and he suggested that I might induce the squire to supply it; as a last extremity I could advance the money. Meanwhile he had engaged to accompany the prince in mufti to England to examine into the working of coal-mines, and hire an overseer and workmen to commence operations on the Sarkeld property. It would be obligatory to entertain him fitly in London.

"Certainly," said I.

"During our absence the margravine will do her best to console you, Richie. The prince chafes at his poverty. We give him a display of wealth in England; here we are particularly discreet. We shall be surer of our ground in time. I set Dettermain and Newson at work. I have written for them to hire a furnished mansion for a couple of months, carriages, horses, lacqueys. But over here we must really be—goodness me! I know how hard it is!—we must hold the reins on ourselves tight. Baroness Turckems is a most estimable person on the side of her duty. Why, the Dragon of Wantley sat on its eggs, you may be convinced! She is a praiseworthy dragon. The side she presents to us is horny, and not so agreeable. Talk German when she is on guard. Further I need not counsel a clever old son. Counsel me, Richie. Would it be advisable to run the prince down to Riversley?—a Prince!"

"Oh! decidedly not," was my advice.

"Well, well," he assented.

I empowered him to sell out Bank stock.

He wrote word from England of a very successful expedition. The prince, travelling under the title of Count Delzenburg, had been suitably entertained, received by Lady Wilts, Serena Marchioness of Edbury, Lady Denewdney, Lady Sampleman, and others. He had visited my grandfather's mine, and that of Miss Penrhys, and was astounded; had said of me that I wanted but a title to be as brilliant a *parti* as any in Europe.

The margravine must have received orders from her brother to be civil to me; she sent me an imperious invitation from her villa, and for this fruit of my father's diplomacy I yielded him up my daintier feelings, my judgement into the bargain.

Snows of early Spring were on the pinewood country I had traversed with Temple. Ottilia greeted me in health and vivacity. The margravine led me up to her in the very saloon where Temple, my father, and I had sat after the finale of the statue scene, saying,—

"Our sea-lieutenant."

"It delights me to hear he has turned University student," she said; and in English: "You have made friends of your books?"

She was dressed in blue velvet to the throat; the hair was brushed from the temples and bound in a simple knot. Her face and speech, fair and unconstrained, had neither shadow nor beam directed specially for me. I replied,—

"At least I have been taught to despise idleness."

"My Professor tells me it is strange for any of your country-men to love books."

"We have some good scholars, princess."

"You have your Bentley and Porson. Oh! I know many of the world's men have grown in England. Who can deny that? What we mean is, your society is not penetrated with learning. But my Professor shall dispute with you. Now you are facile in our German you can defend yourself. He is a deep scholar, broad over tongues and dialects, European, Asiatic—a lion to me, poor little mouse! I am speaking of Herr Professor von Karsteg, lady aunt."

"Speak intelligibly, and don't drum on my ear with that hybrid language," rejoined the margravine.

"Hybrid! It is my Herr Professor's word. But English is the choice gathering of languages, and honey is hybrid, unless you condemn the bee to suck at a single flower."

"Ha! you strain compliments like the poet Fretzel," the margravine exclaimed. "Luckily they're not addressed to human creatures. You will find the villa dull, Herr Harry Richmond. For my part every place is dull to me that your father does not enliven. We receive no company in the prince's absence, so we are utterly cut off from fools; we have simply none about us."

"The deprivation is one we are immensely sensible of!" said the princess.

"Laugh on! you will some day be aware of their import-ance in daily life, Ottilia."

The princess answered: "If I could hate, it would be such persons." A sentence that hung in the memory of one knowing himself to be animated by the wildest genius of folly.

We drove to the statue of Prince Albrecht Wohlgemuth, overlooking leagues of snow-roofed branches. Again Ottilia reverted to Temple,—

"That dear little friend of yours who wandered out with you to seek your father, and is now a sailor! I cannot for-get him. It strikes me as a beautiful piece of the heroism of boys. You both crossed the sea to travel over the whole Continent until you should find him, did you not? What is hard to understand, is your father's not writing to you while he did us the favour to reside at the palace."

"Roy is a butterfly," said the margravine.

"That I cannot think."

"Roy was busy, he was occupied. I won't have him abused. Besides, one can't be always caressing and cajoling one's pretty brats."

"He is an intensely loving father."

"Very well; establish that, and what does it matter whether he wrote or not? A good reputation is the best vindication."

The princess smiled. "See here, dearest aunty, the two boys passed half the night here, until my Aennchen's father gave them shelter."

"Apparently he passes half or all the night in the open air everywhere," said the margravine.

I glanced hurriedly over both faces. The margravine was snuffing her nostrils up contemptuously. The princess had vividly reddened. Her face was luminous over the nest of white fur folding her neck.

"Yes, I must have the taste for it: for when I was a child," said I, plunging at anything to catch a careless topic, "I was out in my father's arms through a winter night, and I still look back on it as one of the most delightful I have ever known. I wish I could describe the effect it had on me. A track of blood in the snow could not be brighter."

The margravine repeated,—

"A track of blood in the snow! My good young man, you have excited forms of speech."

I shuddered. Ottilia divined that her burning blush had involved me. Divination is fiery in the season of blushes, and I, too, fell on the track of her fair spirit, setting out from the transparent betrayal by Schwartz of my night-watch in the pine-wood near the Traun river-falls. My feelings were as if a wave had rolled me helpless to land, at the margravine's mercy should she put another question. She startled us with a loud outburst of laughter.

"No! no man upon this earth but Roy could have sat that horse I don't know how many minutes by the clock, as a figure of bronze," she exclaimed.

Ottilia and I exchanged a grave look. The gentleness of the old time was sweet to us both : but we had the wish that my father's extravagant prominency in it might be forgotten.

At the dinner-table I made the acquaintance of the Herr Professor Dr. Julius von Karsteg, tutor to the princess, a grey, broad-headed man, whose chin remained imbedded in his neckcloth when his eyelids were raised on a speaker. The first impression of him was that he was chiefly neck-cloth, coat-collar, grand head, and gruffness. He had not joined the ceremonial step from the reception to the dining saloon, but had shuffled in from a side-door. No one paid him any deference save the princess. The margravine had the habit of thrumming the table thrice as soon as she heard his voice: nor was I displeased by such an exhibition of impatience, considering that he spoke merely for the purpose of snubbing me. His powers were placed in evidence by her not daring to utter a sarcasm, which was possibly the main cause of her burning fretfulness. I believe there was not a word uttered by me throughout the dinner that escaped him. Nevertheless he did his business of catching and worrying my poor unwary sentences too neatly for me, an admirer of real force and aptitude, to feel vindictive. I behaved to him like a gentleman, as we phrase it, and obtained once an encouraging nod from the margravine. She leaned to me to say that they were accustomed to think themselves lucky if no learned talk came on between the Professor and his pupil. The truth was that his residence in Sarkeld was an honour to the prince, and his acceptance of the tutorship a signal condescension, accounted for by his appreciation of the princess's intelligence. He was a man distinguished even in Germany for scholarship, rather notorious for his political and social opinions too. The margravine, with infinite humour in her countenance, informed me that he wished to fit the princess for the dignity of a Doctor of Laws.

"It says much for her that he has not spoilt her manners; her health, you know, he succeeded in almost totally destroying, and he is at it again. The man is, I suspect, at heart arrant Republican. He may teach a girl whatever nonsensical politics he likes—it goes at the lifting of the bridegroom's little finger. We could not permit him to be near a young prince. Alas! we have none."

The Professor allowed himself extraordinary liberties with strangers, the guests of the margravine. I met him crossing an inner court next day. He interrupted me in the middle of a commonplace remark, and to this effect:—

"You are either a most fortunate or a most unfortunate young man!"

So profoundly penetrated with thoughtfulness was the tone of his voice that I could not take umbrage. The attempt to analyze his signification cost me an aching forehead, perhaps because I knew it too acutely.

CHAPTER XXVIII.

OTTILIA.

SHE was on horseback, I on foot, Schwartz for sole witness, and a wide space of rolling silent white country around us.

We had met in the fall of the winter noon by accident.

"You like my Professor?" said Ottilia.

"I do: I respect him for his learning."

"You forgive him his irony? It is not meant to be personal to you. England is the object; and partly, I may tell you, it springs from jealousy. You have such wealth! You embrace half the world: you are such a little island! All this is wonderful. The bitterness is, you are such a mindless people—I do but quote to explain my Professor's ideas. 'Mindless,' he says, 'and arrogant, and neither in the material nor in the spiritual kingdom of noble or gracious stature, and ceasing to have a brave aspect.' He calls you squat Goths. Can you bear to hear me?"

"Princess!"

"And to his conception, you, who were pioneers when the earth had to be shaped for implements and dug for gold, will turn upon us and stop our march; you are to be over-thrown and left behind, there to gain humility from the only teacher you can understand—from poverty. Will you defend yourself?"

"Well, no, frankly, I will not. The proper defence for a nation is its history.

"For an individual?"

"For a man, his readiness to abide by his word."

"For a woman—what?"

"For a princess, her ancestry."

"Ah! but I spoke of women. There, there is my ground of love for my Professor! I meet my equals, princes, prin-cesses, and the man, the woman, is out of them, gone, flown! They are out of the tide of humanity; they are walking titles. 'Now,' says my Professor, 'that tide is the blood of our being; the blood is the life-giver; and to be cut off from it is to perish.' Our princely houses he esteems as dead wood. Not near so much say I: yet I hear my equals talk, and I think, 'Oh! my Professor, they testify to your wisdom.' I love him because he has given my every sense a face-forward attitude (you will complain of my feebleness of speech) to exterior existence. There is a princely view of life which is a true one; but it is a false one if it is the sole one. In your Parliament your House of Commons shows us real princes, your Throne merely titled ones. I speak what everybody knows, and you, I am sure, are astonished to hear me."

"I am," said I.

"It is owing to my Professor, my mind's father and mother. They say it is the pleasure of low-born people to feel themselves princes; mine it is to share their natural feelings. 'For a princess, her ancestry.' Yes; but for a princess who is no more than princess, her ancestors are a bundle of faggots, and she, with her mind and heart tied fast to them, is, at least a good half of her, dead wood. This is our opinion. May I guess at your thoughts?"

" It's more than I could dare to do myself, princess."

How different from the Ottilia I had known, or could have imagined! That was one thought.

" Out of the number, then, this," she resumed: "you think that your English young ladies have command over their tongues: is it not so ? "

" There are prattlers among them."

" Are they educated strictly ? "

" I know little of them. They seem to me to be educated to conceal their education."

" They reject ideas ? "

" It is uncertain whether they have had the offer."

Ottilia smiled. "Would it be a home in their midst ? "

Something moved my soul to lift wings, but the passion sank.

" I questioned you of English ladies," she resumed, "because we read your writings of us. Your kindness to us is that which passes from nurse to infant; your criticism reminds one of paedagogue and urchin. You make us sorry for our manners and habits, if they are so bad; but most of all you are merry at our simplicity. Not only we say what we feel, we display it. Now, I am so German, this offence is especially mine."

I touched her horse's neck, and said, "I have not seen it."

" Yet you understand me. You know me well. How is that ?"

The murmur of honest confession came from me: " I *have* seen it !"

She laughed. " I bring you to be German, you see. Could you forsake your England ?"

" Instantly, though not willingly."

" Not regrettingly ?"

" Cheerfully, if I had my work and my—my friend."

" No; but well I know a man's field of labour is his country. You have your ambition."

" Yes, now I have."

She struck a fir-branch with her riding-whip, scattering flakes on my head. "Would that extinguish it ?"

" In the form of an avalanche perhaps it would."

" Then you make your aims a part of your life ?"

" I do."

" Then you win! or it is written of you that you never

knew failure! So with me. I set my life upon my aim when I feel that the object is of true worth. I win, or death hides from me my missing it. This I look to; this obtains my Professor's nod, and the approval of my conscience. Worthiness, however!—the mind must be trained to discern it. We can err very easily in youth; and to find ourselves shooting at a false mark uncontrollably must be a cruel thing. I cannot say it is undeserving the scourge of derision. Do you know yourself? I do not; and I am told by my Professor that it is the sole subject to which you should not give a close attention. I can believe him. For who beguiles so much as Self? Tell her to play, she plays her sweetest. Lurk to surprise her, and what a serpent she becomes! She is not to be aware that you are watching her. You have to review her acts, observe her methods. Always be above her; then by-and-by you catch her hesitating at cross-roads; then she is bare: you catch her bewailing or exulting; then she can no longer pretend she is other than she seems. I make self the feminine, for she is the weaker, and the soul has to purify and raise her. On that point my Professor and I disagree. Dr. Julius, unlike our modern Germans, esteems women over men, or it is a further stroke of his irony. He does not think your English ladies have heads: of us he is proud as a laurelled poet. Have I talked you dumb?"

"Princess, you have given me matter to think upon."

She shook her head, smiling with closed eyelids.

I, now that speech had been summoned to my lips, could not restrain it, and proceeded, scarcely governing the words, quite without ideas;—" For you to be indifferent to rank— yes, you may well be; you have intellect; you are high above me in both——" So on, against good taste and common sense.

She cried: " Oh! no compliments from you to me. I will receive them, if you please, by deputy. Let my Professor hear your immense admiration for his pupil's accomplishments. Hear him then in return! He will beat at me like the rainy West wind on a lily. 'See,' he will say, when I am broken and bespattered, 'she is fair, she is stately, is she not!' And really I feel at the sound of praise, though I like it, that the opposite, satire, condemnation, has its good right to pelt me. Look; there is the tower, there's the statue, and under that line of pine-trees the path we ran up ;—' dear English boys!' as I remember saying to myself; and what did you say of me?"

Her hand was hanging loose. I grasped it. She drew a sudden long breath, and murmured, without fretting to disengage herself,—

" My friend, not that!"

Her voice carried an unmistakable command. I kissed above the fingers and released them.

" Are you still able to run?" said she, leading with an easy canter, face averted. She put on fresh speed; I was outstripped.

Had she quitted me in anger? Had she parted from me out of view of the villa windows to make it possible for us to meet accidentally again in the shadow of her old protecting Warhead, as we named him from his appearance, gaunt Schwartz?

CHAPTER XXIX.

AN EVENING WITH DR. JULIUS VON KARSTEG.

IN my perplexity I thought of the Professor's saying: " A most fortunate or a most unfortunate young man." These words began to strike me as having a prophetic depth that I had not fathomed. I felt myself fast becoming bound in every limb, every branch of my soul. Ottilia met me smiling. She moved free as air. She could pursue her studies, and argue and discuss and quote, keep unclouded eyes, and laugh and play, and be her whole living self, unfettered, as if the pressure of my hand implied nothing. Perhaps for that reason I had her pardon. " My friend, not that!" Her imperishably delicious English rang me awake, and lulled me asleep. Was it not too securely friendly? Or was it not her natural voice to the best beloved, bidding him respect her that they might meet with the sanction of her trained discretion? The Professor would invite me to his room after the 'sleep well' of the ladies, and I sat with him much like his pipe-bowl, which burned bright a moment at one sturdy puff, but generally gave out smoke in fantastical wreaths. He told me frankly he had a poor idea of my erudition. My fancifulness he commended as something to be turned to use in writing stories. " Give me time, and I'll do better things," I groaned. He rarely spoke of the princess ; with grave affection always when he did. He was evidently observing me comprehensively. The result was beyond my guessing.

One night he asked me what my scheme of life was.

On the point of improvizing one of an impressive character, I stopped and confessed : " I have so many that I may say I have none." Expecting reproof, I begged him not to think the worse of me for that.

" Quite otherwise," said he. " I have never cared to read deliberately in the book you open to me, my good young man."

" The book, Herr Professor ?"

" Collect your wits. We will call it Shakspeare's book; or Göthe's, in the minor issues. No, not minor, but a narrower volume. You were about to give me the answer of hypocrite. Was it not so ?"

I admitted it, feeling that it was easily to have been perceived. He was elated.

" Good. Then I apprehend that you wait for the shifting of a tide to carry you on ?"

" I try to strengthen my mind."

" So I hear," said he drily.

" Well, as far as your schools of teaching will allow."

" That is, you read and commit to memory like other young scholars. Whereunto ? Have you no aim ? You have, or I am told you are to have, fabulous wealth—a dragon's heap. You are one of the main drainpipes of English gold. What is your object ? To spend it ?"

" I shall hope to do good with it."

" To do good ! There is hardly a prince or millionnaire, in history or alive, who has not in his young days hugged that notion. Pleasure swarms, he has the pick of his market. You English live for pleasure."

" We are the hardest workers in the world."

" That you may live for pleasure ! Deny it !"

He puffed his tobacco-smoke zealously, and resumed :

"Yes, you work hard for money. You eat and drink, and boast of your exercises: they sharpen your appetites. So goes the round. We strive, we fail; you are our frog-chorus of critics, and you suppose that your brek-ek-koax affects us. I say we strive and fail, but we strive on, while you remain in a past age, and are proud of it. You reproach us with lack of common sense, as if the belly were its seat. Now I ask you whether you have a scheme of life, that I may know whether you are to be another of those huge human pumpkins called rich men, who cover your country and drain its blood and intellect—those impoverishers of nature! Here we have our princes ; but they are rulers, they are responsi-ble, they have their tasks, and if they also run to gourds, the scandal punishes them and their order, all in seasonable time. They stand eminent. Do you mark me ? They are not a community, and are not—bad enough ! bad enough !—but they are not protected by laws in their right to do nothing for what they receive. That system is an invention of the commercial genius and the English."

"We have our aristocracy, Herr Professor."

"Your nobles are nothing but rich men inflated with empty traditions of insufferable, because unwarrantable, pride, and drawing substance from alliances with the merchant class. Are they your leaders ? Do they lead you in Letters ? in the Arts ? ay, or in Government ? No, not, I am informed, not even in military service ! and there our titled witlings do manage to hold up their brainless pates. You are all in one mass struggling in the stream to get out and he and wallow and belch on the banks. You work so hard that you have all but one aim, and that is fatness and ease !"

"Pardon me, Herr Professor," I interposed, " I see your drift. Still I think we are the only people on earth who have shown mankind a representation of freedom. And as to our aristocracy, I must, with due deference to you, main-tain that it is widely respected."

I could not conceive why he went on worrying me in this manner with his jealous outburst of Continental bile.

"Widely ! " he repeated. " It is widely respected; and you respect it: and why do you respect it ? "

"We have illustrious names in our aristocracy."

"We beat you in illustrious names and in the age of the lines, my good young man."

"But not in a race of nobles who have stood for the country's liberties."

"So long as it imperilled their own! Any longer?"

"Well, they have known how to yield. They have helped to build our Constitution."

"Reverence their ancestors, then! The worse for such descendants. But you have touched the exact stamp of the English mind :—it is, to accept whatsoever is bequeathed it, without inquiry whether there is any change in the matter. Nobles in very fact you would not let them be if they could. Nobles in name, with a remote recommendation to posterity— that suits you!"

He sat himself up to stuff a fresh bowl of tobacco, while he pursued: "Yes, yes: you worship your aristocracy. It is notorious. You have a sort of sagacity. I am not prepared to contest the statement that you have a political instinct. Here it is chiefly social. You worship your so-called aristocracy perforce in order to preserve an ideal of contrast to the vulgarity of the nation."

This was downright insolence.

It was intolerable. I jumped on my feet. "The weapons I would use in reply to such remarks I cannot address to you, Herr Professor. Therefore, excuse me."

He sent out quick spirts of smoke rolling into big volumes. "Nay, my good young Englishman, but on the other hand you have not answered me. And hear me: yes, you have shown us a representation of freedom. True. But you are content with it in a world that moves by computation some considerable sum upwards of sixty thousand miles an hour."

"Not on a fresh journey—a recurring course!" said I.

"Good!" he applauded, and I was flattered,

"I grant you the physical illustration," the Professor continued, and with a warm gaze on me, I thought. "The mind journeys somewhat in that way, and we in our old Germany hold that the mind advances notwithstanding. Astronomers condescending to earthly philosophy may admit that advance in the physical universe is computable, though not perceptible. Somewhither we tend, shell and spirit. You English, fighting your little battles of domestic policy, and sneering at us for flying at higher game,—you unimpressionable English, who won't believe in the existence of aims that don't drop on the ground before your eyes, and squat and stare at you, you assert that man's labour is completed when the poor are kept from crying out. Now my question is, have you a scheme of life consonant with the spirit of modern philosophy—with the views of intelligent, moral, humane human beings of this period? Or are you one of your robust English brotherhood worthy of a Caligula in his prime, lions in gymnastics—for a time; sheep always in the dominions of mind; and all of one pattern, all in a rut! Favour me with an outline of your ideas. Pour them out pell-mell, intelligibly, or not, no matter. I undertake to catch you somewhere. I mean to know you, hark you, rather with your assistance than without it."

We were deep in the night. I had not a single idea ready for delivery. I could have told him that wishing was a good thing, excess of tobacco a bad, moderation in speech one of the outward evidences of wisdom; but Ottilia's master in the Humanities exacted civility from me.

"Indeed," I said, "I have few thoughts to communicate at present, Herr Professor. My German will fail me as soon as I quit common ground. I love my country, and I do not reckon it as perfect. We are swillers, possibly gluttons; we have a large prosperous middle class; many good men are to be found in it."

His discharges of smoke grew stifling. My advocacy was certainly of a miserable sort.

"Yes, Herr Professor, on my way when a boy to this very place I met a thorough good man."

Here I relate the tale of my encounter with Captain Welsh.

Dr. Julius nodded rapidly for continuations. Further! further!

He refused to dig at the mine within me, and seemed to expect it to unbosom its riches by explosion.

" Well, Herr Professor, we have conquered India, and hold it as no other people could."

" *Vide* the articles in the last file of English newspapers! " said he.

" Suppose we boast of it—— "

" Can you ? " he simulated wonderment.

" Why, surely it's something ! "

" Something for non-commissioned officers to boast of; not

for statesmen.   However, say that you are fit to govern Asiatics.   Go on."

" I would endeavour to equalize ranks at home, encourage the growth of ideas . . . ."

" Supporting a non-celibate clergy, and an intermingled aristocracy ?   Your endeavours, my good young man, will lessen like those of the man who employed a spade to uproot a rock.   It wants blasting.   Your married clergy and mer-chandized aristocracy are coils : they are the ivy about your social tree : you would resemble Laocoon in the throes, if one could imagine you anything of a heroic figure.   Forward."

In desperation I exclaimed, " It's useless !   I have not thought at all.   I have been barely educated.   I only know that I do desire with all my heart to know more, to be of some service."

" Now we are at the bottom, then ! " said he.

But I cried, " Stay ; let me beg you to tell me what you meant by calling me a most fortunate, or a most unfortunate young man."

He chuckled over his pipe-stem, " Aha !"

" How am I one or the other ?"

" By the weight of what you carry in your head."

" How by the weight ?"

He shot a keen look at me.   " The case, I suspect, is singular, and does not often happen to a youth.   You are fortunate if you have a solid and adventurous mind : most unfortunate if you are a mere sensational whipster.   There's an explanation that covers the whole.   I am as much in the dark as you are.   I do not say which of us two has the convex eye."

Protesting that I was unable to read riddles, though the heat of the one in hand made my frame glow, I entreated to have explicit words.   He might be in Ottilia's confidence, probing me—why not ?   Any question he chose to put to me, I said, I was ready to answer.

" But it's the questioner who unmasks," said he.

" Are we masked, Herr Professor.   I was not aware of it."

" Look within, and avoid lying."

He stood up.   " My nights," he remarked, " are not com-monly wasted in this manner.   We Germans use the night for work."

After a struggle to fling myself on his mercy and win his aid or counsel, I took his hand respectfully, and holding it, said, "I am unable to speak out. I would if it involved myself alqne."

"Yes, yes, I comprehend; your country breeds honourable men, chivalrous youngsters," he replied. "It's not enough— not enough. I want to see a mental force, energy of brain. If you had that, you might look as high as you liked for the match for it, with my consent. Do you hear? What I won't have is, flat robbery! Mark me, Germany or Eng- land, it's one to me if I see vital powers in the field running to a grand career. It's a fine field over there. As well there as here, then! But better here than there if it's to be a wasp's life. Do you understand me?"

I replied, "I think I do, if I may dare to;" and catching breath: "Herr Professor, dear friend, forgive my boldness; grant me time to try me; don't judge of me at once; take me for your pupil—am I presumptuous in asking it?—make of me what you will, what you can; examine me; you may find there's more in me than I or anybody may know. I have thoughts and aims, feeble at present—— Good God! I see nothing for me but a choice of the two—'most unfortunate' seems likeliest. You read at a glance that I had no other choice. Rather the extremes!—I would rather grasp the limits of life and be swung to the pits below, be the' most unfortunate of human beings, than never to have aimed at a star. You laugh at me? An Englishman must be horribly in earnest to talk as I do now. But it is a star!" (The image of Ottilia sprang fountain-like into blue night heavens before my eyes memorably.) "She," was my next word. I swallowed it, and with a burning face, petitioned for help in my studies.

To such sight as I had at that instant he appeared laugh- ing outrageously. It was a composed smile. "Right," he said; "you shall have help in a settled course. Certain professors, friends of mine, at your University, will see you through it. Aim your head at a star—your head!—and even if you miss it you don't fall. It's that light dancer, that gambler, the heart in you, my good young man, which aims itself at inaccessible heights, and has the fall—some- what icy to reflect on! Give that organ full play and you may make sure of a handful of dust. Do you hear? It's a mind that wins a mind. That is why I warn you of being most unfortunate if you are a sensational whipster. Good-night. Shut my door fast that I may not have the trouble to rise."

I left him with the warm lamplight falling on his fore-head, and books piled and sloped, shut and open; an enviable picture to one in my condition. The peacefulness it indicated made scholarship seem beautiful, attainable, I hoped. I had the sense to tell myself that it would give me unrotting grain, though it should fail of being a practicable road to my bright star; and when I spurned at consolations for failure, I could still delight to think that she shone over these harvests and the reapers.

CHAPTER XXX.

A SUMMER STORM, AND LOVE.

THE foregoing conversations with Ottilia and her teacher, hard as they were for passion to digest, grew luminous on a relapsing heart. Without apprehending either their exact purport or the characters of the speakers, I was transformed by them from a state of craving to one of intense quietude. I thought neither of winning her, nor of aiming to win her, but of a foothold on the heights she gazed at reverently. And if, sometimes, seeing and hearing her, I thought, Oh, rarest soul! the wish was that brother and sisterhood of spirit might be ours. My other eager thirstful self I shook off like a thing worn out. Men in my confidence would have supposed me more rational: I was simply possessed.

My desire was to go into harness, buried in books, and for recreation to chase visions of original ideas for benefiting mankind. A clear-witted friend at my elbow, my dear Temple, perhaps, could have hit on the track of all this mental vagueness, but it is doubtful that he would have pushed me out of the strange mood, half stupor, half the folding-in of passion; it was such magical happiness. Not to be awake, yet vividly sensible; to lie calm and reflect, and only to reflect; be satisfied with each succeeding hour and the privations of the hour, and, as if in the depths of a

smooth water, to gather fold over patient fold of the sub-
merged self, safe from wounds; the happiness was not noble,
but it breathed and was harmless, and it gave me rest when
the alternative was folly and bitterness.

Visitors were coming to the palace to meet the prince, on
his return with my father from England. I went back to
the University, jealous of the invasion of my ecstatic calm
by new faces, and jealous when there of the privileges those
new faces would enjoy; and then, how my recent deadness
of life cried out against me as worse than a spendthrift, a
destroyer! a nerveless absorbent of the bliss showered on
me—the light of her morning presence when, just before
embracing, she made her obeisance to the margravine, and
kindly saluted me, and stooped her forehead for the baroness
to kiss it; her gestures and her voice; her figure on horseback, with old Warhead following, and I meeting her but
once!—her walk with the Professor, listening to his instructions—I used to see them walking up and down the cypress
path of the villa garden, her ear given to him wholly as she
continued her grave step, and he shuffling and treading out
of his line across hers, or on the path-borders, and never
apologizing, nor she noticing it. At night she sang, sometimes mountain ditties to the accompaniment of the zither,
leaning on the table and sweeping the wires between snatches
of talk. Nothing haunted me so much as those tones of her
zither, which were little louder than summer gnats when
fireflies are at their brightest and storm impends.

My father brought horses from England, and a couple of
English grooms, and so busy an air of cheerfulness that I
had, like a sick invalid, to beg him to keep away from me
and prolong unlimitedly his visit to Sarkeld; the rather so,
as he said he had now become indispensable to the prince
besides the margravine. " Only, no more bronze statues!"
I adjured him. He nodded. He had hired Count Fretzel's
château, in the immediate neighbourhood, and was absolutely independent, he said. His lawyers were busy procuring evidence. He had impressed Prince Ernest with a
due appreciation of the wealth of a young English gentleman by taking him over my grandfather's mine.

" And, Richie, we have advanced him a trifle of thousands
for the working of this coal discovery of his. In six weeks
our schooner yacht will be in the Elbe to offer him enter-

tainment. He graciously deigns to accept a couple of
English hunters at our hands; we shall improve his breed
of horses, I suspect. Now, Richie, have I done well? I
flatter myself I have been attentive to your interests, have I
not?"

He hung waiting for confidential communications on my
part, but did not press for them; he preserved an unvarying
delicacy in that respect.

"You have nothing to tell?" he asked.

"Nothing," I said. "I have only to thank you."

He left me. At no other period of our lives were we so
disunited. I felt in myself the reverse of everything I
perceived in him, and such letters as I wrote to the squire
consequently had a homelier tone. It seems that I wrote of
the pleasures of simple living—of living for learning's sake.
Mr. Peterborough at the same time despatched praises of my
sobriety of behaviour and diligent studiousness, confessing
that I began to outstrip him in some of the higher branches.
The squire's brief reply breathed satisfaction, but too evidently on the point where he had been led to misconceive
the state of affairs. " He wanted to have me near him, as
did another person whom I appeared to be forgetting; he
granted me another year's leave of absence, bidding me
bluffly not to be a bookworm and forget I was an Englishman." The idea that I was deceiving him never entered my
mind.

I was deceiving everybody, myself in the bargain, as a
man must do when in chase of a woman above him in rank.
The chase necessitates deceit—who knows? chicanery of a
sort as well; it brings inevitable humiliations; such that
ever since the commencement of it at speed I could barely
think of my father with comfort, and rarely met him with
pleasure. With what manner of face could I go before the
prince or the margravine, and say, I am an English commoner, the son of a man of doubtful birth, and I claim the
hand of the princess? What contortions were not in store
for these features of mine! Even as affairs stood now,
could I make a confidant of Temple and let him see me
through the stages of the adventure? My jingling of verses,
my fretting about the signification of flowers, and trifling
with symbols, haunted me excruciatingly, taunting me with
I know not what abject vileness of spirit.

In the midst of these tortures an arrow struck me, in the
shape of an anonymous letter, containing one brief line :
" The princess is in need of help."

I threw my books aside, and repaired to Count Fretzel's
château, from which, happily, my father was absent ; but
the countenance of the princess gave me no encouragement
to dream I could be of help to her ; yet a second unsigned
note worded in a quaint blunt manner, insisted that it was
to me she looked.   I chanced to hear the margravine,
addressing Baroness Turckems, say : " The princess's betrothal," what further, escaped me.   Soon after, I heard
that Prince Otto was a visitor at the lake-palace.   My
unknown correspondent plied me a third time.

I pasted the scrap in my neglected book of notes and
reflections, where it had ample space and about equal lucidity.
It drew me to the book, nearly driving me desperate ; I was
now credulous of anything, except that the princess cared
for help from me.   I resolved to go home ; I had no longer
any zeal for study.   The desolation of the picture of
England in my mind grew congenial.   It became imperative
that I should go somewhere, for news arrived of my father's
approach with a French company of actors, and deafening
entertainments were at hand.   On the whole, I thought it
decent to finish my course at the University, if I had not
quite lost the power of getting into the heart of books.   One
who studies is not being a fool : that is an established truth.
I thanked Dr. Julius for planting it among my recollections.
The bone and marrow of study form the surest antidote to
the madness of that light gambler, the heart, and distasteful
as books were, I had gained the habit of sitting down to
them, which was as good as an instinct toward the right
medicine, if it would but work.

On an afternoon of great heat I rode out for a gaze at the
lake-palace, that I chose to fancy might be the last, fore-
seeing the possibility of one of my fits of movement coming
on me before sunset.   My very pulses throbbed " away !"
Transferring the sense of overwhelming heat to my moral
condition, I thought it the despair of silliness to stay baking
in that stagnant place, where the sky did nothing but shine,
gave nothing forth.   The sky was bronze, a vast furnace dome.
The folds of light and shadow everywhere were satin-rich ;
shadows perforce of blackness had light in them, and the

light a sword-like sharpness over their edges. It was inanimate radiance. The laurels sparkled as with frost-points; the denser foliage dropped burning brown : a sickly saint's-ring was round the heads of the pines. That afternoon the bee hummed of thunder, and refreshed the ear.

I pitied the horse I rode, and the dog at his heels, but for me the intensity was inspiriting. Nothing lay in the light, I had the land to myself. "What hurts *me?*" I thought. My physical pride was up, and I looked on the cattle in black corners of the fields, and here and there a man tumbled anyhow, a wreck of limbs, out of the insupportable glare, with an even glance. Not an eye was lifted on me.

I saw nothing that moved until a boat shot out of the bight of sultry lake-water, lying close below the dark promontory where I had drawn rein. The rower was old Schwartz Warhead. How my gorge rose at the impartial brute! He was rowing the princess and a young man in uniform across the lake.

That they should cross from unsheltered paths to close covert was reasonable conduct at a time when the vertical rays of the sun were fiery arrow-heads. As soon as they were swallowed in the gloom I sprang in my saddle with torture, transfixed by one of the coarsest shafts of hideous jealousy. Off I flew, tearing through dry underwood, and round the bend of the lake, determined to confront her, wave the man aside, and have my last word with the false woman. Of the real Ottilia I had lost conception. Blood was inflamed, brain bare of vision : "He takes her hand, she jumps from the boat; he keeps her hands, she feigns to withdraw it, all woman to him in her eyes : they pass out of sight." A groan burst from me. I strained my crazy imagination to catch a view of them under cover of the wood and torture myself trebly, but it was now blank, shut fast. Sitting bolt upright, panting on horseback in the yellow green of one of the open woodways, I saw the young officer raise a branch of chestnut and come out. He walked moodily up to within a yard of my horse, looked up at me, and with an angry stare that grew to be one of astonishment, said,—"Ah ? I think I have had the pleasure—somewhere ? in Würtemberg, if I recollect."

It was Prince Otto. I dismounted. He stood alone. The

spontaneous question on my lips would have been "Where is she?" but I was unable to speak a word.

"English?" he said, patting the horse's neck.

"Yes—the horse? an English hunter. How are you, Prince Otto? Do you like the look of him?"

"Immensely. You know we have a passion for English thoroughbreds. Pardon me, you look as if you had been close on a sunstroke. Do you generally take rides in this weather?"

"I was out by chance. If you like him, pray take him; take him. Mount him and try him. He is yours if you care to have him; if he doesn't suit you send him up to Count Fretzel's. I've had riding enough in the light."

"Perhaps you have," said he, and hesitated. "It's difficult to resist the offer of such a horse. If you want to dispose of him, mention it when we meet again. Shall I try him? I have a slight inclination to go as hard as you have been going, but he shall have good grooming in the prince's stables, and that's less than half as near again as Count Fretzel's place; and a horse like this ought not to be out in this weather, if you will permit me the remark."

"No: I'm ashamed of bringing him out, and shan't look on him with satisfaction," said I. "Take him and try him, and then take him from me, if you don't mind."

"Do you know, I would advise your lying down in the shade awhile?" he observed, solicitously. "I have seen men on the march in Hungary and Italy. An hour's rest under cover would have saved them."

I thanked him.

"Ice is the thing!" he ejaculated. "I'll ride and have some fetched to you. Rest here."

With visible pleasure he swung to the saddle. I saw him fix his cavalry thighs and bound off as if he meant to take a gate. Had he glanced behind him he would have fancied that the sun had done its worst. I ran at full speed down the footpath, mad to think she might have returned homeward by the lake. The two had parted—why? He this way, she that. They would not have parted but for a division of the will. I came on the empty boat. Schwartz lay near it beneath heavy boughs, smoking and perspiring in peace. Neither of us spoke. And it was now tempered by a fit of alarm that I renewed my search. So when I beheld her, intense gratitude broke my passion; when I touched her hand it was trembling for absolute assurance of her safety. She was leaning against a tree, gazing on the ground, a white figure in that iron-moted gloom.

" Otto !" she cried, shrinking from the touch ; but at sight of me, all softly as a sight in the heavens, her face melted in a suffusion of wavering smiles, and deep colour shot over them, heavenly to see. She pressed her bosom while I spoke :—a lover's speech, breathless.

" You love me ?" she said.

My fingers tightened on her wrist,—

" You have known it !"

" Yes, yes !"

" Forgiven me ? Speak, princess."

" Call me by my name."

" My own soul ! Ottilia !"

She disengaged her arms tenderly.

" I have known it by my knowledge of myself," she said, breathing with her lips dissevered. " My weakness has come upon me. Yes, I love you. It is spoken. It is too true. Is it a fate that brings us together when I have just lost my little remaining strength—all power ? You hear me ! I pretend to wisdom, and talk of fate !"

She tried to laugh in scorn of herself, and looked at me with almost a bitter smile on her features, made beautiful by her soft eyes. I feared from the helpless hanging of her underlip that she would swoon ; a shudder convulsed her ; and at the same time I became aware of the blotting out of sunlight, and a strange bowing and shore-like noising of the forest.

" Do not heed me," she said in happy undertones. " I think I am going to cry like a girl. One cannot see one's pride die like this, without—— but it is not anguish of any kind. Since we are here together, I would have no other change."

She spoke till the tears came thick.

I told her of the letters I had received, warning me of a trouble besetting her. They were, perhaps, the excuse for my conduct, if I had any.

Schwartz burst on us with his drill-sergeant's shout for the princess. Standing grey in big rain-drops he was an object of curiosity to us both. He came to take her orders.

"The thunder," he announced, raising a telegraphic arm,
"rolls. It rains. We have a storm. Command me, princess! your highness!"

Ottilia's eyelids were set blinking by one look aloft. Rain
and lightning filled heaven and earth.

"Direct us, you!" she said to me gently.

The natural proposition was to despatch her giant by the
direct way down the lake to fetch a carriage from the stables,
or matting from the boathouse. I mentioned it, but did not
press it.

She meditated an instant. "I believe I may stay with
my beloved?"

Schwartz and I ran to the boat, hauled it on land, and set
it keel upward against a low leafy dripping branch. To
this place of shelter, protecting her as securely as I could, I
led the princess, while Schwartz happed a rough trench
around it with one of the sculls. We started him on foot to
do the best thing possible; for the storm gave no promise
that it was a passing one. In truth, I knew that I should
have been the emissary and he the guard; but the storm
overhead was not fuller of its mighty burden than I of mine.
I looked on her as mine for the hour, and well won.

CHAPTER XXXI.

PRINCESS OTTILIA'S LETTER.

THAT hour of tempest went swift as one of its flashes over
our little nest of peace, where we crouched like insects. The
lightning and the deluge seemed gloriously endless. Ottilia's
harbouring nook was dry within an inch of rushing floods
and pattered mire. On me the torrents descended, and her
gentle efforts drew me to her side, as with a maternal claim
to protect me, or to perish in my arms if the lightning found
us. We had for prospect an ever-outbursting flame of
foliage, and the hubbub of the hissing lake, crimson, purple,
dusky grey, like the face of a passionate creature scourged.
It was useless to speak. Her lips were shut, but I had the
intent kindness of her eyes on me almost unceasingly.

The good hour slipped away. Old Warhead's splashed knees on the level of our heads were seen by us when the thunder had abated. Ottilia prepared to rise.

"You shall hear from me," she said, bending with brows measuring the boat-roof, like a bird about to fly.

"Shall I see you?"

"Ultimately you surely will. Ah! still be patient."

"Am I not? have I not been?"

"Yes; and can you regret it?"

"No; but we separate!"

"Would you have us be two feet high for ever?" she answered smiling.

"One foot high, or under earth, if it might be together!"

"Poor little gnomes!" said she.

The homeliness of our resting-place arrested her for an instant, and perhaps a touch of comic pity for things of such diminutive size as to see nothing but knees where a man stood. Our heads were hidden.

"Adieu! no pledge is needed," she said tenderly.

"None!" I replied.

She returned to the upper world with a burning blush.

Schwartz had borne himself with extraordinary discretion by forbearing to spread alarm at the palace. He saluted his young mistress in the regulation manner while receiving her beneath a vast umbrella, the holiday peasant's invariable companion in these parts. A forester was in attendance carrying shawls, clogs, and matting. The boat was turned and launched.

"Adieu, Harry Richmond. Will you be quite patient till you hear from me?" said Ottilia, and added, "It is my question!" delightfully recalling old times.

I was soon gazing at the track of the boat in rough water.

Shouts were being raised somewhere about the forest, and were replied to by hearty bellow of the rower's lungs. She was now at liberty to join my name to her own or not, as she willed. I had to wait. But how much richer was I than all the world! The future owed me nothing. I would have registered a vow to ask nothing of it. Among the many determined purposes framing which I walked home, was one to obtain a grant of that bit of land where we had sat together, and build a temple on it. The fear that it might be trodden by feet of men before I had enclosed it beset me with anguish. The most absolute pain I suffered sprang from a bewildering incapacity to conjure up a vision of Ottilia free of the glittering accessories of her high birth; and that was the pain of shame; but it came only at intervals, when pride stood too loftily and the shadow of possible mischance threatened it with the axe.

She did not condemn me to long waiting. Her favourite Aennchen brought me her first letter. The girl's face beamed, and had a look as if she commended me for a worthy deed.

"An answer, Aennchen?" I asked her.

"Yes, yes!" said she anxiously; "but it will take more time than I can spare." She appointed a meeting near the palace garden-gates at night.

I chose a roof of limes to read under.

"Noblest and best beloved!" the princess addressed me in her own tongue, doubting, I perceived, as her training had taught her, that my English eyes would tolerate apostrophes of open-hearted affection. The rest was her English confided to a critic who would have good reason to be merciful:—

"The night has come that writes the chapter of the day. My father has had his interview with his head-forester to learn what has befallen from the storm in the forest. All has not been told him! That shall not be delayed beyond to-morrow

"I am hurried to it. And I had the thought that it hung perhaps at the very end of my life among the coloured leaves, the strokes of sunset—that then it would be known! or if earlier, distant from this strange imperative Now. But we have our personal freedom now, and I have learnt from minutes what I did mean to seek from years, and from our forest what I hoped that change of scene, travel, experience, would teach me. Yet I was right in my intention. It was a discreet and a just meaning I had. For things will not go smoothly for him at once: he will have his hard battle. *He* is proved: *he* has passed his most brave ordeal. But I! Shall I see him put to it and not certainly know myself? Even thus I reasoned. One cannot study without knowing that our human nature is most frail. Daily the body changes, daily the mind—why not the heart? I did design to travel and converse with various persons.

" Pardon it to one who knew that she would require super-feminine power of decision to resolve that she would dispose of herself!

"I heard of Harry Richmond before I saw him. My curiosity to behold the two fair boys of the sailor kingdom set me whipping my pony after them that day so remote, which is always yesterday. My thoughts followed you, and I wondered—does he mean to be a distinguished countryman of his Nelson? or a man of learning? Then many an argument with 'my professor,' until—for so it will ever be—the weaker creature did succumb in the open controversy, and thought her thoughts to herself. Contempt of England gained on me still. But when I lay withered, though so young, by the sea-shore, his country's ancient grandeur insisted, and I dreamed of Harry Richmond, imagining that I had been false to my childhood. You stood before me, dearest. You were kind : you were strong, and had a gentle voice. Our souls were caught together on the sea. Do you recollect my slip in the speaking of Lucy Sibley's marriage? —'We change countries.' At that moment I smelt salt air, which would bring you to my sight and touch were you and I divided let me not think how far.

"To-morrow I tell the prince, my father, that I am a plighted woman. Then for us the struggle, for him the grief. I have to look on him and deal it.

" I can refer him to Dr. Julius for my estimate of my husband's worth.

" 'My professor' was won by it. He once did incline to be the young bold Englishman's enemy. 'Why is he here? what seeks he among us?' It was his jealousy, not of the man, but of the nation, which would send one to break and bear away his carefully cultivated German lily. No eye but his did read me through. And you endured the trial that was forced on you. You made no claim for recompense when it was over. No, there is no pure love but strong love! It belongs to our original elements, and of its purity should never be question, only of its strength.

" I could not help you when you were put under scrutiny before the margravine and the baroness. Help from me would have been the betrayal of both. The world has accurate eyes, if they are not very penetrating. The world will see a want of balance immediately, and also too true a balance, but it will not detect a depth of concord between two souls that do not show some fretfulness on the surface.

"So it was considered that in refusing my cousin Otto and other proposed alliances, I was heart-free. An instructed princess, they thought, was of the woeful species of woman. You left us : I lost you. I heard you praised for civil indifference to me—the one great quality you do not possess! Then it was the fancy of people that I, being very cold, might be suffered to hear my cousin plead for himself. The majority of our family favour Otto. He was permitted to woo me as though I had been a simple maid; and henceforth shall I have pity for all poor little feminine things who are so persecuted, asked to inflict cruelty—to take a sword and strike with it. But I—who look on marriage as more than a surrender—I could well withstand surpassing eloquence. It was easy to me to be inflexible in speech and will when I stood there, entreated to change myself. But when came magically the other, who is my heart, my voice, my mate, the half of me, and broke into illumination of things long hidden—oh! then did I say to you that it was my weakness had come upon me ? It was my last outcry of self—the 'I' expiring. I am now yours, 'We' has long overshadowed 'I,' and now engulphs it. We are one. If it were new to me to find myself interrogating the mind of my beloved, relying on his courage, taking many proofs of his devotion, I might pause to re-peruse my words here, without scruple, written. I sign it, before heaven, your Ottilia.

"OTTILIA FREDERIKA WILHELMINA HEDWIG,
"*Princess of Eppenwelzen-Sarkeld.*"

CHAPTER XXXII.

AN INTERVIEW WITH PRINCE ERNEST AND A MEETING WITH PRINCE OTTO.

A MESSENGER from Prince Ernest commanding my immediate attendance at the palace signified that the battle had begun. I could have waited for my father, whose return from one of his expeditions in the prince's service was expected every instant; but though I knew I should have had a powerful coadjutor in him to assist me through such a conference, I preferred to go down alone. Prince Otto met me in the hall. He passed by, glancing an eye sharply, and said over his shoulder,—

"We shall have a word together presently!"

The library door was flung open. Prince Ernest and the margravine were in the room. She walked out with angry majesty. The prince held his figure in the stiff attitude of reception. He could look imposing.

The character of the interview was perceptible at once.

"You have not, I presume, to be informed of the business in hand, Mr. Richmond!"

"Your Highness, I believe I can guess it."

This started him pacing the floor.

"An impossibility! a monstrous extravagance! a thing unheard of! mania! mania!" he muttered. "You are aware, sir, that you have been doing your worst to destroy the settled arrangements of my family? What does it mean? In common reason you cannot indulge any legitimate hope of succeeding. Taking you as a foreigner, you must know that. Judge of the case by your own reigning Families. Such events never happen amongst them. Do you suppose that the possession of immense wealth entitles you to the immeasurable presumption of aspiring to equality of position with reigning Houses? Such folly is more frequently castigated than reasoned with. Why, now—now, were it published that I had condescended—condescend as I am doing, I should be the laughing-stock of every Court in Europe. You English want many lessons. You are taught by your scribes to despise the dignity which is not supported by a multitude of bayonets, guns, and gold. I heard of it when I travelled incognito. You make merry over little potentates. Good. But do not cross their paths. Their dominion may be circumscribed, but they have it; and where we are now, my power equals that of the Kaiser and the Czar. You will do me the favour to understand that I am not boasting, not menacing; I attempt, since it is extraordinarily imposed on me, to instruct you. I have cause to be offended; I waive it. I meet you on common ground, and address myself to your good sense. Have you anything to say?"

" Much, sir."

" Much ?" he said, with affected incredulity.

The painful hardship for me was to reply in the vague terms he had been pleased to use.

" I have much to say, your Highness.   First, to ask pardon of you, without excusing myself."

" A condition, apparently, that absolves the necessity for the grant.   Speak precisely."

But I was as careful as he in abstaining from any direct indication of his daughter's complicity, and said, "I have offended your Highness.   You have done me the honour to suggest that it is owing to my English training.   You will credit my assurance that the offence was not intentional, not preconceived."

" You charge it upon your having been trained among a nation of shopkeepers ?"

" My countrymen are not illiterate or unmannerly, your Highness."

" I have not spoken it ; I may add, I do not think it."

" I feared that your Highness entertained what I find to be a very general, perhaps here and there wilful, error with regard to England."

" When I was in the service I had a comrade, a gallant gentleman, deeply beloved by me, and he was an Englishman. He died in the uniform and under the flag I reverence."

" I rejoice that your Highness has had this experience of us.   I have to imagine that I expressed myself badly.   My English training certainly does not preclude the respect due to exalted rank.   Your Highness will, I trust humbly, pardon my offence.   I do not excuse myself because I cannot withdraw, and I am incapable of saying that I regret it."

" In cool blood you utter that ?" exclaimed the prince.

His amazement was unfeigned.

" What are the impossible, monstrous ideas you —— where —— ?   Who leads you to fancy there is one earthly chance for you when you say you cannot withdraw ?   Cannot ?   Are you requested ?   ·Are you consulted ?   It is a question to be decided in the imperative : you must.   What wheel it is you think you have sufficient vigour to stop, I am profoundly unaware, but I am prepared to affirm that it is not the wheel of my household.   I would declare it, were I a plain citizen.   You are a nullity in the case, in point of your individual will—a nullity swept away with one wave of the hand. You can do this, and nothing else: you can apologize, recognize your station, repair a degree of mischief that I will not say was preconceived or plotted. So for awhile pursue your studies, your travels. In time it will give me pleasure to receive you. Mr. Richmond," he added, smiling and rising; " even the head of a little German principality has to give numberless audiences." His features took a more cordial smile to convince me that the dismissing sentence was merely playful.

As for me, my mind was confused by the visible fact that the father's features resembled the daughter's. I mention it that my mind's condition may be understood.

Hardly had I been bowed out of the room when my father embraced me, and some minutes later I heard Prince Otto talking to me and demanding answers. That he or any one else should have hostile sentiments toward a poor devil like me seemed strange. My gift of the horse appeared to anger him most. I reached the château without once looking back, a dispirited wretch. I shut myself up; I tried to read. The singular brevity of my interview with the prince, from which I had expected great if not favourable issues, affected me as though I had been struck by a cannon shot; my brains were nowhere. His perfect courtesy was confounding. I was tormented by the delusion that I had behaved pusillanimously.

My father rushed up to me after dark. Embracing me and holding me by the hand, he congratulated me with his whole heart. The desire of his life was accomplished; the thing he had plotted for ages had come to pass. He praised me infinitely. My glorious future, he said, was to carry a princess to England and sit among the highest there, the husband of a lady peerless in beauty and in birth, who, in addition to what she was able to do for me by way of elevation in my country, could ennoble in her own territory. I had the option of being the father of English nobles or of German princes; so forth. I did not like the strain; yet I clung to him. I was compelled to ask whether he had news of any sort worth hearing.

" None," said he calmly; " none. I have everything to hear, nothing to relate; and, happily, I can hardly speak for joy." He wept.

He guaranteed to have the margravine at the château within a week, which seemed to me a sufficient miracle. The prince, he said, might require three months of discretionary treatment. Three further months to bring the family round, and the princess would be mine. "But she is yours! she is yours already!" he cried authoritatively. "She is the reigning intellect there. I dreaded her very intellect would give us all the trouble, and behold, it is our ally! The prince lives with an elbow out of his income. But for me it would be other parts of his person as well, I assure you, and the world would see such a princely tatterdemalion as would astonish it. Money to him is important. He must carry on his mine. He can carry on nothing without my help. By the way, we have to deal out cheques?"

I assented.

In spite of myself, I caught the contagion of his exuberant happiness and faith in his genius. The prince had applauded his energetic management of the affairs of the mine two or three times in my hearing. It struck me that he had really found his vocation, and would turn the sneer on those who had called him volatile and reckless. This led me to a luxurious sense of dependence on him, and I was willing to live on dreaming and amused, though all around me seemed phantoms, especially the French troupe, the flower of the Parisian stage: Regnault, Carigny, Desbarolles, Mesdames Blanche Bignet and Dupertuy, and Mdlle. Jenny Chassediane, the most spirituelle of Frenchwomen. "They are a part of our enginery, Richie," my father said. They proved to be an irresistible attraction to the margravine. She sent word to my father that she meant to come on a particular day when, as she evidently knew, I should not be present. Two or three hours later I had Prince Otto's cartel in my hands. Jorian DeWitt, our guest at this season, told me subsequently, and with the utmost seriousness, that I was largely indebted to Mdlle. Jenny for a touching French song of a beau chevalier she sang before Ottilia in my absence. Both he and my father believed in the efficacy of this kind of enginery, but, as the case happened, the beau chevalier was down low enough at the moment his high-born lady listened to the song.

It appeared that when Prince Otto met me after my interview with Prince Ernest, he did his best to provoke a rencontre, and failing to get anything but a nod from my stunned head, betook himself to my University. A friendly young fellow there, Eckart vom Hof, offered to fight him on my behalf, should I think proper to refuse. Eckart and two or three others made a spirited stand against the aristocratic party siding with Prince Otto, whose case was that I had played him a dishonourable trick to laugh at him. I had, in truth, persuaded him to relieve me at once of horse and rival at the moment when he was suffering the tortures of a rejection, and I was rushing to take the hand he coveted; I was so far guilty. But to how great a degree guiltless, how could I possibly explain to the satisfaction of an angry man? I had the vision of him leaping on the horse, while I perused his challenge; saw him fix to the saddle and smile hard, and away to do me of all services the last he would have performed wittingly. The situation was exactly of a sort for one of his German phantasy-writers to image the forest jeering at him as he flew, blind, deaf, and unreasonable, vehement for one fierce draught of speed. We are all dogged by the humour of following events when we start on a wind of passion. I could almost fancy myself an accomplice. I realized the scene with such intensity in the light running at his heels: it may be quite true that I laughed in the hearing of his messenger as I folded up the letter. That was the man's report. I am not commonly one to be forgetful of due observances.

The prospect of the possible eternal separation from my beloved pricked my mechanical wits and set them tracing the consequent line by which I had been brought to this pass as to a natural result. Had not my father succeeded in inspiring the idea that I was something more than something? The tendency of young men is to conceive it for themselves without assistance; a prolonged puff from the breath of another is nearly sure to make them mad as kings, and not so pardonably.

I see that I might have acted wisely, and did not; but that is a speculation taken apart from my capabilities. If a man's fate were as a forbidden fruit, detached from him, and in front of him, he might hesitate fortunately before plucking it; but, as most of us are aware, the vital half of it lies in the seed-paths he has traversed. We are sons of yesterday, not of the morning. The past is our mortal mother, no

dead thing. Our future constantly reflects her to the soul.
Nor is it e er the new man of to-day which grasps his
fortune, good or ill. We are pushed to it by the hundreds
of days we have buried, eager ghosts. And if you have not
the habit of taking counsel with them, you are but an
instrument in their hands.

My English tongue admonishes me that I have fallen
upon a tone resembling one who uplifts the finger of piety in
a salon of conversation. A man's review of the course of
his life grows for a moment stringently serious when he
beholds the stream first broadening perchance under the
light interpenetrating mine just now.

My seconds were young Eckart vom Hof, and the barely
much older, though already famous Gregorius Bandelmeyer,
a noted mathematician, a savage Republican, lean-faced,
spectacled, and long, soft-fingered; a cat to look at, a tiger to
touch. Both of them were animated by detestation of the
Imperial uniform. They distrusted my skill in the management of the weapon I had chosen; for reasons of their own
they carried a case of pistols to the field. Prince Otto was
attended by Count Loepel and a Major Edelsheim of his
army, fresh from the garrison fortress of Mainz, gentlemen
perfectly conversant with the laws of the game, which my
worthy comrades were not. Several minutes were spent in
an altercation between Edelsheim and Bandelmeyer. The
major might have had an affair of his own had he pleased.
My feelings were concentrated within the immediate ring
where I stood : I can compare them only to those of a
gambler determined to throw his largest stake and abide the
issue. I was not open to any distinct impression of the
surrounding scenery; the hills and leafage seemed to wear
an iron aspect. My darling, my saint's face was shut up in
my heart, and with it a little inaudible cry of love and pain.
The prince declined to listen to apologies. "He meant to
teach me that this was not a laughing matter." Major
Edelsheim had misunderstood Bandelmeyer; no offer of an
apology had been made. A momentary human sensation of
an unworthy sort beset me when I saw them standing together again, and contrasted the collectedness and good-humour
of my adversary's representative with the vexatious and
unnecessary naggling of mine, the sight of whose yard-long
pipe scandalized me.

At last the practical word was given. The prince did not reply to my salute. He was smoking, and kept his cigar in one corner of his mouth, as if he were a master fencer bidding his pupil to come on. He assumed that he had to do with a **bou**rgeois Briton unused to arms, such as we are generally held to be on the Continent. After feeling my wrist for a while he shook the cigar out of his teeth.

The 'cliquetis' of the crossed steel must be very distant in memory, and yourself in a most dilettante frame of mind, for you to be accessible to the music of that thin skeleton's clank. Nevertheless it is better and finer even at the time of action, than the abominable hollow ogre's eye of the pistol-muzzle. We exchanged passes, the prince chiefly attacking. Of all the things to strike my thoughts, can you credit me that the vividest was the picture of the old woman Temple and I had seen in our boyhood on the night of the fire dropping askew, like forks of brown flame, from the burning house in London city; I must have smiled. The prince cried out in French : " Laugh, sir; you shall have it !" He had nothing but his impetuosity for an assurance of his promise, and was never able to force me back beyond a foot. I touched him on the arm and the shoulder, and finally pierced his arm above the elbow. I could have done nearly what I liked with him; his skill was that of a common regimental sabreur.

" Ludere qui nescit campestribus abstinet armis !" Bandel-meyer sang out.

" You observed ?" said Major Edelsheim, and received another disconcerting discharge of a Latin line. The prince frowned and made use of some military slang. Was his honour now satisfied ? Not a whit. He certainly could not have kept his sword-point straight, and yet he clamoured to fight on, stamped, and summoned me to assault him, pro-posed to fight me with his left hand after his right had failed; in short, he was beside himself, an example of the predicament of a man who has given all the provocation and finds himself disabled. My seconds could have stopped it had they been equal to their duties; instead of which Bandelmeyer, hearing what he deemed an insult to the order of student and scholar, retorted furiously and offen-sively, and Eckart, out of good-fellowship, joined him. whereat, Major Edelsheim, in the act of bandaging the prince's arm, warned them that he could not pass by an outrage on his uniform. Count Loepel stept politely forward, and gave Eckart a significant bow. The latter remarked mockingly, " With pleasure and condescension !" At a murmur of the name of doctor from Edelsheim, the prince damned the doctor until he or I were food for him. Irritated by the whole scene, and his extravagant vindictiveness, in which light I regarded the cloak of fury he had flung over the shame of his defeat, I called to Bandelmeyer to open his case of pistols and offer them for a settlement. As the proposal came from me it was found acceptable. The major remonstrated with the prince, and expressed to me his regrets and et ceteras of well-meant civility. He had a hard task to keep out of the hands of Bandelmeyer, who had seized my sword, and wanted vi et armis to defend the cause of Learning and the People against military brigands on the spot. If I had not fallen we should have had one or two other prostrate bodies.

A silly business on all sides.

CHAPTER XXXIII.

WHAT CAME OF A SHILLING.

THE surgeon, who attended us both, loudly admired our mutual delicacy in sparing arteries and vital organs : but a bullet cuts a rougher pathway than the neat steel blade, and I was prostrate when the prince came to press my hand on his departure for his quarters at Laibach. The utterly unreasonable nature of a duel was manifested by his declaring to me that he was now satisfied I did not mean to insult him and then laugh at him. We must regard it rather as a sudorific for feverish blood and brains. I felt my wound acutely, seeing his brisk step when he retired. Having overthrown me bodily, it threw my heart back to its first emotions, and I yearned to set eyes on my father, with a haunting sense that I had of late injured him and owed him reparation. It vanished after he had been in my room an hour, to return when he had quitted it, and incessantly and inexplicably it went and came in this manner. He was depressed. I longed for drollery, relieved only by chance allusions to my beloved one, whereas he could not conceal his wish to turn the stupid duel to account.

"Pencil a line to her," he entreated me, and dictated his idea of a moving line, adding urgently that the crippled letters would be affecting to her, as to the Great Frederick his last review of his invalid veterans. "Your name—the signature of your name alone, darling Richie," and he traced a crooked scrawl with a forefinger,—"'Still, dearest angel, in contempt of death and blood, I am yours to eternity, Harry Lepel Richmond, sometimes called Roy—a point for your decision in the future, should the breath everlastingly devoted to the most celestial of her sex, continue to animate the frame that would rise on wings to say adieu! adieu!'— Richie, just a sentence?"

He was distracting.

His natural tenderness and neatness of hand qualified him for spreading peace in a sick room; but he was too full of life and his scheme, and knowing me out of danger, he could not forbear giving his despondency an outlet. I heard him exclaim in big sighs: "Heavens! how near!" and again, "She must hear of it!" Never was man so incorrigibly dramatic.

He would walk up to a bookcase and take down a volume, when the interjectional fit waxed violent, flip the pages, affecting a perplexity he would assuredly have been struck by had he perused them, and read, as he did once,—"Italy, the land of the sun! and she is to be hurried away there, and we are left to groan. The conspiracy is infamous! One of the Family takes it upon himself to murder us! and she is to be hurried out of hearing! And so we are to have the blood of the Roys spilt for nothing?—no!" and he shut up the book with a report, and bounded to my side to beg pardon of me. From his particular abuse of the margravine, the iteration of certain phrases, which he uttered to denounce and defy them, I gathered that an interview had passed between the two, and that she had notified a blockade against all letters addressed to the princess. He half admitted having rushed to the palace on his road to me.

"But, Richie," said he, pressing me again to write the

moving line, "a letter with a broad black border addressed by *me* might pass." He looked mournfully astute. "The margravine might say to herself,—'Here's Doctor Death in full diploma come to cure the wench of her infatuation.' I am but quoting the coarse old woman, Richie; confusion on her and me! for I like her. It might pass in my hand-writing, with a smudge for paternal grief—it might. 'To Her Serene Highness the Margravine of Rippau, &c. &c. &c., in trust for the Most Exalted the Princess of Eppenwelzen-Sarkeld.' I transpose or omit a title or so. 'Aha!' says she, 'there's *verwirrung* in Roy's poor head, poor fellow; the boy has sunk to a certainty. Here (to the princess), it seems, my dear, this is for you. Pray do not communicate the contents for a day or so or a month.'"

His imitation of the margravine was the pleasantest thing I heard from him. The princess's maid and confidante, he regretted to state, was incorruptible, which I knew. That line of Ottilia's writing, "Violets are over," read by me in view of the root-mountain of the Royal House of Princes, scoffed at me insufferably whenever my father showed me these openings of his mind, until I was dragged down to think almost that I had not loved the woman and noble soul, but only the glorified princess—the carved gilt frame instead of the divine portrait! a shameful acrid suspicion, ransack-ing my conscience with the thrusting in of a foul torch here and there. For why had I shunned him of late? How was it that he tortured me now? Did I in no degree participate in the poignant savour of his scheme? Such questionings set me flushing in deadly chills. My brain was weak, my heart exhausted, my body seemed truthful perforce and con-fessed on the rack. I could not deny that I had partly, insensibly clung to the vain glitter of hereditary distinction, my father's pitfall; taking it for a substantial foothold, when a young man of wit and sensibility and, mark you, true pride, would have made it his first care to trample that under heel. Excellent is pride; but oh! be sure of its foun-dations before you go on building monument high. I know nothing to equal the anguish of an examination of the basis of one's pride that discovers it not solidly fixed; an imposing, self-imposing structure, piled upon empty cellarage. It will inevitably, like a tree striking bad soil, betray itself at the top with time. And the anguish I speak of will be the sole healthy sign about you. Whether in the middle of life it is adviseable to descend the pedestal altogether, I dare not say. Few take the precaution to build a flight of steps inside—it is not a labour to be proud of; fewer like to let themselves down in the public eye—it amounts to a castigation; you must, I fear, remain up there, and accept your chance in toppling over. But in any case, delude yourself as you please, your lofty baldness will assuredly be seen with time. Meanwhile, you cannot escape the internal intimations of your unsoundness. A man's pride is the front and head-piece of his character, his soul's support or snare. Look to it in youth. I have to thank the interminable hours on my wretched sick-bed for a singularly beneficial investigation of the ledger of my deeds and omissions and moral stock. Perhaps it has already struck you that one who takes the trouble to sit and write his history for as large a world as he can obtain, and shape his style to harmonize with every development of his nature, can no longer have much of the hard grain of pride in him. A proud puppet-showman blowing into Pandæan pipes is an inconceivable object, except to those who judge of characteristics from posture.

It began to be observed by others that my father was not the most comforting of nurses to me. My landlady brought a young girl up to my room, and introduced her under the name of Lieschen, saying that she had for a long time been interested in me, and had been diligent in calling to inquire for news of my condition. Commanded to speak for herself, this Lieschen coloured and said demurely, "I am in service here, sir, among good-hearted people, who will give me liberty to watch by you for three hours of the afternoon and three of the early part of the night, if you will honour me."

My father took her shoulder between finger and thumb, and slightly shook her to each ejaculation of his emphatic "No! no! no! no! What! a young maiden nurse to a convalescent young gentleman! Why, goodness gracious me! Eh?"

She looked at me softly, and I said I wished her to come.

My father appealed to the sagacity of the matron. So jealous was he of a suggested partner in his task that he had refused my earnest requests to have Mr. Peterborough to share the hours of watching by my side. The visits of college friends and acquaintances were cut very short, he soon reduced them to talk in a hush with thumbs and nods and eyebrows, and if it had not been so annoying to me, I could have laughed at his method of accustoming the regular visitors to make ready, immediately after greeting, for his affectionate dismissal of them. Lieschen went away with the mute blessing of his finger on one of her modest dimples; but, to his amazement, she returned in the evening. He gave her a lecture, to which she listened attentively, and came again in the morning. He was petrified. " Idiots, insects, women, and the salt sea ocean!" said he, to indicate a list of the untameables, without distressing the one present, and, acknowledging himself beaten, he ruefully accepted his holiday.

The girl was like sweet Spring in my room. She spoke of Sarkeld familiarly. She was born in that neighbourhood, she informed me, and had been educated by a dear great lady. Her smile of pleasure on entering the room one morning, and seeing me dressed and sitting in a grandfatherly chair by the breezy window, was like a salutation of returning health. My father made another stand against the usurper of his privileges; he refused to go out.

" Then must I go," said Lieschen, " for two are not allowed here."

" No! don't leave me," I begged of her, and stretched out my hands for hers, while she gazed sadly from the doorway. He suspected some foolishness or he was actually jealous. " Hum—oh!" He went forth with a murmured groan.

She deceived me by taking her seat in perfect repose. After smoothing her apron, " Now I must go," she said.

" What! to leave me here alone?"

She looked at the clock, and leaned out of the window.

" Not alone; oh, not alone!" the girl exclaimed. " And please, please do not mention me——presently. Hark! do you hear wheels? Your heart must not beat. Now farewell. You will not be alone: at least, so I think. See what I wear, dear Mr. Patient!" She drew from her bosom, attached to a piece of blue ribbon, the half of an English shilling, kissed it, and blew a soft farewell to me.

She had not been long gone when the Princess Ottilia stood in her place.

A shilling tossed by an English boy to a couple of little foreign girls in a woodman's hut!—you would not expect it to withstand the common fate of silver coins, and preserve mysterious virtues by living celibate, neither multiplying nor reduced, ultimately to play the part of a powerful magician in bringing the boy grown man to the feet of an illustrious lady, and her to his side in sickness, treasonably to the laws of her station. The little women quarrelled over it, and snatched and hid and contemplated it in secret, each in her turn, until the strife it engendered was put an end to by a doughty smith, their mother's brother, who divided it into equal halves, through which he drove a hole, and the pieces being now thrown out of the currency, each one wore her share of it in her bosom from that time, proudly appeased. They were not ordinary peasant children, and happily for them they had another friend that was not a bird of passage, and was endowed by nature and position to do the work of an angel. She had them educated to read, write, and knit, and learn pretty manners, and in good season she took one of the sisters to wait on her own person. The second went, upon her recommendation, into the household of a professor of a neighbouring University. But neither of them abjured her superstitious belief in the proved merits of the talisman she wore. So when they saw the careless giver again they remembered him; their gratitude was as fresh as on that romantic morning of their childhood, and they resolved without concert to serve him after their own fashion, and quickly spied a way to it. They were German girls.

You are now enabled to guess more than was known to Ottilia and me of the curious agency at work to shuffle us together. The doors of her suite in the palace were barred against letters addressed to the princess; the delivery of letters to her was interdicted, she consenting, yet she found one: it lay on the broad walk of the orange-trees, between one: it lay on the broad walk of the orange-trees, between the pleasure and the fruit-gardens, as if dropped by a falcon in mid air. Ottilia beheld it, and started. Her little maid walking close by, exclaimed, scuttling round in front of her the while like an urchin in sabots, "Ha! what is it? a snake? let me! let me!" The guileless mistress replied, "A letter!" Whereupon the maid said, "Not a window near! and no wall neither! Why, dearest princess, we have walked up and down here a dozen times and not seen it staring at us! Oh, my good heaven!" The letter was seized and opened, and Ottilia read:

"He who loves you with his heart has been cruelly used. They have shot him. He is not dead. He must not die. He is where he has studied since long. He has his medicine and doctors, and they say the bullet did not lodge. He has not the sight that cures. Now is he, the strong young man, laid helpless at anybody's mercy."

She supped at her father's table, and amused the margravine and him alternately with cards and a sonata. Before twelve at midnight she was driving on the road to the University, saying farewell to what her mind reverenced, so that her lover might but have sight of her. She imagined I had been assassinated. For a long time, and most pertinaciously, this idea dwelt with her, I could not dispossess her of it, even after uttering the word "duel" I know not how often. I had flatly to relate the whole of the circumstances.

"But Otto is no assassin," she cried out.

What was that she reverenced? It was what she jeopardized—her state, her rank, her dignity as princess and daughter of an ancient House, things typical to her of sovereign duties, and the high seclusion of her name. To her the escapades of foolish damsels were abominable. The laws of society as well as of her exalted station were in harmony with her intelligence. She thought them good, but obeyed them as a subject, not slavishly: she claimed the right to exercise her trained reason. The modestest, humblest, sweetest of women, undervaluing nothing that she possessed, least of all what was due from her to others, she could go whithersoever her reason directed her, putting anything aside to act justly according to her light. Nor would she have had cause to repent had I been the man she held me to be. Even with me she had not behaved precipitately. My course of probation was severe and long before she allowed her heart to speak.

Pale from a sleepless night and her heart's weariful eagerness to be near me, she sat by my chair, holding my hand, and sometimes looking into my eyes to find the life reflecting hers as in a sunken well that has once been a spring. My books and poor bachelor comforts caught her attention betweenwhiles. We talked of the day of storm by the lake;

we read the unsigned letter. With her hand in mine I slept some minutes, and awoke grasping it, doubting and terrified, so great a wave of life lifted me up.

"No! you are not gone," I sighed.

"Only come," said she.

The nature of the step she had taken began to dawn on me.

"But when they miss you at the palace? Prince Ernest?"

"Hush! they have missed me already. It is done." She said it smiling,

"Ottilia, will he take you away?"

"Us, dear, us."

"Can you meet his anger?"

"Our aunt will be the executioner. We have a day of sweet hours before she can arrive."

"May I see her first?"

"We will both see her as we are now."

"We must have prompt answers for the margravine!"

"None, Harry. I do not defend myself ever."

Distant hills, and folds of receding clouds and skies beyond them, were visible from my window, and beyond the skies I felt her soul.

"Ottilia, you were going to Italy?"

"Yes: or whither they please, for as long as they please. I wished once to go, I have told you why. One of the series" (she touched the letter lying on a reading-table beside her) "turned the channel of all wishes and intentions. My friends left me to fall at the mercy of this one. I consented to the injunction that I should neither write nor receive letters. Do I argue ill in saying that a trust was implied? Surely it was a breach of the trust to keep me ignorant of the danger of him I love! Now they know it. I dared not consult them—not my dear father!—about any design of mine when I had read this odd copybook writing, all in brief sentences, each beginning ' he ' and ' he.' It struck me like thrusts of a sword; it illuminated me like lightning. That ' he ' was the heart within my heart. The writer must be some clever woman or simple friend, who feels for us very strongly. My lover assassinated, where could I be but with him?"

Her little Ann coming in with chocolate and strips of fine

white bread to dip in it stopped my efforts to explain the distinction between an assassination and a duel. I noticed then the likeness of Aennchen to Lieschen.

"She has a sister here," said Ottilia; "and let her bring Lieschen to visit me here this afternoon."

Aennchen, with a blush, murmured, that she heard and would obey. I had a memorable pleasure in watching my beloved eat and drink under my roof.

The duel remained incomprehensible to her. She first frightened me by remarking that duels were the pastime of brainless young men. Her next remark, in answer to my repeated attempts to shield my antagonist from a capital charge: "But only military men and Frenchmen fight duels!" accompanied by a slightly investigating glance of timid surprise, gave me pain, together with a flashing apprehension of what she had forfeited, whom offended, to rush to the succour of a duellist. I had to repeat to her who my enemy was, so that there should be no further mention of assassination. Prince Otto's name seemed to entangle her understanding completely.

"Otto! Otto!" she murmured; "he has, I have heard, been obliged by some so-called laws of honour once or twice to—to—he is above suspicion of treachery! To my mind it is one and the same, but I would not harshly exclude the view the world puts on things; and I use the world's language in saying that he could not do a dishonourable deed. How far he honours himself is a question apart. That may be low enough, while the world is full of a man's praises."

She knew the nature of a duel. "It is the work of soulless creatures!" she broke through my stammered explanations with unwonted impatience, and pressing my hand: "Ah! You are safe. I have you still. Do you know, Harry, I am not yet able to endure accidents and misadventures: I have not fortitude to meet them, or intelligence to account for them. They are little ironical laughter. Say we build so high: the lightning strikes us:—why build at all? The Summer fly is happier. If I had lost you! I can almost imagine that I should have asked for revenge. For why should the bravest and purest soul of my worship be snatched away? I am not talking wisdom, only my shaken self will speak just now! I pardon Otto, though he has behaved basely."

"No, not basely," I felt bound to plead on his behalf, thinking, in spite of a veritable anguish of gathering dread, that she had become enlightened and would soon take the common view of our case; "not basely. He was excessively irritated, without cause in my opinion; he simply misunderstood certain matters. Dearest, you have nations fighting: a war is only an exaggerated form of duelling."

"Nations at war are wild beasts," she replied. "The passions of these hordes of men are not an example for a living soul. Our souls grow up to the light: we must keep eye on the light, and look no lower. Nations appear to me to have no worse than a soiled mirror of themselves in mobs. They are still uncivilized: they still bear a resemblance to the old monsters of the mud. Do you not see their claws and fangs, Harry? Do you find an apology in their acts for intemperate conduct? Men who fight duels appear in my sight no nobler than the first desperate creatures spelling the cruel A B C of the passions."

"No, nor in mine," I assented hastily. "We are not perfect. But hear me. Yes, the passions are cruel. Circumstances however——I mean, there are social usages——Ay, if one were always looking up! But should we not be gentle with our comparisons if we would have our views in proportion?"

She hung studiously silent, and I pursued:

"I trust you so much as my helper and my friend that I tell you what we do not usually tell to women—the facts, and the names connected with them. Sooner or later you would have learnt everything. Beloved, I do not wait to let you hear it by degrees, to be reconciled to it piecemeal."

"And I forgive him," she sighed. "I scarcely bring myself to believe that Harry has bled from Otto's hand."

"It was the accident of the case, Ottilia. We had to meet."

"To meet?"

"There are circumstances when men will not accept apologies; they——we——heaven knows, I was ready to do all that a man could do to avoid this folly—wickedness; give it the worst of titles!"

"It did not occur——accidentally?" she inquired. Her voice sounded strange, half withheld in the utterance.

"It occurred," said I, feeling my strength ebb and despair

set in, " it occurred—the prince compelled me to meet him."

" But my cousin Otto is no assassin ? "

" Compelled, I say : that is, he conceived I had injured him, and left me no other way of making amends."

Her defence of Otto was in reality the vehement cherishing of her idea of me. This caused her bewilderment, and like a barrier to the flowing of her mind it resisted and resisted. She could not suffer herself to realize that I was one of the brainless young savages, creatures with claws and fangs.

Her face was unchanged to me. The homeliness of her large mild eyes embraced me unshadowed, and took me to its inner fire unreservedly. Leaning in my roomy chair, I contemplated her at leisure while my heart kept saying " Mine ! mine ! " to awaken an active belief in its possession. Her face was like the quiet morning of a winter day when cloud and sun intermix and make an ardent silver, with lights of blue and faint fresh rose ; and over them the beautiful fold of her full eyebrow on the eyelid like a bending upper heaven. Those winter mornings are divine. They move on noiselessly. The earth is still, as if awaiting. A wren warbles, and flits through the lank drenched brambles ; hill-side opens green ; elsewhere is mist, everywhere expectancy. They bear the veiled sun like a sangreal aloft to the wavy marble flooring of stainless cloud.

She was as fair. Gazing across her shoulder's gentle depression, I could have desired to have the couchant brow, and round cheek, and rounding chin no more than a young man's dream of women, a picture alive, without the animating individual awful mind to judge of me by my acts. I chafed at the thought that one so young and lovely should meditate on human affairs at all. She was of an age to be maidenly romantic : our situation favoured it. But she turned to me, and I was glad of the eyes I knew. She kissed me on the forehead.

" Sleep," she whispered.

I feigned sleep to catch my happiness about me.

Some disenchanting thunder was coming, I was sure, and I was right. My father entered.

" Princess ! " He did amazed and delighted homage, and forthwith uncontrollably poured out the history of my heroism, a hundred words for one ;—my promptitude in picking the prince's glove up on my sword's point, my fine play with the steel, my scornful magnanimity, the admiration of my fellow-students ;—every line of it; in stupendous language; an artillery celebration of victory. I tried to stop him. Ottilia rose, continually assenting, with short affirmatives, to his glorifying interrogations—a method he had of recapitulating the main points. She glanced to right and left, as if she felt caged.

"Is it known?" I heard her ask, in the half audible strange voice which had previously made me tremble.

"Known? I certify to you, princess,"—the unhappy man spouted his withering fountain of interjections over us anew; known in every Court and garrison of Germany! Known by this time in Old England! And, what was more, the correct version of it was known! It was known that the young Englishman had vanquished his adversary with the small sword, and had allowed him, because he had raged demoniacally on account of his lamed limb, to have a shot in revenge.

"The honour done me by the princess in visiting me is not to be known," I summoned energy enough to say.

She shook her head.

My father pledged himself to the hottest secresy, equiva. lent to a calm denial of the fact, if necessary.

"Pray, be at no trouble," she addressed him.

The "Where am I?" look was painful in her aspect.

It led me to perceive the difference of her published position in visiting a duellist lover instead of one assassinated. In the latter case, the rashness of an hereditary virgin princess avowing her attachment might pass condoned or cloaked by general compassion. How stood it in the former? I had dragged her down to the duellist's level! And as she was not of a nature to practise concealments, and scorned to sanction them, she was condemned, seeing that concealment as far as possible was imperative, to suffer bitterly in her own esteem. This, the cruellest, was the least of the evils. To keep our names disjoined was hopeless. My weakened frame and mental misery coined tears when thoughts were needed.

Presently I found the room empty of our poor unconscious tormentor. Ottilia had fastened her hand to mine again.

"Be generous," I surprised her by saying. "Go back at once. I have seen you! Let my father escort you on the

road.   You will meet the margravine, or some one.   I think,
with you, it will be the margravine, and my father puts her
in good humour.   Pardon a wretched little scheme to save
you from annoyance!   So thus you return within a day, and
the margravine shelters you.   Your name will not be spoken.
But go at once, for the sake of Prince Ernest.   I have hurt
him already; help me to avoid doing him a mortal injury.
It was Schwartz who drove you?   Our old Schwartz! old
Warhead!   You see, we may be safe; only every fresh
minute adds to the danger.   And another reason for going—
another——"

"Ah!" she breathed, "my Harry will talk himself into a
fever."

"I shall have it if the margravine comes here."

"She shall not be admitted."

"Or if I hear her, or hear that she has come!   Consent at
once, and revive me.   Oh! I am begging you to leave me,
and wishing it with all my soul.   Think over what I have
done.   Do not write to me.   I shall see the compulsion of
mere kindness between the lines.   You consent.   Your
wisdom I never doubt—I doubt my own."

"When it is yours you would persuade me to confide in?"
said she, with some sorrowful archness.

Wits clear as hers could see that I had advised well,
except in proposing my father for escort.   It was evidently
better that she should go as she came.

I refrained from asking her what she thought of me now.
Suing for immediate pardon would have been like the applying of a lancet to a vein for blood: it would have burst forth,
meaning mere words coloured by commiseration, kindness,
desperate affection, anything but her soul's survey of herself
and me; and though I yearned for the comfort passion could
give me, I knew the mind I was dealing with, or, rather, I
knew I was dealing with a mind; and I kept my tongue
silent.   The talk between us was of the possible date of my
recovery, the hour of her return to the palace, the writer of
the unsigned letters, books we had read apart or peeped into
together.   She was a little quicker in speech, less meditative.
My sensitive watchfulness caught no other indication of a
change.

My father drove away an hour in advance of the princess
to encounter the margravine.

" By," said he, rehearsing his exclamation of astonishment and delight at meeting her, " the most miraculous piece of good fortune conceivable, dear madam. And now comes the question, since you have condescended to notice a solitary atom of your acquaintance on the public high-road, whether I am to have the honour of doubling the freight of your carriage, or you will deign to embark in mine? But the direction of the horses' heads must be reversed, absolutely it must, if your Highness would repose in a bed to-night. Good. So. And now, at a conversational trot, we may happen to be overtaken by acquaintances."

I had no doubt of his drawing on his rarely-abandoned seven-league boots of jargon, once so delicious to me, for the margravine's entertainment. His lack of discernment in treating the princess to it ruined my patience.

The sisters Aennchen and Lieschen presented themselves a few minutes before his departure. Lieschen dropped at her feet.

" My child," said the princess, quite maternally, " could you be quit of your service with the Mährlens for two weeks, think you, to do duty here?"

" The professor grants her six hours out of the twenty-four already," said I.

" To go where?" she asked, alarmed.

" To come here."

" Here? She knows you? She did not curtsey to you."

" Nurses do not usually do that."

The appearance of both girls was pitiable; but having no suspicion of the cause for it, I superadded,—

" She was here this morning."

" Ah! we owe her more than we were aware of."

The princess looked on her kindly, though with suspense in the expression.

" She told me of my approaching visitor," I said.

" Oh! not told!" Lieschen burst out.

" Did you,"—the princess questioned her, and murmured to me, " These children cannot speak falsehoods,"—they shone miserably under the burden of uprightness—" did you make sure that I should come?"

Lieschen thought—she supposed. But why? Why did she think and suppose? What made her anticipate the princess's arrival? This inveterate why communicated its

terrors to Aennchen, upon whom the princess turned scruti-
nizing eyes, saying,—"You write of me to your sister?"

" Yes, princess."

" And she to you?"

Lieschen answered : "Forgive me, your Highness, dearest
lady!"

" You offered yourself here unasked?"

" Yes, princess."

" Have you written to others besides your sister?"

" Seldom, princess ; I do not remember."

" You know the obligation of signatures to letters?"

" Ah!"

" You have been remiss in not writing to me, child."

" Oh, princess ! I did not dare to."

" You have not written to me?"

" Ah! princess, how dared I ?"

" Are you speaking truthfully?"

The unhappy girls stood trembling. Ottilia spared them
the leap into the gulfs of confession. Her intuitive glance,
assisted by a combination of minor facts, had read the story
of their misdeeds in a minute. She sent them down to the
carriage, suffering her culprits to kiss her fingers, while she
said to one : "This might be a fable of a pair of mice."

When she was gone, after many fits of musing, the signification of it was revealed to my slower brain. I felt that it
could not but be an additional shock to the regal pride of
such a woman that these little maidens should have been
permitted to act forcibly on her destiny. The mystery of
the letters was easily explained as soon as a direct suspicion
fell on one of the girls who lived in my neighbourhood and
the other who was near the princess's person. Doubtless
the revelation of their effective mouse plot had its humiliating
bitterness for her on a day of heavy oppression, smile at it
as she subsequently might. The torture of heart with which
I twisted the meaning of her words about the pair of mice to
imply that the pair had conspired to make a net for an eagle
and had enmeshed her, may have struck a vein of the truth.
I could see no other antithesis to the laudable performance
of the single mouse of fable. Lieschen, when she next appeared in the character of nurse, met my inquiries by sup-
plicating me to imitate her sister's generous mistress, and be
merciful.

She remarked by-and-by, of her own accord : " Princess Ottilia does not regret that she had us educated."

A tender warmth crept round me in thinking that a mind thus lofty would surely be, however severe in its insight, above regrets and recantations.

CHAPTER XXXIV.

I GAIN A PERCEPTION OF PRINCELY STATE.

I HAD a visit from Prince Ernest, nominally one of congratulation on my escape. I was never in my life so much at any man's mercy : he might have fevered me to death with reproaches, and I expected them on hearing his name pronounced at the door. I had forgotten the ways of the world. For some minutes I listened guardedly to his affable talk. My thanks for the honour done me were awkward, as if they came upon reflection. The prince was particularly civil and cheerful. His relative, he said, had written of me in high terms—the very highest, declaring that I was blameless in the matter, and that, though he had sent the horse back to my stables, he fully believed in the fine qualities of the animal, and acknowledged his fault in making it a cause of provocation. To all of which I assented with easy nods.

" Your Shakespeare, I think," said the prince, " has a scene of young Frenchmen praising their horses. I myself am no stranger to the enthusiasm : one could not stake life and honour on a nobler brute. Pardon me if I state my opinion that you young Englishmen of to-day are sometimes rather overbearing in your assumption of a superior knowledge of horseflesh. We Germans in the Baltic provinces and in the Austrian cavalry think we have a right to a remark or two ; and if we have not suborned the testimony of modern history, the value of our Hanoverian troopers is not unknown to one at least of your Generals. However, the odds are that you were right and Otto wrong, and he certainly put himself in the wrong to defend his ground."

I begged him to pass a lenient sentence upon fiery youth. He assured me that he remembered his own. Our interchange of courtesies was cordially commonplace : we walked,

as it were, arm-in-arm on thin ice, rivalling one another's
gentlemanly composure. Satisfied with my discretion, the
prince invited me to the lake-palace, and then a week's
shooting in Styria to recruit. I thanked him in as clear a
voice as I could command: "Your Highness, the mine
flourishes, I trust?"

"It does; I think I may say it does," he replied. "There
is always the want of capital. What can be accomplished,
in the present state of affairs, your father performs, on the
whole, well. You smile—but I mean extraordinarily well.
He has, with an accountant at his elbow, really the genius
of management. He serves me busily, and, I repeat, well.
A better employment for him than the direction of Court
theatricals?"

"Undoubtedly it is."

"Or than bestriding a bronze horse, personifying my good
ancestor! Are you acquainted with the Chancellor von
Redwitz?"

"All I know of him, sir, is that he is fortunate to enjoy
the particular confidence of his master."

"He has a long head. But, now, *he* is a disappointing
man in action; responsibility overturns him. He is the
reverse of Roy, whose advice I do not take, though I'm
glad to set him running. Von Redwitz is in the town. He
shall call on you, and amuse an hour or so of your convalescence."

I confessed that I began to feel longings for society.

Prince Ernest was kind enough to quit me without un-
masking. I had not to learn that the simplest visits and
observations of ruling princes signify more than lies on the
surface. Interests so highly personal as theirs demand from
them a decent insincerity.

Chancellor von Redwitz called on me, and amused me
with secret anecdotes of all the royal Houses of Germany,
amusing chiefly through the veneration he still entertained
for them. The grave senior was doing his utmost to divert
one of my years. The immoralities of blue blood, like the
amours of the Gods, were to his mind tolerable, if not
beneficial to mankind, and he presumed I should find them
toothsome. Nay, he besought me to coincide in his excuses
of a widely charming young archduchess, for whom no
estimable husband of a fitting rank could anywhere be dis-

covered, so she had to be bestowed upon an archducal imbecile; and hence—and hence——Oh, certainly! Generous youth and benevolent age joined hands of exoneration over her. The princess of Satteberg actually married, under covert, a colonel of Uhlans at the age of seventeen; the marriage was quashed, the colonel vanished, the princess became the scandalous Duchess of Ilm-Ilm, and was surprised one infamous night in the outer court of the castle by a soldier on guard, who dragged her into the guard-room and unveiled her there, and would have been summarily shot for his pains but for the locket on his breast, which proved him to be his sovereign's son.—A perfect romance, Mr. Chancellor. We will say the soldier son loved a delicate young countess in attendance on the duchess. The countess spies the locket, takes it to the duchess, is reprimanded, when behold! the locket opens, and Colonel von Bein appears as in his blooming youth, in Lancer uniform.—Young sir, your piece of romance has exaggerated history to caricature. Romances are the destruction of human interest. The moment you begin to move the individuals, they are puppets. "Nothing but poetry, and I say it who do not read it"— (Chancellor von Redwitz is the speaker)—"nothing but poetry makes romances passable: for poetry is the everlastingly and embracingly human. Without it your fictions are flat foolishness, non-nourishing substance—a species of brandy and gruel!—diet for craving stomachs that can support nothing solider, and must have the weak stuff stiffened. Talking of poetry, there was an independent hereditary princess of Leiterstein in love with a poet!—a Leonora d'Este!—This was no Tasso. Nevertheless, she proposed to come to nuptials. *Good*, you observe? I confine myself to the relation of historical circumstances; in other words, facts; and of good or bad I know not."

Chancellor von Redwitz smoothed the black silk stocking of his crossed leg, and set his bunch of seals and watch-key swinging. He resumed, entirely to amuse me,—

" The Princess Elizabeth of Leiterstein promised all the qualities which the most solicitous of paternal princes could desire as a guarantee for the judicious government of the territory to be bequeathed to her at his demise. But, as there is no romance to be extracted from her story, I may as well tell you at once that she did not espouse the poet."

" On the contrary, dear Mr. Chancellor, I am interested in the princess. Proceed, and be as minute as you please."

" It is but a commonplace excerpt of secret historical narrative buried among the archives of the Family, my good Mr. Richmond. The Princess Elizabeth thoughtlessly pledged her hand to the young sonneteer. Of course, she could not fulfil her engagement."

" Why not ?"

" You see, you are impatient for romance, young gentleman."

" Not at all, Mr. Chancellor. I do but ask a question."

" You fence. Your question was dictated by impatience."

" Yes, for the facts and elucidations."

" For the romance, that is. You wish me to depict emotions."

Hereupon this destroyer of temper embrowned his nostrils with snuff, adding,—" I am unable to."

" Then one is not to learn why the princess could not fulfil her engagement ?"

" Judged from the point of view of the pretender to the supreme honour of the splendid alliance, the fault was none of hers. She overlooked his humble, his peculiarly dubious, birth."

" Her father interposed ?"

" No."

" The Family ?"

" Quite inefficacious to arrest her determinations."

" What then—what was in her way ?"

" Germany."

" What ?"

" Great Germany, young gentleman. I should have premised that, besides mental, she had eminent moral dispositions,—I might term it the conscience of her illustrious rank. She would have raised the poet to equal rank beside her had she possessed the power. She could and did defy the Family, and subdue her worshipping father, the most noble prince, to a form of paralysis of acquiescence—if I make myself understood. But she was unsuccessful in her application for the sanction of the Diet."

" The Diet ?"

" The German Diet. Have you not lived among us long enough to know that the German Diet is the seat of domestic legislation for the princely Houses of Germany? A prince or a princess may say, 'I will this or that.' The Diet says, 'Thou shalt not;' pre-eminently, 'Thou shalt not mix thy blood with that of an impure race, nor with blood of inferiors.' Hence, we have it what we see it, a translucent flood down from the topmost founts of time. So we revere it. 'Quâ man and woman,' the Diet says, by implication, 'do as you like, marry in the ditches, spawn plentifully. Quâ prince and princess, No! Your nuptials are nought. Or would you maintain them a legal ceremony, and be bound by them, you descend, you go forth; you are no reigning sovereign, you are a private person.' His Serene Highness the prince was thus prohibited from affording help to his daughter. The princess was reduced to the decision either that she, the sole child born of him in legal wedlock, would render him quâ prince childless, or that she would—in short, would have her woman's way. The sovereignty of Leiterstein continued uninterruptedly with the elder branch. She was a true princess."

"A true woman," said I, thinking the sneer weighty.

The Chancellor begged me to recollect that he had warned me there was no romance to be expected.

I bowed; and bowed during the remainder of the interview.

Chancellor von Redwitz had performed his mission. The hours of my convalescence were furnished with food for amusement sufficient to sustain a year's blockade; I had no further longing for society, but I craved for fresh air intensely.

Did Ottilia know that this iron law, enforced with the might of a whole empire, environed her, held her fast from any motion of heart and will? I could not get to mind that the prince had hinted at the existence of such a law. Yet why should he have done so? The word impossible, in which he had not been sparing when he deigned to speak distinctly, comprised everything. More profitable than shooting empty questions at the sky was the speculation on his project in receiving me at the palace, and that was dark. My father, who might now have helped me, was off on duty again.

I found myself driving into Sarkeld with a sense of a whirlwind round my head; wheels in multitudes were spinning inside, striking sparks for thoughts. I met an orderly in hussar uniform of blue and silver, trotting on his errand. There he was; and whether many were behind him or he stood for the army in its might, he wore the trappings of an old princely House that nestled proudly in the bosom of its great jealous Fatherland. Previously in Sarkeld I had noticed members of the diminutive army to smile down on them. I saw the princely arms and colours on various houses and in the windows of shops. Emblems of a small State, they belonged to the history of the Empire. The Court-physician passed with a bit of ribbon in his button-hole. A lady driving in an open carriage encouraged me to salute her. She was the wife of the Prince's Minister of Justice. Upon what foundation had I been building? A reflection of the ideas possessing me showed Riversley, my undecorated home of rough red brick, in the middle of barren heaths. I entered the palace, I sent my respects to the prince. In return, the hour of dinner was ceremoniously named to me: ceremony damped the air. I had been insensible to it before, or so I thought, the weight was now so crushing. Arms, emblems, colours, liveries, portraits of princes and princesses of the House, of this the warrior, that the seductress, burst into sudden light. What had I to do among them?

The presence of the living members of the Family was an extreme physical relief.

For the moment, beholding Ottilia, I counted her but as one of them. She welcomed me without restraint.

We chattered pleasantly at the dinner-table.

"Ah! you missed our French troupe," said the margravine.

"Yes," said I, resigning them to her. She nodded:

"And one very pretty little woman they had, I can tell you—for a Frenchwoman."

"You thought her pretty? Frenchwomen know what to do with their brains and their pins, somebody has said."

"And exceedingly well said, too. Where is that man Roy? Good things always remind me of him."

The question was addressed to no one in particular. The man happened to be my father, I remembered. A second allusion to him was answered by Prince Ernest:

"Roy is off to Croatia to enrol some dozens of cheap workmen. The strength of those Croats is prodigious, and well looked after they work. He will be back in three or four or more days."

"You have spoilt a good man," rejoined the margravine; "and that reminds me of a bad one—a cut-throat. Have you heard of that creature, the princess's tutor? Happily cut loose from us, though! He has published a book—a horror! all against Scripture and Divine right! Is there any one to defend him now, I should like to ask?"

"I," said Ottilia.

"Gracious me! you have not read the book?"

"Right through, dear aunt, with all respect to you."

"It's in the house?"

"It is in my study."

"Then I don't wonder! I don't wonder!" the margravine exclaimed.

"Best hear what the enemy has to say," Prince Ernest observed.

"Excellently argued, papa, supposing that he be an enemy."

"An enemy as much as the fox is the enemy of the poultry-yard, and the hound is the enemy of the fox!" said the margravine.

"I take your illustration, auntie," said Ottilia. "He is the enemy of chickens, and only does not run before the numbers who bark at him. My noble old professor is a resolute truth-seeker: he raises a light to show you the ground you walk on. How is it that you, adoring heroes as you do, cannot admire him when he stands alone to support his view of the truth! I would I were by him! But I am, whenever I hear him abused."

"I daresay you discard nothing that the wretch has taught you!"

"Nothing! nothing!" said Ottilia, and made my heart live.

The grim and taciturn Baroness Turckems, sitting opposite to her, sighed audibly.

"Has the princess been trying to convert you?" the margravine asked her.

"Trying? no, madam. Reading? yes."

"My good Turckems! you do not get your share of sleep?"

" It is her Highness the princess who despises sleep."

" See there the way with your free-thinkers! They commence by treading under foot the pleasantest half of life, and then they impose their bad habits on their victims. Ottilia! Ernest! I do insist upon having lights extinguished in the child's apartments by twelve o'clock at midnight."

" Twelve o'clock is an extraordinary latitude for children," said Ottilia, smiling.

The prince, with a scarce perceptible degree of emphasis, said,—

" Women born to rule must be held exempt from nursery restrictions."

Here the conversation opened to let me in. More than once the margravine informed me that I was not the equal of my father.

" Why," said she, " why can't you undertake this detestable coal-mine, and let your father disport himself ? "

I suggested that it might be because I was not his equal. She complimented me for inheriting a spark of Roy's brilliancy.

I fancied there was a conspiracy to force me back from my pretensions by subjecting me to the contemplation of my bare self and actual condition. Had there been, I should have suffered from less measured strokes. The unconcerted design to humiliate inferiors is commonly successfuller than conspiracy.

The prince invited me to smoke with him, and talked of our gradual subsidence in England to one broad level of rank through the intermixture by marriage of our aristocracy, squierearchy, and merchants.

" Here it is not so," he said ; " and no democratic ragings will make it so. Rank, with us, is a principle. I suppose you have not read the professor's book ? It is powerful— he is a powerful man. It can do no damage to the minds of persons destined by birth to wield authority—none, therefore, to the princess. I would say to *you*—avoid it. For those who have to carve their way, it is bad. You will enter your Parliament, of course ? There you have a fine career."

He asked me what I had made of Chancellor von Redwitz.

I perceived that Prince Ernest could be cool and sagacious in repairing what his imprudence or blindness had left to occur: that he must have enlightened his daughter as to her actual position, and was most dexterously and devilishly flattering her worldly good sense by letting it struggle and grow, instead of opposing her. His appreciation of her intellect was an idolatrv; he really confided in it, I knew; and this reacted upon her. Did it ? My hesitations and doubts, my fantastic raptures and despair, my loss of the power to appreciate anything at its right value, revealed the madness of loving a princess.

There were preparations for the arrival of an important visitor. The margravine spoke of him emphatically. I thought it might be her farcically pompous way of announcing my father's return, and looked pleased, I suppose, for she added, " Do you know Prince Hermann ? He spends most of his time in Eberhardstadt. He is cousin of the King, a wealthy branch; tant soit peu philosophe, à ce qu'on dit; a traveller. They say he has a South American complexion. I knew him a boy; and his passion is to put together what Nature has unpieced, bones of fishes. and animals. Il faut passer le temps. He adores the Deluge. Anything antediluvian excites him. He can tell us the ' modes ' of those days; and, if I am not very much misinformed, he still expects us to show him the very latest of these. Happily my milliner is back from Paris. Ay, and we have fossils in our neighbourhood, though, on my honour, I don't know where—somewhere; the princess can guide him, and you can help at the excavations. I am told he would go through the crust of earth for the backbone of an idio—ilio—something—saurus."

I scrutinized Prince Hermann as rarely my observation had dwelt on any man. He had the German head, wide, so as seemingly to force out the ears; honest, ready, interested eyes in conversation; parched lips; a rather tropically-coloured skin; and decidedly the manners of a gentleman to all, excepting his retinue of secretaries, valets, and chasseurs —his " blacks," he called them. They liked him. One could not help liking him.

" You study much ? " he addressed the princess at table.

She answered : " I throw aside books, now you have come to open the earth and the sea."

From that time the topics started on every occasion were theirs; the rest of us ran at their heels, giving tongue or not

To me Prince Hermann was perfectly courteous. He had made English friends on his travels; he preferred English comrades in adventure to any other: thought our East Indian empire the most marvellous thing the world had seen, and our Indian Government cigars very smokeable upon acquaintance. When stirred, he bubbled with anecdote. " Not been there," was his reply to the margravine's tentatives for gossip of this and that of the German Courts. His museum, hunting, and the opera absorbed and divided his hours. I guessed his age to be mounting forty. He seemed robust; he ate vigorously. Drinking he conscientiously performed as an accompanying duty, and was flushed after dinner, burning for tobacco and a couch for his length. Then he talked of the littleness of Europe and the greatness of Germany; logical postulates fell in collapse before him. America to America, North and South; India to Europe. India was for the land with the largest sea-board. Mistress of the Baltic, of the North Sea and the East, as eventually she must be, Germany would claim to take India as a matter of course, and find an outlet for the energies of the most prolific and the toughest of the races of mankind,—the purest, in fact, the only true race, properly so called, out of India, to which it would return as to its source, and there create an empire magnificent in force and solidity, the actual wedding of East and West; an empire firm on the ground and in the blood of the people, instead of an empire of aliens, that would bear comparison to a finely fretted cotton-hung palanquin balanced on an elephant's back, all depending on the docility of the elephant (his description of Great Britain's Indian Empire.) " And mind me," he said, " the masses of India are in character elephant all over, tail to proboscis! servile till they trample you, and not so stupid as they look. But you've done wonders in India, and we can't forget it. Your administration of justice is worth all your battles there."

This was the man: a milder one after the evaporation of his wine in speech, and peculiarly moderate on his return, exhaling sandal-wood, to the society of the ladies.

Ottilia danced with Prince Hermann at the grand Ball given in honour of him. The wives and daughters of the notables present kept up a buzz of comment on his personal advantages, in which, I heard it said, you saw his German heart, though he *had* spent the best years of his life abroad

Much court was paid to him by the men.   Sarkeld visibly
expressed satisfaction.   One remark, "We shall have his
museum in the town!" left me no doubt upon the presumed
object of his visit : it was uttered and responded to with a
depth of sentiment that showed how lively would be the
general gratitude toward one who should exhilarate the
place by introducing cases of fish-bones.

So little did he think of my presence that, returning from
a ride one day, he seized and detained the princess's hand.
She frowned with pained surprise, but unresistingly, as
became a young gentlewoman's dignity.   Her hand was
rudely caught and kept in the manner of a boisterous wooer
—a Harry the Fifth or lusty Petruchio.   She pushed her
horse on at a bound.   Prince Hermann rode up head to head
with her gallantly, having now both hands free of the reins,
like an Indian spearing the buffalo :—it was buffalo courtship ; and his shout of rallying astonishment at her resistance, "What ? What ?" rang wildly to heighten the scene,
she leaning constrained on one side and he bending half
his body's length ; a strange scene for me to witness.

They proceeded with old Schwartz at their heels doglike.
It became a question for me whether I should follow in the
bitter track, and further the question whether I could let
them escape from sight.   They wound up the roadway, two
figures and one following, now dots against the sky, now a
single movement in the valley, now concealed, buried under
billows of forest, making the low noising of the leaves an
intolerable whisper of secresy, and forward I rushed again
to see them rounding a belt of firs or shadowed by rocks,
solitary on shorn fields, once more dipping to the forest, and
once more emerging, vanishing.   When I had grown sure of
their reappearance from some point of view or other, I spied
for them in vain.   My destiny, whatever it might be, fluttered over them ; to see them seemed near the knowing of
it, and not to see them, deadly.   I galloped, so intent on the
three in the distance, that I did not observe a horseman face
towards me, on the road : it was Prince Hermann.   He raised
his hat ; I stopped short, and he spoke :—

"Mr. Richmond, permit me to apologize to you.   I have
to congratulate you, it appears.   I was not aware.——However, the princess has done me the favour to enlighten me.
How you will manage I can't guess, but that is not my

affair. I am a man of honour; and, *on* my honour, I conceived that I was invited here to decide, as my habit is, on
the spot, if I would, or if I would not. I speak clearly to
you, no doubt. There could be no hesitation in the mind of
a man of sense. My way is prompt and blunt; I am sorry
I gave you occasion to reflect on it. There! I have been
deceived—deceived myself, let's say. Sharp methods play
the devil with you now and then. To speak the truth,—
perhaps you won't care to listen to it,—family arrangements
are the best; take my word for it, they are the best. And
in the case of princesses of the Blood!——Why, look you,
I happen to be suitable. It's a matter of chance, like your
height, complexion, constitution. One is just what one is
born to be, eh? You have your English notions, I my
German; but as a man of the world in the bargain, and
'gentleman,' I hope, I should say that to take a young
princess's fancy, and drag her from her station is not——
of course, you know that the actual value of the title goes
if she steps down? Very well. But enough said; I thought
I was in a clear field. We are used to having our way
cleared for us, *nous autres.* I will not detain you."

We saluted gravely, and I rcde on at a mechanical pace,
discerning by glimpses the purport of what I had heard,
without drawing warmth from it. The man's outrageously
royal way of wooing, in contempt of minor presences and
flimsy sentiment, made me jealous of him, notwithstanding
his overthrow.

I was in the mood to fall entirely into my father's hands,
as I did by umbosoming myself to him for the first time
since my heart had been under the charm. Fresh from a
rapid course of travel, and with the sense of laying the
prince under weighty obligations, he made light of my
perplexity, and at once delivered himself bluntly: "She
plights her hand to you in the presence of our good Peterborough." His plans were shaped on the spot. "We start
for England the day after to-morrow to urge on the suit,
Richie. Our Peterborough is up at the château. The Frau
Feldmarschall honours him with a farewell invitation: you
have a private interview with the princess at midnight in
the library, where you are accustomed to read, as a student
of books should, my boy: at a touch of the bell, or mere
opening of the door, I see that Peterborough comes to you.

It will not be a ceremony, but a binding of you both by your word of honour before a ghostly gentleman." He informed me that his foresight had enlisted and detained Peterborough for this particular moment and identical piece of duty, which seemed possible, and in a singular manner incited me to make use of Peterborough. For the princess still denied me the look of love's intelligence, she avoided me, she still kept to the riddle, and my delicacy went so far that I was restrained from writing. I agreed with my father that we could not remain in Germany; but how could I quit the field and fly to England on such terms? I composed the flattest letter ever written, requesting the princess to meet me about midnight in the library, that I might have the satisfaction of taking my leave of her; and this done, my spirits rose, and it struck me my father was practically wise, and I looked on Peterborough as an almost supernatural being. If Ottilia refused to come, at least I should know my fate. Was I not bound in manly honour to be to some degree adventurous? So I reasoned in exclamations, being, to tell truth, tired of seeming to be what I was not quite, of striving to become what I must have divined that I never could quite attain to. So my worthier, or ideal, self fell away from me. I was no longer devoted to be worthy of a woman's love, but consenting to the plot to entrap a princess. I was somewhat influenced, too, by the consideration, which I regarded as a glimpse of practical wisdom, that Prince Ernest was guilty of cynical astuteness in retaining me as his guest under manifold disadvantages. Personal pride stood up in arms, and my father's exuberant spirits fanned it. He dwelt loudly on his services to the prince, and his own importance and my heirship to mighty riches. He made me almost believe that Prince Ernest hesitated about rejecting me; nor did it appear altogether foolish to think so, or why was I at the palace? I had no head for reflections.

My father diverted me by levelling the whole battery of his comic mind upon Peterborough, who had a heap of manuscript, directed against heretical German theologians, to pack up for publication in his more congenial country:— how different, he ejaculated, from this nest—this forest of heresy, where pamphlets and critical essays were issued without let or hindrance, and, as far as he could see, no

general reprobation of the Press, such as would most undoubtedly, with one voice, hail *any* strange opinions in our
happy land at home! Whether he really understood the
function my father prepared him for, I cannot say. The
invitation to dine and pass a night at the lake-palace flattered
him immensely.

We went up to the château to fetch him.

A look of woe was on Peterborough's countenance when
we descended at the palace portals: he had forgotten his
pipe.

"You shall smoke one of the prince's," my father said.

Peterborough remarked to me,—"We shall have many
things to talk over in England."

"No tobacco allowed on the premises at Riversley, I'm
afraid," said I.

He sighed, and bade me jocosely to know that he regarded
tobacco as just one of the consolations of exiles and
bachelors.

"Peterborough, my good friend, you are a hero!" cried
my father. "He divorces tobacco to marry!"

"Permit me," Peterborough interposed, with an ingenuous
pretension to subtle waggery, in itself very comical,—"permit me; no legitimate union has taken place between myself
and tobacco!"

"He puts an end to the illegitimate union between himself and tobacco that he may marry according to form!"
cried my father.

We entered the palace merrily, and presently Peterborough, who had worn a studious forehead in the midst of
his consenting laughter, observed, "Well, you know, there is
more in that than appears on the surface."

His sweet simpleton air of profundity convulsed me. I
handed my father the letter addressed to the princess to
entrust it to the charge of one of the domestics, thinking
carelessly at the time that Ottilia now stood free to make
appointments and receive communications, and moreover
that I was too proud to condescend to subterfuge, except
this minor one, in consideration for her, of making it appear
that my father, and not I, was in communication with her.
My fit of laughter clung. I dressed chuckling. The margravine was not slow to notice and comment on my hilarious
readiness.

" Roy," she said, " you have given your son spirit. One sees he has your blood when you have been with him an hour."

" The season has returned, if your Highness will let it be Spring," said my father.

" Far fetched !—from the Lower Danube !" she ejaculated in mock scorn to excite his sprightliness, and they fell upon a duologue as good as wit for the occasion.

Prince Hermann had gone. His departure was mentioned with the ordinary commonplaces of regret. Ottilia was unembarrassed, both in speaking of him and looking at me. We had the Court physician and his wife at table, Chancellor von Redwitz and his daughter, and General Happenwyll, chief of the prince's contingent, a Prussian at heart, said to be a good officer on the strength of a military book of some sort that he had full leisure to compose. The Chancellor's daughter and Baroness Turckems enclosed me.

I was questioned by the baroness as to the cause of my father's unexpected return, " He is generally opportune," she remarked.

" He goes with me to England," I said.

" Oh ! he goes," said she ; and asked why we were honoured with the presence of Mr. Peterborough that evening. There had always been a smouldering hostility between her and my father.

To my surprise the baroness spoke of Ottilia by her name.

" Ottilia must have mountain air. These late hours destroy her complexion. Active exercise by day and proper fatigue by night time—that is my prescription."

" The princess," I replied, envying Peterborough, who was placed on one side of her, " will benefit, I am sure, from mountain air. Does she read excessively ? The sea——"

" The sea I pronounce bad for her—unwholesome," returned the baroness. " It is damp."

I laughed.

" Damp," she reiterated. " The vapours, I am convinced, affect mind and body. That excursion in the yacht did her infinite mischief. The mountains restored her. They will again, take my word for it. Now take you my word for it, they will again. She is not too strong in constitution, but in order to prescribe accurately one must find out whether there is seated malady. To ride out in the night instead of reposing! To drive on and on, and not reappear till the night of the next day! I ask you, is it sensible? Does it not approach mania?"

"The princess——?" said I.

"Ottilia has done that."

"Baroness, can I believe you?—and alone?"

A marvellous twinkle or shuffle appeared in the small slate-coloured eyes I looked at under their roofing of thick black eyebrows.

"Alone," she said. "That is, she was precautious to have her giant to protect her from violence. There you have a glimmering of reason in her; and all of it that I can see."

"Old Schwartz is a very faithful servant," said I, thinking that she resembled the old Warhead in visage.

"A dog's obedience to the master's whims you call faithfulness! Hem!" The baroness coughed drily.

I whispered: "Does Prince Ernest——is he aware?"

"*You* are aware," retorted the baroness, "that what a man idolizes he won't see flaw in. Remember, I am something here, or I am nothing."

The enigmatical remark was received by me decorously as a piece of merited chastisement. Nodding with gravity, I expressed regrets that the sea did not please her, otherwise I could have offered her a yacht for a cruise. She nodded stiffly. Her mouth shut up a smile, showing more of the door than the ray. The dinner, virtually a German supper, ended in general conversation on political affairs, preceded and supported by a discussion between the Prussian-hearted General and the Austrian-hearted margravine. Prince Ernest, true to his view that diplomacy was the weapon of minor sovereigns, held the balance, with now a foot in one scale, now in the other, a politic proceeding, so long as the rival powers passively consent to be weighed.

We trifled with music, made our bow to the ladies, and changed garments for the smoking-room. Prince Ernest smoked his one cigar among guests. The General, the Chancellor, and the doctor, knew the signal for retirement, and rose simultaneously with the discharge of his cigar-end in sparks on the unlit logwood pile. My father and Mr. Peterborough kept their chairs.

There was, I felt with relief, no plot, for nothing had been definitely assented to by me. I received Prince Ernest's proffer of his hand, on making my adieux to him, with a passably clear conscience.

I went out to the library. A man came in for orders; I had none to give. He saw that the shutters were fixed and the curtains down, examined my hand-lamp, and placed lamps on the reading-desk and mantel-piece. Bronze busts of sages became my solitary companions. The room was long, low and dusky, voluminously and richly hung with draperies at the farther end, where a table stood for the prince to jot down memoranda, and a sofa to incline him to the relaxation of romance-reading. A door at this end led to the sleeping apartments of the West wing of the palace. Where I sat the student had ranges of classical volumes in prospect and classic heads; no other decoration to the walls. I paced to and fro and should have flung myself on the sofa, but for a heap of books there covered from dust, perhaps concealed, that the yellow Parisian volumes, of which I caught sight of some new dozen, might not be an attraction to the eyes of chance-comers. At the lake-palace the prince frequently gave audience here. He had said to me, when I stated my wish to read in the library, " You keep to the classical department ? " I thought it possible he might not like the coloured volumes to be inspected; I had no taste for a perusal of them. I picked up one that fell during my walk, and flung it back, and disturbed a heap under cover, for more fell, and there I let them lie.

Ottilia did not keep me waiting.

CHAPTER XXXV.

THE SCENE IN THE LAKE-PALACE LIBRARY.

I WAS humming the burden of Göthe's Zigeunerlied, a favourite one with me whenever I had too much to think of, or nothing. A low rush of sound from the hall-door-way swung me on my heel, and I saw her standing with a silver lamp raised in her right hand to the level of her head, as if she expected to meet obscurity. A thin blue Indian scarf muffled her throat and shoulders. Her hair was loosely

knotted.   The lamp's full glow illumined and shadowed her.
She was like a statue of Twilight.

I went up to her quickly, and closed the door, saying,
" You have come ; " my voice was not much above a breath.

She looked distrustfully down the length of the room ;
" You were speaking to some one ? "

" No."

" You were speaking."

" To myself, then, I suppose."

I remembered and repeated the gipsy burden.

She smiled faintly and said it was the hour for Anna and
Ursel and Käth and Liese to be out.

Her hands were gloved, a small matter to tell of.

We heard the portico-sentinel challenged and relieved.

" Midnight," I said.

She replied : " You were not definite in your directions
about the minutes."

" I feared to name midnight."

" Why ? "

" Lest the appointment of midnight—I lose my knowledge
of you!—should make you reflect, frighten you.   You see, I
am inventing a reason ; I really cannot tell why, if it was
not that I hoped to have just those few minutes more of you.
And now they're gone. I would not have asked you but that
I thought you free to act."

" I am."

" And you come freely ? "

" A ' therefore ' belongs to every grant of freedom."

" I understand : your judgement was against it."

" Be comforted," she said ; " it is your right to bid me
come, if you think fit."

One of the sofa-volumes fell.   She caught her breath ; and
smiled at her foolish alarm.

I told her that it was my intention to start for England in
the morning ; that this was the only moment I had, and
would be the last interview : my rights, if I possessed any,
and 1 was not aware that I did, I threw down.

" You throw down one end of the chain," she said.

" In the name of heaven, then," cried I, " release yourself."

She shook her head.   " That is not my meaning."

Note the predicament of a lover who has a piece of dishonesty lurking in him. My chilled self-love had certainly the right to demand the explanation of her coldness, and I could very well guess that a word or two drawn from the neighbourhood of the heart would fetch a warmer current to unlock the ice between us, but feeling the coldness I complained of to be probably a suspicion, I fixed on the suspicion as a new and deeper injury done to my loyal love for her, and armed against that I dared not take an initiative for fear of unexpectedly justifying it by betraying myself.

Yet, supposing her inclination to have become diverted, I was ready frankly to release her with one squeeze of hands, and take all the pain, and I said: "Pray do not speak of chains."

"But they exist. Things cannot be undone for us two by words."

The tremble as of a strung wire in the strenuous pitch of her voice seemed to say she was not cold, though her gloved hand resting its finger-ends on the table, her restrained attitude, her very calm eyes, declared the reverse. This and that sensation beset me in turn.

We shrank oddly from uttering one another's Christian name. I was the first with it; my "Ottilia!" brought soon after "Harry" on her lips, and an atmosphere about us much less Arctic.

"Ottilia, you have told me you wish me to go to England."

"I have."

"We shall be friends."

"Yes, Harry; we cannot be quite divided; we have that knowledge for our present happiness."

"The happy knowledge that we may have our bone to gnaw when food's denied. It is something. One would like possibly, after expulsion out of Eden, to climb the gates to see how the trees grow there. What I cannot imagine is the forecasting of any joy in the privilege."

"By nature or system, then, you are more impatient than I, for I can," said Ottilia. She added: "So much of your character I divined early. It was part of my reason for wishing you to work. You will find that hard work in England——but why should I preach to you! Harry, you have called me here for some purpose?"

"I must have detained you already too long."

"Time is not the offender. Since I have come, the evil——"

"Evil? Are not your actions free?"

"Patience, my friend. The freer my actions, the more am I bound to deliberate on them. I have the habit of thinking that my deliberations are not in my sex's fashion of taking counsel of the nerves and the blood. In truth, Harry, I should not have come but for my acknowledgement of your right to bid me come."

"You know, princess, that in honouring me with your attachment, you imperil your sovereign rank?"

"I do."

"What next?"

"Except that it is grievously in peril, nothing!"

"Have you known it all along?"

"Dimly—scarcely. To some extent I knew it, but it did not stand out in broad daylight. I have been learning the world's wisdom recently. Would you have had me neglect it? Surely much is due to my father? My relatives have claims on me. Our princely Houses have. My country has."

"Oh, princess, if you are pleading——"

"Can you think that I am?"

The splendour of her high nature burst on me with a shock.

I could have fallen to kiss her feet, and I said indifferently: "Not pleading, only it is evident the claims—I hate myself for bringing you in antagonism with them. Yes, and I have been learning some worldly wisdom; I wish for your sake it had not been so late. What made me overleap the proper estimate of your rank! I can't tell; but now that I know better the kind of creature—the man who won your esteem when you knew less of the world!"——

"Hush! I have an interest in him, and do not suffer him to be spurned," Ottilia checked me. "I, too, know him better, and still, if he is dragged down I am in the dust; if he is abused the shame is mine." Her face bloomed.

Her sweet warmth of colour was transfused through my veins.

"We shall part in a few minutes. I have a mind to beg gift of you."

"Name it."

" That glove."

She made her hand bare and gave me, not the glove, but the hand.

" Ah ! but this I cannot keep."

" Will you have everything spoken ?" she said, in a tone that would have been reproachful had not tenderness melted it. " There should be a spirit between us, Harry, to spare the task. You do keep it, if you choose. I have some little dread of being taken for a madwoman, and more—an actual horror of behaving ungratefully to my generous father. He has proved that he can be indulgent, most trusting and considerate for his daughter, though he is a prince ; my duty is to show him that I do not forget I am a princess. I owe my rank allegiance when he forgets his on my behalf, my friend ! You are young. None but an inexperienced girl hoodwinked by her tricks of intuition, would have dreamed you superior to the passions of other men. I was blind ; I am regretful— take my word as you do my hand—for no one's sake but my father's. You and I are bound fast ; only, help me that the blow may be lighter for him ; if I descend from the place I was born to, let me tell him it is to occupy one I am fitted for, or should not at least feel my Family's deep blush in filling. To be in the midst of life in your foremost England is, in my imagination, very glorious. Harry, I remember picturing to myself when I reflected upon your country's history—perhaps a year after I had seen the 'two young English gentlemen,'—that you touch the morning and evening star, and wear them in your coronet, and walk with the sun West and East ! child's imagery ; but the impression does not wear off. If I rail at England, it is the anger of love. I fancy I have good and great things to speak to the people through you."

There she stopped. The fervour she repressed in speech threw a glow over her face, like that on a frosty bare autumn sky after sunset.

I pressed my lips to her hand.

In our silence another of the fatal yellow volumes thumped the floor.

She looked into my eyes and asked,—

" Have we been speaking before a witness ?"

So thoroughly had she renovated me, that I accused and reproved the lurking suspicion with a soft laugh.

" Beloved ! I wish we had been."

" If it might be," she said, divining me and musing.

" Why not ?"

She stared.

" How ?   What do you ask ?

The look on my face alarmed her.   I was breathless and colourless, with the heart of a hawk eyeing his bird—a fox, would be the truer comparison, but the bird was noble, not one that cowered.   Her beauty and courage lifted me into high air, in spite of myself, and it was a huge weight of greed that fell away from me when I said,—

" I would not urge it for an instant.   Consider—if you had just plighted your hand in mine before a witness !"

" My hand is in yours ; my word to you is enough."

" Enough.   My thanks to heaven for it !   But consider— a pledge of fidelity that should be my secret angel about me in trouble and trial ; my wedded soul !   She cannot falter, she is mine for ever, she guides me, holds me to work, inspirits me !—she is secure from temptation, from threats, from everything—nothing can touch, nothing move her, she is mine !   I mean, an attested word, a form, that is—a betrothal.   For me to say—my beloved and my betrothed ! You hear that ?   Beloved ! is a lonely word :—betrothed ! carries us joined up to death.   Would you ?—I do but ask to know that you would.   To-morrow I am loose in the world, and there's a darkness in the thought of it almost too terrible.   Would you ?—one sworn word that gives me my bride, let men do what they may !   I go then singing to battle—sure !——Remember, it is but the question whether you would."

" Harry, I would, and will," she said, her lips shuddering —" wait "—for a cry of joy escaped me—" I will—look you me in the eyes and tell me you have a doubt of me."

I looked : she swam in a mist.

We had our full draught of the divine self-oblivion which floated those ghosts of the two immortal lovers through the bounds of their purgatorial circle, and for us to whom the minutes were ages, as for them to whom all time was unmarked, the power of supreme love swept out circumstance.   Such embraces cast the soul beyond happiness, into no known region of sadness, but we drew apart sadly, even as that involved pair of bleeding recollections looked on the life lost to them. I knew well what a height she dropped from when the senses took fire. She raised me to learn how little of fretful thirst and its reputed voracity remains with love when it has been met midway in air by a winged mate able to sustain, unable to descend farther.

And it was before a witness, though unviewed by us.

The farewell had come. Her voice was humbled.

Never, I said, delighting in the now conscious bravery of her eyes engaging mine, shadowy with the struggle, I would never doubt her, and I renounced all pledges. To be clear in my own sight as well as in hers, I made mention of the half-formed conspiracy to obtain her plighted troth in a binding manner. It was not necessary for me to excuse myself; she did that, saying, " Could there be a greater proof of my darling's unhappiness ? I am to blame."

We closed hands for parting. She hesitated and asked if my father was awake; then promptly to my answer: " I will see him. I have treated you ill. I have exacted too much patience. The suspicion was owing to a warning I had this evening, Harry; a silly warning to beware of snares; and I had no fear of them, believe me, though for some moments, and without the slightest real desire to be guarded, I fancied Harry's father was overhearing me. He is your father, dearest : fetch him to me. My father will hear of this from my lips—why not he ? Ah ! did I suspect you ever so little ? I will atone for it; not atone, I will make it my pleasure; it is my pride that has hurt you both. O my lover ! my lover ! Dear head, dear eyes ! Delicate and noble that you are ! my own stronger soul ! Where was my heart ? Is it sometimes dead, or sleeping ? But you can touch it to life. Look at me—I am yours. I consent, I desire it; I will see him. I *will* be bound. The heavier the chains, oh ! the better for me. What am I to be proud of anything not yours, Harry ? and I that have passed over to you ! I will see him at once."

A third in the room cried out,—

" No, not that—you do not !"

The tongue was German and struck on us like a roll of unfriendly musketry before we perceived the enemy. " Princess Ottilia ! you remember your dignity or I defend you and it, think of me what you will !"

Baroness Turckems, desperately entangled by the sofa-covering. rushed into the ray of the lamps and laid her hand on the bell-rope. In a minute we had an alarm sounding, my father was among us, there was a mad play of chatter, and we stood in the strangest nightmare-light that ever ended an interview of lovers.

CHAPTER XXXVI.

HOMEWARD AND HOME AGAIN.

THE room was in flames, Baroness Turckems plucking at the bell-rope, my father looking big and brilliant.

"Hold hand!" he shouted to the frenzied baroness.

She counter-shouted; both of them stamped feet; the portico sentinel struck the butt of his musket on the hall-doors; bell answered bell along the upper galleries.

"Foolish woman, be silent!" cried my father.

"Incendiary!" she half-shrieked.

He turned to the princess, begging her to retire, but she stared at him, and I too, after having seen him deliberately apply the flame of her lamp to the curtains, deemed him mad. He was perfectly self-possessed, and said, "This will explain the bell!" and fetched a deep breath, and again urged the princess to retire.

Peterborough was the only one present who bethought him of doing fireman's duty. The risk looked greater than it was. He had but to tear the lighted curtains down and trample on them. Suddenly the baroness called out, "The man is right! Come with me, princess; escape, your High-ness, escape! And you," she addressed me—"*you* rang the bell, you!"

"To repair your error, baroness," said my father.

"I have my conscience pure; have you?" she retorted.

He bowed and said, "The fire will also excuse your presence on the spot, baroness."

"I thank my God I am not so cool as you," said she.

"Your warmth"—he bent to her—"shall always be your apology, baroness."

Seeing the curtains extinguished, Ottilia withdrew. She gave me no glance.

All this occurred before the night-porter, who was going his rounds, could reach the library. Lacqueys and maids were soon at his heels. My father met Prince Ernest with a florid story of a reckless student, either asleep or too anxious to secure a particular volume, and showed his usual consideration by not asking me to verify the narrative. With that, and with high praise of Peterborough, as to whose gallantry I heard him deliver a very circumstantial account, he, I suppose, satisfied the prince's curiosity, and appeased him, the damage being small compared with the uproar. Prince Ernest questioned two or three times, "What set him ringing so furiously?" My father made some reply.

Ottilia's cloud-pale windows were the sole greeting I had from her on my departure early next morning, far wretcheder than if I had encountered a misfortune. It was impossible for me to deny that my father had shielded the princess: she would never have run for a menace. As he remarked, the ringing of the bell would not of itself have forced her to retreat, and the nature of the baroness's alarm demanded nothing less than a conflagration to account for it to the household. But I felt humiliated on Ottilia's behalf, and enraged on my own. And I had, I must confess, a touch of fear of a man who could unhesitatingly go to extremities, as he had done, by summoning fire to the rescue. He assured me that moments such as those inspired him and were the pride of his life, and he was convinced that, upon reflection, "I should rise to his sublime pitch." He deluded himself with the idea of his having foiled Baroness Turckems, nor did I choose to contest it, though it struck me that she was too conclusively the foiler. She must have intercepted the letter for the princess. I remembered acting carelessly in handing it to my father for him to consign it to one of the domestics, and he passed it on with a flourish. Her place of concealment was singularly well selected under the sofa-cover, and the little heaps of paper-bound volumes. I do not fancy she meant to rouse the household; her notion probably was to terrorize the princess, that she might compel her to quit my presence. In rushing to the bell-rope, her impetuosity sent her stumbling on it with force, and while threatening to ring, and meaning merely to threaten, she rang; and as it was not a retractable act, she continued ringing, and the more violently upon my father's appearance. Catching sight of Peterborough at his heels, she screamed a word equivalent to a clergyman. She had lost her discretion, but not her wits. For any one save a lover —thwarted as I was, and perturbed by the shadow falling on the princess—my father's àplomb and promptness in conjuring a check to what he assumed to be a premeditated piece of villany on the part of Baroness Turckems, might have seemed tolerably worthy of admiration. Me the whole scene affected as if it had burnt my skin. I loathed that picture of him, constantly present to me, of his shivering the glass of Ottilia's semi-classical night-lamp, gravely asking her pardon, and stretching the flame to the curtain, with large eyes blazing on the baroness. The stupid burlesque majesty of it was unendurable to thought. Nevertheless, I had to thank him for shielding Ottilia, and I had to brood on the fact that I had drawn her into a situation requiring such a shield. He, meanwhile, according to his habit, was engaged in reviewing the triumphs to come. "We have won a princess!" And what England would say, how England would look, when, on a further journey, I brought my princess home, entirely occupied his imagination, to my excessive torture—a state of mind for which it was impossible to ask his mercy. His sole link with the past appeared to be this notion that he had planned all the good things in store for us. Consequently I was condemned to hear of the success of the plot, until—for I had not the best of consciences—I felt my hand would be spell-bound in the attempt to write to the princess; and with that sense of incapacity I seemed to be cut loose from her, drifting back into the desolate days before I saw her wheeled in her invalid chair along the sands, and my life knew sunrise. But whatever the mood of our affections, so it is with us island wanderers : we cannot gaze over at England, knowing the old country to be close under the sea-line, and not hail it, and partly forget ourselves in the time that was. The smell of sea-air made me long for the white cliffs, the sight of the white cliffs revived pleasant thoughts of Riversley, and thoughts of Riversley thoughts of Janet. which were singularly and refreshingly free from self-accusations.

Some love for my home, similar to what one may have for
Winter, came across me, and some appreciation of Janet as
well, in whose society I was sure to be at least myself, a
creature much reduced in altitude, but without the cramped
sensations of a man on a monument. My hearty Janet! I
thanked her then for seeing me of my natural height.

Some hours after parting with my father in London, I lay
down to sleep in my old home, feeling as if I had thrown off
a coat of armour. I awoke with a sailor's song on my lips.
Looking out of window at the well-known features of the
heaths and dark firs, and waning oak copses, and the shadowy
line of the downs stretching their long whale backs South to
West, it struck me that I had been barely alive of late.
Indeed one who consents to live as I had done, in a hope and
a retrospect, will find his life slipping between the two, like
the ships under the striding Colossus. I shook myself, braced
myself, and saluted every one at the breakfast table with the
frankness of Harry Richmond. Congratulated on my splendid
spirits, I was confirmed in the idea that I enjoyed them,
though I knew of something hollow which sent an echo
through me at intervals. Janet had become a fixed inmate
of the house. "I've bought her, and I shall keep her; she's
the apple of my eye," said the squire, adding with characteristic scrupulousness, "if apple's female." I asked her
whether she had heard from Temple latterly. "No; dear
little fellow!" cried she, and I saw in a twinkling what it
was that the squire liked in her, and liked it too. I caught
sight of myself, as through a rift of cloud, trotting home
from the hunt to a glad, frank, unpretending mate, with just
enough of understanding to look up to mine. For a second
or so it was pleasing, as a glance out of his library across
hill and dale will be to a strained student. Our familiarity
sanctioned a comment on the growth of her daughter-of-the-
regiment moustache, the faintest conceivable suggestion of a
shadow on her soft upper lip, which a poet might have
feigned to have fallen from her dark thick eyebrows.

"Why, you don't mean to say, Hal, it's not to your taste?"
said the squire.

"No," said I, turning an eye on my aunt Dorothy, "I've
loved it all my life."

The squire stared at me to make sure of this, muttered
that it was to his mind a beauty, and that it was nothing

more on Janet's lip than down on a flower, bloom on a plum. The poetical comparisons had the effect of causing me to examine her critically. She did not raise a spark of poetical sentiment in my bosom. She had grown a tall young woman, firmly built, light of motion, graceful perhaps; but it was not the grace of grace: the grace of simplicity, rather. She talked vivaciously and frankly, and gave (to friends) her whole eyes and a fine animation in talking; and her voice was a delight to friends; there was always the full ring of Janet in it, and music also. She still lifted her lip when she expressed contempt or dislike of persons; nor was she cured of her trick of frowning. She was as ready as ever to be flattered; that was evident. My grandfather's praise of her she received with a rewarding look back of kindness; she was not discomposed by flattery, and threw herself into no postures, nor blushed very deeply. ' Thank you for perceiving my merits,' she seemed to say; and to be just I should add that one could fancy her saying, you see them because you love me. She wore her hair in a plain knot, peculiarly neatly rounded away from the temples, which sometimes gave to a face not aquiline a look of swiftness. The face was mobile, various, not at all suggestive of bad temper, in spite of her frowns. The profile of it was less assuring than the front, because of the dark eyebrows' extension and the occasional frown, but that was not shared by the mouth, which was, I admitted to myself, a charming bow, running to a length at the corners like her eyebrows, quick with smiles. The corners of the mouth would often be in movement, setting dimples at work in her cheek, while the brows remained fixed, and thus at times a tender meditative air was given her that I could not think her own. Upon what could she possibly reflect? She had not a care, she had no education, she could hardly boast an idea—two at a time I was sure she never had entertained. The sort of wife for a fox-hunting lord, I summed up, and hoped he would be a good fellow.

Peterborough was plied by the squire for a description of German women. Blushing and shooting a timid look from under his pendulous eyelids at my aunt, indicating that he was prepared to go the way of tutors at Riversley, he said he really had not much observed them.

"They're a whitey-brown sort of women, aren't they?" the squire questioned him, "with tow hair and fish eyes, high o' the shoulder, bony, and a towel skin and gone teeth, so I've heard tell. I've heard that's why the men have all taken to their beastly smoking."

Peterborough ejaculated: "Indeed! sir, really!" He assured my aunt that German ladies were most agreeable, cultivated persons, extremely domesticated, retiring; the encomiums of the Roman historian were as well deserved by them in the present day as they had been in the past; decidedly, on the whole, Peterborough would call them a virtuous race.

"Why do they let the men smoke, then?" said the squire. "A pretty style o' courtship. Come, sit by my hearth, ma'am; I'll be your chimney—faugh! dirty rascals!"

Janet said: "I rather like the smell of cigars."

"Like what you please, my dear—he'll be a lucky dog," the squire approved her promptly, and asked me if I smoked.

I was not a stranger to the act, I confessed.

"Well"—he took refuge in practical philosophy—" a man must bring some dirt home from every journey: only don't smoke me out, mercy's sake."

Here was a hint of Janet's influence with him, and of what he expected from my return to Riversley.

Peterborough informed me that he suffered persecution over the last glasses of Port in the evening, through the squire's persistent inquiries as to whether a woman had anything to do with my staying so long abroad. "A lady, sir?" quoth Peterborough. "Lady, if you like," rejoined the squire. "You parsons and petticoats must always mince the meat to hash the fact." Peterborough defended his young friend Harry's moral reputation, and was amazed to hear that the squire did not think highly of a man's chastity. The squire acutely chagrined the sensitive gentleman by drawling the word after him, and declaring that he tossed that kind of thing into the women's wash-basket. Peterborough, not without signs of indignation, protesting, the squire asked him point-blank if he supposed that Old England had been raised to the head of the world by such as he. In fine, he favoured Peterborough with a lesson in worldly views. "But these," Peterborough said to me, "are not the views, dear Harry—if they are the views of ladies of any description, which I take leave to doubt—not the views of the ladies you and I would esteem. For instance.

the ladies of this household." My aunt Dorothy's fate was plain.

In reply to my grandfather's renewed demand to know whether any one of those High-Dutch women had got hold of me, Peterborough said: "Mr. Beltham, the only lady of whom it could be suspected that my friend Harry regarded her with more than ordinary admiration was hereditary princess of one of the ancient princely Houses of Germany." My grandfather thereupon said, "Oh!" pushed the wine, and was stopped.

Peterborough chuckled over this "Oh!" and the stoppage of further questions, while acknowledging that the luxury of a pipe would help to make him more charitable. He enjoyed the Port of his native land, but he did, likewise, feel the want of one whiff or so of the less restrictive foreigner's pipe; and he begged me to note the curiosity of our worship of aristocracy and royalty; and we, who were such slaves to rank, and such tyrants in our own households,—we Britons were the great sticklers for freedom! His conclusion was, that we were not logical. We would have a Throne, which we would not allow the liberty to do anything to make it worthy of rational veneration: we would have a peerage, of which we were so jealous that it formed almost an assembly of automatons; we would have virtuous women, only for them to be pursued by immoral men. Peterborough feared, he must say, that we were an inconsequent people. His residence abroad had so far unhinged him; but a pipe would have stopped his complainings.

Moved, perhaps, by generous wine, in concert with his longing for tobacco, he dropped an observation of unwonted shrewdness; he said: "The squire, my dear Harry, a most honourable and straightforward country gentleman, and one of our very wealthiest, is still, I would venture to suggest, an example of old blood that requires—I study race—varying, modifying, one might venture to say, correcting; and really, a friend with more privileges than I possess, would or should throw him a hint that no harm has been done to the family by an intermixture . . . . old blood does occasionally need it—you know I study blood—it becomes too coarse, or, in some cases, too fine. The study of the mixture of blood is probably one of our great physical problems."

Peterborough commended me to gratitude for the imaginative and chivalrous element bestowed on me by a father that was other than a country squire; one who could be tolerant of innocent habits, and not of guilty ones—a further glance at the interdicted pipe. I left him almost whimpering for it.

The contemplation of the curious littleness of the lives of men and women lived in this England of ours, made me feel as if I looked at them out of a palace balcony-window; for no one appeared to hope very much or to fear; people trotted in their different kinds of harness; and I was amused to think of my heart going regularly in imitation of those about me. I was in a princely state of mind indeed, not disinclined for a time to follow the general course of life, while despising it. An existence without colour, without anxious throbbing, without salient matter for thought, challenged contempt. But it was exceedingly funny. My aunt Dorothy, the squire, and Janet submitted to my transparent inward laughter at them, patiently waiting for me to share their contentment, in the deluded belief that the hour would come. The principal items of news embraced the death of Squire Gregory Bulsted, the marriage of this and that young lady, a legal contention between my grandfather and Lady Maria Higginson, the wife of a rich manufacturer newly located among us, on account of a right of encampment on Durstan heath, my grandfather taking side with the gipsies, and beating her ladyship—a friend of Heriot's, by the way. Concerning Heriot, my aunt Dorothy was in trouble. She could not, she said, approve his behaviour in coming to this neighbourhood at all, and she hinted that I might induce him to keep away. I mentioned Julia Bulsted's being in mourning, merely to bring in her name tentatively.

"Ay, mourning's her outer rig, never doubt," said the squire. "Flick your whip at her, she's a charitable soul, Judy Bulsted! She knits stockings for the poor. She'd down and kiss the stump of a sailor on a stick o' timber. All the same, she oughtn't to be alone. Pity she hasn't a baby. You and I'll talk it over by-and-by, Harry."

Kiomi was spoken of, and Lady Maria Higginson, and then Heriot.

"M—m—m—m rascal!" hummed the squire. "There's three, and that's not enough for him. Six months back a man comes over from Surreywards, a farm he calls Dipwell,

and asks after you, Harry; rigmaroles about a handsome
lass gone off . . . . some scoundrel! You and I'll talk it
over by-and-by, Harry."

Janet raised and let fall her eyebrows. The fiction that,
so much having been said, an immediate show of reserve on
such topics preserved her in ignorance of them, was one she
subscribed to merely to humour the squire. I was half in
doubt whether I disliked or admired her want of decent
hypocrisy. She allowed him to suppose that she did not
hear, but spoke as a party to the conversation. My aunt
Dorothy blamed Julia. The squire thundered at Heriot;
Janet, liking both, contented herself with impartial comments. "I always think in these cases that the women must
be the fools," she said. Her affectation was to assume a
knowledge of the world and all things in it. We rode over
to Julia's cottage, on the outskirts of the estate now devolved upon her husband. Irish eyes are certainly bewitching
lights. I thought, for my part, I could not do as the captain
was doing, serving his country in foreign parts, while such
as these were shining without a captain at home. Janet
approved his conduct, and was right. "What can a wife
think the man worth who sits down to guard his house-
door?" she answered my slight innuendo. She compared
the man to a kennel-dog. "This," said I, "comes of made-
up matches," whereat she was silent.

Julia took her own view of her position. She asked me
whether it was not dismal for one who was called a grass
widow, and was in reality a salt-water one, to keep fresh,
with a lap-dog, a cook and a maid-servant, and a postman
that passed the gate twenty times for twice that he opened
it, and nothing to look for but this disappointing creature
day after day! At first she was shy, stole out a coy line of
fingers to be shaken, and lisped; and out of that mood came
right-about-face, with an exclamation of regret that she
supposed she must not kiss me now. I projected, she drew
back. "Shall Janet go?" said I. "Then if nobody's present I'll be talked of," said she, moaning queerly. The
tendency of her hair to creep loose of its bands gave her
handsome face an aspect deliriously wild. I complimented
her on her keeping so fresh, in spite of her salt-water widowhood. She turned the tables on me for looking so powerful,
though I was dying for a foreign princess. "Oh! but that'll

blow over," she said; "anything blows over as long as you
don't go up to the altar;" and she eyed her ringed finger,
woebegone, and flashed the pleasantest of smiles with the
name of her William. Heriot, whom she always called Walter
Heriot, was, she informed me, staying at Durstan Hall, the
new great house, built on a plot of ground that the Lan-
cashire millionaire had caught up, while the squire and the
other landowners of the neighbourhood were sleeping. "And
if you get Walter Heriot to come to you, Harry Richmond,
it'll be better for him, I'm sure," she added, and naïvely :
" I'd like to meet him up at the Grange." Temple, she said
had left the Navy and was reading in London for the Bar—
good news to me.

" You have not told us anything about your princess,
Harry," Janet observed on the ride home.

" Do you take her for a real person, Janet ?"

" One thinks of her as a snow-mountain you've been
admiring."

" Very well ; so let her be."

" Is she kind and good ?"

" Yes."

" Does she ride well ?"

" She rides remarkably well."

" She's fair, I suppose ?"

" Janet, if I saw you married to Temple, it would be the
second great wish of my heart."

" Harry, you're a bit too cruel, as Julia would say."

" Have you noticed she gets more and more Irish ?"

" Perhaps she finds it is liked. Some women can adapt
themselves . . . they're the happiest. All I meant to ask
you is, whether your princess is like the rest of us ?"

" Not at all," said I, unconscious of hurting.

" Never mind. Don't be hard on Julia. She has the
making of a good woman—a girl can see that ; only she
can't bear loneliness, and doesn't understand yet what it is
to be loved by a true gentleman. Persons of that class can't
learn it all at once."

I was pained to see her in tears. Her figure was straight,
and she spoke without a quaver of her voice.

" Heriot's an excellent fellow," I remarked.

" He is. I can't think ill of my friends," said she.

" Dear girl, is it these two who make you unhappy ?"

" No ; but dear old grandada ! . . ."

The course of her mind was obvious. I would rather have had her less abrupt and more personal in revealing it. I stammered something.

" Heriot does not know you as I do," she said, strangling a whimper. " I was sure it was serious, though one's accustomed to associate princesses with young men's dreams. I fear, Harry, it will half break our dear old grandada's heart. He is rough, and you have often been against him, for one unfortunate reason. If you knew him as I do you would pity him sincerely. He hardly grumbled at all at your terribly long absence. Poor old man ! he hopes on."

" He's incurably unjust to my father."

" Your father has been with you all the time, Harry ? 1 guessed it."

" Well ?"

" It generally bodes no good to the Grange. Do pardon me for saying that. I know nothing of him ; I know only that the squire is generous, and *that* I stand for him with ill my might. Forgive me for what I said."

" Forgive you ; with all my heart. I like you all the better. You're a brave partisan. I don't expect women to be philosophers."

" Well, Harry, I would take your side as firmly as any. body's."

" Do, then ; tell the squire how I am situated."

" Ah !" she half sighed, " I knew this was coming."

" How could it other than come ? You can do what you like with the squire. I'm dependent on him, and I am betrothed to the Princess Ottilia. God knows how much she has to trample down on her part. She casts off—to speak plainly, she puts herself out of the line of succession, and for whom ? for me. In her father's lifetime she will hardly yield me her hand ; but I must immediately be in a position to offer mine. She may : who can tell ? she is above all women in power and firmness. You talk of generosity ; could there be a higher example of it ?"

" I daresay ; I know nothing of princesses," Janet murmured. " I don't quite comprehend what she has done. The point is, what am I to do ?"

" Prepare him for it. Soothe him in advance. Why, dear Janet, you can reconcile him to anything in a minute."

"Lie to him downright?"

"Now what on earth is the meaning of that, and why can't you speak mildly?"

"I suppose I speak as I feel. I'm a plain speaker, a plain person. You don't give me an easy task, friend Harry."

"If you believe in his generosity, Janet, should you be afraid to put it to proof?"

"Grandada's generosity, Harry? I do believe in it as I believe in my own life. It happens to be the very thing I must keep myself from rousing in him, to be of any service to you. Look at the old house!" She changed her tone. "Looking on old Riversley with the eyes of my head even, I think I'm looking at something far away in the memory. Perhaps the deep red brick causes it. There never was a house with so many beautiful creepers. Bright as they are, you notice the roses on the wall. There's a face for me for ever from every window; and good-by, Riversley! Harry, I'll obey your wishes."

So saying, she headed me, trotting down the heath-track.

CHAPTER XXXVII.

JANET RENOUNCES ME.

An illness of old Sewis, the butler,—amazingly resembling a sick monkey in his bed—kept me from paying a visit to Temple and seeing my father for several weeks, during which time Janet loyally accustomed the squire to hear of the German princess, and she did it with a decent and agreeable cheerfulness that I quite approved of. I should have been enraged at a martyr-like appearance on her part, for I demanded a sprightly devotion to my interests, considering love so holy a thing, that where it existed, all surrounding persons were bound to do it homage and service. We were thrown together a great deal in attending on poor old Sewis, who would lie on his pillows recounting for hours my father's midnight summons of the inhabitants of Riversley, and his little Harry's infant expedition into

the world. Temple and Heriot came to stay at the Grange,
and assisted in some rough scene-painting—torrid colours
representing the island of Jamaica. We hung it at the foot
of old Sewis's bed. He awoke and contemplated it, and
went downstairs the same day, cured, he declared: the fact
being that the unfortunate picture testified too strongly to
the reversal of all he was used to in life, in having those he
served to wait on him. The squire celebrated his recovery
by giving a servants' ball. Sewis danced with the handsomest lass, swung her to supper, and delivered an extraordinary speech, entirely concerning me, and rather to my
discomposure, particularly so when it was my fate to hear
that the old man had made me the heir of his savings.
Such was his announcement in a very excited voice, but
incidentally upon a solemn adjuration to the squire to
beware of his temper—govern his temper and not be a
turncoat. We were present at the head of the supper-table
to hear our healths drunk. Sewis spoke like a half-caste
oblivious of his training, and of the subjects he was at
liberty to touch on as well. Evidently there was a weight
of foreboding on his mind. He knew his master well. The
squire excused him under the ejaculation, " Drunk, by the
Lord !" Sewis went so far as to mention my father. "He
no disgrace, sar, he no disgrace, I say ! but he pull one way,
old house pull other way, and 'tween 'em my little Harry
torn apieces, squire. He set out in the night. ' You not
enter it any more !' Very well. I go my lawyer next day.
You see my Will, squire. Years ago, and little Harry so
high. Old Sewis not the man to change. He no turncoat,
squire. God bless you, my master ; you recollect, and ladies
tell you if you forget, old Sewis no turncoat. You hate
turncoat. You taught old Sewis, and God bless you, and
Mr. Harry, and British Constitution, all Amen !"

With that he bounded to bed. He was dead next morning.

The squire was humorous over my legacy. It amounted
to about seventeen hundred pounds invested in Government
Stock, and he asked me what I meant to do with it ; proposed a Charity to be established on behalf of decayed half-
castes, insisting that servants' money could never be appro-
priated to the uses of gentlemen. All the while he was
muttering " Turncoat ! eh ? turncoat ?"—proof that the word

had struck where it was aimed. For me, after thinking on it, I had a superstitious respect for the legacy, so I determined, in spite of the squire's laughter over " Sixty pounds per annum !" to let it rest in my name. I saw for the first time the possibility that I might not have my grandfather's wealth to depend upon. He warned me of growing miserly. With my father in London, living freely on my property, I had not much fear of that. However, I said discreetly, " I don't mind spending when I see my way."

" Oh ! see your way," said he, " Better a niggard than a chuckfist. Only, there's my girl : she's good at accounts. One'll do for them, Harry ?—ha'n't been long enough at home yet ?"

Few were the occasions when our conversation did not diverge to this sort of interrogation. Temple and Heriot, with whom I took counsel, advised me to wait until the idea of the princess had worn its way into his understanding, and leave the work to Janet. " Though," said Heriot to me aside, " upon my soul, it's slaughter." He believed that Janet felt keenly. But then, she admired him, and so they repaid one another.

I won my grandfather's confidence in practical matters on a trip we took into Wales. But it was not enough for me to be a man of business, he affirmed ; he wanted me to have some ambition ; why not stand for our county at the next general election ? He offered me his Welsh borough if I thought fit to decline a contest. This was to speak as mightily as a German prince. Virtually, in wealth and power, he was a prince ; but of how queer a kind ! He was immensely gratified by my refraining to look out for my father on our return journey through London, and remarked that I had not seen him for some time, he supposed. To which I said, no, I had not. He advised me to let the fellow run his length. Suggesting that he held it likely I contributed to " the fellow's " support : he said generously, " Keep clear of him, Hal : I add you a thousand a year to your allowance," and damned me for being so thoughtful over it. I found myself shuddering at a breath of anger from him. Could he not with a word dash my hopes for ever ? The warning I had taken from old Sewis transformed me to something like a hypocrite, and I dare say I gave the squire to understand that I had not seen my father for a very long period and knew nothing of his recent doings. "Been infernally quiet these last two or three years," the squire muttered of the object of his aversion. "I heard of a City widow last, sick as a Dover packet-boat 'bout the fellow! Well, the women are ninnies, but you're a man, Harry; you're not to be taken in any longer, eh?"

I replied that I knew my father better now, and was asked how the deuce I knew him better. It was the world I knew better after my stay on the Continent.

I contained myself enough to say, "Very well, the world, sir."

"Flirted with one of their princesses?" He winked.

"On that subject I will talk to you some other time," said I.

"Got to pay an indemnity? or what?" He professed alarm, and pushed for explanations with the air of a man of business ready to help me if need were. "Make a clean breast of it, Harry. You're not the son of Tom Fool the Bastard for nothing, I'll swear. All the same you're Beltham; you're my grandson and heir, and I'll stand by you. Out with 't! She's a princess, is she?"

The necessity for correcting his impressions taught me to think the moment favourable. I said, "I am engaged to her, sir."

He returned promptly: "Then you'll break it off."

I shook my head.

"Why you can't jilt my girl at home!" said he.

"Do you find a princess objectionable, sir?"

"Objectionable? She's a foreigner. I don't know her. I never saw her. Here's my Janet I've brought up for you, under my own eyes, out of the way of every damned soft-sawderer, safe and plump as a melon under a glass, and you fight shy of her and go and engage yourself to a foreigner I don't know and never saw! By George, Harry, I'll call in a parson to settle you soon as ever we sight Riversley. I'll couple you, by George, I will! 'fore either of you know whether you're on your legs or your backs."

We were in the streets of London, so he was obliged to moderate his vehemence.

"Have you consulted Janet?" said I.

"Consulted her? ever since she was a chick with half a feather on."

A chick with half a feather on," I remarked, "is not always of the same mind as a piece of poultry of full plumage."

"Hang your sneering and your talk of a fine girl, like my Janet, as a piece of poultry, you young rooster! You toss your head up like a cock too conceited to crow. I'll swear the girl's in love with you. She does you the honour to be fond of you. She's one in a million. A handsome girl, straight-backed, honest, just a dash, and not too much, of our blood in her."

"Consult her again, sir," I broke in. "You will discover she is not of your way of thinking."

"Do you mean to say she's given you a left-hander, Harry?"

"I have only to say that I have not given her the option."

He groaned going up the steps of his hotel, faced me once or twice, and almost gained my sympathy by observing, "When we're boys, the old ones worry us; when we're old ones, the boys begin to tug!" He rarely spoke so humanely, —rarely, at least, to me.

For a wonder, he let the matter drop : possibly because he found me temperate. I tried the system on him with good effect during our stay in London ; that is, I took upon myself to be always cool, always courteous, deliberate in my replies, and not uncordial, though I was for representing the reserved young man. I obtained some praise for my style and bearing among his acquaintances. To one lady passing an encomium on me, he said, " Oh, some foreign princess has been training him," which seemed to me of good augury.

My friends Temple and Heriot were among the Riversley guests at Christmas. We rode over to John Thresher's, of whom we heard that the pretty Mabel Sweetwinter had disappeared, and understood that suspicion had fallen upon one of us gentlemen. Bob, her brother, had gone the way of the bravest English fellows of his class—to America. We called on the miller, a soured old man. Bob's evasion affected him more than Mabel's, Martha Thresher said, in derision of our sex. I was pained to hear from her that Bob supposed me the misleader of his sister ; and that he had, as she believed, left England, to avoid the misery of ever meeting me again, because he liked me so much. She had been seen walking down the lanes with some one resembling me in figure.

Heriot took the miller's view, counting the loss of one stout young Englishman to his country of far greater importance thar the escapades of dozens of girls, for which simple creatures he had no compassion : he held the expression of it a sham. It was given them to exercise the choice whether they would be prey to the natural hawk, man, if they liked it ; pity was waste of breath, nonsense. Temple bantered him capitally by tracing the career of the natural hawk gorged with prey, and the mighty service he was of to his country. Heriot retorted that all great men had, we should find, entertained his ideas about women ; but he was compelled to admit that a vast number of very small ones were similarly to be distinguished. He had grown terribly coxcombical. Without talking of his conquests, he talked largely of the ladies who were possibly in the situation of victims to his grace of person, though he did not do so with any unctuous boasting. On the contrary, there was a rather taking undertone of regret that his enfeebled over-fat country would give her military son no worthier occupation. He laughed at the mention of Julia Bulsted's name. " She proves, Richie, marriage is the best of all receipts for women, just as it's the worst for men. Poor Billy Bulsted, for instance, a first-rate seaman, and his heart's only half in his profession since he and Julia swore their oath ; and no wonder,—he made something his own that won't go under lock and key. No military or naval man ought ever to marry."

" Stop," said Temple, " is the poor old country——How about continuing the race of heroes ? "

Heriot commended him to rectories, vicarages, and curates' lodgings for breeding grounds, and coming round to Julia related one of the racy dialogues of her married life. " The salt-water widow's delicious. Billy rushes home from his ship in a hurry. What's this Greg writes me ?—That he's got a friend of his to drink with him, d'ye mean, William ? —A friend of yours, ma'am.—And will you say a friend of mine is not a friend of yours, William ?—Julia, you're driving me mad !—And is that far from crazy, where you said I drove you at first sight of me, William ? Back to his ship goes Billy with a song of love and constancy."

I said nothing of my chagrin at the behaviour of the pair who had furnished my first idea of the romantic beauty of love.

"Why does she talk twice as Irish as she used to, Heriot?"

"Just to coax the world to let her be as nonsensical as she likes. She's awfully dull; she has only her nonsense to amuse her. I repeat: soldiers and sailors oughtn't to marry. I'm her best friend. I am, on my honour: for I'm going to make Billy give up the service, since he can't give her up. There she is!" he cried out, and waved his hat to a lady on horseback some way down the slope of a road leading to the view of our heathland: "There's the only girl living fit to marry a man and swear she'll stick to him through life and death."

He started at a gallop. Temple would have gone too at any possible speed, for he knew as well as I did that Janet was the girl alone capable of winning a respectful word from Heriot; but I detained him to talk of Ottilia and my dismal prospect of persuading the squire to consent to my proposal for her, and to dower her in a manner worthy a princess. He doled out his yes and no to me vacantly. Janet and Heriot came at a walking pace to meet us, he questioning her, she replying, but a little differently from her usual habit of turning her full face to the speaker. He was evidently startled, and, to judge from his posture, repeated his question, as one would say, '*You* did this?' She nodded, and then uttered some rapid words, glanced at him, laughed shyly, and sank her features into repose as we drew near. She had a deep blush on her face. I thought it might be that Janet and her loud champion had come to particular terms, a supposition that touched me with regrets for Temple's sake. But Heriot was not looking pleased. It happened that whatever Janet uttered struck a chord of opposition in me. She liked the Winter and the Winter sunsets, had hopes of a frost for skating, liked our climate, thought our way of keeping Christmas venerable, rejoiced in dispensing the squire's bounties—called them bounties, joined Heriot in abusing foreign countries to the exaltation of her own: all this with "Well, Harry, I'm sorry you don't think as we do. And we do, don't we?" she addressed him.

"I reserve a point," he said, and not playfully.

She appeared distressed, and courted a change of expression in his features, and I have to confess that never having seen her gaze upon any one save myself in that fashion, which was

with her very winning, especially where some of her contralto
tones of remonstrance or entreaty aided it, I felt as a man does
at a neighbour's shadow cast over his rights of property.

Heriot dropped to the rear : I was glad to leave her with
Temple, and glad to see them canter ahead together on the
sand of the heaths:

"She has done it," Heriot burst out abruptly. "She has
done it!" he said again. "Upon my soul, I never wished in
my life before that I was a marrying man : I might have a
chance of ending worth something. She has won the squire
round with a thundering fib, and you're to have the German
if you can get her. Don't be in a hurry. The squire'll speak
to you to-night : but think over it. Will you? Think what
a girl this is. I believe on my honour no man ever had such
an offer of a true woman. Come, don't think it's Heriot
speaking—I've always liked her, of course. But I have
always respected her, and that's not of course. Depend upon
it, a woman who can be a friend of men is the right sort of
woman to make a match with. Do you suppose she couldn't
have a dozen fellows round her at the lift of her finger ?—
the pick of the land! I'd trust her with an army. I tell
you, Janet Ilchester's the only girl alive who'll double the
man she marries. I don't know another who wouldn't make
the name of wife laugh the poor devil out of house and company. She's firm as a rock ; and sweet as a flower on it!
Will that touch you? Bah! Richie, let's talk like men. I
feel for her because she's fond of you, and I know what it is
when a girl like that sets her heart on a fellow. There," he
concluded, "I'd ask you to go down on your knees and pray
before you decide against her!"

Heriot succeeded in raising a certain dull indistinct image
in my mind of a well-meaning girl, to whom I was bound
to feel thankful, and felt so. I thanked Heriot, too, for his
friendly intentions. He had never seen the Princess Ottilia.
And at night I thanked my grandfather. He bore himself,
on the whole, like the good and kindly old gentleman Janet
loved to consider him. He would not stand in my light, he
said, recurring to that sheet-anchor of a tolerant sentence
whenever his forehead began to gather clouds. He regretted
that Janet was no better than her sex in her preference for
rakes, and wished me to the deuce for bringing Heriot into
the house, and not knowing when I was lucky. "German

grandchildren, eh ! " he muttered. No Beltham had ever
married a foreigner. What was the time fixed between us
for the marriage ? He wanted to see his line safe before he
died. " How do I know this foreign woman'll bear ? " he
asked, expecting an answer. His hand was on the back of a
chair, grasping and rocking it ; his eyes bent stormily on the
carpet ; they were set blinking rapidly after a glance at me.
Altogether his self-command was creditable to Janet's tuition.

Janet met me next day, saying with some insolence (so it
struck me from her liveliness): " Well, it's all right, Harry ?
Now you'll be happy, I hope." I did not shine in my reply.
Her amiable part appeared to be to let me see how brilliant
and gracious the commonplace could be made to look. She
kept Heriot at the Grange, against the squire's remonstrance
and her mother's. " It's to keep him out of harm's way :
the women he knows are not of the best kind for him," she
said, with astounding fatuity. He submitted, and seemed to
like it. She must be teaching Temple to skate figures in the
frost, with a great display of good-humoured patience, and
her voice at musical pitches. But her principal affectation
was to talk on matters of business with Mr. Burgin and Mr.
Trewint, the squire's lawyer and bailiff, on mines and interest,
on money and economical questions ; not shrinking from
politics either, until the squire cries out to the males assisting in the performance, " Gad, she's a head as good as our
half-dozen put together," and they servilely joined their
fragmentary capitals in agreement. She went so far as to
retain Peterborough to teach her Latin. He was idling in
the expectation of a living in the squire's gift. The annoyance for me was that I could not detach myself from a contemplation of these various scenes, by reverting to my life in
Germany. The preposterous closing of my interview with
Ottilia blocked the way, and I was unable to write to her—
unable to address her even in imagination, without pangs of
shame at the review of the petty conspiracy I had sanctioned
to entrap her to plight her hand to me, and without perpetually multiplying excuses for my conduct. So to escape
them I was reduced to study Janet, forming one of her satellites. She could say to me impudently, with all the air of a
friendly comrade, " Had your letter from Germany yet,
Harry ?" She flew—she was always on the chase. I saw
her permit Heriot to kiss her hand, and then the squire

appeared, and Heriot and she burst into laughter, and the
squire, with a puzzled face, would have the game explained
to him, but understood not a bit of it, only growled at me;
upon which Janet became serious and chid him. I was told
by my aunt Dorothy to admire this behaviour of hers. One
day she certainly did me a service: a paragraph in one of
the newspapers spoke of my father, not flatteringly: "Richmond is in the field again," it commenced. The squire was
waiting for her to hand the paper to him. None of us could
comprehend why she played him off and denied him his right
to the first perusal of the news; she was voluble, almost
witty, full of sprightly Roxalana petulance. "This paper,"
she said, "deserves to be burnt," and she was allowed to burn
it—money article, mining column as well—on the pretext of
an infamous anti-Tory leader, of which she herself composed
the first sentence to shock the squire completely. I had
sight of that paper some time afterwards. Richmond was
in the field again, it stated, with mock flourishes. But that
was not the worst. My grandfather's name was down there,
and mine, and Princess Ottilia's. My father's connection
with the court of Eppenwelzen-Sarkeld was alluded to as the
latest, and next to his winning the heiress of Riversley, the
most sucessful of his ventures, inasmuch as his son, if rumour
was to be trusted, had obtained the promise of the hand of
the princess. The paragraph was an excerpt from a gossiping weekly journal, perhaps less malevolent than I thought
it. There was some fun to be got out of a man who, the
journal in question was informed, had joined the arms of
England and a petty German principality stamped on his
plate and furniture.

My gratitude to Janet was fervent enough when I saw
what she had saved me from. I pressed her hand and held
it. I talked stupidly, but I made my cruel position intelligible to her, and she had the delicacy, on this occasion, to
keep her sentiments regarding my father unuttered. We
sat hardly less than an hour side by side—I know not how
long hand in hand. The end was an extraordinary trembling
in the limb abandoned to me. It seized her frame. I would
have detained her, but it was plain she suffered both in her
heart and her pride. Her voice was under fair command—
more than mine was. She counselled me to go to London at
once. "I would be off to London if I were you, Harry,"—

for the purpose of checking my father's extravagances,— would have been the further wording, which she spared me; and I thanked her, wishing, at the same time, that she would get the habit of using choicer phrases whenever there might, by chance, be a stress of emotion between us. Her trembling, and her "I'd be off," came into unpleasant collision in the recollection. I acknowledge to myself that she was a true and hearty friend. She listened with interest to my discourse on the necessity of my being in Parliament before I could venture to propose formally for the hand of the princess, and undertook to bear the burden of all consequent negotiations with my grandfather. If she would but have allowed me to speak of Temple, instead of saying, "Don't, Harry, I like him so much!" at the very mention of his name, I should have sincerely felt my indebtedness to her, and some admiration of her fine spirit and figure besides. I could not even agree with my aunt Dorothy that Janet was handsome. When I had to grant her a pardon I appreciated her better.

CHAPTER XXXVIII.

MY BANKERS' BOOK.

THE squire again did honour to Janet's eulogy and good management of him.

"And where," said she, "would you find a Radical to behave so generously, Harry, when it touches him so?"

He accorded me his permission to select my side in politics, merely insisting that I was never to change it, and this he requested me to swear to, for (he called the ghost of old Sewis to witness) he abhorred a turncoat.

"If you're to be a Whig, or a sneaking half-and-half, I can't help you much," he remarked. "I can pop a young Tory in for my borough, maybe; but I can't insult a number of independent Englishmen by asking them to vote for the opposite crew; that's reasonable, eh? And I can't promise you plumpers for the county neither. You can date your Address from Riversley. You'll have your house in town.

Tell me this princess of yours is ready with her hand, and,"
he threw in roughly, " is a respectable young woman, I'll
commence building. You'll have a house fit for a prince in
town and country, both."

Temple had produced an effect on him by informing him
that " this princess of mine " was entitled to be considered a
fit and proper person, in rank and blood, for an alliance with
the proudest royal Houses of Europe, and my grandfather
was not quite destitute of consolation in the prospect I presented to him. He was a curious study to me of the Tory
mind, in its attachment to solidity, fixity, certainty, its
unmatched generosity within a limit, its devotion to the
family, and its family eye for the country. An immediate
introduction to Ottilia would have won him to enjoy the
idea of his grandson's marriage ; but not having seen her,
he could not realize her dignity, nor even the womanliness
of a foreign woman.

"Thank God for one thing," he said : " we shan't have
that fellow bothering—shan't have the other half of your
family messing the business. You'll have to account for
him to your wife as you best can. I've nothing to do with
him, mind that. He came to my house, stole my daughter,
crazed her wits, dragged us all . . . ."

The excuse to turn away from the hearing of abuse of my
father was too good to be neglected, though it was horribly
humiliating that I should have to take advantage of it—
vexatious that I should seem chargeable with tacit lying in
allowing the squire to suppose the man he hated to be a
stranger to the princess. Not feeling sure whether it might
be common prudence to delude him even passively, I thought
of asking Janet for her opinion, but refrained. A stout
deceiver has his merits, but a feeble hypocrite applying to
friends to fortify him in his shifts and tergiversations must
provoke contempt. I desired that Janet might continue to
think well of me. I was beginning to drop in my own
esteem, which was the mirror of my conception of Ottilia's
view of her lover. Now, had I consulted Janet, I believe
the course of my history would have been different, for she
would not then, I may imagine, have been guilty of her
fatal slip of the tongue that threw us into heavy seas when
we thought ourselves floating on canal waters. A canal
barge (an image to me of the most perfect attainable peace),

suddenly, on its passage through our long fir-woods, with their scented reeds and flowering rushes, wild balsam and silky cotton-grass beds, sluiced out to sea and storm, would be somewhat in my likeness soon after a single luckless observation had passed at our Riversley breakfast-table one Sunday morning.

My aunt Dorothy and Mr. Peterborough were conversing upon the varieties of Christian sects, and particularly such as approached nearest to Anglicanism, together with the strange, saddening fact that the Christian religion appeared to be more divided than, Peterborough regretted to say, the forms of idolatry established by the Buddha, Mahomet, and other impostors. He claimed the audacious merit for us that we did not discard the reason of man : we admitted man's finite reason to our school of faith, and it was found refractory. Hence our many divisions.

"The Roman Catholics admit reason ? " said Janet, who had too strong a turn for showing her keenness in little encounters with Peterborough.

"No," said he ; "the Protestants." And, anxious to elude her, he pressed on to enchain my aunt Dorothy's attention. Janet plagued him meanwhile, and I helped her. We ran him and his schoolboy, the finite refractory, up and down, until Peterborough was glad to abandon him, and Janet said, "Did you preach to the Germans much ? " He had officiated in Prince Ernest's private chapel : not, he added in his egregious modesty, not that he personally wished to officiate.

"It was Harry's wish ?" Janet said, smiling.

"My post of tutor," Peterborough hastened to explain, "was almost entirely supernumerary. The circumstances being so, I the more readily acquiesced in the title of private chaplain, prepared to fulfil such duties as devolved upon me in that capacity, and acting thereon I proffered my occasional services. Lutheranism and Anglicanism are not, doubtless you are aware, divided on the broader bases. We are common Protestants. The Papacy, I can assure you, finds as little favour with one as with the other. Yes, I held forth, as you would say, from time to time. My assumption of the title of private chaplain, it was thought, improved the family dignity—that is, on *our* side."

"Thought by Harry ?" said Janet; and my aunt Dorothy said, " You and Harry had a consultation about it ?"

"Wanted to appear as grand as they could," quoth the squire.

Peterborough signified an assent, designed to modify the implication. "Not beyond due bounds, I trust, sir."

"Oh! now I understand," Janet broke out in the falsetto notes of a puzzle solved in the mind. "It was his father! Harry proclaiming his private chaplain!"

"Mr. Harry's father did first suggest——" said Peterborough, but her quickly-altered features caused him to draw in his breath, as she had done after one short laugh.

My grandfather turned a round side-eye on me, hard as a cock's.

Janet immediately started topics to fill Peterborough's mouth : the weather, the walk to church, the probable preacher. "And, grandada," said she to the squire, who was muttering ominously with a grim under-jaw, "His private chaplain!" and for this once would not hear her,— "Grandada, I shall drive you over to see papa this afternoon." She talked as if nothing had gone wrong. Peterborough, criminal red, attacked a jam-pot for a diversion. "Such sweets are rare indeed on the Continent," he observed to my aunt Dorothy. "Our home-made dainties are matchless."

"Private chaplain!" the squire growled again.

"It's you that preach this afternoon," Janet said to Peterborough. "Do you give us an extempore sermon?"

"You remind me, Miss Ilchester, I must look to it; I have a little trimming to do."

Peterborough thought he might escape, but the squire arrested him. "You'll give me five minutes before you're out of the house, please. D'ye smoke on Sundays?"

"Not on Sundays, sir," said Peterborough, openly and cordially, as to signify that they were of one mind regarding the perniciousness of Sunday smoking.

"See you don't set fire to my ricks with your foreign chaplain's tricks. I spied you puffing behind one t'other day. There," the squire dispersed Peterborough's unnecessary air of abtruse recollection, "don't look as though you were trying to hit on a pin's head in a bushel of oats. Don't set my ricks on fire—that's all."

"Mr. Peterborough," my aunt Dorothy interposed her

voice to soften this rough treatment of him with the offer of some hot-house flowers for his sitting-room.

"Oh, I thank you!" I heard the garlanded victim lowing as I left him to the squire's mercy.

Janet followed me out. "It was my fault, Harry. You won't blame him, I know. But will he fib? I don't think he's capable of it, and I'm sure he can't run and double. Grandada will have him fast before a minute is over."

I told her to lose no time in going and extracting the squire's promise that Peterborough should have his living,—so much it seemed possible to save.

She flew back, and in Peterborough's momentary absence, did her work. Nothing could save the unhappy gentleman from a distracting scene and much archaic English. The squire's power of vituperation was notorious: he could be more than a match for roadside navvies and predatory tramps in cogency of epithet. Peterborough came to me drenched, and wailing that he had never heard such language,—never dreamed of it. And to find himself the object of it!—and, worse, to be unable to conscientiously defend himself! The pain to him was in the conscience,—which is, like the spleen, a function whose uses are only to be understood in its derangement. He had eased his conscience to every question right out, and he rejoiced to me at the immense relief it gave him. Conscientiously he could not deny that he knew the squire's objection to my being in my father's society; and he had connived at it "for reasons, my dearest Harry, I can justify to God and man, but not—I had to confess as much—not, I grieve to say, to your grandfather. I attempted to do justice to the amiable qualities of the absent. In a moment I was assailed with epithets that . . . and not a word is to be got in when he is so violent. One has to make up one's mind to act Andromeda, and let him be the sea-monster, as somebody has said; I forget the exact origin of the remark."

The squire certainly had a whole ocean at command. I strung myself to pass through the same performance. To my astonishment I went unchallenged. Janet vehemently asserted that she had mollified the angry old man, who, however, was dark of visage, though his tongue kept silence. He was gruff over his wine-glass: the blandishments of his favourite did not brighten him. From his point of view he

had been treated vilely, and he was apparently inclined to
nurse his rancour and keep my fortunes trembling in the
balance. Under these circumstances it was impossible for
me to despatch a letter to Ottilia, though I found that I
could write one now, and I sat in my room writing all day,
—most eloquent stuff it was. The shadow of misfortune
restored the sense of my heroical situation, which my father
had extinguished, and this unlocked the powers of speech.
I wrote so admirably that my wretchedness could enjoy the
fine millinery I decorated it in. Then to tear the noble
composition to pieces was a bitter gratification. Ottilia's
station repelled and attracted me mysteriously. I could not
separate her from it, nor keep my love of her from the con-
tentions into which it threw me. In vain I raved, "What
is rank?" There was a magnet in it that could at least set
me quivering and twisting, behaving like a man spell-
bound, as madly as any hero of the ballads under a wizard's
charm.

At last the squire relieved us. He fixed that side-cast
cock's eye of his on me, and said, "Where's your bankers'
book, sir?"

I presumed that it was with my bankers, but did not
suggest the possibility that my father might have it in his
custody; for he had a cheque-book of his own, and regulated
our accounts. Why not? I thought, and flushed somewhat
defiantly. The money was mine.

"Any objection to my seeing that book?" said the squire.

"None whatever, sir."

He nodded. I made it a point of honour to write for the
book to be sent down to me immediately.

The book arrived, and the squire handed it to me to break
the cover, insisting, "You're sure you wouldn't rather not
have me look at it?"

"Quite," I replied. The question of money was to me
perfectly unimportant. I did not see a glimpse of danger
in his perusing the list of my expenses.

"'Cause I give you my word I know nothing about it
now," he said.

I complimented him on his frank method of dealing, and
told him to look at the book if he pleased, but with prudence
sufficiently awake to check the declaration that I had not
once looked at it myself

He opened it. We had just assembled in the hall, where breakfast was laid during Winter, before a huge wood fire. Janet had her teeth on her lower lip, watching the old man's face. I did not condescend to be curious ; but when I turned my head to him he was puffing through thin lips, and then his mouth crumpled in a knob. He had seen sights.

" By George, I must have breakfast 'fore I go into this !" he exclaimed, and stared as if he had come out of an oven.

Dorothy Beltham reminded him that Prayers had not been read.

" Prayers !" He was about to objurgate, but affirmatived her motion to ring the bell for the servants, and addressed Peterborough : " You read 'em abroad every morning ?"

Peterborough's conscience started off on its inevitable jog-trot at a touch of the whip. " A—yes ; that is—oh, it was my office." He had to recollect with exactitude : " I should specify exceptions ; there were intervals . . ."

" Please, open your Bible," the squire cut him short ; " I don't want a damned fine edge on everything."

Partly for an admonition to him, or in pure nervousness, Peterborough blew his nose monstrously : an unlucky note ; nothing went well after it. " A slight cold," he murmured and resumed the note, and threw himself maniacally into it. The unexpected figure of Captain Bulsted on. tiptoe, wearing the ceremonial depressed air of intruders on these occasions, distracted our attention for a moment.

" Fresh from ship, William ?" the squire called out.

The captain ejaculated a big word, to judge of it from the aperture, but it was mute as his footing on the carpet, and he sat and gazed devoutly toward Peterborough, who had waited to see him take his seat, and must now, in his hurry to perform his duty, sweep the peccant little red-bound book to the floor. " Here, I'll have that," said the squire. " Allow me, sir," said Peterborough ; and they sprang into a collision.

" Would you jump out of your pulpit to pick up an old woman's umbrella ?" the squire asked him in anger, and muttered of requiring none of his clerical legerdemain with books of business. Tears were in Peterborough's eyes. My aunt Dorothy's eyes dwelt kindly on him to encourage him, but the man's irritable nose was again his enemy.

Captain Bulsted chanced to say in the musical voice of inquiry: " Prayers are not yet over, are they ?"

" No, nor never will be with a parson blowing his horn at this rate," the squire rejoined. " And mind you," he said to Peterborough, after dismissing the servants, to whom my aunt Dorothy read the morning lessons apart, " I'd not have had this happen, sir, for money in lumps. I've always known I should hang the day when my house wasn't blessed in the morning by prayer. So did my father, and his before him. Fiddle! sir, you can't expect young people to wear decent faces when the parson's hopping over the floor like a flea, and trumpeting as if the organ-pipe wouldn't have the sermon at any price. You tried to juggle me out of this book here."

" On my!—indeed, sir, no !" Peterborough proclaimed his innocence, and it was unlikely that the squire should have suspected him.

Captain Bulsted had come to us for his wife, whom he had not found at home on his arrival last midnight.

" God bless my soul," said the squire, " you don't mean to tell me she's gone off, William ?"

" Oh! dear, no, sir," said the captain, " she's only cruising."

The squire recommended a draught of old ale. The captain accepted it. His comportment was cheerful in a sober fashion, notwithstanding the transparent perturbation of his spirit. He answered my aunt Dorothy's questions relating to Julia simply and manfully, as became a gallant seaman, cordially excusing his wife for not having been at home to welcome him, with the singular plea, based on his knowledge of the sex, that the nearer she knew him to be the less able was she to sit on her chair waiting like Patience. He drank his ale from the hands of Sillabin, our impassive new butler, who had succeeded Sewis, the squire told him, like a Whig Ministry the Tory; proof that things were not improving.

" I thought, sir, things were getting better," said the captain.

" The damnedest mistake ever made, William. How about the Fall of Man, then ? eh ? You talk like a heathen Radical. It's Scripture says we're going from better to worse, and that's Tory doctrine. And stick to the good as long as you can! Why, William, you were a jolly bachelor once."

"Sir, and ma'am," the captain bowed to Dorothy Beltham, "I have, thanks to you, never known happiness but in marriage, and all I want is my wife."

The squire fretted for Janet to depart. "I'm going, grandada," she said. "You'll oblige me by not attending to any matter of business to-day. Give me that book of Harry's to keep for you."

"How d'ye mean, my dear?"

"It's bad work done on a Sunday, you know."

"So it is. I'll lock up the book."

"I have your word for that, grandada," said Janet.

The ladies retired, taking Peterborough with them.

"Good-bye to the frocks! and now, William, out with your troubles," said the squire.

The captain's eyes were turned to the door my aunt Dorothy had passed through.

"You remember the old custom, sir!"

"Ay, do I, William. Sorry for you then; infernally sorry for you now, that I am! But you've run your head into the halter."

"I love her, sir; I love her to distraction. Let any man on earth say she's not an angel, I flatten him dead as his lie. By the way, sir, I am bound in duty to inform you I am speaking of my wife."

"To be sure you are, William, and a trim schooner-yacht she is."

"She's off, sir; she's off!"

I thought it time to throw in a word. "Captain Bulsted, I should hold any man but you accountable to me for hinting such things of my friend."

"Harry, your hand," he cried, sparkling.

"Hum; his hand!" growled the squire. "His hand's been pretty lively on the Continent, William. Here, look at this book, William, and the bundle o' cheques! No, I promised my girl. We'll go into it to-morrow, he and I, early. The fellow has shot away thousands and thousands—been gallivanting among his foreign duchesses and countesses. There's a petticoat in that bank-book of his; and more than one, I wager. Now he's for marrying a foreign princess— got himself in a tangle there, it seems."

"Mightily well done, Harry!" Captain Bulsted struck a
terrific encomium on my shoulder, groaning, "May she be
true to you, my lad!"

The squire asked him if he was going to church that
morning.

"I go to my post, sir, by my fireside," the captain
replied; nor could he be induced to leave his post vacant
by the squire's promise to him of a sermon from the new
rector that would pickle his temper for a whole week's wear
and tear. He regretted extremely that he could not enjoy
so excellent a trial of his patience, but he felt himself bound
to go to his post and wait.

I walked over to Bulstead with him, and heard on the
way that it was Heriot who had called for her and driven
her off. "The man had been, I supposed," Captain Bulsted
said, "deputed by some of you to fetch her over to Riversley.
My servants mentioned his name. I thought it adviseable
not to trouble the ladies with it to-day." He meditated.
"I hoped I should find her at the Grange in the morning,
Harry. I slept on it, rather than startle the poor lamb in
the night."

I offered him to accompany him at once to Heriot's quarters.

"What! and let my wife know I doubted her fidelity.
My girl shall never accuse me of that."

As it turned out, Julia had been taken by Heriot on a
visit to Lady Maria Higginson, the wife of the intrusive
millionnaire, who particularly desired to know her more
intimately. Thoughtless Julia, accepting the impudent
invitation without scruple, had allowed herself to be driven
away without stating the place of her destination. She and
Heriot were in the Higginsons' pew at church. Hearing
from Janet of her husband's arrival, she rushed home, and
there, instead of having to beg forgiveness, was summoned
to grant pardon. Captain Bulsted had drawn largely on
Squire Gregory's cellar to assist him in keeping his post.

The pair appeared before us fondling ineffably next day,
neither one of them capable of seeing that our domestic
peace at the Grange was unseated. "We're the two
wretchedest creatures alive; haven't any of ye to spare a
bit of sympathy for us?" Julia began. "We're like on a
pitchfork There's William's duty to his country, and

there's his affection for me, and they won't go together, because Government, which is that horrid Admiralty, fears pitching and tossing for post-captains' wives. And William away, I'm distracted, and the Admiralty's hair's on end if he stops. And, 'deed, Miss Beltham, I'm not more than married to just half a husband."

The captain echoed her, "Half! but happy enough for twenty whole ones, if you'll be satisfied, my duck."

Julia piteously entreated me, for my future wife's sake, not to take service under Government. As for the Admiralty, she said, it had no characteristic but the abominable one that it hated a woman. The squire laid two or three moderately coarse traps for the voluble frank creature, which she evaded with surprising neatness, showing herself more awake than one would have imagined her. Janet and I fancied she must have come with the intention to act uxorious husband and Irish wife for the distinct purpose of diverting the squire's wrath from me, for he greatly delighted in the sight of merry wedded pairs. But they were as simple as possible in their display of happiness. It chanced that they came opportunely. My bankers' book had been the theme all the morning, and an astonishing one to me equally with my grandfather. Since our arrival in England, my father had drawn nine thousand pounds. The sums expended during our absence on the Continent reached the perplexing figures of forty-eight thousand. I knew it too likely, besides, that all debts were not paid. Self—self— self drew for thousands at a time; sometimes, as the squire's convulsive forefinger indicated, for many thousands within a week. It was incomprehensible to him until I, driven at bay by questions and insults, and perceiving that conceal-ment could not long be practised, made a virtue of the situa-tion by telling him (what he in fact must have seen) that my father possessed a cheque-book as well as I, and likewise drew upon the account. We had required the money; it was mine, and I had sold out Bank Stock and Consols,— which gave very poor interest, I remarked cursorily—and had kept the money at my bankers', to draw upon according to our necessities. I pitied the old man while speaking. His face was livid; language died from his lips. He asked to have little things explained to him—the two cheque-books, for instance,—and what I thought of doing when this money

was all gone : for he supposed I did not expect the same
amount to hand every two years ; unless, he added, I had
given him no more than a couple of years' lease of life when
I started for my tour.   "Then the money's gone !" he
summed up; and this was the signal for redemanding
explanations.   Had he not treated me fairly and frankly in
handing over my own to me on the day of my majority ?
Yes.

"And like a fool, you think—eh ?"

"I have no such thought in my head, sir."

"You have been keeping that fellow in his profligacy, and
you're keeping him now.   Why, you're all but a beggar !
. . . . Comes to my house, talks of his birth, carries off
my daughter, makes her mad, lets her child grow up to lay
hold of her money, and then grips him fast and pecks him,
fleeces him !   . . .   You're beggared—d'ye know that ?
He's had the two years of you, and sucked you dry.   What
were you about ?   What were you doing ?   Did you have
your head on ?   You shared cheque-books ? good !   . . . .
The devil in hell never found such a fool as you !   You had
your house full of your foreign bonyrobers—eh ?   Out with
it !   How did you pass your time ?   Drunk and dancing ?"

By such degrees my grandfather worked himself up to
the pitch for his style of eloquence.   I have given a faint
specimen of it.   When I took the liberty to consider that I
had heard enough, he followed me out of the library into the
hall, where Janet stood.   In her presence he charged the
princess and her family with being a pack of greedy adventurers, conspirators with "that fellow" to plunder me; and
for a proof of it, he quoted my words, that my father's time
had been spent in superintending the opening of a coal-mine
on Prince Ernest's estate.   "That fellow pretending to
manage a coal-mine !"   Could not a girl see it was a shuffle
to hoodwink a greenhorn ?   And now he remembered it was
Colonel Goodwin and his daughter who had told him of
having seen "the fellow" engaged in playing Court-buffoon
to a petty German prince, and performing his antics, cutting capers like a clown at a fair.

"Shame !" said Janet.

"Hear her !"   The squire turned to me.

But she cried : "Oh ! grandada, hear yourself ! or don't,
but be silent.   If Harry has offended you, speak like one

gentleman to another. Don't rob me of my love for you: I haven't much besides that."

"No, because of a scoundrel and his young idiot!"

Janet frowned in earnest, and said: "I don't permit you to change the meaning of the words I speak."

He muttered a proverb of the stables. Reduced to behave temperately, he began the whole history of my bankers' book anew—the same queries, the same explosions and imprecations.

"Come for a walk with me, dear Harry," said Janet.

I declined to be protected in such a manner, absurdly on my dignity; and the refusal, together possibly with some air of contemptuous independence in the tone of it, brought the squire to a climax. "You won't go out and walk with her? You shall go down on your knees to her and beg her to give you her arm for a walk. By God! you shall, now, here, on the spot, or off you go to your German princess, with your butler's legacy, and nothing more from me but good-bye and the door bolted. Now, down with you!"

He expected me to descend.

"And if he did, he would never have my arm." Janet's eyes glittered hard on the squire.

"Before that rascal dies, my dear, he shall whine like a beggar out in the cold for the tips of your fingers!"

"Not if he asks me first," said Janet.

This set him off again. He realized her prospective generosity, and contrasted it with my actual obtuseness. Janet changed her tactics. She assumed indifference. But she wanted experience, and a Heriot to help her in playing a part. She did it badly—overdid it; so that the old man, now imagining both of us to be against his scheme for uniting us, counted my iniquity as twofold. Her phrase, "Harry and I will always be friends," roused the loudest of his denunciations upon me, as though there never had been question of the princess, so inveterate was his mind's grasp of its original designs. Friends! Would our being friends give him heirs by law to his estate and name? And so forth. My aunt Dorothy came to moderate his invectives. In her room the heavily-burdened little book of figures was produced, and the items read aloud; and her task was to hear them without astonishment, but with a business-like desire to comprehend them accurately, a method that softened

the squire's outbursts by degrees.   She threw out hasty
running commentaries: "Yes, that was for a yacht;" and
"They were living at the Court of a prince;" such and such
a sum was "large, but Harry knew his grandfather did not
wish him to make a poor appearance."

"Why, do you mean to swear to me, on your oath, Dorothy
Beltham," said the squire, amazed at the small amazement
he created, "you think these two fellows have been spending
within the right margin?   What'll be women's ideas next!"

"No," she answered demurely.   "I think Harry has been
extravagant, and has had his lesson.   And surely it is better
now than later?   But you are not making allowances for his
situation as the betrothed of a princess."

"That's what turns your head," said he; and she allowed
him to have the notion, and sneer at herself and her sex.

"How about this money drawn since he came home?"
the squire persisted.

My aunt Dorothy reddened.   He struck his finger on the
line marking the sum, repeating his demand; and at this
moment Captain Bulsted and Julia arrived.   The ladies
manœuvred so that the captain and the squire were left
alone together.   Some time afterwards the captain sent out
word that he begged his wife's permission to stay to dinner
at the Grange, and requested me to favour him by conducting his wife to Bulsted: proof, as Julia said, that the two
were engaged in a pretty hot tussle.   She was sure her
William would not be the one to be beaten.   I led her away,
rather depressed by the automaton performance assigned to
me; from which condition I awoke with a touch of horror to
find myself paying her very warm compliments; for she had
been coquettish and charming to cheer me, and her voice
was sweet.   We reached a point in our conversation I know
not where, but I must have spoken with some warmth.
"Then guess," said she, "what William is suffering for your
sake now, Harry;" that is, "suffering in remaining away
from me on your account:" and thus, in an instant, with a
skill so intuitive as to be almost unconscious, she twirled
me round to a right sense of my position, and set me reflecting, whether a love that clad me in such imperfect armour
as to leave me penetrable to these feminine graces—a plump
figure, swinging skirts, dewy dark eyelids, laughing red
lips—could indeed be absolute love.   And if it was not love

of the immortal kind, what was I? I looked back on the
thought like the ship on its furrow through the waters, and
saw every mortal perplexity, and death under. My love of
Ottilia delusion? Then life was delusion! I contemplated
Julia in alarm, somewhat in the light fair witches were
looked on when the faggots were piled for them. The sense
of her unholy attractions abased and mortified me : and it
set me thinking on the strangeness of my disregard of Mdlle.
Jenny Chassediane when in Germany, who was far spright-
lier, if not prettier, and, as I remembered, had done me the
favour to make discreet play with her eyelids in our
encounters, and long eyes in passing. I caught myself
regretting my coldness of that period ; for which regrets I
could have swung the scourge upon my miserable flesh.
Ottilia's features seemed dying out of my mind. " Poor
darling Harry!" Julia sighed. " And d'ye know, the sight of
a young man far gone in love gives me the trembles?" I
rallied her concerning the ladder scene in my old schooldays,
and the tender things she had uttered to Heriot. She
answered, " Oh! I think I got them out of poats and chapters about love-making, or I felt it very much. And that's
what I miss in William ; he can't talk soft nice nonsense. I
believe him, he would if he could, but he's like a lion of the
desert—it's a roar!"

I rejoiced when we heard the roar. Captain Bulsted
returned to take command of his ship, not sooner than I
wanted him, and told us of a fierce tussle with the squire.
He had stuck to him all day, and up to 11 P.M. " By
George! Harry, he had to make humble excuses to dodge
out of eyeshot a minute. Conquered him over the fourth
bottle! And now all's right. He'll see your dad. ' In a
barn?' says the squire. ' Here's to your better health, sir,'
I bowed to him ; ' gentlemen don't meet in barns ; none but
mice and traps make appointments there.' To shorten my
story, my lad, I have arranged for the squire and your
excellent progenitor to meet at Bulsted : we may end by
bringing them over a bottle of old Greg's best. ' See the
boy's father,' I kept on insisting. The point is, that this
confounded book must be off your shoulders, my lad. A
dirty dog may wash in a duck-pond. You see, Harry, the
dear old squire may set up your account twenty times over,
but he has a right to know how you twirl the coin. He says

you don't supply the information. I suggest to him that
your father can, and will. So we get them into a room
together. I'll be answerable for the rest. And now top
your boom, and to bed here: off in the morning and tug the
big vessel into port here! And, Harry, three cheers, and
another bottle to crown the victory, if you're the man for
it ? "

Julia interposed a decided negative to the proposition; an
ordinarily unlucky thing to do with bibulous husbands, and
the captain looked uncomfortably checked; but when he
seemed to be collecting to assert himself, the humour of her
remark, " Now, no bravado, William," disarmed him.

" Bravado, my sweet chuck ? "

" Won't another bottle be like flashing your sword after
you've won the day ? " said she.

He slung his arm round her, and sent a tremendous
whisper into my ear—" A perfect angel ! "

I started for London next day, more troubled æsthetically
regarding the effect produced on me by this order of perfect
angels than practically anxious about material affairs,
though it is true that when I came into proximity with my
father, the thought of his all but purely mechanical power
of making money spin, fly, and vanish, like sparks from a
fire-engine, awakened a serious disposition in me to bring
our monetary partnership to some definite settlement. He
was living in splendour, next door but one to the grand
establishment he had driven me to from Dipwell in the old
days, with Mrs. Waddy for his housekeeper once more,
Alphonse for his cook. Not living on the same scale, however, the troubled woman said. She signified that it was now
the whirlwind. I could not help smiling to see how proud
she was of him, nevertheless, as a god-like charioteer—in
pace, at least. " Opera to-night," she answered my inquiries
for him, admonishing me by her tone that I ought not to be
behindhand in knowing his regal rules and habits. Praising
his generosity, she informed me that he had spent one
hundred pounds, and offered a reward of five times the sum,
for the discovery of Mabel Sweetwinter. " Your papa never
does things by halves, Mr. Harry ! " Soon after she was
whimpering, " Oh, will it last ? " I was shown into the
room called " The princess's room," a miracle of furniture,
not likely to be occupied by her, I thought, the very magni-

ficence of the apartment striking down hope in my heart like cold on a nerve. "Your papa says the whole house is to be for you, Mr. Harry, when the happy day comes." Could it possibly be that he had talked of the princess? I took a hasty meal and fortified myself with claret to have matters clear with him before the night was over.

CHAPTER XXXIX.

I SEE MY FATHER TAKING THE TIDE AND AM CARRIED ON IT MYSELF.

My father stood in the lobby of the Opera, holding a sort of open court, it appeared to me, for a cluster of gentlemen hung round him; and I had presently to bow to greetings which were rather of a kind to flatter me, leading me to presume that he was respected as well as marvelled at. The names of Mr. Serjeant Wedderburn, Mr. Jennings, Lord Alton, Sir Weeton Slater, Mr. Monterez Williams, Admiral Loftus, the Earl of Witlington, were among those which struck my ear, and struck me as good ones. I could not perceive anything of the air of cynical satellites in these gentlemen—on the contrary they were cordially deferential I felt that he was encompassed by undoubted gentlemen, and my warmer feelings to my father returned when I became sensible of the pleasant sway he held over the circle, both in speaking and listening. His sympathetic smile and semi-droop of attention; his readiness, when occasion demanded it, to hit the key of the subject and help it on with the right word; his air of unobtrusive appreciation; his sensibility to the moment when the run of conversation depended upon him—showed inimitable art coming of natural genius; and he did not lose a shade of his superior manner the while. Mr. Serjeant Wedderburn, professionally voluble, a lively talker, brimming with anecdote, but too sparkling, too prompt, too full of personal relish of his point, threw my father's urbane supremacy into marked relief; and so in another fashion did the Earl of Witlington, "a youth in the season of guffaws," as Jorian DeWitt described him, whom a jest would seize by the throat, shaking his sapling frame

Jorian strolled up to us goutily. No efforts of my father's would induce him to illustrate his fame for repartee, so it remained established. "Very pretty waxwork," he said to me of our English beauties swimming by. "Now, those women, young Richmond, if they were inflammable to the fiftieth degree, that is, if they had the fiftieth part of a Frenchwoman in them, would have canvassed society on the great man's account long before this, and sent him to the top like a bubble. He wastes his time on them. That fat woman he's bowing to is Viscountess Sedley, a porcine empress, widow of three, with a soupçon of bigamy to flavour them. She mounted from a grocer's shop, I am told. Constitution has done everything for that woman. So it will everywhere—it beats the world! Now he's on all-fours to Lady Rachel Stokes, our pure aristocracy; she walks as if she were going through a doorway, and couldn't risk an eyelid. I'd like to see her tempting St. Anthony. That's little Wreckham's wife: she's had as many adventures as Gil Blas before he entered the Duke of Lerma's service." He reviewed several ladies, certainly not very witty when malignant, as I remembered my father to have said of him. "The style of your Englishwoman is to keep the nose exactly at one elevation, to show you're born to it. They daren't run a gamut, these women. These English women are a fiction! The model of them is the nursery-miss, but they're like the names of true lovers cut on the bark of a tree—awfully stiff and longitudinal with the advance of time. We've our Lady Jezebels, my boy! They're in the pay of the bishops, or the police, to make vice hideous. The rest do the same for virtue, and get their pay for it somewhere, I don't doubt; perhaps from the newspapers, to keep up the fiction. I tell you, these Englishwomen have either no life at all in them, or they're nothing but animal life. 'Gad, how they dizen themselves! They've no other use for their fingers. The wealth of this country's frightful!"

Jorian seemed annoyed that he could not excite me to defend my countrywomen; but I had begun to see that there was no necessity for the sanguine to encounter the bilious on their behalf, and was myself inclined to be critical. Besides I was engaged in watching my father, whose bearing toward the ladies he accosted did not dissatisfy my critical taste, though I had repeated fears of seeing him overdo it. He summoned me to an introduction to the Countess Szezedy, a merry little Hungarian dame.

"So," said she at once, speaking German, "you are to marry the romantic head, the Princess Ottilia of Eppen- welzen! I know her well. I have met her in Vienna. Schöne Seele and bas bleu! It's just those that are won with a duel. I know Prince Otto too." She prattled away, and asked me whether the marriage was to take place in the Summer. I was too astounded to answer.

"No date is yet fixed," my father struck in.

"It's the talk of London," she said.

Before I could demand explanations of my father with regard to this terrible rumour involving Ottilia, I found myself in the box of the City widow, Lady Sampleman, a grievous person, of the complexion of the autumnal bramble- leaf, whose first words were: "Ah! the young suitor! And how is our German princess?" I had to reply that the theme was more of German princes than princesses in Eng- land. "Oh! but," said she, "you are having a—shall I call it—national revenge on them? 'I will take one of your princesses,' says you; and as soon as said done! I'm dying for a sight of her portrait. Captain DeWitt declares her heavenly—I mean, he says she is fair and nice, quite a lady —that of course! And never mind her not being rich. *You* can do the decoration to the match. H'm," she perused my features; "pale! Lovelorn? Excuse an old friend of your father's. One of his very oldest, I'd say, if it didn't impugn. As such, proud of your alliance. I am. I speak of it every- where—everywhere."

Here she dramatized her circulation of the gossip. "Have you heard the news? No, what? Fitz-George's son marries a princess of the German realm. Indeed! True as gospel. And how soon? In a month; and now you will see the dear, neglected man command the Court. . . ."

I looked at my father: I felt stifling with confusion and rage. He leant over to her, imparting some ecstatic news about a great lady having determined to call on her to regu- late the affairs of an approaching grand Ball, and under cover of this we escaped.

"If it were not," said he, "for the Chassediane—you are aware, Richie, poor Jorian is lost to her?—he has fallen at her quicksilver feet. She is now in London. Half the poor

350 THE ADVENTURES OF HARRY RICHMOND.

fellow's income expended in bouquets! Her portrait, in the character of the widow Lefourbe, has become a part of his dressing apparatus; he shaves fronting her play-bill. His first real affaire de cœur, and he is forty-five! So he is taken in the stomach. That is why love is such a dangerous malady for middle age. As I said, but for Jenny Chasse-diane, our Sampleman would be the fortune for Jorian. I have hinted it on both sides. Women, Richie, are cleverer than the illustrious Lord Nelson in not seeing what their inclinations decline to see, and Jorian would do me any service in the world except that one. You are restless, my son?"

I begged permission to quit the house, and wait for him outside. He, in return, begged me most urgently to allow myself to be introduced to Lady Edbury, the stepmother of Lord Destrier, now Marquis of Edbury; and, using conver-sational pressure, he adjured me not to slight this lady, adding, with more significance than the words conveyed, "I am taking the tide, Richie." The tide took me, and I bowed to a lady of impressive languor, pale and young, with plea-sant manners, showing her character in outline, like a glove on the hand, but little of its quality. She accused my father of coming direct from 'that person's' box. He re-plied that he never forsook old friends. "You should," was her rejoinder. It suggested to me an image of one of the sister Fates cutting a thread.

My heart sank when, from Lady Edbury too, I heard the allusion to Germany and its princess, "Some one told me she was dark?"

"Blonde," my father corrected the report.

Lady Edbury "thought it singular for a German woman of the Blood to be a brunette. They had not much dark mixture among them, particularly in the North. Her name? She had forgotten the name of the princess."

My father repeated: "The Princess Ottilia, Princess of Eppenwelzen-Sarkeld."

"Brunette, you say?"

"The purest blonde."

"A complexion?"

"A complexion to dazzle the righteous!"

Lady Edbury threw a flying glance in a mirror: "The unrighteous you leave to us then?"

They bandied the weariful shuttlecock of gallantry. I bowed and fled. My excuse was that I had seen Anna Penrhys in an upper tier of boxes, and I made my way to her, doubting how I should be welcomed. " The happy woman is a German princess, we hear!" she set me shivering. Her welcome was perfectly unreserved and friendly. She asked the name of the lady whose box I had quitted, and after bending her opera-glass on it for a moment, said with a certain air of satisfaction: " She is young;" which led me to guess that Lady Edbury was reputed to be Anna's successor; but why the latter should be flattered by the former's youth was one of the mysteries for me then. Her aunt was awakened from sleep by the mention of my name. " Is the man here ?" she exclaimed, starting. Anna smiled, and talked to me of my father, saying that she was glad to see me at his right hand, for he had a hard battle to fight. She spoke of him with affectionate interest in his fortunes ; no better proof of his generosity as well as hers could have been given me. I promised her heartily I would not be guilty of letting our intimacy drop, and handed the ladies down to the crush-room, where I saw my father leading Lady Edbury to her carriage, much observed. Destrier, the young marquis, coming in to meet the procession from other haunts, linked his arm to his friend Witlington's, and said something in my hearing of old ' Duke Fitz,' which provoked, I fancied, signs of amusement equivalent to tittering in a small ring of the select assembly. Lady Sampleman's carriage was called. " Another victim," said a voice. Anna Penrhys walked straight out to find her footman and carriage for herself.

I stood alone in the street, wondering, fretting, filled with a variety of ugly sensations, when my father joined me humming an air of the opera. " I was looking for Jorian, Richie. He had our Sampleman under his charge. He is off to the Chassediane. Well ! And well, Richie, you could not bear the absence from your dada ? You find me in full sail on the tide. I am at home, if our fortunes demand it, in a little German principality, but there is," he threw out his chest, " a breadth in London ; nowhere else do I breathe with absolute freedom—so largely: and this is my battlefield. By the way, Lady Edbury accounts you complete ; which is no more to say than that she is a woman of taste. The instance :

she positively would not notice that you wear a dress-coat of
a foreign cut.   Correct it to-morrow; my tailor shall wait on
you.   I meant to point out to you that when a London woman
has not taken note of that, the face and the man have made
the right impression on her.   Richie, dear boy, how shall I
speak the delight I have in seeing you!   My arm in yours,
old Richie! strolling home from the Fashion: this seems to
me what I dreamt of!   All in sound health at the Grange?
She too, the best of women?"

"I have come on very particular business," I interposed
briefly.

He replied, "I am alive to you, Richie; speak."

"The squire has seen my bankers' book.   He thinks I've
been drawing rather wildly: no doubt he's right.   He wants
some sort of explanation.   He consents to an interview with
you.   I have come to ask you to go down to him, sir."

"To-morrow morning, without an hour's delay, my dear
boy.   Very agreeable will be the sight of old Riversley.
And in the daylight!"

"He prefers to meet you at Bulsted.   Captain Bulsted
offers his house for the purpose.   I have to warn you, sir,
that we stand in a very exceptional position.   The squire
insists upon having a full account of the money rendered to
him."

"I invite him to London, Richie.   I refer him to Dettermain and Newson.   I request him to compute the value of a
princess."

"You are aware that he will not come to your invitation."

"Tell me, then, how is he to understand what I have
established by the expenditure, my son?   I refer him to
Dettermain and Newson."

"But you must know that he sets his face against legal
proceedings involving exposure."

"But surely, Richie, exposure is the very thing we court.
The innocent, the unjustly treated, court it.   We *would* be
talked about; you *shall* hear of us!   And into the bargain
an hereditary princess.   Upon my faith, Mr. Beltham, I
think you have mighty little to complain of."

My temper was beginning to chafe at the curb.   "As
regards any feeling about the money, personally, sir, you
know I have none.   But I must speak of one thing.   I have

heard to-night, I confess with as much astonishment as grief, the name . . . I could not have guessed that I should hear the princess's name associated with mine, and quite openly."

"As a matter of course." He nodded, and struck out a hand in wavy motion.

"Well, sir, if you can't feel for her or her family, be good enough to think of me, and remember that I object to it."

"For you all," said he, buoyantly; "I feel for you all, and I will act for you all. I bring the princess to your arms, my dear boy. You have written me word that the squire gives her a royal dowry—have you not? My combinations permit of no escape to any one of you. Nay, 'tis done. I think for you—I feel for you—I act for you. By heaven, you shall be happy! Sigh, Richie, sigh; your destiny is now entrusted to me!"

"I daresay I'm wasting my breath, sir, but I protest against false pretences. You know well that you have made use of the princess's name for your own purposes."

"Most indubitably, Richie, I have; and are they not yours? I must have social authority to succeed in our main enterprise. Possibly the princess's name serves for a temporary chandelier to cast light on us. She belongs to us. For her sake we are bringing the house she enters into order. Thus, Richie, I could tell Mr. Beltham: you and he supply the money, the princess the name, and I the energy, the skilfulness, and the estimable cause. I pay the princess for the use of her name with the dowry, which is royal; I pay you with the princess, who is royal too; and I, Richie, am paid by your happiness most royally. Together, it is past contest that we win.—Here, my little one," he said to a woman, and dropped a piece of gold into her hand, "on condition that you go straight home." The woman thanked him and promised.—"As I was observing, we are in the very tide of success. Curious! I have a slight inclination to melancholy. Success, quotha? Why, hundreds before us have paced the identical way homeward at night under these lamps between the mansions and the park. The bare thought makes them resemble a double line of undertakers. The tomb is down there at the end of them—costly or not. At the age of four, on my birthday, I was informed that my mother lay dead in her bed. I remember to this day my

astonishment at her not moving. 'Her heart is broken,' my
old nurse said. To me she appeared intact. Her sister took
possession of me, and of her papers, and the wedding-ring—
now in the custody of Dettermain and Newson—together
with the portraits of both my parents; and she, poor soul,
to sustain me, as I verily believe—she had a great idea of my
never asking unprofitably for anything in life—bartered the
most corroborative of the testificatory documents, which
would now make the establishment of my case a comparatively light task. Have I never spoken to you of my boyhood? My maternal uncle was a singing-master and master
of elocution. I am indebted to him for the cultivation of my
voice. He taught me an effective delivery of my sentences.
The English of a book of his called *The Speaker* is still to
my mind a model of elegance. Remittances of money came
to him from an unknown quarter; and, with a break or two,
have come ever since up to this period. My old nurse—
heaven bless her—resumed the occupation of washing. I
have stood by her tub, Richie, blowing bubbles and listening
to her prophecies of my exalted fortune for hours. On my
honour, I doubt, I seriously doubt, if I have ever been happier. I depend just now—I have to avow it to you—slightly
upon stimulants . . . of a perfectly innocuous character.
Mrs. Waddy will allow me a pint of champagne. The truth
is, Richie—you see these two or three poor pensioners of
mine, honi soit qui mal y pensé—my mother has had hard
names thrown at her. The stones of these streets cry out
to me to have her vindicated. I am not tired; but I want
my wine."
    He repeated several times before he reached his house-
door that he wanted his wine, in a manner to be almost
alarming. His unwonted effort of memory, the singular pictures of him which it had flashed before me, and a sort of
impatient compassion, made me forget my wrath. I saw
him take his restorative at one draught. He lay down on a
sofa, and his valet drew his boots off and threw a cloak over
him. Lying there, he wished me gaily good-night. Mrs.
Waddy told me that he had adopted this system of sleeping
for the last month. "Bless you, as many people call on him
at night now as in the day," she said; and I was induced to
suppose he had some connection with the Press. She had
implicit faith in his powers of constitution, and would affirm

that he had been the death of dozens whom the attraction had duped to imitate his habits. "He is now a Field-Marshal on his campaign." She betrayed a twinkle of humour. He must himself have favoured her with that remark. The report of the house-door frequently shutting in the night suggested the passage of his aides-de-camp.

Early in the morning, I found him pacing through the open doors of the dining-room and the library dictating to a secretary at a desk, now and then tossing a word to Dettermain and Newson's chief clerk. The floor was strewn with journals. He wore Hessian boots; a voluminous black cloak hung loosely from his shoulders.

"I am just settling the evening papers," he said after greeting me, with a show of formality in his warmth; and immediately added, "That will do, Mr. Jopson. Put in a note—'Mr. Harry Lepel Richmond of Riversley and Twn-y-glas, my son, takes no step to official distinction in his native land save through the ordinary Parliamentary channels.' Your pardon, Richie; presently. I am replying to a morning paper."

"What's this? Why print my name?" I cried.

"Merely the correction of an error. I have to insist, my dear boy, that you claim no privileges: you are apart from them. Mr. Jopson, I beseech you, not a minute's delay in delivering that. Fetch me from the printer's my pamphlet this afternoon. Mr. Jacobs, my compliments to Dettermain and Newson: I request them to open proceedings instanter, and let the world know of it. Good-morning, gentlemen."

And now, turning to me, my father fenced me with the whole weight of his sententious volubility, which was the force of a river. Why did my name appear in the papers? Because I was his son. But he assured me that he carefully separated me from public companionship with his fortunes, and placed me on the side of my grandfather, as a plain gentleman of England, the heir of the most colossal wealth possible in the country.

"I dis-sociate you from me, Richie, do you see? I cause it to be declared that you need, on no account, lean on me. Jopson will bring you my pamphlet—my Declaration of Rights—to peruse. In the Press, in Literature, at Law, and on social ground, I meet the enemy, and I claim my own; by heaven, I do! And I will down to the squire for a distraction, if you esteem it necessary, certainly. Half-a-dozen words to him. Why, do you maintain him to be insensible to a title for you? No, no. And ask my friends. I refer him to any dozen of my friends to convince him I have the prize almost in my possession. Why, dear boy, I have witnesses, living witnesses, to the ceremony. Am I, tell me, to be deprived of money now, once again, for the eleventh time? Oh! And put aside my duty to you, I protest I am bound in duty to her who bore me—you have seen her miniature: how lovely that dear woman was! how gentle!—bound in duty to her to clear her good name. This does not affect you . . . ."

"Oh, but it does," he allowed me to plead.

"Ay, through your love for your dada."

He shook me by both hands. I was touched with pity, and at the same time in doubt whether it was not an actor that swayed me; for I was discontented, and could not speak my discontent; I was overborne, overflowed. His evasion of the matter of my objections relating to the princess I felt to be a palpable piece of artfulness, but I had to acknowledge to myself that I knew what his argument would be, and how overwhelmingly his defence of it would spring forth. My cowardice shrank from provoking a recurrence to the theme. In fact, I submitted consciously to his masterful fluency and emotional power, and so I was carried on the tide with him, remaining in London several days to witness tha I was not the only one. My father, admitting that money erved him in his conquest of society, and defying any other man to do as much with it as he did, replied to a desperate insinuation of mine, "This money I spend I am actually putting out to interest as much as, or more than, your grandad." He murmured confidentially, "I have alarmed the Government. Indeed, I have warrant for saying I am in communication with its agents. They are bribing me; they are positively bribing me, Richie. I receive my stipend annually. They are mighty discreet. So am I. But I push them hard. I take what they offer: I renounce none of my claims."

Janet wrote that it would be prudent for me to return.

"I am prepared," my father said. "I have only to meet Mr. Beltham in a room—I stipulate that it shall be between square walls—to win him. The squire to back us, Richie, we have command of the entire world. His wealth, and my good cause, and your illustrious union—by the way, it is announced definitely in this morning's paper."

Dismayed, I asked what was announced.

"Read," said he. "This will be something to hand to Mr. Beltham at our meeting. I might trace it to one of the embassies, Imperial or Royal. No matter—there it is."

I read a paragraph in which Ottilia's name and titles were set down; then followed mine and my wealthy heirship, and —woe was me in the perusing of it!—a roundabout vindication of me as one not likely to be ranked as the first of English commoners who had gained the hand of an hereditary foreign princess, though it was undoubtedly in the light of a commoner that I was most open to the congratulations of my countrymen upon my unparalleled felicity. A display of historical erudition cited the noble inferiors by birth who had caught princesses to their arms—Charles, Humphrey, William, John. Under this list a later Harry!

The paragraph closed by fixing the nuptials to take place before the end of the season.

I looked at my father to try a struggle with him. The whole man was efflorescent.

"Can't it be stopped?" I implored him.

He signified the impossibility in a burst of gesticulations, motions of the mouth, smiling frowns; various patterns of an absolute negative beating down opposition.

"Things printed can never be stopped, Richie. Our Jorian compares them to babies baptized. They have a soul from that moment, and go on for ever!—an admirable word of Jorian's. And a word to you, Richie. Will you swear to me by the veracity of your lover's heart, that paragraph affords you no satisfaction? He cannot swear it!" my father exclaimed, seeing me swing my shoulder round, and he made me feel that it would have been a false oath if I had sworn it. But I could have sworn that I had rather we two were at the bottom of the sea than that it should come under the princess's eyes. I read it again. It was in print. It looked like reality. It was at least the realization of my dream. But this played traitor and accused me of being crowned with no more than a dream. The sole practical thing I could do was to insist on our starting for Riversley immediately, to make sure of my own position. "Name your hour, Richie," my father said confidently: and we waited.

A rather plainer view of my father's position, as I inclined to think, was afforded to me one morning at his breakfast-table, by a conversation between him and Jorian DeWitt, who brought me a twisted pink note from Mdlle. Chassediane, the which he delivered with the air of a dog made to disgorge a bone, and he was very cool to me indeed. The cutlets of Alphonse were subject to snappish criticism. "I assume," he said, "the fellow knew I was coming?"

"He saw it in my handwriting of yesterday," replied my father. "But be just to him, acknowledge that he is one of the few that perform their daily duties with a tender conscience."

"This English climate has bedevilled the fellow! He peppers his dishes like a mongrel Indian reared on mangoes."

"Ring him up, ring him up, Jorian. All I beg of you is not to disgust him with life, for he quits any service in the world to come to me, and, in fact, he suits me."

"Exactly so: you spoil him."

My father shrugged. "The state of the case is that your stomach is growing delicate, friend Jorian."

"The actual state of the case being, that my palate was never keener, and consequently my stomach knows its business."

"You should have tried the cold turbot with oil and capers."

"Your man had better stick to buttered eggs, in my opinion."

"Say, porridge!"

"No, I'll be hanged if I think he's equal to a bowl of porridge."

"Carème might have confessed to the same!"

"With this difference," cried Jorian in a heat, "that he would never have allowed the thought of any of your barbarous messes to occur to a man at table. Let me tell you, Roy, you astonish me: up till now I have never known you guilty of the bad taste of defending a bad dish on your own board."

"Then you will the more readily pardon me, Jorian."

"Oh, I *pardon* you," Jorian sneered, tripped to the carpet by such ignoble mildness. "A breakfast is no great loss."

My father assured him he would have a serious conversation with Alphonse, for whom he apologized by saying that Alphonse had not, to his knowledge, served as hospital cook anywhere, and was therefore quite possibly not sufficiently solicitous for appetites and digestions of invalids.

Jorian threw back his head as though to discharge a spiteful sarcasm with good aim; but turning to me, said, "Harry, the thing must be done; your father must marry. Notoriety is the season for a pick and choice of the wealthiest and the loveliest. I refuse to act the part of warming-pan any longer; I refuse point blank. It's not a personal feeling on my part; my advice is that of a disinterested friend, and I tell you candidly, Roy, set aside the absurd exhibition of my dancing attendance on that last rose of Guildhall,—egad, the alderman went like Summer, and left us the very picture of a fruity Autumn,—I say you can't keep her hanging on the tree of fond expectation for ever. She'll drop."

"Catch her, Jorian; you are on guard."

"Upwards of three hundred thousand, if a penny, Roy Richmond! Who? I? I am not a fortune-hunter."

"Nor am I, friend Jorian."

"No, it's because you're not thorough: you'll fall between the stools."

My father remarked that he should visit this upon Mr. Alphonse.

"You shook off that fine Welsh girl, and she was in your hand—the act of a madman!" Jorian continued. "You're getting older: the day will come when you're a flat excitement. You know the first Lady Edbury spoilt one of your best chances when you had the market. Now you're trifling with the second. She's the head of the Light Brigade, but you might fix her down, if she's not too much in debt. You're not at the end of your run, I dare say. Only, my good Roy, let me tell you, in life you mustn't wait for the prize of the race till you touch the goal—if you prefer metaphor. You generally come forward about every seven years or so. Add on another seven, and women'll begin to think. You can't beat Time, mon Roy."

"So," said my father, "I touch the goal, and women begin

to think, and I can't beat time to them.   Jorian, your mind
is in a state of confusion.   I do not marry."

"Then, Roy Richmond, hear what a friend says . . ."

"I do not marry, Jorian, and you know my reasons."

"Sentiments!"

"They are a part of my life."

"Just as I remarked, you are not thorough.   You have
genius and courage out of proportion, and you are a dead
failure, Roy; because, no sooner have you got all Covent
Garden before you for the fourth or fifth time, than in go your
hands into your pockets, and you say—No, there's an apple
I can't have, so I'll none of these; and, by the way, the apple
must be tolerably withered by this time.   And you know
perfectly well (for you don't lack common sense at a shaking,
Roy Richmond), that you're guilty of simple madness in
refusing to make the best of your situation.   You haven't to
be taught what money means.   With money—and a wife to
take care of it, mind you—you are pre-eminently the man for
which you want to be recognized.   Without it—H rry'll
excuse me, I must speak plainly—you're a sort of a spectacle
of a bob-cherry, down on your luck, up on your luck, and
getting dead stale and never bitten; a familiar curiosity."
Jorian added, "Oh, by Jove! it's not nice to think of."

My father said: "Harry, I am sure, will excuse you for
talking, in your extreme friendliness, of matters that he and
I have not—and they interest us deeply—yet thought fit to
discuss.   And you may take my word for it, Jorian, that I
will give Alphonse his medical dose.   I am quite of your
opinion that the kings of cooks require it occasionally.   Harry
will inform us of Mddle. Chassediane's commands."

The contents of the letter permitted me to read it aloud.
She desired to know how she could be amused on the Sunday.

"We will undertake it," said my father.   "I depute the
arrangements to you, Jorian.   Respect the prejudices, and
avoid collisions, that is all."

Captain DeWitt became by convenient stages cheerful,
after the pink slip of paper had been made common property,
and from a seriously-advising friend, in his state of spite,
relapsed to the idle and shadow-like associate, when pleased.
I had to thank him for the gift of fresh perceptions.   Surely
it would be as well if my father could get a woman of fortune
to take care of him!

We had at my request a consultation with Dettermain and Newson on the eve of the journey to Riversley, Temple and Jorian DeWitt assisting. Strange documentary evidence was unfolded and compared with the date of a royal decree: affidavits of persons now dead; a ring, *the* ring; fans, and lace, and handkrchiefs with notable initials; jewelry stamped 'To the Divine Anastasia' from an adoring Christian name: old brown letters that shrieked 'wife' when 'charmer' seemed to have palled; oaths of fidelity ran through them like bass notes. Jorian held up the discoloured sheets of ancient paper saying: "Here you behold the mummy of the villain Love." Such love as it was—the love of the privileged butcher for the lamb. The burden of the letters, put in epigram, was rattlesnake and bird. A narrative of Anastasia's sister, Elizabeth, signed and sealed, with names of witnesses appended, related in brief bald English the history of the events which had killed her. It warmed pathetically when dwelling on the writer's necessity to part with letters and papers of greater moment that she might be enabled to sustain and educate her sister's child. She named the certificate; she swore to the tampering with witnesses. The number and exact indication of the house where the ceremony took place was stated—a house in Soho;—the date was given, and the incident on that night of the rape of the beautiful Miss Armett by mad Lord Beaumaris at the theatre doors, aided by masked ruffians, after Anastasia's performance of Zamira.

"There are witnesses I know to be still living, Mr. Temple," my father said, seeing the young student-at-law silent and observant. "One of them I have under my hand; I feed him. Listen to this."

He read two or three insufferable sentences from one of the love-epistles, and broke down. I was ushered aside by a member of the firm to inspect an instrument prepared to bind me as surety for the costs of the appeal. I signed it. We quitted the attorney's office convinced (I speak of Temple and myself) that we had seen the shadow of something.

CHAPTER XL.

MY FATHER'S MEETING WITH MY GRANDFATHER.

MY father's pleasure on the day of our journey to Bulsted was to drive me out of London on a lofty open chariot, with which he made the circuit of the fashionable districts, and caused innumerable heads to turn. I would have preferred to go the way of other men, to be unnoticed, but I was subject to an occasional glowing of undefined satisfaction in the observance of the universally acknowledged harmony existing between his pretensions, his tastes and habits, and his person. He contrived by I know not what persuasiveness and simplicity of manner and speech to banish from me the idea that he was engaged in playing a high stake; and though I knew it, and he more than once admitted it, there was an ease and mastery about him that afforded me some degree of positive comfort still. I was still most securely attached to his fortunes. Supposing the ghost of dead Hector to have hung over his body when the inflamed son of Peleus whirled him at his chariot wheels round Troy, he would, with his natural passions sobered by Erebus, have had some of my reflections upon force and fate, and my partial sense of exhilaration in the tremendous speed of the course during the whole of the period my father termed his Grand Parade. I showed just such acquiescence or resistance as were superinduced by the variations of the ground. Otherwise I was spell-bound; and beyond interdicting any further public mention of my name or the princess's, I did nothing to thwart him. It would have been no light matter.

We struck a station at a point half-way down to Bulsted, and found little Kiomi there, thunder in her brows, carrying a bundle, and purchasing a railway-ticket, not to travel in our direction. She gave me the singular answer that she could not tell me where her people were; nor would she tell me whither she was going, alone, and by rail. I chanced to speak of Heriot. One of her sheet-lightning flashes shot out. " He won't be at Bulsted," she said, as if that had a significance. I let her know we were invited to Bulsted. " Oh, she's at home; " Kiomi blinked, and her features twitched like whip-cord. I saw that she was possessed by one of her furies. That girl's face had the art of making me forget beautiful women, and what beauty was by comparison.

It happened that the squire came across us as we were rounding the slope of larch and fir plantation near a part of the Riversley hollows, leading to the upper heath-land, where, behind a semicircle of birches, Bulsted lay. He was on horseback, and called hoarsely to the captain's coachman, who was driving us, to pull up. "Here, Harry," he sung out to me, in the same rough voice, "I don't see why we should bother Captain William. It's a bit of business, not pleasure. I've got the book in my pocket. You ask—is it convenient to step into my bailiff's cottage hard by, and run through it? Ten minutes 'll tell me all I want to know. I want it done with. Ask."

My father stood up and bowed, bareheaded.

My grandfather struck his hat and bobbed.

"Mr. Beltham, I trust I see you well."

"Better, sir, when I've got rid of a damned unpleasant bit o' business."

"I offer you my hearty assistance."

"Do you? Then step down and come into my bailiff's."

"I come, sir."

My father alighted from the carriage. The squire cast his gouty leg to be quit of his horse, but not in time to check my father's advances and ejaculations of condolence.

"Gout, Mr. Beltham is a little too much a proof to *us* of a long line of ancestry."

His hand and arm were raised in the form of a splint to support the squire, who glared back over his cheek-bone, horrified that he could not escape the contact, and in too great pain from arthritic throes to protest: he resembled a burglar surprised by justice. "What infernal nonsense . . . . fellow talking now?" I heard him mutter between his hoppings and dancings, with one foot in the stirrup and a toe to earth, the enemy at his heel, and his inclination half bent upon swinging to the saddle again. I went to relieve him. "Damn! . . . . Oh, it's you," said he.

The squire directed Uberly, his groom, to walk his horse up and down the turf fronting young Tom Eckerthy's cottage, and me to remain where I was; then hobbled up to the door, followed at a leisurely march by my father. The door opened. My father swept the old man in before him, with a bow and flourish that admitted of no contradiction, and the door closed on them. I caught a glimpse of Uberly screwing his wrinkles in a queer grimace, while he worked his left eye and thumb expressively at the cottage, by way of communicating his mind to Samuel, Captain Bulsted's coachman; and I became quite of his opinion as to the nature of the meeting, that it was comical and not likely to lead to much. I thought of the princess and of my hope of her depending upon such an interview as this. From that hour when I stepped on the sands of the Continent to the day of my quitting them, I had been folded in a dream: I had stretched my hand to the highest things of earth, and here now was the retributive material money-question, like a keen scythe-blade!

The cottage-door continued shut. The heaths were darkening, I heard a noise of wheels, and presently the unmistakable voice of Janet, saying, "That must be Harry." She was driving my aunt Dorothy. Both of them hushed at hearing that the momentous duel was in progress. Janet's first thought was of the squire. "I won't have him ride home in the dark," she said, and ordered Uberly to walk the horse home. The ladies had a ladies' altercation before Janet would permit my aunt to yield her place and proceed on foot, accompanied by me. Naturally the best driver of the two kept the whip. I told Samuel to go on to Bulsted, with word that we were coming: and Janet, nodding bluntly, agreed to direct my father as to where he might expect to find me on the Riversley road. My aunt Dorothy and I went ahead slowly: at her request I struck a pathway to avoid the pony-carriage, which was soon audible; and when Janet, chattering to the squire, had gone by, we turned back to intercept my father. He was speechless at the sight of Dorothy Beltham. At his solicitation she consented to meet him next day; his account of the result of the interview was unintelligible to her as well as to me. Even after leaving her at the park-gates, I could get nothing definite from him, save that all was well, and that the squire was eminently practical; but he believed he had done an excellent evening's work. "Yes," said he, rubbing his hands, "excellent! making due allowances for the emphatically commoner's mind we have to deal with." And then to change the subject he dilated on that strange story of the man who, an enormous number of years back in the date of the world's history, carried his little son on his shoulders one night when the winds were not so boisterous, though we were deeper in Winter, along the identical road we traversed, between the gorse-mounds, across the heaths, with yonder remembered fir-tree clump in sight and the wastewater visible to footfarers rounding under the firs. At night-time he vowed that, as far as Nature permitted it, he had satisfied the squire—"completely satisfied him, I mean," he said, to give me sound sleep. "No doubt of it; no doubt of it, Richie." He won Julia's heart straight off, and Captain Bulsted's profound admiration. "Now I know the man I've always been adoring since you were so high, Harry," said she. Captain Bulsted sighed: "Your husband bows to your high good taste, my dear." They relished him sincerely, and between them and him I suffered myself to be dandled once more into a state of credulity, until I saw my aunt Dorothy in the afternoon subsequent to the appointed meeting. His deep respect and esteem for her had stayed him from answering any of her questions falsely. To that extent he had been veracious. It appeared that, driven hard by the squire, who would have no waving of flags and lighting of fireworks in a matter of business, and whose 'commoner's mind' chafed sturdily at a hint of the necessity for lavish outlays where there was a princess to win, he had rallied on the fiction that many of the cheques, standing for the bulk of the sums expended, were moneys borrowed by him of me, which he designed to repay, and was prepared to repay instantly—could in fact, the squire demanding it, repay as it were on the spot; for behold, these borrowed moneys were not spent; they were moneys invested in undertakings, put out to high rates of interest; moneys that perhaps it would not be advisable to call in without a season of delay; still, if Mr. Beltham, acting for his grandson and heir, insisted, it should be done. The moneys had been borrowed purely to invest them with profit on my behalf: a gentleman's word of honour was pledged to it.

The squire grimly gave him a couple of months to make it good.

Dorothy Beltham and my father were together for about an hour at Eckerthy's farm. She let my father kiss her hand when he was bending to take his farewell of her, but held her face away. He was in manifest distress, hardly master of his voice, begged me to come to him soon, and bowing, with " God bless you, madam, my friend on earth !" turned his heel, bearing his elastic frame lamentably. A sad or a culprit air did not befit him : one reckoned up his foibles and errors when seeing him under a partly-beaten aspect. At least, I did ; not my dear aunt, who was compassionate of him, however thoroughly she condemned his ruinous extravagance, and the shifts and evasions it put him to. She feared that, instead of mending the difficulty, he had postponed merely to exaggerate it in the squire's mind ; and she was now of opinion that the bringing him down to meet the squire was very bad policy, likely to result in danger to my happiness ; for, if the money should not be forthcoming on the date named, all my father's faults would be transferred to me as his accomplice, both in the original wastefulness and the subterfuges invented to conceal it. I recollected that a sum of money had really been sunk in Prince Ernest's coal-mine. My aunt said she hoped for the best.

Mounting the heaths, we looked back on the long yellow road, where the carriage conveying my father to the railway-station was visible, and talked of him, and of the elements of antique tragedy in his history, which were at that period, let me say, precisely what my incessant mental efforts were strained to expel from the idea of our human life. The individual's freedom was my tenet of faith ; but pity pleaded for him that he was well-nigh irresponsible, was shamefully sinned against at his birth, one who could charge the Gods with vindictiveness, and complain of the persecution of natal Furies. My aunt Dorothy advised me to take him under my charge, and sell his house and furniture, make him live in bachelor chambers with his faithful waiting-woman and a single man-servant.

" He will want money even to do that," I remarked.

She murmured, " Is there not some annual income paid to him ?"

Her quick delicacy made her redden in alluding so closely to his personal affairs, and I loved her for the nice feeling.

"It was not much," I said.   The miserable attempt to repair the wrongs done to him with this small annuity angered me; and I remembered, little pleased, the foolish expectations he founded on this secret acknowledgment of the justice of his claims.   "We won't talk of it," I pursued.   "I wish he had never touched it.   I shall interdict him."

"You would let him pay his debts with it, Harry?"

"I am not sure, aunty, that he does not incur a greater debt by accepting it."

"One's wish would be that he might not ever be in need of it."

"Ay, or never be caring to find the key of it."

"That must be waste of time," she said.

I meant something else, but it was useless to tell her so.

CHAPTER XLI.

COMMENCEMENT OF THE SPLENDOURS AND PERPLEXITIES OF MY FATHER'S GRAND PARADE.

JANET, in reply to our inquiries as to the condition of the squire's temper, pointed out in the newspaper a notification of a grand public Ball to be given by my father, the first of a series of three, and said that the squire had seen it and shrugged.   She thought there was no positive cause for alarm, even though my father should fail of his word; but expressed her view decidedly that it was an unfortunate move to bring him between the squire and me, and so she blamed Captain Bulsted.   This was partly for the reason that the captain and his wife, charmed by my father, were for advocating his merits at the squire's table: our ingenuity was ludicrously taxed to mystify him on the subject of their extravagant eulogies.   They told him they had been invited, and were going to the great London Balls.

"Subscription Balls?" asked the squire.

"No, sir," rejoined the captain.

"Tradesmen's Balls, d'ye call 'em, then?"

"No, sir; they are Balls given by a distinguished gentle-man."

"Take care it's not another name for tradesmen's Balls, William."

"I do not attend tradesmen's Balls, sir."

"Take care o' that, William."

The captain was very angry. "What," said he, turning to us, "what does the squire mean by telling an officer of the Royal Navy that he is conducting his wife to a trades-men's Ball?"

Juli threatened malicious doings for the insult. She and the squire had a controversy upon the explication of the word gentleman, she describing my father's appearance and manners to the life. "Now listen to me, squire. A gentle-man, I say, is one you'd say, if he wasn't born a duke, he ought to have been, and more shame to the title! He turns the key of a lady's heart with a twinkle of his eye. He's never mean—what he has is yours. He's a true friend; and if he doesn't keep his word, you know in a jiffy it's the fault of affairs; and stands about five feet eleven: he's a full-blown man:" and so forth.

The squire listened, and perspired at finding the object of his abhorrence crowned thus in the unassailable realms of the abstract. Julia might have done it more elegantly; but her husband was rapturous over her skill in portraiture, and he added: "That's a gentleman, squire; and that's a man pretty sure to be abused by half the world."

"Three-quarters, William," said the squire; "there's about the computation for your gentleman's creditors, I sus-pect."

"Ay, sir; well," returned the captain, to whom this kind of fencing in the dark was an affliction, "we make it up in quality—in quality."

"I'll be bound you do," said the squire; "and so you will so long as you're only asked to dance to the other poor devils' fiddling."

Captain Bulsted bowed. "The last word to you, squire."

The squire nodded. "I'll hand it to your wife, William."

Julia took it graciously. "A perfect gentleman!—per-fect! confound his enemies!"

"Why, ma'am, you might keep from swearing," the squire bawled.

"La! squire," said she, "why, don't you know the National Anthem?"

"National Anthem, ma'am! and a fellow, a velvet-tongued —confound *him*, if you like."

"And where's my last word, if you please?" Julia jumped up, and dropped a provoking curtsey.

"You silly old grandada!" said Janet, going round to him; "don't you see the cunning woman wants to dress you in our garments, and means to boast of it to us while you're finishing your wine?"

The old man fondled her. I could have done the same, she bent over him with such homely sweetness. "One comfort, *you* won't go to these gingerbread Balls," he said.

"I'm not invited," she moaned comically.

"No; nor shan't be, while I can keep you out of bad company."

"But, grandada, I do like dancing."

"Dance away, my dear; I've no objection."

"But where's the music?"

"Oh, you can always have music."

"But where are my partners?"

The squire pointed at me.

"You don't want more than one at a time, eh?" He corrected his error: "No, the fellow's engaged in another quadrille. Mind you, Miss Janet, he shall dance to your tune yet. D'ye hear, sir?" The irritation excited by Captain Bulsted and Julia broke out in fury. "Who's that fellow danced when Rome was burning?"

"The Emperor Nero," said Janet. "He killed Harry's friend Seneca in the eighty-somethingth year of his age; an old man, and—hush, grandada!" She could not check him.

"Hark you, Mr. Harry; dance your hardest up in town with your rips and reps, and the lot of ye; all very fine while the burning goes on: you won't see the fun of dancing on the ashes. A nice king of Rome Nero was next morning! By the Lord, if I couldn't swear you'll be down on your knees to an innocent fresh-hearted girl's worth five hundred of the crew you're for partnering now while you've a penny for the piper."

Janet shut his mouth, kissed him, and held his wine up. He drank, and thumped the table. "We'll have parties here, too. The girl shall have her choice of partners: she shan't be kept in the back-ground by a young donkey. Take any six of your own age, and six sensible men, to try you by your chances. By George, the whole dozen 'd bring you in non-compos. You've only got the women on your side because of a smart face and figure."

Janet exclaimed indignantly, "Grandada, I'm offended with you;" and walked out on a high step.

"Come, if he has the women on his side," said Captain Bulsted, mildly.

"He'll be able to go partnering and gallopading as long as his banker 'll let him, William—like your gentleman! That's true. We shall soon see."

"I leave my character in your hands, sir," said I, rising. "If you would scold me in private, I should prefer it, on behalf of your guests; but I am bound to submit to your pleasure, and under any circumstances I remember, what you appear to forget, that you are my grandfather."

So saying, I followed the ladies. It was not the wisest of speeches, and happened, Captain Bulsted informed me, to be delivered in my father's manner, for the squire pronounced emphatically that he saw very little Beltham in me. The right course would have been for me to ask him then and there whether I had his consent to start for Germany. But I was the sport of resentments and apprehensions; and, indeed, I should not have gone. I could not go without some title beyond that of the heir of great riches.

Janet kept out of my sight. I found myself strangely anxious to console her: less sympathetic, perhaps, than desirous to pour out my sympathy in her ear, which was of a very pretty shape, with a soft unpierced lobe. We danced together at the Riversley Ball, given by the squire on the night of my father's Ball in London. Janet complimented me upon having attained wisdom. "Now we get on well," she said. "Grandada only wants to see us friendly, and feel that I am not neglected."

The old man, a martyr to what he considered due to his favourite, endured the horror of the Ball until supper-time, and kept his eyes on us two. He forgot, or pretended to forget, my foreign engagement altogether, though the announcement in the newspapers was spoken of by Sir Roderick and Lady Ilchester and others.

"How do you like that?" he remarked to me, seeing her twirled away by one of the young Rubreys.

"She seems to like it, sir," I replied.

"Like it!" said he. "In my day you wouldn't have caught me letting the bloom be taken off the girl I cared for by a parcel o' scampish young dogs. Right in their arms! Look at her build. She's strong; she's healthy; she goes round like a tower. If you want a girl to *look* like a princess!——"

His eulogies were not undeserved. But she danced as lightly and happily with Mr. Fred Rubrey as with Harry Richmond. I congratulated myself on her lack of sentiment. Later, when in London, where Mdlle. Jenny Chasse-diane challenged me to perilous sarabandes, I wished that Janet had ever so small a grain of sentiment, for a preservative to me. Ottilia glowed high and distant; she sent me no message; her image did not step between me and disorder. The whole structure of my idea of my superior nature seemed to be crumbling to fragments; and beginning to feel in despair that I was wretchedly like other men, I lost by degrees the sense of my hold on her. It struck me that my worst fears of the effect produced on the princess's mind by that last scene in the lake-palace must be true, and I abandoned hope. Temple thought she tried me too cruelly. Under these circumstances I became less and less resolutely disposed to renew the forlorn conflict with my father concerning his prodigal way of living. "Let it last as long as I have a penny to support him!" I exclaimed. He said that Dettermain and Newson were now urging on his case with the utmost despatch in order to keep pace with him, but that the case relied for its life on his preserving a great appearance. He handed me his division of our twin cheque-books, telling me he preferred to depend on his son for supplies, and I was in the mood to think this a partial security.

"But you can take what there is," I said.

"On the contrary, I will accept nothing but minor sums —so to speak, the fractional shillings; though I confess I am always bewildered by silver," said he.

I questioned him upon his means of carrying on his expenditure. His answer was to refer to the pavement of the city of London. By paying here and there he had, he informed me, made a concrete for the wheels to roll on. He calculated that he now had credit for the space of three new years—ample time for him to fight his fight and win his victory.

"*My* tradesmen are not like the tradesmen of other persons," he broke out with a curious neigh of supreme satisfaction in that retinue. "They believe in me. I have de facto harnessed them to my fortunes; and if you doubt me on the point of success, I refer you to Dettermain and Newson. All I stipulate for is to maintain my position in society to throw a lustre on my Case. So much I must do. My failures hitherto have been entirely owing to the fact that I had not my son to stand by me."

"Then you must have money, sir."

"Yes, money."

"Then what can you mean by refusing mine?"

"I admit the necessity for it, my son. Say you hand me a cheque for a temporary thousand. Your credit and mine in conjunction can replace it before the expiration of the two months. Or," he meditated, "it might be better to give a bond or so to a professional lender, and preserve the account at your bankers intact. The truth is, I have, in my interview with the squire, drawn in advance upon the material success I have a perfect justification to anticipate, and I cannot allow the old gentleman to suppose that I retrench for the purpose of giving a large array of figures to your bankers' book. It would be sheer madness. I cannot do it. I cannot afford to do it. When you are on a runaway horse, —I prefer to say a racehorse,—Richie, you must *ride* him. You dare not throw up the reins. Only last night Wedderburn, appealing to Loftus, a practical sailor, was approved when he offered—I forget the subject-matter—the illustration of a ship on a lee-shore; you are lost if you do not spread every inch of canvas to the gale. Retrenchment at this particular moment is perdition. Count our gains, Richie. We have won a princess . . ."

I called to him not to name her.

He persisted: "Half a minute. She is won; she is ours. And let me, in passing,—bear with me one second,—counsel you to write to Prince Ernest instanter, proposing formally for his daughter, and, in your grandfather's name, state her dowry at fifty thousand per annum."

"Oh, you forget!" I interjected.

"No, Richie, I do not forget that you are off a lee-shore;

you are mounted on a skittish racehorse, with, if you like, a New Forest fly operating within an inch of his belly-girths. Our situation is so far ticklish, and prompts invention and audacity."

"You must forget, sir, that in the present state of the squire's mind, I should be simply lying in writing to the prince that he offers a dowry."

" No, for your grandfather has yielded consent."

" By implication, you know he withdraws it."

" But if I satisfy him that you have not been extravagant?"

" I must wait till he is satisfied."

" The thing is done, Richie, done. I see it in advance—it is done! Whatever befalls me, you, my dear boy, in the space of two months, may grasp your fortune. Besides, here is my hand. I swear by it, my son, that I shall satisfy the squire. I go farther; I say I shall have the means to refund to you—the means, the money. The marriage is announced in our prints for the Summer—say early June. And I undertake that you, the husband of the princess, shall be the first gentleman in England—that is, Europe. Oh! not ruling a coterie : not dazzling the world with entertainments." He thought himself in earnest when he said, " I attach no mighty importance to these things, though there is no harm I can perceive in leading the fashion—none that I see in having a consummate style. I know your taste, and hers, Richie, the noble lady's. She shall govern the intellectual world—your poets, your painters, your men of science. They *reflect* a beautiful sovereign mistress more exquisitely than almost aristocracy does. But you head our aristocracy also. You are a centre of the political world. So I scheme it. Between you, I defy the Court to rival you. This I call distinction. It is no mean aim, by heaven! I protest, it is an aim with the mark in sight, and not out of range."

He whipped himself up to one of his oratorical frenzies, of which a cheque was the common fruit. The power of his persuasiveness in speech, backed by the spectacle of his social accomplishments, continued to subdue me, and I protested only inwardly even when I knew that he was gambling with fortune. I wrote out many cheques, and still it appeared to me that they were barely sufficient to meet the current expenses of his household.   Temple and I calculated that his Grand Parade would try the income of a duke, and could but be a matter of months.   Mention of it reached Riversley from various quarters, from Lady Maria Higginson, from Captain Bulsted and his wife, and from Sir Roderick Ilchester, who said to me, with fine accentuation, " I have *met* your father."   Sir Roderick, an Englishman reputed of good breeding, informed the son that he had actually met the father in lofty society, at Viscountess Sedley's, at Lady Dolchester's, at Bramham DeWitt's, and heard of him as a frequenter of the Prussian and Austrian embassy entertainments ; and also that he was admitted to the exclusive dinner-parties of the Countess de Strode, " which are," he observed, in the moderated tone of an astonishment devoting itself to propagation, " the cream of society."   Indubitably, then, my father was an impostor: society proved it.   The squire listened like one pelted by a storm, sure of his day to come at the close of the two months. I gained his commendation by shunning the metropolitan Balls, nor did my father press me to appear at them.   It was tacitly understood between us that I should now and then support him at his dinner-table, and pass bowing among the most select of his great ladies.   And this I did, and I felt at home with them, though I had to bear with roughnesses from one or two of the more venerable dames, which were not quite proper to good breeding.   Old Lady Kane, great-aunt of the Marquis of Edbury, was particularly my tormentor, through her plain-spoken comments on my father's legal suit; for I had to listen to her without wincing, and agree in her general contempt of the Georges, and foil her queries coolly, when I should have liked to perform Jorian DeWitt's expressed wish to " squeeze the acid out of her in one grip, and toss her to the Gods that collect exhausted lemons." She took extraordinary liberties with me.

" Why not marry an Englishwoman ?   Rich young men ought to choose wives from their own people, out of their own sets.   Foreign women never get on well in this country, unless they join the hounds to hunt the husband."

She cited naturalized ladies famous for the pastime.   Her world and its outskirts she knew thoroughly, even to the fact of my grandfather's desire that I should marry Janet Ilchester.   She named a duke's daughter, an earl's.   Of course I should have to stop the scandal: otherwise the choice I had was unrestricted. My father she evidently disliked, but she just as much disliked an encounter with his invincible bonhomie and dexterous tongue. She hinted at family reasons for being shy of him, assuring me that I was not implicated in them. "The Guelph pattern was never much to my taste," she said, and it consoled me with the thought that he was not ranked as an adventurer in the houses he entered. I learned that he was supposed to depend chiefly on my vast resources. Edbury acted the part of informant to the inquisitive harridan: "Her poor dear good-for-nothing Edbury! whose only cure would be a nice, well-conducted girl, an heiress." She had cast her eye on Anna Penrhys, but considered her antecedents doubtful. Spotless innocence was the sole receipt for Edbury's malady. My father, in a fit of bold irony, proposed Lady Kane for President of his Tattle and Scandal Club,—a club of ladies dotted with select gentlemen, the idea of which Jorian DeWitt claimed the merit of starting, and my father surrendered it to him, with the reservation that Jorian intended an association of backbiters pledged to reveal all they knew, whereas the Club, in its present form, was an engine of morality and decency, and a social safeguard, as well as an amusement. It comprised a Committee of Investigation, and a Court of Appeal; its object was to arraign slander. Lady Kane declined the honour. "I am not a washerwoman," she said to me, and spoke of where dirty linen should be washed, and was distressingly broad in her innuendoes concerning Edbury's stepmother. This Club sat and became a terror for a month, adding something to my father's reputation. His inexhaustible conversational art and humour gave it such vitality as it had. Ladies of any age might apply for admission when well seconded: gentlemen under forty-five years were rigidly excluded, and the seniors must also have passed through the marriage ceremony. Outside tattle and scandal declared that the Club was originated to serve as a club for Lady Edbury, but I chose to have no opinion upon what I knew nothing of.

These matters were all ephemeral, and freaks; they produced, however, somewhat of the same effect on me as on my father, in persuading me that he was born for the sphere he occupied, and rendering me rather callous as to the sources

of ways and means.   I put my name to a bond for several
thousand pounds, in conjunction with Lord Edbury, thinking my father right in wishing to keep my cheque-book un-
worried, lest the squire should be seized with a spasm of
curiosity before the two months were over.   "I promise you
I surprise him," my father said repeatedly.   He did not say
how : I had the suspicion that he did not know.   His confidence
and my growing recklessness acted in unison.   Happily the
newspapers were quiet.   I hoped consequently to find peace
at Riversley; but there the rumours of the Grand Parade
were fabulous, thanks to Captain Bulsted and Julia, among
others.   These two again provoked an outbreak of rage from
the squire, and I, after hearing them, was almost disposed to
side with him; they suggested an inexplicable magnificence,
and created an image of a man portentously endowed with
the capacity to throw dust in the eyes.   No description of
the Balls could have furnished me with such an insight of
their brilliancy as the consuming ardour they awakened in
the captain and his wife.   He reviewed them : "Princely
entertainments!   Arabian Nights!"

She built them up piecemeal : "The company! the dresses!
the band! the supper!"   The host was a personage supernatural.   "Aladdin's magician, if you like," said Julia,
"only—good!   A perfect gentleman! and I'll say again,
confound his enemies."   She presumed, as she was aware
she might do, upon the squire's prepossession in her favour,
without reckoning that I was always the victim.

"Heard o' that new story 'bout a Dauphin?" he asked.

"A Dauphin?" quoth Captain Bulsted.   "I don't know
the fish."

"You've been in a pretty kettle of 'em lately, William.
I heard of it yesterday on the Bench.   Lord Shale, our new
Lord-Lieutenant, brought it down.   A trick they played the
fellow 'bout a Dauphin.   Serve him right.   You heard anything 'bout it, Harry?"

l had not.

"But I tell ye there is a Dauphin mixed up with him.
A Dauphin and Mr. Ik Dine!"

"Mr. Ik Dine!" exclaimed the captain, perplexed.

"Ay, that's German lingo, William, and you ought to
know it if you're a loyal sailor—means 'I serve.'"

"Mr. Beltham," said the captain, seriously, "I give you

my word of honour as a man and a British officer, I don't understand one syllable of what you're saying; but if it means any insinuation against the gentleman who condescends to extend his hospitalities to my wife and me, I must, with regret, quit the place where I have had the misfortune to hear it."

"You stop where you are, William," the squire motioned to him. "'Gad, I shall have to padlock my mouth, or I shan't have a friend left soon . . . . confounded fellow. I tell you they call him Mr. Ik Dine in town. Ik Dine and a Dauphin! They made a regular clown and pantaloon o' the pair, I'm told. Couple o' pretenders to thrones invited to dine together and talk over their chances and show their private marks. Oho! by-and-by, William! You and I! Never a man made such a fool of in his life!"

The ladies retired. The squire continued, in a furious whisper:—

"They got the two together, William. Who are you? I'm a Dauphin; who are you? I'm Ik Dine, bar sinister. Oh! says the other, then I take precedence of you! Devil a bit, says the other; I've got more spots than you. Proof, says one. You first, t'other. Count, one cries. T'other sings out, Measles. Better than a dying Dauphin, roars t'other; and swore both of 'm 'twas nothing but Port-wine stains and pimples. Ha! ha! And, William, will you believe it?—the couple went round begging the company to count spots—ha! ha!—to prove their big birth! Oh, Lord, I'd ha' paid a penny to be there! A Jack o' Bedlam Ik Dine damned idiot!—makes name o' Richmond stink." (Captain Bulsted shot a wild stare round the room to make sure that the ladies had gone.) "I tell ye, William, I had it from Lord Shale himself only yesterday on the Bench. He brought it to us hot from town—didn't know I knew the fellow; says the fellow's charging and firing himself off all day and all night too—can't make him out. Says London's mad about him: lots o' women, the fools! Ha, ha! a Dauphin!"

"Ah, well, sir," Captain Bulsted supplicated feverishly, rubbing his brows and whiskers.

"It's true, William. Fellow ought to be taken up and committed as a common vagabond, and would be anywhere but in London. I'd jail him 'fore you cocked your eye twice.

Fellow came here and talked me over to grant him a couple
o' months to prove he hasn't swindled his son of every scrap
of his money. We shall soon see. Not many weeks to run!
And pretends—fellow swears to me—can get him into Parliament; swears he'll get him in 'fore the two months are
over! An infernal——"

"Please to recollect, sir; the old hereditary shall excuse
you——"

"Gout, you mean, William? By——"

"You are speaking in the presence of his son, sir, and you
are trying the young gentleman's affection for you hard."

"Eh? 'Cause I'm his friend? Harry," my grandfather
faced round on me, "don't you know I'm the friend you can
trust? Hal, did I ever borrow a farthing of you? Didn't
I, the day of your majority, hand you the whole of your
inheritance from your poor broken-hearted mother, with
interest, and treat you like a man? And never played spy,
never made an inquiry, till I heard the scamp had been
fastening on you like a blood-sucker, and singing hymns
into the ears of that squeamish dolt of a pipe-smoking
parson, Peterborough—never thought of doing it! Am I
the man that dragged your grandmother's name through the
streets and soiled yours?"

I remarked that I was sensible of the debt of gratitude
I owed to him, but would rather submit to the scourge, or
to destitution, than listen to these attacks on my father.

"Cut yourself loose, Harry," he cried, a trifle mollified.
"Don't season his stew—d'ye hear? Stick to decent people.
Why, you don't expect he'll be locked up in the Tower for
a finish, eh? It'll be Newgate, or the Bench. He and his
Dauphin—ha! ha! A rascal crow and a Jack Dauphin!"

Captain Bulsted reached me his hand. "You have a great
deal to bear, Harry. I commend you, my boy, for taking it
manfully."

"I say no more," quoth the squire. "But what I said
was true. The fellow gives his little dinners and suppers
to his marchionesses, countesses, duchesses, and plays clown
and pantaloon among the men. He thinks a parcel o'
broidered petticoats 'll float him. So they may till a tradesman sent stark mad pops a pin into him. Harry, I'd as lief
hang on to a fire-ship. Here's Ilchester tells me . . . . and
Ilchester speaks of him under his breath now as if he were

sitting in a pew funking the parson. Confound the fellow! I say he's guilty of treason. Pooh! who cares! He cuts out the dandies of his day, does he? He's past sixty, if he's a month. It's all damned harlequinade. Let him twirl off one columbine or another, or a dozen, and then the last of him! Fellow makes the world look like a farce. He's got about eight feet by five to caper on, and all London gaping at him— geese! Are you a gentleman and a man of sense, Harry Richmond, to let yourself be lugged about in public —by the Lord! like a pair of street-tumblers in spangled haunch-bags, father and boy, on a patch of carpet, and a drum banging, and tossed and turned inside out, and my God! the ass of a fellow strutting the ring with you on his shoulder! That's the spectacle. And you, Harry, now I'll ask you, do you mean your wife—egad, it'd be a pretty scene, with your princess in hip-up petticoats, stiff as bottle-funnel top down'ards, airing a whole leg, and knuckling a tambourine!"

"Not crying, my dear lad?" Captain Bulsted put his arm round me kindly, and tried to catch a glimpse of my face. I let him see I was not going through that process. "Whew!" said he, "and enough to make any Christian sweat! You're in a bath, Harry. I wouldn't expect the man who murdered his godmother for one shilling and fivepence three-farthings the other day, to take such a slinging, and think he deserved it."

My power of endurance had reached its limit.

"You tell me, sir, you had this brutal story from the Lord-Lieutenant of the county?"

"Ay, from Lord Shale. But I won't have you going to him and betraying our connection with a——"

"Halloo!" Captain Bulsted sang out to his wife on the lawn. "And now, squire, I have had my dose. And you will permit me to observe that I find it emphatically what we used to call at school black-jack."

"And you were all the better for it afterwards, William."

"We did not arrive at that opinion, sir. Harry, your arm. An hour with the ladies will do us both good. The squire," he murmured, wiping his forehead as he went out, "has a knack of bringing us into close proximity with hell-fire when he pleases."

Julia screamed on beholding us, "Aren't you two men as pale as death!"

Janet came and looked.

"Merely a dose," said the captain. "We are anxious to play battledore and shuttlecock madly."

"So he shall, the dear!" Julia caressed him. "We'll all have a tournament in the wet-weather shed."

Janet whispered to me, "Was it—the Returning Thanks?"

"The what?" said I, with the dread at my heart of something worse than I had heard.

She hailed Julia to run and fetch the battledores, and then told me she had been obliged to confiscate the newspapers that morning and cast the burden on post-office negligence. "They reach grandada's hands by afternoon post, Harry, and he finds objectionable passages blotted or cut out; and as long as the scissors dont' touch the business, columns and the debates, he never asks me what I have been doing. He thinks I keep a scrap-book. I haven't often time in the morning to run an eye all over the paper. This morning it was the first thing I saw."

What had she seen? She led me out of view of the windows and showed me.

My father was accused of having stood up at a public dinner and returned thanks on behalf of an Estate of the Realm: it read monstrously. I ceased to think of the suffering inflicted on me by my grandfather.

Janet and I, side by side with the captain and Julia, carried on the game of battledore and shuttlecock, in a match to see whether the unmarried could keep the shuttle flying as long as the married, with varying fortunes. She gazed on me, to give me the comfort of her sympathy, too much, and I was too intent on the vision of my father either persecuted by lies or guilty of hideous follies, to allow the match to be a fair one. So Julia could inform the squire that she and William had given the unmarried pair a handsome beating when he appeared peeping round one of the shed-pillars.

"Of course you beat 'em," said the squire. "It's not my girl's fault." He said more, to the old tune, which drove Janet away.

I remembered, when back in the London vortex, the curious soft beauty she won from casting up her eyes to watch the descending feathers, and the brilliant direct beam of those thick-browed firm clear eyes, with her frown, and her set lips and brave figure, when she was in the act of striking to keep up a regular quick fusillade. I had need of calm memories. The town was astir, and humming with one name.

CHAPTER XLII.

THE MARQUIS OF EDBURY AND HIS PUPPET.

I PASSED from man to man, hearing hints and hesitations, alarming half-remarks, presumed to be addressed to one who could supply the remainder, and deduce consequences. There was a clearer atmosphere in the street of Clubs. Jennings was the first of my father's more intimate acquaintances to meet me frankly. He spoke, though not with great serious-ness, of the rumour of a possible prosecution. Sir Weeton Slater tripped up to us with a mixed air of solicitude and restraint, asked whether I was well, and whether I had seen the newspapers that morning; and on my informing him that I had just come up from Riversley, on account of certain rumours, advised me to remain in town strictly for the present. He also hinted at rumours of prosecutions. "The fact is——" he began several times, rendered discreet, I sup-pose, by my juvenility, fierté, and reputed wealth. We were joined by Admiral Loftus and Lord Alton. They queried and counterqueried as to passages between my father and the newspapers, my father and the committee of his Club, preserving sufficient consideration for me to avoid the serious matter in all but distant allusions; a point upon which the breeding of Mr. Serjeant Wedderburn was not so accurate a guide to him. An exciting public scandal soon gathers knots of gossips in Clubland. We saw Wedderburn break from a group some way down the pavement and pick up a fresh crumb of amusement at one of the doorsteps. "Roy Rich-mond is having his benefit to-day!" he said, and repeated this and that, half audible to me. For the rest, he pooh-poohed the idea of the Law intervening. His "How d'ye do, Mr. Richmond, how d'ye do?" was almost congratulatory. "I think we meet at your father's table to-night? It won't be in the Tower, take my word for it. Oh! the papers! There's no Act to compel a man to deny what appears in the papers. No such luck as the Tower!—though Littlepitt (Mr. Wedderburn's nickname for our Premier) would be fool enough for *that*. He would. If he could turn attention from his Bill, he'd do it. We should have to dine off Boleyn's block:—coquite horum obsonia, he'd say, eh?" Jennings espied my father's carriage, and stepped to speak a word to the footman. He returned, saying, with a puff of his cheeks: "The Grand Monarque has been sending his state equipage to give the old backbiting cripple Brisby an airing. He is for horse exercise to-day: they've dropped him in Courtenay Square. There goes Brisby. He'd take the good Samaritan's shilling to buy a flask of poison for him. He'll use Roy's carriage to fetch and carry for that venomous old woman Kane, I'll swear."

"She's a male in Scripture," said Wedderburn, and this reminded me of an anecdote that reminded him of another, and after telling them, he handed round his hat for the laugh, as my father would have phrased it.

"Has her ladyship declared war?" Sir Weeton Slater inquired.

"No, that's not her preliminary to wageing it," Wedderburn replied. These high-pressure smart talkers had a moment of dulness, and he bethought him that he must run into the Club for letters, and was busy at Westminster, where, if anything fresh occurred between meridian and six o'clock, he should be glad, he said, to have word of it by messenger, that he might not be behind his Age.

The form of humour to express the speed of the world was common, but it struck me as a terrible illustration of my father's. I had still a sense of pleasure in the thought that these intimates of his were gentlemen who relished and, perhaps, really liked him. They were not parasites; not the kind of men found hanging about vulgar profligates.

I quitted them. Sir Weeton Slater walked half-a-dozen steps beside me. "May I presume on a friendly acquaintance with your father, Mr. Richmond?" he said. "The fact is—you will not be offended?—he is apt to lose his head, unless the Committee of Supply limits him very precisely. I am aware that there is no material necessity for any restriction." He nodded to me as to one of the marvellously endowed, as who should say, the Gods presided at your birth. The worthy baronet struggled to impart his meaning, which was, that he would have me define something like an allowance to my father, not so much for the purpose of curtailing his expenditure—he did not venture upon private ground—as to bridle my father's ideas of things possible for a private gentleman in this country. In that character none were like him. As to his suit, or appeal, he could assure me that Serjeant Wedderburn, and all who would or could speak on the subject, saw no prospect of success; not any. The worst of it was, that it caused my father to commit himself in sundry ways. It gave a handle to his enemies. It——he glanced at me indicatively.

I thanked the well-meaning gentleman without encouraging him to continue.

"It led him to perform once more as a Statue of Bronze before the whole of gaping London!" I could have added. That scene on the pine-promontory arose in my vision, followed by other scenes of the happy German days. I had no power to conjure up the princess.

Jorian De Witt was the man I wanted to see. After applications at his Club and lodgings I found him dragging his Burgundy leg in the Park, on his road to pay a morning visit to his fair French enchantress. I impeached him, and he pleaded guilty, clearly not wishing to take me with him, nor would he give me Mdlle. Jenny's address, which I had. By virtue of the threat that I would accompany him if he did not satisfy me, I managed to extract the story of the Dauphin, aghast at the discovery of its being true. The fatal after-dinner speech he believed to have been actually spoken, and he touched on that first. "A trap was laid for him, Harry Richmond; and a deuced clever trap it was. They smuggled in special reporters. There wasn't a bit of necessity for the toast. But the old vixen has shown her hand, so now he must fight. He can beat her single-handed on settees. He'll find her a Tartar at long bowls : she sticks at nothing. She blazes out that he scandalizes her family. She has a dozen indictments against him. You must stop in town and keep watch. There's fire in my leg to explode a powder-magazine a mile off !"

"Is it the Margravine of Rippau ?" I inquired. I could think of no other waspish old woman.

"Lady Kane," said Jorian. "She set Edbury on to face him with the Dauphin. You don't fancy it came of the young dog 'all of himself,' do you? Why, it was clever! He trots about a briefless little barrister, a scribbler, devilish clever and impudent, who does his farces for him. Tenby's the fellow's name, and it's the only thing I haven't heard him pun on. Puns are the smallpox of the language;—we're cursed with an epidemic. By gad, the next time I meet him I'll roar out for vaccine matter."

He described the dinner given by Edbury at a celebrated City tavern where my father and this so-called Dauphin were brought together. "Dinner to-night," he nodded, as he limped away on his blissful visit of ceremony to sprightly Chassediane (a bouquet had gone in advance) : he left me stupefied. The sense of ridicule enveloped me in suffocating folds, howling sentences of the squire's Bœotian burlesque by fits. I felt that I could not but take the world's part against the man who allowed himself to be made preposterous externally, when I knew him to be staking his frail chances and my fortune with such rashness. It was unpardonable for one in his position to incur ridicule. Nothing but a sense of duty kept me from rushing out of London, and I might have indulged the impulse advantageously. Delay threw me into the clutches of Lady Kane herself, on whom I looked with as composed a visage as I could command, while she leaned out of her carriage chattering at me, and sometimes over my head to passing gentlemen. She wanted me to take a seat beside her, she had so much to say. Was there not some funny story abroad of a Pretender to the Throne of France? she asked, wrinkling her crow's-feet eyelids to peer at me, and wished to have the particulars. I had none to offer. "Ah! well," said she; "you stay in London? Come and see me. I'm sure you're sensible. You and I can put our heads together. He's too often in Courtenay Square, and he's ten years too young for that, still. He ought to have good advice. Tell me, how can a woman who can't guide herself help a man?—and the most difficult man alive! I'm sure you understand me. I can't drive out in the afternoon for them. They make a crush here, and a clatter of tongues! . . . . That's my private grievance. But he's now keeping persons away who have the first social claim . . . . I know they can't appear. Don't look confused; no one accuses you. Only I do say it's getting terribly hot in London for somebody. Call on me. Will you ?"

She named her hours. I bowed as soon as I perceived my opportunity. Her allusions were to Lady Edbury, and to imputed usurpations of my father's. I walked down to the chambers where Temple was reading Law, for a refuge from these annoyances. I was in love with the modest shadowed life Temple lived, diligently reading, and glancing on the world as through a dusky window, happy to let it run its course while he sharpened his weapons. A look at Temple's face told me he had heard quite as much as was known in the West. Dining-halls of lawyers are not Cistercian ; he was able to give me three distinct versions of the story of the Dauphin. No one could be friendlier. Indeed Temple now urged me forcibly to prevent my father from spending money and wearing his heart out in vain, by stopping the case in Dettermain and Newson's hands. They were respectable lawyers, he said, in a lawyer's ordinary tone when including such of his species as are not black sheep. He thought it possible that my father's personal influence overbore their judgement. In fact, nothing bound them to refuse to work for him, and he believed that they had submitted their views for his consideration. " I do wish he'd throw it up ;" Temple exclaimed. " It makes him enemies. And just examining it, you see he could get no earthly good out of it : he might as well try to scale a perpendicular rock. But when I'm with him, I'm ready to fancy what he pleases—I acknowledge that. He has excess of phosphorus, or he's ultra-electrical; doctors could tell us better than lawyers." Temple spoke of the clever young barrister Tenby as the man whom his father had heard laughing over the trick played upon " Roy Richmond." I conceived that I might furnish Mr. Tenby a livelier kind of amusement, and the thought that I had once been *sur le terrain*, and had bitterly regretted it, by no means deterred me from the idea of a second expedition, so black was my mood. A review of the circumstances, aided by what reached my ears before the night went over, convinced me that Edbury was my man. His subordinate helped him to the instrument, and possibly to the plot, but Edbury was the capital offender. The scene of the prank was not in

itself so bad as the stuff which a cunning anecdotalist could
make out of it. Edbury invited my father to a dinner at a
celebrated City tavern. He kept his guests (Jennings,
Jorian DeWitt, Alton, Wedderburn, were among the few I
was acquainted with who were present) awaiting the arrival
of a person for whom he professed extraordinary respect.
The Dauphin of France was announced. A mild, flabby,
amiable-looking old person, with shelving forehead and
grey locks—excellently built for the object, Jorian said—
entered. The Capet head and embonpoint were there. As
far as a personal resemblance might go, his pretentions to be
the long-lost Dauphin were grotesquely convincing, for,
notwithstanding the accurate picture of the Family presented by him, the man was a pattern bourgeois:—a sturdy
impostor, one would have thought, and I thought so when I
heard of him ; but I have been assured that he had actually
grown old in the delusion that he, carrying on his business
in the City of London, was the identical Dauphin. Edbury
played his part by leading his poor old victim half way to
meet his other most honoured guest, hesitating then and
craving counsel whether he was right in etiquette to advance
the Dauphin so far. The Dauphin left him mildly to decide
the point : he was eminently mild throughout, and seems to
have thought himself in good faith surrounded by believers
and adherents. Edbury's task soon grew too delicate for
that coarse boy. In my father's dexterous hands he at once
lost his assumption of the gallantry of manner which could
alone help him to retain his advantage. When the wine was
in him he began to bawl. I could imagine the sort of dialogue he raised. Bets on the Dauphin, bets on Roy: they
were matched as on a racecourse. The Dauphin remembered incidents of his residence in the Temple, with a
beautiful juvenile faintness: a conscientious angling for
recollection, Wedderburn said. Roy was requested to
remember something, to drink and refresh his memory:
infantine incidents were suggested. He fenced the treacherous host during dinner with superb complacency. The
Dauphin was of an immoveable composure. He " stated
simple facts : he was the Dauphin of France, providentially
rescued from the Temple in the days of the Terror." For
this deliverance, somewhat to the consternation of the others,
he offered up a short prayer of thanksgiving over his plate.

He had, he said, encountered incredulity. He had his proofs. He who had never been on the soil of France since early boyhood, spoke French with a pure accent: he had the physical and moral constitution of the Family: owing to events attending his infant days, he was timid. Jorian imitated him:—"I start at the opening of a door; I see dark faces in my sleep: it is a dungeon; I am at the knees of my Unfortunate Royal Father, with my Beautiful Mother." His French was quaint, but not absurd. He became loquacious, apostrophizing vacancy with uplifted hand and eye. The unwonted invitation to the society of noblemen made him conceive his Dauphinship to be on the high road to a recognition in England, and he was persuaded to drink and exhibit proofs: which were that he had the constitution of the Family, as aforesaid, in every particular; that he was peculiarly marked with testificatory spots; and that his mere aspect inspired all members and branch members of the Family with awe and stupefaction. One of the latter hearing of him, had appointed to meet him in a pastrycook's shop. He met him, and left the place with a cloud on his brow, showing tokens of respectful sympathy. Conceive a monomaniacal obese old English citizen, given to lift hand and eye and address the cornices, claiming to be an Illustrious Boy, and calling on a beautiful historic mother and unfortunate Royal sire to attest it! No wonder the table was shaken with laughter. He appealed to Tenby constantly, as to the one man he knew in the room. Tenby it was who made the discovery of him somewhere in the City, where he earned his livelihood either as a corn-merchant, or a stockbroker, or a chronometer-maker, or a drysalter, and was always willing to gratify a customer with the sight of his proofs of identity. Mr. Tenby made it his business to push his clamorous waggishness for the exhibition. I could readily believe that my father was more than his match in disposable sallies and weight of humour, and that he shielded the old creature successfully, so long as he had a tractable being to protect. But the Dauphin was plied with wine, and the marquis had his fun. Proof upon proof in verification of his claims was proffered by the now-tremulous son of St. Louis—so he called himself. With, Jorian admitted, a real courtly dignity, he stood up and proposed to lead the way to any neighbouring cabinet to show the spots on his person; living witnesses to the truth of his allegations, he declared them to be. The squire had authority for his broad farce, except in so far as he mixed up my father in the swinery of it. I grew more and more convinced that my father never could have lost his presence of mind when he found himself in the net of a plot to cover him with ridicule. He was the only one who did not retire to the Dauphin's ' chamber of testification,' to return convulsed with vinous laughter after gravely inspecting the evidence; for which abstention the Dauphin reproached him violently, in round terms of abuse, challenging him to go through a similar process. This was the signal for Edbury, Tenby and some of the rest. They formed a circle, one-half for the Dauphin, one for Roy. How long the boorish fun lasted, and what exactly came of it, I did not hear. Jorian DeWitt said my father lost his temper, a point contested by Wedderburn and Jennings, for it was unknown of him. Anyhow, he thundered to some effect, inasmuch as he detached those that had gentlemanly feelings from the wanton roysterers, and next day the latter pleaded wine. But they told the story, not without embellishments. The world followed their example.

I dined and slept at Temple's house, not caring to meet my incarnate humiliation. I sent to hear that he was safe. A quiet evening with a scholarly man, and a man of strong practical ability and shrewdness, like Mr. Temple, did me good. I wished my father and I were on the same footing as he and his son, and I may add his daughters. They all talked sensibly; they were at feud with nobody; they reflected their condition. It was a simple orderly English household, of which the father was the pillar, the girls the ornaments, the son the hope, growing to take his father's place. My envy of such a home was acute, and I thought of Janet, and how well she was fashioned to build one resembling it, if only the mate allotted to her should not be a fantastical dreamer. Temple's character seemed to me to demand a wife like Janet on its merits ; an idea that depressed me exceedingly. I had introduced Temple to Anna Penrhys, who was very kind to him; but these two were not framed to be other than friends. Janet, on the contrary, might some day perceive the sterling fellow Temple was, notwithstanding his moderate height. She might, I thought.

I remembered that I had once wished that she would, and I was amazed at myself. But why? She was a girl sure to marry. I brushed these meditations away. They recurred all the time I was in Temple's house.

Mr. Temple waited for my invitation to touch on my father's Case, when he distinctly pronounced his opinion that it could end but in failure. Though a strict Constitutionalist, he had words of disgust for princes, acknowledging, however, that we were not practical in our use of them, and kept them for political purposes often to the perversion of our social laws and their natural dispositions. He spoke of his son's freak in joining the Navy. "That was the princess's doing," said Temple. "She talked of our naval heroes, till she made me feel I had only to wear the anchor-buttons to be one myself. Don't tell her I was invalided from the service, Richie, for the truth is, I believe, I half-shammed. And the time won't be lost. You'll see I shall extract guineas from ' old ocean ' like salt. Precious few barristers understand maritime cases. The other day I was in Court, and prompted a great Q.C. in a case of collision. Didn't I, sir? "

"I think there was a hoarse whisper audible up to the Judge's seat at intervals," said Mr. Temple.

"The Bar cannot confess to obligations from those who don't wear the robe," Temple rejoined.

His father advised me to read for the Bar, as a piece of very good training.

I appealed to Temple whether he thought it possible to read law-books in a cockboat in a gale of wind.

Temple grimaced and his father nodded. Still it struck me that I might one day have the felicity of quiet hours to sit down with Temple and read law—far behind him in the race. And he envied me, in his friendly manner, I knew. My ambition had been blown to tatters.

A new day dawned. The household rose and met at the breakfast-table, devoid of any dread of the morning newspapers. Their talk was like the chirrup of birds. Temple and his father walked away together to chambers, bent upon actual business—upon doing something! I reflected emphatically, and compared them to ships with rudders, while I was at the mercy of wind, tide, and wave. I called at Dettermain and Newson's, and heard there of a discovery of a

witness essential to the case, either in North Wales or in
New South. I did not, as I had intended, put a veto on
their proceedings. The thing to do was to see my father,
and cut the case at the fountain head. For this purpose it
was imperative that I should go to him, and prepare myself
for the interview by looking at the newspapers first. I
bought one, hastily running my eyes down the columns in
the shop. His name was printed, but merely in a fashionable notification that carriages took up and set down for his
costume Ball, according to certain regulations. The relief
of comparative obscurity helped me to breathe freely : not
to be laughed at, was a gain. I was rather inclined to laud
his courage in entering assembly-rooms, where he must be
aware that he would see the Dauphin on every face. Perhaps he was guilty of some new extravagance last night, too
late for scandal to reinforce the reporters !

Mrs. Waddy had a woeful visage when informing me
that he was out, gone to Courtenay Square. She ventured
a murmur of bills coming in. Like everybody else, she
fancied he drew his supplies from my inexhaustible purse ;
she hoped the bills would be paid off immediately : the
servants' wages were overdue. "Never can I get him to
attend to small accounts," she whimpered, and was so ready
to cry outright, that I said, "Tush," and with the one word
gave her comfort. "Of course, you, Mr. Harry, can settle
them, I know that." We were drawing near to poor old
Sewis's legacy, even for the settling of the small accounts !

London is a narrow place to one not caring to be seen.
I could not remain in this creditor-riddled house ; I shunned
the Parks, the Clubs, and the broad, brighter streets of the
West. Musing on the refreshing change it would be to me
to find myself suddenly on board Captain Jasper Welsh's
barque Priscilla, borne away to strange climes and tongues,
the world before me, I put on the striding pace which does
not invite interruption, and no one but Edbury would have
taken the liberty. I heard his shout. "Halloa! Richmond."
He was driving his friend Witlington in his cabriolet.
"Richmond, my hearty, where the deuce have you been ?
I wanted you to dine with me the other night."

I replied, looking at him steadily, that I wished I had been
there.

"Compendious larks !" cried he, in the slang of his dog's

day. "I say; you're one at Duke Fitz's masquerade to-night? Tell us your toggery. Hang it, you might go for the Black Prince. I'm Prince Hal. Got a headache? Come to my Club and try my mixture. Yoicks! it'd make Methuselah and Melchisedec jump up and have a twirl and a fandango. I say, you're thick with that little French actress Chastedian—jolly little woman! too much to say for herself to suit me."

He described the style of woman that delighted him—an ideal English shepherdess of the print-shops, it appeared, and of extremely remote interest to me, I thought at the time. Eventually I appointed to walk round to his Club, and he touched his horse gently, and bobbed his diminutive henchman behind his smart cabriolet, the admiration of the street.

I found him waiting for me on the steps of his Club, puffing a cigar with all his vigour, in the classic attitude of a trumpeter. My first words were: "I think I have to accuse you of insulting me."

"Insulting you, Richmond!" he cried, much surprised, holding his cigar in transit.

"If you insult my father, I make you responsible to me."

"Insult old Duke Fitz! I give you my word of honour, Richmond—why, I like him; I like the old boy. Wouldn't hurt him for the world and all Havannah. What the deuce have you got into your head? Come in and smoke."

The mention of his dinner and the Dauphin crazed him with laughter. He begged me as a man to imagine the scene: the old Bloated Bourbon of London Wall and Camberwell! an Illustrious Boy!—drank like a fish!—ready to show himself to the waiters! And then with "Gee" and "Gaw," the marquis spouted out reminiscences of scene, the best ever witnessed! "Up starts the Dauphin. 'Damn you, sir! and damn me, sir, if I believe you have a spot on your whole body!' And snuffles and puffs—you should have been there, Richmond. I wrote to ask you: did, upon my life! I wanted you there. Lord! why, you won't get such fun in a century. And old Roy! he behaved uncommonly finely: said capital things, by Jove! Never saw him shine so; old trump! Says Dauphin, 'My beautiful mother had a longing for strawberries out of season. I am marked with a strawberry, here.' Says Roy: 'It is an admirable 'and roomy site, but as I am not your enemy, sir, I doubt if I shall often have the opportunity to behold it.' Ha! ha!— gee! Richmond, you've missed the deucedest good scene ever acted."

How could I, after having had an adversary like Prince Otto, call upon a fellow such as Edbury to give me reason for his conduct? He rollicked and laughed until my ungovernable impatience brought him to his senses.

"Dash it, you're a fire-eater, I know, Richmond. We can't fight in this country; ain't allowed. And fighting's infernal folly. By Jove! if you're going to tumble down every man who enjoys old Roy, you've your work cut out for you. He's long chalks the best joke out. 'Twixt you and me, he did return thanks. What does it matter what old Duke Fitz does? I give him a lift on his ladder with all my heart. He keeps a capital table. And I'll be hanged if he hasn't got the secret of the women. How he does it ——old Roy! If the lords were ladies they'd vote him premier peer, double quick. And I'll tell you what, Richmond, I'm thought a devil of a good-tempered fellow for not keeping watch over Courtenay Square. I don't call it my business to be house dog for a pretty stepmother. But there's talking and nodding, and oh! leave all that: come in and smoke, and let me set you up; and I'll shake your hand. Halloa! I'm hailed."

A lady, grasping the veil across her face, beckoned her hand from a closed carriage below. Edbury ran down to her. I caught sight of ravishing golden locks, reminding me of Mabel Sweetwinter's hair, and pricking me with a sensation of spite at the sex for their deplorable madness in the choice of favourites. Edbury called me to come to the carriage window. I moved slowly, but the carriage wheeled about and rolled away. I could just see the outline of a head muffled in furs and lace.

" Queer fish, women !" he delivered himself of the philosophical ejaculation cloudily. I was not on terms with him to offer any remark upon the one in question. His imperturbable good humour foiled me, and I left him, merely giving him a warning, to which his answer was: " Oh! come in and have a bottle of claret."

Claret or brandy had done its work on him by the time I

encountered him some hours later, in the Park. Bramham DeWitt, whom I met in the same neighbourhood, offered me a mount after lunch, advising me to keep near my father as much as I conveniently could; and he being sure to appear in the Park, I went, and heard his name to the right and left of me. He was now, as he said to me once that he should become, "the tongue of London." I could hardly expect to escape from curious scrutiny myself; I was looked at. Here and there I had to lift my hat and bow. The stultification of one's feelings and ideas in circumstances which divide and set them at variance is worse than positive pain. The looks shed on me were rather flattering, but I knew that in the background I was felt to be the son of the notorious. Edbury came trotting up to us like a shaken sack, calling, "Heigh! any of you seen old Roy?" Bramham DeWitt, a stiff, fashionable man of fifty, proud of his blood and quick as his cousin Jorian to resent an impertinence, replied: "Are you the Marquis of Edbury, or a drunken groom, sir?"

"'Gad, old gentleman, I've half a mind to ride you down," said Edbury, and, espying me, challenged me to a race to run down the fogies.

A cavalcade of six abreast came cantering along. I saw my father listen to a word from Lady Edbury, and push his horse to intercept the marquis. They spoke. "Presently, presently," my father said; "ride to the rear, and keep at half a stone's throw—say, a groom's distance."

"Groom be hanged!" Edbury retorted. "I made a bet I'd drive you out of the Park, old Roy!"

"Ride behind, then," said my father, and to my astonishment Edbury obeyed him, with laughter. Lady Edbury smiled to herself; and I experienced the esteem I perceived in her for a masterful manner. A few minutes later my father beckoned me to pay my respects to Graf Kesensky, an ambassador with strong English predilections and some influence among us. He asked me if he was right in supposing I wished to enter Parliament. I said he was, wondering at the interest a foreigner could find in it. The count stopped a quiet-pacing gentleman. Bramham DeWitt joined them, and a group of friends. I was introduced to Mr. Beauchamp Hill, the Government whip, who begged me to call on him with reference to the candidature of a Sussex borough: "that is," said he turning to Graf Kesensky, "if you're sure the place is open? I've heard nothing of Falmouth's accident." The count replied that Falmouth was his intimate friend; he had received a special report that Falmouth was dying, just as he was on the point of mounting his horse. "We shan't have lost time," said Mr. Hill. The Government wanted votes. I went down to the House of Commons at midnight to see him. He had then heard of Falmouth's hopeless condition, and after extracting my political views, which were for the nonce those of a happy subserviency, he expressed his belief that the new writ for the borough of Chippenden might be out, and myself seated on the Government benches, within a very short period. Nor would it be necessary, he thought, for the Government nominee to spend money: "though *that* does not affect you, Mr. Richmond!" My supposed wealth gave me currency even in political circles.

CHAPTER XLIII.

I BECOME ONE OF THE CHOSEN OF THE NATION.

An entire revulsion in my feelings and my way of thinking was caused by this sudden change of prospect. A member of our Parliament, I could then write to Ottilia, and tell her that I had not wasted time. And it was due to my father, I confessed, when he returned from his ball at dawn, that I should thank him for speaking to Graf Kesensky. "Oh!" said he, "that was our luck, Richie. I have been speaking about you to hundreds for the last six months, and now we owe it to a foreigner!" I· thanked him again. He looked eminently handsome in his Henry III. costume, and was disposed to be as luxurious as his original. He had brought Count Lika, Secretary of Legation to the Austrian Embassy, dressed as an Albanian, with him. The two were stretched on couches, and discoursing of my father's reintroduction of the sedan chair to society. My father explained that he had ordered a couple of dozen of these chairs to be built on a pattern of his own. And he added,

"By the way, Richie, there will be sedaniers—porters to pay to-day. Poor men should be paid immediately." I agreed with the monarch. Contemplating him, I became insensible to the sting of ridicule which had been shooting through me, agonizing me for the last eight-and-forty hours. Still I thought: can I never escape from the fascination?— let me only get into Parliament! The idea in me was that Parliament lifted me nearer to Ottilia, and would prompt me to resolute action, out of his tangle of glittering cobwebs. I told him of my interview with Beauchamp Hill. "I have never known Kesensky wrong yet," said he; "except in his backing of Falmouth's horses." Count Lika murmured that he hoped his Chief would be wrong in something else: he spoke significantly. My father raised his eyebrows. "In his opinion," Lika accepted the invitation to pursue, "Prince Ernest will not let that announcement stand uncontradicted."

My father's eyes dwelt on him. "Are *we* accused of it?"

Lika slipped from the question. "Who is accused of a newspaper's doings? It is but the denial of a statement."

"I dare them to deny it!—and Lika, my dear fellow, light me a cigarette," said my father.

"Then," said Lika, touching the flame delicately, "you take the view that Kesensky is wrong in another thing besides horses."

I believe he struck on the subject casually: there was nothing for him to gain or lose in it; and he had a liking for my father.

After puffing the cigarette twice or thrice my father threw it down, resuming his conversation upon the sedan, the appropriate dresses of certain of the great masquerading ladies, and an incident that appeared to charge Jorian DeWitt with having misconducted himself. The moment Lika had gone upstairs for two or three hours' sleep, he said to me: "Richie, you and I have no time for that. We must have a man at Falmouth's house by eight o'clock. If the scrubbing-maid on all fours—not an inelegant position, I have remarked—declares him dead, we are at Bartlett's (money-lender) by ten: and in Chippenden borough before two post meridian. As I am a tactician, there is mischief! but I will turn it to my uses as I did our poor Jorian to-night;—he smuggled in the Chassediane: I led her out on

my arm. Of that by and by. The point is, that from your
oath in Parliament you fly to Sarkeld. I implore you now,
by your love for me and the princess, not to lose precious
minutes. Richie, we will press things so that you shall be
in Sarkeld by the end of the month. My son! my dear
boy! how you loved me once!—you do still! then follow
my directions. I have a head. Ay, you think it wild? 'Tis
true, my mother was a poetess. But I will convince my son
as I am convincing the world—tut, tut! To avoid swelling
talk, I tell you, Richie, I have my hand on the world's
wheel, and now is the time for you to spring from it and
gain your altitude. If you fail *my* success is emptiness."

"Will you avoid Edbury and his like, and protect yourself?" was my form of stipulation, spoken to counteract his
urgency.

He gave no answer beyond a wave of the hand suitable to
his princely one-coloured costume of ruffled lavender silk,
and the magnificent leg he turned to front me. My senses
even up to that period were so impressionable as to be
swayed by a rich dress and a grand manner when circumstances were not too unfavourable. Now they seemed very
favourable, for they offered me an upward path to tread.
His appearance propitiated me less after he had passed
through the hands of his man Tollingby, but I had again
surrendered the lead to him. As to the risk of proceedings
being taken against him, he laughed scornfully at the suggestion. "They dare not. The more I dare, the less dare
they." Again I listened to his curious roundabout reasoning, which dragged humour at its heels like a comical
cur, proclaiming itself imposingly, in spite of the mongrel's barking, to be prudence and common sense. Could I
deny that I owed him gratitude for the things I cherished
most?—for my acquaintance with Ottilia?—for his services
in Germany?—for the prospect of my elevation in England?
I could not; and I tried hard to be recklessly grateful.
As to money, he reiterated that he could put his hand on
it to satisfy the squire on the day of accounts: for the
present we must borrow. His argument upon borrowing—
which I knew well, and wondered that I did not at the
outset disperse with a breath of contempt—gained on me
singularly when reviewed under the light of my immediate
interests: it ran thus:—We have a rich or a barren

future, just as we conceive it. The art of generalship in
life consists in gathering your scattered supplies to suit
a momentous occasion; and it is the future which is chiefly
in debt̩to us, and adjures us for its sake to fight the fight
and conquer.   That man is vile and fit to be trampled on
who cannot count his future in gold and victory. If, as
we find, we are always in debt to the past, we should determine that the future is in our debt, and draw on it. Why
let our future lie idle while we need succour ? For instance,
to-morrow I am to have what saves my reputation in the
battle to-day ; shall I not take it at once ? The military
commander who acts on that principle overcomes his adversary to a certainty. " You, Richie, the member for this
borough of Chippenden, have won solid ground. I guarantee
it to you. And you go straight from the hustings, or the
first taste of parliamentary benches, to Sarkeld : you take
your grandad's proposition to Prince Ernest : you bring back
the prince's acceptance to the squire. Can you hope to have
a princess without a battle for her ?" More and much more
in this strain, until—for he could read me and most human
beings swiftly on the surface, notwithstanding the pressure
of his fancifulness—he perceived that talking influenced me
far less than activity, and so after a hurried breakfast and
an innocuous glance at the damp morning papers, we started
to the money-lender's, with Jennings to lend his name. We
were in Chippenden close upon the hour my father had
named, bringing to the startled electors the first news of
their member's death.

During the heat of the canvass for votes I received a kind
letter from the squire in reply to one of mine, wherein he
congratulated me on my prospects of success, and wound up:
" Glad to see it announced you are off with that princess of
yours. Show them we are as proud as they are, Harry, and
a fig for the whole foreign lot ! Come to Riversley soon,
and be happy." What did that mean ? Heriot likewise
said in a letter : " So it's over ? The proud prince kicks ?
You will not thank me for telling you now what you know I
think about it." I appealed to my father. " Canvass !
canvass !" cried he ; and he persistently baffled me. It was
from Temple I learnt that on the day of our starting for
Chippenden, the newspapers contained a paragraph in large
print flatly denying upon authority that there was any

foundation for the report of an intended marriage between
the Princess of Eppenwelzen-Sarkeld and an English gentleman.   Then I remembered how that morning my father had
flung the papers down, complaining of their dampness.

Would such denial have appeared without Ottilia's sanction?

My father proved that I was harnessed to him; there was
no stopping, no time for grieving.   Pace was his specific.
He dragged me the round of the voters; he gave dinners at
the inn of true Liberals, and ate of them contentedly; he
delivered speeches incessantly.   The whole force of his
serio-comic genius was alive in its element at Chippenden.
From Balls and dinners, and a sharp contest to maintain his
position in town, he was down among us by the first morning train, bright as Apollo, and quite the sun of the place,
dazzling the independent electors and their wives, and even
me somewhat ; amazing me, certainly.   Dettermain, his
lawyer, who had never seen him in action, and supposed he
would treat an election as he did his Case, with fits and
starts of energy, was not less astonished, and tried to curb
him.

" Mr. Dettermain, my dear sir, I apprehend it is the
electoral maxim to woo the widowed borough with the tear
in its eye, and I shall do so hotly, in a right masculine
manner," my father said.   " We have the start ; and if we
beat the enemy by nothing else we will beat him by constitution.   We are the first in the field, and not to reap it is
to acknowledge oneself deficient in the very first instrument
with which grass was cut."

Our difficulty all through the election was to contend with
his humour.   The many triumphs it won for him, both in
speech and in action, turned at least the dialectics of the
argument against us, and amusing, flattering, or bewildering,
contributed to silence and hold us passive.   Political convic-
tions of his own, I think I may say with truth, he had none.
He would have been just as powerful, after his fashion, on
the Tory side, pleading for Mr. Normanton Hipperdon ;
more, perhaps : he would have been more in earnest.   His
store of political axioms was Tory; but he did remarkably
well, and with no great difficulty, in confuting them to the
wives of voters, to the voters themselves, and at public
assemblies.   Our adversary was redoubtable; a promising

Opposition member, ousted from his seat in the North—a handsome man, too, which my father admitted, and wealthy, being junior partner in a City banking firm. Anna Penrhys knew him, and treacherously revealed some of the enemy's secrets, notably concerning what he termed our incorrigible turn for bribery.

"And that means," my father said, "that Mr. Hipperdon does not possess the art of talking to the ladies. I shall try him in repartee on the hustings. I must contrive to have our Jorian at my elbow."

The task of getting Jorian to descend upon such a place as Chippenden worried my father more than electoral anxieties. Jorian wrote, "My best wishes to you. Be careful of your heads. The habit of the Anglo-Saxon is to conclude his burlesques with a play of cudgels. It is his notion of freedom, and at once the exordium and peroration of his eloquence. Spare me the Sussex accent on your return."

My father read out the sentences of this letter with admiring bursts of indignation at the sarcasms, and an evident idea that I inclined to jealousy of the force displayed.

"But we must have him," he said; "I do not feel myself complete without Jorian."

So he made dispositions for a concert to be given in Chippenden town. Jenny Chassediane was invited down to sing, and Jorian came in her wake, of course. He came to suffer tortures. She was obliging enough to transform me into her weapon of chastisement upon the poor fellow for his behaviour to her at the Ball—atrocious, I was bound to confess. On this point she hesitated just long enough to imply a doubt whether, under any circumstances, the dues of men should be considered before those of the sex, and then struck her hands together with enthusiasm for my father, who was, she observed—critical in millinery in the height of her ecstacy—the most majestic, charming, handsome Henri III. imaginable, the pride and glory of the assembly, only one degree too rosy at night for the tone of the lavender, needing a touch of French hands, and the merest trifle in want of compression about the waistband. She related that a certain Prince Henri d'Angleterre had buzzed at his ear annoyingly. "Et Gascoigne, où est-il?" called the King, and the Judge stepped forth to correct the obstreperous youth. The Judge was Jennings, clearly prepared by my father to foil the

Prince—no other than Edbury. It was incomprehensible to me that my father should tolerate the latter's pranks; unless, indeed, he borrowed his name to bonds of which I heard nothing. Mademoiselle Chassediane vowed that her own dress was ravishing. She went attired as a boudoir-shepherdess, or demurely-coquettish Sèvres-china Ninette, such of whom Louis Quinze would chuck the chin down the deadly introductory walks of Versailles. The reason of her desiring to go was the fatal sin of curiosity, and, therefore, her sex's burden, not hers. Jorian was a Mousquetaire, with plumes and ruffles prodigious, and a hen's heart beneath his cock's feathers. " Pourtant j'y allai. I saw your great ladies, how they carry themselves when they would amuse themselves, and, mon Dieu! Paris has done its utmost to grace their persons, and the length of their robes did the part of Providence in bestowing height upon them, parceque, vous savez, Monsieur, c'est extraordinaire comme ils ont les jambes courtes, ces Anglaises ! " Our aristocracy, however, was not so bad in that respect as our bourgeoisie; yet it was easy to perceive that our female aristocracy, though they could ride, had never been drilled to walk : " de belles femmes, oui; seulement, tenez, je n'admire ni les yeux de vache, ni de souris, ni même ceux de verre comme ornament feminin. Avec de l'embonpoint elles font de l'effet, mais maigre il n'y a aucune illusion possible." This vindictive critic smarted, with cause, at the recollection of her walk out of her rooms. Jorian's audacity or infatuation quitted him immediately after he had gratified her whim. The stout Mousquetaire placed her in a corner, and enveloped her there, declaring that her petition had been that she might come to see, not to be seen,— as if, she cried out tearfully, the two wishes must not necessarily exist together, like the masculine and the feminine in this world ! Prince Hal, acting the most profligate period of his career, espied her behind the Mousquetaire's moustache, and did not fail to make much of his discovery. In a perilous moment for the reputation of the Ball, my father handed him over to Gascoigne, and conducted Jenny in a leisurely walk on his arm out of the rooms.

" Il est comme les Romains," she said : " he never despairs of himself. It is a Jupiter! If he must punish you he confers a dignity in doing it. Now I comprehend that with such women as these grandes dames Anglaises I should have done him harm but for his greatness of soul."

Some harm, I fancied, must have been done, in spite of his boast to the contrary. He had to be in London every other night, and there were tales current of intrigues against him which had their sources from very lofty regions. But in Chippenden he threw off London, just as lightly as in London he discarded Chippenden. No symptom of personal discouragement, or of fatigue, was betrayed in his face. I spoke once of that paragraph purporting to emanate from Prince Ernest.

"It may," he said. "Business! Richie."

He set to counting the promises of votes, disdaining fears and reflections. Concerts, cricket-matches, Balls, dinner-parties, and the round of the canvass, and speech-making at our gatherings, occupied every minute of my time, except on Saturday evenings, when I rode over to Riversley with Temple to spend the Sunday. Temple, always willing to play second to me, and a trifle melancholy under his partial eclipse—which, perhaps, suggested the loss of Janet to him —would have it that this election was one of the realizations of our boyish dreams of greatness. The ladies were working rosettes for me. My aunt Dorothy talked very anxiously about the day appointed by my father to repay the large sum expended. All hung upon that day, she said, speaking from her knowledge of the squire. She was moved to an extreme distress by the subject.

"He is confident, Harry; but where can he obtain the money? If your grandfather sees it invested in your name in Government securities, he will be satisfied, not other-wise: nothing less will satisfy him; and if that is not done, he will join you and your father together in his mind; and as he has hitherto treated one he will treat both. I know him. He is just, to the extent of his vision; but he will not be able to separate you. He is aware that your father has not restricted his expenses since they met; he will say you should have used your influence."

She insisted on this, until the tears streamed from her eyes, telling me that my grandfather was the most upright and unsuspicious of men, and precisely on that account the severest when he thought he had been deceived. The fair chances of my election did not console her, as it did me by dazzling me. She affirmed strongly that she was sure my father expected success at the election to be equivalent to

the promised restitution of the money, and begged me to
warn him that nothing short of the sum squandered would
be deemed sufficient at Riversley.   My dear aunt, good
woman though she was, seemed to me to be waxing miserly.
The squire had given her the name of Parsimony; she had
vexed him, Janet told me, by subscribing a miserable sum
to a sailors' asylum that he patronized—a sum he was
ashamed to see standing as the gift of a Beltham; and she
had stopped the building of a wing of her village school-
house, designed upon his plan.   Altogether, she was fretful
and distressful; she appeared to think that I could have
kept my father in better order.   Riversley was hearing new
and strange reports of him.   But how could I at Chippenden
thwart his proceedings in London.   Besides, he was serving
me indefatigably.

It can easily be imagined what description of banter he
had to meet and foil.

"This gentleman is obliging enough to ask me, 'How
about the Royal Arms ?'   If in his extreme consideration he
means to indicate *my* Arms, I will inform him that they are
open to him ; he shall find entertainment for man *and beast;*
so he is doubly assured of a welcome."

Questioned whether he did not think he was entitled to be
rated at the value of half-a-crown, he protested that whatever might be the sum of his worth, he was pure coin, of
which neither party in Chippenden could accuse the silver
of rubbing off; and he offered forthwith an impromptu
apologue of a copper penny that passed itself off for a crown-
piece, and deceived a portion of the country : that was why
(with a wave of the arm over the Hipperdon faction) it had
a certain number of backers; for everybody on whom the
counterfeit had been foisted, praised it to keep it in the
currency.

"Now, gentlemen, I apprehend that Chippenden is not
the pocket-borough for Hipperdon coin.   Back with him to
the Mint ! and, with your permission, we will confiscate the
first syllable of his name, while we consign him to oblivion,
with a hip, hip, hip, hurrah for Richmond !"

The cheers responded thunderingly, and were as loud
when he answered a "How 'bout the Dauphin ?" by saying
that it was the Tory hotel, of which he knew nothing.

" A cheer for old Roy !" Edbury sang out.

My father checked the roar, and turned to him.

"Marquis of Edbury, come to the front!"

Edbury declined to budge, but the fellows round him edged aside to show him a mark for my father's finger.

"Gentlemen, this is the young Marquis of Edbury, a member of the House of Lords by right of his birth, born to legislate for you and me. He, gentlemen, makes our laws. Examine him, hear him, meditate on him."

He paused cruelly for Edbury to open his mouth. The young lord looked confounded, and from that moment behaved becomingly.

"He might have been doing mischief to-morrow," my father said to me, and by letting me conceive his adroitness a matter of design, comforted me with proofs of intelligent power, and made me feel less the melancholy conjunction of a piece of mechanism and a piece of criticism, which I was fast growing to be in the contemplation of the agencies leading to honour in our land. Edbury whipped his four-in-hand to conduct our voters to the poll. We had to pull hard against Tory interest. It was a sharp, dubious, hot day—a day of outcries against undue influence and against bribery—a day of beer and cheers and the insanest of tricks to cheat the polling-booth. Old John Thresher of Dipwell, and Farmer Eckerthy drove over to Chippenden to afford me aid and countenance, disconcerting me by the sight of them, for I associated them with Janet rather than with Ottilia, and it was to Ottilia that I should have felt myself rising when the figures increased their pace in my favour, and the yeasty mob surrounding my father's superb four-horsed chariot responded to his orations by proclaiming me victor.

"I congratulate you, Mr. Richmond," Dettermain said. "Up to this day I have had my fears that we should haul more moonshine than fish in our net. Your father has accomplished prodigies."

My father, with the bloom of success on his face, led me aside soon after a safe majority of upwards of seventy had been officially announced. "Now, Richie," said he, "you are a Member. Now to the squire away! Thank the multitude and off, and as quick to Sarkeld as you well can, and tell the squire from me that I pardon his suspicions. I have landed you a Member—that will satisfy him. I am

willing, tell him . . . . you know me competent to direct
mines . . . . bailiff of his estates—whatever he pleases, to
effect a reconciliation. I must be in London to-night—I am
in the thick of the fray there. No matter: go, my son."

He embraced me. It was not a moment for me to cate-
chize him, though I could see that he was utterly deluded.

Between moonlight and morning, riding with Temple and
Captain Bulsted on either side of me, I drew rein under the
red Grange windows, tired, and in love with its air of sleepy
grandeur. Janet's window was open. I hailed her. "Has
he won?" she sang out in the dark of her room, as though
the cry of delight came upon the leap from bed. She was
dressed. She had commissioned Farmer Eckerthy to bring
her the news at any hour of the night. Seeing me, she
clapped hands. "Harry, I congratulate you a thousand
times." She had wit to guess that I should never have
thought of coming had I not been the winner. I could just
discern the curve and roll of her famed thick brown hair in
the happy shrug of her shoulder, and imagined the full
stream of it as she leaned out of window to talk to us.
Janet herself unfastened the hall-door bolts. She caressed
the horses, feverishly exulting, with charming subdued
laughter of victory and welcome, and amused us by leading
my horse round to stables, and whistling for one of the lads,
playing what may, now and then, be a pretty feature in a
young woman of character—the fair tom-boy girl. She and
her maid prepared coffee and toast for us, and entered the
hall, one after the other, laden with dishes of cold meat;
and not until the captain had eaten well did she tell him
slyly that somebody, whom she had brought to Riversley
yesterday, was abed and asleep upstairs. The slyness and
its sisterly innocence lit up our eyes, and our hearts laughed.
Her cheeks were deliciously overcoloured. We stole I know
not what from the night and the day, and conventional circumstances, and rallied Captain Bulsted, and behaved as
decorous people who treat the night properly, and live by
rule, do not quite do. Never since Janet was a girl had I
seen her so spirited and responsive: the womanly armour of
half-reserve was put away. We chatted with a fresh-
hearted natural young creature that forfeited not a particle
of her ladyship while she made herself our comrade in talk
and frolic.

Janet and I walked part of the way to the station with Temple, who had to catch an early train, and returning— the song of skylarks covering us—joined hands, having our choice between nothing to say, and the excess; perilous both.

CHAPTER XLIV.

MY FATHER IS MIRACULOUSLY RELIEVED BY FORTUNE.

MY grandfather had a gratification in my success, mingled with a transparent jealousy of the chief agent in procuring it. He warned me when I left him that he was not to be hoodwinked : he must see the money standing in my name on the day appointed. His doubts were evident, but he affected to be expectant. Not a word of Sarkeld would be spoken. My success appeared to be on a more visionary foundation the higher I climbed.

Now Jorian DeWitt had affirmed that the wealthy widow Lady Sampleman was to be had by my father for the asking. Placed as we were, I regarded the objections to his alliance with her in a mild light. She could lend me the money to appease the squire : that done, I could speedily repay it. I admitted, in a letter to my aunt Dorothy, the existing objections : but the lady had long been enamoured of him, I pleaded, and he was past the age for passionate affection, and would infallibly be courteous and kind. She was rich. We might count on her to watch over him carefully. Of course, with such a wife, he would sink to a secondary social sphere; was it to be regretted if he did ? The letter was a plea for my own interests, barely veiled. At the moment of writing it, and moreover when I treated my father with especial coldness, my heart was far less warm in the contemplation of its pre-eminent aim than when I was suffering him to endanger it, almost without a protest. Janet and a peaceful Riversley, and a life of quiet English distinction, beckoned to me visibly, and not hatefully. The image of Ottilia conjured up pictures of a sea of shipwrecks, a scene of immeasurable hopelessness. Still, I strove toward that. My strivings were against my leanings, and imagining the latter, which involved no sacrifice of the finer sense of honour, to be in the direction of my lower nature, I repelled them to preserve a lofty aim that led me through questionable ways.

"Can it be you, Harry," my aunt Dorothy's reply ran (I had anticipated her line of reasoning, though not her warmth), "who advise him to this marriage from a motive so inexplicably unworthy? That you will repay her the money, I do not require your promise to assure me. The money is nothing. It is the prospect of her life and fortune which you are consenting, if not urging him, to imperil for your own purposes. Are you really prepared to imitate in him, with less excuse for doing it, the things you most condemn? Let it be checked at the outset. It cannot be. A marriage of inclination on both sides, prudent in a worldly sense, we might wish for him, perhaps, if he could feel quite sure of himself. His wife might persuade him not to proceed in his law-case. There I have long seen his ruin. He builds such expectations on it! You speak of something worse than a mercenary marriage. I see this in your handwriting! —your approval of it! I have to check the whisper that tells me it reads like a conspiracy. Is she not a simpleton? Can you withhold your pity? and pitying, can you possibly allow her to be *entrapped*? Forgive my seeming harshness. I do not often speak to my Harry so. I do now because I must appeal to you, as the one chiefly responsible, on whose head the whole weight of a dreadful error will fall. Oh! my dearest, be guided by the purity of your feelings to shun doubtful means. I have hopes that after the first few weeks your grandfather will—I know he does not expect to find the engagement fulfilled—be the same to *you* that he was before he discovered the extravagance. You are in Parliament, and I am certain that, by keeping as much as possible to *yourself*, and living soberly, your career there will persuade him to meet your wishes."

The letter was of great length. In conclusion, she entreated me to despatch an answer by one of the early morning trains; entreating me once more to cause "any actual deed" to be at least postponed. The letter revealed what I had often conceived might be.

My rejoinder to my aunt Dorothy laid stress on my father's pledge of his word of honour as a gentleman to satisfy the squire on a stated day. I shrank from the idea of the Riversley crow over him. As to the lady, I said we would see that her money was fastened to her securely before she committed herself to the deeps. The money to be advanced to me would lie at my bankers, in my name, untouched: it would be repaid in the bulk after a season. This I dwelt on particularly, both to satisfy her and to appease my sense of the obligation. An airy pleasantry in the tone of this epistle amused me while writing it and vexed me when it had gone. But a letter sent, upon special request, by railway, should not, I thought, be couched in the ordinary strain. Besides one could not write seriously of a person like Lady Sampleman. I consulted my aunt Dorothy's scruples by stopping my father on his way to the lady. His carriage was at the door: I suggested money-lenders: he had tried them all. He begged me to permit him to start: but it was too ignominious to think of its being done under my very eyes, and I refused. He had tried the money-lenders yesterday. They required a mortgage solider than expectations for the sum we wanted. Dettermain and Newson had declined to undertake the hypothecation of his annuity. Providence pointed to Sampleman.

"You change in a couple of nights, Richie," said he. "Now I am always the identical man. I shall give happiness to one sincerely good soul. I have only to offer myself —let me say in becoming modesty, I believe so. Let me go to her and have it over, for with me a step taken is a thing sanctified. I have in fact held her in reserve. Not that I think fortune has abandoned us: but a sagacious schemer will not leave everything to the worthy dame. I should have driven to her yesterday, if I had not heard from Dettermain and Newson that there was a hint of a negotiation for a compromise. Government is fairly frightened." He mused. "However, I slept on it, and arrived at the conclusion this morning that my old Richie stood in imminent jeopardy of losing the fruit of all my toil. The good woman will advance the money to her husband. When I pledged my word to the squire I had reason to imagine the two months a sufficient time. We have still a couple of days. I have heard of men who lost heart at the eleventh hour, and if they had only hung on, with gallant faith in themselves, they would have been |justified by the result. Faith works miracles. At least it allows time for them."

His fertile ingenuity spared mine the task of persuading him to postpone the drive to Lady Sampleman. But that he would have been prompt to go, at a word from me, and was actually about to go when I entered his house, I could not question.

He drove in manifest relief of mind to Dettermain and Newson's.

I had an appointment with Mr. Temple at a great political Club, to meet the gentlemen who were good enough to undertake the introduction of the infant member to the House of Commons. My incessantly twisting circumstances foiled the pleasure and pride due to me. From the Club I bent my steps to Temple's district, and met in the street young Eckart vom Hof, my champion and second on a memorable occasion, fresh upon London, and looking very Germanic in this drab forest of our city people. He could hardly speak of Deutschland for enthusiasm at the sight of the moving masses. His object in coming to England, he assured me honestly, was to study certain editions of Tibullus in the British Museum. When he deigned to speak of Sarkeld, it was to say that Prince Hermann was frequently there. I gave him no chance to be sly, though he pushed for it, at a question of the Princess Ottilia's health.

The funeral pace of the block of cabs and omnibuses engrossed his attention. Suddenly the Englishman afforded him an example of the reserve of impetuosity we may contain. I had seen my aunt Dorothy in a middle line of cabs coming from the City, and was darting in a twinkling among wheels and shafts and nodding cab-horse noses to take her hand and know the meaning of her presence in London. She had family business to do: she said no more. I mentioned that I had checked my father for a day or two. She appeared grateful. Her anxiety was extreme that she might not miss the return train, so I relinquished her hand, commanded the cabman to hasten, and turned to rescue Eckart—too young and faithful a collegian not to follow his friend, though it were into the lion's den—from a terrific entanglement of horseflesh and vehicles brawled over by a splendid collision of tongues. Secure on the pavement again, Eckart humbly acknowledged that the English tongue could come out upon occasions. I did my best to amuse him. Whether it amused him to see me take my seat in the House of Commons, and hear a debate in a foreign language, I cannot say; but the only pleasure of which I was conscious at that period lay in the thought that he or his father, Baron vom Hof, might some day relate the circumstance at Prince Ernest's table, and fix in Ottilia's mind the recognition of my having tried to perform my part of the contract. Beggared myself, and knowing Prince Hermann to be in Sarkeld, all I hoped for was to show her I had followed the path she traced.. My state was lower : besides misfortune I now found myself exalted only to feel my profound insignificance.

" The standard for the House is a man's ability to do things," said Charles Etherell, my friendly introductor, by whom I was passingly, perhaps ironically, advised to preserve silence for two or three sessions.

He counselled the study of Foreign Affairs for a present theme. I talked of our management of them in the strain of Dr. Julius von Karsteg.

" That's journalism, or clippings from a bilious essay; it won't do for the House," he said. " Revile the House to the country, if you like, but not the country to the House."

When I begged him to excuse my absurdity, he replied : " It's full of promise, so long as you're silent."

But to be silent was to be merely an obedient hound of the whip. And if the standard for the House was a man's ability to do things, I was in the seat of a better man. External sarcasms upon the House, flavoured with justness, came to my mind, but if these were my masters surrounding me, how indefinitely small must I be !

Leaving the House on that first night of my sitting, I received Temple's congratulations outside, and, as though the sitting had exhausted every personal sentiment, I became filled with his ; under totally new sensations, I enjoyed my distinction through the perception of my old comrade's friendly jealousy.

" I'll be there, too, some day," he said, moaning at the prospect of an extreme age before such honours would befall him.

The society of Eckart prevented me from urging him to puff me up with his talk as I should have wished, and after I had sent the German to be taken care of by Mrs. Waddy, I had grown so accustomed to the worldly view of my position that I was fearing for its stability. Threats of a petition against me were abroad. Supposing the squire dis-

inherited me, could I stand ? An extraordinary appetite for
wealth, a novel appreciation of it—which was, in truth, a
voluntary enlistment into the army of mankind, and the
adoption of its passions—pricked me with an intensity of
hope and dread concerning my dependence on my grandfather. I lay sleepless all night, tossing from Riversley to
Sarkeld, condemned, it seemed, to marry Janet and gain
riches and power by renouncing my hope of the princess and
the glory belonging to her, unless I should within a few
hours obtain a show of figures at my bankers.

I had promised Etherell to breakfast with him. A note—
a faint scream—despatched by Mrs. Waddy to Mr. Temple's
house informed me that "the men" were upon them. If so,
they were the forerunners of a horde, and my father was as
good as extinguished. He staked everything on success;
consequently, he forfeited pity. Good-bye to ambition, I
thought, and ate heartily, considering robustly the while
how far lower than the general level I might avoid falling.
The report of the debates in morning papers—doubtless,
more flowing and, perhaps, more grammatical than such as
I gave ear to over-night—had the odd effect on me of re-
lieving me from the fit of subserviency into which the
speakers had sunk me. A conceit of towering superiority
took its place, and as Etherell was kind enough to draw me
out and compliment me, I was attacked by a tragic sense of
contrast between my capacities and my probable fortunes.
It was open to me to marry Janet. But this meant the
loosening of myself 'with my own hand for ever from her
who was my mentor and my glory, to gain whom I was in
the very tideway. I could not submit to it, though the view
was like that of a green field of the springs passed by a
climber up the crags. I went to Anna Penrhys to hear a
woman's voice, and partly told her of my troubles. She had
heard Mr. Hipperdon express his confident opinion that he
should oust me from my seat. Her indignation was at my
service as a loan: it sprang up fiercely and spontaneously in
allusions to something relating to my father, of which the
Marquis of Edbury had been guilty. "How you can bear
it !" she exclaimed, for I was not wordy. The exclamation,
however, stung me to put pen to paper—the woman was not
so remote in me as not to be roused by the woman. I wrote to
Edbury, and to Heriot, bidding him call on the young noble-

man. Late at night I was at my father's door to perform the act of duty of seeing him, and hearing how he had entertained Eckart, if he was still master of his liberty. I should have known him better: I expected silence and gloom. The windows were lighted brilliantly. As the hall-door opened, a band of stringed and wood instruments commenced an overture. Mrs. Waddy came to me in the hall; she was unintelligible. One thing had happened to him at one hour of the morning, and another at another hour. He was at one moment suffering the hands of the "officers" on his shoulder. "And behold you, Mr. Harry! a knock, a letter from a messenger, and he conquers Government!" It struck me that the epitome of his life had been played in a day: I was quite incredulous of downright good fortune. He had been giving a dinner followed by a concert, and the deafening strains of the music clashed with my acerb spirit, irritating me excessively. "Where are those men you spoke of?" I asked her. "Gone," she replied,—"gone long ago!"

"Paid?" said I.

She was afraid to be precise, but repeated that they were long since gone.

I singled Jorian DeWitt from among a crowd of loungers on the stairs and landing between the drawing-rooms. "Oh, yes, Government has struck its flag to him," Jorian said. "Why weren't you here to dine? Alphonse will never beat his achievement of to-day. Jenny and Carigny gave us a quarter-of-an-hour before dinner—a capital idea!—'VEUVE ET BACHELIER.' As if by inspiration. No preparation for it, no formal taking of seats. It seized amazingly—floated small talk over the soup beautifully."

I questioned him again.

"Oh, dear yes; there can't be a doubt about it," he answered, airily. "Roy Richmond has won his game."

Two or three urgent men round a great gentleman were extracting his affable approbation of the admirable nature of the experiment of the Chassediane before dinner. I saw that Eckart was comfortably seated, and telling Jorian to provide for him in the matter of tobacco, I went to my room, confused beyond power of thought by the sensible command of fortune my father, fortune's sport at times, seemed really to have.

His statement of the circumstances bewildered me even

more.   He was in no hurry to explain them; when we met next morning he waited for me to question him, and said, "Yes. I think we have beaten them so far!" His mind was pre-occupied, he informed me, concerning the defence of a lady much intrigued against, and resuming the subject: "Yes, we have beaten them up to a point, Richie. And that reminds me: would you have me go down to Riversley and show the squire the transfer paper? At any rate you can now start for Sarkeld, and you do, do you not? To-day: to-morrow at latest."

I insisted: "But how, and in what manner has this money been paid?" The idea struck me that he had succeeded in borrowing it.

"Transferred to me in the Bank, and intelligence of the fact sent to Dettermain and Newson, my lawyers," he replied. "Beyond that, I know as little as you, Richie, though indubitably I hoped to intimidate them. If," he added, with a countenance perfectly simple and frank, "they expect me to take money for a sop, I am not responsible, as I by no means provoked it, for their mistake. I proceed. The money is useful to you, so I rejoice at it."

Five and twenty thousand pounds was the amount.

"No stipulation was attached to it?"

"None. Of course a stipulation was implied: but of that I am not bound to be cognizant."

"Absurd!" I cried: "it can't have come from the quarter you suspect."

"Where else?" he asked.

I thought of the squire, Lady Edbury, my aunt, Lady Sampleman, Anna Penrhys, some one or other of his frantic female admirers. But the largeness of the amount, and the channel selected for the payment, precluded the notion that any single person had come to succour him in his imminent need, and, as it chanced, mine.

Observing that my speculations wavered, he cited numerous instances in his life of the special action of Providence in his favour, and was bold enough to speak of a star, which his natural acuteness would have checked his doing before me, if his imagination had not been seriously struck.

"You hand the money over to me, sir?" I said.

"Without a moment of hesitation, my dear boy," he melted me by answering.

" You believe you have received a bribe ?"

" That is my entire belief—the sole conclusion I can arrive at. I will tell you, Richie : the old Marquis of Edbury once placed five thousand pounds to my account on a proviso that I should—neglect, is the better word, my Case. I inherited from him at his death ; of course his demise cancelled the engagement. He had been the friend of personages implicated. He *knew*. I suspect he apprehended the unpleasant position of a witness."

" But what was the stipulation you presume was implied ?" said I.

" Something that passed between lawyers : I am not bound to be cognizant of it. Abandon my claims for a few thou sands ? Not for ten, not for ten hundred times the sum !"

To be free from his boisterous influence, which made my judgement as unsteady as the weather-glass in a hurricane, I left my house and went straight to Dettermain and Newson, who astonished me quite as much by assuring me that the payment of the money was a fact. There was no mystery about it. The intelligence and transfer papers, they said, had not been communicated to them by the firm they were opposed to, but by a solicitor largely connected with the aristocracy ; and his letter had briefly declared the unknown donator's request that legal proceedings should forthwith be stopped. They offered no opinion of their own. Suggestions of any kind, they seemed to think, had weight, and all of them an equal weight, to conclude from the value they assigned to every idea of mine. The name of the solicitor in question was Charles Adolphus Bannerbridge. It was, indeed, my old, one of my oldest friends ; the same by whom I had been led to a feast and an evening of fun when a little fellow starting in the London streets. Sure of learning the whole truth from old Mr. Bannerbridge, I walked to his office and heard that he had suddenly been taken ill. I strode on to his house, and entered a house of mourning. The kind old man, remembered by me so vividly, had died overnight. Miss Bannerbridge perceived that I had come on an errand, and with her gentle good breeding led me to speak of it. She knew nothing whatever of the sum of money. She was, however, aware that an annuity had been regularly paid through the intervention of her father. I was referred by her to a Mr. Richards, his recently-established partner. This gentleman was ignorant of the whole transaction. Throughout the day I strove to combat the pressure of evidence in favour of the idea that an acknowledgment of special claims had been wrested from the enemy. Temple hardly helped me, though his solid sense was dead against the notions entertained by my father and Jorian DeWitt, and others besides, our elders. The payment of the sum through the same channel which supplied the annuity, pointed distinctly to an admission of a claim, he inclined to think, and should be supposed to come from a personage having cause either to fear him or to assist him. He set my speculations astray by hinting that the request for the stopping of the case might be a blind. A gift of money, he said shrewdly, was a singularly weak method of inducing a man to stop the suit of a life-time. I thought of Lady Edbury; but her income was limited, and her expenditure was not:—of Lady Sampleman, but it was notorious that she loved her purse as well as my aunt Dorothy, and was even more, in the squire's phrase, "a petticoated parsimony." Anna Penrhys appeared the likelier, except for the fact that the commencement of the annuity was long before our acquaintance with her. I tried her on the subject. Her amazement was without a shadow of reserve. "It's Welsh, it's not English," she remarked. I knew no Welshwoman save Anna. "Do you know the whole of his history?" said she. Possibly one of the dozen unknown episodes in it might have furnished the clue, I agreed with her.

The sight of twenty-one thousand pounds placed to my credit in the Funds assuaged my restless spirit of investigation. Letters from the squire and my aunt Dorothy urged me to betake myself to Riversley, there finally to decide upon what my course should be.

"Now that you have the money, pray," St. Parsimony wrote,—"pray be careful of it. Do not let it be encroached on. Remember it is to serve one purpose. It should be guarded strictly against every appeal for aid," &c., with much underlining.

My grandfather returned the papers. His letter said: "I shall not break my word. Please to come and see me before you take steps right or left."

So here was the dawn again.

I could in a day or two start for Sarkeld. Meanwhile, to

give my father a lesson, I discharged a number of bills, and paid off the bond to which Edbury's name was attached. My grandfather, I knew, was too sincerely and punctiliously a gentleman in practical conduct to demand a further inspection of my accounts. These things accomplished, I took the train for Riversley, and proceeded from the station to Durstan, where I knew Heriot to be staying. Had I gone straight to my grandfather, there would have been another story to tell.

CHAPTER XLV.

WITHIN AN INCH OF MY LIFE.

A single tent stood in a gully running from one of the gravel-pits of the heath, near an iron-red rillet, and a girl of Kiomi's tribe leaned over the lazy water at half length, striking it with her handkerchief. At a distance of about twice a stone's-throw from the new carriage-road between Durstan and Bulsted, I fancied from old recollections she might be Kiomi herself. This was not the time for her people to be camping on Durstan. Besides, I feared it improbable that one would find her in any of the tracks of her people. The noise of the wheels brought the girl's face round to me. She was one of those who were babies in the tents when I was a boy. We were too far apart for me to read her features. I lay back in the carriage, thinking that it would have been better for my poor little wild friend if I had never crossed the shadow of her tents. A life caught out of its natural circle is as much in danger of being lost as a limb given to a wheel in spinning machinery; so it occurred to me, until I reflected that Prince Ernest might make the same remark, and deplore the damage done to the superior machinery likewise.

My movements appeared to interest the girl. She was up on a mound of the fast-purpling heath, shading her eyes to watch me, when I called at Bulsted lodge-gates to ask for a bed under Julia's roof that night. Her bare legs twinkled in a nimble pace on the way to Durstan Hall, as if she was determined to keep me in sight. I waved my hand to her.

She stopped. A gipsy girl's figure is often as good an index to her mind as her face, and I perceived that she had not taken my greeting favourably; nor would she advance a step to my repeated beckonings; I tried hat, handkerchief, purse, in vain. My driver observed that she was taken with a fit of the obstinacy of "her lot." He shouted "Silver," and then "Fortune." She stood looking. The fellow discoursed on the nature of gipsies. Foxes were kept for hunting, he said; there was reason in that. Why we kept gipsies none could tell. He once backed a gipsy prize-fighter, who failed to keep his appointment. "Heart sunk too low below his belt, sir. You can't reckon on them for performances. And that same man afterwards fought the gamest fight in the chronicles o' the Ring! I knew he had it in him. But they're like nothing better than the weather; you can't put money on 'em and feel safe." Consequently he saw no good in them.

"She sticks to her post," he said, as we turned into the Durstan grounds. The girl was like a flag-staff on the upper line of heathland.

Heriot was strolling, cigar in mouth, down one of the diminutive alleys of young fir in this upstart estate. He affected to be prepossessed by the case between me and Edbury, and would say nothing of his own affairs, save that he meant to try for service in one of the Continental armies; he whose susceptible love for his country was almost a malady. But he had given himself to women: it was Cissy this, Trichy that, and the wiles of a Florence, the spites of an Agatha, duperies, innocent-seemings, witcheries, reptile-tricks of the fairest of women, all through his conversation. He had so saturated himself with the resources, evasions, and desperate cruising of these light creatures of wind, tide, and tempest, that, like one who has been gazing on the whirligoround, he saw the whole of women running or only waiting for a suitable partner to run the giddy ring to perdition and an atoning pathos. I cut short one of Heriot's narratives by telling him that this picking bones of the dish was not to my taste. He twitted me with turning parson. I spoke of Kiomi. Heriot flushed, muttering, "The little devil!" with his usual contemplative relish of devilry. We parted, feeling that severe tension of the old links keeping us together which indicates the lack of new ones: a point where simple affection must bear the strain of friendship if it can. Heriot had promised to walk half-way with me to Bulsted, in spite of Lady Maria's childish fears of some attack on him. He was now satisfied with a good-bye at the hall-doors, and he talked ostentatiously of a method he had to bring Edbury up to the mark. I knew that same loud decreeing talk to be a method on his own behalf of concealing his sensitive resentment at the tone I had adopted. Lady Maria's carriage had gone to fetch her husband from a political dinner. My portmanteau advised me to wait for its return. Durstan and Riversley were at feud, however, owing to some powerful rude English used toward the proprietor of the former place by the squire; so I thought it better to let one of the grooms shoulder my luggage, and follow him. The night was dark; he chose the roadway, and I crossed the heath, meeting an exhilarating high wind that made my blood race. Egoism is not peculiar to any period of life; it is only especially curious in a young man beginning to match himself against his elders, for in him it suffuses the imagination; he is not merely selfishly sentient, or selfishly scheming: his very conceptions are selfish. I remember walking at my swiftest pace, blaming everybody I knew for insufficiency, for want of subordination to my interests, for poverty of nature, grossness, blindness to the fine lights shining in me; I blamed the Fates for harassing me, circumstances for not surrounding me with friends worthy of me. The central *I* resembled the sun of this universe, with the difference that it shrieked for nourishment, instead of dispensing it. My monstrous conceit of elevation will not suffer condensation into sentences. What I can testify to is, that for making you bless the legs you stand on, a knock-down blow is a specific. I had it before I knew that a hand was up. I should have fancied that I had run athwart a tree, but for the recollection, as I was reeling to the ground, of a hulk of a fellow suddenly fronting me, and he did not hesitate with his fist. I went over and over into a heathery hollow. The wind sang shrill through the furzes; nothing was visible but black clumps, black cloud. Astonished though I was, and shaken, it flashed through me that this was not the attack of a highwayman. He calls upon you to stand and deliver: it is a foe that hits without warning. The blow took me on the forehead, and might have been worse. Not seeing the enemy, curiosity was almost as strong in me as anger; but reflecting that I had injured no one I knew of, my nerves were quickly at the right pitch. Brushing some spikes of furze off my hands, I prepared for it. A cry rose. My impression seemed to be all backward, travelling up to me a moment or two behind time. I recognized a strange tongue in the cry, but too late that it was Romany to answer it. Instantly a voice was audible above the noisy wind:—"I spot him." Then began some good and fair fighting. I got my footing on grass, and liked the work. The fellow facing me was unmistakably gipsy-build. I, too, had length of arm, and a disposition to use it by hitting straight out, with footing firm, instead of dodging and capering, which told in my favour, and is decidedly the best display of the noble art on a dark night. My dancer went over as neatly as I had preceded him; and therewith I considered enough was done for vengeance. The thrill of a salmon on the gut is known to give a savage satisfaction to our original nature; it is but an extension and attenuation of the hearty contentment springing from a thorough delivery of the fist upon the prominent features of an assailant that yields to it perforce. Even when you receive such perfect blows you are half satisfied. Feeling conqueror, my wrath was soothed; I bent to have a look at my ruffian, and ask him what cause of complaint gipsies camping on Durstan could find against Riversley. A sharp stroke on the side of my neck sent me across his body. He bit viciously. In pain and desperation I flew at another of the tawny devils. They multiplied. I took to my heels; but this was the vainest of stratagems, they beat me in nimbleness. Four of them were round me when I wheeled breathless to take my chance at fighting the odds. Fiery men have not much notion of chivalry: gipsies the least of all. They yelled disdain of my summons to them to come on one by one: "Now they had caught me, now they would pay me, now they would pound me;" and, standing at four corners, they commended me to think of becoming a jelly. Four though they were, they kept their positions; they left it to me to rush in for a close; the hinder ones held out of arms' reach so long as I was disengaged. I had perpetually to shift my front, thinking—Oh, for a stick! any stout bit of timber! My fists ached, and a repetition of nasty dull knocks on back and neck, slogging thumps dealt by men getting to make sure of me, shattered my breathing. I cried out for a pause: I offered to take a couple of them at a time: I challenged three—the fourth to bide. I was now the dancer: left, right, and roundabout I had to swing, half-stunned, half-strangled with gorge. Those terrible blows in the back did the mischief. Sickness threatened to undermine me. Boxers know the severity of the flat-fisted stroke which a clever counterfeinting will sometimes fetch them in the unguarded bend of the back to win a rally with. Boxers have breathing-time: I had none. Stiff and sick, I tried to run; I tottered, I stood to be knocked down, I dropped like a log—careless of life. But I smelt earth keenly, and the damp grass and the devil's play of their feet on my chin, chest, and thighs, revived a fit of wrath enough to set me staggering on my legs again. They permitted it, for the purpose of battering me further. I passed from down to up mechanically, and enjoyed the chestful of air given me in the interval of rising: thought of Germany and my father, and Janet at her window, complacently; raised a child's voice in my throat for mercy, quite inaudible, and accepted my punishment. One idea I had was, that I could not possibly fail as a speaker after this—I wanted but a minute's grace to fetch breath for an oration, beginning, " You fools!" for I guessed that they had fallen upon the wrong man. Not a second was allowed. Soon the shrewd physical bracing, acting momentarily on my brain, relaxed; the fitful illumination ceased: all ideas faded out—clung about my beaten body—fled. The body might have been tossed into its grave, for aught I knew.

CHAPTER XLVI.

AMONG GIPSY WOMEN.

I cannot say how long it was after my senses had gone when I began to grope for them on the warmest of heaving soft pillows, and lost the slight hold I had on them with the effort. Then came a series of climbings and fallings, risings to the surface and sinkings fathoms below. Any attempt to speculate pitched me back into darkness. Gifted with a pair of enormous eyes, which threw surrounding objects to a distance of a mile away, I could not induce the diminutive things to approach; and shutting eyes led to such a rolling of mountains in my brain, that, terrified by the gigantic revolution, I lay determinedly staring; clothed, it seemed positive, in a tight-fitting suit of sheet-lead; but why? I wondered why, and immediately received an extinguishing blow. My pillow was heavenly; I was constantly being cooled on it, and grew used to hear a croon no more musical than the unstopped reed above my head; a sound as of a breeze about a cavern's mouth, more soothing than a melody. Conjecture of my state, after hovering timidly in dread of relapses, settled and assured me I was lying baked, half-buried in an old river-bed; moss at my cheek, my body inextricable; water now and then feebly striving to float me out, with horrid pain, with infinite refreshingness. A shady light, like the light through leafage, I could see; the water I felt. Why did it keep trying to move me? I questioned and sank to the depths again.

The excruciated patient was having his wet bandages folded across his bruises, and could not bear a motion of the mind.

The mind's total apathy was the sign of recovering health. Kind nature put that district to sleep while she operated on the disquieted lower functions. I looked on my later self as one observes the mossy bearded substances travelling blind along the under-current of the stream, clinging to this and that, twirling absurdly.

Where was I? Not in a house. But for my condition of absolute calm, owing to skilful treatment, open air, and physical robustness, the scene would have been of a kind to scatter the busy little workmen setting up the fabric of my wits. A lighted oil-cup stood on a tripod in the middle of a tent-roof, and over it the creased neck and chin of a tall old woman, splendid in age, reddened vividly; her black eyes and grey brows, and greyish-black hair fell away in a dusk of their own. I thought her marvellous. Something she held in her hands that sent a thin steam between her and the light. Outside, in the A cutting of the tent's threshold, a heavy-coloured sunset hung upon dark land. My pillow meantime lifted me gently at a regular measure

and it was with untroubled wonder that I came to the knowledge of a human heart beating within it. So soft could
only be feminine; so firm still young. The bosom was
Kiomi's. A girl sidled at the opening of the tent, peeping
in, and from a muffled rattle of subpectoral thunder discharged at her in quick heated snaps, I knew Kiomi's voice.
After an altercation of their monotonous gipsy undertones,
the girl dropped and crouched outside.

It was morning when I woke next, stronger, and aching
worse. I was lying in the air, and she who served for nurse,
pillow, parasol, and bank of herbage, had her arms round
beneath mine cherishingly, all the fingers outspread and flat
on me, just as they had been when I went to sleep.

" Kiomi !"

" Now, you be quiet."

" Can I stand up a minute or two ?"

" No, and you won't talk."

I submitted. This was our duel all day : she slipped from
me only twice, and when she did the girl took her place.

I began to think of Bulsted and Riversley.

" Kiomi, how long have I been here ?"

" You'll be twice as long as you've been."

" A couple of days ?"

" More like a dozen."

" Just tell me what happened."

" Ghm—m—m," she growled admonishingly.

Reflecting on it, I felt sure there must have been searching
parties over the heath.

" Kiomi, I say, how was it they missed me ?"

She struck at once on my thought.

" They're fools."

" How did you cheat them ?"

" I didn't tie a handkercher across their eyes."

" You half smothered me once, in the combe."

" You go to sleep."

" Have you been doctor ?"

The growling tigerish " Ghm—m—m " constrained me to
take it for a lullaby.

" Kiomi, why the deuce did your people attack me ?"

She repeated the sound resembling that which sometimes
issues from the vent of a mine ; but I insisted upon her
answering.

" I'll put you down and be off," she threatened,
" Brute of a girl! I hate you!"

" Hate away."

" Tell me who found me."

" I shan't. You shut your peepers."

The other and younger girl sung out: " I found *you*."

Kiomi sent a volley at her.

" I did," said the girl; " yes, and I nursed you first, I
did; and mother doctored you. Kiomi hasn't been here a
day."

The old mother came out of the tent. She felt my pulse,
and forthwith squatted in front of me. " You're hard to
kill, and oily as a bean," said she. " You've only to lie
quiet in the sun like a handsome gentleman; I'm sure you
couldn't wish for more. Air and water's the doctor for such
as you. You've got the bound in you to jump the ditch:
don't you fret at it, or you'll lose your spring, my good
gentleman."

" Leave off talking to me as a stranger," I bawled. " Out
with it; why have you kept me here? Why did your men
pitch into me? "

" *Our* men, my good gentleman! " the old woman ejaculated. There was innocence indeed! sufficient to pass the
whole tribe before a bench of magistrates. She wheedled:
" What have they against a handsome gentleman like you?
They'd run for you fifty mile a day, and show you all their
tricks and secrets for nothing."

My despot Kiomi fired invectives at her mother. The old
mother retorted; the girl joined in. All three were scowling, flashing, showing teeth, driving the wordy javelin upon
one another, indiscriminately, or two to one, without a
pause; all to a sound like the slack silver string of the
fiddle.

I sang out truce to them; they racked me with laughter;
and such laughter!—the shaking of husks in a half-empty
sack.

Ultimately, on a sudden cessation of the storm of tongues,
they agreed that I must have my broth.

Sheer weariness, seasoned with some hope that the broth
would give me strength to mount on my legs and walk, persuaded me to drink it. Still the old mother declared that
none of her men would ever have laid hands on me. Why

should they? she asked. What had I done to them? Was it their way?

Kiomi's arms tightened over my breast. The involuntary pressure was like an illumination to me.

No longer asking for the grounds of the attack on a mistaken person, and bowing to the fiction that none of the tribe had been among my assailants, I obtained information. The girl Eveleen had spied me entering Durstan. Quite by chance, she was concealed near Bulsted Park gates when the groom arrived and told the lodge-keeper that Mr. Harry Richmond was coming up over the heath, and might have lost his way. "Richmond!" the girl threw a world of meaning into the unexpected name. Kiomi clutched me to her bosom, but no one breathed the name we had in our thoughts. Eveleen and the old mother had searched for me upon the heath, and having haled me head and foot to their tent, despatched a message to bring Kiomi down from London to aid them in their desperate shift. They knew Squire Beltham's temper. He would have scattered the tribe to the shores of the kingdom at a rumour of foul play to his grandson. Kiomi came in time to smuggle me through an inspection of the tent and cross-examination of its ostensible denizens by Captain Bulsted, who had no suspicions, though he was in a state of wonderment. Hearing all this, I was the first to say it would be better I should get out of the neighbourhood as soon as my legs should support me. The grin that goes for a laugh among gipsies followed my question of how Kiomi had managed to smuggle me. Eveleen was my informant when the dreaded Kiomi happened to be off duty for a minute. By a hasty transformation, due to a nightcap on the bandages about the head, and an old petticoat over my feet, Captain William's insensible friend was introduced to him as the sore sick great-grandmother of the tribe, mother of Kiomi's mother, aged ninety-one. The captain paid like a man for doctor and burial fees; he undertook also to send the old lady a pound of snuff to assist her to a last sneeze or two on the right side of the grave, and he kept his word; for, deeming it necessary to paint her in a characteristic, these prodigious serpents told him gravely that she delighted in snuff; it was almost the only thing that kept her alive, barring a sip of broth. Captain William's comment on the interesting piece of longevity whose well-covered length and framework lay exposed to his respectful contemplation, was, that she must have been a devilish fine old lady in her day. "Six foot" was given as her measurement. One pound of snuff, a bottle of rum, and five sovereigns, were the fruits of the captain's sensibility. I shattered my ribs with laughter over the story. Eveleen dwelt on the triumph, twinkling. Kiomi despised laughter or triumph resulting from the natural exercise of craft in an emergency. "But my handsome gentleman he won't tell on us, will he, when we've nursed him, and doctored him, and made him one of us, and as good a stick o' timber as grows in the forest?" whined the old mother. I had to swear I would not. "He!" cried Kiomi. "He may forget us when he's gone," the mother said. She would have liked me to kiss a book to seal the oath. Anxiety about the safety of their 'homes,' that is, the assurance of an untroubled reception upon their customary camping-grounds, is a peculiarity of the gipsies, distinguishing them, equally with their cleanliness and thriftiness, from mumpers and the common wanderers. It is their tribute to civilization, which generally keeps them within the laws. Who that does not know them will believe that under their domestic system I had the best broth and the best tea I have ever tasted! They are very cunning brewers and sagacious buyers too; their maxims show them to direct all their acuteness upon obtaining quality for their money. A compliment not backed by silver is hardly intelligible to the pretty ones: money is a really credible thing to them; and when they have it, they know how to use it. Apparently because they know so well, so perfectly appreciating it, they have only vague ideas of a corresponding sentiment on the opposite side to the bargain, and imagine that they fool people much more often than they succeed in doing. Once duped themselves, they are the wariest of the dog-burnt; the place is notched where it occurred, and for ever avoided. On the other hand, they repose implicit faith in a reputation vouched for by their experience. I was amused by the girl Eveleen's dotting of houses over the breadth of five counties, where for this and that article of apparel she designed to expend portions of a golden guinea, confident that she would get the very best, and a shilling besides. The unwonted coin gave her the joy of supposing she cheated the Mint of that sum. This guinea was a present to the girl (to whom

I owed my thrashing, by the way) that excused itself under
cover of being a bribe for sight of a mirror interdicted by
the implacable Kiomi. I wanted to have a look at my face.
Now that the familiar scenes were beginning to wear their
original features to me, my dread of personal hideousness
was distressing, though Eveleen declared the bad blood in
my cheeks and eyes "had been sucked by pounds of red
meat." I wondered whether, if I stood up and walked to
either one of the three great halls lying in an obtuse triangle
within view, I should easily be recognized. When I did see
myself, I groaned verily. With the silence of profound resignation, I handed back to Eveleen the curious fragment of her
boudoir, which would have grimaced at Helen of Troy.

"You're feeling your nose—you've been looking at a
glass!" Kiomi said, with supernatural swiftness of deduction
on her return.

She added for my comfort that nothing was broken, but
confessed me to be still "a sight;" and thereupon drove
knotty language at Eveleen. The girl retorted, and though
these two would never acknowledge to me that any of their
men had been in this neighbourhood recently, the fact was
treated as a matter of course in their spiteful altercation, and
each saddled the other with the mistake they had committed.
Eveleen snatched the last word. What she said I did not
comprehend, she must have hit hard. Kiomi's eyes lightened and her lips twitched; she coloured like the roofing
smoke of the tent-fire; twice she showed her teeth, as in a
spasm, struck to the heart, unable to speak, breathing in and
out of a bitterly disjoined mouth. Eveleen ran. I guessed
at the ill-word spoken. Kiomi sat eyeing the wood-ashes, a
devouring gaze that shot straight and read but one thing.
They who have seen wild creatures die will have her before
them, saving the fiery eyes. She became an ashen-colour,
I took her little hand. Unconscious of me, her brown fingers
clutching at mine, she flung up her nostrils, craving air.

This was the picture of the woman who could not weep in
her misery.

"Kiomi, old friend!" I called to her. I could have cursed
that other friend, the son of mischief; for she, I could have
sworn, had been fiercely and wantonly hunted. Chastity of
nature, intense personal pride, were as proper to her as the
free winds are to the heaths: they were as visible to dull

divination as the milky blue about the iris of her eyeballs. She had actually no animal vileness, animal though she might be termed, and would have appeared if compared with Heriot's admirable Cissies and Gwennies, and other ladies of the Graces that run to fall, and spend their pains more in kindling the scent of the huntsman than in effectively flying.

There was no consolation for her.

The girl Eveleen came in sight, loitering and looking, kicking her idle heels.

Kiomi turned sharp round to me.

"I'm going. Your father's here, up at Bulsted. I'll see him. He won't tell. He'll come soon. You'll be fit to walk in a day. You're sound as a nail. Good-bye—I shan't say good-bye twice," she answered my attempt to keep her, and passed into the tent, out of which she brought a small bundle tied in a yellow handkerchief, and walked away, without nodding or speaking.

"What was that you said to Kiomi?" I questioned Eveleen, who was quickly beside me.

She replied, accurately or not: "I told her our men'd give her as good as she gave me, let her wait and see."

Therewith she pouted; or, to sketch her with precision, "snouted" would better convey the vivacity of her ugly flash of features. It was an error in me to think her heartless. She talked of her aunt Kiomi affectionately for a gipsy girl, whose modulated tones are all addressed to the soft public. Eveleen spoke with the pride of bated breath of the ferocious unforgivingness of their men. Perhaps if she had known that I traced the good repute of the tribes for purity to the sweeter instincts of the women, she would have eulogized her sex to amuse me. Gipsy girls, like other people, are fond of showing off; but it would have been a victory of education to have helped her to feel the distinction of the feminine sense of shame half as awfully and warmly as she did the inscrutable iron despotism of the males. She hinted that the mistake of which I had been the victim would be rectified.

"Tell your men I'll hunt them down like rats if I hear of it," said I.

While we were conversing my father arrived. Eveleen, not knowing him, would have had me accept the friendly covering of a mat.

"Here's a big one! he's a clergyman," she muttered to

herself, and ran to him and set up a gipsy whine, fronting me up to the last step while she advanced ; she only yielded ground to my outcry.

My father bent over me. Kiomi had prepared him for what he saw. I quieted his alarm by talking currently and easily. Julia Bulsted had despatched a messenger to inform him of my mysterious disappearance ; but he, as his way was, revelling in large conjectures, had half imagined me seized by a gust of passion, and bound for Germany. " Without my luggage ?" I laughed.

" Ay, without your lugguge, Richie," he answered seriously. His conceit of a better knowledge of me than others possessed, had buoyed him up. " For I knew," he said, " we two do nothing like the herd of men. I thought you were off to her, my boy. Now !" he looked at me, and this look of dismay was a perfect mirror. I was not a presentable object.

He stretched his limbs on the heather and kept hold of my hand, looking and talking watchfully, doctor-like, doubting me to be as sound in body as I assured him I was, despite aches and pains. Eveleen hung near.

" These people have been kind to you ?" he said.

" No, the biggest brutes on the earth," said I.

" Oh ! you say that, when I spotted you out in the dark where you might have lied to be eaten, and carried you and washed your bloody face, and watched you, and never slept, I didn't, to mother you and wet your head !" cried the girl.

My father beckoned to her and thanked her appreciably in the yellow tongue.

" So these scoundrels of the high-road fell upon you and robbed you, Richie ?"

I nodded.

" You let him think they robbed you, and you had your purse to give me a gold guinea out of it !" Eveleen cried, and finding herself in the wrong track, volubly resumed : " That they didn't for they hadn't time, whether they meant to, and the night black as a coal, whoever they were."

The mystery of my not having sent word to Bulsted or to Riversley perplexed my father.

" Comfortable here !" he echoed me, disconsolately, and glanced at the heath, the tent, the black circle of the broth-pot, and the wild girl.

CHAPTER XLVII.

MY FATHER ACTS THE CHARMER AGAIN.

KIOMI's mother was seen in a turn of the gravel-cutting, bearing purchases from Durstan village. She took the new circumstances in with a single cast up of her wary eyelids; and her, and her skill in surgery and art in medicine, I praised to lull her fears, which procured me the denomination of old friend, as well as handsome gentleman : she went so far as to add, in a fit of natural warmth, nice fellow; and it is the truth that this term effected wonders in flattering me : it seemed to reveal to me how simple it was for Harry Richmond, one whom gipsies could think a nice fellow, to be the lord of Janet's affections—to be her husband. My heart throbbed; yet she was within range of a mile and a half, and I did not wish to be taken to her. I did wish to smell the piney air about the lake-palace; but the thought of Ottilia caused me no quick pulsations.

My father remained an hour. He could not perceive the drift of my objection to go either to Bulsted or to Riversley, and desire that my misadventure should be unknown at those places. However, he obeyed me, as I could always trust him to do scrupulously, and told a tale at Bulsted. In the afternoon he returned in a carriage to convey me to the seaside. When I was raised I fainted, and saw the last of the camp on Durstan much as I had come to it first. Sickness and swimming of the head continued for several days. I was persecuted with the sensation of the carriage journey, and an iteration of my father's that ran : "My son's inanimate body in my arms," or "Clasping the lifeless body of my sole son, Harry Richmond," and other variations. I said nothing about it. He told me aghast that I had spat blood. A battery of eight fists, having it in the end all its own way, leaves a deeper indentation on its target than a pistol-shot that passes free of the vital chords. My convalescence in Germany was a melody compared with this. I ought to have stopped in the tent, according to the wise old mother's advice, given sincerely, for prudence counselled her to strike her canvas and be gone. There I should have lain, interested in the progress of a bee, the course of a beetle or a cloud, a spider's business, and the shaking of the gorse and the heather, until good health had grown out of thoughtlessness. The very sight of my father was as a hive of humming troubles. His intense anxiety about me reflected in my mind the endless worry I had concerning him. It was the intellect which condemned him when he wore a joyful air, and the sensations when he waxed over-solicitous. Whether or not the sentences were just, the judges should have sometimes shifted places. I was unable to divine why he fevered me so much. Must I say it?—He had ceased to entertain me. Instead of a comic I found him a tragic spectacle; and his exuberant anticipations, his bursting hopes that fed their forcing-bed with the blight and decay of their predecessors, his transient fits of despair after a touch at my pulses, and exclamation of "Oh, Richie, Richie, if only I had my boy up and well!"—assuming that nothing but my tardy recovery stood in the way of our contentment—were examples of downright unreason such as contemplation through the comic glass would have excused; the tragic could not. I knew, nevertheless, that to the rest of the world he was a progressive comedy: and the knowledge made him seem more tragic still. He clearly could not learn from misfortune; he was not to be contained. Money I gave him freely, holding the money at my disposal his own; I chafed at his unteachable spirit, surely one of the most tragical things in life; and the proof of my love for him was that I thought it so, though I should have been kinder had he amused me, as in the old days. Conceive to yourself the keeping watch over a fountain choked in its spouting, incessantly labouring to spirt a jet into the air; now for a moment glittering and towering in a column, and once more straining to mount. My father appeared to me in that and other images. He would have had me believe him shooting to his zenth, victorious at last. I likewise was to reap a victory of the highest kind from the attack of the mysterious ruffians; so much, he said, he thought he could assure me of. He chattered of an intimidated Government, and Dettermain and Newson; duchesses, dukes, most friendly; innumerable invitations to country castles; and among other things one which really showed him to be capable of conceiving ideas and working from an initiative. But this, too,

though it accomplished a temporary service, he rendered
illusory to me by his unhappy manner of regarding it as an
instance of his now permanent social authority. He had
instituted what he called his JURY OF HONOUR COURT, composed of the select gentlemen of the realm, ostensibly to
weigh the causes of disputes between members of their
class, and decree the method of settlement: but actually, my
father admitted, to put a stop to the affair between Edbury
and me. "That was the origin of the notion, Richie. I
carried it on. I dined some of the best men of our day.
I seized the opportunity when our choicest 'emperor' was
rolling on wheels to propound my system. I mention the
names of Bramham DeWitt, Colonel Hibbert Segrave, Lord
Alonzo Carr, Admiral Loftus, the Earl of Luton, the Marquis of Hatchford, Jack Hippony, Monterez Williams,—I
think you know him?—and little Dick Phillimore, son of a
big-wig, a fellow of a capital wit and discretion; I mention
them as present to convince you we are not triflers, dear
boy. My argument ran, it is absurd to fight; also it is
intolerable to be compelled to submit to insult. As the
case stands, we are under a summary edict of the citizens,
to whom chivalry is unknown. Well, well, I delivered a
short speech. Fighting, I said, resembled butting,—a performance proper to creatures that grow horns instead of
brains . . . not to allude to a multitude of telling remarks;
and the question 'Is man a fighting animal?' my answer
being that he is not born with spurs on his heels or horns to
his head: and that those who insisted on fighting should be
examined by competent anatomists, 'ologists' of some sort,
to decide whether they have the excrescences, and proclaim
them . . . touching on these lighter parts of my theme with
extreme delicacy. But—and here I dwelt on my point:
Man, if not a fighting animal in his glorious—I forgot what
—is a sensitive one, and has the idea of honour. 'Hear,'
from Colonel Segrave, and Sir Weeton Slater—he was one
of the party. In fine, Richie, I found myself wafted into a
breathing oration. I cannot, I confess it humbly, hear your
'hear, hear,' without going up and off, inflated like a balloon.
'Shall the arbitration of the magistracy, indemnifications in
money awarded by the Law-courts, succeed in satisfying,'—
but I declare to you, Richie, it was no platform speech. I
know your term—'the chain-cable sentence.' Nothing of

the kind, I assure you. Plain sense, as from gentlemen to gentlemen. We require, I said, a protection that the polite world of Great Britain does not now afford us against the aggressions of the knave, the fool, and the brute. We establish a Court. We do hereby—no, no, not the 'hereby;' quite simply, Richie—pledge ourselves—I said some other word not 'pledge' to use our utmost authority and influence to exclude from our circles persons refusing to make the reparation of an apology for wanton common insults: we renounce intercourse with men declining, when guilty of provoking the sentiment of hostility, to submit to the jurisdiction of our Court. All I want you to see is the notion. We raise the shield against the cowardly bully which the laws have raised against the bloody one. 'And gentlemen,'" my father resumed his oration, forgetting my sober eye for a minute—"'Gentlemen, we are the ultimate Court of Appeal for men who cherish their honour, yet abstain from fastening it like a millstone round the neck of their commonsense.' Credit me, Richie, the proposition kindled. We cited Lord Edbury to appear before us, and I tell you we extracted an ample apology to you from that young nobleman. And let me add, one that I, that we, must impose it upon an old son to accept. He does! Come, come. And you shall see, Richie, society shall never repose an inert mass under my leadership. I cure it; I shake it and cure it."

He promenaded the room, repeating: "I do not say I am possessed of a panacea," and bending to my chin as he passed; "I maintain that I can and do fulfil the duties of my station, which is my element, attained in the teeth of considerable difficulties, as no other man could, be he prince or Prime Minister. Not one," he flourished, stepping onward. "And mind you, Richie, this," he swung round, conscious as ever of the critic in me, though witless to correct his pomp of style, "this is not self-glorification. I point you facts. I have a thousand schemes—projects. I recognize the value of early misfortune. The particular misfortune of princes born is that they know nothing of the world —babies! I grant you, babies. Now I do. I have it on my thumbnail. I know its wants. And just as I succeeded in making you a member of our Parliament in assembly, and the husband of an hereditary princess—hear me—so will I

make good my original determination to be in myself the
fountain of our social laws, and leader. I have never, I
believe—to speak conscientiously—failed in a thing I have
once determined on."

The single wish that I might be a boy again, to find
pleasure in his talk, was all that remained to combat the
distaste I had for such oppressive deliveries of a mind apparently as little capable of being seated as a bladder
charged with gas. I thanked him for getting rid of Edbury,
and a touch of remorse pricked me, it is true, on his turning
abruptly and saying: "You see me in my nakedness, Richie.
To you and my valet, the heart, the body!" He was too
sympathetic not to have a keen apprehension of a state of
hostility in one whom he loved. If I had inclined to melt,
however, his next remark would have been enough to harden
me: "I have fought as many battles, and gained as startling
victories as Napoleon Buonaparte; he was an upstart." The
word gave me a jerk.

Sometimes he would indulge me transparently in a political controversy, confessing that my dialectical dexterity
went far to make a Radical of him. I had no other amusement, or I should have held my peace. I tried every
argument I could think of to prove to him that there was
neither honour, nor dignity, nor profit in aiming at titular
distinctions not forced upon us by the circumstances of our
birth. He kept his position with much sly fencing, approaching shrewdness; and, whatever I might say, I could
not deny that a vile old knockknee'd world, tugging its
forelock to the look of rank and chink of wealth, backed
him, if he chose to be insensible to radical dignity. "In my
time," said he, "all young gentlemen were born Tories.
The doctor no more expected to see a Radical come into the
world from a good family than a radish. But I discern you,
my dear boy. Our reigning Families must now be active;
they require the discipline I have undergone; and I also
dine at aldermen's tables, and lay a foundation-stone—as
Jorian says—with the facility of a hen-mother: that should
not suffice them. 'Tis not sufficient for me. I lay my stone,
eat my dinner, make my complimentary speech—and that is
all that is expected of us; but I am fully aware we should
do more. We must lead, or we are lost. Ay, and—to quote
you—a Lord Mayor's barge is a pretty piece of gilt for the

festive and luxurious to run up the river Thames in and mark their swans. I am convinced there is something deep in that. But what am I to do? - Would you have me frown upon the people? Richie, it is prudent—I maintain it righteous, nay, it is, I affirm positively, sovereign wisdom—to cultivate every flower in the British bosom. Riposte me —have you too many? Say yes, and you pass my guard. You cannot. I fence you there. This British loyalty is, in my estimation, absolutely beautiful. We grow to a head in our old England. The people have an eye! I need no introduction to them. We reciprocate a highly cordial feeling when they line the streets and roads with respectful salutations, and I acknowledge their demonstrative good-will. These things make us a nation. By heaven, Richie, you are, on this occasion, if your dad may tell you so, wrong. I ask pardon for my bluntness; but I put it to you, could we, not travelling as personages in our well-beloved country, count on civility to greet us everywhere? Assuredly not. My position is, that by consenting to their honest enthusiasm, we—the identical effect you are perpetually crying out for—we civilize them, we civilize them. Goodness!—a Great Britain without Royalty!"

He launched on a series of desolate images. In the end, he at least persuaded himself that he had an idea in his anxiety to cultivate the primary British sentiment.

We moved from town to town along the South coast; but it was vain to hope we might be taken for simple people. Nor was he altogether to blame, except in allowing the national instinct for 'worship and reverence' to air itself unrebuked. I fled to the island. Temple ran down to meet me there, and I heard that Janet had written to him for news of me. He entered our hotel a private person; when he passed out, hats flew off before him. The modest little fellow went along a double line of attentive observers on the pier, and came back, asking me in astonishment who he was supposed to be.

"I petitioned for privacy here!" exclaimed my father. It accounted for the mystery.

Temple knew my feelings, and did but glance at me.

Close upon Temple's arrival we had a strange couple of visitors. "Mistress Dolly Disher and her husband," my father introduced them. She called him by one of his

Christian names inadvertently at times. The husband was a confectioner, a satisfied shade of a man, who reserved the exercise of his will for his business, we learnt; she, a bustling, fresh-faced woman of forty-five, with still expressive dark eyes, and, I guessed, the ideal remainder of a passion in her bosom. The guess was no great hazard. She was soon sitting beside me, telling me of the "years" she had known my father, and of the most affectionate friend and perfect gentleman he was : of the ladies who had been in love with him; "no wonder:" and of his sorrows and struggles, and his beautiful voice, and hearts that bled for him; and of one at least who prayed and trusted he would be successful at last. Temple and the pallid confectioner spent the day on board a yacht with my father. Mrs. Dolly stayed to nurse me and persuade me to swallow medicine. She talked of her youth, when, as a fashionable bootmaker's daughter, she permitted no bills to be sent in to Mr. Richmond, alleging, as a sufficient reason for it to her father, that their family came from Richmond in Yorkshire. Eventually, the bills were always paid. She had not been able to manage her husband so well ; and the consequence was that (she breathed low) an execution was out; "though I tell him," she said tremulously, " he's sure to be paid in the long run, if only he'll wait. But no; he is you cannot think how obstinate in his business. And my girl Augusta waiting for Mr. Roy Richmond, the wish of our hearts! to assist at her wedding; and can we ask it, and have an execution hanging over him? And for all my husband's a guest here, he's as likely as not to set the officers at work, do what I will, to-morrow or any day. Your father invited us, Mr. Harry. I forced my husband to come, hoping against hope; for your papa gave the orders, relying on me, as he believed he might, and my husband undertook them, all through me. There it stops; he hears reports, and he takes fright: in goes the bill : then it's law, and last—— Oh! I'm ashamed."

Mr. Disher's bill was for supplying suppers to the Balls. He received my cheque for the amount in full, observing that he had been confident his wife was correct when she said it would be paid, but a tradesman's business was to hasten the day of payment; and, for a penance, he himself would pacify the lawyers.

On hearing of the settlement of Mr. Disher's claim, my father ahem'd, speechless, which was a sign of his swallowing vexation. He remarked that I had, no doubt with the best intentions, encroached on his liberty. "I do not like to have my debts disturbed." He put it to me whether a man, carrying out a life-long plan, would not be disconcerted by the friendliest intervention. This payment to Disher he pronounced fatal in policy. "You have struck a heavy blow to my credit, Richie. Good little Mistress Dolly brought the man down here—no select addition to our society—and we were doing our utmost to endure him, as the ladies say, for the very purpose . . . but the error stands committed! For the future, friend Disher will infallibly expect payments within the year. Credit for suppers is the guarantee of unlimited entertainments. And I was inspiring him with absolute confidence for next year's campaign. Money, you are aware, is no longer a question to terrify me. I hold proofs that I have conclusively frightened Government, and you know it. But this regards the manipulation of the man Disher. He will now dictate to me. A refresher of a few hundreds would have been impolitic to this kind of man; but the entire sum!—and to a creditor in arms! You reverse the proper situations of gentleman and tradesman. My supper-man, in particular, should be taught to understand that he is bound up in my success. Something frightened him; he proceeded at law; and now we have shown him that he has frightened *us*. An execution? My dear boy, I have danced an execution five years running, and ordered, consecutively, at the same house. Like other matters, an execution depends upon how you treat it. The odds are that we have mortally offended Mistress Dolly." He apologized for dwelling on the subject, with the plea that it was an essential part of his machinery of action, and the usual comparison of "the sagacious General" whose forethought omitted no minutiæ. I had to listen.

The lady professed to be hurt. The payment, however, put an end to the visit of this couple. Politic or not, it was a large sum to disburse, and once more my attention became fixed on the probable display of figures in my bankers' book. Bonds and bills were falling due: the current expenses were exhausting. I tried to face the evil, and take a line of con-

duct, staggering, as I did on my feet. Had I been well
enough, I believe I should have gone to my grandfather, to
throw myself on his good-nature; such was the brain's wise
counsel: but I was all nerves and alarms, insomuch that I
interdicted Temple's writing to Janet, lest it should bring
on me letters from my aunt Dorothy, full of advice that
could no longer be followed, well-meant cautions that might
as well be addressed to the mile-posts behind me. Moreover,
Janet would be flying on the wind to me, and I had a craving for soft arms and the look of her eyebrows that warned
me to keep her off if I intended to act as became a man of
good faith.

Fair weather, sunny green sea-water speckled with yachts
shooting and bounding, and sending me the sharp sense of
life there is in dashed-up fountains of silvery salt-spray,
would have quickened my blood sooner but for this hot-bed
of fruitless adventure, tricksy precepts, and wisdom turned
imp, in which my father had again planted me. To pity
him seemed a childish affectation. His praise of my good
looks pleased me, for on that point he was fitted to be a
judge, and I was still fancying I had lost them on the heath.
Troops of the satellites of his grand parade surrounded
him. I saw him walk down the pier like one breaking up a
levée. At times he appeared to me a commanding phantasm
in the midst of phantasm figures of great ladies and their
lords, whose names he told off on his return like a drover
counting his herd; but within range of his eye and voice
the reality of him grew overpowering. It seduced me, and,
despite reason, I began to feel warm under his compliments.
He was like wine. Gaiety sprang under his feet. Sitting
at my window, I thirsted to see him when he was out of
sight, and had touches of the passion of my boyhood. I
listened credulously, too, as in the old days, when he repeated,
"You will find I am a magician, and very soon, Richie,
mark me." His manner hinted that there was a surprise in
store. "You have not been on the brink of the grave for
nothing." He resembled wine in the other conditions
attached to its rare qualities. Oh for the choice of having
only a little of him, instead of having him on my heart!
The unfilial wish attacked me frequently: he could be, and
was, so ravishing to strangers and light acquaintances. Did
by chance a likeness exist between us? My sick fancy

rushed to the Belthams for a denial. There did, of some sort, I knew; and the thought partitioned my dreamy ideas, of which the noblest, taking advantage of my physical weakness, compelled me to confess that it was a vain delusion for one such as I to hope for Ottilia. This looking at the roots of yourself, if you are possessed of a nobler half that will do it, is a sound corrective of an excessive ambition. Unfortunately it would seem that young men can do it only in sickness. With the use of my legs, and open-air breathing, I became compact, and as hungry and zealous on behalf of my individuality, as proud of it as I had ever been: prouder and hungrier.

My first day of outing, when, looking at every face, I could reflect on the miraculous issue of mine almost clear from its pummelling, and above all, that my nose was safe—not stamped with the pugilist's brand—inspired a lyrical ebullition of gratitude. Who so intoxicated as the convalescent catching at health?

I met Charles Etherell on the pier, and heard that my Parliamentary seat was considered in peril, together with a deal of gossip about my disappearance.

My father, who was growing markedly restless, on the watch for letters and new arrivals, started to pay Chippenden a flying visit. He begged me urgently to remain for another few days, while he gathered information, saying my presence at his chief quarters did him infinite service, and I always thought that possible. I should find he was a magician, he repeated, with a sort of hesitating fervour.

I had just waved my hand to him as the boat was bearing him away from the pier-head, when a feminine voice murmured in my ear, "Is not this our third meeting, Mr. Harry Richmond?—Venice, Elbestadt, and the Isle of Wight?" She ran on, allowing me time to recognize Clara Goodwin, "What was your last adventure? You have been ill. *Very* ill? Has it been serious?"

I made light of it. "No: a tumble."

"You look pale," she said quickly.

"That's from grieving at the loss of my beauty, Miss Goodwin."

"Have you really not been seriously ill?" she asked with an astonishing eagerness.

I told her mock-loftily that I did not believe in serious

illnesses coming to godlike youth, and plied her in turn
with inquiries.

"You have not been laid up in bed?" she persisted.

"No, on my honour, not in bed."

"Then," said she, "I would give much to be able to stop
that boat."

She amazed me. "Why?"

"Because it's going on a bad errand," she replied.

"Miss Goodwin, you perplex me. My father has started
in that boat."

"Yes, I saw him." She glanced hastily at the foam in a
way to show indifference. "What I am saying concerns
others . . . who have heard you were dangerously ill. I
have sent for them to hasten across."

"My aunt and Miss Ilchester?"

"No."

"Who are they? Miss Goodwin, I'll answer any question. I've been queerish, that's true. Now let me hear who
they are, when you arrived, when you expect them. Where
are they now?"

"As to me," she responded with what stretched on my
ears like an insufferable drawl, "I came over last night to
hire a furnished house or lodgings. Papa has an appointment attached to the fortifications yonder. We'll leave the
pier, if you please. You draw too much attention on ladies
who venture to claim acquaintance with so important a
gentleman."

We walked the whole length of the pier, chatting of our
former meetings.

"Not here," she said, as soon as I began to question.

I was led farther on, half expecting that the accessories of
time and place would have to do with the revelation.

The bitter creature drew me at her heels into a linen-
draper's shop. There she took a seat, pitched her voice
to the key of a lady's at a dinner-table, when speaking to
her cavalier of the history or attire of some one present, and
said, "You are sure the illness was not at all feigned?"

She had me as completely at her mercy in this detestable
shop as if I had been in a witness-box.

"Feigned!" I exclaimed.

"That is no answer. And pray remember where you are."

"No, the illness was not feigned."

" And you have not made the most of it ?"

" What an extraordinary thing to say !"

" That is no answer.   And please do not imagine yourself under the necessity of acting every sentiment of your heart before these people."

She favoured a shopman with half-a-dozen directions.

" My answer is, then, that I have *not* made the most of it," I said.

" Not even by proxy ? "

" Once more I'm adrift."

" You are certainly energetic.   I must address you as a brother, or it will be supposed we are quarrelling.   Harry, do you like that pattern ? "

" Yes.   What's the meaning of proxy ? "

" With the accent you give it, heaven only knows what it means.   I would rather you did not talk here like a Frenchman relating his last love-affair in company.   *Must* your voice escape control exactly at the indicatory words ?   Do you think your father made the most of it ? "

" Of my   illness ?   Oh ! yes ;   the   utmost.   I should undoubtedly think so.   That's his way."

" Why did you permit it ? "

"I was what they call ' wandering ' half the time.   Besides, who could keep him in check ? I rarely know what he is doing."

" You don't know what he wrote ? "

" Wrote ? "

" That you were dying."

" Of me ?   To whom ? "

She scrutinized me, and rose from her chair.   " I must try some other shop.   How is it that, if these English people cannot make a ' berthe ' fit to wear, they do not conceive the idea of importing such things from Paris ?   I will take your arm, Harry."

" You have bought nothing," I remarked.

" I have as much as I went for," she replied, and gravely thanked the assistant leaning on his thumbs across the counter ;   after which, dropping the graceless play of an enigma, she inquired whether I had forgotten the Frau von Dittmarsch.

I had, utterly ; but not her maiden name of Sibley.

" Miss Goodwin, is she one of those who are coming to the island ? "

"Frau von Dittmarsch? Yes. She takes an interest in you. She and I have been in correspondence ever since my visit to Sarkeld. It reminds me, you may vary my maiden name with the Christian, if you like. Harry, I believe you are truthful as ever, in spite—— "

"Don't be unjust," said I.

"I wish I could think I was!" she rejoined. "Frau von Dittmarsch was at Sarkeld,'and received terrible news of you. She called on me, at my father's residence over the water yonder, yesterday afternoon, desiring greatly to know —she is as cautious as one with a jewel in her custody—how it fared with you, whether you were actually in a dying state. I came here to learn; I have friends here: you were not alone, or I should have called on you. The rumour was that you were very ill; so I hired a furnished place for Frau von Dittmarsch at once. But when I saw you and him together, and the parting between you, I began to have fears; I should have countermanded the despatch I sent by the boat had it been possible."

"It has gone! And tell me the name of the other."

"Frau von Dittmarsch has a husband."

"Not with her now. Oh! cruel! speak: her name?"

"Her name, Harry? Her title is Countess von Delzenburg."

"Not princess?"

"Not in England."

Then Ottilia was here!

My father was indeed a magician!

CHAPTER XLVIII.

THE PRINCESS ENTRAPPED.

"Not princess in England" could betoken but one thing —an incredible act of devotion, so great that it stunned my senses, and I thought of it, and of all it involved, before the vision of Ottilia crossing seas took possession of me.

"The Princess Ottilia, Miss Goodwin?"

"The Countess of Delzenburg, Harry."

"To see me? She has come!"

"Harry, you talk like the boy you were when we met

before you knew her. Yes and yes to everything you have to say, but I think you should spare her name."

" She comes thinking me ill ?"

"Dying."

"I'm as strong as ever I was."

"I should imagine you are, only rather pale."

" Have you, tell me, Clara, seen her yourself ? Is she well ?"

" Pale : not unwell : anxious."

" About me ?"

" It may be about the political affairs of the Continent; they are disturbed."

" She spoke of me ?"

" Yes."

" She is coming by the next boat ?"

" It's my fear that she is."

" Why do you fear ?"

" Shall I answer you, Harry ? It is useless now. Well, because she has been deceived. That is why. You will soon find it out."

" Prince Ernest is at Sarkeld ?"

" In Paris, I hear."

" How will your despatch reach these ladies in time for them to come over by the next boat ?"

" I have sent my father's servant. The General—he is promoted at last, Harry—attends the ladies in person, and is now waiting for the boat's arrival over there, to follow my directions."

" You won't leave me ?"

Miss Goodwin had promised to meet the foreign ladies on the pier. We quarrelled and made it up a dozen times like girl and boy, I calling her aunt Clara, as in the old days, and she calling me occasionally son Richie : an imitation of my father's manner of speech to me when we formed acquaintance first in Venice. But I was very little aware of what I was saying or doing. The forces of my life were yoked to the heart, and tumbled as confusedly as the world under Phaëthon charioteer. We walked on the heights above the town. I looked over the water to the white line of shore and batteries where this wonder stood, who was what poets dream of, deep-hearted men hope for, none quite believe in. Hardly could I ; and though my relenting

spinster friend at my elbow kept assuring me it was true
that she was there, my sceptical sight fixed on the stale
prominences visible in the same features which they had
worn day after empty day of late. This deed of hers was
an act of devotion great as death. I knew it from experience
consonant to Ottilia's character; but could a princess, hereditary, and bound in the league of governing princes, dare
so to brave her condition? Complex of mind, simplest in
character, the uncontrollable nobility of her spirit was no
sooner recognized by me than I was shocked throughout by a
sudden light, contrasting me appallingly with this supreme
of women, who swept the earth aside for truth. I had never
before received a distinct intimation of my littleness of
nature, and my first impulse was to fly from thought, and
then, as if to prove myself justly accused, I caught myself
regretting—no, not regretting, gazing, as it were, on a picture
of regrets—that Ottilia was not a romantic little lady of
semi-celestial rank, exquisitely rash, wilful, desperately
enamoured, bearing as many flying hues and peeps of fancy
as a love-ballad, and not more roughly brushing the root-
emotions. If she had but been such an one, what sprightly
colours, delicious sadness, magical transformations, tenderest intermixture of earth and heaven; what tears and sun-
beams, divinest pathos: what descents from radiance to
consolatory twilight, would have surrounded me for poetry
and pride to dwell on! What captivating melody in the
minor key would have been mine, though I lost her—the
legacy of it all for ever! Say a petulant princess, a star of
beauty, mad for me, and the whisper of our passion and
sorrows traversing the flushed world! Was she coming?
Not she, but a touchstone, a relentless mirror, a piercing
eye, a mind severe as the Goddess of the God's head: a
princess indeed, but essentially a princess above women: a
remorseless intellect, an actual soul visible in the flesh. She
was truth. Was I true? Not so very false, yet how far
from truth! The stains on me (a modern man writing his
history is fugitive and crepuscular in alluding to them, as a
woman kneeling at the ear-guichet) burnt like the blood-
spots on the criminal compelled to touch his victim by
savage ordinance, which knew the savage and how to search
him. And these were faults of weakness rather than the
sins of strength. I might as fairly hope for absolution of

them from Ottilia as from offended laws of my natural being, gentle though she was, and charitable.

Was I not guilty of letting her come on to me hoodwinked at this moment? I had a faint memory of Miss Goodwin's saying that she had been deceived, and I suggested a plan of holding aloof until she had warned the princess of my perfect recovery, to leave it at her option to see me.

"Yes," Miss Goodwin assented: "if you like, Harry."

Her compassion for me only tentatively encouraged the idea. "It would, perhaps, be right. You are the judge. If you can do it. You are acting bravely." She must have laughed at me in her heart. I shook my head perusingly, murmuring "No;" and then a decisive negative and a deep sigh. The moods of half-earnest men and feeble lovers narrowly escape the farcical, if they do at all.

She adopted my plan in a vigorous outline of how to proceed.

"I think it would be honourable, Harry."

"It would be horrible, horrible! No, since she has come . . . . . I wish!—but the mischief is done."

"You are quite a boy."

I argued that it was not to be a boy to meet and face a difficult situation.

She replied that it was to be a boy of boys not to perceive that the sacrifice would never be accepted.

"Why, an old maid can teach you," she said, scornfully, and rebuked me for failing to seize my opportunity to gain credit with her for some show of magnanimous spirit. "Men are all selfish in love," she concluded most logically.

The hours wore on. My curse of introspection left me, and descending through the town to the pier, amid the breezy blue skirts and bonnet-strings, we watched the packet-boat approaching. There was in advance one of the famous swift island wherries. Something went wrong with it, for it was overtaken, and the steamer came in first. I jumped on board, much bawled at. Out of a crowd of unknown visages, Janet appeared: my aunt Dorothy was near her. The pair began chattering of my paleness, and wickedness in keeping my illness unknown to them. They had seen Temple on an excursion to London; he had betrayed me, as he would have betrayed an archangel to Janet.

" Will you not look at us, Harry ?" they both said.

The passengers were quitting the boat, strangers every one.

" Harry, have we really offended you in coming?" said Janet.

My aunt Dorothy took the blame on herself.

I scarcely noticed them, beyond leading them on to the pier-steps and leaving them under charge of Miss Goodwin, who had, in matters of luggage and porterage, the practical mind and aplomb of an Englishwoman that has passed much of her time on the Continent.   I fancied myself vilely duped by this lady.   The boat was empty of its passengers ; a grumbling pier-man, wounded in his dignity, notified to me that there were fines for disregard of the Company's rules and regulations.   His tone altered ; he touched his hat : "Didn't know who you was, my lord."   Janet overheard him, and her face was humorous.

" *We* may break the rules, you see," I said to her.

" We saw him landing on the other side of the water," she replied ; so spontaneously did the circumstance turn her thoughts on my father.

" Did you speak to him ?"

" No."

" You avoided him ?"

" Aunty and I thought it best.   He landed . . . . . there was a crowd.

Miss Goodwin interposed : " You go to Harry's hotel ?"

" Grandada is coming down to-morrow or next day," Janet prompted my aunt Dorothy.

" If we could seek for a furnished house ; Uberly would watch the luggage," Dorothy murmured in distress.

" Furnished houses, even rooms at hotels, are doubtful in the height of the season," Miss Goodwin remarked.   " Last night I engaged the only decent set of rooms I could get, for friends of Harry's who are coming."

" No wonder he was disappointed at seeing us—he was expecting them !" said Janet, smiling a little.

" They are sure to come," said Miss Goodwin.

Near us a couple of yachtsmen were conversing.

" Oh, he'll be back in a day or two," one said.   " When you've once tasted that old boy, you can't do without him. I remember when I was a youngster—it was in Lady Betty

Bolton's day; she married old Edbury, you know, first wife
—the Magnificent was then in his prime. He spent his
money in a week: so he hired an eighty-ton schooner; he
laid violent hands on a Jew, bagged him, lugged him on
board, and sailed away."

" What the deuce did he want with a Jew ?" cried the other.

" Oh, the Jew supplied cheques for a three months' cruise
in the Mediterranean, and came home, I heard, very good
friends with his pirate. That's only one of dozens."

The unconscious slaughterers laughed.

" On another occasion"—I heard it said by the first
speaker, as they swung round to parade the pier, and passed
on narrating.

"Not an hotel, if it is possible to avoid it," my aunt
Dorothy, with heightened colour, urged Miss Goodwin.
They talked together.

"Grandada is coming to you, Harry," Janet said. " He
has business in London, or he would have been here now.
Our horses and carriages follow us: everything you would
like. He does love you! he is very anxious. I'm afraid his
health is worse than he thinks. Temple did not say your
father was here, but grandada must have suspected it when
he consented to our coming, and said he would follow us.
So that looks well perhaps. He has been much quieter
since your money was paid back to you. If they should
meet .... no, I hope they will not: grandada hates noise.
And, Harry, let me tell you: it may be nothing: if he questions you, do not take fire; just answer plainly: I'm sure
you understand. One in a temper at a time I'm sure's
enough: you have only to be patient with him. He has
been going to London, to the City, seeing lawyers, bankers,
brokers, and coming back muttering. Ah! dear old man.
And when he ought to have peace! Harry, the poor will
regret him in a thousand places. I write a great deal for
him now, and I know how they will. What are you looking
at ?"

I was looking at a man of huge stature, of the stiffest
build, whose shoulders showed me their full breadth while
he stood displaying frontwards the open of his hand in a
salute.

" Schwartz !" I called. Janet started, imagining some
fierce interjection. The giant did not stir.

But others had heard. A lady stepped forward. "Dear
Mr. Harry Richmond! Then you are better? We had
most alarming news of you."

I bowed to the Frau von Dittmarsch, anciently Miss
Sibley.

"The princess?"

"She is here."

Frau von Dittmarsch clasped Miss Goodwin's hand. I
was touching Ottilia's. A veil partly swathed her face.
She trembled: the breeze robbed me of her voice.

Our walk down the pier was almost in silence. Miss
Goodwin assumed the guardianship of the foreign ladies.
I had to break from them and provide for my aunt Dorothy
and Janet.

"They went over in a little boat, they were so impatient.
Who is she?" Dorothy Beltham asked.

"The Princess Ottilia," said Janet.

"Are you certain? Is it really, Harry?"

I confirmed it, and my aunt said, "I should have guessed
it could be no other; she has a foreign grace."

"General Goodwin was with them when the boat came in
from the island," said Janet. "He walked up to Harry's
father, and you noticed, aunty, that the ladies stood away,
as if they wished to be unobserved, as we did, and pulled
down their veils. They would not wait for our boat. We
passed them crossing. People joked about the big servant
over-weighting the wherry."

Dorothy Beltham thought the water too rough for little
boats.

"She knows what a sea is," I said.

Janet gazed steadily after the retreating figures, and then
commended me to the search for rooms. The end of it was
that I abandoned my father's suite to them. An accommo-
dating linen-draper possessed of a sea-view, and rooms which
hurled the tenant to the windows in desire for it, gave me
harbourage.

Till dusk I scoured the town to find Miss Goodwin, without
whom there was no clue to the habitation I was seeking, and
must have passed blindly again and again. My aunt Dorothy
and Janet thanked me for my consideration in sitting down
to dine with them; they excused my haste to retire. I heard
no reproaches except on account of my not sending them

word of my illness. Janet was not warm. She changed in colour and voice when I related what I had heard from Miss Goodwin, namely, that " some one" had informed the princess I was in a dying state. I was obliged to offer up my father as a shield for Ottilia, lest false ideas should tarnish the image of her in their minds. Janet did not speak of him. The thought stood in her eyes; and there lies the evil of a sore subject among persons of one household: they have not to speak to exhibit their minds.

After a night of suspense I fell upon old Schwartz and Aennchen out in the earliest dawn, according to their German habits, to have a gaze at sea, and strange country and people. Aennchen was all wonder at the solitary place, Schwartz at the big ships. But when they tried to direct me to the habitation of their mistress, it was discovered by them that they had lost their bearings. Aennchen told me the margravine had been summoned to Rippau just before they left Sarkeld. Her mistress had informed Baroness Turckems of her intention to visit England. Prince Ernest was travelling in France.

The hour which brought me to Ottilia was noon. The arrangements of the ladies could only grant me thirty minutes, for Janet was to drive the princess out into the country to view the island. She and my aunt Dorothy had been already introduced. Miss Goodwin, after presenting them, insisted upon ceremoniously accompanying me to the house. Quite taking the vulgar view of a proceeding such as the princess had been guilty of, and perhaps fearing summary audacity and interestedness in the son of a father like mine, she ventured on lecturing me, as though it lay with me to restrain the fair romantic head, forbear from calling up my special advantages, advise, and stand to the wisdom of this world, and be the man of honour. The princess had said: "Not see him when I have come to him ?" I reassured my undiscerning friend partly, not wholly."

" Would it be commonly sensible or civil, to refuse to see me, having come ?"

Miss Goodwin doubted.

I could indicate forcibly, because I felt, the clear-judging brain and tempered self-command whereby Ottilia had gained her decision.

Miss Goodwin nodded and gave me the still-born affirmative of politeness. Her English mind expressed itself willing to have exonerated the rash great lady for visiting a dying lover, but he was not the same person now that he was on his feet, consequently her expedition wore a different aspect: —my not dying condemned her. She entreated me to keep the fact of the princess's arrival unknown to my father, on which point we were one. Intensely enthusiastic for the men of her race, she would have me, above all things, by a form of adjuration designed to be a masterpiece of persuasive rhetoric, "prove myself an Englishman." I was to show that "the honour, interests, reputation and position of any lady (demented or not," she added) "were as precious to me as to the owner:" that "no woman was ever in peril of a shadow of loss in the hands of an English gentleman," and so forth, rather surprisingly to me, remembering her off-hand manner of the foregoing day. But the sense of responsibility thrown upon her ideas of our superior national dignity had awakened her fervider naturalness—made her a different person, as we say when accounting, in our fashion, for what a little added heat may do.

The half hour allotted to me fled. I went from the room and the house, feeling that I had seen and heard her who was barely of the world of humankind for me, so strongly did imagination fly with her. I kissed her fingers, I gazed in her eyes, I heard the beloved voice. All passed too swift for happiness. Recollections set me throbbing, but recollection brought longing. She said, "Now I have come I must see you, Harry." Did it signify that to see me was a piece of kindness at war with her judgement? She rejoiced at my perfect recovery, though it robbed her of the plea in extenuation of this step she had taken. She praised me for abstaining to write to her, when I was stammering a set of hastily-impressed reasons to excuse myself for the omission. She praised my step into Parliament. It did not seem to involve a nearer approach to her. She said, "You have not wasted your time in England." It was for my solitary interests that she cared, then.

I brooded desperately. I could conceive an overlooking height that made her utterance simple and consecutive: I could not reach it. Topics which to me were palpitating, had no terror for her. She said, "I have offended my father; I have written to him; he will take me away." In speaking of the letter which had caused her to offend, she did not blame the writer. I was suffered to run my eyes over it, and was ashamed. It read to me too palpably as an outcry to delude and draw her hither :—pathos and pathos : the father holding his dying son in his arms, his sole son, Harry Richmond ; the son set upon by enemies in the night : the lover never daring to beg for a sight of his beloved ere he passed away :—not an ill-worded letter ; read uncritically, it may have been touching : it must have been, though it was the reverse for me. I frowned, broke down in regrets, under sharp humiliation. She said, " You knew nothing of it. A little transgression is the real offender. When we are once out of the way traced for us, we are in danger of offending at every step ; we are as lawless as the outcasts." That meant, " My turning aside to you originally was the blameable thing." It might mean, " My love of you sets my ideas of duty at variance with my father's." Might it also mean, " I am still in that road extra muros ?" She smiled ; nothing was uttered in a tone of despondency. Her high courage and breeding gave her even in this pitfall the smoothness which most women keep for society. Why she had not sent me any message or tidings of herself to Riversley was not a matter that she could imagine to perplex me : she could not imagine my losing faith in her. The least we could do, I construed it, the religious bond between us was a faith in one another that should sanctify to our souls the external injuries it caused us to commit. But she talked in no such strain. Her delight in treading English ground was her happy theme. She said, " It is as young as when we met in the forest;" namely, the feeling revived for England. How far off we were from the green Devonshire coast, was one of her questions, suggestive of our old yacht-voyage lying among her dreams. Excepting an extreme and terrorizing paleness, there was little to fever me with the thought that she suffered mortally. Of reproach, not a word ; nor of regret. At the first touch of hands, when we stood together, alone, she said, " Would hearing of your recovery have given me peace ?" My privileges were the touch of hands, the touch of her fingers to my lips, a painless hearing and seeing, and passionate recollection. She said, " Impatience is not for us, Harry :"—I was not to see her again before the evening. These were the last words she said, and seemed the lightest until my hot brain made a harvest of them transcending thrice-told vows of love. Did they not mean, 'We two wait:' therefore, 'The years are bondmen to our steadfastness." Could sweeter have been said? They might mean nothing!

She was veiled when Janet drove her out; Janet sitting upright in her masterly way, smoothing her pet ponies with the curl of her whip, chatting and smiling; the princess slightly leaning back. I strode up to the country roads, proud of our land's beauty under a complacent sky. By happy chance, which in a generous mood I ascribed to Janet's good nature, I came across them at a seven miles' distance. They were talking spiritedly: what was wonderful, they gave not much heed to me: they seemed on edge for one another's conversation: each face was turned to the other's, and after nodding an adieu they resumed the animated discourse. I had been rather in alarm lest Ottilia should think little of Janet. They passed out of sight without recurring to a thought of me behind them.

In the evening I was one among a group of ladies. I had the opportunity of hearing the running interchange between Ottilia and Janet, which appeared to be upon equal terms; indeed, Janet led. The subjects were not very deep. Plain wits, candour, and an unpretending tongue, it seemed, could make common subjects attractive, as fair weather does our English woods and fields. The princess was attracted by something in Janet. I myself felt the sway of something, while observing Ottilia's rapt pleasure in her talk and her laughter, with those funny familiar frowns and current dimples twisting and melting away like a play of shadows on the eddies of the brook.

" I'm glad to be with her," Janet said of Ottilia.

It was just in that manner she spoke in Ottilia's presence. Why it should sound elsewhere unsatisfactorily blunt, and there possess a finished charm, I could not understand.

I mentioned to Janet that I feared my father would be returning.

She contained herself with a bridled " Oh!"

We were of one mind as to the necessity for keeping him absent, if possible.

" Harry, you'll pardon me; I can't talk of him," said she.

I proposed half-earnestly to foil his return by going to London at once.

"That's manly; that's nice of you," Janet said.

This was on our walk from the house at night. My aunt Dorothy listened, pressing my arm. The next morning Janet urged me to go at once. "Keep him away, bring down grandada, Harry. She cannot quit the island, because she has given Prince Ernest immediate rendezvous here. You must not delay to go. Yes, the Countess of Delzenburg shall have your excuses. And no, I promise you I will run nobody down. Besides, if I do, aunty will be at hand to plead for the defence, and she can! She has a way that binds one to accept everything she says, and Temple ought to study with her for a year or two before he wears his gown. Bring him back with you and grandada. He is esteemed here at his true worth. I love him for making her in love with English boys. I leave the men for those who know them, but English boys are unrivalled, I declare. Honesty, bravery, modesty, and nice looks! They are so nice in their style and their way of talking. I tell her, our men may be shy and sneering,— awkward, I daresay; but our boys beat the world. Do bring down Temple. I should so like her to see a cricket-match between two good elevens of our boys, Harry, while she is in England! We could have arranged for one at Riversley."

I went, and I repressed the idea, on my way, that Janet had manœuvred by sending me off to get rid of me, but I felt myself a living testimony to her heartlessness: for no girl of any heart, acting the part of friend, would have allowed me to go without a leave-taking of her I loved: few would have been so cruel as to declare it a duty to go at all, especially when the chances were that I might return to find the princess wafted away. Ottilia's condescension had done her no good. "Turn to the right, that's your path; on." She seemed to speak in this style, much as she made her touch of the reins understood by her ponies. "I'll take every care of the princess," she said. Her conceit was unbounded. I revelled in contemptuous laughter at her assumption of the post of leader with Ottilia. However, it was as well that I should go: there was no trusting my father.

CHAPTER XLIX.

WHICH FORESHADOWS A GENERAL GATHERING.

At our Riversley station I observed the squire, in company
with Captain Bulsted, jump into a neighbouring carriage.
I joined them, and was called upon to answer various inquiries. The squire gave me one of his short tight grasps
of the hand, in which there was warmth and shyness, our
English mixture. The captain whispered in my ear: " He
oughtn't to be alone."

" How's the great-grandmother of the tribe? " said I.

Captain Bulsted nodded, as if he understood, but was at
sea until I mentioned the bottle of rum and the remarkable
length of that old lady's measurement.

" Ay, to be sure! a grand old soul," he said. " You know
that scum of old, Harry."

I laughed, and so did he, at which I laughed the louder.

" He laughs, I suppose, because his party's got a majority
in the House," said the squire.

" We gave you a handsome surplus this year, sir."

" Sweated out of the country's skin and bone, ay!"

" You were complimented by the Chancellor of the Ex-
chequer."

" Yes, that fellow's compliments are like a cabman's, and
cry fool:—he never thanks you but when he's overpaid."

Captain Bulsted applauded the sarcasm.

" Why did you keep out of knowledge all this time, Hal?"
my grandfather asked.

I referred him to the captain.

" Hang it," cried Captain Bulsted, " do you think I'd have
been doing duty for you if I'd known where to lay hold of
you?"

" Well, if you didn't shake hands with me, you touched
my toes," said I, and thanked him with all my heart for his
kindness to an old woman on the point of the grave. I had
some fun to flavour melancholy with.

My grandfather resumed his complaint: " You might have
gone clean off, and we none the wiser."

" Are we quite sure that his head's clean on? " said the
mystified captain.

"Of course we should run to him, wherever he was, if he was down on his back," the squire muttered.

"Ay, ay, sir; of course," quoth Captain William, frowning to me to reciprocate this relenting mood. "But, Harry, where did you turn off that night. We sat up expecting you. My poor Julia was in a terrible fright, my lad. Eh? speak up."

I raised the little finger.

"Oh, oh," went he, happily reassured; but, reflecting, added: "A bout of it?"

I dropped him a penitent nod.

"That's bad, though," said he.

"Then why did you tip me a bottle of rum, Captain William?"

"By George, Harry, you've had a crack o' the sconce," he exclaimed, more sagaciously than he was aware of.

My grandfather wanted to keep me by his side in London until we two should start for the island next day; but his business was in the city, mine toward the West. We appointed to meet two hours after reaching the terminus.

He turned to me while giving directions to his man.

"You've got *him* down there, I suppose?"

"My father's in town, sir. He shall keep away," I said.

"Humph! I mayn't object to see him."

This set me thinking.

Captain Bulsted—previously asking me in a very earnest manner whether I was really all right and sound—favoured me with a hint:

"The squire has plunged into speculations of his own, or else he is peeping at somebody else's. No danger of the dad being mixed up with Companies? Let's hope not. Julia pledged her word to Janet that I would look after the old squire. I suppose I can go home this evening? My girl hates to be alone."

"By all means," said I; and the captain proposed to leave the squire at his hotel, in the event of my failing to join him in the city.

"But don't fail, if you can help it," he urged me; "for things somehow, my dear Harry, appear to me to look like the compass when the needle gives signs of atmospheric disturbance. My only reason for saying so is common observation. You can judge for yourself that he is glad to have you with him."

I told the captain I was equally glad; for, in fact, my grandfather's quietness and apparently friendly disposition tempted me to petition for a dower for the princess at once, so that I might be in the position to offer Prince Ernest on his arrival a distinct alternative; supposing—it was still but a supposition—Ottilia should empower me. Incessant dialogues of perpetually shifting tendencies passed between Ottilia and me in my brain—now dark, now mildly fair, now very wild, on one side at least. Never, except by downright force of will, could I draw from the phantom of her one purely irrational outcry, so deeply-rooted was the knowledge of her nature and mind; and when I did force it, I was no gainer: a puppet stood in her place—the vision of Ottilia melted out in threads of vapour. "And yet she has come to me; she has braved everything to come." I might say that, to liken her to the women who break rules and read duties by their own light, but I could not cheat my knowledge of her. Mrs. Waddy met me in the hall of my father's house, as usual, pressing, I regretted to see, one hand to her side. "Her heart," she said, "was easily set pitty-pat now." She had been, by her master's orders, examined by two of the chief physicians of the kingdom, "baronets both." They advised total rest. As far as I could apprehend, their baronetcies and doings in high regions had been of more comfort than their prescriptions.

"What I am I must be," she said, meekly; "and I cannot quit his service till he's abroad again, or I drop. He has promised me a monument. I don't want it; but it shows his kindness."

A letter from Heriot informed me that the affair between Edbury and me was settled: he could not comprehend how. "What is this new Jury of Honour? Who are the jurymen?" he asked, and affected wit.

I thanked him for a thrashing in a curt reply.

My father had left the house early in the morning. Mrs. Waddy believed that he meant to dine that evening at the season's farewell dinner of the Trump-Trick Club: "Leastways, Tollingby has orders to lay out his gentlemen's-dinners' evening-suit. Yesterday afternoon he flew down to Chippenden, and was home late. To-day he's in the City, or one of the squares. Lady Edbury's—ah!—detained in town with the jaundice, or toothache. He said he was sending to France for a dentist—or was it Germany, for some lady's eyes? I am sure I don't know. Well or ill, so long as you're anything to him, he will abound. Pocket and purse! You know him by this time, Mr. Harry. Oh, my heart!"

A loud knock at the door had brought on the poor creature's palpitations.

This visitor was no other than Prince Ernest. The name on his card was Graf von Delzenburg, and it set my heart leaping to as swift a measure as Mrs. Waddy's.

Hearing that I was in the house, he desired to see me. We met, with a formal bow.

"I congratulate you right heartily upon being out of the list of the nekrōn," he said, civilly. "I am on my way to one of your watering-places, whither my family should have preceded me. Do you publish the names and addresses of visitors daily, as it is the custom with us?"

I relieved his apprehensions on that head: "Here and there, rarely; and only at the hotels, I believe." The excuse was furnished for offering the princess's address.

"Possibly, in a year or two, we may have the pleasure of welcoming you at Sarkeld," said the prince, extending his hand. "Then, you have seen the Countess of Delzenburg?"

"On the day of her arrival, your Highness. Ladies of my family are staying on the island."

"Ah?"

He paused, and invited me to bow to him. We bowed thus in the room, in the hall, and at the street-door.

For what purpose could he have called on my father? To hear the worst at once? That seemed likely, supposing him to have lost his peculiar confidence in the princess, of which the courtly paces he had put me through precluded me from judging.

But I guessed acutely that it was not his intention to permit of my meeting Ottilia a second time. The blow was hard: I felt it as if it had been struck already, and thought I had gained resignation, until, like a man reprieved on his road to execution, the narrowed circle of my heart opened out to the breadth of the world in a minute. Returning from the city, I hurried to my father's house, late in the afternoon, and heard that he had started to overtake the

prince, leaving word that the prince was to be found at his
address in the island. No doubt could exist regarding the
course I was bound to take. I drove to my grandfather,
stated my case to him, and by sheer vehemence took the
wind out of his sails; so that when I said, "I am the only
one alive who can control my father," he answered mildly,
"Seems t'other way," and chose a small snort for the indul-
gence of his private opinion.

"What! this princess came over alone, and is down driving
out with my girl under an alias?" he said, showing sour
aversion at the prospect of a collision with the foreign
species, as expressive as the ridge of a cat's back.

Temple came to dine with us, so I did not leave him quite
to himself, and Temple promised to accompany him down to
the island.

"Oh, go, if you like," the fretted old man dismissed me:
"I've got enough to think over. Hold him fast to stand up
to me within forty-eight hours, present time; you know who
I mean; I've got a question or two for him. How he treats
his foreign princess and princesses don't concern me. I'd
say, like the Prevention-Cruelty-Animal's man to the keeper
of the menagerie, 'Lecture 'em, wound their dignity, hurt
their feelings, only don't wop 'em.' I don't wish any harm
to them, but what the deuce they do here nosing after my
grandson! . . . . There, go; we shall be having it out and
ha' done with to-morrow or next day. I've run the badger
to earth, else I'm not fit to follow a scent."

He grumbled at having to consume other than his
Riversley bread, butter, beef, and ale for probably another
fortnight. One of the boasts of Riversley was that while
the rest of the world ate and drank poison, the Grange
lived on its own solid substance, defying malefactory Radical
tricksters.

Temple was left to hear the rest. He had the sweetest of
modest wishes for a re-introduction to Ottilia.

CHAPTER L.

WE ARE ALL IN MY FATHER'S NET.

JOURNEYING down by the mail-train in the face of a great sunken sunset broken with cloud, I chanced to ask myself what it was that I seriously desired to have. My purpose to curb my father was sincere and good; but concerning my heart's desires, whitherward did they point? I thought of Janet—she made me gasp for air; of Ottilia, and she made me long for earth. Sharp, as I write it, the distinction smote me. I might have been divided by an electrical shot into two halves, with such an equal force was I drawn this way and that, pointing nowhither. To strangle the thought of either one of them was like the pang of death; yet it did not strike me that I loved the two: they were apart in my mind, actually as if I had been divided. I passed the Riversley station under sombre sunset fires, saddened by the fancy that my old home and vivacious Janet were ashes, past hope. I came on the smell of salt air, and had that other spirit of woman around me, of whom the controlled sea-deeps were an image, who spoke to my soul like star-light. Much wise counsel, and impatience of the wisdom, went on within me. I walked like a man with a yawning wound, and had to whip the sense of passion for a drug. Toward which one it strove I know not; it was blind and stormy as the night.

Not a boatman would take me across. The lights of the island lay like a crown on the water. I paced the ramparts, eyeing them, breathing the keen salt of thundering waves, until they were robbed of their magic by the coloured East.

It is, I have learnt, out of the conflict of sensations such as I then underwent that a young man's brain and morality, supposing him not to lean overmuch to sickly sentiment, becomes gradually enriched and strengthened, and himself shaped for capable manhood. I was partly conscious of a better condition in the morning; and a sober morning it was to me after my long sentinel's step to and fro. I found myself possessed of one key—whether the right one or not—wherewith to read the princess, which was never possible to me when I was under stress of passion, or of hope or despair;

my perplexities over what she said, how she looked, cease to
trouble me. I read her by this strange light: that she was
a woman who could only love intelligently—love, that is, in
the sense of giving herself. She had the power of passion,
and it could be stirred; but he who kindled it wrecked his
chance if he could not stand clear in her intellect's un-
sparing gaze. Twice already she must have felt herself
disillusioned by me. This third time, possibly, she blamed
her own fatally credulous tenderness, not me; but it was her
third awakening, and could affection and warmth of heart
combat it? Her child's enthusiasm for my country had prepared her for the impression which the waxen mind of the
dreamy invalid received deeply; and so, aided by the emotional blood of youth, she gave me place in her imagination,
probing me still curiously, as I remembered, at a season
when her sedate mind was attaining to joint deliberations
with the impulsive overgenerous heart. Then ensued for
her the successive shocks of discernment. She knew me to
have some of the vices, many follies, all the intemperateness
of men who carve a way for themselves in the common roads,
if barely they do that. And resembling common men (men,
in a judgement elective as hers, common, however able), I
was not assuredly to be separated by her from my associa-
tions; from the thought of my father, for example. Her
look at him in the lake-palace library, and her manner in
unfolding and folding his recent letter to her, and in one or
two necessitated allusions, embraced a kind of grave, pitiful
humour, beyond smiles or any outward expression, as if the
acknowledgement that it was so quite obliterated the wonder
that it should be so—that one such as he could exercise
influence upon her destiny. Or she may have made her
reckoning generally, not personally, upon our human destinies : it is the more likely, if, as I divine, the calm oval of
her lifted eyelids contemplated him in the fulness of the
recognition that this world, of which we hope unuttered
things, can be shifted and swayed by an ignis-fatuus. The
father of one now seen through, could hardly fail of being
transfixed himself. It was horrible to think of. I would
rather have added a vice to my faults than that she should
have penetrated him.

Nearing the island, I was reminded of the early morning
when I landed on the Flemish flats. I did not expect a

similar surprise, but before my rowers had pulled in, the tall beaconhead of old Schwartz notified that his mistress might be abroad. Janet walked with her. I ran up the steps to salute them, and had Ottilia's hand in mine.

"Prince Ernest has arrived?"

"My father came yesterday evening."

"Do you leave to-day?"

"I cannot tell; he will decide."

It seemed a good omen, until I scanned Janet's sombre face.

"You will not see us out for the rest of the day, Harry," said she.

"That is your arrangement?"

"It is."

"Your own?"

"Mine, if you like."

There was something hard in her way of speaking, as though she blamed me, and the princess were under her protection against me. She vouchsafed no friendly significance of look and tone.

In spite of my readiness to criticize her (which in our language means condemn) for always assuming leadership with whomsoever she might be, I was impressed by the air of high-bred friendliness existing between her and the princess. Their interchange was pleasant to hear. Ottilia had caught the spirit of her frank manner of speech; and she, though in a less degree, the princess's fine ease and sweetness. They conversed, apparently, like equal minds. On material points, Janet unhesitatingly led. It was she who brought the walk to a close.

"Now, Harry, you had better go and have a little sleep. I should like to speak to you early."

Ottilia immediately put her hand out to me.

I begged permission to see her to her door.

Janet replied for her, indicating old Schwartz: "We have a protector, you see, six feet and a half."

An hour later, Schwartz was following her to the steps of her hotel. She saw me, and waited. For a wonder, she displayed reluctance in disburdening herself of what she had to say. "Harry, you know that he has come? He and Prince Ernest came together. Get him to leave the island at once: he can return to-morrow. Grandada writes of wishing to see him. Get him away to-day."

" Is the prince going to stay here ?" I asked.

" No. I daresay I am only guessing; I hope so. He has threatened the prince."

" What with ?"

" Oh ! Harry, can't you understand ? I'm no reader of etiquette, but even I can see that the story of a young princess travelling over to England alone to visit . . . . and you . . . ., and her father fetching her away ! The prince is almost at his mercy, unless you *make* the man behave like a gentleman. This is exactly the thing Miss Goodwin feared!"

" But who's to hear of the story ?" said I.

Janet gave an impatient sigh.

" Do you mean that my father has threatened to publish it, Janet ?"

" I won't say he has. He has made the prince afraid to move : that I think is true."

" Did the princess herself mention it to you ?"

" She understands her situation, I am sure."

" Did she speak of ' the man,' as you call him ?"

" Yes : not as I do. You must try by-and-by to forgive me. Whether he set a trap or not, he has decoyed her— don't frown at words—and it remains for you to act as I don't doubt you will; but lose no time. Determine. Oh ! if I were a man !"

" You would muzzle us ?"

" Muzzle, or anything you please; I would make any one related to me behave honourably. I would give him the alternative . . ."

" You foolish girl ! suppose he took it ?"

" I would make him feel my will. He should not take it. Keep to the circumstances, Harry. If you have no control over him—I should think I was not fit to live, in such a position ! No control over him at a moment like this ? and the princess in danger of having her reputation hurt ! Surely, Harry ! But why should I speak to you as if you were undecided !"

" Where is he ?"

" At the house where you sleep. He surrendered his rooms here very kindly."

" Aunty has seen him ?"

Janet blushed : I thought I knew why. It was for subtler reasons than I should have credited her with conceiving.

"She sent for him, at my request, late last night. She believed her influence would be decisive. So do I. She could not even make the man perceive that he was acting— to use her poor dear old-fashioned word—reprehensibly in frightening the prince to further your interests. From what I gathered he went off in a song about them. She said he talked so well! And aunty Dorothy, too! I should nearly as soon have expected grandada to come in for his turn of the delusion. How I wish he was here! Uberly goes by the first boat to bring him down. I feel with Miss Goodwin that it will be a disgrace for all of us—the country's disgrace. As for our family! . . . Harry, and your name! Good-bye. Do your best."

I was in the mood to ask, "On behalf of the country?" She had, however, a glow and a ringing articulation in her excitement that forbade trifling; a minute's reflection set me weighing my power of will against my father's. I nodded to her.

"Come to us when you are at liberty," she called.

I have said that I weighed my power of will against my father's. Contemplation of the state of the scales did not send me striding to meet him. Let it be remembered—I had it strongly in memory—that he habitually deluded himself under the supposition that the turn of all events having an aspect of good fortune had been planned by him of old, and were offered to him as the legitimately-won fruits of a politic life. While others deemed him mad, or merely reckless, wild, a creature living for the day, he enjoyed the conceit of being a profound schemer, in which he was fortified by a really extraordinary adroitness to take advantage of occurrences: and because he was prompt in an emergency, and quick to profit of a crisis, he was deluded to imagine that he had created it. Such a man would be with difficulty brought to surrender his prize.

Again, there was his love for me. · 'Pater est, Pamphile; —difficile est.' How was this vast conceit of a not unreal paternal love to be encountered? The sense of honour and of decency might appeal to him personally; would either of them get a hearing if he fancied them to be standing in opposition to my dearest interests? I, unhappily, as the case would be sure to present itself to him, appeared the living example of his eminently politic career. After establishing me the heir of one of the wealthiest of English commoners, would he be likely to forego any desperate chance of ennobling me by the brilliant marriage? His dreadful devotion to me extinguished the hope that he would, unless I should happen to be particularly masterful in dealing with him. I heard his nimble and overwhelming volubility like a flood advancing. That could be withstood, and his arguments and persuasions. But by what steps could I restrain the man himself? I said "the man," as Janet did. He figured in my apprehensive imagination as an engine more than as an individual. Lassitude oppressed me. I felt that I required every access of strength possible, physical besides moral, in anticipation of our encounter, and took a swim in sea-water, which displaced my drowsy fit, and some alarming intimations of cowardice menacing a paralysis of the will: I had not altogether recovered from my gipsy drubbing. And now I wanted to have the contest over instantly. It seemed presumable that my father had slept at my lodgings. There, however, the report of him was that he had inspected the rooms, highly complimented the owner of them, and vanished. Returning to the pier, I learnt that he had set sail in his hired yacht for the sister town on the Solent, at an early hour:—for what purpose? I knew of it too late to intercept it. One of the squire's horses trotted me over; I came upon Colonel Hibbert Segrave near the Club-house, and heard that my father was off again: "But your German prince and papa-in-law shall be free of the Club for the next fortnight," said he, and cordially asked to have the date of the marriage. My face astonished him. He excused himself for speaking of this happy event so abruptly. A sting of downright anger drove me back at a rapid canter. It flashed on me that this Prince Ernest, whose suave fashion of depressing me, and philosophical skill in managing his daughter, had induced me to regard him as a pattern of astuteness, was really both credulous and feeble, or else supremely unsuspecting: and I was confirmed in the latter idea on hearing that he had sailed to visit the opposite harbour and docks on board my father's yacht. Janet shared my secret opinion.

"The prince is a gentleman," she said.

Her wrath and disgust were unspeakable. My aunt

Dorothy blamed her for overdue severity. " The prince, I suppose, goes of his own free will where he pleases."

Janet burst out, " Oh! can't you see through it, aunty? The prince goes about without at all knowing that the person who takes him—Harry sees it—is making him compromise himself: and by-and-by the prince will discover that he has no will of his own, whatever he may wish to resolve upon doing."

" Is he quite against Harry?" asked my aunt Dorothy.

" Dear aunty, he's a prince, and a proud man. He will never in his lifetime consent to . . . to what you mean, without being hounded into it. I haven't the slightest idea whether anything will force him. I know that the princess would have too much pride to submit, even to save her name. But it's her name that's in danger. Think of the scandal to a sovereign princess! I know the signification of that now; I used to laugh at Harry's ' sovereign princess.' She is one, and thorough! there is no one like her. Don't you understand, aunty, that the intrigue, plot—I don't choose to be nice upon terms—may be perfectly successful, and do good to nobody. The prince may be tricked; the princess, I am sure, will not."

Janet's affectation of an intimate and peculiar knowledge of the princess was a show of her character that I was accustomed to: still, it was evident they had conversed much, and perhaps intimately. I led her to tell me that the princess had expressed no views upon my father. " He does not come within her scope, Harry." ' Scope' was one of Janet's new words, wherewith she would now and then fall to seasoning a serviceable but savourless outworn vocabulary of the common table. In spite of that and other offences, rendered prominent to me by the lifting of her lip and her frown when she had to speak of my father, I was on her side, not on his. Her estimation of the princess was soundly based. She discerned exactly the nature of Ottilia's entanglement, and her peril.

She and my aunt Dorothy passed the afternoon with Ottilia, while I crossed the head of the street, looking down at the one house, where the princess was virtually imprisoned, either by her father's express injunction or her own discretion. And it was as well that she should not be out. The yachting season had brought many London men to the island. I met several who had not forgotten the newspaper-paragraph assertions and contradictions. Lord Alton, Admiral Loftus, and others were on the pier and in the outfitters' shops, eager for gossip, as the languid stretch of indolence inclines men to be. The Admiral asked me for the whereabout of Prince Ernest's territory. He too said that the prince would be free of the Club during his residence, adding: " Where is he ? "—not a question demanding an answer. The men might have let the princess gc by, but there would have been questions urgently demanding answers had she been seen by their women.

Late in the evening my father's yacht was sighted from the pier. Just as he reached his moorings, and his boat was hauled round, the last steamer came in. Sharp-eyed Janet saw the squire on board among a crowd, and Temple next to him, supporting his arm.

" Has grandada been ill ? " she exclaimed.

My chief concern was to see my father's head rising in the midst of the crowd, uncovering repeatedly. Prince Ernest and General Goodwin were behind him, stepping off the lower pier-platform. The General did not look pleased. My grandfather, with Janet holding his arm in the place of Temple, stood waiting to see that his man had done his duty by the luggage.

My father, advancing, perceived me, and almost taking the squire into his affectionate salutation, said : " Nothing could be more opportune than your arrival, Mr. Beltham."

The squire rejoined : " I wanted to see you, Mr. Richmond, and not in public."

" I grant the private interview, sir, at your convenience."

Janet went up to General Goodwin. My father talked to me, and lost a moment in shaking Temple's hand and saying kind things.

" Name any hour you please, Mr. Beltham," he resumed ; " meantime, I shall be glad to effect the introduction between Harry's grandfather and his Highness Prince Ernest of Eppenwelzen-Sarkeld."

He turned. General Goodwin was hurrying the prince up the steps, the squire at the same time retreating hastily. I witnessed the spectacle of both parties to the projected introduction swinging round to make their escape. My father glanced to right and left. He covered in the airiest fashion what would have been confusion to another by carrying on a jocose remark that he had left half spoken to Temple, and involved Janet in it, and soon—through sheer amiable volubility and his taking manner—the squire himself for a minute or so.

"Harry, I have to tell you she is not unhappy," Janet whispered rapidly. "She is reading of one of our great men alive now. She is glad to be on our ground." Janet named a famous admiral, kindling as a fiery beacon to our blood. She would have said more: she looked the remainder; but she could have said nothing better fitted to spur me to the work she wanted done. Mournfulness dropped on me like a cloud in thinking of the bright little princess of my boyhood, and the Ottilia of to-day, faithful to her early passion for our sea-heroes and my country, though it had grievously entrapped her. And into what hands! Not into hands which could cast one ray of honour on a devoted head. The contrast between the sane service-giving men she admired, and the hopping skipping social meteor, weaver of webs, thrower of nets, who offered her his history for a nuptial acquisition, was ghastly, most discomforting. He seemed to have entangled us all.

He said that he had. He treated me now confessedly as a cipher. The prince, the princess, my grandfather, and me —he had gathered us together, he said. I heard from him that the prince, assisted by him in the part of an adviser, saw no way of cutting the knot but by a marriage. All were at hand for a settlement of the terms:—Providence and destiny were dragged in.

"Let's have no theatrical talk," I interposed.

"Certainly, Richie; the plainest English," he assented.

This was on the pier, while he bowed and greeted passing figures. I dared not unlink my arm, for fear of further mischief. I got him to my rooms, and insisted on his dining there.

"Dry bread will do," he said.

My anticipations of the nature of our wrestle were correct. But I had not expected him to venture on the assertion that the prince was for the marriage. He met me at every turn with this downright iteration. "The prince consents: he knows his only chance is to yield. I have him fast."

"How?" I inquired.

"How, Richie? Where is your perspicuity? I have him here. I loosen a thousand tongues on him. I——"

"No, not on him; on the princess, you mean."

"On him. The princess is the willing party; she and you are one. On him, I say. 'Tis but a threat: I hold it in terrorem. And by heaven, son Richie, it assures me I have not lived and fought for nothing. 'Now is the day and now is the hour.' On your first birthday, my boy, I swore to marry you to one of the highest ladies upon earth: she was, as it turns out, then unborn. No matter: I keep my oath. Abandon it? pooh! you are—forgive me—silly. Pardon me for remarking it, you have not that dashing courage—never mind. The point is, I have my prince in his trap. We are perfectly polite, but I have him, and he acknowledges it; he shrugs: love has beaten him. Very well. And observe: I permit no squire-of-low-degree insinuations; none of that. The lady—all earthly blessings on her!—does not stoop to Harry Richmond. I have the announcement in the newspapers. I maintain it the fruit of a life of long and earnest endeavour, legitimately won, by heaven it is! and with the constituted authorities of my native land against me. Your grandad proposes formally for the princess to-morrow morning."

He quite maddened me. Merely to keep him silent I burst out in a flux of reproaches as torrent-like as his own could be; and all the time I was wondering whether it was true that a man who talked as he did, in his strain of florid flimsy, had actually done a practical thing.

The effect of my vehemence was to brace him and make him sedately emphatic. He declared himself to have gained entire possession of the prince's mind. He repeated his positive intention to employ his power for my benefit. Never did power of earth or of hell seem darker to me than he at that moment, when solemnly declaiming that he was prepared to forfeit my respect and love, die sooner than "yield his prince." He wore a new aspect, spoke briefly and pointedly, using the phrases of a determined man, and in voice and gesture signified that he had us all in a grasp of iron. The charge of his having plotted to bring it about he accepted with exultation.

"I admit," he said, "I did not arrange to have Germany present for a witness besides England, but since he is here, I take advantage of the fact, and to-morrow you will see young Eckart down."

I cried out, as much enraged at my feebleness to resist him, as in disgust of his unscrupulous tricks.

" Ay, you have not known me, Richie," said he. " I pilot you into harbour, and all you can do is just the creaking of the vessel to me. You are in my hands. I pilot you. I have you the husband of the princess within the month. No other course is open to her And I have the assurance that she loses nothing by it. She is yours, my son."

" She will not be. You have wrecked my last chance. You cover me with dishonour."

" You are a youngster, Richie. 'Tis the wish of her heart. Probably while you and I are talking it over, the prince is confessing that he has no escape. He has not a loophole! She came to you ; you take her. I am far from withholding my admiration of her behaviour ; but there it is—she came. Not consent ? She is a ruined woman if she refuses !"

" Through you, through you !—through my father !"

" Have you both gone mad ?"

" Try to see this," I implored him. " She will not be subjected by any threats. The very whisper of one will make her turn from me . . . ."

He interrupted. " Totally the contrary. The prince acknowledges that you are master of her affections."

" Consistently with her sense of honour and respect for us."

" Tell me of her reputation, Richie."

" You pretend that you can damage it !"

" Pretend ? I pretend in the teeth of all concerned to establish her happiness and yours, and nothing human shall stop me. I have you grateful to me before your old dad lays his head on his last pillow. And that reminds me : I surrender my town house and furniture to you. Waddy has received the word. By the way, should you hear of a good doctor for heart-disease, tell me : I have my fears for the poor soul."

He stood up, saying, " Richie, I am not like Jorian, to whom a lodging-house dinner is no dinner, and an irreparable loss, but I must have air. I go forth on a stroll."

It was impossible for me to allow it. I stopped him.

We were in the midst of a debate as to his right of per-

sonal freedom, upon the singularity of which he commented
with sundry ejaculations, when Temple arrived and General
Goodwin sent up his card.   Temple and I left the General
closeted with my father, and stood at the street-door.   He
had seen the princess, having at her request been taken to
present his respects to her by Janet.   How she looked, what
she said, he was dull in describing; he thought her lively,
though she was pale.   She had mentioned my name,
"kindly," he observed.   And he knew, or suspected, the
General to be an emissary from the prince.   But he could
not understand the exact nature of the complication, and
plagued me with a mixture of blunt inquiries and the delicate
reserve proper to him so much that I had to look elsewhere
for counsel and sympathy.   Janet had told him everything;
still he was plunged in wonder, tempting me to think the
lawyer's mind of necessity bourgeois, for the value of a
sentiment seemed to have no weight in his estimation of the
case.   Nor did he appear disinclined to excuse my father.
Some of his remarks partly swayed me, in spite of my seeing
that they were based on the supposition of an "all for love"
adventure of a mad princess.   They whispered a little hope,
when I was adoring her passionately for being the reverse
of whatever might have given hope a breath.

General Goodwin, followed by my father, came down and
led me aside after I had warned Temple not to let my
father elude him.   The General was greatly ruffled.   "Clara
tells me she can rely on you," he said.   "I am at the end
of my arguments with that man, short of sending him to the
lock-up.   You will pardon me, Mr. Harry; I foresaw the
scrapes in store for you, and advised you."

"You did, General," I confessed.   "Will you tell me what
it is Prince Ernest is in dread of?"

"A pitiable scandal, sir; and if he took my recommendation, he would find instant means of punishing the man
who dares to threaten him.   You know it."

I explained that I was aware of the threat, not of the
degree of the prince's susceptibility; and asked him if he
had seen the princess.

"I have had the honour," he replied, stiffly.   "You gain
nothing with her by this infamous proceeding."

I swallowed my anger, and said, "Do you accuse me,
General?"

"I do not accuse you," he returned, unbendingly. "You chose your path some ten or twelve years ago, and you must take the consequences. I foresaw it; but this I will say, I did not credit the man with his infernal cleverness. If I speak to you at all, I must speak my mind. I thought him a mere buffoon and spendthrift, flying his bar-sinister story for the sake of distinction. He has schemed up to this point successfully: he has the prince in his toils. I would cut through them, as I have informed Prince Ernest. I daresay different positions lead to different reasonings; the fellow appears to have a fascination over him. Your father, Mr. Harry, is guilty now—he is guilty, I reiterate, now of a piece of iniquity that makes me ashamed to own him for a countryman."

The General shook himself erect. "Are you unable to keep him in?" he asked.

My nerves were pricking and stinging with the insults I had to listen to, and conscience's justification of them.

He repeated the question.

"I will do what I can," I said, unsatisfactorily to myself and to him, for he transposed our situations, telling me the things he would say and do in my place; things not dissimilar to those I had already said and done, only more toweringly enunciated; and for that reason they struck me as all the more hopelessly ineffectual, and made me despair.

My dumbness excited his ire. "Come," said he; "the lady is a spoilt child. She behaved foolishly; but from your point of view you should feel bound to protect her on that very account. Do your duty, young gentleman. He is, I believe, fond of you, and if so, you have him by a chain. I tell you frankly, I hold you responsible."

His way of speaking of the princess opened an idea of the world's, in the event of her name falling into its clutches.

I said again, "I will do what I can," and sang out for Temple.

He was alone. My father had slipped from him to leave a card at the squire's hotel. General Goodwin touched Temple on the shoulder kindly, in marked contrast to his treatment of me, and wished us good-night.

Nothing had been heard of my father by Janet, but while I was sitting with her, at a late hour, his card was brought up, and a pencilled entreaty for an interview the next morning.

"That will suit grandada," Janet said. "He commissioned me before going to bed to write the same for him."

She related that the prince was in a state of undisguised distraction. From what I could comprehend—it appeared incredible—he regarded his daughter's marriage as the solution of the difficulty, the sole way out of the meshes.

"Is not that her wish?" said Temple; perhaps with a wish of his own.

"Oh, if you think a lady like the Princess Ottilia is led by her wishes," said Janet. Her radiant perception of an ideal in her sex (the first she ever had) made her utterly contemptuous toward the less enlightened.

We appointed the next morning at half-past eleven for my father's visit.

"Not a minute later," Janet said in my ear, urgently. "Don't—don't let him move out of your sight, Harry! The princess is convinced you are not to blame."

I asked her whether she had any knowledge of the squire's designs.

"I have not, on my honour," she answered. "But I hope . . . It is so miserable to think of this disgraceful thing! She is too firm to give way. She does not blame you. I am sure I do not; only, Harry, one always feels that if one were in another's place, in a case like this, I could and would command him. I would have him obey me. One is not born to accept disgrace even from a father. I should say, 'You shall not stir, if you mean to act dishonourably.' One is justified, I am sure, in breaking a tie of relationship that involves you in dishonour. Grandada has not spoken a word to me on the subject. I catch at straws. This thing burns me! Oh, good-night, Harry. I can't sleep."

"Good night," she called softly to Temple on the stairs below. I heard the poor fellow murmuring good-night to himself in the street, and thought him happier than I. He slept at a room close to the hotel.

A note from Clara Goodwin adjured me, by her memory of the sweet, brave, gracious fellow she loved in other days, to be worthy of what I had been. The General had unnerved her reliance on me.

I sat up for my father until long past midnight. When he came his appearance reminded me of the time of his altercation with Baroness Turckems under the light of the blazing curtains : he had supped and drunk deeply, and he very soon proclaimed that I should find him invincible, which, as far as insensibility to the strongest appeals to him went, he was.

"Deny you love her, deny she loves you, deny you are one —I knot you fast !"

He had again seen Prince Ernest ; so he said, declaring that the prince positively desired the marriage ; would have it. "And I," he dramatized their relative situations, "consented."

After my experience of that night, I forgive men who are unmoved by displays of humour. Commonly we think it should be irresistible. His description of the thin-skinned sensitive prince striving to run and dodge for shelter from him, like a fever-patient pursued by a North-easter, accompanied by dozens of quaint similes full of his mental laughter, made my loathing all the more acute. But I had not been an equal match for him previous to his taking wine ; it was waste of breath and heart to contend with him. I folded my arms tight, sitting rigidly silent, and he dropped on the sofa luxuriously.

"Bed, Richie!" he waved to me. "You drink no wine, you cannot stand dissipation as I do. Bed, my dear boy ! I am a God, sir, inaccessible to mortal ailments ! Seriously, dear boy, I have never known an illness in my life. I have killed my hundreds of poor devils who were for imitating me. This I boast—I boast constitution. And I fear, Richie, you have none of my superhuman strength. Added to that, I know I am watched over. I ask—I have : I scheme—the tricks are in my hand ! It may be the doing of my mother in heaven ; there is the fact for you to reflect on. ' Stand not in my way, nor follow me too far,' would serve me for a motto admirably, and you can put it in Latin, Richie. Bed ! You shall turn your scholarship to account as I do my genius in your interest. On my soul, that motto in Latin will require me. Now to bed.'"

"No," said I. "You have got away from me once. I shall keep you in sight and hearing, if I have to lie at your door for it. You will go with me to London to-morrow. I shall treat you as a man I have to guard, and I shall not let you loose before I am quite sure of you."

"Loose !" he exclaimed, throwing up an arm and a leg.

" I mean, sir, that you shall be in my presence wherever you are, and I will take care you don't go far and wide. It's useless to pretend astonishment. I don't argue and I don't beseech any further : I just sit on guard, as I would over a powder-cask."

My father raised himself on an elbow, " The explosion," he said, examining his watch, " occurred at about five minutes to eleven—we are advancing into the morning—last night. I received on your behalf the congratulations of friends Loftus, Alton, Segrave, and the rest, at that hour. So, my dear Richie, you are sitting on guard over the empty magazine."

I listened with a throbbing forehead, and controlled the choking in my throat, to ask him whether he had touched the newspapers.

" Ay, dear lad, I have sprung my mine in them," he replied.

" You have sent word—— ?"

" I have despatched a paragraph to the effect that the prince and princess have arrived to ratify the nuptial preliminaries."

" You expect it to appear this day ?"

" Or else my name and influence are curiously at variance with the confidence I repose in them, Richie."

" Then I leave you to yourself," I said. " Prince Ernest knows he has to expect this statement in the papers ?"

" We trumped him with that identical court-card, Richie."

" Very well. To-morrow, after we have been to my grandfather, you and I part company for good, sir. It costs me too much."

" Dear old Richie," he laughed, gently. " And now to bye-bye ! My blessing on you now and always."

He shut his eyes.

CHAPTER LI.

AN ENCOUNTER SHOWING MY FATHER'S GENIUS IN A STRONG LIGHT.

THE morning was sultry with the first rising of the sun. I knew that Ottilia and Janet would be out. For myself, I dared not leave the house. I sat in my room, harried by the most penetrating snore which can ever have afflicted wakeful ears. It proclaimed so deep-seated a peacefulness in the bosom of the disturber, and was so arrogant, so ludicrous, and inaccessible to remonstrance, that it sounded like a renewal of our midnight altercation on the sleeper's part. Prolonged now and then beyond all bounds, it ended in the crashing blare whereof utter wakefulness cannot imagine honest sleep to be capable, but a playful melody twirled back to the regular note. He was fast asleep on the sitting-room sofa, while I walked fretting and panting. To this twinship I seemed condemned. In my heart nevertheless there was a reserve of wonderment at his apparent astuteness and resolution, and my old love for him whispered disbelief in his having disgraced me. Perhaps it was wilful self-deception. It helped me to meet him with a better face.

We both avoided the subject of our difference for some time: he would evidently have done so altogether, and used his best and sweetest manner to divert me: but when I struck on it, asking him if he had indeed told me the truth last night, his features clouded as though with an effort of patience. To my consternation he suddenly broke away, with his arms up, puffing and stammering, stamping his feet. He would have a truce—he insisted on a truce, I understood him to exclaim, and that I was like a woman, who would and would not, and wanted a master. He raved of the gallant downrightedness of the young bloods of his day, and how splendidly this one and that had compassed their ends by winning great ladies, lawfully, or otherwise. For several minutes he was in a state of frenzy, appealing to his pattern youths of a bygone generation as to moral principles—stuttering, and of a dark red hue from the neck to the temples. I refrained from a scuffle of tongues. Nor did he excuse himself after he had cooled. His hand touched instinctively for his pulse, and, with a glance at the ceiling, he exclaimed, " Good Lord ! " and brought me to his side. " These wigwam houses check my circulation," said he. " Let us go out—let us breakfast on board."

The open air restored him, and he told me that he had been merely oppressed by the architect of the inferior classes, whose ceiling sat on his head. My nerves, he remarked to me, were very excitable. " You should take your wine, Richie,—you require it. Your dear mother had a low-toned nervous system." I was silent, and followed him, at once a captive and a keeper.

This day of slackened sails and a bright sleeping water kept the yachtsmen on land ; there was a crowd to meet the morning boat. Foremost among those who stepped out of it was the yellow-haired Eckart, little suspecting what the sight of him signalled to me. I could scarcely greet him at all, for in him I perceived that my father had fully committed himself to his plot, and left me nothing to hope. Eckart said something of Prince Hermann. As we were walking off the pier, I saw Janet conversing with Prince Ernest, and the next minute Hermann himself was one of the group. I turned to Eckart for an explanation.

" Didn't I tell you he called at your house in London, and travelled down with me this morning ! " said Eckart.

My father looked in the direction of the princes, but his face was for the moment no index. They bowed to Janet, and began talking hurriedly in the triangle of road between her hotel, the pier, and the way to the villas : passing on, and coming to a full halt, like men who are not reserving their minds. My father stept out toward them. He was met by Prince Ernest. Hermann turned his back.

It being the hour of the appointment, I delivered Eckart over to Temple's safe-keeping, and went up to Janet. " Don't be late, Harry," she said.

I asked her if she knew the object of the meeting appointed by my grandfather.

She answered impatiently : " Do get him away from the prince." And then : " I ought to tell you the princess is well, and so on—pardon me just now: Grandada is kept waiting, and I don't like it."

Her actual dislike was to see Prince Ernest in dialogue with my father, it seemed to me; and the manner of both, which was, one would have said, intimate, anything but the manner of adversaries. Prince Ernest appeared to affect a pleasant humour; he twice, after shaking my father's hand, stepped back to him, as if to renew some impression. Their attitude declared them to be on the best of terms. Janet withdrew her attentive eyes from observing them, and threw a world of meaning into her abstracted gaze at me. My father's advance put her to flight. Yet she gave him the welcome of a high-bred young woman when he entered the drawing-room of my grandfather's hotel-suite. She was alone, and she obliged herself to accept conversation graciously. He recommended her to try the German Baths for the squire's gout, and evidently amused her with his specific probations for English persons designing to travel in company, that they should previously live together in a house with a collection of undisciplined chambermaids, a musical footman, and a mad cook: to learn to accommodate their tempers. "I would add a touch of earthquake, Miss Ilchester, just to make sure that all the party know one another's edges before starting." This was too far a shot of nonsense for Janet, whose native disposition was to refer to lunacy, or stupidity, or trickery, whatsoever was novel to her understanding. "I, for my part," said he, "stipulate to have for comrade no man who fancies himself a born and stamped chieftain, no inveterate student of maps, and no dog with a turn for feeling himself pulled by the collar. And that reminds me you are amateur of dogs. Have you a Pomeranian boar-hound?"

"No," said Janet; "I have never even seen one."

"That high." My father raised his hand flat.

"Bigger than our Newfoundlands!"

"Without exaggeration, big as a pony. You will permit me to send you one, warranted to have passed his distemper, which can rarely be done for our human species, though here and there I venture to guarantee my man as well as my dog."

Janet interposed her thanks, declining to take the dog, but he dwelt on the dog's charms, his youth, stature, appearance, fitness, and grandeur, earnestly. I had to relieve her apprehensions by questioning where the dog was.

"In Germany," he said.

It was not improbable, nor less so that the dog was in Pomerania likewise.

The entry of my aunt Dorothy, followed by my grandfather, was silent.

"Be seated," the old man addressed us in a body, to cut short particular salutations.

My father overshadowed him with drooping shoulders.

Janet wished to know whether she was to remain.

"I like you by me always," he answered, bluff and sharp.

"We have some shopping to do," my aunt Dorothy murmured, showing she was there against her will.

"Do you shop out of London?" said my father; and for some time he succeeded in making us sit for the delusive picture of a comfortable family meeting.

My grandfather sat quite still, Janet next to him. "When you've finished, Mr. Richmond," he remarked.

"Mr. Beltham, I was telling Miss Beltham that I join in the abuse of London exactly because I love it. A paradox! she says. But we seem to be effecting a kind of insurance on the life of the things we love best by crying them down violently. You have observed it? Denounce them—they endure for ever! So I join any soul on earth in decrying our dear London. The naughty old City can bear it."

There was a clearing of throats. My aunt Dorothy's foot tapped the floor.

"But I presume you have done me the honour to invite me to this conference on a point of business, Mr. Beltham?" said my father, admonished by the hint.

"I have, sir," the squire replied.

"And I also have a point. And, in fact, it is urgent, and with your permission, Mr. Beltham, I will lead the way."

"No, sir, if you please. I'm a short speaker, and go to it at once, and I won't detain you a second after you've answered me."

My father nodded to this, with the conciliatory comment that it was business-like.

The old man drew out his pocket-book.

"You paid a debt," he said deliberately, "amounting to twenty-one thousand pounds to my grandson's account."

"Oh! a debt! I did, sir. Between father and boy, dad and lad; debts! . . . . but use your own terms, I pray you."

"I don't ask you where that money is now. I ask you to tell me where you got it from."

"You speak bluntly, my dear sir."

"You won't answer, then?"

"You ask the question as a family matter? I reply with alacrity, to the best of my ability: and with my hand on my heart, Mr. Beltham, let me assure you, I very heartily desire the information to be furnished to me. Or rather—why should I conceal it? The sources are irregular, but a child could toddle its way to them: you take my indication. Say that I obtained it from my friends. *My* friends, Mr. Beltham, are of the kind requiring squeezing. Government, as my chum and good comrade, Jorian DeWitt, is fond of saying, is a sponge—a thing that when you dive deep enough to catch it gives liberal supplies, but will assuredly otherwise reverse the process by acting the part of an absorbent. I get what I get by force of arms, or I might have perished long since."

"Then you don't know where you got it from, sir?"

"Technically you are correct, sir."

"A bird didn't bring it, and you didn't find it in the belly of a fish."

"Neither of these prodigies. They have occurred in books I am bound to believe; they did *not* happen to me."

"You swear to me you don't know the man, woman, or committee, who gave you that sum?"

"I do not know, Mr. Beltham. In an extraordinary history, extraordinary circumstances! I have experienced so many that I am surprised at nothing."

"You suppose you got it from some fool?"

"Oh! if you choose to indict Government collectively?"

"You pretend you got it from Government?"

"I am termed a Pretender by some, Mr. Beltham. The facts are these: I promised to refund the money, and I fulfilled the promise. There you have the only answer I can make to you. Now to my own affair. I come to request you to demand the hand of the Princess of Eppenwelzen-Sarkeld on behalf of my son Harry, your grandson; and I possess the assurance of the prince, her father, that it will be granted. Doubtless you, sir, are of as old a blood as the prince himself. You will acknowledge that the honour brought to the family by an hereditary princess is considerable : it is something. I am prepared to accompany you to his Highness, or not, as you please : his English is of a falter in character. Still it is but a question of dotation, and a selection from one of two monosyllables."

Janet shook her dress.

The squire replied : "We'll take that up presently. I haven't quite done. Will you tell me what agent paid you the sum of money ?"

"The usual agent—a solicitor, Mr. Beltham; a gentleman whose business lay amongst the aristocracy; he is defunct ; and a very worthy old gentleman he was, with a remarkable store of anecdotes of his patrons, very discreetly told : for you never heard a name from him."

"You took him for an agent of Government, did you ? why ?"

"To condense a long story, sir, the kernel of the matter is, that almost from the hour I began to stir for the purpose of claiming my rights—which are transparent enough—this old gentleman—certainly from no sinister motive, I may presume—commenced the payment of an annuity ; not sufficient for my necessities, possibly, but warrant of an agreeable sort for encouraging my expectations ; although oddly, this excellent old Mr. Bannerbridge invariably served up the dish in a sauce that did not agree with it, by advising me of the wish of the donator that I should abandon my Case. I consequently, in common with my friends, performed a little early lesson in arithmetic, and we came to the one conclusion open to reflective minds—namely, that I was feared."

My aunt Dorothy looked up for the first time.

"Janet and I have some purchases to make," she said.

The squire signified sharply that she must remain where she was.

"I think aunty wants fresh air ; she had a headache last night," said Janet.

I suggested that, as my presence did not seem to be required, I could take her on my arm for a walk to the pierhead.

Her face was burning; she would gladly have gone out,

but the squire refused to permit it, and she nodded over her crossed hands, saying that she was in no hurry.

"Ha! I am," quoth he.

"Dear Miss Beltham!" my father ejaculated solicitously.

"Here, sir, oblige me by attending to me," cried the squire, fuming and blinking. "I sent for you on a piece of business. You got this money through a gentleman, a solicitor, named Bannerbridge, did you?"

"His name was Bannerbridge, Mr. Beltham."

"Dorothy, you knew a Mr. Bannerbridge?"

She faltered: "I knew him. . . . . Harry was lost in the streets of London when he was a little fellow, and the Mr. Bannerbridge I knew found him and took him to his house, and was very kind to him."

"What was his Christian name?"

I gave them: "Charles Adolphus."

"The identical person!" exclaimed my father.

"Oh! you admit it," said the squire. "Ever seen him since the time Harry was lost, Dorothy?"

"Yes," she answered, "I have heard he is dead."

"Did you see him shortly before his death?"

"I happened to see him a short time before."

"He was your man of business, was he?"

"For such little business as I had to do."

"You were sure you could trust him, eh?"

"Yes."

My aunt Dorothy breathed deeply.

"By God, ma'am, you're a truthful woman!"

The old man gave her a glare of admiration.

It was now my turn to undergo examination, and summoned by his apostrophe to meet his eyes, I could appreciate the hardness of the head I had to deal with.

"Harry, I beg your pardon beforehand; I want to get at facts; I must ask you what you know about where the money came from?"

I spoke of my attempts to discover the whence and wherefore of it.

"Government? eh?" he sneered.

"I really can't judge whether it came from that quarter," said I.

"What do you think?—think it likely?"

I thought it unlikely, and yet likelier than that it should have come from an individual.

"Then you don't suspect any particular person of having sent it in the nick of time, Harry Richmond?"

I replied: "No, sir; unless you force me to suspect you."

He jumped in his chair, astounded and wrathful, confounded me for insinuating that he was a Bedlamite, and demanded the impudent reason of my suspecting him to have been guilty of the infernal folly.

I had but the reason to instance that he was rich and kind at heart.

"Rich! kind!" he bellowed. "Just excuse me—I must ask for the purpose of my inquiry;—there, tell me, how much do you believe you've got of that money remaining? None o' that Peterborough style of counting in the back of your pate. Say!"

There was a dreadful silence.

My father leaned persuasively forward.

"Mr. Beltham, I crave permission to take up the word. Allow me to remind you of the prize Harry has won. The prince awaits you to bestow on him the hand of his daughter——"

"Out with it, Harry," shouted the squire.

"Not to mention Harry's seat in Parliament," my father resumed, "he has a princess to wife, indubitably one of the most enviable positions in the country! It is unnecessary to count on future honours; they may be alluded to. In truth, sir, we make him the first man in the country. Not necessarily Premier: you take my meaning: he possesses the combination of social influence and standing with political achievements, and rank and riches in addition——"

"I'm speaking to my grandson, sir," the squire rejoined, shaking himself like a man rained on. "I'm waiting for a plain answer, and no lie. You've already confessed as much as that the money you told me on your honour you put out to interest;—psh!—for my grandson was smoke. Now let's hear him."

My father called out: "I claim a hearing! The money you speak of *was* put out to the very highest interest. You have your grandson in Parliament, largely acquainted with the principal members of society, husband of an hereditary princess! You have only at this moment to propose for her hand. I guarantee it to you. With that money I have won him everything. Not that I would intimate to you that princesses are purchaseable. The point is, I knew how to employ it."

"In two months' time, the money in the Funds in the boy's name—you told me that."

"You had it in the Funds in Harry Richmond's name, sir."

"Well, sir, I'm asking him whether it's in the Funds now."

"Oh! Mr. Beltham."

"What answer's that?"

The squire was really confused by my father's interruption, and lost sight of me.

"I ask where it came from: I ask whether it's squandered?" he continued.

"Mr. Beltham, I reply that you have only to ask for it to have it; do so immediately."

"What's he saying?" cried the baffled old man.

"I give you a thousand times the equivalent of the money, Mr. Beltham."

"Is the money there?"

"The lady is here."

"I said money, sir."

"A priceless honour and treasure, I say emphatically."

My grandfather's brows and mouth were gathering for storm. Janet touched his knee.

"Where the devil your understanding truckles, if you have any, I don't know," he muttered. "What the deuce—lady got to do with money!"

"Oh!" my father laughed lightly, "customarily the alliance is, they say, as close as matrimony. Pardon me. To speak with becoming seriousness, Mr. Beltham, it was duly imperative that our son should be known in society, should be, you will apprehend me, advanced in station, which I had to do through the ordinary political channel. There could not but be a considerable expenditure for such a purpose."

"In Balls, and dinners!"

"In everything that builds a young gentleman's repute."

"You swear to me you gave your Balls and dinners, and the lot, for Harry Richmond's sake?"

"On my veracity, I did, sir!"

"Please don't talk like a mountebank. I don't want any of your roundabout words for truth; we're not writing a Bible essay. I try my best to be civil."

My father beamed on him.

"I guarantee you succeed, sir. Nothing on earth can a man be so absolutely sure of as to succeed in civility, if he honestly tries at it. Jorian DeWitt,—by the way, you may not know him—an esteemed old friend of mine, says—that is, he said once—to a tolerably impudent fellow whom he had disconcerted with a capital retort, 'You may try to be a gentleman, and blunder at it, but if you will only try to be his humble servant we are certain to establish a common feoting.' Jorian, let me tell you, is a wit worthy of our glorious old days."

My grandfather eased his heart with a plunging breath. "Well, sir, I didn't ask you here for your opinion or your friend's, and I don't care for modern wit."

"Nor I, Mr. Beltham, nor I! It has the reek of stable straw. We are of one mind on that subject. The thing slouches, it sprawls. It—to quote Jorian once more—is like a dirty, idle, little stupid boy who cannot learn his lesson and plays the fool with the alphabet. You smile, Miss Ilchester: you would appreciate Jorian. Modern wit is emphatically degenerate. It has no scintillation, neither thrust nor parry. I compare it to boxing, as opposed to the more beautiful science of fencing."

"Well, sir, I don't want to hear your comparisons," growled the squire, much oppressed. "Stop a minute . . ."

"Half a minute to me, sir," said my father, with a glowing reminiscence of Jorian DeWitt, which was almost too much for the combustible old man, even under Janet's admonition.

My aunt Dorothy moved her head slightly toward my father, looking on the floor, and he at once drew in.

"Mr. Beltham, I attend to you submissively."

"You do? Then tell me what brought this princess to England?"

"The conviction that Harry had accomplished his oath to mount to an eminence in his country, and had made the step she is about to take less, I will say, precipitous: though I personally decline to admit a pointed inferiority."

" You wrote her a letter."

" That, containing the news of the attack on him and his desperate illness, was the finishing touch to the noble lady's passion."

"Attack ? I know nothing about an attack. You wrote her a letter and wrote her a lie. You said he was dying."

" I had the boy inanimate on my breast when I despatched the epistle."

" You said he had only a few days to live."

" So in my affliction I feared."

"Will you swear you didn't write that letter with the intention of drawing her over here to have her in your power, so that you might threaten you'd blow on her reputation if she or her father held out against you and all didn't go as you fished for it ?"

My father raised his head proudly.

"I divide your query into two parts. I wrote, sir, to bring her to his side. I did not write with any intention to threaten."

" You've done it, though."

" I have done this," said my father, toweringly : " I have used the power placed in my hands by Providence to over-come the hesitations of a gentleman whose illustrious rank predisposes him to sacrifice his daughter's happiness to his pride of birth and station. Can any one confute me when I assert that the princess loves Harry Richmond ?"

I walked abruptly to one of the windows, hearing a pitiable wrangling on the theme. My grandfather vowed she had grown wiser, my father protested that she was willing and anxious; Janet was appealed to. In a strangely-sounding underbreath, she said, " The princess does not wish it."

" You hear that, Mr. Richmond ?" cried the squire.

He returned : " Can Miss Ilchester say that the Princess Ottilia does not passionately love my son Harry Richmond ? The circumstances warrant me in beseeching a direct answer."

She uttered : " No."

I looked at her ; she at me.

" You can conduct a case, Richmond," the squire re-marked.

My father rose to his feet. " I can conduct my son to happiness and greatness, my dear sir; but to some extent I require your grandfatherly assistance; and I urge you now to present your respects to the prince and princess, and judge yourself of his Highness's disposition for the match. I assure you in advance that he welcomes the proposal."

"I do not believe it," said Janet, rising.

My aunt Dorothy followed her example, saying: "In justice to Harry the proposal should be made. At least it will settle this dispute."

Janet stared at her, and the squire threw his head back with an amazed interjection.

"What! You're for it now? Why, at breakfast you were all t'other way! You didn't want this meeting because you pooh-poohed the match."

"I do think you should go," she answered. "You have given Harry your promise, and if he empowers you, it is right to make the proposal, and immediately, I think."

She spoke feverishly, with an unsweet expression of face, that seemed to me to indicate vexedness at the squire's treatment of my father.

"Harry," she asked me in a very earnest fashion, "is it your desire? Tell your grandfather that it is, and that you want to know your fate. Why should there be any dispute on a fact that can be ascertained by crossing a street? Surely it is trifling."

Janet stooped to whisper in the squire's ear.

He caught the shock of unexpected intelligence apparently; faced about, gazed up, and cried: "You too! But I haven't done here. I've got to cross-examine . . . . Pretend, do you mean? Pretend I'm ready to go? I can release this prince just as well here as there."

Janet laughed faintly.

"I should advise your going, grandada."

"*You* a weathercock woman!" he reproached her, quite mystified, and fell to rubbing his head. "Suppose I go to be snubbed?"

"The prince is a gentleman, grandada. Come with me. We will go alone. You can relieve the prince, and protect him."

My father nodded: "I approve."

"And grandada—but it will not so much matter if we are alone, though," Janet said.

"Speak out."

"See the princess as well; she must be present."

"I leave it to you," he said, crestfallen.

Janet pressed my aunt Dorothy's hand.

"Aunty, you were right, you are always right. This state of suspense is bad all round, and it is infinitely worse for the prince and princess."

My aunt Dorothy accepted the eulogy with a singular trembling wrinkle of the forehead.

She evidently understood that Janet had seen her wish to get released.

For my part, I shared my grandfather's stupefaction at their unaccountable changes. It appeared almost as of my father had won them over to baffle him. The old man tried to insist on their sitting down again, but Janet perseveringly smiled and smiled until he stood up. She spoke to him softly. He was one black frown; displeased with her; obedient, however.

Too soon after, I had the key to the enigmatical scene. At the moment I was contemptuous of riddles, and heard with idle ears Janet's promptings to him and his replies. "It would be so much better to settle it here," he said. She urged that it could not be settled here without the whole burden and responsibility falling upon him.

"Exactly," interposed my father triumphing.

Dorothy Beltham came to my side, and said, as if speaking to herself, while she gazed out of window: "If a refusal, it should come from the prince." She dropped her voice: "The money has not been spent? Has it? Has any part of it been spent? Are you sure you have more than three parts of it?"

Now, that she should be possessed by the spirit of parsimony on my behalf at such a time as this, was to my conception insanely comical, and her manner of expressing it was too much for me. I kept my laughter under to hear her continue: "What numbers are flocking on the pier! and there is no music yet. Tell me, Harry, that the money is all safe; nearly all; it is important to know; you promised economy."

"Music did you speak of, Miss Beltham?" My father bowed to her gallantly. "I chanced to overhear you. My private band performs to the public at midday."

She was obliged to smile to excuse his interruption.

"What's that? whose band?" said the squire, bursting out of Janet's hand. "A private band?"

Janet had a difficulty in resuming her command of him. The mention of the private band made him very restive.

"I'm not acting on my own judgement at all in going to these foreign people," he said to Janet. "Why go? I can have it out here and an end to it, without bothering them and their interpreters."

He sung out to me: "Harry, do you want me to go through this form for you? —mn'd unpleasant!"

My aunt Dorothy whispered in my ear: "Yes! yes!"

"I feel tricked!" he muttered, and did not wait for me to reply before he was again questioning my aunt Dorothy concerning Mr. Bannerbridge, and my father as to "that sum of money." But his method of interrogation was confused and pointless. The drift of it was totally obscure.

"I'm off my head to-day," he said to Janet, with a side-shot of his eye at my father.

"You waste time and trouble, grandada," said she.

He vowed that he was being bewildered, bothered by us all; and I thought I had never seen him so far below his level of energy; but I had not seen him condescend to put himself upon a moderately fair footing with my father. The truth was, that Janet had rigorously schooled him to bridle his temper, and he was no match for the voluble easy man without the freest play of his tongue.

"This prince!" he kept ejaculating.

"Won't you understand, grandada, that you relieve him, and make things clear by going?" Janet said.

He begged her fretfully not to be impatient, and hinted that she and he might be acting the part of dupes, and was for pursuing his inauspicious cross-examination in spite of his blundering, and the "Where am I now?" which pulled him up. My father, either talking to my aunt Dorothy, to Janet, or to me, on ephemeral topics, scarcely noticed him, except when he was questioned, and looked secure of success in the highest degree consistent with perfect calmness.

"So you say you tell me to go, do you?" the squire called to me. "Be good enough to stay here and wait. I don't see that anything's gained by my going: it's damned hard on me, having to go to a man whose language I don't know, and he don't know mine, on a business we're all of us in a muddle about. I'll do it if it's right. You're sure?"

He glanced at Janet. She nodded.

I was looking for this quaint and, to me, incomprehensible interlude to commence with the departure of the squire and Janet, when a card was handed in by one of the hotel-waiters.

"Another prince!" cried the squire. "These Germans seem to grow princes like potatoes—dozens to a root! Who's the card for? Ask him to walk up. Show him into a quiet room. Does he speak English?"

"Does Prince Hermann of—I can't pronounce the name of the place—speak English, Harry?" Janet asked me.

"As well as you or I," said I, losing my inattention all at once with a mad leap of the heart.

Hermann's presence gave light, fire, and colour to the scene in which my destiny had been wavering from hand to hand without much more than amusedly interesting me, for I was sure that I had lost Ottilia; I knew that too well, and worse could not happen. I had besides lost other things that used to sustain me, and being reckless, I was contemptuous, and listened to the talk about money with sublime indifference to the subject: with an attitude, too, I daresay. But Hermann's name revived my torment. Why had he come? to persuade the squire to control my father? Nothing but that would suffer itself to be suggested, though conjectures lying in shadow underneath pressed ominously on my mind.

My father had no doubts.

"A word to you, Mr. Beltham, before you go to Prince Hermann. He is an emissary, we treat him with courtesy, and if he comes to diplomatize we, of course, give a patient hearing. I have only to observe in the most emphatic manner possible that I do not retract one step. I will have this marriage: I have spoken! It rests with Prince Ernest."

The squire threw a hasty glare of his eyes back as he was hobbling on Janet's arm. She stopped short, and replied for him.

"Mr. Beltham will speak for himself, in his own name. We are not concerned in any unworthy treatment of Prince Ernest. We protest against it."

"Dear young lady!" said my father, graciously. "I meet you frankly. Now tell me. I know you a gallant horse-woman: if you had lassoed the noble horse of the desert would you let him run loose because of his remonstrating? Side with me, I entreat you! My son is my first thought. The pride of princes and wild horses you will find wonder-fully similar, especially in the way they take their taming when once they feel they are positively caught. We show him we have him fast—he falls into our paces on the spot! For Harry's sake—for the princess's, I beg you exert your universally-deservedly acknowledged influence. Even now —and you frown on me!—I cannot find it in my heart to wish you the sweet and admirable woman of the world you are destined to be, though you would comprehend me and applaud me, for I could not—no, not to win your favourable opinion!—consent that you should be robbed of a single ray of your fresh maidenly youth. If you must misjudge me, I submit. It is the price I pay for seeing you young and lovely. Prince Ernest is, credit me, not unworthily treated by me, if life is a battle, and the prize of it to the General's head. I implore you"—he lured her with the dimple of a lurking smile—" do not seriously blame your afflicted senior, if we are to differ. I am vastly your elder: you instil the doubt whether I am by as much the wiser of the two; but the father of Harry Richmond claims to know best what will ensure his boy's felicity. Is he rash? Pronounce me guilty of an excessive anxiety for my son's welfare; say that I am too old to read the world with the accuracy of a youthful intelligence: call me indiscreet: stigmatize me unlucky; the severest sentence a judge"—he bowed to her deferentially—" can utter; only do not cast a gaze of rebuke on me because my labour is for my son—my utmost devo-tion. And we know, Miss Ilchester, that the princess honours him with her love. I protest in all candour, I treat love as love; not as a weight in the scale; it is the heavenly power which dispenses with weighing! its ascendancy . . ."

The squire could endure no more, and happily so, for my father was losing his remarkably moderated tone, and threatening polysyllables. He had followed Janet, step for step, at a measured distance, drooping toward her with his winningest air, while the old man pulled at her arm to get her out of hearing of the obnoxious flatterer. She kept her long head in profile, trying creditably not to appear discourteous to one who addressed her by showing an open ear, until the final bolt made by the frenzied old man dragged her through the doorway. His neck was shortened behind his collar as though he shrugged from the blast of a bad wind. I believe that, on the whole, Janet was pleased. I will wager that, left to herself, she would have been drawn into an answer, if not an argument. Nothing would have made her resolution swerve, I admit.

They had not been out of the room three seconds when my aunt Dorothy was called to join them. She had found time to say that she hoped the money was intact.

CHAPTER LII.

STRANGE REVELATIONS, AND MY GRANDFATHER HAS HIS LAST OUTBURST.

My father and I stood at different windows, observing the unconcerned people below.

"Did you scheme to bring Prince Hermann over here as well?" I asked him.

He replied laughing: "I really am not the wonderful wizard you think me, Richie. I left Prince Ernest's address as mine with Waddy in case the Frau Feld-Marschall should take it into her head to come. Further than that you must question Providence, which I humbly thank for its unfailing support, down to unexpected trifles. Only this—to you and to all of them: nothing bends me. I will not be robbed of the fruit of a life-time."

"Supposing I refuse?"

"You refuse, Richie, to restore the princess her character and the prince his serenity of mind at their urgent supplication? I am utterly unable to suppose it. You are married in the papers this morning. I grieve to say that the position of Prince Hermann is supremely ridiculous. I am bound to add he is a bold boy. It requires courage in one of the pretenders to the hand of the princess to undertake the office of intercessor, for he must know—the man must know in his heart that he is doing her no kindness. He does not appeal to me, you see. I have shown that my arrangements are unalterable. What he will make of your grandad! . . . Why on earth he should have been sent to—of all men in the world—your grandad, Richie!"

I was invited to sympathetic smiles of shrewd amusement.

He caught sight of friends, and threw up the window, saluting them.

The squire returned with my aunt Dorothy and Janet to behold the detested man communicating with the outer world from his own rooms. He shouted unceremoniously, " Shut that window !" and it was easy to see that he had come back heavily armed for the offensive. " Here, Mr. Richmond, I don't want all men to know you're in my apartments."

" I forgot, sir, temporarily," said my father, " I had vacated the rooms for your convenience—be assured."

An explanation on the subject of the rooms ensued between the old man and the ladies ;—it did not improve his temper.

His sense of breeding, nevertheless, forced him to remark, " I can't thank you, sir, for putting me under an obligation I should never have incurred myself."

" Oh, I was happy to be of use to the ladies, Mr. Beltham, and require no small coin of exchange," my father responded, with the flourish of a pacifying hand. " I have just heard from a posse of friends that the marriage is signalled in this morning's papers—numberless congratulations, I need not observe."

" No, don't," said the squire. " Nobody'll understand them here, and I needn't ask you to sit down, because I don't want you to stop. I'll soon have done now ; the game's played. Here, Harry, quick ; has all that money been spent—no offence to you, but as a matter of business ?"

" Not all, sir," I was able to say.

" Half ?"

" Yes, I think so."

" Three parts ?"

" It may be."

" And liabilities besides ?"

" There are some."

" You're not a liar. That'll do for you."

He turned to my aunt : her eyes had shut.

"Dorothy, you've sold out twenty-five thousand pounds' worth of stock. You're a truthful woman, as I said, and so I won't treat you like a witness in a box. You gave it to Harry to help him out of his scrape. Why, short of staring lunacy, did you pass it through the hands of this man? He sweated his thousands out of it at the start. Why did you make a secret of it to make the man think his nonsense?— Ma'am, behave like a lady and my daughter," he cried, fronting her, for the sudden and blunt attack had slackened her nerves; she moved as though to escape, and was bewildered. I stood overwhelmed. No wonder she had attempted to break up the scene.

"Tell me your object, Dorothy Beltham, in passing the money through the hands of this man? Were you for helping him to be a man of his word? Help the boy—that I understand. However, you were mistress of your money! I've no right to complain, if you will go spending a fortune to whitewash the blackamoor! Well, it's your own, you'll say! So it is: so's your character!"

The egregious mildness of these interjections could not long be preserved.

"You deceived me, ma'am. You wouldn't build schoolhouses, you couldn't subscribe to Charities, you acted parsimony, to pamper a scamp and his young scholar! You went to London—you did it in cool blood; you went to your stockbroker, and from the stockbroker to the Bank, and you sold out stock to fling away this big sum. I went to the Bank on business, and the books were turned over for my name, and there at 'Beltham' I saw quite by chance the cross of the pen, and I saw your folly, ma'am; I saw it all in a shot. I went to the Bank on my own business, mind that. Ha! you know me by this time; I loathe spying; the thing jumped out of the book; I couldn't help seeing. Now I don't reckon how many positive fools go to make one superlative humbug; you're one of the lot, and I've learnt it."

My father airily begged leave to say: "As to positive and superlative, Mr. Beltham, the three degrees of comparison are no longer of service except to the trader. I do not consider them to exist for ladies. Your positive is always particularly open to dispute, and I venture to assert I cap you your superlative ten times over."

He talked the stuff for a diversion, presenting in the

midst of us an incongruous image of smiles that filled me
with I knew not what feelings of angry alienation, until I
was somewhat appeased by the idea that he had not apprehended the nature of the words just spoken.

It seemed incredible, yet it was true; it was proved to be
so to me by his pricking his ears and his attentive look at
the mention of the word prepossessing him in relation to the
money: Government.

The squire said something of Government to my aunt
Dorothy, with sarcastical emphasis.

As the observation was unnecessary, and was wantonly
thrown in by him, she seized on it to escape from her com-
promising silence: " I know nothing of Government or its
ways."

She murmured further, and looked at Janet, who came to
her aid, saying: " Grandada, we've had enough talk of
money, money! All is done that you wanted done. Stocks,
Shares, Banks—we've gone through them all. Please finish!
Please, do. You have only to state what you have heard
from Prince Hermann."

Janet gazed in the direction of my father, carefully
avoiding my eyes, but evidently anxious to shield my
persecuted aunty.

" Speaking of Stocks and Shares, Miss Ilchester," said my
father, " I myself would as soon think of walking into a
field of scytheblades in full activity as of dabbling in them.
One of the few instances I remember of our Jorian stooping
to a pun, is upon the contango: ingenious truly, but objectionable, because a pun. I shall not be guilty of repeating
it. ' The stock-market is the national snapdragon bowl,' he
says, and is very amusing upon the Jews; whether quite
fairly, Mr. Beltham knows better than I, on my honour."

He appealed lightly to the squire, for thus he danced on
the crater's brink, and had for answer,—

" You're a cool scoundrel, Richmond."

" I choose to respect you, rather in spite of yourself, I
fear, sir," said my father, bracing up.

" Did you hear my conversation with my daughter ?"

" I heard, if I may say so, the lion taking his share of it."

" All roaring to you, was it ?"

" Mr. Beltham, we have our little peculiarities; I am
accustomed to think of a steam-vent when I hear you

indulging in a sentence of unusual length, and I hope it is for our good, as I thoroughly believe it is for yours, that you should deliver yourself freely."

" So you tell me ; like a stage lacquey !" muttered the old man, with surprising art in caricaturing a weakness in my father's bearing, of which I was cruelly conscious, though his enunciation was flowing. He lost his naturalness through forcing for ease in the teeth of insult.

" Grandada, aunty and I will leave you," said Janet, waxing importunate.

" When I've done," said he, facing his victim savagely. " The fellow pretends he didn't understand. She's here to corroborate. Richmond, there, my daughter, Dorothy Beltham, there's the last of your fools and dupes. She's a truthful woman, I'll own, and she'll contradict me if what I say is not the fact. That twenty-five thousand from ' Government ' came out of her estate."

" Out of—— ?"

" Out of——be damned, sir! She's the person who paid it."

" If the ' damns ' have set up, you may as well let the ladies go," said I.

He snapped at me like a rabid dog in career.

" She's the person—one of your petticoat ' Government ' —who paid—do you hear me, Richmond?—the money to help you to keep your word: to help you to give your Balls and dinners too. She—I won't say she told you, and you knew it—she paid it. She sent it through her Mr. Banner-bridge. Do you understand now ? *You* had it from *her*. My God! look at the fellow !"

A dreadful gape of stupefaction had usurped the smiles on my father's countenance; his eyes rolled over, he tried to articulate, and was indeed a spectacle for an enemy. His convulsed frame rocked the syllables, as with a groan, unpleasant to hear, he called on my aunt Dorothy by succes-sive stammering apostrophes to explain, spreading his hands wide. He called out her Christian name. Her face was bloodless.

" Address my daughter respectfully, sir, will you! I won't have your infernal familiarities !" roared the squire.

" He is my brother-in-law," said Dorothy, reposing on the courage of her blood, now that the worst had been spoken

" Forgive me, Mr. Richmond, for having secretly induced you to accept the loan from me."

" Loan !" interjected the squire. " They fell upon it like a pair of kites. You'll find the last ghost of a bone of your loan in a bill, and well picked. They've been doing their bills: I've heard that."

My father touched the points of his fingers on his forehead, straining to think, too theatrically, but in hard earnest, I believe. He seemed to be rising on tiptoe.

" Oh, madam ! Dear lady ! my friend ! Dorothy, my sister ! Better a thousand times that I had married, though I shrank from a heartless union ! This money ?—it is not——"

The old man broke in : " Are you going to be a damned low vulgar comedian and tale of a trumpet up to the end, you Richmond ? Don't think you'll gain anything by standing there as if you were jumping your trunk from a shark. Come, sir, you're in a gentleman's rooms ; don't pitch your voice like a young jackanapes blowing into a horn. Your gasps and your spasms, and howl of a yawning brute ! Keep your menagerie performances for your pantomime audiences. What are you meaning? Do you pretend you're astonished? She's not the first fool of a woman whose money you've devoured, with your ' Madam,' and ' My dear ' and mouthing and elbowing your comedy tricks ; your gabble of ' Government' protection, and scandalous advertisements of the by-blow of a star-coated rapscallion. If you've a recollection of the man in you, show your back, and be off, say you've fought against odds—I don't doubt you have, counting the constables—and own you're a villain : plead guilty, and be off and be silent, and do no more harm. Is it ' Government' still ? "

My aunt Dorothy had come round to me. She clutched my arm to restrain me from speaking, whispering : " Harry, you can't save him. Think of your own head."

She made me irresolute, and I was too late to check my father from falling into the trap.

" Oh ! Mr. Beltham," he said, " you are hard, sir. I put it to you : had you been in receipt of a secret subsidy from Government for a long course of years—— "

" How long ? " the squire interrupted.

Prompt though he would have been to dismiss the hateful person, he was not, one could see, displeased to use the whip upon so excitable and responsive a frame. He seemed to me to be basely guilty of leading his victim on to expose himself further.

"There's no necessity for 'how long,'" I said.

The old man kept the question on his face.

My father reflected.

"I have to hit my memory, I am shattered, sir. I say, you would be justified, amply justified——"

"How long?" was reiterated.

"I can at least date it from the period of my marriage."

"From the date when your scoundrelism first touches my family, that's to say! So, 'Government' agreed to give you a stipend to support your wife!"

"Mr. Beltham, I breathe with difficulty. It was at that period, on the death of a nobleman interested in restraining me—I was his debtor for kindnesses. . . . . my head is whirling! I say, at that period, upon the recommendation of friends of high standing, I began to agitate for the restitution of my rights. From infancy——"

"To the deuce, your infancy! I know too much about your age. Just hark, you Richmond! none of your 'I was a child' to provoke compassion from women. I mean to knock you down and make you incapable of hurting these poor foreign people you trapped. They defy you, and I'll do my best to draw your teeth. Now for the annuity. You want one to believe you thought you frightened 'Government,' eh?"

"Annual proof was afforded me, sir."

"Oh! annual! through Mr. Charles Adolphus Bannerbridge, deceased!"

Janet stepped up to my aunt Dorothy to persuade her to leave the room, but she declined, and hung by me, to keep me out of danger, as she hoped, and she prompted me with a guarding nervous squeeze of her hand on my arm to answer temperately when I was questioned: "Harry, do you suspect Government paid that annuity?"

"Not now, certainly."

"Tell the man who 'tis you suspect."

My aunt Dorothy said: "Harry is not bound to mention his suspicions."

"Tell him yourself, then."

"Does it matter—— ?"

"Yes, it matters. I'll break every plank he walks on, and strip him stark till he flops down shivering into his slough—a convicted common swindler, with his dinners and Balls and his private bands! Richmond, you killed one of my daughters; t'other fed you, through her agent, this Mr. Charles Adolphus Bannerbridge, from about the date of your snaring my poor girl and carrying her off behind your postillions—your trotting undertakers!—and the hours of her life reckoned in milestones. She's here to contradict me, if she can. Dorothy Beltham was your 'Government' that paid the annuity."

I took Dorothy Beltham into my arms. She was trembling excessively, yet found time to say: "Bear up, dearest; keep still." All I thought and felt foundered in tears.

For a while I heard little distinctly of the tremendous tirade which the vindictive old man, rendered thrice venomous by the immobility of the petrified large figure opposed to him, poured forth. My poor father did not speak because he could not; his arms drooped; and such was the torrent of attack, with its free play of thunder and lightning in the form of oaths, epithets, short and sharp comparisons, bitter home thrusts and most vehement imprecatory denunciations, that our protesting voices quailed. Janet plucked at my aunt Dorothy's dress to bear her away.

"I can't leave my father," I said.

"Nor I you, dear," said the tender woman; and so we remained to be scourged by this tongue of incarnate rage.

"You pensioner of a silly country spinster!" sounded like a return to mildness. My father's chest heaved up.

I took advantage of the lull to make myself heard: I did but heap fuel on fire, though the old man's splenetic impetus had partly abated.

"You Richmond! do you hear him? he swears he's your son, and asks to be tied to the stake beside you. Disown him, and I'll pay you money and thank you. I'll thank my God for anything short of your foul blood in the family. You married the boy's mother to craze and kill her, and guttle her property. You waited for the boy to come of age to swallow what was settled on him. You wait for me to lie in my coffin to pounce on the strong-box you think me the fool to toss to a young donkey ready to ruin all his belongings for you! For nine-and-twenty years you've sucked the veins of my family, and struck through my house like a rotting-disease. Nine-and-twenty years ago you gave a singing-lesson in my house: the pest has been in it ever since! You breed vermin in the brain, to think of you! Your wife, your son, your dupes, every soul that touches you, mildews from a blight! You were born of ropery, and you go at it straight, like a webfoot to water. What's your boast?—your mother's disgrace! You shame your mother. Your whole life's a ballad o' bastardy. You cry up the woman's infamy to hook at a father. You swell and strut on her pickings. You're a cock forced from the smoke of the dunghill! You shame your mother, damned adventurer! You train your boy for a swindler after your own pattern; you twirl him in your curst harlequinade to a damnation as sure as your own. The day you crossed my threshold the devils danced on their flooring. I've never seen the sun shine fair on me after it. With your guitar under the windows, of moonlight nights! your Spanish fopperies and trickeries! your French phrases and toeings! I was touched by a leper. You set your traps for both my girls: you caught the brown one first, did you, and flung her second for t'other, and drove a tandem of 'em to live the spangled hog you are; and down went the mother of the boy to the place she liked better, and my other girl here— the one you cheated for her salvation—you tried to cajole her from home and me, to send her the same way down. She stuck to decency. Good Lord! you threatened to hang yourself, guitar and all. But her purse served your turn. For why? You're a leech. I speak before ladies or I'd rip your town-life to shreds. Your cause! your romantic history! your fine figure! every inch of you's notched with villany! You fasten on every moneyed woman that comes in your way. You've outdone Herod in murdering the innocents, for he didn't feed on 'em and they've made you fat. One thing I'll say of you: you look the beastly thing you set yourself up for. The kindest blow to you's to call you impostor."

He paused, but his inordinate passion of speech was unsated: his white lips hung loose for another eruption.

I broke from my aunt Dorothy to cross over to my father, saying on the way: "We've heard enough, sir. You forget the cardinal point of invective, which is, not to create sympathy for the person you assail."

" Oh ! you come in with your infernal fine language, do you !" the old man thundered at me. " I'll just tell you at once, young fellow——"

My aunt Dorothy supplicated his attention. " One error I must correct." Her voice issued from a contracted throat, and was painfully thin and straining, as though the will to speak did violence to her weaker nature. " My sister loved Mr. Richmond. It was to save her life, because I believed she loved him much and would have died, that Mr. Richmond—in pity—offered her his hand, at my wish :" she bent her head : " at my cost. It was done for me. I wished it; he obeyed me. No blame——" her dear mouth faltered. " I am to be accused, if anybody."

She added more firmly : " My money would have been his. I hoped to spare his feelings, I beg his forgiveness now, by devoting some of it, unknown to him, to assist him. That was chiefly to please myself, I see, and I am punished."

" Well, ma'am," said the squire, calm at white heat ; " a fool's confession ought to be heard out to the end. What about the twenty-five thousand ?"

" I hoped to help my Harry."

" Why didn't you do it openly ? "

She breathed audible long breaths before she could summon courage to say : " His father was going to make an irreparable sacrifice. I feared that if he knew this money came from me he would reject it, and persist."

Had she disliked the idea of my father's marrying ?

The old man pounced on the word sacrifice. " What sacrifice, ma'am ? What's the sacrifice ?"

I perceived that she could not without anguish, and perhaps peril of a further exposure, bring herself to speak, and explained : " It relates to my having tried to persuade my father to marry a very wealthy lady, so that he might produce the money on the day appointed. Rail at me, sir, as much as you like. If you can't understand the circumstances without a chapter of statements, I'm sorry for you. A great deal is due to you, I know ; but I can't pay a jot of it while you go on rating my father like a madman."

" Harry !" either my aunt or Janet breathed a warning.

I replied that I was past mincing phrases. The folly of giving the tongue an airing was upon me : I was in fact invited to continue, and animated to do it thoroughly, by the old man's expression of face, which was that of one who says, "I give you rope," and I dealt him a liberal amount of stock irony not worth repeating; things that any cultivated man in anger can drill and sting the Bœotian with, under the delusion that he has not lost a particle of his self-command because of his coolness. I spoke very deliberately, and therefore supposed that the words of composure were those of prudent sense. The error was manifest. The women saw it. One who has indulged his soul in invective will not, if he has power in his hand, be robbed of his climax with impunity by a cool response that seems to trifle, and scourges.

I wound up by thanking my father for his devotion to me: I deemed it, I said, excessive and mistaken in the recent instance, but it was for me.

Upon this he awoke from his dreamy-looking stupefaction.

"Richie does me justice. He is my dear boy. He loves me: I love him. None can cheat us of that. He loves his wreck of a father. You have struck me to your feet, Mr. Beltham."

"I don't want to see you there, sir; I want to see you go, and not stand rapping your breast-bone, sounding like a burst drum, as you are," retorted the unappeasable old man.

I begged him in exasperation to keep his similes to himself.

Janet and my aunt Dorothy raised their voices.

My father said: "I am broken."

He put out a swimming hand that trembled when it rested, like that of an aged man grasping a staff. I feared for a moment he was acting, he spoke so like himself, miserable though he appeared: but it was his well-known native old style in a state of decrepitude.

"I am broken," he repeated. "I am like the ancient figure of mortality entering the mouth of the tomb on a sepulchral monument, somewhere, by a celebrated sculptor: I have seen it: I forget the city. I shall presently forget names of men. It is not your abuse, Mr. Beltham. I should have bowed my head to it till the storm passed. Your facts. . . . Oh! Miss Beltham, this last privilege to call you dearest of human beings! my benefactress! my blessing! Do not scorn me, madam."

"I never did; I never will; I pitied you," she cried, sobbing.

The squire stamped his foot.

"Madam," my father bowed gently, "I was under heaven's special protection—I thought so. I feel I have been robbed —I have not deserved it! Oh! madam, no: it was your generosity that I did not deserve. One of the angels of heaven persuaded me to trust in it. I did not know. . . . Adieu, madam. May I be worthy to meet you!—Ay, Mr. Beltham, your facts have committed the death-wound. You have taken the staff out of my hand: you have extinguished the light. I have existed—ay, a pensioner, unknowingly, on this dear lady's charity; to her I say no more. To you, sir, by all that is most sacred to a man—by the ashes of my mother! by the prospects of my boy! I swear the annuity was in my belief a tangible token that my claims to consideration were in the highest sources acknowledged to be just. I cannot speak! One word to you, Mr. Beltham: put me aside, I am nothing:—Harry Richmond!—his fortunes are not lost; he has a future! I entreat you—he is your grandson—give him your support; go this instant to the prince—no! you will not deny your countenance to Harry Richmond:—let him abjure my name; let me be nameless in his house. And I promise you I shall be unheard of both in Christendom and Heathendom: I have no heart except for my boy's nuptials with the princess: this one thing, to see him the husband the fairest and noblest lady upon earth, with all the life remaining in me I pray for! I have won it for him. I have a moderate ability, immense devotion. I declare to you, sir, I have lived, actually subsisted, on this hope! and I have directed my efforts incessantly, sleeplessly, to fortify it. I die to do it!—I implore you, sir, go to the prince. If I" (he said this touchingly)—"if I am any further in anybody's way, it is only as a fallen tree." But his inveterate fancifulness led him to add: "And that may bridge a cataract."

My grandfather had been clearing his throat two or three times.

"I'm ready to finish and get rid of you, Richmond."

My father bowed.

"I am gone, sir. I feel I am all but tongue-tied. Think

that it is Harry who petitions you to ensure his happiness. To-day I guarantee it."

The old man turned an inquiring eyebrow upon me. Janet laid her hand on him. He dismissed the feline instinct to prolong our torture, and delivered himself briskly.

"Richmond, your last little bit of villany's broken in the egg. I separate the boy from you: he's not your accomplice there, I'm glad to know. You witched the lady over to pounce on her like a fowler, you threatened her father with a scandal, if he thought proper to force the trap; swore you'd toss her to be plucked by the gossips, eh? She's free of you! You got your English and your Germans here to point their bills, and stretch their necks, and hiss, if this gentleman—and your newspapers!—if he didn't give up to you like a funky traveller to a highwayman. I remember a tale of a clumsy Turpin, who shot himself when he was drawing the pistol out of his holsters to frighten the money-bag out of a market farmer. You've done about the same, you Richmond; and, of all the damned poor speeches I ever heard from a convicted felon, yours is the worst—a sheared sheep'd ha' done it more respectably, grant the beast a tongue! The lady is free of you, I tell you. Harry has to thank you for that kindness. She—what is it, Janet? Never mind, I've got the story—she didn't want to marry; but this prince, who called on me just now, happened to be her father's nominee, and he heard of your scoundrelism, and he behaved like a man and a gentleman, and offered himself, none too early nor too late, as it turns out; and the princess, like a good girl, has made amends to her father by accepting him. I've the word of this Prince Hermann for it. Now you can look upon a game of stale-mate. If I had gone to the prince, it wouldn't have been to back your play; but, if you hadn't been guilty of the tricks of a blackguard past praying for, this princess would never have been obliged to marry a man to protect her father and herself. They sent him here to stop any misunderstanding. He speaks good English, so that's certain. Your lies will be contradicted, every one of 'em, seriatim, in to-morrow's newspapers, setting the real man in place of the wrong one; and you'll draw no profit from them in your fashionable world, where you've been grinning lately, like a blackamoor's head on a conjuror's plate—the devil alone able to account for the body and joinings. Now you can be off."

I went up to my father. His plight was more desperate than mine, for I had resembled the condemned before the firing-party, to whom the expected bullet brings a merely physical shock. He, poor man, heard his sentence, which is the heart's pang of death; and how fondly and rootedly he had clung to the idea of my marriage with the princess was shown in his extinction after this blow.

My grandfather chose the moment as a fitting one to ask me for the last time to take my side.

I replied, without offence in the tones of my voice, that I thought my father need not lose me into the bargain, after what he had suffered that day.

He just as quietly rejoined with a recommendation to me to divorce myself for good and all from a scoundrel.

I took my father's arm: he was not in a state to move away unsupported.

My aunt Dorothy stood weeping; Janet was at the window, no friend to either of us.

I said to her, "You have your wish."

She shook her head, but did not look back.

My grandfather watched me, step by step, until I had reached the door.

"You're going, are you?" he said. "Then I whistle you off my fingers!"

An attempt to speak was made by my father in the door-way. He bowed wide of the company, like a blind man. I led him out.

Dimness of sight spared me from seeing certain figures, which were at the toll-bar of the pier, on the way to quit our shores. What I heard was not of a character to give me faith in the sanity of the companion I had chosen. He murmured it at first to himself:

"Waddy shall have her monument!"

My patience was not proof against the repetition of it aloud to me. Had I been gentler I might have known that his nature was compelled to look forward to something, and he discerned nothing in the future, save the task of raising a memorial to a faithful servant.

CHAPTER LIII.

THE HEIRESS PROVES THAT SHE INHERITS THE FEUD AND I GO DRIFTING.

MY grandfather lived eight months after a scene that had afforded him high gratification at the heaviest cost a plain man can pay for his pleasures : it killed him.

My father's supple nature helped him to survive it in apparently unimpeded health, so that the world might well suppose him unconquerable, as he meant that it should. But I, who was with him, knew, though he never talked of his wounds, they had been driven into his heart. He collapsed in speech, and became what he used to call " one of the ordinary nodding men," forsaken of his swamping initiative. I merely observed him ; I did not invite his confidences, being myself in no mood to give sympathy or to receive it. I was about as tender in my care of him as a military escort bound to deliver up a captive alive.

I left him at Bulsted on my way to London to face the creditors. Adversity had not lowered the admiration of the captain and his wife for the magnificent host of those select and lofty entertainments which I was led by my errand to examine in the skeleton, and with a wonder as big as theirs, but of another complexion. They hung about him, and perused and petted him quaintly; it was grotesque; they thought him deeply injured : by what, by whom, they could not say ; but Julia was disappointed in me for refraining to come out with a sally on his behalf. He had quite intoxicated their imaginations. Julia told me of the things he did not do as marvellingly as of the things he did or had done ; the charm, it seemed, was to find herself familiar with him to the extent of all but nursing him and making him belong to her. Pilgrims coming upon the source of the mysteriously-abounding river, hardly revere it the less because they love it more when they behold the babbling channels it issues from ; and the sense of possession is the secret, I suppose. Julia could inform me rapturously that her charge had slept eighteen hours at a spell. His remarks upon the proposal to fetch a doctor, feeble in themselves, were delicious to her, because they recalled his old humour

to show his great spirit, and from her and from Captain
William in turn I was condemned to hear how he had said
this and that of the doctor, which in my opinion might have
been more concise. " Really, deuced good indeed!" Captain
William would exclaim. " Don't you see it, Harry, my boy ?
He denies the doctor has a right to cast him out of the
world on account of his having been the official to introduce
him, and he'll only consent to be visited when he happens
to be as incapable of resisting as upon their very first
encounter."

The doctor and death and marriage, I ventured to remind
the captain, had been riddled in this fashion by the whole
army of humourists and their echoes. He and Julia fancied
me cold to my father's merits. Fond as they were of the
squire, they declared war against him in private, they
criticized Janet, they thought my aunt Dorothy slightly
wrong in making a secret of her good deed : my father was
the victim. Their unabated warmth consoled me in the
bitterest of seasons. He found a home with them at a time
when there would have been a battle at every step. The
world soon knew that my grandfather had cast me off, and
with this foundation destroyed, the entire fabric of the
Grand Parade fell to the ground at once. The crash was
heavy. Jorian DeWitt said truly that what a man hates in
adversity is to see " faces " ; meaning that the humanity has
gone out of them in their curious observation of you under
misfortune. You see neither friends nor enemies. You are
too sensitive for friends, and are blunted against enemies.
You see but the mask of faces : my father was sheltered
from that. Julia consulted his wishes in everything ; she
set traps to catch his whims, and treated them as birds of
paradise ; she could submit to have the toppling crumpled
figure of a man, Bagenhope, his pensioner and singular comforter, in her house. The little creature was fetched out of
his haunts in London purposely to sooth my father with
performances on his ancient clarionet, a most querulous
plaintive instrument in his discoursing, almost the length of
himself ; and she endured the nightly sound of it in the
guest's blue bedroom, heroically patient, a model to me.
Bagenhope drank drams : she allowanced him. He had
known my father's mother, and could talk of her in his
cups : his playing, and his aged tunes, my father said, were

a certification to him that he was at the bottom of the
ladder. Why that should afford him peculiar comfort, none
of us could comprehend. "He was the humble lover of my
mother, Richie," I heard with some confusion, and that he
adored her memory. The statement was part of an entreaty
to me to provide liberally for Bagenhope's pension before we
quitted England. "I am not seriously anxious for much
else," said my father. Yet was he fully conscious of the
defeat he had sustained and the catastrophe he had brought
down upon me: his touch of my hand told me that, and his
desire for darkness and sleep. He had nothing to look to,
nothing to see twinkling its radiance for him in the dim
distance now; no propitiating Government, no special Providence. But he never once put on a sorrowful air to press
for pathos, and I thanked him. He was a man endowed to
excite it in the most effective manner, to a degree fearful
enough to win English sympathies despite his un-English
faults. He could have drawn tears in floods, infinite pathetic
commiseration, from our grangousier public, whose taste is
to have it as it may be had to the mixture of one-third of
nature in two-thirds of artifice. I believe he was expected
to go about with this beggar's petition for compassion, and
it was a disappointment to the generous, for which they
punished him, that he should have abstained. And moreover his simple quietude was really touching to true-hearted
people. The elements of pathos do not permit of their being
dispensed from a stout smoking bowl. I have to record
no pathetic field-day. My father was never insincere in
emotion.

I spared his friends, chums, associates, excellent men of a
kind, the trial of their attachment by shunning them. His
servants I dismissed personally, from M. Alphonse down to
the coachman Jeremy, whose speech to me was, that he
should be happy to serve my father again, or me, if he
should happen to be out of a situation when either of us
wanted him, which at least showed his preference for employment: on the other hand, Alphonse, embracing the
grand extremes of his stereotyped national oratory, where
"SI JAMAIS," like the herald Mercury new-mounting, takes
its august flight to set in the splendour of "JUSQU'À LA
MORT," declared all other service than my father's repug-
nant, and vowed himself to a hermitage, remote from

condiments. They both meant well, and did but speak the diverse language of their blood. Mrs. Waddy withdrew a respited heart to Dipwell; it being, according to her experiences, the third time that my father had relinquished house and furniture to go into eclipse on the Continent after blazing over London. She strongly recommended the Continent for a place of restoration, citing his likeness to that animal the chameleon, in the readiness with which he forgot himself among them that knew nothing of him. We quitted Bulsted previous to the return of the family to Riversley. My grandfather lay at the island hotel a month, and was brought home desperately ill. Lady Edbury happened to cross the channel with us. She behaved badly, I thought; foolishly, my father said. She did as much as obliqueness of vision and sharpness of feature could help her to do to cut him in the presence of her party: and he would not take nay. It seemed in very bad taste on his part; he explained to me off-handedly that he insisted upon the exchange of a word or two for the single purpose of protecting her from calumny. By and by it grew more explicable to me how witless she had been to give gossip a handle in the effort to escape it. She sent for him in Paris, but he did not pay the visit.

My grandfather and I never saw one another again. He had news of me from various quarters, and I of him from one; I was leading a life in marked contrast with the homely Riversley circle of days: and this likewise was set in the count of charges against my father. Our Continental pilgrimage ended in a course of riotousness that he did not participate in, and was entirely innocent of, but was held accountable for, because he had been judged a sinner.

"I am ordered to say," Janet wrote, scrupulously obeying the order, "that if you will leave Paris, and come home, and not delay in doing it, your grandfather will receive you on the same footing as heretofore."

As heretofore! in a letter from a young woman supposed to nourish a softness toward me!

I could not leave my father in Paris, alone; I dared not bring him to London. In wrath at what I remembered, I replied that I was willing to return to Riversley if my father should find a welcome as well.

Janet sent a few dry lines to summon me over in April, a pleasant month on heath-lands when the South-west sweeps them. The squire was dead. I dropped my father at Bulsted. I could have sworn to the terms of the Will; Mr. Burgin had little to teach me. Janet was the heiress; three thousand pounds per annum fell to the lot of Harry Lepel Richmond, to be paid out of the estate, and pass in reversion to his children, or to Janet's should the aforesaid Harry die childless.

I was hard hit, and chagrined, but I was not at all angry, for I knew what the Will meant. My aunt Dorothy supplied the interlining eagerly to mollify the seeming cruelty. "You have only to ask to have it all, Harry." The sturdy squire had done his utmost to forward his cherished wishes after death. My aunt received five-and-twenty thousand pounds, the sum she had thrown away. "I promised that no money of mine should go where the other went," she said.

The surprise in store for me was to find how much this rough-worded old man had been liked by his tenantry, his agents and servants. I spoke of it to Janet. "They loved him," she said. "No one who ever met him fairly could help loving him." They followed him to his grave in a body. From what I chanced to hear among them, their squire was the man of their hearts : in short, an Englishman of the kind which is perpetually perishing out of the land. Janet expected me to be enthusiastic likewise, or remorseful. She expected sympathy; she read me the long list of his charities. I was reminded of Julia Bulsted commenting on my father, with her this he did and that. "He had plenty," I said, and Janet shut her lips. Her coldness was irritating.

What ground of accusation had she against me? Our situation had become so delicate that a cold breath sundered us as far as the Poles. I was at liberty to suspect that now she was the heiress, her mind was simply obedient to her grandada's wish; but, as I told my aunt Dorothy, I would not do her that injustice.

"No," said Dorothy; "it is the money that makes *her* position so difficult, unless you break the ice."

I urged that having steadily refused her before, I could hardly advance without some invitation now.

"What invitation?" said my aunt.

"Not a corpse-like consent," said I.

"Harry," she twitted me, "you have not forgiven her."

That was true.

Sir Roderick and Lady Ilchester did not conceal their elation at their daughter's vast inheritance, though the lady appealed to my feelings in stating that her son Charles was not mentioned in the Will. Sir Roderick talked of the squire with personal pride:—"Now as to his management of those unwieldy men, his miners : they sent him up the items of their complaints. He took them one by one, yielding here, discussing there, and holding to his point. So the men gave way; he sent them a month's pay to reward them for their good sense. He had the heart of moulding the men who served him in his own likeness. His capacity for business was extraordinary ; you never expected it of a country gentleman. He more than quadrupled his inheritance—much more!" I state it to the worthy Baronet's honour, that although it would have been immensely to his satisfaction to see his daughter attracting the suitor proper to an heiress of such magnitude, he did not attempt to impose restriction upon my interviews with Janet : Riversley was mentioned as my home. I tried to feel at home; the air of the place seemed foreign, and so did Janet. I attributed it partly to her deep mourning dress that robed her in so sedate a womanliness, partly, in spite of myself, to her wealth. "Speak to her kindly of your grandfather," said my aunt Dorothy. To do so, however, as she desired it, would be to be guilty of a form of hypocrisy, and I belied my better sentiments by keeping silent. Thus, having ruined myself through anger, I allowed silly sensitiveness to prevent the repair.

It became known that my father was at Bulsted.

I saw trouble one morning on Janet's forehead.

We had a conversation that came near to tenderness ; at last she said: "Will you be able to forgive me if I have ever the misfortune to offend you ?"

"You won't offend me," said I.

She hoped not.

I rallied her: "Tut, tut, you talk like any twelve-years-old, Janet."

"I offended you then !"

"Every day ! it's all that I care much to remember."

She looked pleased, but I was so situated that I required

passion and abandonment in return for a confession damaging to my pride. Besides, the school I had been graduating in of late unfitted me for a young English gentlewoman's shades and intervolved descents of emotion. A glance up and a dimple in the cheek, were pretty homely things enough, not the blaze I wanted to unlock me, and absolutely thought I had deserved.

Sir Roderick called her to the library on business, which he was in the habit of doing ten times a day, as well as of discussing matters of business at table, ostentatiously consulting his daughter, with a solemn countenance and a transparently reeling heart of parental exultation. "Janet is supreme," he would say: "my advice is simple advice; I am her chief agent, that is all." Her chief agent, as director of three Companies and chairman of one, was perhaps competent to advise her, he remarked. Her judgement upon ordinary matters he agreed with my grandfather in thinking consummate.

Janet went to him, and shortly after drove him to the station for London. My aunt Dorothy had warned me that she was preparing some deed in my favour, and as I fancied her father to have gone to London for that purpose, and supposed she would now venture to touch on it, I walked away from the East gates of the park as soon as I heard the trot of her ponies, and was led by an evil fate (the stuff the fates are composed of in my instance I have not kept secret) to walk Westward. Thither my evil fate propelled me, where accident was ready to espouse it and breed me mortifications innumerable. My father chanced to have heard the particulars of Squire Beltham's will that morning: I believe Captain William's coachman brushed the subject despondently in my interests; it did not reach him through Julia.

He stood outside the Western gates, and as I approached I could perceive a labour of excitement on his frame. He pulled violently at the bars of the obstruction.

"Richie, I am interdicted house and grounds!" he called, and waved his hand toward the lodge: "they decline to open to me."

"Were you denied admission?" I asked him.

" — Your name, if you please, sir? — Mr. Richmond Roy. — We are sorry we have orders not to admit you.

And they declined; they would not admit me to see my son."

"Those must be the squire's old orders," I said, and shouted to the lodge-keeper.

My father, with the forethoughtfulness which never forsook him, stopped me.

"No, Richie, no; the good woman shall not have the responsibility of letting me in against orders; she may be risking her place, poor soul! Help me, dear lad."

He climbed the bars to the spikes, tottering, and communicating a convulsion to me as I assisted him in the leap down: no common feat for one of his age and weight.

He leaned on me, quaking.

"Impossible! Richie, impossible!" he cried, and reviewed a series of interjections.

It was some time before I discovered that they related to the Will. He was frenzied, and raved, turning suddenly from red to pale under what I feared were redoubtable symptoms, physical or mental. He came for sight of the Will; he would contest it, overthrow it. Harry ruined? He would see Miss Beltham and fathom the plot;—angel, he called her, and was absurdly exclamatory, but in dire earnest. He must have had the appearance of a drunken man to persons observing him from the Grange windows.

My father was refused admission at the hall-doors.

The butler, the brute Sillabin, withstood me impassively. Whose orders had he?

Miss Ilchester's.

"They are afraid of me!" my father thundered.

I sent a message to Janet.

She was not long in coming, followed by a footman who handed a twist of note-paper from my aunt Dorothy to my father. He opened it and made believe to read it, muttering all the while of the Will.

Janet dismissed the men-servants. She was quite colourless.

"We have been stopped in the doorway," I said.

She answered: "I wish it could have been prevented."

"You take it on yourself then?"

She was inaudible.

"My dear Janet, you call Riversley my home, don't you?"

"It is yours."

"**Do** you intend to keep up this hateful feud now my grandfather is dead ?"

" No, Harry, not I."

" Did you give orders to stop my father from entering the house and grounds ?"

" I did."

" You won't have him here ?"

" Dear Harry, I hoped he would not come just yet."

" But you gave the orders ?"

" Yes."

" You're rather incomprehensible, my dear Janet."

" I wish you could understand me, Harry."

" You arm your servants against him !"

" In a few days———" she faltered.

" You insult him and me *now*," said I, enraged at the half indication of her relenting, which spoiled her look of modestly-resolute beauty, and seemed to show that she meant to succumb without letting me break her. " You are mistress of the place."

" I am. I wish I were not."

" You are mistress of Riversley, and you refuse to let my father come in !"

" While I am the mistress, yes."

" Why ?"

" Anywhere but here, Harry ! If he will see me or aunty, if he will kindly appoint any other place, we will meet him, we shall be glad."

" I request you to let him enter the house. Do you consent or not ?"

" No."

" He was refused once at these doors. Do you refuse him a second time ?"

" I do."

" You mean that ?"

" I am obliged to."

" You won't yield a step to me ?"

" I cannot."

The spirit of an armed champion was behind those mild features, soft almost to supplication to me that I might know her to be under a constraint. The nether lip dropped in breathing, the eyes wavered : such was her appearance in open war with me, but her will was firm.

Of course 1 was not so dense as to be unable to perceive her grounds for refusing.

She would not throw the burden on her grandada, even to propitiate me—the man she still loved.

But that she should have a reason, and think it good, in spite of me, and cling to it, defying me, and that she should do hurt to a sentient human creature, who was my father, for the sake of blindly obeying to the letter the injunction of the dead, were intolerable offences to me and common humanity. I, for my own part, would have forgiven her, as I congratulated myself upon reflecting. It was on her account—to open her mind, to enlighten her concerning right and wrong determination, to bring her feelings to bear upon a crude judgment—that I condescended to argue the case. Smarting with admiration, both of the depths and shallows of her character, and of her fine figure, I began: —She was to consider how young she was to pretend to decide on the balance of duties, how little of the world she had seen; an oath sworn at the bedside of the dead was a solemn thing, but was it Christian to keep it to do an unnecessary cruelty to the living? if she had not studied philosophy, she might at least discern the difference between just resolves and insane—between those the soul sanctioned, and those hateful to nature; to bind oneself to carry on another person's vindictiveness was voluntarily to adopt slavery; this was flatly-avowed insanity, and so forth, with an emphatic display of patience.

The truth of my words could not be controverted. Unhappily I confounded right speaking with right acting, and conceived, because I spoke so justly, that I was specially approved in pressing her to yield.

She broke the first pause to say, " It's useless, Harry. 1 do what I think I am bound to do."

" Then I have spoken to no purpose! "

" If you will only be kind, and wait two or three days ? "

" Be sensible! "

" I am, as much as I can be."

" Hard as a flint—you always were! The most grateful woman alive, I admit. I know not another, I assure you, Janet, who, in return for millions of money, would do such a piece of wanton cruelty. What! You think he was not punished enough when he was berated and torn to

shreds in your presence ? They would be cruel, perhaps—
we will suppose it of your sex—but not so fond of their consciences as to stamp a life out to keep an oath. I forget the
terms of the Will. Were you enjoined in it to force him
away ? "

My father had stationed himself in the background.
Mention of the Will caught his ears, and he commenced
shaking my aunt Dorothy's note, blinking and muttering at
a great rate, and pressing his temples.

"I do not read a word of this," he said,—"upon my
honour, not a word; and I know it is her handwriting.
That Will!—only, for the love of heaven, madam,"—he
bowed vaguely to Janet—"not a syllable of this to the princess, or we are destroyed. I have a great bell in my head,
or I would say more. Hearing is out of the question."

Janet gazed piteously from him to me.

To kill the deer and be sorry for the suffering wretch is
common.

I begged my father to walk along the carriage-drive. He
required that the direction should be pointed out accurately,
and promptly obeyed me, saying : "I back you, remember.
I should certainly be asleep now but for this extraordinary
bell." After going some steps, he turned to shout "Gong,"
and touched his ear. He walked loosely, utterly unlike the
walk habitual to him even recently in Paris.

"Has he been ill ? " Janet asked.

"He won't see the doctor; the symptoms threaten
apoplexy or paralysis, I'm told. Let us finish. You were
aware that you were to inherit Riversley ? "

"Yes, Riversley, Harry; I knew that; I knew nothing
else."

"The old place was left to you that you might bar my
father out ? "

"I gave my word."

"You pledged it—swore ? "

"No."

"Well, you've done your worst, my dear. If the axe
were to fall on your neck for it, you would still refuse,
would you not ? "

Janet answered softly : "I believe so."

"Then, good-bye," said I.

That feminine softness and its burden of unalterable

firmness pulled me two ways, angering me all the more that
I should feel myself susceptible to a charm which came of
spiritual rawness rather than sweetness; for she needed not
to have made the answer in such a manner; there was pride
in it; she liked the soft sound of her voice while declaring
herself invincible: I could see her picturing herself meek
but fixed.

"Will you go, Harry? Will you not take Riversley?"
she said.

I laughed.

"To spare you the repetition of the dilemma?"

"No, Harry; but this might be done."

"But—my fullest thanks to you for your generosity:
really! I speak in earnest:—it would be decidedly against
your grandada's wishes, seeing that he left the Grange to
you, and not to me."

"Grandada's wishes! I cannot carry out all his wishes,"
she sighed.

"Are you anxious to?"

We were on the delicate ground, as her crimson face
revealed to me that she knew as well as I.

I, however, had little delicacy in leading her on it. She
might well feel that she deserved some wooing.

I fancied she was going to be overcome, going to tremble
and show herself ready to fall on my bosom, and I was
uncertain of the amount of magnanimity in store there.

She replied calmly: "Not immediately."

"You are not immediately anxious to fulfil his wishes?"

"Harry, I find it hard to do those that are thrust on me."

"But, as a matter of serious obligation, you would hold
yourself bound by and by to perform them all?"

"I cannot speak any further of my willingness, Harry."

"The sense of duty is evidently always sufficient to make
you act upon the negative—to deny, at least?"

"Yes, I daresay," said Janet.

We shook hands like a pair of commercial men.

I led my father to Bulsted. He was too feverish to
remain there. In the evening, after having had a fruitless
conversation with my aunt Dorothy upon the event of the
day, I took him to London that he might visit his lawyers,
who kindly consented to treat him like doctors, when I had
arranged to make over to them three parts of my annuity,

and talked of his Case encouragingly; the effect of which should not have astonished me. He closed a fit of reverie resembling his drowsiness, by exclaiming: "Richie will be indebted to his dad for his place in the world after all!" Temporarily, he admitted, we must be fugitives from creditors, and as to that eccentric tribe, at once so human and so inhuman, he imparted many curious characteristics ga:ned of his experience. Jorian DeWitt had indeed compared them to the female ivy that would ultimately kill its tree, but inasmuch as they were parasites, they loved their debtor; he was life and support to them, and there was this remarkable fact about them : by slipping out of their clutches at critical moments when they would infallibly be pulling you down, you were enabled to return to them fresh, and they became inspired with another lease of lively faith in your future: et cetera. I knew the language. It was a flash of himself, and a bad one, but I was not the person whom he meant to deceive with it. He was soon giving me other than verbal proof out of England that he was not thoroughly beaten. We had no home in England. At an hotel in Vienna, upon the close of the aristocratic season there, he renewed an acquaintance with a Russian lady, Countess Kornikoff, and he and I parted. She disliked the Margravine of Rippau, who was in Vienna, and did not recognize us. I heard that it was the Margravine who had despatched Prince Hermann to England as soon as she discovered Ottilia's flight thither. She commissioned him to go straightway to Roy in London, and my father's having infatuatedly left his own address for Prince Ernest's in the island, brought Hermann down : he only met Eckart in the morning train. I mention it to show the strange working of events.

Janet sent me a letter by the hands of Temple in August. It was moderately well written for so blunt a writer, and might have touched me but for other news coming simultaneously that shook the earth under my feet.

She begged my forgiveness for her hardness, adding characteristically that she could never have acted in any other manner. The delusion that what she was she must always be, because it was her nature, had mastered her understanding, or rather it was one of the doors of her understanding not yet opened : she had to respect her grandada's wishes. She made it likewise appear that she was ready for further sacrifices to carry out the same.

" At least you will accept a division of the property, Harry. It should be yours. It is an excess, and I feel it a snare to me. I was a selfish child : I may not become an estimable woman. You have not pardoned my behaviour at the island last year, and I cannot think I was wrong : perhaps I might learn. I want your friendship and counsel. Aunty will live with me : she says that you would complete us. At any rate I transfer Riversley to you. Send me your consent. Papa *will* have it before the transfer is signed."

The letter ended with an adieu, a petition for an answer, and " yours affectionately."

On the day of its date, a Viennese newspaper lying on the Salzburg Hotel table chronicled Ottilia's marriage with Prince Hermann.

I turned on Temple to walk him off his legs if I could.

Carry your fever to the Alps, you of minds diseased : not to sit down in sight of them ruminating, for bodily ease and comfort will trick the soul and set you measuring our lean humanity against yonder sublime and infinite ; but mount, rack the limbs, wrestle it out among the peaks ; taste danger, sweat, earn rest : learn to discover ungrudgingly that haggard fatigue is the fair vision you have run to earth, and that rest is your uttermost reward. Would you know what it is to hope again, and have all your hopes at hand ?—hang upon the crags at a gradient that makes your next step a debate between the thing you are and the thing you may become. There the merry little hopes grow for the climber like flowers and food, immediate, prompt to prove their uses, sufficient if just within the grasp, as mortal hopes should be. How the old lax life closes in about you there ! You are the man of your faculties, nothing more. Why should a man pretend to more ? We ask it wonderingly when we are healthy. Poetic rhapsodists in the vales below may tell you of the joy and grandeur of the upper regions, they cannot pluck you the medical herb. He gets that for himself who wanders the marshy ledge at nightfall to behold the distant Sennhüttchen twinkle, who leaps the green-eyed crevasses, and in the solitude of an emerald alp stretches a salt hand to the mountain kine.

CHAPTER LIV.

MY RETURN TO ENGLAND.

I PASSED from the Alps to the desert, and fell in love with the East, until it began to consume me. History, like the air we breathe, must be in motion to keep us uncorrupt: otherwise its ancient homes are infectious. My passion for the sun and his baked people lasted awhile, the drudgery of the habit of voluntary exile some time longer, and then, quite unawares, I was seized with a thirst for England, so violent that I abandoned a correspondence of several months, lying for me both at Damascus and Cairo, to catch the boat for Europe. A dream of a rainy morning, in the midst of the glowing furnace, may have been the origin of the wild craving I had for my native land and Janet. The moist air of flying showers and drenched spring buds surrounded her; I saw her plainly lifting a rose's head; was it possible I had ever refused to be her yokefellow? Could so noble a figure of a fair young woman have been offered and repudiated again and again by a man in his senses? I spurned the intolerable idiot, to stop reflection. Perhaps she did likewise now. There was nothing to alarm me save my own eagerness. The news of my father was perplexing, leading me to suppose him re-established in London, awaiting the coming on of his Case. Whence the money?

Money and my father, I knew, met as they divided, fortuitously; in illustration of which, I well remembered, while passing in view of the Key of the Adige along the Lombard plain, a circumstance during my Alpine tour with Temple, of more importance to him than to me, when my emulous friend, who would never be beaten, sprained his ankle severely on the crags of a waterfall, not far from Innsbruck, and was invited into a house by a young English lady, daughter of a retired Colonel of Engineers of our army. The colonel was an exile from his country for no grave crime: but, as he told us, as much an exile as if he had committed a capital offence in being the father of nine healthy girls. He had been, against his judgement, he averred, persuaded to fix on his Tyrolese spot of ground by the two elder ones. Five were now married to foreigners; thus they repaid him, by scattering good English blood on the race of Counts and Freiherrs! "I could understand the decrees of Providence before I was a parent," said this dear old Colonel Heddon. "I was looking up at the rainbow when I heard your steps, asking myself whether it was seen in England at that instant, and why on earth I should be out of England!" He lived abroad to be able to dower his girls. His sons-in-law were gentlemen; so far he was condemned to be satisfied, but supposing all his girls married foreigners? His primitive frankness charmed us, and it struck me that my susceptible Temple would have liked to be in a position to re-assure him with regard to the Lucy of the four. We were obliged to confess that she was catching a foreign accent. The old colonel groaned. He begged us to forgive him for not treating us as strangers; his heart leapt out to young English gentlemen.

My name, he said, reminded him of a great character at home, in the old days: a certain Roy-Richmond, son of an actress and somebody, so the story went: and there was an old Lord Edbury who knew more about it than most. "Now Roy was an adventurer, but he had a soul of true chivalry, by gad, he had! Plenty of foreign whiffmajigs are to be found, but you won't come upon a fellow like that. Where he got his money from none knew: all I can say is, I don't believe he ever did a dirty action for it. And one matter I'll tell you of:—pardon me a moment, Mr. Richmond, I haven't talked English for half a century, or, at least, a quarter. Old Lord Edbury put him down in his will for some thousands, and he risked it to save a lady, who hated him for his pains. Lady Edbury was of the Bolton blood, none of the tamest; they breed good cavalry men. She ran away from her husband once. The old lord took her back. 'It's at your peril, mind!' says she. Well, Roy hears by-and-by of a fresh affair. He mounted horse; he was in the saddle, I've been assured, a night and a day, and posted himself between my lady's park-gates, and the house, at dusk. The rumour ran that he knew of the marquis playing spy on his wife. However, such was the fact; she was going off again, and the marquis did play the mean part. She walked down the park-road, and, seeing the cloaked figure of a man, she imagined him to be her Lothario, and very naturally, you will own, fell into his arms. The gentleman in question was an acquaintance of mine; and the less you follow our example the better for you. It was a damnable period in morals! He told me that he saw the scene from the gates, where he had his carriage-and-four ready. The old lord burst out of an ambush on his wife and her supposed paramour; the lady was imprisoned in her rescuer's arms, and my friend retired on tiptoe, which was, I incline to think, the best thing he could do. Our morals were abominable. Lady Edbury would never see Roy-Richmond after that, nor the old lord neither. He doubled the sum he had intended to leave him, though. I heard that he married a second young wife. Roy, I believe, ended by marrying a great heiress, and reforming. He was an eloquent fellow, and stood like a General in full uniform, cocked hat and feathers; most amusing fellow at table; beat a Frenchman for anecdote."

I spared Colonel Heddon the revelation of my relationship to his hero, thanking his garrulity for interrupting me.

How I pitied him when I drove past the gates of the main route to Innsbruck! For I was bound homeward: I should soon see England, green cloudy England, the white cliffs, the meadows, the heaths! And I thanked the colonel again in my heart for having done something to reconcile me to the idea of that strange father of mine.

A banner-like stream of morning-coloured smoke rolled North-eastward as I entered London, and I drove to Temple's chambers. He was in Court, engaged in a case as junior to his father. Temple had become that radiant human creature, a working man, then? I walked slowly to the Court, and saw him there, hardly recognizing him in his wig. All that he had to do was to prompt his father in a case of collision at sea; the barque Priscilla had run foul of a merchant brig, near the mouth of the Thames, and though I did not expect it on hearing the vessel's name, it proved to be no other than the barque Priscilla of Captain Jasper Welsh. Soon after I had shaken Temple's hand, I was going through the same ceremony with the captain himself, not at all changed in appearance, who blessed his heart for seeing me, cried out that a beard and mustachios made a foreign face of a young Englishman, and was full of the 'providential' circumstance of his having confided his case to Temple and his father.

"Ay, ay, Captain Welsh," said Temple, "we have pulled you through, only another time mind you keep an eye on that look-out man of yours. Some of your men, I suspect, see double with an easy conscience.   A close net makes slippery eels."

"Have you anything to say against my men?" the captain inquired.

Temple replied that he would talk to him about it presently, and laughed as he drew me away.

" His men will get him into a deuce of a scrape some day, Richie.   I shall put him on his guard.   Have you had all my letters?   You look made of iron.   I'm beginning capitally, not afraid of the Court a bit, and I hope I'm not pert.   I wish your father had taken it better!"

" Taken what?" said I.

" Haven't you heard from him?"

" Two or three times : a mass of interjections."

" You know he brought his Case forward at last?   Of course it went as we all knew it would."

" Where is he?   Have you seen Janet lately?"

" He is at Miss Ilchester's house in London."

" Write the address on a card."

Temple wrote it rather hesitatingly, I thought.

We talked of seeing one another in the evening, and I sprang off to Janet's residence, forgetting to grasp my old friend's hand at parting.   I was madly anxious to thank her for the unexpected tenderness to my father.   And now nothing stood between us!

My aunt Dorothy was the first to welcome me.   " He must be prepared for the sight of you, Harry.   The doctors say that a shock may destroy him.   Janet treats him so wonderfully."

I pressed her on my heart and cheered her, praising Janet. She wept.

" Is there anything new the matter?" I said.

" It's not new to us, Harry.   I'm sure you're brave?"

" Brave! what am I asked to bear?"

" Much, if you love her, Harry!"

" Speak."

" It is better you should hear it from me, Harry.   I wrote you word of it.   We all imagined it would not be disagreeable to you.   Who could foresee this change in you?   She least of all!"

" She's in love with some one?"

" I did not say in love."

"Tell me the worst."

"She is engaged to be married."

Janet came into the room—another Janet for me. She had engaged herself to marry the Marquis of Edbury. At the moment when she enslaved me with gratitude and admiration she was lost to me. I knew her too well to see a chance of her breaking her pledged word.

My old grandfather said of Janet, "She's a compassionate thing." I felt *now* the tears under his speech, and how late I was in getting wisdom. Compassion for Edbury in Janet's bosom was the matchmaker's chief engine of assault, my aunt Dorothy told me. Lady Ilchester had been for this suitor, Sir Roderick for the other, up to the verge of a quarrel between the most united of wedding couples. Janet was persecuted. She heard that Edbury's life was running to waste; she liked him for his cricketing and hunting, his frankness, seeming manliness, and general native English enthusiasm. I permitted myself to comprehend the case as far as I could allow myself to excuse her.

Dorothy Beltham told me something of Janet that struck me to the dust.

"It is this, dear Harry; bear to hear it! Janet and I and his good true woman of a housekeeper, whose name is Waddy, we are, I believe, the only persons that know it. He had a large company to dine at a City tavern, she told us, on the night after the decision—when the verdict went against him. The following morning I received a note from this good Mrs. Waddy addressed to Sir Roderick's London house, where I was staying with Janet; it said that he was ill; and Janet put on her bonnet at once to go to him."

"The lady didn't fear contagion any longer?"

"She went, walking fast. He was living in lodgings, and the people of the house insisted on removing him, Mrs. Waddy told us. She was cowering in the parlour. I had not the courage to go upstairs. Janet went by herself."

My heart rose on a huge swell.

"She was alone with him, Harry. We could hear them."

Dorothy Beltham looked imploringly on me to waken my whole comprehension.

"She subdued him. When I saw him he was white as death, but quiet, not dangerous at all."

"Do you mean she found him raving?" I cried out on our Maker's name, in grief and horror.

"Yes, dear Harry, it was so."

"She stepped between him and an asylum?"

"She quitted Sir Roderick's house to lodge your father safe in one that she hired, and have him under her own care. She watched him day and night for three weeks, and governed him, assisted only at intervals by the poor frightened woman, Mrs. Waddy, and just as frightened me. And I am still subject to the poor woman's way of pressing her hand to her heart at a noise. It's over now. Harry, Janet wished that you should never hear of it. She dreads any excitement for him. I think she is right in fancying her own influence the best: he is used to it. You know how gentle she is though she is so firm."

"Oh! don't torture me, ma'am, for God's sake," I called aloud.

CHAPTER LV.

I MEET MY FIRST PLAYFELLOW AND TAKE MY PUNISHMENT.

THERE came to me a little note on foreign paper, unaddressed, an enclosure forwarded by Janet, and containing merely one scrap from the playful XENIEN of Ottilia's favourite brotherly poets, of untranslatable flavour:—

> Who shuns true friends flies fortune in the concrete :
> Would he see what he aims at ? let him ask his heels.

It filled me with a breath of old German peace.

From this I learnt that Ottilia and Janet corresponded. Upon what topics ? to what degree of intimacy ?

Janet now confessed to me that their intimacy had never known reserve. The princess had divined her attachment for Harry Richmond when their acquaintance was commenced in the island, and knew at the present moment that I had travelled round to the recognition of Janet's worth.

Thus encouraged by the princess's changeless friendship, I wrote to her, leaving little to be guessed of my state of mind, withholding nothing of the circumstances surrounding me. Imagination dealt me all my sharpest misery, and now that Ottilia resumed her place there, I became infinitely peacefuller, and stronger to subdue my hungry nature. It caused me no pang, strangely though it read in my sight when written, to send warm greetings and respects to the prince her husband.

Is it any waste of time to write of love ? The trials of life are in it, but in a narrow ring and a fierier. You may learn to know yourself through love, as you do after years of life, whether you are fit to lift them that are about you, or whether you are but a cheat, and a load on the backs of your fellows. The impure perishes, the inefficient languishes, the moderate comes to its autumn of decay—these are of the kinds which aim at satisfaction to die of it soon or late. The love that survives has strangled craving; it lives because it lives to nourish and succour like the heavens.

But to strangle craving is indeed to go through a death before you reach your immortality.

But again, to write of a love perverted by all the elements contributing to foolishness, and foredoomed to chastisement, would be a graceless business. Janet and I went through our trial, she, you may believe, the braver under the most to bear.

I was taken by Temple down to the ship-smelling East of London, for the double purpose of trying to convince Captain Welsh of the extravagance of a piece of chivalry he was about to commit, and of seeing a lady with a history, who had recently come under his guardianship. Temple thought I should know her, but he made a mystery of it until the moment of our introduction arrived, not being certain of her identity, and not wishing to have me disappointed. It appeared that Captain Welsh questioned his men closely after he had won his case, and he arrived at the conclusion that two or three of them had been guilty of false swearing in his interests. He did not dismiss them, for, as he said, it was twice a bad thing to turn sinners loose : it was to shove them out of the direct road of amendment, and it was a wrong to the population. He insisted, however, on paying the legal costs and an indemnity for the collision at sea ; and Temple was in great distress about it, he having originally

suggested the suspicion of his men to Captain Welsh. " I
wanted to put him on his guard against those rascals,"
Temple said, " and I suppose," he sighed, " I wanted the old
captain to think me enormously clever all round." He
shook himself, and assumed a bearish aspect, significant of
disgust and recklessness. " The captain 'll be ruined,
Richie; and he's not young, you know, to go on sailing his
barque Priscilla, for ever. If he pays, why, I ought to pay,
and then you ought to pay, for I shouldn't have shown off
before him alone, and then the wind that fetched you ought
to pay. Toss common sense overboard, there's no end to
your fine-drawings ; that's why it's always safest to swear
by the Judge."

We rolled down to the masts among the chimneys on the
top of an omnibus. The driver was eloquent on cricket-
matches. Now, cricket, he said, was fine manly sport ; it
might kill a man, but it never meant mischief : foreigners
themselves had a bit of an idea that it was the best game in
the world, though it was a nice joke to see a foreigner playing at it ! None of them could stand to be bowled at.
Hadn't stomachs for it; they'd have to train for soldiers
first. On one occasion he had seen a Frenchman looking on
at a match. " Ball was hit a shooter twixt the slips : off
starts Frenchman, catches it, heaves it up, like his head,
half-way to wicket, and all the field set to bawling at him,
and sending him, we knew where. He tripped off : ' You no
comprong politeness in dis country.' Ha ! ha !"

To prove the aforesaid Frenchman wrong, we nodded to
the driver's laughter at his exquisite imitation.

He informed us that he had backed the Surrey Eleven
last year, owing to the report of a gentleman-bowler, who
had done things in the way of tumbling wickets to tickle the
ears of cricketers. Gentlemen-batters were common : gentle-
men-bowlers were quite another dish. Saddlebank was the
gentleman's name.

" Old Nandrew Saddle ?" Temple called to me, and we
smiled at the supposition of Saddlebank's fame, neither of
us, from what we had known of his bowling, doubting that
he deserved it.

" Acquainted with him, gentlemen ?" the driver inquired,
touching his hat. " Well, and I ask why don't more gentlemen take to cricket ? 'stead of horses all round the year !

Now, there's my notion of happiness," said the man condemned to inactivity, in the perpetual act of motion; "cricket in cricket season! It comprises—count: lots o' running; and that's good: just enough o' taking it easy; that's good: a appetite for your dinner, and your ale or your Port, as may be the case; good, number three. Add on a tired pipe after dark, and a sound sleep to follow, and you say good morning to the doctor and the parson; for you're in health body and soul, and ne'er a parson 'll make a better Christian of ye, that I'll swear."

As if anxious not to pervert us, he concluded: "That's what I think, gentlemen."

Temple and I talked of the ancient raptures of a first of May cricketing-day on a sunny green meadow, with an ocean of a day before us, and well-braced spirits for the match. I had the vision of a matronly, but not much altered Janet, mounted on horseback, to witness the performance of some favourite Eleven of youngsters with her connoisseur's eye; and then the model of an English lady, wife, and mother, waving adieu to the field and cantering home to entertain her husband's guests. Her husband!

Temple was aware of my grief, but saw no remedy. I knew that in his heart he thought me justly punished, though he loved me.

We had a long sitting with Captain Welsh, whom I found immovable, as I expected I should. His men, he said, had confessed their sin similarly to the crab in a hole, with one claw out, as the way of sinners was. He blamed himself mainly. "Where you have accidents, Mr. Richmond, you have faults; and where you have faults aboard a ship you may trace a line to the captain. I should have treated my ship's crew like my conscience, and *gone through them nightly*. As it is, sir, here comes round one of your accidents to tell me I have lived blinded by conceit. That is my affliction, my young friend. The payment of the money is no more so than to restore money held in trust."

Temple and I argued the case with him, as of old on our voyage, on board the barque Priscilla, quite unavailingly.

"Is a verdict built on lies one that my Maker approves of?" said he. "If I keep possession of that money, my young friends, will it clothe me? Ay, with stings! Will it feed me? Ay, with poison. And they that should be having it shiver and want!"

He was emphatic, as he would not have been, save to read as an example, owing to our contention with him. "The money is Satan in my very hands!" When he had dismissed the subject he never returned to it.

His topic of extreme happiness, to which Temple led him, was the rescue of a beautiful sinner from a life of shame. It appeared that Captain Welsh had the habit between his voyages of making one holiday expedition to the spot of all creation he thought the fairest, Richmond Hill, overlooking the Thames; and there, one evening, he espied a lady in grief, and spoke to her, and gave her consolation. More, he gave her a blameless home. The lady's name was Mabel Bolton. She was in distress of spirit rather than of circumstances, for temptation was thick about one so beautiful, to supply the vanities and luxuries of the father of sin. He described her.

She was my first play-fellow, the miller's daughter of Dipwell, Mabel Sweetwinter, taken from her home by Lord Edbury during my German university career, and now put away by him upon command of his family on the eve of his marriage.

She herself related her history to me, after telling me that she had seen me once at the steps of Edbury's Club. Our meeting was no great surprise to either of us. She had heard my name as that of an expected visitor; she had seen Temple, moreover, and he had prompted me with her Christian name and the praise of her really glorious hair, to anticipate the person who was ushered into the little cabin-like parlour by Captain Welsh's good old mother.

Of Edbury she could not speak for grief, believing that he loved her still and was acting under compulsion. Her long and faithful attachment to the scapegrace seemed to preserve her from the particular regrets Captain Welsh supposed to occupy her sinner's mind; so that, after some minutes of the hesitation and strangeness due to our common recollections, she talked of him simply and well—as befitted her situation, a worldling might say. But she did not conceal her relief in escaping to this quaint little refuge (she threw a kindly-comical look, not overtoned, at the miniature ships on the mantelpiece, and the picture of Joseph leading Mary with her babe on the ass) from the temptations I could imagine a face like hers would expose her to. The face was splendid, the figure already overblown. I breathed some thanks to my father while she and I conversed apart. The miller was dead, her brother in America. She had no other safe home than the one Captain Welsh had opened to her. When I asked her (I had no excuse for it) whether she would consent to go to Edbury again, she reddened and burst into tears. I cursed my brutality. "Let her cry," said Captain Welsh on parting with us at his street door. "Tears are the way of women and their comfort."

To our astonishment he told us he intended to take her for a voyage in the Priscilla. "Why?" we asked.

"I take her," he said, "because not to do things wholly is worse than not to do things at all, for it's waste of time and cause for a chorus below, down in hell, my young friends. The woman is beautiful as Solomon's bride. She is weak as water. And the man is wicked. He has written to her a letter. He would have her reserved for himself, a wedded man : such he is, or is soon to be. I am searching, and she is not deceitful; and I am a poor man again and must go the voyage. I wrestled with her, and by grace I conquered her to come with me of a free will, and be out of his snares. Aboard I do not fear him, and she shall know the mercy of the Lord on high seas."

We grimaced a little on her behalf, but had nothing to reply.

Seeing Janet after Mabel was strange. In the latter one could perceive the palpably suitable mate for Edbury. I felt that my darling was insulted—no amends for it ! I had to keep silent and mark the remorseless preparations going forward. Not so Heriot. He had come over from the camp in Ireland on leave at this juncture. His talk of women still suggested the hawk with the downy feathers of the last little plucked bird sticking to his beak; but his appreciation of Janet and some kindness for me made him a vehement opponent of her resolve. He took licence of his friendship to lay every incident before her to complete his persuasions. She resisted his attacks, as I knew she would, obstinately, and replied to his entreaties with counter-supplications that he should urge me to accept old Riversley. The conflicts went on between those two daily, and I heard of them from

Heriot at night. He refused to comprehend her determination under the head of anything save madness. Varied by reproaches of me for my former inveterate blindness, he raved upon Janet's madness incessantly, swearing that he would not be beaten. I told him his efforts were useless, but thought them friendly, and so they were, only Janet's resistance had fired his vanity, and he stalked up and down my room talking a mixture of egregious coxcombry and hearty good sense that might have shown one the cause he meant to win had become personal to him. Temple, who was sometimes in consultation with him, and was always amused by his quasi-fanfaronnade, assured me that Heriot was actually scheming. The next we heard of him was that he had been seen at a whitebait hotel down the river drunk with Edbury. Janet also heard of that, and declined to see Heriot again.

Our last days marched frightfully fast. Janet had learnt that any the most distant allusion to her marriage-day was an anguish to the man who was not to marry her, so it was through my aunt Dorothy that I became aware of Julia Bulsted's kindness in offering to take charge of my father for a term. Lady Sampleman undertook to be hostess to him for one night, the eve of Janet's nuptials. He was quiet, unlikely to give annoyance to persons not strongly predisposed to hear sentences finished and exclamations fall into their right places.

Adieu to my darling! There have been women well won; here was an adorable woman well lost. After twenty years of slighting her, did I fancy she would turn to me and throw a man over in reward of my ultimate recovery of my senses?—or fancy that one so tenacious as she had proved would snap a tie depending on her pledged word? She liked Edbury; she saw the best of him, and liked him. The improved young lord was her handiwork. After the years of humiliation from me, she had found herself courted by a young nobleman who clung to her for help, showed improvement, and brought her many compliments from a wondering world. She really felt that she was strength and true life to him. She resisted Heriot: she resisted a more powerful advocate, and this was the princess Ottilia. My aunt Dorothy told me that the princess had written. Janet either did or affected to weigh the princess's reasonings;

and she did not evade the task of furnishing a full reply. Her resolution was unchanged. Loss of colour, loss of light in her eyes, were the sole signs of what it cost her to maintain it. Our task was to transfer the idea of Janet to that of Julia in my father's whirling brain, which at first rebelled violently, and cast it out like a stick thrust between rapidly revolving wheels.

The night before I was to take him away, she gave me her hand with a "good-bye, dear Harry." My words were much the same. She had a ghastly face, but could not have known it, for she smiled, and tried to keep the shallow smile in play, as friends do. There was the end.

It came abruptly, and was schoolingly cold and short.

It had the effect on me of freezing my blood and setting what seemed to be the nerves of my brain at work in a fury of calculation to reckon the minutes remaining of her maiden days. I had expected nothing, but now we had parted I thought that one last scene to break my heart on should not have been denied to me. My aunt Dorothy was a mute; she wept when I spoke of Janet, whatever it was I said.

The minutes ran on from circumstance to circumstance of the destiny Janet had marked for herself, each one rounded in my mind of a blood colour like the edge about prismatic hues. I lived through them a thousand times before they occurred, as the wretch who fears death dies multitudinously.

Some womanly fib preserved my father from a shock on leaving Janet's house. She left it herself at the same time that she drove him to Lady Sampleman's, and I found him there soon after she had gone to her bridesmaids. A letter was for me:—

"DEAR HARRY—

"I shall not live at Riversley, never go there again; do not let it be sold to a stranger; it will happen unless you go there. For the sake of the neighbourhood and poor people, I cannot allow it to be shut up. I was the cause of the chief misfortune. You never blamed me. Let me think that the old place is not dead. Adieu,

"Your affectionate,
"JANET."

I tore the letter to pieces, and kept them.

The aspect of the new intolerable world I was to live in after to-morrow, paralyzed sensation. My father chattered, Lady Sampleman hushed him; she said I might leave him to her, and I went down to Captain Welsh to bid him good-bye and get such peace as contact with a man clad in armour proof against earthly calamity could give.

I was startled to see little Kiomi in Mabel's company. They had met accidentally at the head of the street, and had been friends in childhood, Captain Welsh said, adding: "She hates men."

"Good reason, when they're beasts," said Kiomi.

Amid much weeping of Mabel and old Mrs. Welsh, Kiomi showed as little trouble as the heath when the woods are swept.

Captain Welsh wanted Mabel to be on board early, owing, he told me, to information. Kiomi had offered to remain on board with her until the captain was able to come. He had business to do in the City.

We saw them off from the waterside.

"Were I to leave that young woman behind me, on shore, I should be giving the devil warrant to seize upon his prey," said Captain Welsh, turning his gaze from the boat which conveyed Kiomi and Mabel to the barque Priscilla. He had information that the misleader of her youth was hunting her.

He and I parted, and for ever, at a corner of crossways in the central city. There I saw the last of one who deemed it as simple a matter to renounce his savings for old age, to rectify an error of justice, as to plant his foot on the pavement; a man whose only burden was the folly of men.

I thought to myself in despair, under what protest can I also escape from England and my own intemperate mind? It seemed a miraculous answer:—There lay at my chambers a note written by Count Kesensky; I went to the embassy, and heard of an Austrian ship of war being at one of our ports upon an expedition to the East, and was introduced to the captain, a gentlemanly fellow, like most of the officers of his Government. Finding in me a German scholar, and a joyful willingness, he engaged me to take the post of secretary to the expedition in the place of an invalided Freiherr von Redwitz. The bargain was struck immediately:

I was to be ready to report myself to the captain on board not later than the following day. Count Kesensky led me aside : he regretted that he could do nothing better for me : but I thought his friendliness extreme and astonishing, and said so ; whereupon the count assured me that his intentions were good, though he had not been of great use hitherto— an allusion to the borough of Chippenden : he had only heard of von Redwitz's illness that afternoon. I thanked him cordially, saying I was much in his debt, and he bowed me out, letting me fancy, as my father had fancied before me, and as though I had never observed and reflected in my life, that the opportuneness of this intervention signified a special action of Providence. The flattery of the thought served for an elixir. But with whom would my father abide during my absence ? Captain Bulsted and Julia saved me from a fit of remorse ; they had come up to town on purpose to carry him home with them, and had left a message on my table, and an invitation to dinner at their hotel, where the name of Janet was the Marino Faliero of our review of Riversley people and old times. The captain and his wife were indignant at her conduct. Since, however, I chose to excuse it, they said they would say nothing more about her, and she was turned face to the wall. I told them how Janet had taken him for months. " But I'll take him for years," said Julia. " The truth is, Harry, my old dear ! William and I are never so united—for I'm ashamed to quarrel with him—as when your father's at Bulsted. He belongs to us, and other people shall know you're not obliged to depend on your family for help, and your aunt Dorothy can come and see him whenever she likes." That was settled. Captain Bulsted went with me to Lady Sample-man's to prepare my father for the change of nurse and residence. We were informed that he had gone down with Alderman Duke Saddlebank to dine at one of the great City Companies' halls. I could hardly believe it. " Ah ! my dear Mr. Harry," said Lady Sampleman, " old friends know one another best, believe that, now. I treated him ꜱs if he was as well as ever he was, gave him his turtle and madeira lunch ; and Alderman Saddlebank, who lunched here—your father used to say, he looks like a robin hopping out of a larder—quite jumped to dine him in the City like old times ; and he will see a great spread of plate !"

She thought my father only moderately unwell, wanting novelty. Captain Bulsted agreed with me that it would be prudent to go and fetch him. At the door of the City hall stood Andrew Saddlebank, grown to be simply a larger edition of Rippenger's head boy, and he imparted to us that my father was "on his legs" delivering a speech. It alarmed me. With Saddlebank's assistance I pushed in.

"A prince! a treacherous lover! an unfatherly man!"

Those were the words I caught:—a reproduction of many of my phrases employed in our arguments on this very subject.

He bade his audience. to beware of princes, beware of idle princes; and letting his florid fancy loose on these eminent persons, they were at one moment silver lamps, at another poising hawks, and again sprawling pumpkins; anything except useful citizens. How could they be ? They had the attraction of the lamp, the appetite of the hawk, the occupation of the pumpkin: nothing was given them to do but to shine, destroy, and fatten. Their hands were kept empty: a trifle in their heads would topple them over; they were monuments of the English system of compromise. Happy for mankind if they were monuments only! Happy for them! But they had the passions of men. The adulation of the multitude was raised to inflate them, whose self-respect had not one prop to rest on, unless it were contempt for the flatterers and prophetic foresight of their perfidy. They were the monuments of a compromise between the past and terror of the future; puppets as princes, mannikins as men, the snares of frail women, stop-gaps of the State, feathered nonentities!

So far (but not in epigram) he marshalled the things he had heard to his sound of drum and trumpet, like one repeating a lesson off-hand. Steering on a sudden completely round, he gave his audience an outline of the changes He would have effected had he but triumphed in his cause ; and now came the lashing of arms, a flood of eloquence. Princes with brains, princes leaders, princes flowers of the land, he had offered them! princes that should sway assemblies, and not stultify the precepts of a decent people "by making you pay in the outrage of your morals for what you seem to gain in policy." These or similar words. The whole scene was too grotesque and afflicting. But his command of his hearers was extraordinary, partly a consolation I thought, until, having touched the arm of one of the gentlemen of the banquet and said, "I am his son; I wish to remove him," the reply enlightened me: "I'm afraid there's danger in interrupting him; I really am."

They were listening obediently to one whom they dared not interrupt for fear of provoking an outburst of madness.

I had to risk it. His dilated eyes looked ready to seize on me for an illustration. I spoke peremptorily, and he bowed his head low, saying, "My son, gentlemen," and submitted himself to my hands. The feasters showed immediately that they felt released by rising and chatting in groups. Alderman Saddlebank expressed much gratitude to me for the service I had performed. "That first half of your father's speech was the most pathetic thing I ever heard!" I had not shared his privilege, and could not say. The remark was current that a great deal was true of what had been said of the Fitzs. My father leaned heavily on my arm with the step and bent head of an ancient pensioner of the Honourable City Company. He was Julia Bulsted's charge, and I was on board the foreign vessel weighing anchor from England before dawn of Janet's marriage-day.

CHAPTER LVI.

CONCLUSION.

THE wind was high that morning. The rain came in gray rings, through which we worked on the fretted surface of crumbling seas, heaving up and plunging, without an outlook.

I remember having thought of the barque Priscilla as I watched our lithe Dalmatians slide along the drenched decks of the Verona frigate. At night it blew a gale. I could imagine it to have been sent providentially to brush the torture of the land from my mind, and make me feel that men are trifles.

What are their passions, then? The storm in the clouds —even more short-lived than the clouds.

I philosophized, but my anguish was great.

Janet's " Good-bye, Harry," ended everything I lived for, and seemed to strike the day, and bring out of it the remorseless rain. A featureless day, like those before the earth was built; like night under an angry moon; and each day the same until we touched the edge of a southern circle and saw light, and I could use my brain.

The matter most present to me was my injustice regarding my poor father's speech in the City hall. He had caused me to suffer so much that I generally felt for myself when he appealed for sympathy, or provoked some pity : but I was past suffering, and letting kindly recollection divest the speech of its verbiage, I took it to my heart. It was true that he had in his blind way struck the key-note of his position, much as I myself had conceived it before. Harsh trials had made me think of my own fortunes more than of his. This I felt, and I thought there never had been so moving a speech. It seemed to make the world in debt to us. What else is so consolatory to a ruined man ?

In reality the busy little creature within me, whom we call self, was digging pits for comfort to flow in, of any kind, in any form; and it seized on every idea, every circumstance, to turn it to that purpose, and with such success that when by-and-by I learnt how entirely inactive special Providence had been in my affairs, I had to collect myself before I could muster the conception of gratitude toward the noble woman who clothed me in the illusion. It was to the Princess Ottilia, acting through Count Kesensky, that I owed both my wafting away from England at a wretched season, and that chance of a career in Parliament! The captain of the Verona hinted as much when, after a year of voyaging, we touched at an East Indian seaport, and von Redwitz joined the vessel to resume the post I was occupying. Von Redwitz (the son of Prince Ernest's Chancellor, I discovered) could have told me more than he did, but he handed me a letter from the princess, calling me home urgently, and even prescribing my route, and bidding me come straight to Germany and to Sarkeld. The summons was distasteful, for I had settled into harness under my scientific superiors, and had proved to my messmates that I was neither morose nor over-conceited. Captain

Martinitz persuaded me to return, and besides, there lay between the lines of Ottilia's letter a signification of welcome things better guessed at than known. Was I not bound to do her bidding? Others had done it: young von Redwitz, for instance, in obeying the telegraph wires and feigning sickness to surrender his place to me, when she wished to save me from misery by hurrying me to new scenes with a task for my hand and head;—no mean stretch of devotion on his part. Ottilia was still my princess; she my providence. She wrote:—

"Come home, my friend Harry: you have been absent too long. He who intercepts you to displace you has his career before him in the vessel, and you nearer home. The home is always here where I am, but it may now take root elsewhere, and it is from Ottilia you hear that delay is now really loss of life. I tell you no more. You know me, that when I say come, it is enough."

A simple adieu and her name ended the mysterious letter. Not a word of Prince Hermann. What had happened? I guessed at it curiously and incessantly, and only knew the nature of my suspicion by ceasing to hope as soon as I seemed to have divined it. I did not wrong my soul's high mistress beyond the one flash of tentative apprehension which in perplexity struck at impossibilities. Ottilia would never have summoned me to herself. But was Janet free? The hope which refused to live in that other atmosphere of purest calm, sprang to full stature at the bare thought; and would not be extinguished though all the winds beset it. Had my girl's courage failed, to spare her at the last moment? I fancied it might be: I was sure it was not so. Yet the doubt pressed on me with the force of a world of unimagined shifts and chances, and just kept the little flame alive, at times intoxicating me, though commonly holding me back to watch its forlorn conflict with probabilities known too well. It cost me a struggle to turn aside to Germany from the Italian highroad. I chose the line of the Brenner, and stopped half a day at Innsbruck to pay a visit to Colonel Heddon, of whom I had the joyful tidings that two of his daughters were away to go through the German form of the betrothal of one of them to an Englishman. The turn of the tide had come to him. And it comes to me, too, in a fresh spring tide whenever I have to speak of others instead of this everlastingly recurring I of the autobiographer, of which the complacent penman has felt it to be his duty to expose the mechanism when out of action, and which, like so many of our sins of commission, appears in the shape of a terrible offence when the occasion for continuing it draws to a close. The pleasant narrator in the first person is the happy bubbling fool, not the philosopher who has come to know himself and his relations toward the universe. The words of this last are one to twenty ; his mind is bent upon the causes of events rather than their progress. As you see me on the page now, I stand somewhere between the two, approximating to the former, but with sufficient of the latter within me to tame the delightful expansiveness proper to that coming hour of marriage-bells and bridal-wreaths. It is a sign that the end, and the delivery of reader and writer alike, should not be dallied with. The princess had invited Lucy Heddon to Sarkeld to meet Temple, and Temple to meet me. Onward I flew. I saw the old woods of the lake-palace, and, as it were, the light of my past passion waning above them. I was greeted by the lady of all nobility with her gracious warmth, and in his usual abrupt manful fashion by Prince Hermann. And I had no time to reflect on the strangeness of my stepping freely under the roof where a husband claimed Ottilia, before she led me into the library, where sat my lost and recovered, my darling ; and, unlike herself, for a moment, she faltered in rising and breathing my name. We were alone. I knew she was no bondwoman. The question how it had come to pass lurked behind everything I said and did; speculation on the visible features, and touching of the unfettered hand, restrained me from uttering or caring to utter it. But it was wonderful. It thrust me back on Providence again for the explanation—humbly this time. It was wonderful and blessed, as to loving eyes the first-drawn breath of a drowned creature restored to life. I kissed her hand. "Wait till you have heard everything, Harry," she said, and her voice was deeper, softer, exquisitely strange in its known tones, as her manner was, and her eyes. She was not the blooming, straight-shouldered, high-breathing girl of other days, but sister to the day of her "Good-bye, Harry," pale and worn. The eyes had wept. This was Janet, haply widowed. She wore no garb nor a shade of widowhood. Perhaps she had thrown it off, not to offend an implacable temper in me. I said, " I shall hear nothing that can make you other than my own Janet— if you will ?"

She smiled a little. " We expected Temple's arrival sooner than yours, Harry."

" Do you take to his Lucy ?"

" Yes, thoroughly."

The perfect ring of Janet was there.

Mention of Riversley made her conversation lively, and she gave me moderately good news of my father, quaint, out of Julia Bulsted's latest letter to her.

" Then how long," I asked astonished, "how long have you been staying with the princess ?"

She answered, colouring, " So long, that I can speak fairish German."

" And read it easily ?"

" I have actually taken to reading, Harry."

Her courage must have quailed, and she must have been looking for me on that morning of miserable aspect when I beheld the last of England through wailful showers, like the scene of a burial. I did not speak of it, fearing to hurt her pride, but said, " Have you been here—months ?"

" Yes, some months," she replied.

" Many ?"

" Yes," she said, and dropped her eyelids, and then, with a quick look at me, " Wait for Temple, Harry. He is a day behind his time. We can't account for it."

I suggested, half in play, that perhaps he had decided, for the sake of a sea voyage, to come by our old route to Germany on board the barque Priscilla, with Captain Welsh.

A faint shudder passed over her. She shut her eyes and shook her head.

Our interview satisfied my heart's hunger no further. The Verona's erratic voyage had cut me off from letters.

Janet might be a widow, for aught I knew. She was always Janet to me ; but why at liberty ? why many months at Sarkeld, the guest of the princess ? Was she neither maid nor widow—a wife flown from a brutal husband ? or separated, and forcibly free ? Under such conditions Ottilia would not have commanded my return : but what was I to imagine ? A boiling couple of hours divided me from the time for dressing, when, as I meditated, I could put a chance question or two to the man commissioned to wait on me, and hear whether the English lady was a Fräulein. The Margravine and Prince Ernest were absent. Hermann worked in his museum, displaying his treasures to Colonel Heddon. I sat with the ladies in the airy look-out tower of the lake-palace, a prey to intense speculations, which devoured themselves and changed from fire to smoke, while I recounted the adventures of our ship's voyage, and they behaved as if there were nothing to tell me in turn, each a sphinx holding the secret I thirsted for. I should not certainly have thirsted much if Janet had met me as far half-way as a delicate woman may advance. The mystery lay in her evident affection, her apparent freedom and unfathomable reserve, and her desire that I should see Temple before she threw off her feminine armour, to which, judging by the indications, Ottilia seemed to me to accede.

My old friend was spied first by his sweetheart Lucy, winding dilatorily over the hill away from Sarkeld, in one of the carriages sent to meet him. He was guilty of wasting a prodigious number of minutes with his trumpery " How d'ye do's," and his glances and excuses, and then I had him up in my room, and the tale was told ; it was not Temple's fault if he did not begin straightforwardly.

I plucked him from his narrator's vexatious and inevitable commencement : " Temple, tell me, did she go to the altar ?"

He answered " Yes."

" She did ?   Then she's a widow ?"

" No, she isn't," said Temple, distracting me by submitting to the lead I distracted him by taking.

" Then her husband's alive ?"

Temple denied it, and a devil seized him to perceive some comicality in the dialogue.

" Was she married ?"

Temple said " No," with a lurking drollery about his lips. He added, " It's nothing to laugh over, Richie."

" Am I laughing ?   Speak out. Did Edbury come to grief overnight in any way ?"

Again Temple pronounced a negative, this time wilfully enigmatical : he confessed it, and accused me of the provo-

cation. He dashed some laughter with gravity to prepare
for my next assault.

"Was Edbury the one to throw up the marriage? Did
he decline it?"

"No," was the answer once more.

Temple stopped my wrath by catching at me and begging
me to listen. "Edbury was drowned, Richie."

"Overnight?"

"No, not overnight. I can tell it all in half-a-dozen
words, if you'll be quiet; and I know you're going to be as
happy as I am, or I shouldn't trifle an instant. He went
overnight on board the barque Priscilla to see Mabel Sweetwinter, the only woman he ever could have cared for, and he
went the voyage, just as we did. He was trapped, caged,
and transported; it's a repetition, except that the poor old
Priscilla never came to land. She foundered in a storm in
the North Sea. That's all we know. Every soul perished,
the captain and all. I knew how it would be with that crew
of his some day or other. Don't you remember my saying
the Priscilla was the kind of name of a vessel that would go
down with all hands, and leave a bottle to float to shore? A
gin-bottle was found on our East coast—the old captain must
have discovered in the last moments that such things were
on board—and in it there was a paper, and the passengers'
and crew's names in his handwriting, written as if he had
been sitting in his parlour at home; over them a line—
'*The Lord's will is about to be done;*' and underneath—'*We
go to His judgement resigned and cheerful.*' You know the old
captain, Richie?"

Temple had tears in his eyes. We both stood blinking
for a second or two.

I could not but be curious to hear the reason for Edbury's
having determined to sail.

"Don't you understand how it was, Richie?" said Temple.
"Edbury went to persuade her to stay, or just to see her for
once, and he came to persuasions. He seems to have been
succeeding, but the captain stepped on board, and he treated
Edbury as he did us two: he made him take the voyage for
discipline's sake and 'his soul's health.'"

"How do you know all this, Temple?"

"You know your friend Kiomi was one of the party. The
captain sent her back on shore because he had no room for

her. She told us Edbury offered bribes of hundreds and
thousands for the captain to let him and Mabel go off in the
boat with Kiomi, and then he took to begging to go alone.
He tried to rouse the crew. The poor fellow cringed, she
says; he threatened to swim off. The captain locked· him up."

My immediate reflections hit on the Bible lessons Edbury
must have had to swallow, and the gaping of the waters
when its truths were suddenly and tremendously brought
home to him.

An odd series of accidents! I thought.

Temple continued : "Heriot held his tongue about it next
morning. He was one of the guests, though he had sworn
he wouldn't go. He said something to Janet that betrayed
him, for she had not seen him since."

" How betrayed him ?" said I.

"Why," said Temple, "of course it was Heriot who put
Edbury in Kiomi's hands. Edbury wouldn't have known of
Mabel's sailing, or known the vessel she was in, without her
help. She led him down to the water and posted him in
sight before she went to Captain Welsh's; and when you
and Captain Welsh walked away, Edbury rowed to the
Priscilla. Old Heriot is not responsible for the consequences.
What he supposed was likely enough. He thought that
Edbury and Mabel were much of a pair, and thought, I
suppose, that if Edbury saw her he'd find he couldn't leave
her, and old Lady Kane, who managed him, would stand
nodding her plumes for nothing at the altar. And so she
did : and a pretty scene it was. She snatched at the
minutes as they slipped past twelve like fishes, and snarled
at the parson, and would have kept him standing till one
P.M., if Janet had not turned on her heel. The old woman
got in front of her to block her way. 'Ah, Temple,' she
said to me, 'it would be hard if I could not think I had
done all that was due to them.' I didn't see her again till
she was starting for Germany. And, Richie, she thinks you
can never forgive her. She wrote me word that the princess
is of another mind, but her own opinion, she says, is based
upon knowing you."

" Good heaven ! how little !" cried I.

Temple did me a further wrong by almost thanking me on
Janet's behalf for my sustained love for her, while he praised
the very qualities of pride and a spirited sense of obligation

which had reduced her to dread my unforgivingness. Yet he and Janet had known me longest. Supposing that my idea of myself differed from theirs for the simple reason that I thought of what I had grown to be, and they of what I had been through the previous years? Did I judge by the flower, and they by root and stem? But the flower is a thing of the season; the flower drops off: it may be a different development next year. Did they not therefore judge me soundly?

Ottilia was the keenest reader. Ottilia had divined what could be wrought out of me. I was still subject to the relapses of a not perfectly right nature, as I perceived when glancing back at my thought of 'An odd series of accidents!' which was but a disguised fashion of attributing to Providence the particular concern in my fortunes: an impiety and a folly! This is the temptation of those who are rescued and made happy by circumstances. The wretched think themselves spited, and are merely childish, not egregious in egoism. Thither on leads to a chapter—already written by the wise, doubtless. It does not become an atom of humanity to dwell on it beyond a point where students of the human condition may see him passing through the experiences of the flesh and the brain. Meantime, Temple and I, at two hand-basins, soaped and towelled, and I was more discreet toward him than I have been to you, for I reserved from him altogether the pronunciation of the council of senators in the secret chamber of my head. Whether, indeed, I have fairly painted the outer part of myself waxes dubious when I think of his spluttering laugh and shout; "Richie, you haven't changed a bit—you're just like a boy!" Certain indications of external gravity, and a sinking of the natural springs within characterized Temple's approach to the responsible position of a British husband and father. We talked much of Captain Welsh, and the sedate practical irony of his imprisoning one like Edbury to discipline him on high seas, as well as the singular situation of the couple of culprits under his admonishing regimen, and the tragic end. My next two minutes alone with Janet were tempered by it. Only my eagerness for another term of privacy persuaded her that I was her lover instead of judge, and then, having made the discovery that a single-minded gladness animated me in the hope that she and I would travel together one in body and soul, she surrendered, with her last bit of pride broken; except, it may be, a fragment of reserve traceable in the confession that came quaintly after supreme self-blame, when she said she was bound to tell me that possibly—probably, were the trial to come over again, she should again act as she had done. Happily for us both, my wits had been sharpened enough to know that there is more in men and women than the stuff they utter. And blessed privilege now! if the lips were guilty of nonsense, I might stop them. Besides, I was soon to be master upon such questions. She admitted it, admitting with an unwonted emotional shiver, that absolute freedom could be the worst of perils. " For women?" said I. She preferred to say, " For girls," and then " Yes, for women, as they are educated at present." Spice of the princess's conversation flavoured her speech. The signs unfamiliar about her for me were marks of the fire she had come out of; the struggle, the torture, the determined sacrifice, through pride's conception of duty. She was iron once. She had come out of the fire finest steel.

" Riversley! Harry," she murmured, and my smile, and word, and squeeze in reply, brought back a whole gleam of the fresh English morning she had been in face, and voice, and person.

Was it conceivable that we could go back to Riversley single?

Before that was answered she had to make a statement; and in doing it she blushed, because it involved Edbury's name, and seemed to involve her attachment to him; but she paid me the compliment of speaking it frankly. It was that she had felt herself bound in honour to pay Edbury's debts. Even by such slight means as her saying, " Riversley, Harry," and my kiss of her fingers when a question of money was in debate, did we burst aside the vestiges of mutual strangeness, and recognize one another, but with an added warmth of love. When I pleaded for the marriage to be soon, she said, " I wish it, Harry."

Sentiment you do not obtain from a Damascus blade. She most cordially despised the ladies who parade and play on their sex, and are for ever acting according to the feminine standard:—a dangerous stretch of contempt for one less strong than she.

Riding behind her and Temple one day with the princess, I said, " What takes you most in Janet ?"

She replied, "Her courage. And it is of a kind that may knot up every other virtue worth having. I have impulses, and am capable of desperation, but I have no true courage: so I envy and admire, even if I have to blame her; for I know that this possession of hers, which identifies her and marks her from the rest of us, would bear the ordeal of fire I can imagine the qualities I have most pride in withering and decaying under a prolonged trial. I cannot conceive her courage failing. Perhaps because I have it not myself I think it the rarest of precious gifts. It seems to me to imply one half, and to dispense with the other."

I have lived to think that Ottilia was right. As nearly right, too, in the wording of her opinion as one may be in three or four sentences designed to be comprehensive.

My Janet's readiness to meet calamity was shown ere we reached home upon an evening of the late autumn, and set eye on a scene, for her the very saddest that could have been devised to test her spirit of endurance, when, driving up the higher heath-land, we saw the dark sky ominously reddened over Riversley, and, mounting the ridge, had the funeral flames of the old Grange dashed in our faces. The blow was evil, sudden, unaccountable. Villagers, tenants, farm-labourers, groups of a deputation that had gone to the railway-station to give us welcome, and returned, owing to a delay in our arrival, stood gazing from all quarters. The Grange was burning in two great wings, that soared in flame-tips and columns of crimson smoke, leaving the central hall and chambers untouched as yet, but alive inside with mysterious ranges of lights, now curtained, now made bare —a feeble contrast to the savage blaze to right and left, save for the wonder aroused as to its significance. These were soon cloaked. Dead sable reigned in them, and at once a jet of flame gave the whole vast building to destruction. My wife thrust her hand in mine. Fire at the heart, fire at the wings —our old home stood in that majesty of horror which freezes the limbs of men, bidding them look and no more. " What has Riversley done to deserve this ?" I heard Janet murmur to herself. " His room !" she said, when at the South-east wing, where my old grandfather had slept, there burst a glut of flame. We drove down to the park and along the carriage-road to the first red line of gazers. They told us that no living creatures were in the house. My aunt

Dorothy was at Bulsted.   I perceived my father's man Tollingby among the servants, and called him to me; others came, and out of a clatter of tongues, and all eyes fearfully askant at the wall of fire, we gathered that a great reception had been prepared for us by my father : lamps, lights in all the rooms, torches in the hall, illuminations along the windows, stores of fireworks, such a display as only he could have dreamed of.   The fire had broken out at dusk, from an explosion of fireworks at one wing and some inexplicable mismanagement at the other.   But the house must have been like a mine, what with the powder, the torches, the devices in paper and muslin, and the extraordinary decorations fitted up to celebrate our return in harmony with my father's fancy.   Gentlemen on horseback dashed up to us.   Captain Bulsted seized my hand.   He was hot from a ride to fetch engines, and sang sharp in my ear, "Have you got him ?"   It was my father he meant. The cry rose for my father, and the groups were agitated and split, and the name of the missing man, without an answer to it, shouted.   Captain Bulsted had left him bravely attempting to quench the flames after the explosion of fireworks.   He rode about, interrogating the frightened servants and grooms holding horses and dogs.   They could tell us that the cattle were safe, not a word of my father; and amid shrieks of women at fresh falls of timber and ceiling into the pit of fire, and warnings from the men, we ran the heated circle of the building to find a loophole and offer aid if a living soul should be left; the night around us bright as day, busier than day, and a human now added to elemental horror.   Janet would not quit her place.   She sent her carriage-horses to Bulsted, and sat in the carriage to see the last of burning Riversley.   Each time that I came to her she folded her arms on my neck and kissed me silently.

We gathered from the subsequent testimony of men and women of the household who had collected their wits, that my father must have remained in the doomed old house to look to the safety of my aunt Dorothy.   He was never seen again.

THE END.

Appendixes

APPENDIX A

A NOTE ON THE TEXT

THE textual history of *Harry Richmond* is of interest in showing something of the evolution of this novel from an early manuscript draft through manuscript revisions to serialization and later revisions, and in addition it throws some general light on these processes in the Victorian age.

As mentioned in the present Introduction (p. xiii), Meredith's letters show that he had the novel which became *Harry Richmond* in mind, whether or not he had committed anything to paper, in August, 1861, nine years before it began as a serial in the *Cornhill*. He referred to it as an "autobiographic," that is, first-person, tale, and he was definitely working on it in May, 1864, along with *Vittoria* (serialized during 1866). The early title was "The Adventures of Richmond Roy and his friend Contrivance Jack: Being the History of Two Rising Men," "a spanking bid for popularity."[1] What appears to be a manuscript draft of the story at this stage, in the form of brief chapter summaries (Chapters I and IV–XV), is preserved in the Altschul Collection of Meredith at the Yale University Library. Richard B. Hudson's useful discussion, with quotations, of this draft, "Meredith's Autobiography and 'The Adventures of Harry Richmond,' "[2] makes detailed consideration here unnecessary. As Hudson points out, the "popularity" Meredith was aiming at was to be obtained through a reliance on Dickensian eccentrics, intrigues, and low comedy. But the spicing of the story with mystery, exciting adventure, even murder, with continual

---

[1] C. L. Cline, ed., *The Letters of George Meredith*, 3 vols. (Oxford, in press), I, 225.

[2] *Nineteenth-Century Fiction*, IX (June 1954), 38–49.

547

emphasis on action in terms of external event, also suggests the influence of Wilkie Collins and the sensation novel as well as of Dickens.

Samuel Lucas, editor of *Once a Week*, had complained about the slowness and dullness of *Evan Harrington* (serialized in that journal in 1861) and had urged Meredith without success to concentrate more on action in the style of Smollett and Wilkie Collins. Meredith found himself unable to follow this advice. To him "mysteries of the W. Collins" kind tended to be "false and evanescent," whereas interest "ought to centre more in character—out of which incidents should grow."[3] However, he felt that his desire to show the reason for things was "a perpetual obstruction to movement. I *do* want the dash of Smollet and know it."[4] The popular *The Woman in White* was serialized concurrently with *Evan*.

As we shall see, the draft-summary of the "autobiographic" story, or a development of it, was offered to Samuel Lucas in order to win his assent to serializing the completed novel in *Once a Week*, so Meredith appears to have decided in this instance to follow Lucas's recipe for the popular novel.

It would not have escaped Meredith's attention that the successor of the unpopular *Evan Harrington* in *Once a Week*, Shirley Brooks's successful *The Silver Cord*, was written very much in the Wilkie Collins vein, with strong "sensation" elements and the author explicitly omitting "as far as possible, Description, physical as well as moral [in order] to tell his story by means of action and of Dialogue."[5] It is interesting that, probably with a view to publicity, Meredith later thought Shirley Brooks might be interested in reading *Harry Richmond*, and so considered sending him a copy.[6]

Richmond Roy, originally designed as the autobiographic hero, was in Hudson's words "to be a kind of young Nicholas Nickleby trying to make his way in the cruel city accompanied at least part of the time by his friend Contrivance Jack, a Dickensian eccentric of many resources with a 'Contrivance'

---

[3] Letter to Samual Lucas, *Letters*, I, 49.
[4] Letter to Lucas, *Letters*, I, 57.
[5] Preface to *The Silver Cord*, 1st ed. (1861).
[6] *Letters*, I, 454.

to meet every exigency."[7] The following brief samples from the draft-summary suggest its flavor:

> Chapter 7. *A Message from Jack in Jeopardy.*
> (Roy receives a curious letter, crumpled and soiled on the outside, in Jack's handwriting, containing simply the description of a house in a low neighbourhood by the river's side. . . . Roy fancies Jack in trouble and discovers the house. After watching it an hour a man [*sic*] comes up to him . . . begs him to enter the house, takes him upstairs and thrusts him into the room with Jack. They find themselves common prisoners.)

> Chapter 8. *Jack's relation of his adventure and of his Contrivances.*
> (He has witnessed a murder: has been caught, threatened, and caged. He lures the sparrows to his windows with crumbs . . . finally catches one in a loop of thread to which his letter to Roy is attached.)

> Chapter 9. *The Escape*
> (After innumerable contrivances)—Jack's ingenuity finds a counterpoise in one called The Fox. . . .

The draft bears no resemblance at all to the final version, except for two minor details that were to be developed in the presentation of Roy: In Chapter IV Roy "goes to the great house of which he believes his father to be the master, and discovers that his father is but a singing master there, acting a part"; and a marginal note to Chapter VI includes "one who believes himself Dauphin of France" among Jack's motley series of masters. In the final version the squire was to accuse Roy of using his position at Riversley as singing master as a means of winning the affections of his daughters and bringing ruin to his family (present text, p. 497), and in Chapters XLI and XLII, through the intriguing of Edbury, Roy is held up to ridicule by being confronted with his "double," a poor deluded creature who believes himself Dauphin of France.

The failure of Jack Raikes in *Evan Harrington* had shown that Meredith was well advised not to attempt the presentation of any more Dickensian eccentrics, and in his changes to the final manuscript version (see below) he pruned away similar elements by restricting the comic roles of the minor

---

[7] Hudson, "Meredith's Autobiography," p. 44.

characters: Peterborough, Alphonse, and the Margravine. The "Dauphin" is shown briefly and indirectly.

The early draft-summary and the final revisions to the extant manuscript suggest that Meredith had at first decided to exploit the fashionable sensation contrivances of the novel of "action" at the expense of his more serious aims in one novel at least, but that he later curbed and changed the "adventurous" element to effect a compromise.

In a letter of June, 1864, Meredith wrote that he was "just engaging to do a serial for *Once a Week*,"[8] and a month later he recorded that the editor, Samuel Lucas, was "charmed with the sketch of the autobiography, but owing to certain changes in relation to *O[nce] a W[eek]* he has not yet sent word for me to start away. Thus we are in a little uncertainty."[9] Hudson may be right in suggesting that the surviving manuscript summary was a "fragment of what was probably a rough draft of the sketch sent to Lucas or an early version of it,"[10] probably written in 1864, on the evidence of the relevant letters.

Of some interest as showing the possible germinal beginnings of the final *Harry Richmond* is a page of manuscript not commented on by Hudson and at present grouped with the manuscript chapter summary in the Yale University Library. This is a sketch of a character called Mastodon:

> *Mastodon:* The great man come. He knows not himself whether part impostor. [In the margin here "Mrs Annabel Mastodon" is written.] The wife of his bosom knows not. Copious in eloquence, grand in schemes, patriotic, universal, so great is his devotedness that he can boast of thinking never of himself, yet has to question himself whether at times his mean personal appetites have not directed the mighty engine for good and evil that he is. [In the margin against the above passage is written: "He admires: 'the two eminent ladies, the Lady Euphemia, the Lady Virginia Davidney. Misses Wildey Thomas, Pifford' "—and some other names hard to decipher.]
>
> He is haunted by this half-consciousness till his passion for action (or his greed?) is on him, then it flies, to return.
>
> His infinite pretension to all excellences puts him in antagonism with an unavowedly sensual nature.

8 *Letters*, I, 260.
9 *Letters*, I, 275.
10 Hudson, p. 43.

Though this sketch may not have been intended for *Harry Richmond*, there is a striking similarity of some of the elements in his projected character to those developed in Richmond Roy. These elements include the doubt about whether Mastodon is an impostor (though Roy has no self-doubts), his qualities of being copious in eloquence, grand in schemes, patriotic, "universal," boasting of "thinking never of himself," "passion for action," and "infinite pretension." In the same group of manuscripts in the Yale University Library is a list of the names for comedies, including "The Impostor."

In a letter of May, 1867,[11] Meredith speaks of having "one novel nearly finished and another advancing; but *Vittoria* has made the publishers' faces cold." One of these novels must have been *Harry Richmond*. Two months later he writes that Fredrick Greenwood (editor of the *Pall Mall Gazette*) had advised that the manuscript be sent to him and "he will forward it with a strong recommendation to George Smith [publisher of the *Cornhill*]. . . . I am to name the day when the book will be ready and ask for what I want now."[12] Smith accepted the work, and by January, 1870, Meredith was still finishing the novel, "one of three or four that are carved out, and waiting."[13]

In view of the importance of fire imagery in the completed novel,[14] it is interesting that at this stage Meredith witnessed a fire: "The drama of a household burnt out under my eye here, has given me some excitement . . . and I giving a touch to *Richmond*."[15] This seems to imply that Meredith felt the actual fire was a coincidence, but one may wonder whether the event influenced the fire scenes in the completing and the rewriting of the novel, especially the ending, if it did not originate the imagery and scenes.

---

[11] *Letters*, I, 358.

[12] *Letters*, I, 384.

[13] *Letters*, I, 412–413.

[14] See Barbara Hardy, " 'A Way to Your Hearts through Fire and Water': The Structure of Imagery in *Harry Richmond*," *Essays in Criticism*, X (April 1960), 163–180; reprinted in Barbara Hardy, *The Appropriate Form* (London, 1964).

[15] *Letters*, I, 415.

Meredith admitted to rewriting "a large portion of the work before it appeared in the *Cornhill* [it began as a serial in September, 1870]: so as to make it an almost entirely different thing from what you [George Smith] read in MS."[16] Whether this rewriting was undertaken because of Meredith's own dissatisfaction with the work, or at Smith's suggestion, is uncertain.

THE EXTANT FINAL MANUSCRIPT

The final manuscript from which the novel was printed is preserved in the Yale University Library. We know for certain that the novel had originally existed in rough draft in a very different form, and that near publication date it was substantially rewritten. The extant manuscript was substantially altered, but at proof stage, and as we shall see, not in such a way "as to make it an almost entirely different thing." There is also an additional piece of evidence for taking the extant manuscript as a substantial rewriting of the version first submitted to Smith. Apparently no manuscript evidence of the penultimate draft survives, but the letters point to one particular area that was revised:

> I was here and there hand-tied too, in relation to the royal reigning House . . . or I should (and did on paper) have launched out. The speech at the City Banquet would have satisfied a Communist Red originally. And I had planned startling doings for the season of the Grand Parade. But I constrained myself . . . .[17]

Professor C. L. Cline in his edition of the *Letters* cites Chapter XLI, "Commencement of the Splendours and Perplexities of My Father's Grand Parade," as the chapter in which the City Banquet speech occurs, and adds that the speech was reduced in revision "to a single sentence." Cline appears to have confused the episode of "the dinner given by Edbury at a celebrated City tavern," (present text, p. 384) where Roy and the Dauphin were brought together, with Roy's dining at Alderman Saddlebank's request at "one of the great City Companies' halls" (present text, p. 531). The former event is reported twice, in Chapters XLI and XLII, and in

---

16 *Letters*, I, 457.
17 *Letters*, I, 454.

the latter a sentence indirectly reports the general tenor of what Roy was supposed to have said (present text, p. 388). However it is in the second episode, the dinner at the City Company's hall, that Roy makes his radical speech attacking the aristocracy (Chapter LV, "I meet My First Playfellow," present text, p. 532), and this is surely the one Meredith referred to as having been revised under "constraint." The speech as printed takes up a paragraph and agrees exactly with the extant manuscript text, thus providing further evidence that it was the rewritten version. Its republican sentiments are modified by being spoken by a deranged Roy explicitly echoing Harry's own embittered disappointment. Harry's sentiments in turn are borrowed from Dr. Julius, a part-comic, part-serious figure.

THE USE OF THE FINAL MANUSCRIPT FOR THE PRESENT EDITION

A full collation of the manuscript and printed texts has not been attempted in preparing this edition of *Harry Richmond*. Definitive editions which involve a full list of variants and a complete coverage of textual history are usually and appropriately reserved for works which have been accorded a crucial or "classic" literary importance and a wide currency. Meredith's works, especially the less well known *Harry Richmond*, and with the possible exceptions of *Richard Feveral* and *The Egoist*, have not reached this stage yet, though they may well do so in the future. Furthermore, definitive editions are necessarily removed by price from normal use by student and general reader, and usually presuppose the existence of other accessible editions. *Harry Richmond* has been long out of print. For the purpose of the present edition (see Introduction, p. xii), it seemed most appropriate to aim at a reliable and full text, with the main variants, and with some careful attention to textual history, while stopping short of a definitive edition. (However, a collation of printed texts has been undertaken.) The general procedure followed in preparing the present edition was to work through the complete manuscript fairly quickly, making frequent checks against printed texts. The areas where substantial alterations were made, and others where alteration was suspected, have been worked over in detail and the results are presented below. Some substantial sections of the manuscript that were collated in detail with the printed texts were not altered, but of course only a full collation can reveal the extent and importance of the smaller alterations. On the whole, and with one notable exception, those picked up by rapid checking were not of great importance, and samples will be given. Though the manuscript seems to have been a "final" draft, containing few canceled and rewritten passages, insertions in the margin are numerous, and include the marking of chapter divisions and titles, which apparently Meredith left partly open until a late stage, possibly during serialization.

REVISIONS OF THE FINAL MANUSCRIPT

Interesting light on the method of the changes made between manuscript and first serial printing is afforded by nine pages of corrected *Cornhill* proof, which accompany the relevant manuscript pages. These proofs cover Chapter XLV of the serial (*Cornhill*, XXIV, 129–136, Chapter XLIV of the present revised text; the relevant pages in the second part of the manuscript are 246–271). The proofs reveal that slight changes were introduced between corrected page proofs (probably first proofs) and the printed serial, so that Meredith could contemplate and effect alterations up to the last minute before printing, as well as making later changes to the printed text. (The proofs also contained a marginal instruction showing the end of the serialized section for July, 1871, and the beginning of the section for August, a chapter division that was changed back to the manuscript division, except for an added opening paragraph, only with the second edition of 1886.) The changes to the proofs consist of some minor deletions (mainly concerning Eckhart's impressions of London), and small additions (mainly technical details concerning financial arrangements), which need not concern us here; the main importance of the proofs is to suggest how and when other more important and substantial changes were made between manuscript and serial. The fact that alterations were made in the middle of substantial paragraphs suggests that Meredith was not inhibited by the resetting charges, which can be expensive in modern printing.

The most substantial changes to the manuscript version consist mainly of omissions from manuscript Chapters XXX–XXXIX (reduced to Chapters XXX–XXXIV in the printed texts). These omissions were probably made either at the same stage as the alterations above, or in first proof, for the relevant pages of manuscript show no cuts and bear the names of compositors in the appropriate place, thus suggesting they were originally set up in type. The general trend of the deletions, to the mind of the present editor, is to tighten up the account of Harry's second trip to Germany, which centers around his relationship with Ottilia, without omitting anything essential, and less importantly, to reduce the "adventurous" or "romance" element. Indeed, what was pruned away included some inferior as well as unnecessary material. The German episode, thus abridged, took up two monthly installments, March and April, 1871 (though the February installment included Harry's second meeting with Ottilia at Ostend, their growing attraction to one another, and his trip to Germany, Chapters XXIV–XXVI); and Meredith may have thought that to extend this German section into a third installment would retard both the "adventurous" external movement and the linked inner development of the protagonist. His letters show that he was afraid of such slowing-up in this section (see Introduction, p. xix), and it may have been that he only came to full realization of its extent during serialization. In writing the manuscript Meredith may not have been working with any exact idea of serial apportioning. The marginal insertions of the beginnings of Chapters XIV, XVII (which begins in the middle of a manuscript paragraph), XXI, XXXIII, XXXVII, and many later ones suggest that he was relying on the printed stage to some extent as part of the process of composition.

Of the manuscript chapters, Chapter XXX, "Shows the troubles of Love coming On"; Chapter XXXI, "She is an Enigma"; and Chapter XXXII, "A Summer Storm and Love"; only the last-named was retained as Chapter XXX of the printed version. Much of the matter of the other two chapters was omitted, but some of the more important material appeared in condensed form, and several passages were retained at the beginning of Chapter XXXI (most of the present

text, Chapter XXX, pp. 253–255, was retained from manuscript Chapter XXX).

Manuscript Chapter XXX centered around a "preparatory"
meeting of Harry and Ottilia in the forest and their talk together. The chapter opens with the Margravine praising the
superior fortunes of "the young persons of exalted station,"
for they enjoy the advantages of having their careers marked
out in advance and need not have, indeed they are "bound,"
not to have, any ideas or will of their own (manuscript 521).
This "hereditary pride" is gently mocked by Ottilia, but
Harry still feels the barrier of rank dividing them. Typically
vacillating, he sees no future for their lives, yet does not
despair. Next, Harry hears a report of how his father has
been pushing his "case" in England and impressing the Prince
with Harry's wealth, a section that was drastically condensed
(see present text, p. 254: "He had hired . . . grandfather's
mine"). The exaggeration of Roy's having the effrontery to
take the Prince to Riversley while the squire was away was
one of the deleted details along with Roy's diatribe against
"study." In the discarded chapter Harry now studies for a
year in reaction against his father, then has an "accidental"
meeting with Ottilia in the forest in which much is made of
the romantic setting. Ottilia speaks of the greater advantages
for achieving independence, flexibility, and self-knowledge
that men enjoy over women with their "evil reputation for
constancy," because for one thing men have easier access to
"change of scene, shifting of habitation, changes of fortunes"
(manuscript 534–535). Her ideas have an unconscious irony
in view of Harry's limitations. From the drawbacks of women
Ottilia moves on to discuss the drawbacks of rank which lead
to isolation, selfishness, and stagnation. These ideas echo
views she has already expressed (for example, present text
Chapter XXVII, p. 243), and along with her views on women
they also explicitly echo, here and later, her tutor Dr. Julius,
to whom Meredith had already devoted a complete chapter
(XXIX). Meredith's pruning down of the social criticism,
here and in other deletions, is also perhaps explicable in terms
of a desire to keep this subsidiary element from looming too
largely—of preventing some of the concerns of his next novel,
Beauchamp's Career, from spilling over into *Harry Rich-*

mond. (See Introduction, p. xxix, for comment on the role of social criticism in *Harry Richmond*.) In summary of deleted Chapter XXX, then, we may say that the ideas and situations serve little to develop what has already been established, though the treatment is interesting.

Manuscript Chapter XXX ended (manuscript 542) with an anonymous letter to Harry warning him briefly and vaguely that the Princess is in need of help. Manuscript Chapter XXXI, "She is an Enigma," deals with Harry at Sarkeld, trying to work out Ottilia's state of mind and inclined to attribute his own uncertainty to her, as he does in the printed version. In the same manuscript Chapter XXXI (558) a second anonymous letter of greater length and urgency arrives to distress Harry, but the chapter ends with his dismissing the advice of Aennchen, Ottilia's maid, for him to act. A third letter reached him in a deleted part of manuscript Chapter XXXII (567). The title of manuscript Chapter XXXI pointing to "enigma," the letters, and the uncertainty they evoke, set the tone for much of the chapter and show a tendency to build up mystery and tension, to heighten this kind of "romance" contrivance. Apparently Meredith later thought this dispensable as not in keeping with the rest of the novel, which does not depend on such synthetic elements, though doubt and mystery of a different kind hang over Roy. Perhaps these deletions provide a clue to at least one trend in the rewriting of the novel after the first submission to George Smith.

In the printed version Meredith used the text of the first brief letter, closely followed in the same condensing paragraph (present text, p. 256, "I threw my books . . .") by a further two letters of unspecified contents, simply to help unsettle Harry's mind and urge him on to another meeting with Ottilia. In the rewriting this is all managed briefly without fuss and portentiousness. The letters are again introduced briefly in a passage additional to the manuscript text (present text, p. 259, "I told her . . . if I had any") to help to explain and excuse Harry's fervid declaration of his love.

Dr. Julius makes another, redundant appearance in manuscript Chapter XXXI, voicing the same republican ideas, and he is ironically mystifying about Ottilia. Mr. Peterborough,

Meredith's lifeless caricature of a dull-witted, small-minded English clergyman, and a piece of novelistic furniture, also appears here and in later omitted sections, where the small talk of his clerical insularity is offset in the next chapter (in a passage of manuscript also deleted) by the distaste for German manners displayed by another "exile," Alphonse, Roy's French cook. These passages show Meredith trying unsuccessfully and unnecessarily to extend the novel's range, but he was never successful in imitating Dickens.

In manuscript Chapter XXXI in a scene of drawing room conversation at a low ebb Harry draws out Mr. Peterborough on "the riches of Oxford University"; the Prince and Margravine approve its "age" and "dignity," while Ottilia "murmurs" "Overwealthy! Overwealthy!" (Manuscript 562). The Margravine also figures in the same manuscript chapter as Ottilia's watchdog and a conversational fencer who succeeds in entrapping Harry into a show of feeling during a rather artificial episode as he is singing a song (manuscript 553–554). In general Meredith seemed here to be trying to widen the interest but succeeding rather in dispersing it. However, he did well to retain, with slight changes, Harry's diagnosis of his self-deception and posturings (present text, p. 255, "I was deceiving nobody . . . vileness of spirit"). Manuscript Chapter XXXII, "A Summer Storm and Love," important for bringing the lovers to a mutual declaration and for showing Harry's turbulent, jealous state of mind, was little changed except for the material from the omitted two chapters introduced at the beginning. The two main omissions of half a dozen (manuscript 571–572) and a dozen (manuscript 576–577) lines show Meredith dispensing with Harry's wildest flights of feeling, of what is elsewhere called his "freneticism," a trend that is followed in later deletions from the manuscript. Even with these cuts Harry's exaggerated passions, pampering his ego and delaying action, emerge forcefully, so Meredith may have been concerned to show his hero's foolishness sufficiently yet without exaggeration. The first omission compares him to a "man of Southern blood spying the shady hesitations and ultimate evanishings of his gross olive mistress" (manuscript 571); the second omission expresses Harry's sentimental outpourings when he comes upon Ottilia. For the latter Meredith substituted the brief ironic phrase "a lover's speech, breathless" (present text, p. 259).

Chapter XXXII of the printed texts, "An Interview with Prince Ernest and a Meeting with Prince Otto," represents a condensing, with substantial omissions, of two manuscript chapters: XXXIV, "An Interview with Prince Ernest: My Father's French Company of Actors," and XXXV, "The Duel." The deletions from manuscript Chapter XXXIV follow the pattern already established of condensing what amounted to an unimportant "by-play" of the minor characters or accessories, though some of Roy's small talk is also dispensed with. Jorian De Witt's presence becomes a token one instead of his being presented as yet another type of "exile" (one contemptuous of his own country) who provokes a defense from Peterborough. Roy's French company of actors also becomes more strictly functional, and the role of actress Jenny Chassediane here and in the next manuscript chapter was severely cut down. Jenny was of course to be retained and Harry was to have an affair with her, but she was always to appear more fragmentarily than even Heriot and Kiomi. (In revision of the printed texts she became still more functional.) But in manuscript Chapter XXXIV her favoring of Harry appeals to his vanity and sentimentality and she helps to spur him on to the duel with Otto by encouraging him in his role as lovelorn, but gallant "Chevalier." The chapter ended somewhat melodramatically: the two "shook hands like men, and kissed on the right cheek and the left at parting" (manuscript 614), and while he is on his way to the duel, to help Harry's cause she sings before Ottilia a song "from the great French repertoire" that was more applicable than she imagined: while his lady battled with love and pride her knight "has been assailed and lies in his blood. He dies. 'Il est beau, le chevalier' " (manuscript 615). In the printed version the French troupe and Jenny's action were drastically condensed into a paragraph (present text, p. 268, "In spite of myself . . . listened to the song") in which Harry speaks only ironically and laconically of Jenny's song as the "kind of enginery" in which Roy and Jorian believed.

In the next manuscript Chapter XXXV Jenny's part in urging Harry to the duel is recapitulated, but Meredith omitted
this in the printed version, in which Harry's motivation is
based more firmly and exclusively in the pride fanned by his
father, though this is not so enlarged upon as in the manuscript. Such enlargment may have seemed unnecessary and
retarding, especially as Harry's talk with Ottilia in the next
chapter, "What Came of a Shilling," throws important and
supporting retrospective light on the motivation of the duel.
The change in motivation may have been made for several
reasons: to prevent Jenny from figuring on a scale incon-
sistent with her very minor role and diverting the focus from
the relationship of father and son; to avoid some rather artificial melodrama; and even perhaps to keep Harry's foolishness, still palpable enough in the printed text, within bounds.
(Some of the more exaggerated phrases about Harry's "crazy
pride," for example, "preposterously majestic like a drunken
Sultan in his seraglio" [manuscript 621], were also omitted.)

Harry's ironic excuse to the reader for his moralizing and
self-analysis (present text, p. 270, "My English tongue . . .")
is more sustained in the manuscript (624), where he calls himself back to his "audience and business": "Why indeed should
I present you a tract when you came to me for haberdashery!"

Some details of the duel itself were omitted from the manuscript, and in revision of the printed text it was further condensed. These alterations and the avoidance of devoting a
chapter to the duel give the event itself a less important place
and left Meredith free to concentrate on its causes and effects
in Chapter XXXIII, "What Came of a Shilling," retained in
the printed text. Perhaps Meredith was chary of letting the
externally "adventurous" (the conventional romance) element
loom too large, as also seemed to be his motive in curbing
the mysteries of manuscript Chapter XXXI, "She is an
Enigma."

Manuscript Chapters XXXVIII, "Prince Hermann"; and
XXXIX, "I am in My Father's Hands," were condensed and
incorporated into Chapter XXXIV, "I Gain a Perception of
a Princely State," in the printed text (Chapter XXXVII in
manuscript). Sections of the last-named manuscript chapter
were also omitted, especially some of Harry's wilder emotional

moments of hurt pride (manuscript 672, 679–682). These included the writing of three angry letters to Ottilia, none of them sent, and his shamed revulsion when Aennchen avoids him, and feeling like a "forlorn yelping brute," he locks himself up "and wept—whined!" (manuscript 681). In the printed version Meredith substituted a sentence referring generally to Harry's "fantastic raptures and despair, my loss of the power to appreciate anything at its right value" revealing to him "the madness of loving a Princess" (present text, p. 295).

The manuscript Chapter XXXVIII, "Prince Hermann," shows Harry giving on emphasis to Hermann's rivalry similar to that originally given to Otto and the duel. Besides bringing out Harry's "animal nervousness" in manuscript, Meredith originally envisaged a sequel episode for Ottilia's rebuff of Hermann and Harry's attendant feeling of humiliation. In this sequel (manuscript 694–697) Ottilia waits for Harry at the spot where they first met, but he refuses to go to her and instead rides to the Bella Vista promontory, the scene of Roy's pretentious acting of a memorial statue of royalty. This passage, with its obvious symbolism, and the consequent analysis of Harry's motives and freneticism, were omitted along with an accompanying episode in which he is summoned by Ottilia, only to "act the impassive English gentleman of continental tradition" (manuscript 699), still refusing to speak out honestly. Meredith may have felt these parts added needless convolutions and repetitions—after all he gives sufficient evidence in the retained text of the whole German episode of Harry's allowing his injured pride and egotism to distort and delay the expression of his true feelings. As we have seen in the Introduction, Harry's growth proceeds by oscillations and circlings, but one of Meredith's problems was not to overemphasize this movement to the point of losing the reader's interest. The analysis of Harry's motives in the omitted passages covers familiar ground except perhaps for Harry's admission that he had "been indulging a feeble spirit of revenge" (manuscript 698) against Ottilia, his meanest motive, so there is the added possibility already suggested by other omissions that unheroic as his hero was, Meredith may have wished to keep his folly within limits. (The deletion of four chapters in the revision of the printed texts also included much mean-spirited behavior on Harry's part.) It is arguable, however, that the omitted passages do not make Harry out to be much, or even any, worse than is shown or intimated elsewhere in the printed text. His next step of entrapping Ottilia into a pledge of love at his father's suggestion is ungenerous enough. The omitted passages in manuscript Chapter XXXVIII included Harry's defense of his autobiographic honesty in baring his weaknesses, on the grounds that most people have times in their lives which they "hate and abjure" in retrospect because they represent departures from "sound reason and straight feeling" to play instead ridiculous puppet roles (manuscript 695–697). He held up such honesty as preferable to "glorified heroes" in a passage (manuscript 697) in which Meredith's strained, didactic style intrudes to an extent not often felt in the printed novel.

Meredith condensed the fourteen pages of manuscript, arranging the fully dramatized step of the entrapping of Ottilia in the next manuscript Chapter XXIX, "I am in My Father's Hands," into a substantial passage of printed text in Chapter XXXIV (see present text, pp. 298–300, "I was in the mood . . . flattering him immensely"). In the condensation Meredith omitted more of Peterborough and emphasized Harry's crucial step of shifting his burden of decision onto his father by confiding in him in return for the soothing of his hurt pride and the revival of his false hopes. If this switch is reported rather than demonstrated in the printed text, we have seen enough of Harry's ways of surrendering to his father.

Besides the foregoing substantial omissions and condensations of manuscript material there are a number of smaller discrepancies between the manuscript and printed text, though none that the present editor has noted seems of major importance, with one exception to be discussed below. Two examples may be of interest. In Chapter XXXV, "The Scene in the Lake Palace Library," in the middle of the paragraph describing the embrace between the lovers (present text, p. 308, "We had our full draught . . .") which, in an omitted manuscript passage, explicitly took the place of a pledge, Meredith also omitted a sentence describing "the fervour of her yielding . . . the grace of her dear head turned up to me, the languid pressure of her hands and abandonment of her proud spirit" (manuscript 746). Though this description is not highly sensual, Meredith may have thought that it was not quite in harmony with the balance between generous feeling and rational control that he tries to maintain in Ottilia, and with her raising of Harry "beyond fretful thirst and its reputed voracity" in the same passage.

Perhaps the most interesting of the shorter changes was made to the very end of the manuscript and shows that Meredith was capable of adding a major touch at the very last minute. The second from the last sentence of the present text revealing that Roy must have remained in burning Riversley to save Aunt Dorothy, a restrained touch that a number of commentators have pointed to as nicely combining and summing up Roy's strange blend of opposing qualities of foolishness and generous feeling, of the heroic and the theatrical, does not appear in the manuscript. In addition, the cause of the fire, an explosion of fireworks which ignited the highly combustible and "extraordinary decorations" Roy had arranged for the grand homecoming, another detail that makes the manner of his death so in keeping with his life and character, was written into the manuscript as a marginal insertion (". . . from an explosion . . . in harmony with my father's fancy," present text, p. 544, ll. 9–14).

ALTERATIONS TO THE SERIAL TEXT, AND THE "SECOND EDITION"

Bibliography and Various Readings (volume XXXVI of the de Luxe Edition, XXVII of the Memorial Edition, both published in 1911) does not record alterations to the serial text (*Cornhill*, XXII–XXIV, September, 1870–November, 1871), but they are not of great importance, and several only are included in the present list of variants. It may be that these alterations, mainly clarification of details of expression, are the ones Meredith referred to in a letter to George Smith, November 19, 1871:

This is good news [Professor Cline adds: "that a second edition of *Harry Richmond* has been called for"], and it is very good of you to be so prompt in sending the cheque.

As to a preface, I can hardly bring myself to write one.

Will it not be enough to say "Revised, corrected"?—

What I did was to rewrite a large portion of the work before it appeared in the *Cornhill* so as to make it an almost entirely different thing from what you read in MS. It has been touched subsequently, but not enough to make mention of it and trip the practice of the library people.

As there has been little reviewing upon it hitherto, will it not be as well to keep the press open if you only print an extra 250 copies?—You will know best as to this point. . . .[18]

The alterations Meredith refers to here ("touched subsequently") and the reference to "trip[ping] the practice of the library people" become clearer if they are related to the nature of the "second edition" and an earlier letter to Smith. The concluding section of the letter suggests that what is being discussed is a further issue, or second impression, of the first edition, rather than a second edition in the sense of a different text and/or second printing. This suggestion has been confirmed by what I have been able to discover about the "second edition."

M. B. Forman in his *Bibliography of George Meredith*[19] lists such an edition, differing from the first of three volumes only in the adding of "second edition" to the title page, but Forman explicitly relied on Smith, Elder's records rather than a perusal of an actual copy. The edition is in fact made up of "extra" sheets of the first three-volume edition run off for the purpose and bound into one volume in a dark blue binding (the first edition had been "in crimson cloth boards"[20]), and with a price of thirty-one shillings and sixpence, the same price as the first edition, stamped on the spine. The words "Second Edition" are overstamped on the title page, which is in effect the title page of Volume I of the first edition (the title pages of Volumes II and III, and their separate Contents lists of chapters, appearing later in the appropriate places). The text is thus the same as that of the first edition, and a collation of the relevant parts with other editions has confirmed that this "second edition" contains the same few altera-

---

18 *Letters*, I, 457.

19 Edinburgh, 1922, p. 48.

20 Forman, *Bibliography*, p. 46. Forman lists the price of the first edition as thirty-one shillings and sixpence.

tions of the serial text as the first edition and, like it, also lacks the more substantial revisions appearing in the next (1886) edition. However, the "second edition" of 1871 contains one significant addition, not to the actual text, but to the pre-liminaries. An inserted page following the title page declares that: "The Story Is Laid On The Foundation Of A Young Man's Love For His Father." This is obviously a reading direction, suggested either by Meredith or his publishers, but probably at least agreed to by Meredith. It may have been prompted by the fact that half of the reviewers up to the time of the appearance of the "second edition" (December 11, 1871),[21] had found it difficult to trace any satisfying and uni-fying coherence in the narrative, and some later reviewers (of the first edition) expressed the same dissatisfaction. The direction of the readers' attention to the central thread of the relations between father and son, emphasizing the son's love, may also have been meant to offset the strong moral disap-proval of the *Examiner* and the *Daily Telegraph*[22] by suggest-ing a different emphasis. The reviewers of these organs had disapproved of the way the autobiographic hero appeared to dally selfishly with the affections of two women at the one time, even when one (Janet) was betrothed to another man. *The Ordeal of Richard Feverel* (1859) had been subtitled "A History of Father and Son," but the similar reading direction added to the "second edition" (1871) of *Harry Richmond* does not appear to have been carried over to later editions.

Two weeks prior to writing to Smith about the proposed "second edition" (in the letter quoted above), Meredith had been despondent about the novel's reception: "I sup-pose I am unlucky, for the novel does not move. It is confounded by Mudie with the quantity coming out."[23] It is puzzling then, that a limited "second edition" was published

[21] See *Athenaeum* (A. J. Butler), November 4, 1871; *Echo*, November 10, 1871; *Examiner*, November 11, 1871. Later reviews which expressed the same criticism are: *Academy*, December 15, 1871; *Queen*, December 30, 1871; *Spectator* (R. H. Hutton), January 20, 1872; *Vanity Fair*, March 23, 1872; *Blackwood's Edinburgh Magazine*, June, 1872, pp. 755 ff.
[22] *Examiner*, November 11, 1871; *Daily Telegraph*, November 20, 1871. The later *Spectator* notice, January 20, 1872, expressed a similar disapproval.
[23] *Letters*, I, 454.

(December 11, 1871) just over a month after this was written and seven weeks after the first edition (October 26, 1871),[24] unless the novel had suddenly become sought after. This does not seem to be the case, and a clue to the main reason for the "second edition" is provided by a letter Meredith wrote to George Smith nearly three weeks after the publication of the first edition:

> I am told that W. H. Smith's Library gives the bound-up copies of the *Cornhill* containing *Richmond* in the place of the three volumes [of the first book edition; Smith, Elder the publishers were not connected with W. H. Smith & Son]. You are the principal party concerned in it. Are you aware of the fact and is it worth a remonstrance?[25]

If Meredith's letter about the "second edition" is a reply to Smith's answer to this query, then the letters, along with the bibliographical evidence, help to provide a possible explanation for the nature of the "second edition." The issuing of the *Cornhill* version instead of the first edition by W. H. Smith's Library appears to have prompted Meredith's publisher, George Smith, into the defensive action of issuing a "second edition" without any lowering of price in spite of the different binding and the three volumes in one and perhaps serving to increase sales by suggesting a popular demand. Meredith's willingness to add "revised, corrected" to the "extra copies" of the "second edition" suggests a further tactic for competing with W. H. Smith's by providing an edition that superseded the serial version. When Meredith wrote to Smith that the novel "has been touched subsequently, but not enough to trip the practice of the library people," he must have been referring to the slight alterations made to the serial text (for the text of the "second edition" did not differ from that of the first). These alterations were insufficient for the purpose of frustrating W. H. Smith's by-passing of the first edition, by offering a text which superseded the serial version, a tactic presumably suggested by Smith.

---

24 Both dates from Forman, *Bibliography*, p. 46, and the latter are confirmed by advertisements.
25 November 14, 1871, *Letters*, I, 456.

Meredith's correspondence with Smith shows that the latter was being cautious about the number of copies he printed, both of the first and "second" editions. If an "extra 250" copies were printed in so short a time, then the first edition seems to have been restricted, even though the serial seems to have been reasonably well received. This caution was no doubt prompted by the financial failure of Meredith's two preceding novels, *Rhoda Fleming* (1864) and *Vittoria* (1866).[26] He complained that "*Vittoria* has made the publishers' faces cold. I knock at many doors."[27]

Whether or not Smith did "keep the press open" at Meredith's suggestion after printing the "250 extra copies," it is unlikely that substantial numbers were printed, for although Meredith was expecting later reviews to boost sales, these notices were unfavorable and even discouraging.[28] One wonders why a *Cornhill* novel, which was on the whole favorably received by reviewers of the serial installments if it did not go uncriticized,[29] was "confounded by Mudie with the quantity coming out," to the point of either not being stocked or given much circulation,[30] and was not in demand by W. H. Smith's Library. Such treatment by these two powerful organizations was probably sufficient to spoil *Harry Richmond*'s chance of wide sales and readership. A possible clue is provided by the moral disapproval which led some reviewers to disparage the novel. *Richard Feverel* had been banned from

---

[26] See the present writer's "Meredith's Attempts to Win Popularity," *Studies in English Literature*, IV (Autumn 1964), 637–651.

[27] May 26 (1867), *Letters*, I, 358.

[28] See footnote 26 above and the present writer's "Meredith's Revisions of 'Harry Richmond,'" *Review of English Studies*, XIV (February 1963), 24–32.

[29] For details of the reception of the serial installments by a variety of newspapers and journals, see the present writer's unpublished Ph.D. dissertation, "The Contemporary Reception of the Novels of George Meredith, from *The Shaving of Shagpat* to *The Egoist*," in the Library of London University (Senate House), pp. 307–311, 565–566, and a list of the reviews, pp. 589–590. Criticism of the serial was directed mainly at a lack of coherence, a complaint that was taken up by reviewers of the first edition.

[30] Mudie's published lists in periodicals show that the novel was not advertised. Covert criticism of the reigning Royal House of the monarchical system may have offended some readers and influenced the libraries, but it was not mentioned by reviewers.

Mudie's eleven years before, *Modern Love* had been condemned, and *Vittoria* had been frowned upon by the influential *Spectator*, for similar reasons. If such disapproval did hamper the novel's reception, then it is possible that some of Meredith's later revisions may have been made in an attempt to remove these grounds of objection. Such revisions could include the four deleted chapters containing Harry's most "ungentlemanly" treatment of the opposite sex (Janet), a paring down of the illicit love of Heriot and Kiomi and of Harry's affair with the actress Jenny Chassediane, and also some deletions of minor "sensual" passages.

Available evidence seems to suggest, then, that the "second edition" or issue of *Harry Richmond* testifies not to its popularity, as some commentators have assumed,[31] but to difficulties of circulation and restricted sales. The novel was not reprinted again until its appearance in the first collected edition of the novels in 1886. Since the "second edition" of 1871 was a further issue of the first rather than a second edition in any firm sense, I have reserved this term for the 1886 edition, which was not only a separate printing but a substantially revised text.

For the purposes of the present edition a verbal collation of the *Cornhill* text with the final revised printed version was undertaken with the kind assistance of my wife. The revised text used was the Memorial Edition (volumes IX and X, Constable & Co., London, 1910), a reprint of the finally revised text first published in the de Luxe Edition (volumes 11 and 12, Constable & Co., 1897). The Memorial Edition was used because of its accessibility, but reference was made where it seemed necessary, to the de Luxe Edition, to the first and second (1886) editions, and to the published list of the alterations made to the text of the first edition. This published list appears in the volumes *Bibliography and Various Readings*, (volume XXXVI of the de Luxe Edition and volume XXVII

---

31 Hudson, "Meredith's Autobiography," p. 49, grants the novel "at least a small success" on the basis of the "second edition." See also Jack Lindsay, *George Meredith* (London, 1956), p. 188. Siegfried Sasson finds the "unprecedented event" (for Meredith up to this stage) of a second edition due to the serialization in the *Cornhill*, which "meant success for a novelist" (*Meredith* [London, 1948], p. 106).

of the Memorial Edition, both published in 1911), and my collation shows that with several exceptions, it provides a full and accurate record of the important revisions. Consequently the section "Revisions of the Original Text" in the present edition largely coincides with the one in *Bibliography and Various Readings*. Only those additional alterations that seemed important to the present editor have been added, and trivial alterations have not been recorded. Unless otherwise specified, the listed alterations were made to the text of the first edition for the preparation of the second (1886) edition.

REVISIONS OF THE TEXT OF THE FIRST EDITION AND CHOICE OF COPY-TEXT

The novel's republication in the First Collected Edition of the Novels, by Chapman and Hall and Roberts Brothers, Boston, in 1886, marked "New Edition" on the title page, was reprinted by Chapman and Hall more cheaply in a number of impressions in 1889–1895, still marked "New Edition." The Yale University Library holds a copy of the 1894 impression of this edition containing revisions and corrections in blue pencil, mostly in Meredith's hand in preparation for the finally revised text, the de Luxe Edition of 1897. The Lilly Library of the University of Indiana at Bloomington holds a copy of the same reprint, revised and corrected and forwarded to Scribners for inclusion in the 1897–1899 American edition of the works. These two copies, almost identical in their markings, have been consulted in the preparation of the present edition. They reveal that nearly all the revisions listed in *Bibliography and Various Readings*, and all the important revisions, were undertaken for the 1886 edition and its impressions, that is, the alterations were made to the text of the first edition of 1871. The few alterations of any importance made to the present text for the finally revised text of 1897 may be found under "Revisions of the Original Printed Text" in the present edition under entries for pp. 14, 259, 311, 326, 419, 443, 449, 506. I have also supplied a list of "Misprints and Errors" contained in the present text. The insignificant changes of punctuation, consisting mostly of the addition or rearrangement of commas and the introduction of new paragraphs, are not listed because they in no way affect the meaning.

The slightness of the final revisions made to the present text for the 1897 de Luxe Edition hardly bears out Meredith's statement to Gissing that he was "slashing at the novels"[32] so far as *Harry Richmond* is concerned. Of the other novels, *Richard Feverel* underwent a more extensive revision, though the more substantial revisions to its text had been made earlier, as with *Harry Richmond*. One may wonder, then, if, and how far, the revisions for the 1897 de Luxe Edition, were token ones, made to increase circulation of Meredith's works by offering a final, authorized text that would become standard and replace existing ones. By this time Meredith had transferred his copyrights from Chapman and Hall to Constable and Company, and his son, William Maxse Meredith, had taken a position with the latter firm. William took a prominent part in arranging for Scribners to gain the American copyright of the finally revised works.[33] It is significant that Scribners were able to take out a new copyright because of the final revisions to the texts, which provided an opportunity for transferring the American rights of some of the early novels from Roberts Brothers, from a conservative to a more enterprising firm. The surviving correspondence at the Princeton University Library concerning the arrangement with Scribners shows that William Meredith was eager for Scribners to acquire American copyright of the revised works because he foresaw great advantages to both parties, and he laid emphasis on the revisions which made the acquisition possible, admitting that while in the case of some novels they were not important, they were more considerable in some of the most popular novels, including *Richard Feverel*. It may be significant that *Richard Feverel* was the first novel of the de Luxe Edition and the first to be offered to Scribners for American copyright. A letter to Scribners from O. Kyllman of Constable and Company[34] also stresses the final revisions

---

[32] Statement quoted by Lionel Stevenson, *The Ordeal of George Meredith* (London, 1954), p. 329.

[33] Correspondence in the Princeton University Library.

[34] Correspondence in the Princeton University Library, September 2, 1896.

and the importance of the circulation of a standard edition of the works in America.

Since the 1897 finally revised text was physically unsuitable for reprinting in the present format, the text of the second, revised edition of 1886 (in the form of an 1889 Chapman and Hall impression) was chosen as copy-text for the present edition. Besides its physical suitability, it has the advantages of containing very nearly all the revisions, and certainly the most important, and in addition of being the last version actually corrected and revised by Meredith himself. Hence the misprints and errors in this edition, though reproduced, have been located with the help of the author.

GENERAL SURVEY OF REVISIONS TO THE PRINTED TEXT

An editorial principle observed by some editors is that the copy-text should approximate as closely as possible to the author's final intentions. However, it would be unreasonable to apply this rule in every case regardless of its suitability to particular circumstances. An editor may consider that on literary grounds an unrevised text is preferable to the revision, though in this case he will do well to offer readers both, or all, versions, if that is possible, so that they can choose for themselves and use the variants to reach a deeper understanding of a writer and his methods. The present edition follows this procedure.

As I have given elsewhere my reasons for preferring the unrevised (first edition and serial) texts of *Harry Richmond* to the revised version,[35] and have also touched upon reasons for this question in the present Introduction, there is no need to argue it at length here. The question must remain to some extent an open one, and unfortunately we have no statement of authorial intention to guide us in our choice.

The advantages of the unrevised text, as I see them, are that the deleted chapters allow Janet to assume a greater substantiality, in keeping with her important role in assisting Harry's development towards the end of the novel, and at the same time in these chapters Harry's growth reaches a more satis-

---

[35] See footnote 28 above, and also "Alterations to the Serial Text and the 'Second Edition,' " above, p. 568.

factory, if not a final, climax which draws its strength from its relationship to what has gone before—to similar and contrasting situations. In condensing the Heriot-Kiomi relationship, originally present in slight, fragmentary glimpses, Meredith succeeds only in taxing the reader's understanding unnecessarily. Some of the revisions to *Richard Feverel* make the plot harder to follow in a similar way, and perhaps in both instances Meredith may have acted out of impatient resentment at the failure of contemporary readers to understand his work even at the level of plot. Harry's affair with Jenny Chassediane, which is of some importance to his growth, is also made harder to piece together in the revised version. In addition, Meredith cut out some of the details which help to prepare and account for the gypsies' mistaken attack on Harry (present text, p. 416), and one of the reasons why Harry "invited" this attack is changed and becomes less convincing and meaningful in revision: instead of going straight to Heriot because he cannot face Janet and commit himself to her, we are told that the choice was between Heriot and his grandfather (present text, p. 415). However, several details of the Heriot-Kiomi relationship that were discarded could well be dispensed with: the rather melodramatic, if brief, details of their deaths originally worked into the second from the last paragraph. These show an untypical conventionality in Meredith (the illicit lovers punished by death) and detract from the more moving and significant death of Roy. The dropping of the brief allusion to Kiomi's illegitimate child in revision along with the condensing of the Harry–Jenny Chassediane and Heriot-Kiomi relationships, and the omission of Harry's "ungentlemanly" behavior to Janet in the deleted chapters, may have been prompted by the moral disapproval the novel provoked in its first appearance, though such a view must remain speculative. Another trend in the revisions is to exclude some of Harry's more "frenetic" moments in specific passages (for example, pp. 516, 521). Excesses of this kind present in the manuscript were omitted from the printed texts, as we have seen, and they also figure importantly in the three chapters deleted from the end of the novel.

APPENDIX B

REVISIONS OF THE ORIGINAL PRINTED TEXT

THE following list shows the revisions made to the original printed text, that is, the serial version in the *Cornhill*. The revisions made to the serial text for the first edition of 1871 are indicated by "(1871)" at the end of an entry. The revisions made to the second edition text of 1886 for the finally revised text, the de Luxe Edition of 1897, are indicated by "(1897)" at the end of an entry. All other revisions listed were made to the text of the first edition in three volumes, 1871, for the second edition of 1886. This list of revisions supplements previous ones by adding sixteen additional entires (see "A Note on the text," p. 569), but trivial alterations of punctuation (insertion and removal of commas, new paragraphs, changes from lower to upper case) have not been added, and a list of "Misprints, Punctuation, and Author's Errors in the Present Edition Corrected for the Finally Revised de Luxe Edition of 1897" is given separately (p. 610).

p. 14, *l.* 20. *After* "Hamlet" *deleted*: I cannot say why, but . . . . (1897)

p. 122, *l.* 37. path of living: *altered from* path of right living.

p. 130, *l.* 29 "light" was originally "life" in previous texts, but though "life" was retained in the final revision (1897) it may be an uncorrected misprint as suggested in *Bibliography & Various Readings.*

p. 200, *l.* 15. *After* "creature's name" *deleted*: Previously they had reckoned on my father for sparing her, and had done as they liked.

p. 200, *l.* 18. *After* "cavalier" *deleted*: Mervyn Penrhys,

p. 210, *l.* 36. natural guardian has left the annual interest of your money to accumulate *altered from* natural guardian has put out the annual interest of your money to considerable profit. (1871)

p. 201, *l.* 2. *After* Lady Wilts *deleted*:

My reply to this attack was mixed up with the broad vowels of eloquent discomposure:

573

"Really, Miss Penrhys, you are under a delusion; I shall be happy; I like the mountains, I——"

"No delusion at all. But will you wait before you form a positive opinion of me?"

"I can't, for I've formed it already, and it's exactly the reverse of what you seem to have heard."

"Who calls you shy!" she returned, leaving me dissatisfied, I was sure.

p. 213, *l.* 31. *After* "father" *deleted*: and have been myself a prince deserving curses.

p. 214, last line. *Added*: She had suffered in life miserably.

p. 224, *l.* 10. *After* women rascals *omitted*: Your English vaurien is indeed un ange déchu—we will not say from what side of Paradise." (1871)

p. 246, *l.* 26. pressure of my hand: *altered from* pressure of my lips on her hand.

p. 251, *l.* 16. After "then" *deleted*: and it's sound.

p. 259, *l.* 11. *After* she said *deleted*: Her fingers tightened on my wrist. (1897)

p. 261, *l.* 20. *After* "I replied" *deleted*: and gained it by abnegation.

p. 265, *l.* 11. *After* at once *deleted*:

"Be seated," he said.

I bowed my head, and sat—a disadvantageous thing to do before an irritated man, erect and prepared to put harsh questions. My deliberate method of obeying him served for a reminder of what was due from him to me in courtesy, and he placed a chair in front of me, but could not persuade himself to occupy it immediately.

p. 266, *l.* 1. *Before* "Much, sir" *deleted*: I rose.

p. 266, *l.* 1. *After* Much, sir *deleted*:

"Then, pray be seated."

He set me the example, repeating "Much?"

From the excitement he was quite unable to conceal it was evident to me that the princess had done her part bravely and fully. I could not suffer myself to be beaten down.

p. 266, *l.* 2. *After* "he said" *deleted*: again.

p. 269, *l.* 26. *After* "observances" *deleted*: if I did laugh it was involuntarily.

p. 272, *l.* 18. *After* prostrate bodies *deleted*: I walked my part of the twenty-five paces' interval at a quick step, showing a parade front, irresolute about employing the disgusting little instrument I had in my clutch at all. Suddenly I felt a shock as of ice-cold water upon heated lungs. I remember staring at Bandelmeyer's spectacles and nodding like a bulrush. Eckart caught me. "Give it him off the ground," he cried in a frenzy. "You have a shot! a shot! a shot!" screamed Bandelmeyer, jumping. I could plainly see Prince Otto standing ready to receive my fire. I looked up, and was invited by the swimming branch of a tree to take aim in that direction. Down came the sky. I made several attempts to speak for the purpose of telling Bandelmeyer that it was foolish of him in the open air to smoke a pipe half as long as himself, but nothing seemed to matter much;—*adding*:

A silly business on all sides.

p. 272. *Beginning of* Chapter XXXIII. *deleted*:

Otto's bullet found its way right through me, as harmless as a comet in our atmosphere—the most considerate of intruders.

p. 273, *l.* 23. *After* "hear of it" *deleted*: by-and-by. "But the means?"

p. 277, *l.* 28. *After* "way to it" *deleted*: Remember that.

p. 278, *l.* 36. *After* speak *deleted*: My devotion and qualities of mind were not tested by herself only. It was not because she thought lightly of the treasure, but highly of the vessel that she embarked in it. And how much she had prepared herself to cast away I had still to learn.

p. 280, *l.* 6. with a blush *altered from*: in a burning blush.

p. 282, *l.* 13. *After* Leaning *deleted*: towards her.

p. 297, *l.* 14. *After* "at a bound" *deleted*: and I reversed my hold of my riding-whip.

p. 297, *l.* 20. *After* to witness *deleted*: I raced up closer, but I had to await the lady's orders before I dared strike between them.

Ottilia drew rein. "Now!" she said, and her hand was suffered to fall.

Then to me: "Mr. Richmond, I have my servant."

This was enough.

p. 311, *l.* 29. *After* rise to his *deleted*: sublime. (1897)

p. 326, *l.* 5. *After* "sham" *deleted*: It was given them to exercise the choice whether they would be prey to the natural hawk, man, if they liked it; pity was waste of breath, nonsense. Temple bantered him capitally by tracing the career of the natural hawk gorged with prey, and the mighty service he was of to his country. Heriot retorted that all great men had, we should find, entertained his ideas about women; but he was compelled to admit that a vast number of very small ones were similarly to be distinguished. (1897)

p. 326, *l.* 13. *After* grown *deleted*: terribly. (1897)

p. 326, *l.* 28. *After* "country" *deleted*: to be denied a chance of heirs of their gallant bodies?

p. 340, *l.* 8. *After* "sermon" *deleted*: from the new rector.

p. 345, *l.* 24. *After* "desert" *deleted*: not made for cookery.

p. 363, *l.* 1. *After* "whipcord" *deleted*: The reply came quick and keen to my thought. I suspected a mishap to one or the other of my friends, little guessing which one claimed my sympathy. My father desired her to enlighten him upon his fortune at an extreme corner of the station, where martins flew into sand-holes, which was his device to set her up in money for her journey. After we had seen her off, he spoke of her, and puffed, remarking that he had his fears; but he did not specify them.

p. 374, *l.* 16. "an imposter" was "no imposter" in the MS and serial, and "no imposter" seems to fit the context better. Though "an imposter" was retained in the final revision (1897), it may be an uncorrected misprint.

p. 375, *l.* 37. serve as a club: First Edition and MS: serve as a tub ("club" may be an uncorrected misprint still retained in the final revision of 1897).

p. 377, *l.* 10. *After* "town" *deleted*: Ik Deen, some say. That's the worst of a foreign language: no two people speak it alike.

p. 382, *l.* 18. "me" was originally "him" in previous texts, and though "me" was retained in the final revision (1897) it may be an uncorrected misprint as suggested in *Bibliography & Various Readings*.

p. 399, *l.* 28. *After* "confess" *deleted*: in my opinion, very much worse towards my father.

p. 401, *l.* 20. *After* "greatness" *deleted*: Heriot did not come to help me through my contest, for the reason, scarcely credible to his friends, that he was leading some wealthy lady to the altar. Janet's brows were gloomy at his name. That he, who was her model of gallantry, should marry in hot haste for money, degraded also her, who admired and liked him, and had, it may be, in a fit of natural rallying from grief, borne her part in a little game of trifling with him. The sentiments of Julia Bulsted were not wounded, by any means. She rejoiced to hear of Walter Heriot's having sense at last: to marry for money was the best thing he could do; and she rather twitted Janet for objecting, as a woman, to what was a compliment, and should be a comfort, to a jealous mind.

p. 405, *l.* 5. *After* perilous both *deleted*: We did not part without such a leave-taking as is held to be the privilege of lovers.

Then deleted as under: Chapter II, Volume III, First Edition; Chapter XLIV, *Cornhill* version.

A FIRST STRUGGLE WITH MY FATHER

JANET's desire that her grandada should taste of her happiness, sent her to intercept him on his way to the breakfast-table. The blush of her cheek sufficed. I knew what had occurred when he hailed me freshly, rubbing his hands. "So you're one of the Commons, Hal? Whacking majority? No? You're in, though, like the thief who filched St. Peter's keys.—'Come out,' says Peter. 'No,' says Bob Thief, 'I was a first-rate thief, more than your match t'other side the gate, and now I'm here for the reward of my craft,' says he, 'I'm washed white in a jiffy.'—All he had to do was to learn to sing. Lord forgive us! and let's to prayers. Harry there's a seat for you next to Janet. Captain and his wife'll take chairs opposite. Dorothy, my dear, we can't wait for them. Sooner breakfast's over the better; I want to have a talk with Mr. Hal. Harry, boy, I shall drink your health to-night. We'll scrape together a party. Janet, my girl, I don't mind a dance. The pleasure of life is to feel at home in your own house, and deuced few who do."

Notwithstanding the continued absence of Captain Bulsted and Julia, the squire insisted on my taking a chair beside Janet's; and I certainly felt a difference in being seated near, or away, from her. The hot flush of yesterday's triumph had not cooled. At a little distance, I yearned to have her within reach of an arm, but I could weigh her looks and actions. Close to her, close upon touching her, the temptation was lightly resisted, but my senses accepted everything she did, uncritically. And they might well do so. She supposed that we were one at heart, and betrothed; and a marvelously alluring, faintly-shadowed impossibility for her eyes to dwell hard or long on mine in the newness of her happiness, would have pleased even the critic I no more could be. Nor was there too much of this, as with damsels and dames inclining to push their prettinesses by overacting the delicate emotion. Her smile was not the accustomed staring daylight one, and had narrowed and gentler dimples. The frown of her marked eyebrows was rare, and when it came quivered. It never had been a frown of darkness; now it was like a bird alighting. She talked of the election: she wished she had been there.

"Just as well go to battle," said the squire; and eyeing her: "I believe you, my dear. You're the girl to back a husband. No; you keep out of the dust. Don't you be henchman to your lord and master till the house is attacked. Tough work yesterday, Hal?"

"And, Harry, why were you all in white?" Janet interposed.

"Oho! they floured him, did they?" the squire laughed.

"There was an idea in it, I am sure," said Janet.

"Meant, 'I'm a clean-looking fellow, the right sort of man for you'; eh, Hal?"

"Something the Romans did, or the Greeks, grandada, depend upon it."

She nodded knowingly at a turn of mine for tiny pedantries.

"What was it, Hal? Let's hear."

Well, sir, it was a white suit in the morning."

Top to toe? Hat and all?"

"Cap-à-pie, sir."

"Humph," he put on a right English pucker of the features. "Ha! All in white. Why, 'mn it! that's a penitent's dress. Was that the idea? Long sheet and candles? Didn't they call you a crowing chorister? I think I should have chaffed you, Mr. Hal. Froth's white, so's goose, curate, eggflip, give-up-the-ghost, oysters, and the liver that hoists the feather. I'd have been down upon you; couldn't ha' kept my tongue off you, if I'd been there. White! by the Lord, I'd ha' clapped a round of orange-blossoms on you. Why, you must have looked as if Lot's wife had dropped you after she turned her head back. All in white, by George! like a candidate for the sepulchre. Did you go about horizontal? Vote for the corpse! Be dished, Hal, if that white suit was your own idea!"

"There I'm against you, grandada," said Janet, and appealed to my aunt Dorothy, who was of her opinion that the squire had better not be allowed to catch scent of my father in Chippenden, and observed: "Harry always had a liking for light colours; so had his mother."

"A little ballast won't do him harm. A pitcher o' common sense at his elbow!" rejoined the squire. "Hang that 'all in white!' I shall have a nightmare o' that. It's not English. I hate a fellow in a Tom Fool's uniform. Fancy how you'd look in a caricature. Wonder the mob didn't borrow you to chalk their ale-house scores! White! why, election time's the time for showing your colours."

"Yellow and blue stand out well on white," said Janet.

We saw that he was scenting hard in the track of my father, for sign of which he asked first: "Were you the only one in white?" And then: "How much did this election cost you?"

I stopped him by saying: "To begin with, we may put down the cost of the white hat for five-and-twenty shillings."

"Oh, I shall pay all the costs, and I mean to look at the items for myself," said he.

Inspired by Janet, he recovered his cheerfulness, but it was a fleeting glimpse of domestic sunshine. He carried me off to the library, where, telling me he had seen by his girl's face that all was right, he wished to know whether I objected to his driving over to Ilchester at once: nothing but a formality, he remarked. The formality terminated, a word to his lawyer, and the parson had only to publish the banns. It was painful to see him waving his flag of contentment from the summit of his house of cards, which a breath from me was to overturn instantly. I tempered it as well as I could; and indeed I was guilty of something more. We were threatened with a repetition of previous scenes between us. "I'm an old man," he said, almost tremblingly, but frowning, at my request to him not to hurry me. "That princess of yours has thrown you over, what do you want to wait for? A month's enough. I mean to see my family floated in a cradle before I'm off, and a girl like my Janet to look after it. She won't breed dolts nor cowards. I can leave her, with a heart content, to suckle Englishmen. You're not going to keep me in suspense now you're come to your senses? It seems to be you that's for playing the girl."

To my mind it seemed that Janet might have played her sex's part, if but a very little. Not reflecting on her natural impulse (for she loved him) to make him happy in his heart's dearest wish, my vision of her was ruffled and darkened by the unfeminine precipitancy. I admitted that a kiss was as good as a pledge in the estimation of a frankly-natured girl who respected the man she loved, but considering that no distinct word had been spoken by me, I thought she should also have delayed her confidences. It was true that she had betrayed herself by no more than a blush and altered eyes; the old man dwelt on it to prove his penetration. I blamed her because it was necessary to me that she should appear blameworthy, and worthy merely of such esteem as the wording of his praises of her kindled in the imagination of a most exquisitely-refining idiot. We entered upon the well-known wrangle; the misunderstandings, the explications, the highly-seasoned phrasings of wrath: with this difference, that I did consent slightly to temporize, and he to coax and bribe. He hinted at the matter of the banker's book as a thing of small account, supposing I now meant to behave like a man. I was tempted. A reflux of sentiment brought Ottilia's voice to my ear. I said bluntly: "I can't be bound. I can do nothing until I hear from the princess herself that she refuses me."

He seized on the salient feature promptly: "So you stick 'twixt two women, do you, ready for one or t'other!" His exclamation, for a comment on a man in such a position, was withering.

He offered to pay my father's debts under five thousand pounds.

I could not help smiling.

"Sneer away," said he. "The fellow lets you think he snaps his fingers at money. He's a hound by day and a badger by night after it. Come now, quick, Harry, you! are we where we stood when he tried to palaver me in my bailiff's cottage? or does all go easy, with a shake o' the hand? I'm a man of my word. I gave you my word about your princess, but not if you turn out a liar, the fellow's confederate, hunting in couples with him, and waiting for my death to shoot up my money in fireworks. And you can't have her!—she's rejected you; we have it printed. Janet showed it to me. What are you lifting your eyebrows at? She had a right to show it. She smuggles a lot, I wager; I don't always see my own newspapers! Come: do you take her, or not?"

I stated my regret that, as I stood at present . . . He cut me short. "Then tell him I expect to hear from him on the day appointed—five days from the present, that is. I won't have excuses. I'll have the money down. It's for you, not for me—it's your money. But he shall be as good as his word to me—fiddle his word!—or I draw back mine to you, and you may go courting your princess on your own funds. There, go, or I shall be in for a fit of the gout. I generally have a twinge whenever I catch sight of you now."

Janet was walking on the lawn. We both glanced at the window, and he muttered, "None of that game of yours of two at a time. I won't have my girl worried. You think she can't feel—you don't know her yet. She has felt your conduct all her life: she grows straight and strong because she never pities herself. Girl's as sweet as a nut—she's straight as a lily. She's a compassionate thing. You don't think she's not been proposed for? I've kept her out of the way of every other young fellow as much as I could. I haven't been kind—I haven't been kind to her. May God bless her! and I hope she'll forgive me." The old man's voice came through tears—I had not to look in his face to be aware of it. The pain of evading Janet was sharp, and stung pride as well as tenderness. Her figure on the lawn, while my old grandfather spoke of her, wore the light of individual character which defined her clearly from other women. She was raising the head of a rose at her arm's length, barely bending her neck to it,

nor the line of her back. "A compassionate thing," as he who
loved her said of her, the act and the attitude combined to sym-
bolize the orderly, simple unpretendingness of her nature. A
flower had a flower's place in her regard, and, I knew, a man a
man's. She could stoop low to me,—to me this stately girl could
bend, and take the shapes and many colours of a cloud running up
the wind. Her heart was mine. I felt as though I were tossing
and catching, and might, at one moment, miss it, when I had
left the house.

I felt, too, that I must sound my nature for the cause of these
perpetual slippings from self-respect, and, while following out the
Platonic inquiry as to Temperance, determined to ensure it, in
the modern sense, for the beginning of a new scheme of life that
should tame my blood, and help me to be my own master.

Grievously dissatisfied with myself, I was rendered more competent to deal with my father. The blow had to be struck at
once; so I told him that the squire expected the money to be paid,
adding that if it was not paid, I should have to consider myself
disinherited. "And this is final, sir, you may be sure of it." I had
come prepared for verbosity. He looked profoundly grave, and
was silent. Casting an eye on him after a while, I saw that he was
either meditating to a great depth, or was in a collapse of his
powers. He breathed heavily, his hands resting on the length of
an armchair, lifted and fell. Was this an evidence of feeling, of
reflection, or of stupefaction? I pressed him:—"Borrowing a sum
like that is out of the question; besides, I won't consent to the
attempt. Would it be as well to write to Prince Ernest for the
amount sunk over there?"

Without hearing a word from him, my quickly-lighted suspicions gathered that this sum had been repaid, in which case it
had, to a certainty, been spent.

"Then we can't reckon upon it. We have nothing, as far as
I can see. I don't know what I have been fancying possible. I
believed you when you said you would be ready for the day.
Are there still any resources you have unknown to me?"

He tapped on the arm-chair. "Let me think, Richie,—let me
think."

His act of thinking resembled that of sleeping. I stated my
intention to return to him at dinner-time, and went off in search
of my consoler, Temple, of whom I asked the favour of a bed
under his happy roof.

"It's your own room there," said Temple. "Do you go to the
House to-night? I'll sit up for you. Heriot was here this morning."

He was too full of a catastrophe that had overwhelmed Heriot's marriage-ceremony to listen much to me. The gist of it was, that a gipsy girl known to us two had presented herself—he was not sure whether before the altar or at the bride's house—and effectually stopped the marriage. Heriot came to him in a laughing fury, to say that he stood released. He was mortally dreading to behold the affair in newspaper print—which seemed to be his principal concern; and I was not sorry I had a companion in that most melancholy of apprehensions. Sorry for Heriot himself no friend of his could well be. He had a way of his own regarding things, and a savage humour defying sympathy. He confided to Temple his modest wish to catch and "thrash" the black girl, out of compliment to her predilection for a beating with hands rather than wordy abuse. Her fiery boldness had captured his admiration, though it made him smart.

"No, but just fancy!" Temple continued saying, even after I had related my weightier circumstances.

Like others who contrive always to keep the plain straight lines of the working world, he enjoyed from compassionate amusement the deviations of his friends, and he obtained his recreation in that manner, with a certain abuse of his natural delicacy, for he would go on speculating: "What can she have meant by it?" when a thought might have told him that she must have had, by her interpretation, a right to act as she had done. Perceiving this at last, his feast on the startling and the dramatic was displaced by a sense of outraged propriety, and he was hardly like my old friend at all in the way he spoke of the girl.

My father had been thinking to very little purpose during my absence. He denounced the squire's hardness and obstinacy in not being satisfied with a princess and a Member of Parliament. The interval had restored his tongue to him. Yet he had a scheme, he said, a plan, a method: but he was impatient for the dinner-bell, and would not communicate it. He looked exhausted, several times he begged me to preserve my good spirits, declaring that I suffered my health to droop, and there was no occasion for it, none whatever: I did not take wine enough.

The mention of wine as a resource in a situation like ours revolted me. I conjured him to abandon his house, society, the whole train of his extravagances, all excepting, if he pleased, the legal proceedings, which were, I ventured to observe, hopeless in the opinion of most unprejudiced persons fit to judge of them.

"Dettermain and Newson," he rejoined, "have opened a battery that will have immediate effect."

Collecting himself, as if he felt that he had been guilty of talking reason to one bordering upon lunacy—"Wine, Richie, wine is what you want."

"I shall drink none, sir," was my reply.

"Richie, your pulse," said he, and was for insisting on the physician's sagest exhibition of his science. "I have despatched a letter to Sarkeld this afternoon. *Now* you light up, my dear boy. A taste of our empress—not margravine! I remember Mr. Temple's excellent word—and and a bottle of emperor will bring you round. Why, one would suppose we were beaten. The world has never yet said that to me."

Resolutions coming on a spur of disgust may be reckoned upon to endure for an evening. I was challenged to drink at table, and declined. Temple responded to the invitation manfully.

My father complimented him.

"I was telling Richie upstairs in my dressing-room I bear in mind your capital 'margravine of wines,' Mr. Temple. It brings back the day, the sunset, and the two dear lads wondering and happy, and making me happy. Not to drink good wine is to cut yourself violently from every glorious day you have lived, and intend to live. My wine is my friend, my prime minister, my secret cabinet, my jewel-case, my Aladdin's garden. I gain my cause fifty times over on wine. On the bare notion of water, by heaven! it floats drowned, like a young woman I saw once, a pretty creature, stretched out on straw: she had dressed herself with great care. I have detested water ever since: 'tis a common assassin, Richie!"

He challenged me again. My mind being now set against him, I heard nonsense in everything he uttered, and I reviewed the days when I had treasured his prolific speech, then marvelled, then admired and partly envied, then tolerated, then striven to tolerate. It had become scarcely bearable to my nerves to hear him out.

"I once, Mr. Temple," he took refuge with his wine-drinking ally, "while affording shelter far from conveyances to a lady under an umbrella, during a thunderstorm in this identical London— which led, by the way, to an agreeable intimacy considerably more to my profit than I could have anticipated in my dreams—Kellington, her name was, now departed—behold the very poorest, squalid, refuse-wretch of all mankind opposite in the street receiving on his shoulders the contents of the house-spout. It has never been known to me why he preferred the house-spout to the shower. We may *say* we do. The instinct of humanity is entirely opposed to it in practice. Mistress Kellington—she was a maiden lady of some seven-and-thirty: we do not, Mr. Temple, ever place a lady's age exactly on the banks of forty, for fear she should fall over on the other side, where the river is: I commend you to the rule through life—fumbled after her purse. I stated at the time that it would be to pay for a shiver. I am not uncharitable. I contended then, and do still, the wretch committed a deed of unmitigated wantonness; I would have had him castigated: an infinitely worse act than that of the unhappy girl who cast herself into the water headlong! But the effect on me of a man drinking water where there is wine is to remind me of both. The horrors of an insane destitution pour down my back."

He shivered in earnest, calling to me: "Come, Richie," with his wine-glass in hand.

I nodded, and touched the wine with my lips.

He sent his man Tollingby for the oldest wine in his cellar: a wine by no possibility paid for, I reflected in the midst of his praises of the wine. This buying and husbanding of choice wine upon a fictitious credit struck me as a key to his whole career, and I begged firmly to be excused from touching it.

"He doubts me," my father addressed Temple—"Richie doubts me. He doubts my devotion to him; he doubts my cause; he doubts my ability to perform my obligations and my particular promise."

Drawing a breath like one who has taken a blow, he talked excitedly, forgetting the men in attendance, and then subsided, only to renew his florid self-justifications and proofs of his affection for a son that would not drink wine with him. He made a better case of it in the delivery, from his own point of view, than I am doing, and succeeded in impressing it upon Temple, whose responding "Yes" and "Yes" between appreciative sips of the old wine, showed how easily two lively spirits, at work upon him in unison, could unsettle a sedate judgment. But I was dumb. My father grew agitated. The footmen were evidently unused to see him in that condition. He kept away from family subjects until the table had been cleared, and the decanters went round.

"One glass, Richie, of the very lightest and purest claret ever shipped. Will you now, to humour me?"

I shook my head.

He struck the table, declaring that I did him injury. Unjust, unfilial, ungrateful, blind, were some of his epithets. I heard him speak of going into bondage for my sake, of his having reserved that bitter cup to toss it off in case of necessity on my behalf, and of a lady of wealth whom he respected and would swear to love for her service to his son. While Woman lived, he-said he had unlimited resources, and snapped his fingers at fate; Woman was his treasury of happy accidents, his guardian goddess, his guarantee of rosiest possibilities. All with a barely intelligible volubility speeded along by incoherent conjunctions, dashes, parentheses. I feared for his reason—such as was native to him. The wine was somewhat to blame. He drank copiously. I did not rebut his accusation that I meant to read him a lesson. I would have had it a sharper one.

It was only when Temple and I were in the street, walking to his house, my sweeter home, that I discovered, upon a comparison of notes, my father to have signified his intention to repair our circumstances by marrying a wealthy woman; which lady, Temple and I gathered from sundry intimations, could be no other than Lady Sampleman.

p. 405. *Beginning of* Chapter XLIV, *added*:

My grandfather had a gratification . . . the higher I climbed (*l.* 6).

p. 406, *l.* 26. *After* "will fall" *deleted*: The fatal mistake of not trusting to your grandfather's affection, and the working of a merciful Providence, is to blame.

p. 406, *l.* 40. *Begins* Chapter III. ("My Father is miraculously relieved by Fortune") vol. III of First Edition; Chapter XLV, *Cornhill* version.

p. 408, *l.* 7. *After* Newson's *deleted*: An ignoble-looking rascal, calling himself Kellington, ran some steps after his carriage. Unable to obtain the shedding of a single glance, he slunk back to me, and gabbled a tale of his sister's having bequeathed all her money to Roy Richmond to live in splendour, leaving him destitute. A tale delivered in alcoholic breath under a tipsy hat does not inspire confidence. I tossed him a sovereign, fancying I had heard my father mention his sister's name.

"If you're Roy Richmond's son, sir," he said, "tell him from me Mrs. Disher can't keep her husband's bills in the ledger much longer, and old Bagenhope's drinking himself to death; and there's his last witness gone. I'm no enemy to him, nor to you, sir, as long as I get my pension. That's mine, I say."

Mrs. Waddy knew of this man Kellington as being "one of the pensioners."

p. 409, *l.* 13. *After* "passingly" *added*: perhaps ironically.

p. 411, *l.* 36. *After* "dinner" *deleted*: I heard laudation of the dinner and the Chassediane, the music and the cook, down even to the sherry, which must have been answerable for the discussion among certain younger male guests of Lady Edbury's conduct in coming. I gathered that she had defied some opposition of her family. Edbury joined this knot of talkers, saying: "He's a Jupiter! I shall take to swearing by him." Apparently they were aware of what had happened in the house at a particular hour of the morning. "Richmond!" Edbury nodded to me, with a queer semi-interrogation in his look, very like a dog's weighing the disposition of the hand that holds the stick. Otherwise it was not a face to betray secrets, for there was nothing but a sheet behind it. The ladies present were not, I could judge, such as my father would have surrounded Lady de Strode with, though they had titles, and were in the popular eye great ladies.

p. 414, *l*. 30. *After* "investigation" *deleted*: My father's necessities had extracted four thousand. He pleaded for an excuse an unconscionable creditor, and was lightly exonerated by me, considering that I had determined to make a round of payments as soon as the notification had fulfilled its mission at Riversley. My pending affair with Edbury kept me awaiting an answer from Heriot, and when that came I found that I had to run down to see a patient under nursing charge of Lady Maria Higginson over Durstan ridges.

p. 415, *l*. 6. *After* "I took the train" *deleted*: to see Heriot, instead of my own people; for he, I said to myself, was unwell, and Janet, I did not say to myself, was in suspense; moreover, I had a strong objection to being interrogated as to whether I had sold stock and spent a farthing of the money by Dorothy Beltham. She had written two letters of a painfully miserly tone, warning me not to touch it. My heart was moved when driving within eyeshot of Riversley, but I cheated it, and set my face to Durstan, little imagining that adventures to change and colour the course of one's life may spring across the passage of a heath.—*adding after* "I took the train" (*p*. 415, *l*. 6): for Riversley, and proceeded from the station to Durstan, where I knew Heriot to be staying. Had I gone straight to my grandfather, there would have been another story to tell.

p. 416, *l*. 20. *After* heathland *deleted*:

Heriot had promised to meet me at the station. His hostess signified, in the inimitable running half-sentences of her sex and class, when bent upon explaining something to make it equal to nothing, that she had not let him go because it was as well that he should not go, on account of the state of his arm, lest the horses should take fright, in which case, or any other, he would be totally helpless, and she, as his nurse, had exercised authority over her patient—one of the worst of patients—having reason to think it best to keep him under her eye. They were' related, I learnt; subsequently I learnt that the match recently broken off was of Lady Maria's making. She just alluded to it under a French term. She came behind me in a newly-planted walk of evergreens, and called Heriot's name: I was very like him in figure, she said.

p. 416, *l.* 22. *After* "estate" *deleted*: He carried his right arm in a sling. I glanced at it once or twice.

p. 416, *l.* 36. *After* atoning pathos *deleted*: He was still too young and healthy for more than a transient affectation of the cynical survey of their escapades. Pathos was imperiously called for at the close; it covered them over prettily, "tucked them up," as it were, for the final slumber: pathos was necessary, otherwise the ever-execrable husband appeared to triumph. Cissy is now the tall pale woman who is seen walking at a regular hour in the shade of the fashionable gardens, with a female attendant at her elbow and a strong man behind; she cannot pass a beggar. Isabella, still beautiful, nurses day and night her injured liege lord, the crusty incurable. That unvisited cottage by the Thames with the blinds down is the home of Georgina and the last child of her living three. To be just to him, Heriot brushed the pathos softly, and as if to escape from a sneer; but he could not have done well without it, for without it the tales of the ladies would have been rank fox-and-goose play, spider and fly; tales of rampant animalism decorated with jewellery and millinery and upholstery, and flavoured with idiotcy. Now I can listen to a story of a fool and a woman even when a husband intervenes, so long as the passion, apart from circumstances, continues respectable; that is, true to itself. Let the woman take herself off with her fool, and them make the best of it together; it is not impossible for them to do well, though it is hard. But I thank my training I behold the pair under no sentimental light when the husband is retained.

p. 416, *l.* 38. *After* "parson" *deleted*: The fretful feminine ocean incessantly tossing him had knocked the common sense out of him in whatsoever concerned women: he talked of me to Edbury shrewdly enough. I could not sit and listen to him when he hinted that Julia Bulsted might have made another man of him. We had no very amicable five minutes after Lady Maria's departure from the dessert. One's duty is to warn a friend when there is danger of a rising disgust, and I spoke out.

p. 416, *l.* 39. *After* "Kiomi" *deleted*: too.

p. 416, *l.* 40. *After* "devilry" *deleted*: He did not open his mind to me, for he could only have done it by leading through sentimental innuendoes—the stuff he had taken to feed on.

p. 417, *l.* 8. *After* "adopted" *deleted*: and I was comforted by the larger charity—so large that it embraced pitiful contempt—afforded to me by my insight.

p. 417, *l.* 27. *After* "worthy of me" *deleted*: Why had I not gone to one of our Universities, to have a wider choice of discriminating friends among the land's elect! I exacted as much compliance from men as from the earth I trod.

p. 418, *l.* 3. *After* "pitch" *deleted*: to retaliate.

p. 419, *l.* 7. *After* "undermine me" *deleted*: Boxers know the severity of the flat-fisted stroke which a clever counter-feinting will sometimes fetch them in the unguarded bend of the back to win a rally with. (1897)

p. 420, *l.* 24. total apathy *altered from*: total solitude.

p. 426, *l.* 7. *After* for her *deleted*: I thought of the old ballad of the slain knight and the corbies, when

> "Down there came a fallow doe . . ."

She was nothing to me, and as little romantic a creature as could be, but her state was that of "such a leman" whom every gentleman in evil case might pray for to cherish him: and she had nursed me on her bosom. I said the best I could think of. I doubt if she heard me.

p. 426, *l.* 21. *After* wait and see *deleted*:

To some chiding on my part, she rejoined: "Shall I take a slap in the face from one of mine because she's an aunt and can't show herself all for walking off the line?"

p. 426, *l.* 26. *After* "public" *deleted*: letting me at the same time understand that she thought their men right in making the tents uninhabitable to a rye guilty of spoiling the blood. Nevertheless it is the delicacy of the slipped woman which condemns her to be an outcast. Her women will receive her though she often has to smart for it, as Eveleen worked on poor Kiomi's sensitiveness; and I fancy the men would come round by degrees, though they should smite and wither her at first.

p. 433, *l.* 24. he at least persuaded himself: *altered from* I was almost persuaded.

p. 443, *l.* 13. *After* her heart *deleted*: I shook my head perusingly, murmuring "No"; and then a decisive negative and a deep sigh. The moods of half-earnest men and feeble lovers narrowly escape the farcical, if they do at all.

She adopted my plan in a vigorous outline of how to proceed.

"I think it would be honourable, Harry."

"It would be horrible, horrible! No, since she has come . . .
I wish!—but the mischief is done."

"You are quite a boy."

I argued that it was not to be a boy to meet and face a difficult
situation.

She replied that it was to be a boy of boys not to perceive that
the sacrifice would never be accepted.

"Why, an old maid can teach you," she said, scornfully, and
rebuked me for failing to seize my opportunity to gain credit with
her for some show of magnanimous spirit. "Men are all selfish in
love," she concluded, most logically. (1897)

p. 449, *l.* 17. *After* father's *deleted*: Might it also mean, "I am
still in that road extra muros?" (1897)

p. 463, *l.* 18. *After* "her" *deleted*: no one living is like her.

p. 478, *l.* 5. *After* "please" *deleted*: his English is of a faltering
character. Still it . . . . (1897)

p. 485, *ls.* 9–10. *Added*: she evidently understood that Janet had
seen her wish to get released. (1871)

p. 489, (Chapter heading). His Last Outburst: *altered from* His
Last Innings.

p. 496, *l.* 19. "dropped" was "drooped" in previous texts and in
manuscript, and "drooped" seems to fit the context better. Though
"dropped'" was retained in the final revision (1897), it may be an
uncorrected misprint, as suggested in *Bibliography & Various
Readings.*

p. 496, *l.* 19. *After* "drooped" *deleted*: he reminded me of the
figure he had sketched to Temple of the man under the house-
spout, he looked so resigned to his drenching.

p. 498, *l.* 38. *After* madman *deleted*: A madman? it's rather a
compliment to Bedlam.

p. 506, *l.* 36. *After* softness *deleted*: towards me! (1897)

p. 506, *l.* 40. *After* "as well" *deleted*: The correspondence ceased
absolutely.

Janet's formal, stiff, spiritless writing produced the effect on
the mind of a series of maxims done in round-hand. How different
were they from the chirruping rosy notes of Jenny Chassediane, a
songstress in prose! I compared them, and yelled derision of the
austere and frozen, graceless women of my country. Good-night
to them! Jenny met me when I was as low as a young man can
imagine himself to fall, or the nether floors of mortal life to extend. All but at one blow disinherited by my grandfather,

unseated for Parliament, discarded of the soul I loved, I was perfectly stripped: which state presents to a young man's logical
sensations a sufficient argument for beginning life again upon the
first pattern that offers. I determined to live, as we say when we
are wasting life. It is burlesque to write that my Ilium was in
flames, but it was heavy fact that I had Anchises on my back.
Forked heads of the hydra, Credit, glared horrid in the background; scandal devoured our reputations; our history was common property for any publisher, with any amount of embellishments. These things were a terrible conflagration to gaze behind
upon. The future appeared under no direction of celestial powers,
but merely a straight way paved with my poor old Sewis's legacy
to the edge of a cliff. My father meanwhile lived almost in solitude, in complete obscurity, blameless towards me certainly; I
had robbed him of his friend Jorian, and his one daily course was
from our suite of rooms to his second-class restaurant and back:
a melancholy existence, I thought. He declared it to be the contrary, and that he had no difficulty whatever in wearing that air
of cheerfulness which, according to his dictum, "it should be a
man's principle of duty to wear in contempt of rain and thunder,
as though it were his nuptial morning—even under sentence of
death."

I might as well have been at the Riversley death-bed.

p. 507, *l.* 1. *After* "them" *added*: The squire was dead.

p. 507, *l.* 2. *After* "Bulsted" *deleted*: where we heard that the
squire was dead.

p. 507, *l.* 16. *After* "she said" *deleted*: and intimated that my
father's behaviour in Paris would not make the promise difficult
to keep. I could not persuade her of his innocence.

p. 515, *l.* 23. *After* "parted" *deleted*: She was middle-aged, rich,
laughter-loving, and no stranger to the points of his history which
he desired to have notorious.

p. 515, *l.* 32. *After* events *deleted*:

Lady Edbury was in Vienna, too. My father's German life
and his English were thus brought in reflection upon the episode
he was commencing, and as I would not take part in it, and he
sprang in one of his later frenzies from the choice of the obscure
ways offered him by my companionship, we no longer went together now that there might have been good in it.

p. 516, *l.* 2. *After* "the same" *deleted*: Very submissive! I could
see that modesty bewrayed expression, but the want of clearness
had a corresponding effect on my sentiments.

p. 516, *l.* 16. *After* Prince Hermann *deleted*:

I replied in a series of commendably temperate and philosophical lines, as much the expression of my real self as the public execution of a jig on the Salzach Brücke would have been. We two were evidently not only diverse, but adverse, I said. She had a strong will: so had I, and unfortunately our opinions always differed. We would be friends, of course. As to her nature, she would learn that it is the especially human task to discern in what it is bad, and in what it is good, and to shape it ourselves. (I was still more prolix and pedantic than I dared to show: even worse than impertinent. "The dog cannot change its nature: how are we to judge of the dog's master upon that plea?") It was an unpardonable effusion. But one who would write like a high philosopher when he feels like a wounded savage, commits these offences. The letter was despatched to do its work.

p. 517, *l.* 19. *After* "now" *deleted*: No, she was faithful to the death! This I repeated hotly, in the belief that it was only to support her praises. My aunt Dorothy and Temple had kept me informed of her simple daily round of life, sometimes in London, mainly at Riversley: she was Janet still. Temple in his latest letter had mentioned "a Lady Kane" vaguely in connexion with Janet.

p. 520, *l.* 25. *After* "between us" *deleted*: I would reward her for this! Or to phrase it becomingly, and more in harmony with my better feelings, I would claim, beg for, the honour and happiness of dedicating my life to her. She was mine, the very image of fidelity. I loved her person, her mind, her soul: I could not but be sure of it now.

Could I be less fierily sure of myself when I beheld her at last? It was sweeter than the dream of seeing her tending roses. She was seated beside an arm-chair, soothing a sleeper with a hand on his, and he was my father.

p. 520, *l.* 26. My aunt Dorothy . . . engaged to be married (*p.* 655, *l.* 18) *is a condensation of the following deleted passage*: My aunt Dorothy came up to me and embraced me, murmuring a hush. Janet did not move. The curtains of the room were down: there was a dull red fire in the grate: I heard my father's heavy breathing.

"Harry!" Janet said softly.

I knelt to her.

"My own and only Janet!"

"Do not awaken him," she whispered.

"No, but I am home."

"I am glad."

One hand she was obliged to surrender. I kissed it. She seemed startled at my warmth.

"I cannot wait to say how I love you, my Janet! You have not written to me once. I do not blame you; all the faults are mine. I have learnt to know myself. Why do you take back your hands?"

An exchange of glances, like a flash over a hidden terror, shot between Janet and my aunt Dorothy.

"Did you read aunty's last letter?" Janet asked.

"No recent letters," said I, checked by the tone of her voice. "Why should I? My truest Janet! I came home for you. On the faith of a man, I love you with all my soul."

"Do not touch me," she said, shrinking from my arm.

The sleeper stirred and muttered.

"We are expecting Harry," my aunt Dorothy said to him.

"Eight Harrys have reigned in England," he ejaculated.

"It is time for your drive," said Janet.

My aunt Dorothy led me out of the room. "He must be prepared for the sight of you, Harry. The doctors say that a shock may destroy him. Janet treats him so wonderfully."

"She's a little cold to me, aunty. I deserve it, I know. I love her with my whole heart, that's the truth. I believe I have only just woke up."

"You did not receive my last letter, Harry?"

"I've had no letters for nine months and more. By the way, my father's case is over, and that's a good thing; he went like a ship on the rocks. Tell me how it was Janet brought him here. I could swear she has not taken him to Riversley! Has she? And I love her for her obstinacy: anything that's a part of her character!"

"Harry, remember, you wrote cruelly to her!"

"I wrote only once."

"The silence was cruel."

"I will pay all penalties. I will wait her pleasure, be the humblest of wooers."

From the windows of the front drawing-room, where we stood, I saw Janet accepting my father's hand to mount to a seat in her carriage, and he stepped after her, taking her help in return, indebted to it for some muscular assistance, it was plain from the compression of her lips and knitted brows.

"Why does she go without speaking to me again, aunty?"

"She gives him his drive every day, so that he may say he has shown himself. He cannot bear to think people should suppose him beaten, and she is so courted that they have to pay court to him as well."

"How good of her!"

My aunt Dorothy fell to weeping. I pressed her on my heart and cheered her, still praising Janet. She wept the faster.

"Is there anything new the matter?" I said.

"It is not new to us, Harry. I'm sure you're brave?"

"Brave! what am I asked to bear?"

"Much, if you love her, Harry!"

"Speak."

"It is better you should hear it from me, Harry. I wrote you word of it. We all imagined it would not be disagreeable to you. Who could foresee this change in you? She least of all!"

"She's in love with some one?"

"I did not say exactly in love."

"Tell me the worst."

"She is engaged to be married."

p. 521, *l.* 2. *After* engaged to be married *deleted* (Chapter LVI *Cornhill*; Volume III, Chapter XIV first edition) *as under*:

JANET AND I

JANET and I were alone.

When your mistress is faithless to you in your absence, and you hear of the infamy, your prompt inquiry is for the name of the man. His name!—just that. Unto what monster has the degraded wretch sunk to link herself?

And that was the question of my mouth after hearing my aunt Dorothy's tidings. But men are not all made alike, and I, burning to ask for it, was silent, dreading a name that would give shape and hue to my hate and envy; for the man chosen by Janet would be pre-eminently manful, not one to be thought little of: and I had no wish to think of him. I very soon escaped from the house, promising to return in the evening or next day. I could not quit the street. So Janet, driving my father back from the park, surprised me pacing up and down; my father had me by the hand, and I was compelled to go in with them.

The prescription of an hour's rest before dinner withdrew my father; Dorothy Beltham went to dress: Janet remained.

We exchanged steady looks. She was not one to wince from a look.

Whoever the man, the act of the ceremony was as good as performed when Janet gave him her word to wed him.

Her comely face was like marble. She stood upright; I could

not fancy it challengingly, but I had expected an abashed or partly remorseful air in the woman who took advantage of my absence to plight herself to another, and my nerves had revelled since the touch of her hand (this unknown man's absolute possession), in descending from the carriage, all the way up to the drawing-room, anticipating the shrewd bitterness of seeing that dim taint of guilt on her conscious figure. She stood gravely attentive.

"Janet, I have to thank you for your great kindness to my father."

"You feel, Harry, that I had to make amends for old unkindness."

"I thank you with all my heart."

"It is my happiness to please you even in trifles."

"This is not a trifle."

"It was no effort to me."

"You found him involved in debts?"

She jerked her shoulders slightly.

"There were debts, which do not exist now."

"You were determined to bind me hand and foot in gratitude?"

"No; only to do what you would have done, as far as it lay in my power."

"I came home imagining you were disengaged."

"Aunty wrote——"

"She did: the letter never reached me; otherwise I should not be here now. Or, who knows? I should have been here earlier."

"You have come, Harry."

"This I can say, Janet, that, through those old days when I was pulled to pieces, and unjust and unkind to you, and Heriot praised you as one who would be the loyalest woman to her husband in all England, I echoed him."

"Well, Harry, I won't thank you for compliments. I think I can keep my word."

"To this man? You are not married yet."

"No," she uttered mechanically.

"Has the marriage been delayed? Pardon me, you seem to speak of it in a tone——"

"I put it off from the winter to summer, Harry, hoping that you would come and be by me at the altar."

"I? Why, what character did you assign to me in it?"

"A friend's, I hoped: my old and best friend's!"

"Why, you and I were as good as betrothed!"

"Surely never!"

"You would have had me help to give you away?"

"I thought I might look to Harry for that."

"Give away what has been mine longer than I can recollect! Give you?—Oh! I talk; I wish I could only feel you the Janet I could have taken and doubled myself with her, as Heriot said. It was, I believe, in my heart, you that I loved, Janet. Stand by you, and *see* you given away? But I have had you in my arms! I have kissed you! You can't forget me! And to be true, you cannot give yourself except to me. Unless you confess to me that you have quite changed. Make that confession, and there's the end. If you are true you are mine. What is this keeping of the word? You pledge your pride, and are afraid to break it for pride's sake. You love, you must love me; you love none but me. I'm as used to it as the air I breathe. Why, good heaven, I could not treat you as the wife of any but myself. I laugh at a marriage-service that pretends to bind you to a law and exclude me. Not only it can't be, but, supposing it were, I would not hesitate to break it: and because I have the right; and because I would do right by you. We have been betrothed almost since we were born; certainly since we were children. I know the ways, the turn of your mind, your moods, your habits, from the plainest to the sweetest. Do you not half drop your eyelids—? But answer me: can a man with such memories as I have let you go? I claim you for the very reason that you are true and can't swerve."

Her straightforward intellect was bewildered by these raving sophistries. The marvel of the transformation of me, too, must have added to her momentary sense of helplessness.

"Harry! your last letter!" she said, breathing in pain.

"The letter of a fool, a coxcomb! Is it to punish me for that?"

"Not to punish. But that letter: I searched for a word of love, the smallest sign; I had it on my heart all night to see if I could dream of something better than I found in it:—not one!"

"But I was ruined at the time I wrote it. Reflect! Had I lost such a little? And to fill the cup you shut your doors on my father! I could have excused and accounted for your doing so at a moment when I was less sharply wounded and he less inoffensive. How can I explain my situation to you—you don't understand it? Yet I see myself in your eyes. I'm not a stranger there. Janet, come to me!"

Her voice was hoarse in uttering some protest.

"Is this marriage-day fixed then?" I demanded.

"It is. Let me go now, Harry. Your father likes to see me grandly dressed."

"Does this man dine with you who is to marry you?"

"Not to-day."

"Not he to-day, but I! Your father and mother approve the match?"

"Yes."

"Then it's a nobleman. Am I right?"

"He is of noble birth."

"You speak like a ballad. And it was you that fixed the day?"

"Yes."

"Then you belong to the man!"

"I cannot but think that I do indeed. And now, Harry, let me go."

"One word,—you love him?"

"You must read me by my deeds."

"Come, your deeds have not been of the kindest to me; do you love me?"

"I loved my dear friend Harry, who would once have spared me such a question, if it distressed me," said Janet, and my aunt Dorothy entering the room with my father helped her to fly.

Dining with my shattered father was a dismal feast: dining as Janet's guest after such a conversation as ours had been was no happy privilege. The strangeness of the thought that she was not to belong to me numbed my senses. At intervals a dark flash of fancy pictured her the bride of another, but it seemed too dark, impossible to realize: she talked and smiled too pleasantly to make it credible. She was a woman who would talk and smile while stepping to the altar, perhaps be a little paler; how give her finger to be ringed? Why, the hateful creature would extend it with matter-of-fact simplicity, as she did her hand to the wine-glass: but to whom? who was the man? She was giving it for a title. Her love unsatisfied, she had grown ambitious. The idea of her marrying for social rank cooled and relieved my distemper, but at her expense, for, though she complimented me, I must despise her! She had resolved that I should owe her much: her management of my father was a miracle of natural sweetness and tact; she helped out his sentences, she divined his unfinished ones. Could it have been predicted that we should ever have sat together on these terms? She affected to relish him. On whose account but Harry Richmond's? Was it merely to do me friendly service? No, she was mine still!

My self-cajoling heart rushed out to her adoringly, more hopelessly captive from every effort to escape. For she was not mine; she never would be. The qualities I loved in her, that made her

stand side by side with my bravest manhood, and had once preserved her for me in defiance of coldness, were against me now:
my chance had gone.

And studying her acutely in the careless looks one throws at
table, I perceived what had not been so visible when we were
alone, a singular individual tone in her developed womanliness,
a warmth of grace in her temperate nature: the frown was very
rare, and the lips would be at play under it. The soft-shut lips had
a noble repose. She had gained the manner of a perfect young
English gentlewoman, without being fashioned after a pattern,
without the haunting shadow of primness, which has been charged
to the lack of the powers of educated speech in the reputed fairest
of earth's ladies. She had learnt the art of dressing, and knew her
tricks of colour, my Janet.

"Will you go to the opera for an hour to-night, Harry?" she
asked me.

It sounded to me: "Will you run with me and see the man I
am plighted to?"

"Yes," I said.

The solemnity of the affirmative amazed her.

My father spoke.

"Richie has a dress-suit in the right-hand drawer of the third
compartment of my rosewood wardrobe, and the family watch
bequeathed me by my mother lies on it, stopped at a quarter to
ten."

His voice broke.

Janet put her hand out to him.

"Yes! Do I not remember? You told us you would keep his
'uniform' for him, so that if he liked he might go into society the
moment of his return."

My father said he was a general.

I went up to Janet.

"Will you give me that letter?"

"What letter?"

"The letter you had on your heart all night."

She blushed: she shook her head.

I knew the blush innocent, but it was a blush, and my heart
burst out on it like a hound, chasing it through all the shifts and
windings of feminine flight. I felt that I was master.

How if the man should be the manly good fellow I supposed
him of necessity to be, sincerely fond of her? Why, then I pitied
him and loved her none the better for surrendering to me. And

in truth, she would certainly have chosen no other kind of man than the best of our English blood.

She liked my half-indifferent manner on the road to the opera; I was able to prattle, and we laughed and chatted. My father appeared somewhat agitated: he sat erect, saying: "I show myself; I show myself." Janet laid her hand in his. "Ay, the most absolute self-command," said he; and with a look on me: "Old Richie!"

My aunt Dorothy accounted for the observation we attracted upon entering the box.

"Janet has been much noticed."

"Do you see the man she is engaged to, aunty?"

She gazed round the house.

"No."

I quitted the box to look at her myself from the outside, and strolled about the lobby only to fall into the clutches of Lady Kane.

"Here, come with me," said this detestable old woman; "I want to talk to you and taste you after your travels."

I had to enter her box and sit beside her.

"I can take liberties with you now; we're almost relatives," said she.

"Really?" said I.

"Don't acknowledge it, if you don't like it," she ran on; "I find it quite enough to be great-aunt to one young man. That's a fardel pretty nearly off my shoulders. Well and how have you been? and what have you seen? Are you going to write a book? Don't. It's bad style. Are you not ashamed of yourself to have put us back six months? I begged, I implored. No. A will of iron! All the better, though we feel the pinch of it just at present. I like a young woman with plenty of will, though it's nasty to find it in opposition. Got rid of your disappointments, poor boy? You mustn't play high stakes without good backing. I shall take you in hand, and train you and set you up. Do you like this opera-shouting? You haven't brought back a Circassian, eh, sir? Hm'm, there's no knowing your tricks. If I'm to do anything for you in the market I must have a full confession. So I said to my monkey, and he went on his knees, and I listened. You are Calibans! You all of you want washing and combing to make you decent."

Her sick old stale-milk-shot eyes wavered across me nimbly while she rattled her licensed double-dowager's jargon, suitable to Edbury's ears.

"You're gloomy," she said, peering intently. One could have imagined her fluttering in suspense like a kite over the fallows.

"I'll tell you what, my lady," said I, for she pressed me obstinately to open my mind to her. "I've been so long out of England that I hardly remember the language, and I am going round the house to take lessons."

"Very well, go along"; she dismissed me: "and call on me to-morrow early. Yes, there he is"; she glanced at Janet's box. "We don't object to her showing him about; I don't mind it a bit for my part; I have no bourgeois prejudices—if she's quite sure he won't break out again. But you've had enough of scandal, eh? You'll take him in hand now you are back. Go, you bronzed boy, and try and finish your toilet early to-morrow morning: I will see you at eleven. I think I've a match for you in my head."

Janet's eyes dwelt on me a half instant when I resumed my place behind her seat.

"Do you ever see that old woman, Lady Kane?" said I.

She answered: "You have been talking to her."

I threw my remarks into the form of a meditation:

"Some of those old women of society are as intolerable as washing-tub shrews. She couldn't have been more impudent to me or concerning you if she had been bred in the fish-market. Why does one come to be stared at and overhauled in public by a gabbling harridan!"

"We have to consider whether it is good medicine for our patient," said Janet. "Your father likes it, Harry."

"My dearest, my friend!" I whispered, and saw the edge of the cheek before me burn with crimson colour that stole on like a flood tide round among the short spare wisps of curls free of the up-driving comb on her bare neck. A sight heavenly sweet to see; convincing of my mastery!

I touched her dress. The trial of so true a heart as hers had my sympathy, and I was soothed by the thought that I could in my soul respect her even after I had subdued her, for supposing we had not been in public, I would still have refrained from a lover's privileges, and rather have helped her to reflect upon what we, who were under a common spell of love, could best do in reason than have struck her senses.

But it was too hard to sit near that divinely-flaming tell-tale neck and face, merely to speak and hear short replies. I fled to an upper circle, where Temple met me and drew me into the box of Anna Penrhys.

She exclaimed: "I am so glad to see you not unhappy!"

"Why should I be?" said I.

"Men change. I wished it once, but if you are satisfied now, we won't any of us complain. I like you the more, Harry, for not being like the majority."

I guessed at her meaning: "Hunting the heiress? no, that's not my pursuit."

"But I'm in love with Janet Ilchester," said Anna, warmly. "She has improved him wonderfully."

"My father? yes."

"I was speaking for the moment of a more fortunate person, Harry. Look down there."

I looked down at Janet's box, and beheld the Marquis of Edbury occupying my place.

Anna replied to the look I levelled at her.

"Didn't you know? Lady Kane managed it cleverly, they say. I was one of the surprised, but I am still under thirty."

Temple did me a similar service.

"I wrote you word of the engagement, Richie."

"You told me she had engaged herself to Edbury?" said I, and shut my eyes; for if ever a man had devils within him I had. She must have caught sight of her betrothed lover in the house when she threw me on such an ocean of conceit with her treacherous blush.

Chapter LVII, *Cornhill*; Chapter XV, Vol. III, first edition

JANET'S HEROISM

I WENT to the dear peaceful home of Temple that night, and should have been glad if his sisters had kissed me as they did him.

Next day, having, with Mr. Temple's help, procured a set of furnished chambers, I sent a note to my father by messenger, in which I requested him to come to me immediately.

The answer was Janet's. It ran:—

"MY DEAR HARRY—

"We do not think it prudent to let your father be away from us.

"He watches the door for you. Bear in mind that he has passed through an illness.

"We hope you will not allow it to be later than to-morrow before you visit us.

"Your affectionate,

"JANET."

So she attached no idea of shame to her approaching alliance
with Edbury. She wrote to me as though she had not in the
slightest degree degraded herself!

Janet was a judge of what men were; she must have read him
through. Was it that she was actually in secret of the order of
women who are partial to rakes, and are moved by the curiosity of
their inexperienced kinship? Or had the monstrous old intriguer
Lady Kane hoodwinked and spellbound my girl?

I was not to be later than to-morrow in visiting her:—therefore Edbury was expected to-day. It would be as well to see them
together, measure them and consider how they were sorted. "With
all my heart I'm sorry for her!" I said. I thought I was cured.

Presently—and this is the bitter curse of love—the whole condition of things passed into imagination, holding proportionate
relations to reality, but intense as though I walked in fire, and
shivering me with alternate throbs of black and bright.

I despised her: I envied him.

I felt certain that I could outrun him, and I loathed the bestial
rivalry.

Her choice of the man painted him insufferably fair to me:
the shadow of him upon her distorted her features.

But that shadow gave her a vile attractiveness, and thereof
begat a sense of power in me to crush his pretences.

I won her; she was tasteless. I lost her; she was all human life.

Was it not a duty towards the dead as well as the living that
I should take her in contempt of reluctance?

Would it not be stirring a devilry for me to interpose?

And so forth; lovers can colour the sketch. It wants the cunning of the hand that sweeps the lyre to sound the incessant
revolutions which made day or night for me upon a recurring
breath; shocks that were changes of the universe.

The pain of this contest in imagination when passion pre-
dominates is, that you can get no succour of trivial material
circumstances: things are reduced to their elements. The idea of
Edbury, such as he was, would have afflicted me with no jealous
pangs: but I had to contemplate him through the eyes of the
woman who had chosen him: I could not divorce him from her.

I tried recourse to my brain; I thought calmly—she has a poor
mind; I have always known it. The word "always" seized me on
a whirlwind, sweeping me backward through the years of our
common life to the multitude of incidents, untasted in their
sweetness then, to pour it out now like gall.

Ottilia's worldly and intellectual rank both had been con-

stantly present to temper my cravings; but Janet was on my level—
mentally a trifle below it, morally above—hard as metal if she
liked. She invited conflicts, she defied subjugation. My old grandfather was right: she would be a true man's mate. All the more
reason for withdrawing her from that loose-lipped Edbury. He
had the Bolton blood: I remembered Colonel Heddon's anecdote
of the mother.

p. 521, *l.* 2. *After* engaged to be married *added:* Janet came into
. . . her pledged word (*l.* 7).

p. 521, *l.* 9. *After* I felt *added:* now.

p. 521, *l.* 11. the matchmaker's: *altered from* Lady Kane's.

p. 521, *l.* 19. *After* excuse her *deleted as under:*

I went to her house after the lapse of a day. She met me
quietly and kindly, but with I know not what hostility of reserve,
whose apparent threat of resistance challenged an attack.

"Why do you frown at me?" I commenced.

"Have you forgotten my old habit, Harry? I'm not quite cured
of it," she answered.

"You will soon have nothing to frown at."

She smiled.

"That sounds like a promise of heaven. Do you mean that I
shall not see you, Harry?"

"My dear Janet, I have to tell you this. But first let me ask
you: You hold yourself irrevocably plighted to this man Edbury?"

"Yes."

"You have sworn your oath?"

"I do not swear oaths."

"Then you are exceedingly unlike the partner you have selected. You fancy you are bound in honour?"

"I am."

"If you were to learn that you had committed an error, you
would still hold yourself bound to take the step?"

"I should hold myself bound not to punish him for my mistake."

"It would not be to punish him to marry him without respecting him!"

"I don't know," said she, suddenly letting her wits break
down, and replying like a sullen child at a task; a swing of her
skirts would have completed the nice resemblance.

"Well then, Janet, let me tell you I don't respect, and have
strong reasons for disliking, the man you propose to yourself for
your husband, and therefore, if you become the man's wife——"

"You knew him years ago, Harry. He is different——"

"You imagine you have performed miracles!"

"No, I think most young men are alike." She added softly, "in some things."

This was her superior knowledge of mankind, entirely drawn from my old grandfather's slips of conversation regarding the ways of men, in the presence of the countrybred girl.

"You know nothing whatever of him or us," said I.

She answered, "I know as much as I care to hear."

"Concerning the remainder, it doesn't matter?"

"At least, he has not deceived me."

"He must have pushed his confidences beyond the customary limit!"

"Harry, can you say that he is much worse than other young men?"

It was in the attitude of an inquisitor that I received the thrust full in the breast from my own weapon. Is there, indeed, a choice for purely-trained young women among the flock of males? —if we would offer ourselves to their discriminating eyes as fitting mates upon the ground of purity!

"Oh, quite as intelligent—quite as noble!" I covered my retreat, feeling myself trotting in couples with Edbury and his like, as though at her command.

It enraged me. My conduct grew execrable. I made hot love to her, merely to win one clasp of the lost figure in my arms. She listened, fenced, frowned, reddened, and, perhaps, learnt to know more of men in a minute than she had through the course of her life. Who could respect Edbury's betrothed?

She seemed to apprehend what was overshadowing me: she said: "Harry, it's the loss of my respect for you that's the cruellest."

But she could not rob me of my savage consolation in having fixed a permanent blush on her face. Let the wretch redden for her idiot lover; this bit of crimson was mine. I had stolen a trifle.

The trifle became a boundless treasure, a relic, a horrible back-thought, a thing with a sting, all in the space of a few breathings. I had no pleasure of it, no more than a wild beast has of its bolted meal. Passion has none when you let it run counter to love.

"Harry, I leave you," she said, not ungently; rather to provoke my gentleness.

"Good-by, Janet," I replied.

"We shall see you to-day? to-morrow?"

"Hardly."

She sighed:

"You know your power."

"Power! if I could keep you from throwing yourself away on this fellow, I would renounce every chance of my own. Don't speak to me in those undertones. If you look at me in that manner I won't answer for myself. You tempt me to believe you the faithfullest woman alive; I go abroad, I return to you to lay my life at your feet, and I find I am not to touch you, only to see you at stated hours; you've ring-fenced yourself with the coronet of the loosest titled dog in the country. Was I right or wrong in coming to you, supposing you always true to me; who taught me to think her faithful unto death?"

Janet bent her head.

"I may be a little guilty," she said.

My bounding paradoxes, which were like reason playing contortionist with its cranium between its heels, gained that confession from her. So there had been a struggle and a sense of infidelity in her heart! But the confession of "a little guilt" coloured her to my blacker taste: the wild beast sprang for another meal.

She submitted; I paid the cost of it. Dead lips, an unyielding shape and torture on the forehead, make up a vulture's feast.

She left me without a word.

What could she think of me! Madness must have stricken me, and none of the illusions of madness to divert the pain.

I went to my chambers. Behold the carriage of Lady Kane at the door of the house!

"Oh! you really were out!" cried she, staccato. "Why didn't you keep your appointment, naughty fellow? Here, step in, and you shall tell me fie-fie stories of the harem, if you like."

I excused myself for declining the honour, bluntly: whereupon she proceeded to business:—My father was very much in the way in Janet's house. Did I not think it severe upon an ardent lover that neither his relatives nor he himself were permitted to call on her except at hours when it pleased a broken invalid to have a nap. That was all she had to say: I had looked after him so long, that in her opinion I was the best nurse possible for him.

I told her I shared the opinion, and I referred her to Janet.

"Oh! dear me, no, I've had enough of that," she said, shuddering ludicrously.

I felt myself a sharer in her particular sentiments likewise.

Her fury for my delightful society was not to be appeased save by the "positive" promise that I would at once take my father under my own care.

Again I sent for him, hoping to see Janet's handwriting, and taste a new collision.

My aunt Dorothy came.

"Harry, you meant your letter for a command?"

She pressed her bosom for breath.

"The simplest in the world, aunty. My father ought to be with me. He is well-cared for, but he is liable to insult."

"No one is allowed to call but when he is upstairs."

"Yes, so I've heard. I suppose he wishes me to be near him, and as things are you must be aware that I can't well be visiting Janet. And, finally, I have decided on it."

"Do you forget Janet's good influence over him, Harry?"

"On the whole, I don't think it better than mine."

"You are resolved?"

"Quite resolved."

"Then I must let you know the truth. I disobey Janet——"

"A miraculous tyrant, upon my honour!"

"In anything that touches your happiness, Harry, yes; as far as she may be now."

p. 521, *l.* 20. Dorothy Beltham told me something of Janet that struck me to the dust: *altered from* Dorothy Beltham waxed strangely agitated. I kissed her and held both her hands.

p. 522, *l.* 17. *After* called aloud *deleted as under*:

Chapter LVIII, *Cornhill*; Chapter XVI, Volume III, first edition.

MY SUBJECTION

My aunt Dorothy required good proof that the malady she spoke of had not fallen upon me likewise.

The state of her feelings upon that subject could barely be hidden when she took my arm to walk back to Janet's house. My outcries of misery and perdition had unnerved her.

I said as calmly as possible: "'You mentioned her gentleness and firmness, aunty; that set me off. Don't you understand? You needn't be alarmed."

"I understand there is a contrast," Dorothy Beltham said.

Explanations were fruitless to reveal to her how such a contrast so simply spoken would act upon a lover situated as I was, hearing what I heard.

Janet gave me her hand again. I took it with bloodless fingers. I could not but tell her of the load of debt she laid me under.

"Since you know of it, dear Harry," she said, "you will agree with me that I am likely to be the best nurse for the present."

You cannot continue it long."

"While I can."

So long as she was free, that meant.

She could scarcely have discovered a method of phrasing it so as not to imply the grievous indication. I was but half cured in spirit, and in heart all one wound: any breath blowing on me from her did me a hurt.

I held a fair way for a time between gentleness and brutality, and then said abruptly: " 'While you can.' I don't know the date."

"What date, Harry?"

"Of your marriage."

"It is named for next month.

"It is? that is to say, *you* have named next month and the day of it. I'm thinking of my father. He will have to come to me some days before. You will have to look to your dresses, et cætera. The Marquis of Edbury had the habit, owing to an infantine fondness for amusement, of treating your patient upstairs to his notions of fun."

"They do not meet."

"I know they do not. But while my father is here—'while you can' look after him, he may instigate the Marquis's lively mind to talk of him—volubly, is quite within his capacity."

Irony was loss of pains: she might have been susceptible to the irony of thunder not too finely distilled.

So I thought, seeing her unmoved.

She answered to the point.

"He is not what he was. I hoped you would be friendly to him, Harry, to please me."

"And I will be, to please you."

Soft delight shone through fresh surprise in her face.

These must have been the first kind words I had spoken to her since my return to England.

Happily for myself, I had not to accuse my heart of intending them two-edged.

I dropped into a flat sincerity like a condition of stupor.

The description of the bond of alliance between Janet and Edbury—could it by any ingenuity be analyzed? Not without once beholding them together. I waited for that dreary spectacle to gain the bitter advance in wisdom for which I thirsted. Even to so low a condition did I descend, who had once made of each day a step in philosophy, dragging a heart, it was true, but not the slave of my burden.

p. 523, *l.* 7. *After* her husband *deleted as under*:

I could afterwards meet the Marquis of Edbury with sufficient self-containment to make civility an easy matter, nay, to be glad of the improvement manifest in him. He paid his betrothed a morning visit. I had been summoned early to the house to see my father, and had stepped down from his bed-room. The meeting was a surprise. Janet stood up to make the best of it. Edbury came to me affably, much less in his reeling style, with the freshest of faces, "jocund," if you like; a real morning air, allowing for the redolent cosmetics and tobacco upon his person.

"Delighted to see you, Richmond. Brown as a Turk, by Jove! How are you? Fellows that go to the East come back like brown-paper parcels marked 'fireworks': you never can get anything out of them except with a lighted cigar. Lots to tell? We had jolly hunting this year. If ever I go it won't be in the winter; I'm headlong for winter in England; so's Janet. She and I usually lead the field, and when you're alone with a woman at the tail of the hounds on a straight scent, by Jove, it's awfully jolly!"

These were his memorable words. He had not yet mastered the whole of our alphabet, certain consonants of which I supply for him.

Janet talked rapidly with him. She treated him as a lad.

Expression of any ulterior sentiment regarding him in her bosom she showed me none. Many a high-flying young lady similarly situated would, I suspect, have propitiated the critical third person of the three with some slight token of individual loftiness. I should have relished her better at the moment had she done so. She appeared to me like a humane upper-boy, who has an odd liking for a lively dolt—to be accounted for by the latter having a pretty sister at home.

He succeeded, however, in persuading her to drive to the North and South Cricket-Match. Perhaps she wished to give me a sign of her dependency: I could not tell.

At night she sent for me. The hour was late, the case urgent. I sympathized with Lady Ilchester in her desire that Janet should be spared the task of watching my father; it inflicted a grave and ceaseless anxiety, and as he constantly cried for me in my absence. I thought I might take him; but my aunt Dorothy said his call for Janet was wilder.

I found that Janet had soothed him to sleep. All the household were at rest. We sat together on the central ottoman of the drawing-room, conversing at intervals with low voices. The physicians declared my father's affliction to be one of the nerves, not of the brain, she said; and confirmed their opinion from her own experience. She was very tired, but could not sleep—was happy, she said, now that I was in the house, and between-whiles shut her eyes, breathing deeply, and opened them wide to listen. No sound disturbed us. The nurse attending on him came down once to inform us that he slept still.

"Harry, this is nice, our sitting so quiet here," Janet said.

"You sigh

"I am tired, Harry."

"Why not go to bed?"

"I can't: I shall not sleep."

"He will soon be on my hands."

"Let me think you will not have trouble, Harry."

Her look was sorrowful: I steeled my heart to endurance.

p. 523, *l.* 20. *After* immortality *deleted*:

Janet and I sat long into the night, not uttering one word of love.

"Morning's outside," I said.

She answered, "I don't know what morning is."

"You have a dark line under your eyes."

"My own doing."

"Mine."

"Then it will not disfigure me."

We gazed at the clock on the mantelpiece, named the hour, and forgot the hour.

When we parted she kissed me—she bent over to me at half arm's-length, and put her lips to my cheek.

Might I then have overcome her resolution by taking advantage of the thankful tenderness which blessed me for respecting her?

Forms of violation that trample down another's will are pardonable—can well be justified in the broad working world, considering what it is composed of. If you admit the existence of a more delicate and a higher world, you understand that I did not lose by abnegation. My love for my Janet partly slipped the senses into reason, and pity and esteem brought back hers for me. In plainer words, I began to love her as an honest man should love; she me, as a plighted woman should not, and the struggle in me diminished, in her was greater.

p. 523, *l.* 20. *After* "immortality" *added*: But again . . . most to bear (*l.* 25).

p. 523, *l.* 26 *begins* Chapter LIX, *Cornhill*, Chapter XVII, of Volume III of First Edition ("I meet my First Playfellow and take my Punishment").

p. 526, *l.* 22. his family: *altered from* Lady Kane.

p. 528, *l.* 16. *After* "again" *deleted*: I received a smart letter on the subject from Lady Kane, glad that in my conscience I could despise it. The old woman worked zealously for her monkey, as she called him. I contrasted her labours with those of my friends; Temple with a wig on half his time, and Heriot the boastful emptying bottles. Other friends, notably Charles Etherell, were kind in what they said of the prospects of a future career for me; but a young man does not commonly realize a prospect without the vision of himself in it, and the Harry Richmond of the days to come appeared a stricken wretch, a bare half of a man, a sight from which one gladly turns one's face to the wall.

p. 529, *l.* 7. *After* "wheels" *deleted*. He said things that would have melted another than iron Janet.

p. 530, *l.* 11. *After* Kiomi *deleted*:

He looked at the babe in her arms.

Kiomi sucked her throat in at a question of mine.

"I shan't do you mischief this time," she said.

p. 530, *l.* 35. *After* "Kesensky" *deleted*: stating that his chief wished to see me urgently and . . . .

p. 530, *l.* 42. *After* "von Redwitz" *deleted*: whose short experience of sea-voyaging down the Adriatic and across our channel had sickened him.

p. 532, *l.* 9. *After* "caught" *deleted*: conceive my amazement to hear the . . . .

p. 533, *l.* 16. *After* "say" *deleted*: it may have been good.

p. 534, *l.* 33. *After* "year" *deleted*: and nine months.

p. 536, *l.* 36. *After* hand *deleted*: passionately.

p. 539, *l.* 12, the barque Priscilla *altered from*: the Priscilla.

p. 539, *l.* 22. gin-bottle *altered from*: bottle.

p. 540, *l.* 26. *After* "Lady Kane" *added*: who managed him.

p. 540, *l.* 32. *After* "way" *deleted*: Janet said "Well?" Lady Kane muttered a word or two. "Have you to accuse *me* of anything?" said Janet, and walked by.

p. 541, *l.* 12. right nature *altered from*: ripened nature.

p. 544, *l.* 34. *After* "silently" *deleted*: She wept more when little Kiomi was found after a winter night stretched over the grave of her child, frozen dead; more when news came to us that our friend Heriot had fallen on an Indian battlefield.

APPENDIX C

MISPRINTS, PUNCTUATION, AND AUTHOR'S ERRORS IN THE PRESENT EDITION CORRECTED FOR THE FINALLY REVISED DE LUXE EDITION OF 1897

THIS list is based on Meredith's own corrections of the 1886, second edition, that is, the present text (see "A Note on the Text," p. 547), though several have been added by the present editor. Trivial changes of punctuation are not listed.

p. 3, *l.* 32.	challenging *changed to* challengeing.
p. 6, *l.* 39.	Before stronger *added:* the.
p. 12, *l.* 2.	mightly *changed to* mighty.
p. 70, *l.* 14.	*After* dinner *added:* ?
p. 83, *last line.*	*Residenc* changed to Resident.
p. 155, *l.* 1.	the *changed to* de.
p. 156, *l.* 41.	thus set *changed to* set thus.
p. 229, *l.* 25.	proposition *changed to* proposal.
p. 247, *l.* 21.	*After* answer of *omitted:* a.
p. 259, *l.* 6.	sight *changed to* light.
p. 260, *l.* 7.	proposition *changed to* proposal.
p. 285, *l.* 2.	*After* her *added:* "by.
p. 320, *l.* 19.	*After* stand for *deleted:* him.
p. 324, *l.* 8.	Semicolon substituted for full stop after "better"; "i" in ("It") changed to lower case.
p. 325, *l.* 1.	Double inverted commas missing from the beginning of the line.
p. 337, *l.* 37.	Anger *changed to* wrath.
p. 340, *ls.* 8–9.	*After* sermon *deleted:* from the new rector.
p. 346, *l.* 8.	proposition *changed to* proposal.
p. 358, *l.* 6.	"d" *omitted from:* Mdlle.
p. 360, *l.* 29.	same as previous entry.
p. 363, *l.* 10.	sung *changed to* sang.
p. 363, *l.* 40.	*After* Uberly *added:* acting as.
p. 383, *l.* 26.	"d" *omitted from:* Mdlle.
p. 386, *l.* 1.	anecdotalist *change to* anedotist.

610

p. 399, *l.* 31.	the sex *changed to* her sex.
p. 404, *l.* 40.	that *changed to* who.
p. 405, *l.* 19.	could *changed to* might.
p. 405, *l.* 20.	could *changed to* would.
p. 411, *l.* 10.	Full stop after "shoulder" changed to a colon.
p. 419, *l.* 2.	*After* pause *deleted*: I; comma substituted for colon after "pause."
p. 446, *l.* 39.	*After* passed *omitted*: her
p. 447, *l.* 35.	double inverted commas deleted after "wholly."
p. 458, *l.* 1.	cease *changed to* ceased.
p. 486, *l.* 9.	sung *changed to* sang.
p. 508, *l.* 12.	heart *changed to* art.

See also the following entries under "Revisions of the Original Printed Text," which may concern misprints overlooked by Meredith in revision rather than his own alterations: *p.* 130, *l.* 29; *p.* 374, *l.* 16; *p.* 375, *l.* 37; *p.* 382, *l.* 18; *p.* 496, *l.* 19.

ACKNOWLEDGMENTS

It is a pleasure to make the following acknowledgments of the assistance I have received in compiling this edition: to Professor Geoffrey Tillotson of Birkbeck College, University of London, for his encouragement and guidance when I was preparing my Ph.D. dissertation (1960), from which this edition grew; a postgraduate seminar on *Harry Richmond* at Birkbeck College, University of London, held by Mrs. Barbara Hardy, in 1959, added much to my understanding of the novel; Professor C. L. Cline for his generous help in discussion and correspondence and in making his edition of the Meredith *Letters* available to me in page proof and to the Oxford University Press for permission to quote from his edition; to the Yale University Library for permission to use and quote from Meredith manuscripts from the Altschul Collection of George Meredith; to the Lilly Library, Indiana University; to the Princeton University Library for use of manuscripts; to the University of Tasmania for making available research funds; to the Carnegie Corporation of New York for making possible a visit to the United States of which research at libraries was an important by-product; and finally my deepest thanks go to my wife, who helped me in the time-consuming collations of texts and other chores.

L. T. Hergenhan